PENGUIN BOOKS

THE EMIGRANTS

Vilhelm Moberg (1898–1973) was born in the parish of
Algutsboda, a province of Småland, Sweden. He worked
as a forester and a farm hand before becoming a journalist
and then an author. In 1929 he moved to Stockholm, and
his first triumph was the *Knut Töring* trilogy (1935–9),
which was published in English in 1940 as *The Earth is
Ours*. He wrote over twenty novels and thirty plays, and
his books have been translated into eighteen languages. Of
these Penguin also publishes *Unto a Good Land*, *Settlers*
and *Last Letter Home*. Vilhelm Moberg was married and
the father of five children.

VILHELM MOBERG

THE EMIGRANTS
PARTS I & II

THE EMIGRANTS
AND
UNTO A GOOD LAND

PENGUIN BOOKS

PENGUIN BOOKS

Published by the Penguin Group
Penguin Books Ltd, 27 Wrights Lane, London W 8 5 TZ, England
Penguin Putnam Inc., 375 Hudson Street, New York, New York 10014, U S A
Penguin Books Australia Ltd, Ringwood, Victoria, Australia
Penguin Books Canada Ltd, 10 Alcorn Avenue, Toronto, Ontario, Canada M 4 V 3 B 2
Penguin Books (NZ) Ltd, Private Bag 102902, NSMC, Auckland, New Zealand

Penguin Books Ltd, Registered Offices: Harmondsworth, Middlesex, England

The Emigrants first published in Sweden under the title *Utvandrarna* 1951
This English translation first published in the USA by Simon & Schuster, New York
Published in Penguin Books 1991

Copyright 1951 by Vilhelm Moberg

Unto a Good Land first published in Sweden under the title *Invandrarna* 1954
This English translation first published in the USA by Simon & Schuster, New York
Published in Penguin Books 1991

Copyright 1954 by Vilhelm Moberg
English translation copyright © renewed Gustaf Lannestock, 1982

This edition published by Penguin Books 1999

A NOTE ON THE PRONUNCIATION OF THE SWEDISH NAMES
å is pronounced like the *a* in *small* (cf. *Småland*, literally *Small Land*)
ä is pronounced like the *a* in *add*
ö is pronounced like the *ea* in *heard*
j is pronounced like *y*

The Emigrants

To all my relatives in the United States,
and to the translator of this book,
Gustaf Lannestock from Sweden.

By Way of Introduction

THE PEASANTS

This is the story of a group of people who in 1850 left their homes in Ljuder Parish, in the province of Småland, Sweden, and emigrated to North America.

They were the first of many to leave their village. They came from a land of small cottages and large families. They were people of the soil, and they came of a stock which for thousands of years had tilled the ground they were now leaving. Generation had followed generation, sons succeeded fathers at harrow and plow, and daughters took their mothers' place at spinning wheel and loom. Through ever-shifting fortunes the farm remained the home of the family, the giver of life's sustenance. Bread came from the rye field and meat from the cattle. Clothing and shoes were made in the home by itinerant tailors and cobblers, out of wool from the sheep, flax from the ground, skins from the animals. All necessary things were taken from the earth. The people were at the mercy of the Lord's weather, which brought fat years and lean years—but they depended on no other power under the sun. The farm was a world of its own, beholden to no one. The cottages nestled low and gray, timbered to last for centuries, and under the same roof of bark and sod the people lived their lives from birth to death. Weddings were held, christening and wake ale was drunk, life was lit and blown out within these same four walls of rough-hewn pine logs. Outside of life's great events, little happened other than the change of seasons. In the field the shoots were green in spring and the stubble yellow in autumn. Life was lived quietly while the farmer's allotted years rounded their cycle.

And so it was, down through the years, through the path of generations, down through centuries.

About the middle of the nineteenth century, however, the order of unchangeableness was shaken to its very foundations. Newly discovered powers came into use, wagons moved without horses, ships without sails, and distant parts of the globe were brought closer together. And to a new generation, able to read, came the printed word with tales of a land far away, a land which emerged from the mists of the saga and took on the clearing, tempting aspects of reality.

The new land had soil without tillers and called for tillers
without soil. It opened invitingly for those who longed for a
freedom denied them at home. The urge to emigrate stirred
in the landless, in the debt-bound, the suppressed and the dis-
contented. Others again saw no mirage of special privilege or
wealth in the new land, but wanted to escape entanglements
and dilemmas in the old country. They emigrated, not *to*
something but *from* something. Many, and widely different,
were the answers to the question: Why?

In every community there were some men and women who
obeyed the call and undertook the uncertain move to another
continent. The enterprising made the decision, the bold were
the first to break away. The courageous were the first to undertake the forbidding voyage across the great ocean. The dis-
contented, as well as the aggressive, not reconciling themselves to their lot at home, were emigrants from their home
communities. Those who stayed—the tardy and the unimagina-
tive—called the emigrants daredevils.

The first emigrants knew little of the country awaiting them,
and they could not know that more than a million people
would follow them from the homeland. They could not fore-
see that, a hundred years hence, one-fourth of their own people were to inhabit the new country; that their descendants
were to cultivate a greater expanse of land than the whole
arable part of Sweden at that time. They could not guess that
a cultivated land greater than their whole country would be
the result of this undertaking—a groping, daring undertaking,
censured, ridiculed by the ones at home, begun under a cloud
of uncertainty, with the appearance of foolhardiness.

Those men and women, whose story this is, have long ago
quitted life. A few of their names can still be read on crum-
bling tombstones, erected thousands of miles from the place
of their birth.

At home, their names are forgotten—their adventures will
soon belong to the saga and the legend.

THE COUNTRY WHICH THEY LEFT

The Parish

Ljuder Parish in Konga County is about twelve miles long
and three miles wide. The soil is black loam, interspersed with

sandy mold. Only smaller bodies of water exist—two brooks and four lakes or tarns. Dense pine forests still remained a hundred years ago, and groves of deciduous trees and thickets spread over wide areas which now are used as pasture.

On January 1, 1846, Ljuder Parish had 1,925 inhabitants: 998 males, and 927 females. During the century after 1750, the population had increased almost threefold. The number of nonassessed persons—retired old people, cottagers, squatters, servants, parish dependents, and people without permanent homes—during the same time had increased five-fold.

How the People Earned Their Living

According to the assessment books Ljuder Parish originally consisted of 43 full homesteads which in 1750 were divided among 87 owners. Through further division of property at times of death, the number of independent farms had by 1846 increased to 254, two-thirds of which were one-eighth of an original homestead, or smaller. Only four farms now included more than one homestead: the freeholds of Kråkesjö and Gösamåla, Ljuder parsonage, and the sheriff's manse at Alebäck.

The means of livelihood a hundred years ago were mainly agriculture and cattle raising and to a small degree handicraft. Included in agriculture was the distillation of brännvin; the price of grain was so low that the peasants must distill their produce in order to farm profitably. In the eighteen-forties the number of stills in the parish was around 350. About every sixth person had his own vessel for producing the drink. The size of the still was decided by law, according to the size of the farm; if a one-half homestead farm possessed a thirty-gallon still, then a one-quarter homesteader had only a fifteen-gallon one. The biggest still was at the freehold of Kråkesjö, and the next largest at the parsonage, which came as number two in homestead size. All distillers sold part of their product in order to earn their living. However, when Pastor Enok Brusander in 1833 became dean of the parish, he ordered that no brännvin be sold or served in the parsonage on Sundays, except to people of the household or workmen on the place. At a parish meeting in 1845 it was further decided that no brännvin should be sold during church services at a distance of less than six hundred yards from God's house. It was also

stated that any parishioner who gave brännvin to a child who
had not yet received Holy Communion must pay a fine of one
riksdaler banko to the poor purse (in present-day currency,
one krona and fifty öre, or approximately twenty-nine cents).
The same meeting admonished parents not to let their children
get into the habit of drinking "drop by drop." Only in those
cases where the children showed "decided inclination for the
drink" should they be allowed to "enjoy the drink in so great
quantities that they might get sick and thereby lose their taste
for brännvin."

Those Who Governed the Parish

The most important man in Ljuder during the eighteen-
forties was the dean, Enok Brusander, who in his capacity as
minister represented the Almighty, King in heaven and on
earth. Next to him in power was the sheriff, Alexander Lön-
negren in Alebäck, who had his office from the Crown and
represented worldly majesty, Oskar I, King of Sweden and
Norway. The foremost man in the parish as to birth and riches
was Lieutenant Sir Paul Rudeborg, owner of Kråkesjö freehold. He and his lady were the only people of noble birth and
corresponding rights. Representing the parish on the county
council was Per Persson in Åkerby, churchwarden and storekeeper, and next to Lieutenant Rudeborg the wealthiest man
in the community.

These four men governed the parish, holding the spiritual
and worldly offices in accordance with Romans 13, verses one
to three: ". . . For there is no power but of God. . . ."

The Others Who Lived in the Parish

Besides the 254 peasants and cotters who owned and lived
on assessed land, there were 39 persons listed as artisans and
apprentices, 92 squatters, 11 enlisted soldiers, 6 innkeepers,
5 horse traders, 3 house-to-house peddlers. There were also
274 farm servants, 23 bedesmen and bedeswomen, 104 "ordinary poor," 18 sick and crippled, 11 deaf and dumb, 8 blind,
6 nearly blind, 13 almost lame, 4 lame, 5 near idiots, 3 idiots,
1 half idiot, 3 whores and 2 thieves. On the last page of the
church book, under the heading "End of the Parish," were

listed 27 persons who had moved away and never been further heard from.

The poor, "the ordinary poor," and other old and ill and incompetent people, were divided into three groups and cared for according to special regulations passed by the parish council. The first group included the old and crippled who were entirely incapacitated. They received first-class poor help, or "complete sustenance," which might amount to as much as three riksdaler in cash per year—about eighty-seven cents—plus four bushels of barley.

In the second group were those only partly disabled, who could to a certain degree earn a living for themselves and their children. They were helped with sums of cash ranging from twelve shillings to one riksdaler a year—from six to twenty-nine cents—and at the most two bushels of barley.

The third group included people who only temporarily needed help. They received alms from a special fund known as the Ljuder Parish Poor Purse, under the supervision of the parish council. This last group included also "profligate and lazy people who had themselves caused their poverty." They, according to the council's decision, "should be remembered with the smallest aid from the Poor Purse, thereby getting accustomed to sobriety and industry."

Destitute orphans were auctioned off by the parish council to "suitable homes at best bid." For these "parish boys" and "parish girls" the council sought to find foster homes where the children would receive "fatherly care and in good time instruction in honest habits and work."

Conditions were similar in other parishes in Sweden at that time.

The Spiritual Care of the Inhabitants

The people were fostered in the pure evangelical-Lutheran religion in accordance with the church law of 1686, and were protected from heretical and dangerous new ideas by the royal "Resolution and Order" of January 12, 1726, "this wholesome Resolution aiming at good order in the parish, and Christian unity in teaching."

In the church law the clergy were admonished to "see to it that the children learn to read so that they may with their own eyes see God's holy laws and commands." This instruction in reading, advisable only for salvation of the soul, was administered by schoolmaster or by parents. Each fall the minister held an examination in the tenets of the faith according to the Little Catechism of Luther. All unmarried parishioners at this time were probed concerning their reading ability, and were fined for failure to attend.

The parish in 1836 engaged its own schoolmaster, Rinaldo, an ex-enlisted cavalry soldier who, having lost an eye, had been permitted to leave the military service. The schoolmaster received a yearly fee of twelve bushels of rye, and one shilling (half a cent) per day for each child he taught. The parents gave him room and firewood besides. Rinaldo wandered from one end of the parish to the other, and held his school in the homes of the peasants, who each in turn allowed him the use of some spare room or attic for this purpose. The length of the term in each house was decided by the schoolmaster. He had been engaged to teach the children to read well enough to learn Luther's Little Catechism by heart. He ventured sometimes to include such wordly and useless subjects as arithmetic, writing, Swedish history, and geography. Most men and women could read fairly well; some could sign their names; few could write more than this, and very few of the women could write at all: no one knew what use a female could make of the art of writing.

Religious Sects

The so-called Akian heresy had started in the neighboring parish of Elmeboda about 1780, and soon spread also to Ljuder. The adherents to the sect were called Akians after the founder, Ake Svensson of Östergöhl, Elmeboda. They tried to copy the early Christian church and return to the ways of the apostles. The Akians separated from the state church and recognized neither temporal nor spiritual powers in their community. All differences between people as to caste or property ownership were to them contrary to God's word, and so within their own sect they lived a completely communal life. None of them called a single object his own. They conducted their own services and held their own Holy Communion.

Some forty persons in Elmeboda and Ljuder Parishes had joined the new sect. Many of them belonged to Ake Svensson's family, which was scattered throughout both parishes. The home of the sect in Ljuder was Kärragärde, owned by Ake's brother-in-law Andreas Månsson.

The Åkians were soon called in for questioning by the bishopric of Växiö and were given strong warnings. But they were inflexible and met the dignitaries of the church with unpropitious words. The church pronounced its ban but the Åkians retained their convictions. They were then sued in civil court and were brought to Konga County Court in Ingelstad,* where the court admonished them to abide by the law and follow the regulations of the established church. Ake Svensson and his followers could not be persuaded to recant their heretical opinions; they refused to return to the fold of the only true church.

In order to maintain church peace and civil security the case was reviewed by the Göta Crown Court.† This court found the members of the sect "completely fallen into insanity, having lost the use of their sound minds," and held that, to maintain peace, and for the welfare of the dissenters, they should be confined in an asylum. Ake Svensson and seven other leaders of the sect "who had shown their insanity in many instances" were ordered transported to Danvik's asylum in Stockholm, "there to receive such attention as their condition warranted."

The eight sectarians who had fallen under the Crown Court's order were turned over to the sheriff. In 1786 they were taken to Danvik's asylum in Stockholm. Ake Svensson, Andreas Månsson, and two others died within two years, after having received "the attention their condition warranted." Ake was at the time of his death thirty-five years of age.

The other dissenters were gradually liberated and returned as cured to their respective homes, where the one-time asylum inmates lived tranquilly and harmoniously, and for many years it seemed as if the firebrand of Akianism was for ever smothered. But in the eighteen-forties this dangerous heresy reappeared in Ljuder Parish. The circumstances, however, belong to the story.

V. M.

* Konga County Records for 1785.
† Göta Crown Court Proceedings, December 12, 1785.

PART ONE

Gates on the Road to America

I

KING IN HIS STONE KINGDOM

1

Mjodahult is one of Ljuder's most ancient homesteads. Its name is mentioned in a court record two hundred years before the discovery of America.

The Nilsa family had tilled and lived on this farm as far back in history as paper is preserved, as far as the memory of generations can reach. The first known owner was Nils in Mjodahult after whom the family got its name. About Nils in Mjodahult it is further known that he had an unusually large and grotesque nose, which was said to have resembled a well-grown rutabaga. This nose was inherited by his descendants, and someone in each generation possessed it. It became a mark of the Nilsa family. Called the Nilsa-nose, it was believed to be endowed with the same magic powers as a birth cowl, and brought luck to its owner. Children born with the Nilsa-nose became the most fortunate and most successful members of the family, and, even though it was hardly a mark of beauty in a woman, it is not known to have been an obstacle in securing advantageous marriages.

The assessment book indicates that Nils' Mjodahult was still a full homestead in the eighteenth century. The farm was later split up several times, lastly in 1819 when two brothers, Olov Jakob's Son and Nils Jakob's Son, received equal shares. The records list four more brothers and three sisters. The new farms were by now only one-sixteenth of the original homestead Nils, the younger brother, obtained the split-off piece: three arable acres on the outskirts where he built his house among the straggling pines. The new farm is recorded as "one-sixteenth crown assessment Korpamoen under the mother homestead Mjodahult."

Nils Jakob's Son was short of build—only five feet—and he had not been endowed with the Nilsa-nose. He was nevertheless a capable man, strong-armed and persevering; his hands did not willingly rest if there was aught to do. Marta, his wife, was a strong and stately woman, a full head taller than her husband.

Korpamoen was at first hardly more than a cotter's place, but Nils developed his inheritance into a farm. The soil was sandy, strewn with stones. It looked as if it had rained stones from heaven here during all the six days of the creation. But Nils searched out every patch of soil that could be cultivated and attacked the stones with his iron bar and lever—the latter a long pole with a horseshoe nailed to the heavy end. His best tools, however, were his hands; with these he went after the stones deep in their holes, wrestled with them, turned them, finally rolled them away. And when Nils encountered a stone which he couldn't manage with his hands or his tools, he called for his wife. Marta was almost as strong as her husband; she hung on to the small end of the lever while Nils used the iron bar.

It was a silent struggle between Nils and the stone, a fight between an inert mass and the living muscles and sinews of a patient, persevering man.

This fight continued during all of Nils' farming years; each year he broke a new quarter of an acre, until at last there were more stone piles in Korpamoen than on any other farm in the parish. When Nils turned his field the plow circled stone piles; he used to say he became giddy from the ring-around-the-rosy dance in his fields.

Nils Jakob's Son was also handy with wood, and worked sometimes as a timberman in the neighborhood. He had built his own house. Even as a boy he had started to follow the woodmen and before he was grown he could join the corner timbers of a house, that most difficult task in carpentry. He was also a cabinetmaker and a smith. Throughout the winters he stood at his workbench and made all kinds of farming tools.

When he had moved to Korpamoen he had been forced to mortgage the farm, so that his brothers and sisters might receive their inheritance share in cash; the yearly interest on this loan required that he work as timberman and carpenter.

Of the marriage between Nils and Marta three children were born: two sons, Karl Oskar and Robert, and a daughter, Lydia. Twice Marta's pregnancy had ended in miscarriage; once on the same day she had been in the field helping her husband dig up a boulder.

Karl Johan, the new King of Sweden and Norway, had ascended the throne the year before Nils and Marta were mar-

ried; their first-born son was named after him; the child's
second name was for the new Crown Prince, Oskar. It was
thought to be good luck to name one's children after people
of high station—kings, princes, queens, princesses; even the
poorest squatter could afford royal names for his offspring.

The first-born son, Karl Oskar, was also born with the
lucky big nose of the Nilsa family.

Karl Oskar grew up strong of limb and body. Soon he
helped his father at building and stone breaking. But early the
boy showed a mind of his own; in work he would not do as
his father told him, but rather followed his own way, though
eating his parents' bread. No chastisement improved the stubborn child; Nils was many times angered over his son's independent ways.

One day when Karl Oskar was fourteen years old he was
asked by his father to make slats for a new hayrick; they
should be five feet long. Karl Oskar thought the hayrick
would be too low with such short slats; he made them six feet,
instead.

Nils measured the slats and said: "Do as I tell you, or go!"

Karl Oskar kept silent for a while, then haughtily answered: "I shall go."

The same day he hired himself as farmhand to a man in
Idemo, where he was to remain seven years.

Taken at his word, Nils regretted it; his son had been a
help to him. But he could not retract: a boy who had not yet
received Holy Communion could not rule his father in his
work. On the whole, however, all went well for Nils and
Marta in Korpamoen for some twenty-five years.

Then, one day in the early spring of 1844, Nils Jakob's Son
was alone in an outlying glade, breaking new land. Here he
encountered a stone which caused him much trouble. It was
smaller than many a one he had removed alone, but it lay
deep in earth and was round as a globe so that neither bar
nor lever got hold of it. Nils used all his tricks and soon the
stone was halfway up. He now wedged it with the iron bar,
intending to roll it away with his hands; but as he bent down
to get a good hold for the final battle the earth slid away
from under his foot and he fell on his face. In the fall he
moved the iron bar that held the stone, which rolled back into
its hole—over one of his thighs.

Nils lay where he fell. When he didn't come home for his

afternoon meal, Marta went out to look for him. She found her husband in the hole next to the stone, and lifted him onto her back and carried him home. Berta in Idemo, whose aid was solicited for hurts and ailments, was sent for, and she told him that the hipbone was broken and the joint injured.

Nils remained in bed for several months while Berta attended him with her herb concoctions and salves. The bone healed and he could again stand on his feet, but some injury was left in the joint and it remained incurable; he could not move without crutches; from now on he could do chores with his hands only, while seated.

Nils Jakob's Son was a cripple. His farmer's life was over. For twenty-five years he had fought the stones, and in the last battle the stones had won.

Korpamoen was no longer a cotter's place. The size of the manure pile tells the size of the farm: it was not a mean dunghill outside the stable barns at Korpamoen. The farm now had seven arable acres; it could feed seven head of cattle through summer and winter. Nils and Marta had more than doubled the plot they first occupied twenty-five years before. Now they must cede it.

The farm was too small to divide; a one-sixteenth could not be split. And Nils did not wish to sell it to an outsider; one of his children must reap the benefit of his many years of clearing. Karl Oskar was still in service in Idemo, and barely of age. Robert, their second son, was only eleven, and the daughter Lydia fourteen years old. Even the oldest son was rather young to become his own master, but Nils offered Korpamoen to him, nevertheless. The father by now had more respect for the headstrong boy who had left home at fourteen because he couldn't have his way about a few hayrick slats.

After seven years as a farmhand Karl Oskar was weary of working for others, and would rather be master of the homestead; he was ready to buy.

"If you become a farmer, you'll need a wench," said Nils.

"I'll find one," said Karl Oskar, sure of himself.

"Braggart!"

A few days later, however, Karl Oskar announced that the banns would be read for him the following Sunday. The parents were so much astonished they could not say a word: the son had even arranged his marriage without their advice! Indeed, the boy did have a will of his own. But they were also concerned; in the long run such a headstrong son would succeed only with difficulty.

2

On an autumn day a few years earlier Karl Oskar had brought a load of his master's firewood to Berta, the Idemo woman with healing knowledge. Berta offered him a dram in the kitchen, and there sat a young girl, unknown to him, spooling yarn. She had thick, light yellow hair, and a pair of mild eyes—green, blue, or perhaps both. Her face, with its soft, pink skin, pleased him, in spite of a few freckles on her nose. The girl sat quietly at the spooling wheel while Karl Oskar was in the kitchen, and none of them spoke. But when he was ready to leave he turned to her and said: "My name is Karl Oskar."

"Mine is Kristina," she answered.

Then she sat silent, and spooled as before. But she had given him her name, she who was to become his wife.

Kristina was a farmer's daughter from Duvemala, in Algutsboda Parish, and she was only seventeen when they first met. But her body was well developed, with the first marks of womanhood; her hips showed well-rounded curves and her maidenly breasts were cramped inside the blouse which she had long ago outgrown. In her mind, however, she was still a child. She loved to swing. A few weeks before she met Karl Oskar she had taken the ox-thong and set up a swing in the barn at Duvemala. During her play she had fallen out of the swing and broken her kneecap. The injury was poorly looked after, and gangrene set in. Her parents had then sent her to Berta in Idemo, who was known through many parishes for her healing ability, and Kristina was staying with the old woman while the gangrene mended.

Kristina still limped, and that was why she didn't rise from the spooling wheel while Karl Oskar was in the kitchen.

But he found excuses for calling on Berta to see the girl again, and next time he found her standing outside on the porch. He noticed then that she was a tall girl, as tall as he.

She was lithe and slender around the waist. Her eyes were bashful and tempting.

They met now and then while Kristina remained in Idemo. Her knee healed and she limped no more; no longer was she ashamed to walk about when Karl Oskar saw her.

The evening before she was to return home they met and sat outside Berta's cellar on an upturned potato basket. He said he liked her and asked if she liked him. She did. He then asked if she would marry him. She answered that she thought both of them too young, that at least he ought to be of age. He said he could write to the King and get permission to marry. Then she said they had no place to live, nor did she know how they could feed and clothe themselves. To this he had no answer, for it was true. He had nothing to promise her, therefore he kept still; a spoken word and a promise carried weight; one had to answer for it, it could never be taken back.

They had since met at the Klintakrogen fair three times, two springs and one autumn, and each time Karl Oskar had said that he still liked her and no one else was in his thoughts.

Karl Oskar was sure of what he wanted. As soon as he had been offered Korpamoen by his father, he went to Kristina's parents in Duvemala. They were much surprised by this visit from an unknown youth who asked leave to speak with their daughter alone.

Karl Oskar and Kristina stood under the gable of her home and talked to each other for twenty minutes.

Karl Oskar thought:

Their hour to get married had now arrived, he was of age, he was to take over his father's farmstead, they had house and home and means to earn food and clothing.

Kristina thought:

As they had met only a half-score times, they had hardly had opportunity to get to know each other. At nineteen she was still too young to become a farm wife; he must ask her parents if they wanted him for a son-in-law.

It turned out as Karl Oskar had thought it would. He was accepted into the family when her parents learned that his suit was earnest and that he owned a farm. He stayed in their house overnight and slept with his wife-to-be, fully dressed, in all honor. Six weeks later the wedding was held in Duvemala between Karl Oskar Nilsson and Kristina Johansdotter.

Karl Oskar said to his young wife: There was no person in the whole world he liked as well as her, because she never criticized him or pointed out his shortcomings as others did. He was sure he would be happy with her through his whole life.

3

King Oskar I ascended the throne of Sweden and Norway in 1844, and the same year Karl Oskar Nilsson (the old-fashioned spelling of Nils' Son was discarded by Karl Oskar, who had learned to write) took possession of "one-sixteenth of one homestead, Korpamoen." He still carried the names of the King and the Crown Prince, but now the order of the names was reversed: the new King's name was Oskar and the Crown Prince was Karl.

The price agreed upon for Korpamoen, with cattle and farming equipment, was seventeen hundred riksdaler. This sum (amounting to a little less than five hundred dollars in American money today) included the mortgage of eight hundred riksdaler. Nils and Marta also kept their "reserved rights" to the end of their days: living quarters in the spare room, winter and summer fodder for one cow and one sheep, three-quarters of an acre of arable land for their own sowing, with use of the owner's team, and twelve bushels of grain yearly, half rye and half barley. In the preserved deed it can still be read: "The reserved rights to begin July 1, 1844, this agreement entered into with sound mind and ripe considera-tion has taken place in Korpamoen, June nineteenth of this year, in the presence of witnesses." The deed bears the cross marks of Nils and Marta, who had never learned to write.

As was usual when parents ceded their farm with reserved rights, a division of inheritance was now undertaken. Each of the children received two hundred and ten riksdaler and twenty-four shillings. Robert and Lydia, not yet of age, let their shares remain as claims against their brother.

Karl Oskar had got what he wanted; and how was it with

him as a beginner? During his seven years in service he had saved one hundred and fifty riksdaler; with his wife he had received as dowry two hundred riksdaler; his inheritance was two hundred and ten riksdaler. But this money amounted to only one-quarter of the sales price. The other three-quarters remained as debt, debt which carried interest. He must pay fifty riksdaler a year in interest on the mortgage. And his greatest debt was the reserved rights to his parents. Indeed, the reserved rights were heavy for so small a farm—but they must be sufficient for the parents' maintenance. Karl Oskar's obligation to them was a debt on the farm which he must continue to pay as long as they lived; and Nils was only fifty-one years of age, Marta forty-eight. It was hardly a farm that Karl Oskar had taken over—it was debts to pay, with interest. But debt could be blotted out through work, and so he did not worry: he knew how to work.

Thus life continued in Korpamoen: Nils and Marta moved into the little spare room where they were to live out their years; Kristina arrived with her dowry chest and took Marta's place. It was a young farm wife who moved in. But with her own hands she had stitched the bridal cover which she now, the first evening, spread over the nuptial bed. It was the blue of cornflowers, and Marta had said it was nice; Kristina was proud.

Karl Oskar was pleased that his mother and wife could live in harmony; otherwise they might have caused each other great irritation. The contract stated that his mother had the right to cook in the kitchen and bake in the big bake oven; had they been unfriendly they could have been in each other's way in every corner.

But one day Kristina was discovered by her mother-in-law in the threshing barn, where she was playing in a swing which she had secretly hung from the rafters. Marta excused it and said nothing; Kristina was still a child in her ways, with a desire for play still in her body. It was peculiar, however, that Kristina would want to play with a swing since she had once fallen from one, injuring her knee. Besides, the wild play did not suit a married woman. Luckily no outsider saw her in the barn, hence no rumors spread in the neighborhood.

There was, however, something in regard to Kristina which Nils and Marta did not like: on her mother's side she was related to descendants of Ake Svensson, the founder of the

Akian sect. Her mother was Ake's niece. And her uncle, Danjel Andreasson, was owner of Karragarde, the meeting place for the Akians in Ljuder. Of course, more than fifty years had elapsed since the instigator of this heresy, the troublemaker from Ostergohl, had died in Danvik's asylum. As far as was generally known, nothing had survived in Karragarde of the horrible Akianist contagion. But the original ill feeling toward the founder had been so deeply rooted among a great many of the parishioners that it still survived —kinfolk of Ake Svensson did not brag about their relationship.

Nils and Marta said nothing to their daughter-in-law, but one day they did broach the question to Karl Oskar: "Do you know your wife is related to Ake of Ostergohl?"

"I'm aware of it—and I defy anyone to hold it against her."

There was nothing more to be said. Marta and Nils only hoped that Kristina's kinship with the Akian founder wasn't generally known in the village. In Korpamoen it was never mentioned again.

4

Early every weekday morning Nils emerged from the spare room, hobbling along on his crutches, slowly reaching his old workbench outside in the woodshed, where he remained through the day. He cut spokes for wagon wheels, he made rakes, and handles for axes and scythes. He could still use plane and chisel; his hands were in good health, and their dexterity remained. He taught Karl Oskar what he could of this handicraft.

During most of the summer days one could find Nils and his tools outside in the yard, where he sat in the shade of an old maple tree. From there he had a good view over the fields with all the piles of stone which his hands had gathered. His twenty-five farming years had indeed left marks; all the heaps of stone and all the stone fences which he had built remained in their places, and no doubt would long remain.

The invalid was not bitter. His belief was that all things happened according to God's preordination. It was his convic-

tion that God in the beginning had decided that a stone in his
field—on a certain day, at a certain hour—would roll back
into its hole. He would miss his foothold and fall, the stone
would break his hip joint, and he would ever after crawl
about like a wing-broken magpie. It would be presumptuous
of him to question the Creator. Nils Jakob's Son did not burden his brain with questions.

Now his son plowed and sowed the fields which he had
cleared. He had fought the stones to the best of his ability;
now his son reaped the benefit.

But Karl Oskar worried about debts and interest. If he only
had a horse, then he could hire himself out and earn some
money hauling timbers. But a one-sixteenth was too small to
feed a horse, who chewed several barrels of oats during the
winter; he needed three acres more to keep a horse. As it was
he had to feed his parents and his wife and himself on seven
acres, most of which was poor, sandy soil.

Soon he realized that he must clear more land.

He went out to inspect the unbroken ground belonging to
Korpamoen. There were spruce woods and knolls, there were
desolate sandy plains with juniper and pine roots, there were
low swamplands with moss and cranberries, there were hillocks and tussock-filled meadows. The rest was strewn with
stone. He carried an iron bar which he now and then stuck
into the ground, and always he heard the same sound: stone.
He went through pastures and meadows, through woodlands
and moors, and everywhere the same sound: stone, stone,
stone. It was a monotonous tune, a sad tune for a man who
wanted to clear more acres.

Karl Oskar did not find a tenth of an acre within his
boundaries left to clear; his father had done his work well; all
arable ground was cultivated. What he now possessed to till
and sow was all he would have. Until acres could be stretched
and made broader than God created them, there would be no
more arable land in Korpamoen.

And because the young farmer couldn't continue creation
where God had left off, he must be satisfied with his seven
acres, and all the stones wherever he looked: broken stones,
stones in piles, stone fences, stone above ground, stone in the
ground, stone, stone, stone. . . .

King Oskar had ascended the throne of the kingdoms of

Sweden and Norway; Karl Oskar Nilsson had become king in a stone kingdom.

5

His first year as a farmer—1845—was a good year. The crops were ample, he was able to pay the mortgage interest on time, and all was well. And in the spring Kristina had given birth to their first child, a daughter, christened Anna after Kristina's mother.

The second year also they had good crops in Korpamoen, but the harvesting was poor. The rye sprouted in the shocks, and bread baked from the flour was soggy. They sold a calf and half of the pig to help pay interest on the mortgage, and the twenty riksdaler he was short Karl Oskar borrowed from his crippled father: it was money the old one had earned through his handiwork. In the midst of the August harvest Kristina bore a son; he was named Johan after his mother's father in Duvemala.

The third year was filled with anxiety. When the meadow hay was cut in July such a heavy rain fell that the swaths were floating in water. When the flood had subsided some of the hay remained, fox-red, rotten and spoiled. It had a musty smell, no nourishment, and the animals refused to eat it. Karl Oskar and Kristina were forced to sell one cow. More bad luck followed: another cow had a stillborn calf, and a sheep went astray in the woods to become food for wild beasts. In the autumn it was discovered that potato rot had spread to their field—when picked, almost every second potato was spoiled; for one filled basket of good, an equally large one had to be discarded, hardly good enough for fodder for the animals. During the following winter more than one day went by without the potato pot over the fire. It was said the potato rot came from foreign countries, where it caused famine.

This year—1847—Karl Oskar went still deeper into debt. He had to borrow money for the whole amount of the mortgage interest. Nils had no more to lend him, and Karl Oskar did not wish to ask his father-in-law in Duvemala. Kristina thought he should try her uncle, Danjel Andreasson, in Karra-

garde, who was fairly well off. He was known as a quiet and
kind man, although he was the nephew of the despised Akian
founder—but it would be foolish to pay heed to happenings
of fifty years ago. No sooner had Karl Oskar made the request than Danjel gave him fifty riksdaler for the mortgage
interest.

The day before Christmas Eve, that year, Kristina gave
birth to twins, a boy and a girl. The boy was sickly and was
given emergency baptism by Dean Brusander; he died within
a fortnight. The girl lived and was christened Marta, after
Karl Oskar's mother. She would afterwards be known as Lill-
Marta.

After three years in Korpamoen Karl Oskar had now one
cow less in the byre and seventy riksdaler more debt than at
the time of taking over. And yet during every day of the
three years both he and Kristina had worked and drudged to
their utmost ability. They had struggled to get ahead, yet it
had gone backwards for them. They could not sway the Lord's
weather, nor luck with the animals. Karl Oskar had thought
they would be able to get along if they had health and
strength to work; now they were aware that man in this
world could not succeed through his work alone.

"It's written, 'In the sweat of thy brow shalt thou eat thy
bread,' " said Nils.

"Aye—nor am I even sure to get bread through work and
sweat," retorted Karl Oskar.

Karl Oskar, as well as his father, knew the story of the Fall
from his Biblical history; the dean used to praise him for his
quick answers at the yearly examinations.

Karl Oskar had got what he wanted, but it wasn't good for
a person always to have his will. Most people thought he was a
man with luck and of good fortune. He had two royal names,
given him at baptism and formally recorded. He had the big
Nilsa-nose—"Your nose is your greatest heritage," his father
used to say. But what help now were the names of kings and
princes? What help now was a nose that extended a little further into the world than another's? The day still seemed approaching when Sheriff Lonnegren might arrive at the farm
and take something in pawn.

During his younger years Karl Oskar had often been teased
by other boys about the big nose which distorted his face. He
had always answered that it was the best nose he had. And he

had believed his parents' stories about members of the family
in generations gone by from whom his nose had been inherited—he had always believed it would bring him good fortune
in life. Kristina did not think his nose was ugly; it would have
been different in a woman, she thought, but menfolk it suited.
She did not believe, however, that his big nose would have
anything to do with his success in life. That would be a
heathenish thought. Kristina sprang from a religious home,
and she knew that God shifted people as He saw fit, according to His inscrutable and wise ways. Since they now
suffered adversity in Korpamoen, this was only in accord with
God's will.

6

So began the year 1848. Karl Oskar had bought an almanac
from the schoolmaster, Rinaldo, for four shillings. He now
read that the year was the five thousand eight hundred and
fiftieth from the creation of the world. It was also the forty-
eighth since "the High Birth of Oskar the First's Majesty and
the fourth since Its Ascendance on the Throne." It was also
the fourth of Karl Oskar's possession and farming of Korpamoen.

He read about the movements and appearance of the
greater planets in the new year. He was familiar with the constellations whose signs were printed in the almanac for each
day: the ram, with his great bowed horns, the scorpion, with
its horrible claws, the lion, with his wide and beastly jaws, and
the virgin, so narrow around the waist and holding a wreath
of flowers. Weather and wind and perhaps also the destiny of
man depended on the meeting of the wandering planets with
these constellations.

Before the close of the old year people had already noticed
alarming signs: wide parts of the Milky Way where the stars
used to shine clear and brilliant were now nebulous and dark
—the heavenly lights had disappeared. This could mean war
and unrest, rebellion and dire times, sickness and pestilence.
Intense cold and a "crow's winter" set in before Christmas;
those who ventured out to the early service on Christmas
morning came home with frozen ears. New Year's Day

opened with high winds; the steeple in Elmeboda blew down, and also the great mountain ash at Akerby Junction, and this the thickest tree along the whole church road. On the exposed wastelands where the spruce were poorly rooted in the sandy soil the wind mowed along like a sharpened scythe in morning-dewed grass. And Noah's Ark, which had not been seen since the dry year of 1817, appeared again in the heavens, with all its sinister majesty. The Ark was formed by clouds stretching from east to west, thereby obstructing all running waters and streams and preventing rainfall for the coming year.

Throughout the winter and spring there were strange portents in the weather. February was warm, while the spring month of March was windy, dry, and cold. The winter rye fared ill: wide gaping stretches appeared in otherwise green fields after the winter snow had melted.

During the last week of April—the grass month—it seemed as if at last spring had arrived. And early in the morning of May Day Eve Karl Oskar pulled out the wooden harrow from its shed, intending to begin the preparation of the fields for the sowing. Then it started to snow; it snowed the whole day; in the evening a foot of snow covered the ground. The cattle recently had been let out to graze; they must now be put in their stalls again. The April snow covered flowers and grass which had only begun to grow. Again, the spring had frozen away.

Karl Oskar pulled the harrow back into the shed. He sat silent at the food table this May Day Eve, and went to bed with a heavy heart. As far back as men could remember it had never boded so ill for the crops as during this peculiar spring.

The young couple in Korpamoen lay together under the cover, the one Kristina had stitched. It had now warmed them at their rest during four years—more than a thousand nights. Many of these nights Karl Oskar had lain awake, thinking about the mortgage interest, and in many of these nights Kristina had risen to quiet the children when they awoke and cried. Four springs had stood green, four autumnal stubble fields had been turned since for the first time they enjoyed the embrace of man and woman under the cornflower-blue bridal quilt.

That evening in the autumn, when they had sat together on the potato basket in Idemo, now seemed so long ago—it might have been an experience in another world. It belonged to their youth, and they spoke of their youth as something long gone by; they had been young before they were married, and that was once upon a time.

Karl Oskar had recently had his twenty-fifth birthday; Kristina would soon be twenty-three. Not so long ago she was a child herself; now she had brought four children into the world. Three lived and slept now in this room; she listened to their breathing, ever anxious.

Kristina thought at times about the happenings of her young life and the relation of events. If she hadn't fallen from the swing in the barn at home in Duvemala, and injured her knee, she would never have gone to Berta in Idemo to seek a cure for gangrene. Then she would never have met Karl Oskar and they would never have become a married couple. They would not have owned and farmed Korpamoen together, and she would not have had four children by him. Nor would they lie together here tonight under the bridal cover which she had made. She would not have Anna, Johan, and Lill-Marta, those three small beings sleeping so close to them.

Everything important in her life had happened because once she had made a swing from an ox-thong, at home with her parents, and had fallen from it. God surely had willed that she put up the swing; He it was who had directed all this for her.

And she still enjoyed swinging; a little while ago she had made a swing again in the threshing barn, when no one saw her. She knew that her mother-in-law thought it was ill done by a farm wife who had borne four children—thought she should think of other things.

Kristina had blown out the tallow candle when she went to bed. Through the window she could see the glittering snow which had fallen the last day of April and—as it seemed— might remain.

Karl Oskar lay quietly at her side, but she could hear that he was still awake. She asked: "Are you thinking about something?"

"Aye. About spring. It looks ill for the crops."

"It's true. It seems ugly."

Kristina's eyes wandered through the window; when she and her husband arose tomorrow morning the month of May would be here—yet it was snowlight outside.

She said: "We must believe God will let things grow—this year as all years."

"Believe! Yes—if faith were of help, we'd harvest a hundred barrels of rye this fall."

He had never before shown such anxiety; now he seemed dejected, disheartened. His low spirits were contagious; she too began to worry about the coming days.

He continued: Including his parents there were now seven people who must find their food on this small farmstead—a one-sixteenth. If the year were lean and the crops failed, he would not know what to do.

Kristina thought of the children, now sleeping their sweet sleep in this room. Those who had brought the children into the world were responsible for them and must see to it that their stomachs were satisfied and their bodies clothed. The children's welfare was much more important to Kristina than her own, and she knew Karl Oskar felt as she did.

Kristina folded her hands and said her usual evening prayer: "Turn Thy Grace to me and let me sweetly go to sleep this night. . . ." Before she said her Amen she added tonight a few sentences she remembered from "A Prayer for the Fruit of the Earth": "Give us favorable weather and protect the crops from all destruction. Bless us with corn and kernel. Through Jesum Christum, our Lord, Amen."

Karl Oskar seldom said his evening prayer any more; he usually was too tired after he went to bed. But as Kristina prayed and he listened, it might be for both of them. God must look kindly on a farmer in a stone country.

He turned over on his side to go to sleep, and Kristina felt for his hand, for she went to sleep sooner if she held it in her own.

They both lay quiet; Karl Oskar kept hold of his wife's hand. At her touch the desire of the body was awakened in him. He put his arm around her to pull her closer.

"No-oo, Karl Oskar, I do-on't know . . ." She struggled a little.

"What is it, Kristina?"

"I—I was thinking of the children."

"They are asleep, all three."

"I meant something else; I think of the food for the children."

"The food?"

She whispered close to his ear: "If we didn't—I thought—Then there wouldn't be any more."

There was a sense of shame in her voice. But now she had said it.

"If we didn't? For the rest of our whole lives? Is that what you mean?"

Kristina wondered herself what she meant. God created as many people as He desired; as many children as He decided were born. That she knew. But she knew this just as surely: if no man came near her, then she would bear no more children. It seemed as if in one way God decided, in another she herself could make the decision. The conflicting thoughts disturbed her.

Karl Oskar went on to say that he could not leave her alone when he had her next to him in bed during the night; no man who slept with his wife was built in such a way; at least not before he became so old that moss grew in his ears.

Kristina had no reply. No, she thought, they could not stay apart throughout life. She too had her desire, which she could not resist forever. But she would never fall so low as to let Karl Oskar know this.

He continued to seek her; he clasped her breasts, which swelled and hardened in his hands. Her own desire awakened. She opened up as a mollusk opens its shells; she gave in.

They were silent during their embrace, as they always were. In the moment of fulfillment she had entirely forgotten what she had said before.

About a month later Kristina knew that she was carrying her fifth child.

II

THE FARMHAND WHO
DROWNED IN THE MILL BROOK

1

Robert, Nils' and Marta's second son, was ten years younger than Karl Oskar. When he was little he had caused his parents a great deal of trouble by running away as soon as he was outside the house. He would disappear into the woodlands and they might spend hours looking for him among the junipers. They hung a cowbell round his neck so they could locate him, but even this did not always help, for they could not hear the tinkle when the child sat quietly. He did not change as he grew older: if he was not watched he would disappear into the woods and hide; if he was asked to do chores he might run away. And as the boy grew older they were ashamed to hang a bell on him as if he were an animal.

When his parents ceded Korpamoen, Robert was given employment during the summers as herdboy for Akerby *rote* (a *rote* is a parish district with common grazing rights, etc.). Thus there was one mouth less to be fed from the porridge bowl in the spare room. Robert received food from the farmers, and two daler a year in wages (fifty-eight cents). Every fall he received also a cheese and a pair of woolen stockings. He liked it well out in the wastelands, alone with the cattle. During the long summer days, while cows and sheep grazed lazily, he would lie on his back in some glade and stare into the heavens. He learned to whistle, and he sang without even thinking of it. Later, when his shepherd days were over, he realized why he had done these things: he had felt free.

For six weeks every year during three succeeding years he attended the school held by Rinaldo. Schooling came easily to him; the very first year he learned to read and write. Though Rinaldo had only one eye, he had seen more of this world than most of the parishioners with two. Once he had been as far away as Gothenburg, where he had seen the sea, and he told the children about his life's adventures. They enjoyed this more than the Little Catechism and the Biblical history put together.

The day Robert finished school he received a book as a gift from the schoolmaster. It was a *History of Nature*. Rinaldo said that when school days were finished, children seldom touched a book; but if they never improved their reading ability, they would soon lose it. He gave this book to Robert so that he might continue reading when he finished school.

The *History of Nature* was Robert's first possession. But for more than a year it happened that he didn't open his book. During the winter he attended confirmation class at the dean's, and also helped his brother Karl Oskar fell oaks. The oak timbers would later be brought to Karlshamn to be used for shipbuilding. They cut pines, too, the tallest in the forest, for masts on ships. While Robert helped with tree felling and the sawing of timbers which were to travel on the sea, he followed the ships-to-be in thought. The harbor town of Karlshamn was fifty miles away, and the peasants bringing timbers there needed two days and a night for the round trip. Robert thought that he would like to ride with the timbermen to Karlshamn in order to see the sea with his own eyes.

Nils and Marta churned and sold some ten pounds of butter from their own cow in order to raise money for a Bible to give their son at his first Communion. The Bible he received was bound in leather and cost one riksdaler and thirty-two shillings—the same amount as the price of a newborn calf. But it was a Bible that would stand wear and tear; the Holy Writ must be bound in leather to last a lifetime.

Robert now owned two books, one worldly and one religious. Rinaldo had said that all people ought to read these books—from one they learned about the body and all earthly things, from the other about the soul and things spiritual. The *History of Nature* contained all Robert needed to know about this world; the Bible, about the world hereafter.

But Robert was still in this world, and he must now go out and earn his living. His father made all the decisions for his minor son. Nils had arranged for him to serve one year as farmhand in Nybacken, about a mile from Korpamoen. But Robert did not wish to serve. He argued with his parents that he did not like to have a master; couldn't he somehow avoid the service in Nybacken?

Nils and Marta were disturbed to hear their younger son

speak thus, and reprimanded him soundly: What kind of poor
wretch was he, unwilling to work for food and clothing when
hale and hearty? Would he like to become one of the tramps
on the roads, or a beggar from the squatters' sheds in the
wastelands? Or did he want to remain at home, a burden to
his parents who lived but on reserved rights? And he soon
fifteen! He ought to be ashamed of himself! His sister Lydia
had been a maidservant for several years now. They were too
many here in Korpamoen; Karl Oskar could not feed him, he
could not afford a servant. Moreover, his father had hired
him to Aron in Nybacken, and received the earnest money,
according to the servant law—the contract could not be torn
up and changed. Aron was to pay good wages: the first year
Robert would receive thirty daler in money, one wadmal suit,
and one pair of short-legged boots. He should be pleased, and
he should also be thankful to his parents who had arranged
this service for him.

So one May morning in 1848, at sunup, Robert Nilsson left
his parental home to start his first service as farmhand. His
mother had made a bundle of his belongings, tied in a woolen
kerchief. She had gathered together his leather shoes, his
wadmal pants, one Sunday shirt, and one pair of Sunday
stockings. In one hand he carried the bundle, in the other
three books, the Bible, the *History of Nature,* and the prayerbook which his mother had given him. The books were
wrapped in paper so as not to become soiled.

It had rained during the night but now the sun shone down
on the village road. A wet odor rose from the meadows on
either side of the road where the rain had fallen on the fresh,
new grass. The birches had just burst into leaf and shone
green, and from the bushes came the twitter of birds at play.
But the boy who wandered along the road with his two bundles felt no joy in the beauty of the spring morning around
him. He was on his way to Nybacken, to begin the life of a
farmhand, but he had never been asked if he wanted to become a hired hand in Nybacken. He dreaded the confinement
of the service, he did not want to have a master. He was
walking on the road to Nybacken but he did not wish to arrive. Now that he was grown older he was being pushed out
from the home like a fledgling from the nest. He was the
younger son, one of those without portion. And still, he did

not envy his elder brother, who must poke between the
stones, burdened with worries about the mortgage interest.

Robert stopped as he reached the bridge over the mill
brook. What did it matter if he began his service half an hour
earlier or later, at five o'clock or half-past? There would be
ample time for work during the whole long year. He left the
road and sat down at the edge of the brook. He took off his
wooden shoes and his stockings and dangled his feet in the
water. The brook rushed by, swollen with the spring rains. At
last spring had come, and the water felt warm. It rippled
around his feet, it whirled and bubbled between his toes, and
he sat and watched it run away, passing by him, flowing
under the bridge and hastening farther on. He saw the white
bubbles of foam float on and disappear in the thicket of willows where the brook's bed made a curve. This water was
free; the water in the brook was not hired in Nybacken; it
needn't stay in the same place a whole year. It never remained in one place, it could travel anywhere. It could run all
the way down to the sea, and then the way was open around
the world, around the whole globe.

There would be no harm if he sat half an hour and
watched the brook, a last half-hour before he became a hired
hand.

In front of him in the creek bed there was a deep, black
pool near a large stone. In this pool he had once drowned a
cat, a gruesome memory. And there, beside the stone, a maid
from Nybacken had drowned a few years ago. She had not
drowned by will, she had slipped and fallen into the water as
she stood on the stone and rinsed washing. The stone was so
steep that she was unable to crawl up; her body was found in
the pool. On the stone they had seen marks made by her
fingernails: she had scratched and scraped with her nails, unable to get hold anywhere. Afterwards Robert had seen the
marks and he could never forget them; the scratches told him
of human terror at death.

A manservant could drown in that pool as well as a maid.
When a hired hand sank into the water of the brook, no service contract would hold, and no earnest money which the
servant had accepted on earth would have to be accounted
for. A drowned farmhand had no master.

Robert considered this.

He unfolded the paper around his books. His mother had laid a little myrtle branch between the leaves of the prayer-book, and the book opened where the green branch lay: "A Servant's Prayer."

"O Lord Jesus Christe, God's Son. You humbled Yourself in a servant's shape. . . . Teach me to fear and love You in my daily work, and to be faithful, humble, and devoted to my temporal lords in all honesty. . . . What worldly good may fall to me I leave all to Your mild and fatherly pleasure. Teach me only to be godly at all times, and satisfied, and I will gain sufficiency. . . . Let me also find good and Christian masters who do not neglect or mistreat a poor servant, but keep me in love and patience. . . ."

Through the myrtle branch between the leaves his mother spoke to the young servant: Read this prayer! And Dean Brusander required at the yearly examinations that farm-hands and maids should "so act in their poor situation that they could say by heart 'A Servant's Prayer.'"

But now Robert had in mind to read a piece from his *History of Nature*. He had turned the corner of the page and he found the place immediately:

"About the Size of the Sea:
"Many might wonder why the Creator has left so little space on the earth as home for man and beasts. For almost three-quarters of the earth's surface is covered by water. But he who learns to understand why water takes so much space shall therein see another proof of the Creator's omnipotence and kindness.

"These great bodies of water which surround the firm land on all sides, and which have salt water, are called Sea. . . ."

Robert looked up from his book. He thought of the sea which was three times bigger than the firm land on which he sat. No one owned the sea. But the land was divided in homesteads, in quarters, eighths, sixteenths, and the farmers owned them. The one who owned no land became a servant to a landowner.

He thought: On land there were many roads to follow. There were others besides the one which led to Nybacken. There was a parting of the ways close by, at the bridge over

the mill brook: the right one led to Nybacken, the left one
brought you to Abro mill—and if you continued on that road
you would never reach Nybacken.

If you turned to the left you could disappear from the
neighborhood. There were people who had disappeared from
the parish; their names were still in the church book, written
down under "End of the Parish." The dean called their names
at the yearly examination, and inquired about them. Every
year he called the name of the farmhand Fredrik Emanuel
Thron from Kvarntorpet; not heard from since 1833. Someone always answered that no one in the village knew where
he was. And the dean wrote about him in his book: Whereabouts unknown. This was repeated every year: Fredrik from
Kvarntorpet was not heard from. For fifteen years—the
whole span of Robert's life—the lost farmhand's whereabouts
had been unknown. This was the only thing Robert knew
about Fredrik Thron from Kvarntorpet, and because he knew
naught else he wondered about the lost one's fate.

It had happened before that a farmhand had disappeared,
had taken the wrong road.

When Robert was ready to pull on his stockings he missed
one of his wooden shoes. It had fallen into the brook; now it
floated on the water near the willow thicket, far out of reach.
He stood there, startled that his wooden shoe could float.
Now it caught on the branches of the willows where the brook
turned. The water gushed and swirled round the shoe and
Robert stood there and saw his own foot kick and splash; he
saw himself lying there, drowning in the brook.

What he had just now vaguely thought of had begun to
happen by itself. It only remained for him to complete it.

He stuffed his stockings into the remaining shoe and threw
it into the brook. Then he took off his jacket and let it follow
after and was pleased when he saw it float on the water. Then
he picked up his two bundles and went up on the bridge. At
the parting of the roads on the other side of the bridge he
turned to the left; he took the road that did not lead to Nybacken, he took the wrong road.

Caught on a branch of the big willow at the bend of the
brook there now could be seen a boy's little jacket. As the
running water in the brook swung the branches back and
forth, the arms of the jacket would wave to anyone passing
the bridge, telling what had become of the hired hand on his

way to Nybacken to begin his service: he had drowned in the mill brook, as the maid had done a few years earlier.

2

The ground under Robert's feet felt cold in the shadow of the wood: it was too early in the year to go barefooted. He had walked only a short distance when someone pulled up behind him. Robert prayed in his heart that it might be a timberman on his way to Karlshamn; then he would ask if he could ride with him. But it was only Jonas Petter of Hasteback, their nearest neighbor in Korpamoen, on his way to the mill with grain. He stopped. Yes, Robert could sit up on the sacks beside him and ride with him to Abro mill.

Robert crawled onto the wagon and sat down next to the farmer. Jonas Petter of Hasteback was a kind man: he did not ask where Robert was going; he said only that it was dangerous to walk barefooted so early in the spring. Robert answered that he walked easier without shoes and stockings. Apparently Jonas Petter had not noticed the jacket as he passed the bridge.

In the mill room at Abro there were already three farmers, waiting for their grind. They were unknown to Robert. He remained with them in the mill room, where it was nice and warm; a big fire burned in the stove, and the air smelled sweetly of flour and grain.

The peasants ate food which they had brought along and drank brannvin with it, and one of them gave Robert a slice of bread and a dram. He dunked the bread in the brannvin as children were wont to do, and he was a little conscious of this, now that he was almost grown.

The men had driven their grain wagons far alone, and now in company they were conversing loudly and noisily. Jonas Petter of Hasteback stretched himself full length on some empty sacks in front of the fire. He was a tall-grown man with fine black side whiskers.

Below the mill room the grindstones went their even pace and rumbled softly, like thunder at a distance; it was otherwise peaceful and quiet in here. Robert sat in front of the fire next to Jonas Petter. He was not going to work as a hired man, and his heart was light.

"We all remember old Axelina here at Abro," said Jonas Petter, "but does anyone remember how she got the mill and became the richest wench in the parish?"

The answers from the other peasants all were negative. No one had such a good memory as Jonas Petter; he knew all the old stories of the region, and now he must tell about Axelina, whom he remembered as the owner of the mill while he was still a youth.

She was an ingenious and clever woman, this Axelina. She came as a maid to Frans the Miller, who had owned the mill for many years and had had time to steal so much flour from the sacks that he had become as rich as ten trolls. At this time he was old and sickly, and Axelina made up her mind that she was to inherit from him. And now she went about it in the only way a woman can under such circumstances: she tried to inveigle him into carnal connections with her. In the evenings after he had gone to bed she would come into his room in her shift, and as often as she could she displayed her attractions. But Frans was played out, slow in the blood—no longer to be tempted.

One cold winter evening, however, as he returned from a Christmas party where he had drunk more brannvin than was good for him, he happened to fall into a snowdrift. When he did not turn up, Axelina took a lantern and went out to look for him. She found him frozen through and through. She helped him home, put him to bed, and gave him a pint of brannvin to revive his body warmth. Frans drank the brannvin but complained that he still felt cold. Then, said Axelina, she knew only one more remedy which could help him, and that one he probably wouldn't use. Frans was afraid he might contract a deadly sickness and he asked what kind of remedy she knew. Well, replied the maid, she must lie next to him and warm him with her own body. She had heard this was the best remedy against chills. Frans was a little startled, but he had drunk a lot of brannvin and said that if she believed she could help him in this way she might come and lie next to him. She would do it only to save his life, she insisted, and he must promise not to touch her. This he promised willingly— he had no such thoughts while shaking and shivering in his bed.

So Axelina lay down with her master, and she knew how to manage: it ended with the master and the maid being as close to each other as is possible. She used to say later that it took only half an hour until Frans the Miller lost the chills, and she could leave him.

Forty weeks after this happening Axelina bore a son who so much resembled Frans that no one needed to ask the father's name. Frans never forgave his maid who had taken advantage of him, and marriage between them was never talked of. But he was much attached to his boy, and when he died a few years later he left all he owned to the child, with a relative as guardian. Axelina did not get a penny.

However, the boy caught smallpox and died when he was four years old. Axelina then inherited from her son. She received the Abro mill and all Frans' other possessions, and became the richest woman in the parish: owner of more than forty thousand riksdaler. And she bragged later that she had earned it all in one half-hour, the half-hour when she lay in Frans the Miller's bed and warmed him after his exposure in the snow. Nor was it difficult work—she had lain quite still. No woman in the whole world, not even a queen or an empress, had earned so great an hourly pay as Axelina in her master's bed that evening.

Yes, said Jonas Petter, and sighed, women could earn easy money if they liked: only to lie quite still.

Robert stared at Jonas Petter; he always told such unkind stories about women. It was said that he did this because he himself was tormented by a wicked wife. The couple in Hasteback lived so ill together, and quarreled so loudly, that people could stand on the road outside the house and hear every word they said; horses had become frightened and bolted from the hubbub. It sometimes happened that Jonas Petter had to sleep in a stall in the byre because he could not sleep within the same four walls where his wife Brita-Stafva slept.

Robert stretched out on the floor before the fire and contemplated the cracked, sooty beams in the ceiling of the mill room. Again he thought of the farmhand who had chosen the left road instead of the right one.

Presently he asked Jonas Petter: "Do you remember Fredrik of Kvarntorpet who disappeared from home?"

"Fredrik Thron? Yes, I remember him, that cuckoo!"

He was a rascal, continued Jonas Petter. He was as lazy as a well-fed Christmas pig, and would rather steal than work. If anything was lost it was easy to know who had found it. Fredrik stole for pleasure rather than gain, but in either case it was unpleasant for the loser. And he was given to all kinds of pranks: he broke down gates, let the horses out of the church stables while people were in church, brought snakes into the church on Sundays. Every farmer in the parish was disgusted with the knave from Kvarntorpet.

The boy's father was a cotter under the manse, and he had persuaded the owner, Lieutenant Rudeborg, to hire his son as a farmhand and try to make a man of him. When Fredrik had been in Krakesjo for a week, he was asked by the lieutenant to fetch a pair of oxen bought at the Klintakrogen fair. They were fine animals, well broken in, and a child could have driven them this short distance with a loose thong. But Fredrik, who was twenty, could not manage it; he arrived at the manse with another pair. The lieutenant had never seen these animals before; the ones he had bought had measured seventy-eight inches around the chest, and now his farmhand brought a pair of steers measuring hardly sixty-six. These animals were not worth half the price he had paid for the oxen at the fair. Lieutenant Rudeborg was in a red-hot rage at his new man.

On the way home from the fair Fredrik had done some trading of his own, and had exchanged the master's oxen for the smaller ones—with money in his own pocket, of course. But the damned fool swore up and down that these were the same beasts he had received: their color was identical, red with a white spot on the forehead. Fredrik was clever. These looked somewhat smaller, he admitted, but they had shrunk because they had been without fodder the whole day—that was all, they were indeed the same oxen.

Nevertheless, Lieutenant Rudeborg had witnesses who said the animals were not his, so Fredrik couldn't wriggle himself free that time. Rudeborg, however, felt sorry for the boy's parents. He didn't want to put his servant in jail, but he couldn't stand the sight of the fellow. He therefore suggested to his neighbors that they send Fredrik to North America; he would pay half the fare if they chipped in and paid the other half.

That country would suit Fredrik perfectly, said the lieuten-

ant. America was a land for all rogues and misfits who could
not live in law and order at home. Out there he could trade
oxen with other villains to his heart's content. If he remained
at home and they put him into prison, he would be on their
hands again as soon as his sentence was over. But once in
North America, they would be rid of him for time and eternity.

The farmers quite willingly contributed a couple of riksdaler each to free themselves from Thron's boy, who had
been such a nuisance to them. So the money was collected, he
was put on the coach at Klintakrogen, and Lieutenant Rudeborg even came down in person to see that his scoundrel servant started off to North America.

A few months passed by and all was well. No mischief was
heard of and everyone said this was the wisest thing they had
ever done—to send Fredrik to North America.

But one day the news spread that the American traveler
was home in Kvarntorpet again.

He had never boarded the ship for North America. He had
gone only as far as Gothenburg, and in Gothenburg he had
remained the whole time. There he had stayed at an inn, and
had drunk and caroused and lived like a lord as long as the
money lasted. When it was spent he returned home, and now
this debased youth looked honest people in the face as if expecting them to be happy to see him back again in good
health. He had put on weight and he looked fine. On the
money he had received from honest folk he had lived in idleness, gluttony, and debauchery. And the rogue said that if you
wanted to live well you should not work. He was so shameless
that he went around the village and thanked people for their
contributions toward the journey, saying he had used them as
well as he could, he had had much pleasure. And if they
should have it in mind again, he would be most willing to undertake another American journey. He had always longed to
get out and see the world, it was so useful and instructive for
a person. And this parish was a dirty little hole not at all
befitting decent, sensible people. He hoped that the contributions next time would be sufficient to take him a bit farther
on his voyage to America.

By now people were so angry at the inveterate scamp from
Kvarntorpet that they spit at him whenever they saw him.
Evil was within him, and it "inclined him to evil, and disinc-

lined him to good," as it is written. And Lieutenant Rudeborg, who had paid half his American fare and himself seen
him board the Gothenburg coach, had no mercy on him this
time: he reported him to the sheriff for theft of the oxen.
However, when Lonnegren arrived at Kvarntorpet to fetch
Fredrik, he had disappeared, and the authorities had not been
able to lay hands on him since.

"That's fifteen years ago, now. No one here has seen Fredrik since that time. They say he took to the sea," Jonas Petter concluded.

Angry words were mumbled by the peasants as the farmer
from Hasteback finished his tale. Probably, thought Robert,
some of them had contributed toward Fredrik's American
journey at the Gothenburg tavern..

A few words in Jonas Petter's story had especially impressed Robert and he pondered them: the lieutenant from
Krakesjo had said that a land existed which fitted all those
who misbehaved at home.

If one disappeared from one's service and from the
neighborhood, one was written down under "End of the
Parish." He could hear the dean call a name at the examination next autumn: Farmhand Robert Nilsson from Korpamoen. No one present knows where he is. And the dean
writes: Whereabouts unknown. So it would be written next
year, and the following. And ten years, fifteen years later the
dean would still write in the church book about the farmhand
Robert Nilsson: Whereabouts unknown. Not heard from since
1848. For all time it would appear about him in "End of the
Parish": Whereabouts unknown.

It was thus written about those who were free.

How many miles might it be to North America? He dared
not ask anyone present, they might begin to wonder about
him. Perhaps he could learn from some book.

But America was the land for one who had taken the
wrong road.

3

Robert became drowsy from the heat in the mill room and
from the monotonous din of the millstones; he went to sleep

on some empty sacks in a corner. It was late afternoon when he awoke. Jonas Petter and the other peasants were gone with their grind, and in their place two other farmers who had arrived were waiting for their flour and eating their provisions. They no doubt thought Robert was a farmhand who was waiting for his grind. And one of them noticed that he had no food and handed him a slice of bread and a piece of pork.

The same farmer told about a death which had occurred that very morning: a young farmhand on his way to service in Nybacken had drowned in the mill creek. It appeared he had fallen off the bridge. They had found his jacket, and Aron of Nybacken had dragged the pool, but his body had not yet been recovered. Strangely enough, a maid from Nybacken had drowned in the same pool a few years ago.

The farmer also knew that the drowned servant was son to Nils in Korpamoen. He was only recently confirmed. As a child he had been somewhat peculiar: he would run away from home, and his parents had been forced to hang a cowbell around his neck to locate him.

A young person's sudden death—a horrible occurrence, the farmer sighed. He added that fortunately the victim was old enough to have received the Lord's Holy Supper, so one might hope he was now with his Saviour in eternal bliss.

The last bite of bread stuck in Robert's windpipe; he coughed for a moment: the same man who had given him the bread believed he deserved a blissful heaven. He was a kind man, he must be thanked sometime.

Here at the mill Robert felt he might be recognized any moment; he must remain here no longer.

He knew in which direction he must go: he wanted to reach Karlshamn, the town by the sea; he must reach the sea.

He intended to ask if perchance anyone of the peasants came from the southern part of the parish; perhaps he could get a ride part of the way. But just as he opened his mouth to ask, the miller himself came into the room, covered from head to foot with white flour dust. He seemed to be looking for someone; he eyed Robert sharply.

"Are you Nils of Kopramoen's son?"

As he looked closer he added: "You're barefooted, and you haven't any jacket. You must be the one."

It was too late to ask for a ride.

"Your master is here. He heard about you from the other farmers."

Up the steps into the mill room came a big man with thick, fox-red hair covering his forehead. His cheeks were smooth and shone as if greased with pork fat, and he had small, piercing eyes. It was Aron of Nybacken.

Robert crawled backwards into his corner.

Aron smiled with a broad grin as he espied the lost farmhand.

"Well, well, if it isn't my boy, that little helper of mine!"

And he extended his hands toward Robert, a pair of hands covered with long, coarse, red hair. They were heavy and rough as gnarled birch clubs, they were the biggest hands Robert had ever seen. And they were fastened to a pair of powerful arms, the arms of Aron of Nybacken; they hung from the man who was his master.

Robert tried to pull himself into his shirt, into his trousers, he wanted to become small, so small that the master could not get hold of him, could not see him.

But Aron sounded very kind now, his voice was mild and soft as sweet cream: "Too bad you lost your way! My little boy, you didn't find Nybacken this morning—now I'll show you the way. Outside the coach awaits you."

And he stretched out his big hand and grabbed the boy by the shoulder.

"Pick up your bundles and come."

Robert walked out of the mill room followed by the farmer. He was hired according to law, he was bound to the man who had the biggest hands he had ever seen.

Outside the mill stood the horse and wagon from Nybacken, and here the master and the hired hand were alone. Aron got a good hold of Robert's ear, while his broad smile vanished: So-o, the little farmhand was of that sort of wool! So, he wanted to run away, did he! And he had tried to make people believe he had drowned! And had caused his master great trouble—the whole morning had been spent in dragging for the lost farmhand! Now, in the midst of the most pressing time of spring! So he was of that ugly breed that wanted to leave his service before he began it! Was it in this way that the little hired man honored his father and mother and revered and obeyed his masters? His poor parents had today mourned him as drowned and dead, tomorrow they would be

ashamed of him as living. He was confirmed and grown, but
he couldn't walk a mile from home without disappearing. He,
Aron, would tell his parents they must still hang the cowbell
on their boy before they let him leave home.

"You've earned a good thrashing, my little hired fellow.
But I shall let you off with a small box on the ear."

And he gave his servant a box on the ear.

Robert was pushed backwards against the wagon wheel,
and the world around him shook for half a minute, but he did
not fall. The master's hand could no doubt have hit him much
harder, Aron could have given him a real box on the ear.
Robert could hear, and he understood: it was only a small
box he had received.

And so the farmhand rode back with his master, the whole
stretch of road he shouldn't have taken this morning, the
whole road wrongly followed.

And when they arrived at the bridge over the mill brook,
where in the morning he had taken the left road, the wagon
now followed the right one.

So ended the day when Robert Nilsson tried to take his first
steps on the road to America.

III

WHAT THE BEDBUGS IN A STABLE ROOM MUST LISTEN TO

1

The farmstead Nybacken had a master and mistress, plus an
old mistress on reserved rights, three maids in the maids'
room, and two farmhands in the stable room. Aron's hired
men lived in the barn next to the horses' stalls. Their room
had a deal table, a bench for each of them, two beds filled
with straw, and a horse blanket each. In walls and beds lived
bedbugs in great numbers, and they increased in undisturbed
bliss, filling all holes and cracks.

Arvid, the elder farmhand, was grown, and sturdy and
strong of limb, although a light, silky boy-beard still covered

his chin. He had a reddish skin and old frostbites on his nose, which bled in cold weather. Aron called him his big hand; Robert was his little hand.

Arvid seemed slow of speech and shy with people, but the very first evening after they had gone to bed on their straw bundles in the stable room Robert began to ask his comrade in service about the master and mistress. What kind of place was Nybacken for a servant?

Before he went to sleep that night Robert had obtained from the elder boy a fair picture of their situation: Aron was hot-tempered, and if he became angry he might give his hands a box on the ear or a kick in the pants. Otherwise he was really a kind, decent soul who would harm no one. The mistress was less considerate: she hit the maids, and her husband as well, and Aron was afraid of her and dared not hit back. Both master and mistress were afraid of the wife's mother, the old mistress who lived in a "reserved room" in the attic. She was so old she should have been in her grave long ago, if the devil had attended to his business; but apparently he too was afraid of her.

The service was demanding because the master was lazy; the hired men had to do nearly all the chores. The food wasn't restricted in good years and they could eat as much bread as they wished. During lean years the farmhands and the maids must live on what they could get, here as everywhere else.

It was salt herring at every second meal—but in many places they had to eat herring every meal the year round, except Christmas Eve, and in many places the mistress herself cut the bread and portioned out the slices. So you couldn't complain about the fare in Nybacken. Of course, it might happen that the bread was mildewed, the herring rancid, the milk blue sour, and the cheese rat-eaten, so they could see the marks of the small teeth. But only once had they found rat-dirt in the flour porridge; Aron himself had picked out the small black pebbles. Arvid had served at other farms where the bread was nearly always mildewed, the herring always rancid, the milk always sour, and neither the mistress nor the master had bothered to pick out the rat-dirt from the porridge. So one need not belittle the fare at Nybacken, he said.

So much the "little hand" learned from the big one during the first evening. And every evening thereafter Robert tumbled into bed tired and exhausted, and slept like a gopher in his hole, unconscious even of the biting bedbugs, until morning came and Aron awakened him, shaking him by the shoulders: "My little hired man, hurry on up! It's four o'clock! My little hand, you know idleness is perdition! Don't lie there and be lazy. Hurry up to your work!"

Arvid was accustomed to the ways of the farm, and when he said that the service was hard he might as well have said it was hard to harness a horse or to carry a bucket of water.

Robert was the youngest on the farm, and all had chores for him to do: Aron, the mistress, the old mistress, the maids. All lorded it over him, sent him hither and yon, corrected him, hurried him, scolded him. Everyone on the farm was his master. Even the animals: the farm's four horses needed constant attention. He had to get up early in the morning to fill their mangers with fodder, in the evening he must fill them again before going to bed. And the horses must be curried, they must have their stalls cleaned, hay must be brought down from the loft for them, oats fetched from the granary, fodder cut in the barn, and water carried from the well. Robert lived his farmhand's life in close quarters with horses, smelling horses, horse manure, horse sweat, leather and harness. Sundays and weekdays alike, the horses required attention.

The animals were bound in their stalls and the farmhands were bound to the animals. And the service year of a hired hand was three hundred and fifty-eight days, discounting his one free week a year.

During the very first week of his service at Nybacken Robert made the decision that h~ must escape from all his masters, human as well as animal.

2

The little hand who was bossed by all had good ears and quick eyes. He listened to and observed all that happened on the farm, and picked up its secrets. He heard all insinuations, he saw all winking eyes, as when there were hints and whispers about the white heifer which had been butchered at Nybacken last fall; a fine heifer—ready to calve—had gone to the slaughter bench because Aron dared not let her live. Why dared he not let her live?

Robert collected one word here, another there: *The white heifer was with calf without having been with a bull.* It was said to have happened that cows had borne calves with human heads and faces—horrible monsters, half beast, half man. That was why they had slaughtered the white heifer before her calving time was near.

Robert now wondered how the heifer had become pregnant without having been with a bull. It was answered, he had better ask Arvid. No one but Arvid knew, and he could surely give information.

So he learned gradually that the farm folk were directing a horrible accusation against his comrade in service.

Nothing was ever said in the open, everything was half said. All sentences ended in the middle, they were broken off as soon as they touched the accusation itself. The maids whispered and tittered; no one could speak aloud about such things. Robert asked, and he too made a half sentence: "Did they accuse Arvid of . . . ?" No—no one accused Arvid of anything; but anyone wanting to know more must go to him; he was the only person who knew the truth about the white heifer. They repeated only what the old mistress had said.

It had all originated with the old woman in the reserved room in the attic. One day last summer she had happened to see Arvid drive the white heifer into the cow barn. It was in the middle of the day, no other person was in the byre, no one had asked the hired man to drive in the heifer, and she could not understand why the animal should be taken into its stall at that hour. The old mistress had seen nothing more, nothing more than this: Arvid had driven the animal into the stable. She had not accused him of any forbidden or horrible deed with the heifer, she had merely said this to the maids: what he did with the white heifer in her stall, only he and God knew.

The old mistress had said no more than she could stand by.

From the time he was a little boy Robert had gone with his father when he brought cows to the bull, and when he was herdboy he had more than once seen a bull and cow mate. There was nothing unusual about that, he knew how animals acted and he could imagine how people acted. But he couldn't imagine people and animals together, not a man and a cow together—he did not believe his roommate guilty of the horrible deed.

Only God and Arvid knew how the white heifer had gotten with calf . . . it was the old mistress who had started the ugly rumor, and the maids had believed it. They treated Arvid as if he were leprous, they pulled away from him quickly if they happened to touch him, and they refused to be left alone with him. Furthermore, the rumor about the farmhand in Nybacken and the white heifer had begun to spread through the neighborhood, and other girls now shunned Arvid. For a while he had gone visiting with a maid on the neighboring farm; now he was unable to see her. No one wanted to have anything to do with a youth accused of so shameful a deed.

Robert could not make himself speak to his friend about the horrible accusation, but he knew Arvid was aware of its existence. Arvid had earlier been cheerful and sociable, lately he had become morbidly shy of people, and taciturn. One could easily understand why.

After having been in service for one month Robert asked leave to visit his parents in Korpamoen one Sunday, but was refused. The master had not yet sufficient confidence in his little hand to allow him away from the farm. Arvid said that perhaps Aron thought he would go home and complain about the service and belittle his master. And now Robert learned that his elder comrade had not been away from the premises in half a year, though his parents' home was only three miles distant. But Robert understood why he kept away from people: no one accused of connection with a heifer would wish to show himself more than necessary. It was a loathsome accusation if true, and still more loathsome if untrue.

Aron said that Robert would have no free days during the year because he had failed to report on time and had had to be fetched to service by the master. He also wondered why his little hand need run home to his mother: did he still nurse?

A hired man was no suckling; he could not leave the farmstead without permission of the master.

But the farmhands in Nybacken had some free moments in the stable room during Sunday afternoons in summer, when the horses were let out to graze and needed neither fodder, water, nor rubbing down. Then Robert brought forth his *History of Nature* and read aloud to his friend.

Arvid had attended school only two weeks, and had never

learned to read. He pretended he could; he would take the *History of Nature* and stare into the book with a thoughtful, studied expression as if reading. After a suitable time had elapsed he would turn the page slowly and seriously, as if he had deeply considered its contents. The same was repeated with the next page. But Robert had caught him once holding the book upside down.

Arvid did not "read" for very long, he complained it hurt his eyes; the words in the book were so small and crooked that they were hard to see; his eyes never had been strong; after reading for a while they began to smart as if he had been looking into a fire. He had had to stop school, he said, because his eyes were so poor.

And so he handed the *History of Nature* to Robert. "You read! Your eyes can stand it."

So the elder servant pretended that he could read, and the younger one pretended that he believed him.

And Robert read aloud from the *History of Nature*, about the air and the water, about the animals and the plants, about crocodiles and rattlesnakes, about silkworms and butterflies, sea lions and flying fish, spice trees and coffee bushes, about hot deserts and polar seas, about leaf lice and planets, about geysers and volcanoes. Arvid learned about all the amazing objects and phenomena which existed on the globe but which he had never seen. And when Robert closed the book, Arvid said what a pity he couldn't read as much as he wanted to, because of his poor eyes; his sight was good otherwise, but it was of little value when it came to words in a book.

Now, among all the foods in the world, Arvid liked rice porridge best. Rice porridge he could enjoy only once a year —at Yuletide. One Sunday Robert was reading about rice in the *History of Nature*. As he finished, Arvid said: "Read it again!"

Robert read:

"*About Rice*.

"Rice is a grain which is grown in unbelievable quantities in warm countries. The shelled seeds are shipped to us and are then called rice grains. From them is cooked with milk the white and delicious sweet porridge. The best rice comes from Carolina in North America. . . ."

Arvid listened with open mouth, dreaming his thoughts of sweet porridge. It was almost half a year to Christmas; between now and the plate of rice porridge were many hundred salt herrings which he must eat; Aron had lately been to Karlshamn and had brought home a barrel of herring, and they were expected to reach the bottom of it before the sweet white porridge would be cooked.

Robert went on with a new chapter:

"*About Sugar Cane*
"Nearly all sugar consumed in our country is made from sugar cane; this is a tall grass, eight to ten feet high, which grows in warm countries like the East Indies and America. . . ."

The elder farm boy scratched the back of his neck where there were a few fresh bites from last night's bedbugs. Then he looked out through the window, thoughtfully. A land existed where both rice and sugar grew, both the grain and the sweetening for the porridge. But he knew this was far away in the world, separated from his country by a great water. Neither he nor Robert had seen any greater bodies of water than the tarns here in the parish, and these were so small that a man could row around the shores in an hour. Arvid began to wonder about the sea which separated this country from America.

Suddenly, as if he had spoken too himself, he asked: "I wonder how broad the ocean might be?"

Robert looked up, startled. He could have answered the question, he could have told Arvid many things pertaining to the ocean. But he carried a secret which he guarded well; he must act wisely and carefully, he must not confide in anyone, not even his comrade in service.

Thus, on Sundays, Arvid and Robert sat there, looking out through the single window of their stable room. The small panes were spotted and unwashed, in the corners were cobwebs filled with dead flies, the whitewash on the sash had long ago disintegrated. A dirty, small, poor window let in the light to the hired men in Nybacken. But through this window they could see out into the world, they could look across the stable yard and see the farmland beyond, they could see the village road that passed by. And beyond their eyes' reach their thoughts struggled further, their thoughts ventured on roads never traveled, down to a sea never seen, and across the waters of the ocean.

One of them had made his decision, and he was the first in the parish to do so.

3

Arvid drew part of his pay in brannvin from the farm's still. One Saturday evening as the boys were sitting in their stable room after the day's toil Arvid brought out his keg, which had just been filled by Aron, and offered a drink to his friend. Robert had not yet learned to drink brannvin alone; he still dunked bread in it. In order to please Arvid he accepted a mug and drank it, and afterward he felt as if a juniper twig was stuck in his throat.

Aron had today mentioned that the yearly catechism examination would be held at Nybacken, and Arvid, who last year had been strongly reprimanded by the dean because he was unable to recite the Fourth Commandment, anticipated this day with apprehension.

"The dean asked who our masters were and I couldn't answer," he said.

"Our masters are all those who by God's ordinance are placed over us in the *home*, in the *state*, at *school*, and at the *place where we work*," Robert recited glibly.

"Oh, Jesus!" Arvid stared with admiration at his young friend, who gloated in his display of superior knowledge.

"God has given our parents and masters power over us so that they as God's servants may take fatherly care of us, and each in his station watch over our true welfare. Let every soul be subject unto the higher powers. For there is no power but of God: the powers that be are ordained by God. Wilt thou then not be afraid of the power? Do that which is good, and thou shalt have praise of the same."

"God Almighty!" exclaimed Arvid, and in his amazement he drank so much from his brannvin mug that he choked.

Robert could rattle off the old lessons indefinitely. He could also teach a little to his friend. "Do you know how many superiors and masters we have, Arvid? In the whole world, I mean."

"No-o."

Robert held up his right hand and counted on his fingers. For every lord and master he bent one finger. First was the King, then the Governor, below the King; the third was the Crown Sheriff, who came under the Governor. The fourth was Sheriff Lonnegren, and the fifth was the sheriff's hired man. The sixth was the dean, their spiritual authority, and the seventh their own master, Aron of Nybacken. The sheriff watched over them to see that they remained in their place of service, the dean watched over them at the yearly examinations, Aron watched over them to see that they worked and earned their pay. There were seven superiors and masters in all.

"Jesus Christ! What a lot of masters!"

"Now you can name them to the dean at the examination," said Robert.

"I'll try to remember." And Arvid began to count on his own fingers: "The King, the first master . . . What is his name?"

Robert explained: The King who by God's ordinance sat on the thrones of Sweden and Norway was named Oskar I, and through him all other authority derived.

He went through the list of masters with his comrade many times, and at last Arvid could name all those seven who according to God's ordinance had fatherly power over them.

After a time Robert tired of this holding school; he had drunk several mugs of brannvin and he felt drowsy; he undressed and crawled under the horse blanket. Arvid sat alone with the keg in front of him; he continued to drink; he had drunk more often of late. The stable lantern, swinging from a nail on the wall, spread a dim light over the room. From the other side of the wall could be heard the puffing of the horses and the sound of horseshoes against the stable floor. The hunters of the night—the bedbugs—emerged from their cracks and holes and hurried on their way to suck blood.

Robert went to sleep with the odor of brannvin in his nose.

Suddenly he was awakened by a noise. He had been asleep only a short time. The lantern on the wall was still lit, the door was open and banged in the gusty wind; the sound of it had awakened him. But Arvid was not in his bed, he had vanished.

Robert shook the keg on the table: it was empty. He was seized with anxiety for his friend.

Quickly he pulled on his trousers and hurried into the stable yard. Outside, in the clear moonlight, he could make out someone moving near the door of the woodshed. He went closer: it was Arvid, leaving the shed, staggering. He had an ax in his hand.

"What are you up to?"

Arvid weaved back and forth, his breath came quickly, his head was bare, his tousled hair blowing in all directions, and his mouth wide open. His upper lip was thick and swollen, his cheek bloody; he had fallen and hurt himself. In the moonlight his eyes were bloodshot and staring. From the woodshed he had fetched the heavy wedge ax.

"Are you going to split wood? In the middle of the night?"

"No . . . not wood . . . Something else."

"Are you walking in your sleep?"

"Someone . . . someone is going to die . . . now, tonight."

"Arvid!"

"The old mistress is going to die tonight."

"Arvid! Put back the ax!"

Arvid was drunk and apparently unconscious of his actions. His eyes were flaming, burning with rage. Robert shouted: "Drop the ax!"

"I'll kill the bitch!"

"You're crazy!"

"I'll split her snout, the old sow!"

"Arvid, please . . . please . . ."

"She's ruined my life. She must die!"

And Arvid staggered off toward the house.

Robert ran after. He grabbed his comrade by the arm, seizing the ax handle. "Arvid, please . . ."

"Let go the ax!"

"Listen to me. You'll ruin your whole life."

"It's ruined already."

"But listen, you don't know what you're doing!"

"Let go the ax, I say. Let go!"

The two farmhands fought over the ax. Robert was afraid

he might cut himself on the sharp edge; and Arvid was bigger and stronger and soon had the ax away from him. But Arvid's legs were unsteady from all the brannvin, and he slipped and fell on his back, dropping his weapon to the ground. Quickly Robert snatched it, unnoticed by Arvid, and threw it as far away as he was able; it fell among the gooseberry bushes near the barn. Arvid turned over and felt among the debris, searching for the ax. Robert tried to talk sense to him: "We're friends. I want to help you. Please, Arvid."

And soon the drunken man calmed down; he no longer searched for the ax, he only repeated, again and again: "I'm so unhappy . . . so unhappy . . ."

Robert was frightened by the rage which had come to the surface so suddenly in his good-natured comrade. He shivered in the cold wind, and from the fright he had experienced.

"I'm cold. Let's go to bed now."

And after a time he was able to persuade Arvid to go back into the stable room. The drunken man threw himself full length onto his bed; all his strength seemed to have left him; he lay there, limp and exhausted, and kept mumbling, "At times I feel like killing her . . . that devil's bitch in the attic."

Robert thought it best to leave his comrade alone until he grew more calm. And presently Arvid's stupor began to wear off and his head cleared. He sat up in his bed and his voice was normal as he asked: "Do you know what she accuses me of?"

"Ye-es."

"Hm . . . I thought so. It's the old bitch's evil invention—all of it! You know that, don't you?"

"I know that, Arvid."

The elder boy mumbled something incoherent, then said nothing for a time; apparently he was sleeping. But suddenly he sat up and continued, and now he seemed fully to have regained his senses. He had never done anything horrible or forbidden with the white heifer. If this were his deathbed and he were unable to say aught else, this he would say to the dean, to the sheriff, to the authorities—to all people on earth he would say this: he had never mixed with any animal. The old woman had said that only God and he knew what he had done with the white heifer in the barn. And God in His Heaven knew that he, Arvid, was innocent. But what joy did he get from this when people thought him guilty, when people believed he had done it?

Robert didn't know how to reply, except to say that he himself had never believed the accusation.

Moreover, said Arvid, the heifer had not been with calf, it was a lie, a lie which the hag in the attic had invented, long after the heifer had been butchered. The heifer would never have calved any monster with a human head if she had been spared.

"Why don't you sue the old woman in court?"

Yes, Arvid had thought of clearing himself that way, but he was afraid of the court; he didn't like to have to stand there, gaped at by all people; and the rumor might spread still worse if it were brought to the county court and the old woman found not guilty—after all, she had never accused him outright, she had only said that God and he alone knew what he had done.

Robert had seldom seen her outside the house, the little woman in the gray shawl and the black kerchief, a shriveled-up creature who didn't seem to have the strength to hurt a fly. Yet she had ruined Arvid's life, a terrible injustice had been done to him. Why couldn't God, Who was omnipotent, reveal the truth, so Arvid could be cleared?

"Do you know what they call me?" asked Arvid.

"No."

"Listen . . ."

Walking along the road the other day he had met some boys who mocked him. He had heard their words—something about the bull in Nybacken. They referred to *him*. People called him "The Bull of Nybacken."

They were silent again in the stable room. Robert felt sudden twitches in his eyes; he understood why his comrade had filled his brannvin keg so often of late.

Arvid resumed, and now his voice trembled. He was called the Bull. No wonder all women shunned him, no wonder the girls shied away from him. Who would want to be seen in the company of one called the Bull? And he would always be referred to by that name, although he had not harmed man or animal. He had tried to endure it, but the loathsome name would cling to him forever; he would be treated as fool and scoundrel, an outcast whom people would abhor. He could show himself nowhere in this countryside.

So Robert could understand why he went out and got the ax.

Arvid lay down again, but his body shook: he cried. He cried silently, his whole frame shaking. He lay so for some time.

By now Robert knew enough: Arvid could not bear being called the Bull of Nybacken; indeed, no one in his predicament could endure to remain in the neighborhood. Anyone suffering what Arvid did must move away.

And so Robert knew also what he must do: he must confide in his friend.

The next evening he disclosed his secret. The two farmhands sat as usual on their beds, ready to retire, alone in the stable room. Everyone on the farmstead slept. But Robert acted as if Sheriff Lonnegren had been standing outside the window listening to them. He moved over to Arvid's bed and sat down close to him; he spoke in whispers although no living being could hear him, except his friend and the bedbugs in their cracks and hiding places. And now he uncovered his criminal intentions: "I carry a heavy secret, Arvid. You're the only one I'll confide in. Can I rely on you?"

"If my head is chopped off for it I shall say nothing!"

They shook hands, and the younger one unburdened himself: he intended to escape from service. But this time he would not act as foolishly as he had done in the spring on entering service. He would wait till fall, when they carried oak timbers to Karlshamn. He could drive now, and he would no doubt have to join the timbermen, driving Aron's old mare. But once Aron had let him out of sight with the beast he would never see him again: the mare would return alone to Nybacken. By that time the driver would be far away. In Karlshamn he would board a ship which was to sail to North America—to the New World.

"Are you coming along, Arvid? You'll get rid of your name —the Bull."

Arvid found nothing to say; he just stared, such was his surprise; he could only look at his comrade, this fifteen-year-old boy so recklessly plotting to escape with his master's timber load—a daredevil planning to venture the ocean!

For Arvid knew nothing of what had transpired in Robert's mind since that day in spring when he had taken the wrong road at the bridge over the mill creek, on his way to service.

And Robert had discovered something which had helped him along on this road; he now took from its secret hiding place—under the straw of his bed—a little book in narrow, brown-specked covers and gold-stamped back: *Description of the United States of North America.*

Here was his secret help; through this book he had obtained all the information he needed.

When Robert worked on the dunghill with his manure fork, when he carried his scythe at harvest-time, when he stood in the hayrick or chopped straw in the barn, when he sat here in the room and looked out through the window—always his thoughts carried him across the sea. And little by little another land arose on the other shore. Like a flower which sprouts in black soil, puts forth buds and opens its crown, so that land grew in his imagination. By now he had crossed the ocean and become familiar with the land beyond: America.

There were two worlds—nature's world and the Bible's world, this world and the coming world. But *this* world was again divided into two parts: an old and a new. His home was in the Old World, in the world that was frail, worn-out, and full of years. Its people were worn-out, decrepit, old and weak and finished. In their ancient villages time stood still; in their old moss-grown cottages nothing happened which had not happened before; the children obeyed their parents and imitated them, and did the same thing again which their parents had done before them. The Old World could not go on for many years more; it would not be long before it tumbled and fell with all the decrepit people who lived there.

But far away, on the other side of the globe, there was a New World, recently discovered, recently settled. The New World was young and fresh, and full of splendor and riches beyond imagination. And those who had emigrated and settled there were young and swift and nimble people whose whole lives lay ahead of them. The New World was populated by the most daring and the most intelligent people from the Old World: by those who had left their lords and masters behind them. It was populated by all those who wanted to be free, who did not want to serve under masters. To the New World all those emigrated who at home were poor and oppressed, all those who were harrassed and suffering, the destitute and those full of sorrow, the hunted ones and those full of despair.

The one who was not satisfied with his lot in the Old World moved to the New World. America was the right land for Robert—and for Arvid!

4

When Rinaldo had held his school at Nybacken in the spring, Robert had asked him if he knew of some book with a truthful description of North America. The schoolmaster said he had recently seen such a book advertised in the newspaper *Barometern* for forty-eight shillings—one riksdaler—including postage. Rinaldo ordered the book for Robert, and advanced him the price until such time as the boy should receive his pay. The schoolmaster helped him willingly: Robert was his only pupil who read books of his own free will.

Robert had since—in his room during the summer nights—read the *Description of the United States of North America* three times over from cover to cover. It was written for simple uneducated folk who intended to emigrate to the New World. And it assured readers, even on the first page, that it was a true description: it said that to the innocent and the ignorant much of the contents might seem unbelievable, exaggerated, fabulous, but all was clear, clean, beautiful truth. Nothing was changed, added, or fabricated; all was set down in honesty.

Robert knew the most important chapters by heart, or almost by heart, and now Arvid could get all the information he wanted about the New World. The little farmhand related the facts, and the big one listened. There were in Sweden people of the ruling classes who spread lies about the United States of America. They said that the country was fit only for scamps. The lieutenant in Krakesjo had sent over Fredrik of Kvarntorpet, who was ill-liked in the parish (only Fredrik had turned back at Gothenburg). The lieutenant had maintained that mostly bandits, rascals, thieves, and other evil people lived in America. But this was a lie. The Americans were honest and upright in their doings and dealings, they were neat and clean in their homes and in their appearance, they were brave, generous, helpful, and moral. Of course, among them was an occasional evildoer. It was also a lie that America was so unbearably hot that only Indians, Negroes, and the heathen could endure the climate. People from the Old World could breathe the air, eat the food, and drink the water; no one suffocated or was poisoned. In the most healthy places the Indians lived to so ripe an age that they didn't die in the same way as people did here at home: they dried up and shrank in their old age, and became so light that they blew away and disappeared into the air. But what the masters kept secret was that the people of the New World were not divided into gentry and ordinary folk, as was the case in the kingdom of Sweden. In America no one had precedence over anyone else, for all were equals. Emperors and kings were forbidden; the Americans tolerated no masters; one need neither bow nor curtsy, because there was no one to bow or curtsy to. And no false pride existed among Americans; no one was looked down upon or snubbed because he had dirty or mean employment. All work was considered equally important; a farmer who owned a thousand acres of farmland worked himself all day with his hired men. When had anyone ever seen the lieutenant at Krakesjo go into the field with his men and spread manure? And he was the owner of barely a hundred and thirty acres! In America there was no servant law or earnest money, and hired men and maids could leave their service whenever they wanted without punishment. Nor need they slave as here from early to late: in North America no one worked longer than twelve hours a day.

The money was called dollars, and one dollar equaled two or three riksdaler—maybe more. A good farmhand could earn as much as a hundred and twenty-five dollars a year, and that was more than three hundred riksdaler. Arvid worked here in Nybacken for forty riksdaler a year and a suit of wadmal. If one counted the wadmal at ten riksdaler, one still earned more in one year in America than in six years at Aron's. And the food was seven times better. The Americans had good solid fare: all people ate pork and white bread every day, and Sundays they had double portions of pork to the bread. Salt herring was forbidden as food. The cattle in America were better fed than the servants in Sweden. The fare Aron in Nybacken gave to his servants would be rejected by the pigs in America, for they were very particular. A pig in the New World lived as well as a count in Sweden.

Robert related what he remembered from the book, the

words came pouring from his lips, and perhaps, in his enthusiasm, he added a little here and deducted a little there, but it evened out so that the truth about the United States of America did not suffer from it.

And he carried his comrade away so that Arvid trembled at the revelations. Now and then he put in his "No! No! God! God Almighty! The devil it is! Christ in hell!" and other expressions which he daily carried on his lips and which meant nothing in particular. Arvid had never read a description of heaven, since he could not read, and he had never heard the dean describe it from the pulpit, either, for the dean only spoke of happenings in hell; but if only half the contents of Robert's book were true, and the other half a lie, then the book must describe a heaven on earth.

But Arvid asked about other things, as for example the wild heathen, Indians who flayed people on the head with their knives and were unfriendly toward Christians. There was nothing in the book about Indians' scalping people, said Robert. Arvid then wondered if the wild animals in North America were dangerous. Were there any angry snakes there? He had always been afraid of crawling animals, never daring to kill a snake, and avoiding small quadrupeds Robert admitted that in America great wild animals did live, and they could kill people, and were consequently a little annoying. The fiercest beast was the gray bear, who attacked all who tried to take his life. But if you lay down on the ground and pretended you were dead, the bear would leave you in peace There were also lions and tigers and wolves there, but they had a natural fear of people and attacked only if wounded or frightened. There were poisonous rattlesnakes but they rattled and made a noise when they crawled in the woods and could be heard at great distances, so it was easy to run away from them. America had also some irritating small creatures, grasshoppers, blowflies, cankerworms on the fruit trees and others, but they were unable to kill people. The grasshoppers ate only crops, they were quite satisfied with this. No, no one need be afraid to live in America on account of wild animals.

No, Arvid wasn't afraid of them either, he had only asked for the fun of it. And now he knew how it was: when the bears came, one was to lie flat on the ground and pretend to be dead. And he had good hearing; no doubt he would hear when the snakes came rattling and have time to run away.

About those who were called Negroes and had black woolly hair, it said in the book that they were kept as slaves, and were bought and sold as if they were cattle. Robert did not think this was being fair to them. Otherwise they seemed to have it decent and comfortable enough, and he read for Arvid about them: "Many slaves have better living quarters, food, clothing, care, working conditions and old-age security than most of England's factory workers or the peasants in Europe. They have their own chickens and pigs, their own piece of land where they can cultivate whatever they wish and sell the yield for their own profit. A half-year may pass without abuse from their owner. It has therefore happened that liberated slaves—dissatisfied with their newfound liberty and its consequent responsibilities—have again sold themselves as slaves."

Arvid listened in amazement: the slaves had their own chickens and their own pigs? And their own piece of land? And better food and clothing than most peasants at home? Then the best one could do on arriving in America would be to sell oneself as a slave; it would be the wisest thing a farmhand could do. Here in Sweden he would never be able to acquire his own patch of land, or chickens or pigs.

Robert said it was forbidden in America for white-skinned people to sell themselves as slaves.

"Forbidden?" retorted Arvid. "But you said America was a free land, that all people could do as they pleased. You just said so."

"Yes, yes, but that kind of trade is forbidden anyway. For whites."

"But why should it be forbidden to sell oneself? When all have the right to do as they please?"

Robert was confused, he couldn't answer this. And Arvid thought that probably there was a difference between people in America, after all, if the whites did not have the same rights as the blacks to become slaves and have their own land with chickens and pigs.

He would have liked to read a few chapters in the book, Arvid would, if he had been able to, with his weak eyes; but he got such an eyesmart when he read; wouldn't his friend continue?

Robert turned the page to a new chapter, describing the life of the inmates of an asylum in the New World—an asy-

lum in Pennsylvania: "In this house the weak-minded work in
their clear moments with weaving, wood chopping, sewing,
spinning, knitting, etc., to shorten the time and occupy their
minds, besides which for the same reason there are available
books, newspapers, chess games, musical instruments, like the
flute and the pianoforte. . . ."

"For the crazy?" exclaimed Arvid.

"It says 'the weak-minded.' "

"They have newspapers? And play flutes?" For the first
time Arvid voiced doubt.

"Well—look for yourself."

"God Almighty!"

But it was the truth, Robert's eyes were too good to make
a mistake in his reading. And when everything was so fine and
expensive for insane people in America, one could easily
imagine how the sane lived.

Arvid agreed immediately to go with his comrade to the
New World.

In the United States of America no one could have heard
the ugly rumor which the old woman in Nybacken had spread
about him. There no one knew of the horrible deed with the
white heifer which he was accused of here at home. In America no one would call him the Bull behind his back; there the
girls wouldn't shun him; there he could look all people freely
in the eyes and be held in regard like other menfolk.

And on this the big servant shook hands with the little one:
together they would cross the ocean.

5

The lantern in the stable room burned late into the night
while Arvid and Robert planned their future emigration. And
none but the bedbugs in the rotten walls shared their secret
deliberations.

Robert had been clever when he figured on driving Aron's
timber wagon to Karlshamn; thus the master would contrib-
ute, as it were, toward the fare for the journey to America. In
the harbor town they would later come to agreement with
some captain to sail them across the sea.

Arvid wondered: "How much is the fare across the ocean?"

Robert knew: The transportation from the port of embarkation in Sweden to New York in America, including provisions for the voyage, firewood, and fresh water, cost one hundred and fifty riksdaler* for a grown person. To this was added ten riksdaler entrance fee to America, and some other expenses, so that every emigrant needed about two hundred riksdaler. He himself had that sum—his inheritance—remaining with his brother in Korpamoen.

"Two hundred daler!" Arvid had risen, now he sat down again, so heavily that the bench creaked in every joint.

Two hundred riksdaler was five years' wages. And he had not one shilling saved. If he should save every penny, and didn't even allow himself a pinch of snuff during the whole time, he would have to remain here in Nybacken and serve for five years before he could save that much money.

He sat dejected and avoided looking at his friend; he had never dreamed that the transportation to North America would cost such an incredible sum of money. He must stay at least five service years more—during five more years he would be forced to remain here as the Bull of Nybacken.

A long silence ensued. The bedbugs thought their nightly victims had finally gone to sleep and emerged cautiously from their holes and corners.

Two hundred riksdaler! That boy there was lucky to have an inheritance to draw on. But Robert must go alone, even though a moment ago they had decided to keep company and had sealed it by a handshake.

"You mean you cannot raise the transportation?"

"No—I couldn't manage."

"Not in any way?" Robert was almost as disappointed as Arvid.

"No, there isn't any way out."

"There must be some way. Perhaps we can help each other."

And again they sat silent, and brooded and pondered.

Suddenly Arvid jumped up, his eyes gleaming. "I've got it! We may get across some other way!"

"What do you mean?"

Arvid grabbed hold of Robert's shoulder, intense, breathless. "The highway, of course—we hadn't thought of that!"

* 43.50 in today's currency.

Surely, there must be some road over firm land. They could
walk *around* the ocean, and in this way reach America
dryshod. They would have to take a roundabout way, it
would take them longer, but in his case that would make no
difference; he would rather walk the long road to America
than remain here and be shunned like a villain. If he could arrive dryshod, on foot, he would willingly take a roundabout
road; he had strong, sturdy legs and was a good walker, he
needn't risk his life at sea. He was sure he could walk to
America. It might take a few years, that couldn't be helped.
He would not take too much with him that might be a burden
to carry, he couldn't take his servant chest, he'd manage with
a knapsack. He might take the keg too, he would need something to encourage him on the long journey if his legs alone
must pay the transportation.

He couldn't believe anything else but that in some way they
could walk around the ocean.

"It's impossible. No one can walk to America."

"It's impossible? There is no way?" Arvid's eyes were
pleading for any little hope, the barest possibility, even if it
meant the longest and most difficult road.

Robert answered definitely: No one could walk dryshod to a
land which was surrounded on all sides by water. Arvid could
see that on the map at schoolmaster Rinaoldo's. America lay
there like a vast island in the world sea; they could not walk
around that body of water.

"Under no circumstances?"

"Under no circumstances."

Arvid's face fell. Robert continued: In any case, that way
was so long that if Arvid were to walk it he would not arrive
until he was eighty, just in time to lie down in his grave. And
he must take the village shoemaker with him to prepare him
a new pair of boots a couple of times a year to replace the
worn-out ones.

Arvid sat silent again, very long. Then he mumbled something between his teeth—four words: "That God-damned
ocean!"

At last he crawled into bed, still cursing the ocean which
separated the Old and the New Worlds. That evening he
swore himself to sleep.

IV

KARL OSKAR AND KRISTINA

1

In this year—"the 5,850th since the creation of the world," according to the almanac—the early summer was the driest in thirty-one years.

During the month of June not a drop of rain fell. Dry, harsh winds from east and north blew constantly, but never the west wind, the wind of rain. The sun glared day after day from a cloudless sky. The grass in glades and meadows turned coarse and rough, rustling underfoot. The winter rye stopped growing at knee-height; grazing ended, and the cows went dry.

Haying commenced before June had passed; to leave the ready ripened grass standing would risk its strength. Hillocks and knolls turned brown-red—the color of animal blood, foretelling death under the knife for cattle, with fodder shortage ahead.

Karl Oskar and Kristina harvested the meager hay grown in their meadow. The straws were so short and spindly that the rake could hardly catch them; one could almost count the straws, Karl Oskar said.

He was angry and bitter as he raked; last year was a wet year and hay rotted in the swaths or washed away in the flood. This year it was drought, and the hay burned up. Which was the better for the farmer? Which one could satisfy him?

This year the only moisture in Karl Oskar's field was his own sweat. The Lord's weather was either too wet or too dry. Of what help was it, then, to bend one's back and toil and struggle? The Lord's weather ruined everything for him, all his labor was in vain.

"It's all the fault of the Lord's weather!"

Kristina stopped raking and looked at him gravely.

"Don't be impious, Karl Oskar."

"But—is this hay, or is it cats' hair? Is it worth our work?"

And Karl Oskar was gripped by sudden anger: he seized a

69

wisp of hay on his rake and threw it up into the air while he shouted heavenwards: "As you have taken the rest of the hay you might as well have this, too!"

Kristina let out a shriek, terror-stricken: Karl Oskar had challenged the Lord in heaven and on earth. Her eyes followed the wisp of hay as if she expected it to reach the heavens. But the straws did not get high above the earth, they were separated from each other by the wind and, scattering over the meadow, they fell slowly to the ground. No one up there in heaven would accept the hay.

"Karl Oskar. You have blasphemed."

Kristina stood there, her cheeks white, her hands clutching the rake handle. Her husband had thrown their hay back to Him above because he was not satisfied. What was he doing? How dared he? Did he no longer fear his Creator? He must know that God would not allow mockery. Frightened, she looked toward the sky as if she expected that the presumptuous one would receive his punishment immediately.

"May God forgive you! May God forgive what you did!"

Karl Oskar did not answer. Silently he began to rake together a new swath. He had indeed learned God's commandments, he knew the Lord endured no mockery, and he felt a pang within him. He had lost his temper, the gesture with the hay would have been better undone, those words should not have been uttered.

The clear words of the Bible proclaimed that man on earth should eat his bread in the sweat of his brow; he asked no better than to be allowed to do this. But as he gave his sweat, so would he like also to receive in return the bread. He did not think it too much to ask that all might happen according to God's own words.

In silence they continued to harvest their hay. But the meadow hay barn which in good years was too small was this year not half filled.

The drought continued.

Their well dried up and the people in Korpamoen carried water from an old spring in the forest. Hungry and thirsty, the cattle stood all day long at the stile, lowing plaintively. The fields were scorched as if fire had passed over them. In the beginning of August the birches turned yellow and began to lose their leaves. The summer had never had time to bloom and ripen before the autumn set in; this summer had died in its youth.

Karl Oskar had a stiff neck from looking for rain clouds. At times clouds did appear, dry clouds, empty smoke rings that passed across the heavens, visions of deceit, a cruel mockery. A few tiny scattered drops fell at times; they were like scorn.

The rye stood overripe, the grains ready to drop from the heads. At the cutting they must be careful not to lose some of the invaluable kernels. Karl Oskar and Kristina brought the quilted bedcover with them into the field, and spread it on the stubble before the swath of the scythe. They moved the quilt gradually, for the cut straws to fall on it and remain there while being tied into sheaves. Thus grains which might fall from the heads were collected on the quilt and saved. From the ground Kristina gleaned the broken heads, gathering them in her apron; when evening came they had collected in the cover a tenth of a bushel of the drop-rye, sufficient for a few loaves of bread. The rye field yielded only a third of its usual crop in this year of drought: what would one loaf of bread count when winter came?

Kristina tied the corners of the quilt into a sack and carried it home under her arm. Four years ago it had been her bridal spread, her cover during the first night with her mate, when she was transformed from maid to wife. Now the bridal cover was with them in their field and helped to garner their bread; it belonged closely to their lives.

Kristina thought: Four years ago, when this cover was new, Karl Oskar had more to say to me. Why is he nowadays so silent? She mused: Now he spoke mostly of work to be done; in the morning about what must be done that day, in the evening about tomorrow's work. And at least once a day either he or she said: Still no rain!

During this summer all people, it seemed, had become serious and sullen and short-tempered; the weather affected their minds. Talk was about the dire winter ahead, as though no one had a right to be joyous now because of the crop failure. Not even children dared show happiness: when a child laughed some older person at hand spoke harshly and silenced it. And all continued to speak of this: What would happen next winter?

Karl Oskar blamed everything on the drought. When he returned empty-handed from a day in the woods with gun and dog, this was because of the dried-up ground: the dog could get no scent of game. When he pulled nets and lines empty from the tarn, he blamed this on the drought: heat drove the fish into the depths. And three times he had brought a cow to the bull with no result: this too because of the drought. Such an opinion did not seem reasonable, as part of the blame might be laid on the bull. But Karl Oskar said that his neighbor, Jonas Petter of Hasteback, was also unable to get his cows with calf because of the heat.

One night toward the end of August Kristina was awakened by a great thunder. She was afraid of storms and she called her husband.

Karl Oskar sat up in bed and listened. It rumbled and thundered, and lightning flashed past the window. Shirt-clad only, he ran to stand on the porch, hands outstretched. An occasional fat raindrop fell; once it began there would be heavy showers. He could go back to bed and sleep again in the blissful knowledge that there would be rain.

He returned inside. Kristina was comforting the children, awake and frightened by the lightning and thunder.

Anna, the oldest child, was now in her fourth year and all were of the opinion that she had a mind far ahead of her years. She was wont to follow Karl Oskar in his work outside, close to him everywhere; if he drove or walked, the child was with him. He called her his big helper. Wise as an eight-year-old, he said.

The thunder boomed again, and Anna asked: "Will the lightning kill us tonight, Mother?"

"No! What nonsnsense! Who has given you such an idea?"

"Father. He said we are to die—all of us."

"Yes, yes, but not tonight."

"When will we die, Mother?"

"No one knows, no one except God. Go back to sleep now!"

And Kristina's eyes turned questioningly to Karl Oskar: What had he said to the child? He smiled and explained. When he had gone with Anna through the pastures recently they had found a dead baby rabbit, and then she had asked if they were to become like the rabbit, if they were all to die.

He had replied in the affirmative. He could not lie about such things to a child. But ever after the girl asked whomsoever she met when they were to die. The other day she had embarrassed her grandmother with the same question. He had had to assure his mother that the question was the child's own idea. She was a strange child, Anna.

Karl Oskar was very proud of this daughter, his big girl.

A clap of thunder sounded, louder than before, and the lightning pierced their eyes, sharp and blinding.

Kristina let out a shriek.

"Did it strike?"

"If so, it was near."

But the heavy rain was slow in coming; only an occasional few drops smote the windowpanes. Karl Oskar could not help the rain to fall, and he went back to bed. Before he was asleep the window was again brilliant, with a new light; but this time it was not lightning cutting through the dark and disappearing. This time the light remained, mobile and flickering.

The young farmer leapt up.

"There is a fire!"

"My dear God!"

"It's burning somewhere!"

As Karl Oskar reached the window he could see that the light came from the hay meadow.

"The meadow barn! The meadow barn has caught on fire!"

He ran outside, only half dressed, followed by his wife. By now Nils and Marta also had awakened in their room, and Kristina called to them to look after the children.

Karl Oskar ran to the well where two water buckets stood filled from the forest spring; he thrust one bucket at his wife and they rushed down the meadow with a pail each in their hands. The water splashed to and fro, and when they arrived at the burning hay barn hardly more than half of it was left. Nor did it matter; the fire by now had reached such proportions that a couple of buckets of water would be of no help. The whole barn was burning, flames leaping high from the dry shingled roof which went up like tinder. A fierce, voracious lightning-fire was burning, and it had found delicious fare: an old dry barn filled with the harvested hay.

The owners of the hay barn—the young farm couple—approached the fire as closely as they could for the heat. They stood there, water pails in their hands, and watched the fire; they just stood and watched, like a pair of surprised, amazed children listening to a cruel and horrible tale which—God be praised—could not be true.

People from neighboring farms had already seen the fire and come running. They too soon realized it would be hopeless to try to stop this fire. The conflagration had the barn within its scorching jaws—no one could hinder it from swallowing its prey.

Luckily, there was no wind. But the neighbors remained to see that the fire did not spread; what might not happen once it were loose in the drought-dry woods?

Already the rain was over; a few heavy drops had fallen, hardly enough to wet the stones on the ground.

Swiftly the meadow barn was burned, and hay and all became embers and sullen ashes. Karl Oskar and Kristina walked back to the farmhouse; there had been nothing for them to do, they had done nothing. On the way home they walked quite slowly, they did not run, nothing was urgent any more. In their hands they still carried their buckets, half full of water; without thinking, they carried the water home again.

At the meadow stile they met Nils on his way to the fire, hobbling on his crutches. He had managed half the way when his son and daughter-in-law told him to turn back. But he sat down on the stile to rest; for many years he had not walked so far from the house.

Watching the fire, Karl Oskar and Kristina had not exchanged a single word. They had only looked at each other a few times; perhaps they had been thinking the same thoughts.

Now on the way home Kristina said, "Do you remember the harvest this summer? When you threw the hay upwards?"

"Yes."

"It happened as you asked."

Karl Oskar kept silent; he could find no answer.

She continued: "It was the punishment. God allows no mockery."

Karl Oskar in Korpamoen walked back to his home carrying his bucket. He walked with bent head and looked at the ground. What Kristina had said was true. This time the Lord had answered his prayer—He had taken the rest of the hay.

2

The east wind blew and no rain fell. Those who could read in
the book of the future predicted that rain would never fall
again. Last time the Lord had wished to destroy mankind
through flood, now He intended to do it through dought, and
this time no Noah would be saved with wife and children to
propagate a new race.

Karl Oskar sowed his winter rye on the fallow land, strewn
with hard clods of earth—gray, lumpy, and unfertile as a field
of crushed stone. Even below the topsoil the earth was
scorched. It seemed futile planting here, he might as well sow
in the ashes of his hearth. Last spring he had sown four bushels of barley in one field; now in autumn he harvested four
bushels in return. What did he gain by all his work? Why
should he plant seed corn in the earth when the earth did not
multiply it? Nothing would germinate here before the rains
came and loosed the hard crust of the field.

He entrusted the seed rye to his field without confidence; he
had lost his confidence in the earth. Who could tell if it would
bring him one single grain in return? It might have been wiser
to grind the seed corn and make bread of it.

When God drove the first man from paradise He said:
Cursed is the ground for thy sake; in sorrow shalt thou eat of
it all the days of thy life. No words in the Bible were more
true than these, for Karl Oskar. The Lord had also said to
Adam that the earth would bring forth to him thorns and
thistles. Hadn't he pulled up thistles in every field of this his
stone kingdom until his back ached? The Bible's words were
still in force, at least as far as the local fields were concerned.

It was rumored that rain had fallen in other places, in
other parishes and counties. But here the earth was accursed.

Every evening Kristina read the "Prayer Against Persistent
Drought" and sometimes he himself joined in. She was frightened by the lightning-fire which had burned down their
meadow barn, and she believed the drought also was a chastisement from the Lord. Now she wished Karl Oskar would
go to the dean and pray for absolution because he had
blasphemed that time during the harvest; he must do it before
they went to Holy Communion together again.

But he paid no heed to her admonition.

"Doesn't your conscience bother you?" she asked.

"Not because of that sin."

No. Karl Oskar would not turn to the dean: he had not committed murder, nor was he lying on his deathbed. What he had done in the field was done in sudden anger, which he had regretted, and God would by now have had time to forgive him such a small trespass and needn't plague man and beast with drought because of it. Nor was God so petty that He burned down the barn because of that small tuft of hay. One mustn't think the Highest One was an incendiary.

But Karl Oskar must know, retorted Kristina, that no one except the Omnipotent decided where lightning was to strike. And she continued urging: he ought to seek absolution before he prepared himself for his next Communion. No one except Dean Brusander could decide whether his sin was great or small. And they were on good terms with the dean, who commanded them both as frequent churchgoers.

But she could not persuade Karl Oskar to seek out the dean; he was so obstinate he would not unbend even for God. And as Kristina looked back over the years of their marriage, she wondered if she ever had managed to sway him. What he wanted to do, he did; what he didn't want to do was never done. His sister Lydia had said that her brother was difficult because of this stubbornness, but Kristina had never thought of him as being so before they married. Persistence was right for useful undertakings and good deeds. But Karl Oskar was equally stubborn in useless and foolish undertakings; large-nosed people were held to be stubborn.

"Your obstinacy is in your nose; that's why it is so large."

Until God gave him another nose he must use the old one, was Karl Oskar's answer. But he had noticed that it extended far enough to annoy some people.

Otherwise Kristina had no reason to complain of her husband. He seldom drank more brannvin than he could handle, and he could handle a great deal; she never had to drag a drink-fouled husband from Christmas parties, as did other wives. And there were married men who went to Ulrika of Vastergohl, the "Glad One," the most sought-after whore in Ljuder. To poor men she sold herself for twelve shillings or a quart of brannvin, but to homeowners her price was a whole riksdaler. In her youth Ulrika had been a beautiful woman, and she was not ugly yet. It was said that the churchwarden himself, Per Persson in Akerby, had frequented the whore in her better days. Karl Oskar would never degrade himself to such an extent that he would stir in other pots.

But Kristina worried because lately he had been so closed-up, and at last she asked him point-blank what was on his mind.

"Worries about living," he said. Where would food come from? And with more and more of them to feed.

Kristina was in her fifth month, soon they would be eight people in Korpamoen. The people increased, but not the land; the number of acres would never be more than seven.

Kristina did not like the reference to her pregnancy. "Leave the worries about the unborn to God."

"If I only could!"

"Do you think you are wiser than God?"

"No. But I don't think He would feed our children if we sat with our arms in our laps."

Her temper flared up and she exclaimed angrily: "Is God supposed to feed all children you make?"

"Kristina! What do you mean?"

"I mean you must not blame the Lord when you make your wife with child!"

He gazed at her. "But, my dearest—I have never denied my part in it."

She burst into tears. "You complain because we get to be more and more. Exactly as if it were my fault—because the lives come from me."

"I've never blamed you!"

"I don't want it! I've told you so! You mustn't think that!"

"I do not think anything."

"But now—when you walk about in silence, as if you ac-cused me—what am I to believe?"

And she cried into her apron.

A pregnant woman was sensitive and easily hurt; he forgot it at times, and didn't watch his words.

He left her alone till she quieted, then he asked: How could she imagine that he disapproved of her? He kept to himself because he was depressed from worries, that was all. And how could she think that he reproached her for being preg-nant again? He was not so unfair! She must realize how happy he was over the children she had borne him before. His children and his wife were his dearest possessions on earth. This he had shown her. She must have noticed, for example, how attached he was to Anna. And he would surely be as devoted to the new one as he was to the other three. But it was natural that he worried about food for the children in years of adversity and crop failure.

Kristina was drying her tears. "Do you mean that you like me as well as you used to?"

"You must know that I do!"

"Is it the truth you tell me, Karl Oskar?"

"Tell me the time I ever lied to you."

She could not. And he said they must remain friends, and stick together in adversity. For there was no other person in the world who would help them; they must help themselves.

Kristina realized she had acted foolishly; why she had behaved in such a way she didn't know; if you took exception, any word led to a quarrel. But she sensed that she did it from fear, fear of diminishing attention from him.

His assurances made her almost glad of their quarrel.

3

Karl Oskar went deeper into debt. This autumn also he went to Danjel Andreasson in Karragarde and asked to borrow fifty daler for the mortgage interest.

He wore a solemn expression when he returned. Kristina asked anxiously: "Did Uncle refuse you the money?"

"No. I got every penny I asked for."

"But why do you look so queer?"

"Something strange is going on in Karragarde."

"With Uncle Danjel?"

"Yes. Something has happened to him."

Karl Oskar had been startled today as he stepped over the threshold at Danjel Andreasson's. The house was full of paupers and loose people. Strangers sat at table with the house folk. There was Severius Pihl, a dishonorably discharged soldier, a notorious fighter and drunkard; the disabled maid, Sissa Svensdotter, the impoverished thief who now depended on the parish; but Karl Oskar had been most surprised to discover among these people Ulrika of Vastergohl, the old whore, as well as her illegitimate daughter. At first he thought that they must all, in their rounds of begging, have happened to reach the farm at the same time. But it came as a box on the ear when Danjel said that these people from now on would be living with him in Karragarde. Inga-Lena, his wife, confirmed it: they all lived there together.

Kristina burst out in loud laughter. "Are you telling April-fool jokes in October, Karl Oskar?"

"Do you think I lie?" he asked, a little hurt.

"You must have made up a story to see if you could fool me."

"It's the truth—all of it! Go to your uncle's house and see for yourself."

Now Kristina approached him and smelled his breath: had he perchance been drinking today, so that he didn't know what he was saying? Did he reek of brannvin?

"I've taken just two drinks the whole day."

"But you say Ulrika of Vasterghol, the whore, has moved in with my uncle?"

"He said so himself."

"And Aunt Inga-Lena, what was she doing?"

"They had been slaughtering, and she was boiling blood sausage for her guests."

"Did the Glad One eat, the old whore? Did my aunt boil sausage for her?"

"Yes. Go and ask yourself, if you don't believe me."

Now Kristina was truly concerned. What could all this mean? What had happened in Karragarde?

Karl Oskar continued: The strangest of all was the way Danjel acted when he handed over the fifty daler. When asked if they should count the interest as before, he had answered that he did not desire interest on the money. And when Karl Oskar asked for a delay in the interest on the old debt, Danjel had said that he would nevermore accept interest on loaned money. He said it twice, for clarity.

Now Kristina realized that something serious had happened to her uncle. Karl Oskar guessed that some mental disturbance must have affected him.

And not many days passed before rumors began to spread from Danjel Andreasson's farm. From house to house, from

village to village, the news was told: Ake Svensson's heresy,
supposed to be dead with himself more than fifty years ago,
had been revived by his sister's son in Karragarde.

V

AKE RETURNS FROM THE INSANE ASYLUM

1

Danjel Andreasson, at forty-four years of age, was the nearest surviving relative of the Akian founder. He was known as
a good-natured man, and until now his life had been quiet
and blameless. He had piously accepted the only right and
true faith, thus showing a sound religious concept. His home,
Karragarde, at one time sorely tainted by Akianism, had
many years ago been declared cleansed.

But one night in the fall of 1848 a strange happening took
place in Karragarde.

Before Danjel went to bed that night he was seized by an
undefinable anxiety, and to his wife Inga-Lena he expressed
apprehension about some approaching illness: at moments he
felt a queer dizziness. During the night he was awakened by
someone knocking heavily at the door and calling his name in
a loud voice. Thinking that maybe a fire had broken out, and
his help was needed, he hurried out of bed. When he opened
the door the room became illuminated by a brilliant light.
Two men stood outside. One of them was a youth dressed in
outmoded wadmal clothes and unknown to Danjel. But the
second man he recognized instantly from the altarpiece in the
church: it was the Saviour, Jesus Christ. Jesus carried a lantern in His hand, and it was this lantern that spread the
strangely clear illumination widely into the night. The
Saviour looked as Danjel had imagined Him. From His face
radiated such a strong light that Danjel could not look at it:
he had to drop his eyes.

The man in the wadmal coat at the side of the Saviour had
awakened Danjel, and now he called him again by name, say-

ing: "I am Ake Svensson, your mother's brother. I died young
and came to my Saviour in heaven."

Danjel now saw that the man had the likeness of his uncle
as described by old villagers. People were still alive who remembered Ake as he was before the sheriff fetched him to
Danvik's asylum.

The Saviour studied Danjel with compassion, but remained
silent.

Ake Svensson spoke again and said: "Your Saviour has
awakened you this night that you may resume my work here
on earth. The Spirit will tell you what you must do. Danjel,
go out and complete my misssion! Your Saviour has called
you!"

Twice, in a clear voice, Ake repeated this exhortation to his
sister's son. Then the nocturnal visitors were gone, the light
from Christ's lantern disappeared, and all was dark around
Danjel.

He found himself on his knees at his threshold, praying, but
quite calm. He had not been frightened by what he had seen
and heard at his door, and kneeling there he was not conscious of anxiety. His breast was full of a peace which he had
never before experienced.

He awakened his wife, Inga-Lena, and told her that the
Saviour this night had visited his house in the company of
Ake, his uncle who had died at Danvik's asylum. She thought
he had had a dream. But he knew he had been awake the
whole time. His ears had heard the knocks on the door when
Ake called him by name, his eyes had seen the face of the
Saviour. He could well describe the lantern which Christ had
carried in His hand: it was in every detail identical with the
one He carried in the picture above the church altar.

This was what had happened to Danjel Andreasson, and
from that moment his life on earth changed.

Ake had spoken barely twenty words to Danjel, but he
knew what he must do: the Spirit spoke in his heart. And
after that night all his actions were dictated by the Spirit.
Nevermore did he hesitate in his undertakings, nor worry
about their outcome. Each time he felt in his heart that he
was right. Christ had called him; he had become a follower of
the Saviour, and from now on he would lead the same life
here on earth as the apostles and the first Christians. He
would preach Ake's teachings, which already were forgotten

in the neighborhood. The Spirit guided him when he read the
Bible, and moved his hand to those places which had commands for him: "Thy word is a lamp unto my feet, and a light
upon my path." He had seen the light from Christ's lantern,
he knew the path.

In that autumnal night when Danjel heard his name called,
he was reborn into the world. Until he was forty-four years of
age he had lived in the flesh; now began his life in the spirit.

And so he resumed the teachings of Ake. Every Sunday he
gave Bible talks to his house folk—wife, children, and servants—and if some neighbor happened by, he was welcomed.
He went to church every time it was Holy Communion, to
enjoy the blessed sacrament. Even during his work he said his
prayers—in the field, at plow or harrow, in the barn with the
flail in his hand. He always bent his knees while praying.
Sometimes he cried aloud during his prayers, which caused
people near by to rush to him, thinking help was needed.

Danjel threw the farm's still on the scrap pile; not only did
he discontinue the manufacture and sale of brännvin, he also
stopped using alcoholic drinks, nor did he offer them in his
home. He forbore swearing and the use of all profane language. Earlier he had sometimes been irritable and quickly
angered—now his speech was always mild and gentle. Only
about the clergy who had persecuted his uncle did he use hard
words.

From now on Danjel considered all his possessions as gifts
from God which, while they lasted, he must share with poorer
brethren. He took into his house a few helpless creatures and
gave them a permanent home in Karragårde, where they received both food and clothing. Two of them were the most
notorious people in the parish, known for whoring, drunkenness, idleness, and general debauchery.

Danjel used no more bolts or locks in his house, but left all
doors unlocked at night. Why would he need locks and latches
when the Lord stood guard over his house? Could a weak
lock, made by human hands, protect his abode better than the
hand of the Omnipotent? Those who locked their doors did
not trust in God; they committed the trespasses of doubt and
disbelief, man's greatest sins.

To Danjel, as earlier to Ake, there were neither high nor
low classes, neither exalted nor simple people—all were
equal, equal as children in God's family. He discriminated

only between those who continued to live in their old bodies and those who were reborn in Christ, between those who lived in the flesh and those who lived in the spirit.

After his rebirth he no longer shared his bed with his wife. Because Inga-Lena still lived in the flesh, they were no longer a true married couple. Those marriages where the mates lived in their old bodies were joined by the devil, and the same was true if only one of the couple was reborn. If Danjel now had sought his wife, he would have committed adultery. He therefore told her that they no longer could have marital relations.

They must also abstain because of future children. A clean offspring must be conceived without lust, therefore it must be conceived by sin-free, reborn parents. Danjel and Inga-Lena already had three children, born while they themselves still lived in the flesh, and he felt great anguish for the sake of these children. As they had not been conceived in a true marriage, they must be considered the result of adultery, he thought. But he prayed continually that his offspring might through God's grace be purified and accepted as clean.

Inga-Lena, the housewife of Karragarde, was in a difficult dilemma. She was devoted to her husband—next to God he was dearer to her than anyone. She lived only to serve him, and followed his will in everything: by nature she was irresolute, relying on him for decisions; he was the lord and master. After his conversion she still tried to please him but found it difficult to accept his new ideas, and the consequent changes in their lives. She would willingly share her loaf of bread with a hungry beggar who might come to the farm. But she was filled with sadness and anxiety when the number of house folk increased by four people whom her husband invited and whom the house must feed. And when she also must receive into her home Ulrika of Vastergohl, the most detested woman in the parish, she spoke to her husband with mild reproach. She wished to do naught against his will, nor say that he was wrong when he allowed Ulrika and her illegitimate daughter to live with them, but what would others think or say when he housed in their home the Glad One, the great whore herself? Danjel answered: We must obey God above man. Let that woman who is without sin come here and throw the first stone at Ulrika.

Inga-Lena was greatly disturbed, too, when her husband repeated the doings and actions of the Akians. Ake Svensson

had aimed to establish a kingdom in which the Holy Ghost
and not the King reigned, and where no one called anything
his own, but all earthly possessions were common property.
No wonder he had been sent to the insane asylum, where he
had suffered a pitiful death after a few years—despite his
being a young and hale person. (Though there were those who
thought injustice had been done to him, who were convinced
he had been tortured to death at Danvik.)

The fate of Ake had terrified all in the region, but no one
was surprised; he who insisted that all were equal, and that
they must hold their possessions in common and share them
as brothers and sisters, such a one must come to an ill end;
people were right in this.

Inga-Lena feared now that Danjel's path in his uncle's footsteps would lead to an equally horrible end. If you set yourself up against the ordinance of authority, you angered the
clergy and came to no good.

But Danjel said that if you walked in Christ's bloody footsteps you were bound to cause anger and be persecuted by
the church, the clergy, and worldly powers as well.

She began to worry about their belongings when her husband no longer locked the house. One night thieves went into
the unlocked larder and stole pork and flour. Danjel said they
kept a greater store of food than God allowed them, and that
was why He had not prevented the theft. But Inga-Lena did
not comprehend this. God Himself in His fifth commandment
had forbidden theft. It was her responsibility that the food in
the house should suffice for all; henceforth, unbeknownst to
her husband, she locked the larder door in the evening.

But her conscience bothered her each time she disobeyed
him. The Bible's words in Ephesians were clear and distinct:
"For the husband is the head of the wife, even as Christ is the
head of the church. . . . Therefore as the church is subject
unto Christ, so let the wives be to their own husbands in every
thing."

Inga-Lena, furthermore, had a feeling of being a defiled
and unclean woman when her husband deserted the marital
bed. She had disturbing and painful dreams during her lonely
nights; she awakened, and called on God for advice and help.
She confessed in her prayers that she was a woman of only
poor understanding; her knowledge was insufficient to com-

prehend Ake's religion. She prayed God to enlighten her. Danjel prayed the same prayer.

And after a while the couple's prayers were heard: the Spirit came to Inga-Lena and she experienced her rebirth. She came to understand that she must obey her husband, not her own inadequate intelligence. Danjel was right in spiritual things, she had been wrong. And so their marriage became a true marriage. Danjel returned to the marital bed, and again knew his wife.

By now there was a small flock of Akians in Karragarde. The paupers who made their home on the farm, as well as a few of the neighbors, embraced the Akian teachings and saw in Danjel Andreasson a new Lord's apostle on earth.

But his wife Inga-Lena still committed, in secret every evening, the gross sin of doubt when she locked the farm's larder for the night.

2

The happenings in Karragarde were soon brought to the attention of Dean Brusander. It was said that people under pretext of devotion met at Danjel Andreasson's, where he preached the Akian faith—this heresy had again begun to spread its horrible poison in the parish.

Dean Brusander was a powerful clergyman who guarded the dignity and sanctity of his office well. Always he had maintained the purity of the evangelical-Lutheran church with unflagging zeal; never sparing himself, he watched over the flock God had entrusted to him, protecting it from heterodoxy. Now he sent promptly for the churchwarden, Per Persson of Akerby, who confirmed the story of the unlawful meetings in Karragarde. It was said throughout the parish that Ake Svensson had returned in the shape of his nephew. And Per Persson could affirm that Danjel used evil words about the dean, and called him a neglectful shepherd, because brannvin was distilled and sold in the parsonage.

Brusander was provoked that a parishioner should question his lawful right, shared by all the clergy who cultivated land. And on the King's estates too brannvin was distilled and sold, as well as on the Prince's manor at Backaskog. The farmer in Karragarde had therefore, through his criticism, committed a serious crime against the Crown. The sale and serving of brannvin in the parsonage was nowadays allowed only on weekdays; the drink was stimulating to laborers and servants after a day's toil. It was true that the well-known Dean Wieselgren in Vasterstad wanted to abolish brannvin altogether, and that in un-Christian hatred he persecuted his colleagues who only enjoyed their legal rights. Wieselgren in his blindness wanted to rob the peasants of their lawful trade; if they were not permitted to distill their grain to brannvin, the agriculture of the country would in a short time be ruined and the farmers impoverished. The price of grain would drop so low that the farmers would be bankrupt, which in turn would make the poor people more insolent; it would be difficult then to obtain servants and day laborers. Who would want to do day labor if a bushel of barley could be bought at six shillings?

Dean Brusander called Danjel Andreasson of Karragarde to appear at the parsonage, and in the presence of his assistant, Pastor Krusell, and the churchwardens of the parish, he questioned the farmer at length.

3

At this inquiry the assistant pastor made notes which were signed by the churchwardens as unbiased witnesses and deposited in the archives of the parish.

"Summoned homeowner Danjel Andreasson was first questioned briefly in religion by Dean Brusander; he showed satisfactory knowledge in the foundation and order of the salvation tenets. Questioned specifically, Danjel Andreasson admitted that at the present time several loose people maintained their residence in his house, to wit: court-martialed soldier Severius Pihl, disabled servant wench Sissa Svensdotter, unmarried female Ulrika of Vastergohl and her illegitimate daughter Elin. Ulrika being known since her youth for her lewd and immoral life, during which she had conceived four illegitimate children of whom three died in infancy. Danjel

Andreasson admitted that he fed and protected these people in his house.

"Questioned Dean Brusander: 'Is it true that in your house you conduct meetings with your housefolk and neighbors?'

"Answered Danjel Andreasson: 'It is true, Mr. Dean.'

"Asked Dean B.: 'What do you do at these meetings?'

"Answered Danjel A.: 'I explain the Bible word to my listeners.'

"Asked Dean B.: 'You admit then that you are practicing the office of the ministry?'

"Answered Danjel A.: 'I do what the ministers do not: I preach God's true word.'

"Asked Dean B.: 'Who has given you power to do this?'

"Answered Danjel A.: 'God's Spirit has given me that power in my heart.'

"Said Dean B.: 'You are seized by an evil spirit. No one is allowed to be minister unless called and ordained according to the church law. In the presence of these honest and trusted men I herewith command you, Danjel Andreasson, to forgo all ministering pretensions in the future!'

"Answered Danjel A.: 'You, Mr. Dean, have no power to forbid me this.'

"Said Dean B.: 'God has entrusted your soul to me. I am your spiritual authority. In all spiritual things you must obey me and no one else.'

"Answered Danjel A.: 'The Bible teaches that I must obey God before man. You are a man, Mr. Dean.'

"Said Dean B.: 'In Romans, Chapter 13, verse 2, the Bible says, "Whosoever therefore resisteth the power, resisteth the ordinance of God: and they that resist shall receive to themselves damnation." Do you not admit that my power is from God?'

"Answered Danjel A.: 'No, Mr. Dean.'

"Asked Dean B.: 'Do you refuse to obey law and order?'

"Answered Danjel A.: 'There is no law over the righteous.'

"Asked Dean B.: 'Are you obsessed by such religious vanity that you call yourself righteous?'

"Answered Danjel A.: 'I am possessed by God's Spirit. The guide for my conduct is the Bible and my conscience.'

"Asked Dean B.: 'Can you tell me: What is conscience?'

"Answered Danjel A.: 'He who is reborn will find out what conscience is. I hear that you are not reborn, Mr. Dean.'

"Said Dean B.: 'The devil, the soul-destroyer, is whispering his answers into your ears! Have you preached that no man has a right to keep possessions for himself alone?'

"Answered Danjel A.: 'Yes. You, Mr. Dean, should have preached the same, if you had preached God's true word.'

"Asked Dean B.: 'Do you accuse me of false teachings?'

"Answered Danjel A.: 'In Acts 4, verse 32, it is written of Christ's church: "And the multitude of them that believed were of one heart and of one soul: neither said any of them that ought of the things which he possessed was his own; but they had all things in common." You, Mr. Dean, have never preached Christianity for this parish.'

"Said Dean B.: 'You lean on some words in the Bible while you tear down others. You also have said that I am a negligent shepherd and lead my flock headlong to hell when they are drunk. Is it true you have said this at your unlawful meetings?'

"Answered Danjel A.: 'It is true, Mr. Dean.'

"Asked Dean B.: 'How can you defend this false testimony about your spiritual guide?'

"Answered Danjel A.: 'Is it not true, Mr. Dean, that you sell brannvin from the parsonage still?'

"Answered Dean B.: 'I use my possessions as I see fit. What right have you to deny me my income, to which I am lawfully entitled during my tenure of office?'

"Answered Danjel A.: 'People get drunk from your brannvin, Mr. Dean, and in their drunkenness they commit violence and adultery and other crimes against the Ten Commandments. Doesn't he who breaks God's command earn hell, Mr. Dean?'

"Said Dean B.: 'You are called in for questioning, not I.'

"Said Danjel A.: 'As long as I served the devil I received praise from you, Mr. Dean. Now when I serve God I am called in for questioning and receive blame and censure.'

"Said Dean B.: 'Your case is now clear, Danjel Andreasson. You have here admitted—in the presence of unbiased witnesses—that you have broken the law by practicing the ministry. You should now receive your punishment in civil court. But I wish your repentance, not your ruin. If you retract your heresy, and promise no longer to preach or to spread your false and ungodly doctrines, I will grant you grace and forgiveness for what you have done.'

"Answered Danjel A.: 'The grace belongs to God alone. Accordingly, you, Mr. Dean, have no grace to bestow on me, nor can I receive grace from you.'

"Said Dean B.: 'In the presence of these witnesses I have forbidden you to preach. If you still pursue your illegal activities you will be sued in civil court and be fined or sentenced to bread and water in prison. On a third offense you are liable to two years' exile.'

"Answered Danjel A.: 'Mr. Dean, you cannot exile me from the kingdom of God, not even for one moment.'

"In spite of strong admonishments from Dean Brusander, the interrogated Andreasson adhered to his heresy, and refused obstinately to retract any of his false doctrines. The dean consequently administered his first warning against the spreading of heretical doctrines tending to undermine church unity and threaten the order, welfare, and security of the country. The dean instructed the strayed one to remain at his calling and pursue lawful work. Andreasson was then allowed to leave."

4

This interrogation by Dean Brusander had extracted the truth from the very mouth of the questioned one himself.

Danjel Andreasson, a simple man of the rough peasantry, was blown up by self-righteousness and vanity, and in his heart was angry and malicious toward church and clergy. In his arguments he showed a certain cunning and shrewdness not uncommon among peasants. He harbored the most insane opinions concerning man's spiritual and temporal well-being. And his heresy was particularly dangerous because it attacked the bond of unity between authority and subjects; he incited disobedience of the holy church laws. And even foolish thoughts were easily accepted by an ignorant peasantry, as witnessed in the time of Ake Svensson. Danjel had as yet no proselytes besides a few loose and notorious persons; but well-thought-of people *might* be enticed into his false religious fold.

Brusander felt his high and holy duty: the only true religion must not be besmirched. No blemish must stain it. The evangelical-Lutheran religion—the faith of his fathers—must be preserved untarnished within his parish henceforth as hitherto. During the reign of the devout King Charles XI deviation from the pure religion had been punished by the gauntlet, and sometimes loss of life. Though to a later era this might seem severe, one must keep in mind that it concerned the Augsburg Confession and the purity of evangelical-Lutheran religion. At the present time Sweden had a milder monarch, her inhabitants lived in a tolerant and enlightened century, and milder means must be used against recalcitrant subjects. It would have boded ill for Danjel Andreasson in other times. The dean had thought to bring him to his senses through warnings and kind admonishments alone. He did not wish the poor man's ruin. He would pray God to enlighten his darkened senses. He wished to force the man to repentance, and free his parish from the abominable contagion of Akianism, without having to call in the secular authorities.

Dean Brusander duly warned his entrusted flock: three Sundays in succession he read from the pulpit the "wholesome ordinance" which prescribed fines, prison, or exile, for male or female, old or young, few or many, who gathered together in private houses under pretext of devotion. And all parishioners were warned about the farm Karragarde, which had once more become a forbidden meeting place.

After a short while it was again reported to the dean that Danjel Andreasson persisted in his unlawful Bible explanations. Brusander then resorted to the church ban: homeowner Danjel Andreasson of Karragarde and all his house folk were excluded from the Lord's Holy Communion and banished from the sacraments and fellowship of the church. It was the church's ban against the man who had returned from the insane asylum.

VI

"SUITABLE CHASTISEMENT"

1

The wagonloads of oak timbers began rolling toward Karlshamn in the autumn, but Aron of Nybacken himself went with his team. He said that he was so concerned about his little hand that he dared not let him out on long journeys. A door which had seemed open was shut in Robert's face. There were many closed gates on the road to America.

His master still had no confidence in him. And yet, ever since Robert began his service, he had been obedient and attentive and done all he had been asked to do. Only once during the whole summer had the master been impelled to discipline him: then, when he was told to fetch water for the horses, Aron had thought he didn't move fast enough or obey quickly enough, and he gave his little hand a kick in the groin. It could have been a harder kick; but as it was it hit his scrotum which swelled up and became sensitive. For a few days he walked slowly and with difficulty, and the maids poked fun at him and wondered what kind of sickness ailed the little man. But that was the only time Aron had been dissatisfied.

One morning about Michaelmas Robert was sent to clean a ditch in a field near the house. He loosed the stones with an iron bar and threw up the earth with a shovel; the ditch was deep, and when he bent down in his work his head was barely visible above the edge. After a few hours' work he felt hungry. Wouldn't it soon be time for breakfast? No call for food was heard, he became sweaty and thirsty, his back ached from the bending, the earth became heavier with each shovelful. The drudgery was heavy—interminable. He grew depressed, realizing he hadn't labored through half his service year; this period with Aron was endless. He saw all his future years as service years with farmers, and all were endless; everything in the world seemed to him wretched and endless. And he wondered if it were worth while to live, if he must remain a farmhand.

At last he put the shovel aside and lay down on his back in the bottom of the ditch, with his arms under his head, and watched the sailing clouds in the sky. During his herdboy days he used to lie like this, sometimes for half a day at a stretch; he enjoyed it now no less.

But in order to rest undisturbed by Aron it must look from the house as if he were still working.

Robert therefore took off his cap and hung it on the spade handle, which he held in such a position that the cap was visible above the ditch's edge; as he lay there he moved the spade a little now and then, back and forth, up and down, as one might imagine the head of a busy farmhand would move while he cleaned a ditch.

The notion scattered his depressing thoughts, he grew cheerful, almost gay: he could remain lying here, resting and enjoying himself, while from the farm his master kept an eye on his splendid little fellow, working in the ditch. Aron was satisfied and so was he. One could get a rest period now and then if one were clever.

Robert thoroughly enjoyed his rest. Above him was the expanse of the high heaven, stretched out like a blue sea of freedom over all the ditches on earth and over all farmhands who labored in them. He was so filled with joy that he began to whistle and sing.

This, however, he was soon to regret; a master would easily understand that all was not as it should be when one of his hands kept singing and whistling while he worked.

Suddenly the farmer from Nybacken appeared above him. "Are you playing dollhouse, my little fellow?"

Robert had not heard the master's approach. There he stood and looked down upon his servant, stretched out full length at the bottom of the ditch.

The boy jumped from the ditch in one leap, shovel in hand. He wanted to say that he had taken only five minutes' rest because breakfast was delayed. But he did not find time to say anything. Aron's jaws clenched, and he shook his fists in front of him. "So, you are loafing, you damned lazybones!"

And Robert encountered two gnarled clumps, the biggest hands he had ever seen on a human being. Terror-struck, he dropped the shovel and tried to escape; but he took only one step.

The master's right fist landed on his left ear. He bent like a jackknife from the blow and fell face down on a pile of dirt. His face was buried in the earth from the impact. The pain cut through his head, red stars sparkled before his eyes, the whole world around him whirled. He heard someone shriek; he did not recognize the voice—could it be his own?

He did not faint; the whole time his head was bursting with pain. He thought his skull was broken, split in two like a piece of wood under the chopping ax; he thought he couldn't live with his head in two pieces; he wanted to die to escape the pain. He had stopped shrieking and now he heard someone else shouting: the mistress stood on the stoop calling Aron to breakfast.

The master left, and the beaten farmhand rose slowly to a sitting position. His face dirt-covered, he tried to pick pieces of earth from his eyes. A sharp stone had scratched his nose; his mouth was full of dirt—he spat. He was still dizzy, the world around him still heaved, but the pain had abated a little.

Only once before had he received a box on the ear from the master—that day when he had entered the service. That time it was only a small box; today he had experienced a big box on the ear.

As soon as the pain from the blow had subsided, hunger returned. He stood up and attempted a few steps: the ground lay almost still under his feet; he followed his master home to breakfast.

Robert did not mention the box on the ear to anyone. He had been chastised, he was ashamed of it, it was nothing to talk about. He had been lazy in his work and punished for it. He had received what he had earned; there was nothing more to say. If a servant was lazy and disobedient, then his master had the right to discipline him. He knew this well, all others knew it, and if they hadn't known it, much less work would have been accomplished for the farmers. So it was according to the servant law which Dean Brusander reiterated at the yearly examinations: "If a servant is inclined to laziness" the master must correct this through "suitable chastisement." There was no other remedy.

Aron of Nybacken was his master, who according to God's ordinance had fatherly power over him. It was Aron's right and duty to administer suitable punishment; the little farmhand had nothing to complain about. He was not wronged by anyone; he had been given the box on the ear according to God's ordinance.

He carried no hatred toward the master who had hit him. Once, when he was standing behind the barn, he had seen Aron beaten by his wife: she gave him a heavy blow across his neck with the byre besom; it was a big, rough besom, filled with cow dung, but Aron endured the blow without attempting to defend himself; he had looked frightened. Robert pitied his master rather than hated him.

When he went to bed that evening he could still hear a buzz in his ear from the hard blow; there was no sound around him, but there was a buzz in his ear. He lay there and listened to the humming sound and wondered what caused it. Outside in the yard as well as inside in the stable room complete silence reigned, but from inside his ear came a strange noise. He lay absolutely quiet and only listened within himself; he did not cause any sound; what could it be that buzzed and hummed so?

He let Arvid put his ear next to his own and listen. But Arvid couldn't hear anything, not a sound. It was inexplicable: Robert heard a sound which did not exist.

He awoke in the middle of the night. His left ear throbbed and ached intensely, and the noise inside had increased, and sounded by now like the roar of a storm. And his heartbeats were felt in his ear like the piercing of a pointed knife. He lay there on his bed and turned and twisted in agony. Something must have broken inside to cause the throbbing. He counted his heartbeats: the knife's edge cut and cut and cut in his ear; it felt like the sting in a fresh, open sensitive wound. The stings did not cease, the ache did not abate. He counted and waited and hoped, but it did not diminish. He was alone in the whole world with his pain and he did not know what to do about it. He began to moan; he didn't cry but he groaned quietly and at intervals. He folded his hands and prayed to God. He realized that the earache was in punishment for his laziness in the ditch, and he prayed for forgiveness. If God granted absolution He would also remove the earache. He had been a disloyal servant and he also remembered now that he had lately omitted reading "A Servant's Prayer." Tonight he recited it again in deep remorse: "Teach me to be faithful, humble, and devoted to my temporal lords. . . . Let me also find good and Christian masters who do not neglect or mistreat a poor servant, but keep me in love and patience. . . ."

After the prayer he lay in darkness and waited. But the ache did not leave him, it throbbed and throbbed and he felt the sting of the knife edge in his sensitive ear a hundred times each minute. God would not remove the ache, he fought his pain alone, and he was helpless and could do nothing to alleviate it. Deep inside his ear in a roaring storm his pain lived on.

He arose and lit the stable lantern. Arvid woke and wondered sleepily what had happened.

"I've a bad earache."

"The hell you have!"

"What shall I do?" Robert moaned pitifully.

The elder farmhand sat up in his bed and scratched his straggly hair. He cogitated.

The best remedy for earache was mother's milk, he said. But where would they get hold of a suckling woman who had some milk left in her breasts this time of night? The mistress had never even had a child; she was a dried-up woman. And the maids were virgins with unopened breasts.

But Arvid rose and brought forth his brannvin keg. "We'll try with brannvin on a wool wad."

He searched for a while in his servant chest and found some sheep's wool which he soaked in brannvin and put into his friend's aching ear.

"It will smart at first, but not for long."

The brannvin-soaked wool wad did smart so intensely that Robert almost pulled it out; he held his hands closed, cramplike, so as not to shriek. And after a moment the throbbing pain abated, as Arvid had said it would. No enjoyment can be greater than diminishing pain. He understood now that God had sent Arvid to help him; luckily there had been some brannvin left in the keg. Soon he glided into sleep, but some pain remained, mingling with his dreams: his left ear was filled with stinging wasps, a whole swarm of them, and they

crowded each other inside and stung, only stung. And his ear
swelled up and became one big sensitive boil where all the
wasps' stingers remained and hurt.

The pain in the ear was almost gone when Robert awakened the following morning, and within the next few days it
disappeared altogether, but a thick, yellowish, malodorous
fluid ran from his ear: it was the pain coming out. Something
did remain inside, however: the strange sound which no one
else could hear.

Yes, the buzzing and humming was still there; sometimes
he heard it more loudly, sometimes lower, but he was always
aware of it, inside the ear. It did not pain him, but he became
tired and disheartened at hearing it follow him night and day.
He put a bandage over his ear, he held his hand against it, he
struck a piece of wool into it, but the sound remained; nothing could silence it.

One night as he lay there and listened to his own ear he
realized what this strange sound meant which existed for him
only: he was listening to the rumbling of a great water, it was
the roar and din of the sea itself; it was the voice of the sea in
his ear, calling him, and him alone: he was chosen. The ocean
called him, urged him, and the hum in his ear became a word,
a word which always followed him, through night and day,
calling: Come!

Not yet could he come; all gates on the road still remained
closed.

                               2

One Sunday morning Robert appeared unexpected at his parents' home in Korpamoen. He had not been to see them since
he began his service, and Nils and Marta were pleased. Last
spring when he threw his clothes into the brook and rode to
the mill instead of going to Nybacken the boy had become
the laughingstock of the neighborhood, but since they had not
seen him the whole summer they would not mention that
now. Marta thought he was thin and his cheekbones sharp,
but when she asked him how he fared with Aron he gave no
reply.

Robert stayed home the whole Sunday, and when, after

supper, he still remained in his chair, Nils wondered if he shouldn't go back to his place of service before bedtime. The boy answered he had come home without his master's permission; he would never again go back to Nybacken.

Nils and Marta exchanged perplexed blances. Nils said: "When one has received earnest money, one must stay to the end of the year."

Robert said that if they wished to send him back to Nybacken they must first bind him hand and foot and tie him onto a wagon like a beast on its way to slaughter.

The parents did not know what to do; the son remained on his chair and said nothing more.

The mother called Karl Oskar: his brother refused to return to service of his own will.

"Did you leave Aron without permission?" asked Karl Oskar.

Robert removed his jacket and showed his bare back. Broad red streaks extended from one side to the other; the skin was broken and it had been bleeding.

Marta let out a cry: "You've been flogged, poor child!"

"Who has beaten you?" asked his brother.

Robert told the story. Yesterday he was bringing home a wagonload of rutabagas and had to pass a narrow gate; there was a curve in the road just before he reached the gate, the mare was hard to hold and didn't obey the rein quickly enough, he wagon hit the gatepost and broke its shaft; he couldn't help it, he had held the reins as firmly as he could. But Aron had grabbed a fence stake and hit him many times across his back. The stake had protruding knots which tore into his flesh. His back had ached the whole night, and in the morning he had left for home without letting anyone know. Not long ago, too, Aron had given him so hard a box on his ear that it still rang and buzzed. He would never again return to Nybacken.

Karl Oskar inspected the red streaks on his brother's back. "You needn't return. No one in our family need accept flogging. We are as good as Aron."

"Do you think Aron will release him without trouble?" wondered the mother.

"He can do as he pleases. The boy does not go back."

But Nils was worried. If Robert left service without permission, Aron would have the right to send the sheriff after him, and according to the servant law Robert would then lose half his pay and must defray Aron's expenses. Wouldn't it be better to settle amicably?

"I'll go and speak to him," Karl Oskar said firmly. But it didn't sound as if he were thinking of reconciliation.

Robert regretted he had not returned home earlier and confided in his elder brother. Marta brought out some pork bile and covered her son's wounds with it.

His brother's bloody back was an insult to Karl Oskar and to the whole Nilsa family. Since the father was lame and broken-down, and not able to defend his younger son, it thus became his duty.

Karl Oskar picked up his cap and went straight to Nybacken. At a distance he caught sight of Aron, who stood at the cattle well and hauled up water. Karl Oskar approached the farm cautiously, looking around as he crossed the barnyard. No one was in sight. It seemed he might have luck on this visit.

Aron did not notice Karl Oskar until the visitor stood next to him; he was so surprised that he almost dropped the well bucket which he was just removing from the hook. As he looked the unexpected caller in the face he began to retreat around the well curb, at the same time looking about as if in search of help.

"Are you coming to take your brother's place? Then I'll have a real hand!" He attempted a weak smile, timidly.

Karl Oskar went up close to the farmer of Nybacken. Aron could not move, his back was already against the wall around the well; he acted as if he intended to call for help.

"You've beaten my brother. You bastard! Do you realize he's only fifteen?"

"He got a little chastisement, he was lazy and careless."

"Drawing blood is not a little chastisement. You'd better get yourself another hand to flog. You'll get none from my family."

"Your brother had better be here tomorrow morning! Otherwise the sheriff will get him."

"Come and get him yourself! You'll get a welcome in Korpamoen!"

Aron's face grew whiter.

Karl Oskar took another half step, forcing his antagonist still closer to the well curb. He looked quickly about: no one was in sight. Aron became panicky, dropped the pail, and was just going to call for help when Karl Oskar grabbed him by the neck, choking the words in his throat.

Karl Oskar pushed him slowly backward until he was extended across the well opening; Aron was a living lid over the well, he lay there kicking and struggling, terror-stricken. With Karl Oskar's viselike grip at his throat he was unable to produce any sound but puffs and grunts. He did not know if Karl Oskar intended to choke him to death, or drown him, or both, but he was convinced he was going to die.

And Karl Oskar let him think so for a few minutes.

He pressed the farmer's throat a suitably long time before relaxing his grip. Aron collapsed like an empty sack against the well wall. Karl Oskar warned him that it would be enough for this time. They would undoubtedly meet soon again; it happened sometimes while they hauled timber during the winter. They had met more than once in out-of-the-way places—they might meet again, far from people. They would then continue their conversation. For he was most anxious to meet alone anyone who laid hands on a member of his family. And any bastard who attacked a fifteen-year-old was easy to handle.

Then Karl Oskar turned about and went home to Korpamoen. Robert met him at the gate.

"You'll have no more trouble from Aron, that much I can promise."

Robert had never been intimate with Karl Oskar, who was ten years older. If anything, he had been a little afraid of his big brother. For the first time today they felt really close. Shyness prevented Robert from telling his brother what he wished to, but someday he would show Karl Oskar that he thought more of him than of any other person in the world.

3

Robert remained in Korpamoen; but as he was a deserter, no one knew whether he would be left in peace at home. Karl Oskar advised him to be prepared to hide in the woods when visitors came.

A few days went by and nothing happened. Karl Oskar had suggested that Aron come to Korpamoen and get Robert, but he didn't show up and Karl Oskar did not expect him; as he scanned the road now and then he feared other callers. And one evening before dusk as he was standing near the gate the bitch began barking. Karl Oskar looked down the village road: an open carriage was approaching the farm. Two men were sitting in the wagon, and one of them wore a cap with broad yellow bands which glittered at a distance.

Robert was at the sawhorse next to the woodpile and Karl Oskar ran to warn him. But as soon as the dog started barking his brother had thrown away the saw; he now saw Robert disappear into the wood lot near the byre.

The carriage stopped at the gate, and Karl Oskar went to meet his callers.

"Good day, Karl Oskar Nilsson."

The long, wide uniform coat hampered Sheriff Lonnegren in his movements; he almost tripped as he stepped down from the carriage. He told his man to tie the horse to the gatepost.

Lonnegren was an unusually tall man. At fairs his head could be seen above all others. He was as strong as he was tall. When he had to stop a fight, he often grabbed one combatant and used him as a weapon against the other. When he corrected some wrongdoer he invariably said: You scoundrel! This was his word of greeting in the community when he executed his office. If he spoke to a more hardened person he would say: You big scoundrel! And when he dealt with thieves and criminals: You damned scoundrel! Lonnegren was severe in his office, but folk were agreed that he was not a bad man.

"I'm looking for your brother, the farmhand Robert Nilsson," he said.

"He's not in this house," answered Karl Oskar.

"Where is he?"

"I don't know where he is at the moment."

Sheriff Lonnegren gave the farmer of Korpamoen a piercing look. Karl Oskar looked back equally firmly.

The sheriff ordered his man to look around the farm and see if he could find the deserter.

He continued: "Aron of Nybacken has asked the assistance of authorities in bringing your brother back to his service. I presume you know he left last Sunday morning?"

"He left because the farmer flogged him."

Lonnegren nodded: Aron had said that he had corrected his hand with suitable chastisement, as was the right of masters, according to paragraph 5 of the servant law. But this chastisement was intended to improve the servant: the boy ought to have accepted it in mild submission. It did not give him the right to desert.

"My brother has shown me his bloody back."

The sheriff gave Karl Oskar another searching look.

"You've met, then? Has he been here?"

"Yes, but he isn't here any longer."

"Is he close by?"

"I don't know how close he might be."

Karl Oskar tried to evade the truth without lying.

The sheriff stroked his chin in deep thought. From his coat pocket he pulled a large stamped paper which he now unfolded. According to paragraph 52 of the servant law, and Chapter 16, paragraph 7, of the land code, a master had the right to enforce the return of a deserted servant. In the name of the law he now asked Karl Oskar to divulge his brother's whereabouts.

"I am not responsible for my brother."

"The boy has once before tried to get away. It's a second offense."

The sheriff's man returned: the escaped one could not be found outside the house.

The sheriff's patience was coming to an end. "You are harboring the deserter, you scoundrel! Turn him over!"

Karl Oskar answered: According to the law he did not consider himself duty-bound to help the authorities apprehend his own brother. In any case, he would first like to see the paper concerning such duty.

The sheriff did not answer; this big-nosed peasant was not born on the porch, he knew his rights. And if it were up to him alone, the boy might well go. It was a most unpleasant task to hunt poor farmhands who evaded the servant law. But law was law and duty was duty; it was his business to see to it that the servant law was followed.

Karl Oskar watched the sheriff's face and became bolder. If the sheriff himself had a brother who had escaped from his master because of flogging, would he then report his brother for apprehension?

The sheriff shouted in answer: "If you cannot tell the truth, you might at least shut up, you scoundrel!"

But he looked up toward the sky for a moment, and Karl Oskar thought: What people said about him was true; if he hadn't been sheriff he might have been almost a good man.

Lonnegren turned his back on Karl Oskar and called his man to accompany him; they went into the house. The sheriff and his servant searched the main room, they went into the kitchen where Kristina stood with the frightened children hanging on to her skirts. They looked into the reserved room where Nils and Marta sat silent and immovable on their chairs, and felt the shame of the search; no sheriff had ever before been to this house. They went up the stepladder into the attic, where they felt in a pile of old clothes; the dust rose from the rags and the sheriff came down angry and coughing. They had looked through the house, and the search continued now through the barns. Lonnegren remained in the yard while his helper went through a heap of unwashed wool in the byre, ascended the hay loft and kicked here and there in the hay, went down into the cellar, through the wagon cover, the woodshed, and the outhouse.

The authorities had to leave, their errand unsuccessful. Karl Oskar escorted the sheriff to his carriage. When Loonegren was seated he said: "I'll get the rascal if he remains in this district. Do you hear me, Karl Oskar Nilsson? I'll catch up with your brother if he remains *in my district!*"

The young farmer in Korpamoen looked thoughtfully after the sheriff's departing carriage: he had got the implication; he understood.

4

Karl Oskar stayed up late that evening and waited for his brother. Toward midnight Robert knocked on the window and was admitted. He had been over in a neighbor's field, and had hidden in Jonas Petter's meadow barn the whole evening. The night frosts had set in, and he shivered and shook. There was still some fire on the hearth and Karl Oskar put on a pot and warmed milk for his brother.

The sheriff's statement, he said, must be interpreted to

mean that Robert need not worry about being returned to Nybacken if he stayed outside the sheriff's district. He could therefore not remain at home any longer. Kristina had suggested that he stay for some time with her parents in Duvemala. The parish of Algutsboda was outside Lonnegren's district. He could safely remain there until some other opening turned up; Kristina's parents needed a hand, they were both considerate and would treat him well, not on account of the relationship only. Few of the farmers hereabouts treated their help as badly as Aron in Nybacken.

Robert said he was glad to obey his brother and sister-in-law: early in the morning he would set out for Duvemala.

Still feeling cold after the many hours in Jonas Petter's windy barn, he moved closer to the hearth; across from him sat Karl Oskar and stirred the embers with the fire tongs. The brothers had seldom been together at home; Karl Oskar had been away in service while Robert grew up; they had been strangely foreign to each other until last Sunday, when Robert came home with his wounded back.

Robert was thinking: He had been a lazy and negligent farmhand; perhaps it was his inborn sinful nature which inclined him to idleness and disobedience. He had, according to the ordinances of God and man, received chastisement, and he was now a deserter, hunted by the sheriff. But he was no longer afraid of anything in this world because he had a big, protective brother. He need keep no secrets from this brother. Now as he sat here alone with him in the night was the right moment. Now it must out, now it must be said, what he ought to have said long ago, what he regretted not having said last spring.

He could hear the echo of Aron's hard box in his ear, that eternal hum, the sound of that water which covered three-quarters of the globe's surface, the great sea's message to him, the ocean's command: Come!

It was dark in the room, only a small section near the fireplace was lighted by the flickering embers. Now it must be said, now when they sat here together, as intimate brothers.

Robert did not look up as he began: "You've been good to me, Karl Oskar. I want to ask something of you."

"Yes? If I can give it to you."

"I would like to get my inheritance from the farm. I intend to go to North America."

He had managed it, he had spoken, it was done. He inhaled deeply, then he waited.

A few minutes passed and Karl Oskar had not yet answered. He had heard big words from his brother, he had heard the fifteen-year-old speak as a grown man, he had heard him say boldly, challengingly, like a man: I intend to move to North America. But he did not answer.

Several more minutes elapsed and still nothing was said between the brothers. The elder kept silent, the younger one waited for him to speak. The grandfather's clock in the corner creaked and snapped, the dying embers crackled on the hearth. And in Robert's ear was heard the humming, roaring sound of the great water, challenging him to come and sail upon it.

Rays from the fire lit up Karl Oskar's face. The younger brother sat close to the hearth and stared into the glowing ashes; he dared not look at his brother just now.

What could he expect? He knew in advance what he was going to hear. Through his one healthy ear he would hear his brother speak of childish ideas, notions of a fifteen-year-old. What possesses you, Robert? You know very well, my little brother, that you cannot handle your inheritance before you are of age, before you are twenty-one. And you think a boy like you can travel to the other end of the world? Much is still lacking in your head; you must stay at home and eat many loaves of bread before you can leave the country. You must ripen in your notions, my little brother. Your big brother knows more about the world than you. Listen now to what he has to say, this your elder, wiser brother.

But the surprising thing was that Robert couldn't hear his brother say anything at all. Karl Oskar sat with the fire tongs in his hands, his elbows on his knees, and poked in the embers and kept silent. Robert dared not even look toward his face. Had his tongue become paralyzed from shock when he heard his brother say: I intend to go to North America?

Robert   began   again: "You   were   startled,   Karl Oskar . . . ?"

"Ye-es."

"I understand."

"Never before in all my life have I been so startled!"

Now Karl Oskar raised his head and looked at his brother

with a broad smile. "Because—I could never in the world have guessed that you had the same thoughts as I!"

"You too—Karl Oskar?"

"Yes. Those ideas have been my own lately. But I haven't mentioned a word to anyone except Kristina."

What was this that Robert's healthy ear heard tonight? Weren't Karl Oskar's words a hearing-illusion, like the storm of the sea in the other ear?

Had two brothers ever before so surprised each other as Karl Oskar and Robert did this night, sitting together round the dying embers of the fire? When before had two brothers so promptly agreed in a great, life-important decision, as these two now did—before the embers on the hearth had even blackened?

Karl Oskar said: Robert need not move alone; he would have the company of his brother and sister-in-law and their children, he would have the company of all who were young on the farm.

The hum in Robert's ear was intense and persistent tonight, louder than usual. Now he could answer "Yes!" to the message and the challenge in his sick ear: I come!

He had opened his first gate on the road to America.

VII

ABOUT A WHEAT FIELD AND A BOWL OF BARLEY PORRIDGE

1

The first ships have already crossed the ocean, bearing emigrants away from the land.

There is a stir in peasant communities which have been the home of unchangeableness itself for thousands of years. To the earth folk, seeing their plots diminish while their offspring increase, tidings have come of a vast land on another continent where fertile soil was to be had almost for the taking by all who wished to come and till it. Into old gray cottages in

tranquil hamlets where food is scarce for folk living according
to inherited customs and traditions, a new restlessness is
creeping over the threshold. Rumors are spread, news is
shared, information is carried from neighbor to neighbor,
through vales and valleys, through parishes and counties.
These germs of unrest are like seeds scattered by the wind:
one takes root somewhere deep in a man's soul and begins its
growth unknown to others; the sowing has been done in secret, thus the sprouting surprises neighbors and friends.

At first the movement is slow and groping. The only evi-
dence of this new land is supplied by pictures and rumors.
None in the home communities had seen or explored it. And
the unknown ocean is forbidding. All that is unknown is uncertain—the home community is familiar and safe. Argument
is rife, for and against; some hesitate, some dare; the daring
stand against the hesitating, men against women, youth
against age. The cautious and the suspicious always have their
objections: *For sure*, we know nothing. . . .

Only the bold and enterprising have sufficient courage: they
are the instruments which stir up the tranquil hamlets and
shake the order of unchangeableness.

These separate from the multitude and fill a few small ships
—a trickle here and there starts the running stream which in
due time swells to a mighty river.

2

Karl Oskar Nilsson had seen a picture. He had called one day
on the churchwarden, Per Persson in Akerby, and had borrowed a newspaper; there he had seen the picture.

That same day, after he came home, he plowed his rye
stubble. He drove an ox and a cow; he had been forced to sell
one ox, so now he hitched the cow under the yoke; the two
beasts made a poor and uneven team. From time immemorial
farmers had driven oxen—he felt ashamed to drive a cow
along the roads, it was in some way degrading. And he felt
sorry for his cow, who had to pull the plow as well as to give
milk. The pull cow was with calf also, he could see the calf
stir in her. She walked heavily in the furrow, her udder already so swollen she moved her hind legs with difficulty. The

team dragged at a snail's pace across the field because of the poor cow. Karl Oskar had not the heart to prod an animal who had to carry a calf as well as drag a plow.

God was hard on the people, and the people were hard on the animals. He suffered because he must use the poor cow, but he couldn't pull the plow himself, and he must plow the field lest his children be without bread next year. His children, too, were innocent beings. But according to God's world order, which he had never been able to understand despite much thought, the innocent must suffer with the guilty. Drought and crop failure hit the righteous and the unrighteous alike.

Suddenly the plow hit an earth-bound stone which threw it from the furrow. Karl Oskar looked closer and saw that part of the plow remained in the ground: the wooden plowshare was broken, split in two.

He unhitched the team and went home. He knew enough about carpentry to make a new plowshare, but he did not go to the workbench. Instead, he went inside the house and sat down. It was the middle of the day and Kristina was surprised: was he already back from the field? He answered that he had broken the plow; it was a damned earth-bound stone; all the fields round here were damned.

He wouldn't curse and carry on so because of some such small mishap, she thought; it wasn't like him. And, she added in her thoughts, neither was it like him to sit here inside in the middle of the day, and neglect his work.

Karl Oskar looked out through the window at the unplowed rye stubble; his brow wrinkled in discouragement. After a time he picked up the paper he had brought from the churchwarden's. It was borrowed property, and he wiped his fingers on his trousers before he touched it; he handled the sheet carefully, as if it had been a valuable deed. Then his eyes fell on the picture: "A Wheat Field in North America."

It was a field at harvest-time, and the crop was still standing in shocks. An even field was visible, an endless field without borders or fences. The wheat field had no end at the horizon, it stretched beyond the place where sky met the earth. Not a single stone or heap of stones, no hillock or knoll was visible on this whole wide field of wheat stubble. It lay even and smooth as the floor boards of his own cottage. And in this field shock stood by shock so close they almost touched each other, so close a rick could hardly pass between them. The strong sheaves rose from the shocks, spreading out their long, swollen, full-developed heads of wheat, like golden crowns. A powerful, strong-grown seed was shocked on this field. Every head of wheat was like a mighty blossom, every straw like a sapling, every sheaf like a shrub.

From a clear sky the sun shone down on this multitude of golden grain. The sun shown down on a fertile field, a field to which had been given grain and kernel. The shocks were as innumerable as the billows on the sea; here surged a sea of golden grain, a tremendous granary of endless dimensions. It was the fruit of the earth that he saw here, an unmeasurable quantity of bread for man: "A Wheat Field in North America."

A story could be invented, people's word could be inaccurate, a description could be imaginary. But a picture could not be false, a picture could not lie. It could only show things as they were. What he saw must be somewhere before it could be pictured; what his eyes beheld was not illusion: this field of wheat existed. This ground without stones and hillocks was somewhere in the world. These potent sheaves, these golden heads of wheat, had grown; no one could step forward and deny it. Everything he saw in this picture, all this splendor to a farmer's eye, it existed, it *was* somewhere—in another world, in the New World.

Karl Oskar Nilsson, owner of seven stony acres in stone-country Korpamoen, sat quietly for long, his eyes lingering upon the picture. His mind's eye reveled in this grandeur. He held up the paper reverently before him, as if he were sitting on a church bench of a Sunday, following the hymn with the psalmbook in his hand.

It was in the Old World that God once had cursed the soil because of man; in the New World the ground still was blessed.

3

A few words were printed under the picture: "It has been said that work-willing farmers have great prospects of future success in the United States."

It happened the day when Karl Oskar plowed his rye stubble and broke the plowshare. That was the beginning; then it went on through many days and—as he lay awake—through the nights.

He wasn't actually slow when it came to making up his mind; but this was the greatest decision of his life, and more than one day was needed for it; it must be made with "common sense and ripe consideration," as is stated in bills of sale and other important documents. He needed a few weeks to think it over.

So far he had shown the picture of the North American wheat field only to Kristina, and she had looked at it casually. She could not know that her husband carried that picture in his mind wherever he went.

Through the long autumn evenings they sat in front of the fire, busy with their indoor activities. Karl Oskar whittled ax handles and wooden teeth for the rakes, and Kristina carded wool and spun flax. At last, one evening after the children had gone to sleep and it was quiet in the room, he began to talk. In advance he had thought over what he should say, and in his mind he had fought all the obstacles and excuses his wife might make.

As for himself, he had decided on the move and now he would like to hear what she thought of it.

She asked first: "Are you making fun of me?"

What was she to think? Here he sat and suddenly announced that he intended to sell his farm, and all he owned. Then with his whole family—a wife and three children and a fourth not yet born—he would move away; not to another village or parish, nor to another place in this country, or to any country on this continent. But to a new continent! He might just as well have stretched it a little further, it would have made no difference to her had he announced that he intended to move them all to the moon; he must be jesting with her.

But as he continued to talk, she realized he spoke in earnest. This new idea was exactly like Karl Oskar, like no one else. He never let well enough alone, he was not satisfied with what others considered sufficient. He was never satisfied with anything in this world; he reached for the impossible, the little-known. He had told her once before he would sell Korpamoen; then he wanted to be a timberman. Another time it

had been a horse trader, and again, enlistment as a soldier.
And when he decided to move, of course nothing less than
North America would do—the other end of the world! If he
had been satisfied with less he would not have been Karl
Oskar.

But now Kristina must answer with innermost sincerity and
let him know what she felt in her heart. So they talked, and
exchanged their opinions, evening after evening, while the
crackling fire alone interrupted their conversation and at
times was even louder than they.

Why did Karl Oskar want to move?

For four years now they had lived in Korpamoen, and
today they were several hundred riksdaler poorer than when
they started. Four years they had spilled the strength of their
youth here, to no purpose. If they remained they would have
to continue struggling and slaving until they could move neither hand nor foot, until they finally sat there, worn out,
worked out, limp and broken. No one would then thank them
for having ruined themselves for no earthly good. They could
mirror themselves in his father, who sat crippled in his room.
In this place they had nothing more to look forward to than
the reserved room; it would be ready for them one day, when
they were able-bodied no more, and from then on they would
sit there, like his father and mother now, and reproach themselves all through their old age; health and strength would be
gone, but from all the work through all the years they would
have naught to show but the reserved room with its meager
bread.

*However much they struggled and toiled, they could never
improve their situation here in Korpamoen.*

He didn't know much about conditions in the United
States, but he did know that once there he would be given,
for next to nothing, fertile, stone-free soil which was now
only waiting for the plowshare. Things which he had no
money to purchase here could be obtained for very little in
North America. They were both of them strong and healthy
and accustomed to hard work, and that was all that they need
bring along: their ability to work; it was all America asked of
them. Perhaps they must face as much drudgery as here, but

they would do it in another spirit, with another hope, another joy. Because the great difference between the two countries was this: *In America they could improve their lot through their own work.*

He for his part was weary of the struggle which led nowhere. Nonetheless he could continue his work with a happy heart if he believed he could improve the situation for himself and his. People liked to fight for a goal, at least while still young, as they both were. What else was there to live for? But one day their children would be grown and shifting for themselves, and what sort of future awaited them here? One child would inherit the farm, but what about the others? They would have to work as hired farmhands or become squatters. No third choice existed. There were already so many hired hands that they competed in offering their services to farmers; there were too many cottagers already, soon every opening in the forest would have its rotten, rickety shack with the black earth for floor. The people in these huts seldom had meat with their bread—and many days no bread. Karl Oskar and Kristina did not want their children to become hired farmhands or crofters; but they could do nothing better for them unless they took them from this impoverished place. If they felt responsibility for their children, they must move away.

On one point all information from North America agreed: the people had in every way more liberty in that country. The four classes were long ago abolished there, they had no king who sat on a throne and drew a high salary. The people themselves elected a President who could be thrown from office if they didn't like him. They had no high officials who annoyed the people, no sheriff who came and took the farmers' belongings. And at the community meeting everyone spoke as freely as his neighbor, for all had equal rights.

If he now sold his farm with everything on it, chattels and kine included, Karl Oskar would have enough money to pay the transportation for all of them with some small part left over for the settling in the new country.

He had long turned it over in his mind, thought about it, weighed arguments for and against, but this conviction remained with him: a farm couple still in their youth, hale and hearty, could undertake nothing wiser than to emigrate to the United States of America.

Why Kristina wanted to remain at home:

Karl Oskar had drawn a beautiful and sanguine picture. If Kristina could believe it all as he painted it for her, she would not for one moment hesitate to follow him.

But she was afraid it might turn out to be a wild-goose chase. Her husband believed all he heard and saw about America. But who could guarantee its truth? What did they have to rely on? Who had promised them tillable soil in the United States? Those who ruled over there had not written him a letter or given him a promise. He had no deed to a piece of land that would await them on arrival. One taking such a journey needed written words and agreements before starting.

They had never met a single person who had been to North America; they knew of no one who had set foot in that country, no one who could tell them what the land was like. If a reliable human being who had seen the country with his own eyes had advised emigration, that would be different. In the printed words of newspapers and books she had no confidence.

If moving to North America was so advisable for young farm folk, then there must be some who had already done so. But they knew no such folk. He could not mention the name of a single farmer—young or old—who had emigrated with wife and children; the wisdom of such a move existed only in his head.

He had also forgotten to mention the fact that they must sail on a fragile ship across the ocean; he had said nothing about the dangerous voyage. How often had they heard about ships wrecked and sunk? No one knew if they would ever reach America alive. Even if exposing themselves to all these dangers were advisable, had they the right to venture the lives of their children on a voyage which wasn't necessary, which they weren't forced to undertake? The children were too young to consult, and perhaps they would rather remain at home, even as squatters, than be pulled down into the depth of the ocean; perhaps it were better to earn one's bread as a farmhand, and live, than to be a corpse on the bottom of the sea, eaten by whales and other sea-faring monsters.

Karl Oskar wanted to emigrate because he felt responsibility for his children; Kristina wanted to remain at home for the same reason.

And what did he know about the children's lot in the foreign country? Had someone there written him that Anna would become a lady, or that Johan would be a gentleman of leisure?

He hadn't mentioned, either, that they must separate from their parents, brothers and sisters, relatives and friends—in short, all those they knew. Had he realized they would come to places where every human being they met was a stranger? They might have to live in communities where people were ill-natured and cruel; they were to live in a land where they would be unable to speak one word of the language, unable to ask a single soul for a drink of water if they needed it; where they might have to die without their tongues being able to cry for help. In such a land they would wander about like changelings, alien and lost. Had he never thought that their life might be lonely and bleak?

If she moved so far away she might never be able to return home; she might never see her nearest and dearest again;
ever meet parents, brothers and sisters. At once she would lose them all, and even though they lived they would be dead to her; they would be alive and yet dead.

True enough, things had gone backwards for them and they had had bad luck. But it might soon change, they might have a good year, they might have good fortune. At least they had the necessary food each day, and even though—as it looked for the moment—they might have to starve a bit this winter, they would most likely eat so much the better next year. They weren't dressed in silk and satin, of course, but at least they were able to cover their bodies and keep their children warm. Surely they would gain their sufficiency at home in future as they had in the past, as other people did.

All wise and thoughtful men whose advice he might seek would answer him as she had.

Kristina wanted to remain at home.

4

Through many autumnal evenings, while busy with their respective handiwork before the fire, the husband and wife in Korpamoen exchanged their divergent views on this decision which would determine their future. Karl Oskar held out the prospect of new advantages and possibilities through emigration; Kristina saw only drawbacks. When she came to the end of her objections, she always had this argument to fall back on: "If only someone we know had emigrated before. But none in these parts has ever gone."

His answer was always the same: "Let us be the first; someone must be first, in everything."

"And you're willing to shoulder the responsibility?"

"Yes. Someone must be responsible, in all undertakings."

She knew her husband by now: he had never relinquished what once he had decided upon, and hitherto he had always had his will, defying her and his parents. But this time he must fall in with her; this time she would not give in; this time he must change his mind.

She spoke to Nils and Marta: they must help her to dissuade Karl Oskar from this dangerous project.

But the parents only felt sorry for their foolhardy son and could give his wife no assistance. Nils said: Ever since Karl Oskar was able to button up his trousers alone in the outhouse, he had never asked advice or help from his parents. He would persist even more stubbornly if his father and mother tried to influence him.

Kristina began to realize that this time more than ever Karl Oskar knew what he wanted. And so did she.

5

After the drought and crop failure came winter now, and famine. The summer had been short, had died in its youth; the winter would last so much longer with its starvation.

The sheriff's carriage was seen more often on the roads. His errands concerned the poorest farms, and the carriage remained long at the gates. The sheriff's horses were seldom in their stalls this winter: they were tied to gateposts, waiting for their master, who had much to do inside the houses; the horses were covered by blankets but still cold: they had to wait so long.

> "Hurry up and hide your mittens!
> The sheriff comes to take each pittance."

Even before the snow had set in, little children could be seen along the roads, pale, with sunken cheeks, their running noses blue. Once arrived at a farm, they didn't go to the main entrance; they went to the refuse pile near the kitchen door, where they remained awhile, scratching in the debris, searching. Then they went inside the house but stayed close to the door. The boys bowed, the girls would curtsy. With their forefingers they would try to dry their noses; then they would stand there, in the corner near the door, silent, timid.

They had no errand. They had already brought their message to anyone who looked closely: the mute testimony of hunger.

Parents sent their children begging, ashamed to be seen themselves. To the small ones, begging was no shame. For wretched, starving children begging was a natural occupation, the only one they were able to perform, their only help.

Perhaps some time might elapse before anyone in the house paid notice to the unknown children, huddling in their corner at the door. Perhaps the house folk sat at table; then the children waited until all had eaten, inhaling the smell of food, the savory odor of boiled potatoes, beef soup, fried pork. They stood there watching, their eyes growing big, their nostrils extended. The longer the meal lasted, the bigger grew their nostrils, and sometimes it happened, when they had stood there a long time, smelling the food, that one of them might faint and fall to the floor.

At length they would be spoken to, then they would ask if they might pick up the herring heads and beef bones which they had seen outside on the refuse pile. The bones could be crushed to get the marrow which their mother would boil to soup. And if there was something for the refuse pile in the house, might they have it? It could be used at home. Father and Mother had taught them what to say.

The parents had told them not to ask too much. They must beg for such as the people in the house had no use for themselves; they must not boldly ask for bread. For he who asked least often obtained most. But if they sometimes happened to receive a slice of bread, they would gulp it immediately; Father and Mother must never know.

The children trudged along, sucking their salt herring heads, dragging their bundles of clean-gnawed bones. They went to the next farm, searched the next refuse pile; no one snubbed them when they came inside and asked for herring heads which they saw glittering outside.

The small children were famine's pure witnesses. No one had the heart to hurl at them the word which adults feared: Shame!

Each one was supposed to beg in the parish where he lived. But those who felt ashamed would rather go to distant parishes, would rather beg from unknown people. The hunger tore and dug in stomach and bowels, but the humiliation of begging dug itself into the crevices of the soul.

Even older persons walked along the roads, big, full-grown men who carried on their backs brooms, brushes, baskets, or wooden vessels which they offered for sale. They pursued an honest calling, no one could accuse them of begging, but if they were told in some house that no trade would take place, they still remained sitting. They kept their errand secret under the burden on their backs but after sitting for a while it would escape: Give me a piece of bread! I'm too weak to go farther. It smarted deep in the soul of many a wanderer before those words escaped. Therefore the pale children were sent upon the roads.

6

Kristina baked famine bread; when the rye flour did not suffice she added chaff, beechnuts, heather seed, and dried berries of the mountain ash. She also tried to grind acorns and mix them in the dough, but such bread caused constipation and the bowels would not move for many days. She boiled an edible porridge from hazelnut kernels, and used it instead of the clear rye porridge which they had to do without this winter. No real nourishment was found, though, in famine food: sprouts, seeds, nuts, and other products from the wastelands did fill the stomach but gave no lasting satisfaction. One left the table because the meal was over, not because one was satisfied. And however much they stretched and added, all the bins and foodboxes would be empty long before the next crop was ripe.

In the middle of the winter the time was up for Kristina,

and she bore a son. They were now eight people in Korpamoen.

Owing to the meager fare this winter the mother had not sufficient milk for the newborn; her breasts were dry long before he was satisfied, and a suckling could not stand the bitter milk from their starved cows. This was a bad winter for a new arrival into the world. Kristina must now choose the most nourishing pieces for herself, in order to give milk to the little one. But the other children needed food too; she noticed that Anna, the eldest, had fallen off and grown very thin. Kristina felt as if she stole food from three of her children to give to the fourth.

The newborn was to be given the name Anders Harald, and was to be called Harald. But whom should they ask to carry him at the baptism? When Kristina wished as godparents her relatives in Karragarde, Danjel and Inga-Lena, this caused great consternation in Nils and Marta: Danjel was preaching the heresy of Ake Svensson, and the dean had excluded him from the Lord's Supper because of his unlawful Bible explanations. This impious man was not to carry their grandchild to his baptism.

Karragarde had once more a bad reputation. Kristina did not understand how her uncle could take loose, bad people into his home, but she had known Danjel since she was a little girl, and he had always been good to her. Nor had he done harm to any other person; she knew of no man more kind than he. So she thought that the dean had done him a great injustice: only the greatest sinners were excluded from the Lord's Supper table. Ulrika of Vastergohl had long been forbidden the body and blood of Christ, and it was only right that one who for gain lay on her back with any man should be forbidden to kneel with honest people at the altar. But Uncle Danjel had neither whored nor murdered, neither defrauded nor stolen. In Ljunder Parish there were many much greater sinners who enjoyed the holy sacraments. He was mistaken in spiritual things, but he did not deserve to be pointed out and avoided as a robber and evildoer. Kristina wanted to show all people that she considered her uncle an honest man —and therefore she wished to invite him to be godfather to her newborn son.

Marta asked: Was she prepared to leave her innocent child

to be carried to baptism by a man possessed of the Evil
Spirit? Was she willing to hand over her own offspring to the
devil?

Danjel had said that he no longer accepted interest on
money which he lent, and from this Karl Oskar deduced his
wits were failing; the peasant of Karragarde had been
stricken by a disturbance of his senses when he embraced
Ake's teachings. But no one should be punished because of illness, even though it were illness of the mind. The dean therefore had no right to exclude Danjel from gatherings of
Christian people, and give a bad name to his home, for anyone who passed through the gate of his farm, now, was almost considered eternally lost. It was foolish of Danjel to
gather whores and drunkards into his house, but God would
hardly punish him because he fed and protected paupers.

Karl Oskar agreed with Kristina; they would show the dean
what they thought of Danjel, and invite him to godfather
their little one. Karl Oskar himself bore the invitation to
Karragarde.

He returned home disappointed; Danjel had said he was excluded from christenings as well as communion; he could be
neither godfather nor witness to a baptism in the church; he
was forbidden to carry their child to its christening.

Kristina was downcast, but Karl Oskar was angry at the
dean who prevented them from choosing godparents for their
own child. He felt a strong desire to go and tell the dean that
he interfered too much. But Brusander was his pastor, and
for the sake of one's salvation one should not be on bad terms
with one's spiritual guide. This much, though, he was sure of:
in North America, no minister had power to prevent any person from carrying a child to Christian baptism.

Instead, they now asked their neighbors in Hasteback,
Jonas Petter and his wife Brita-Stafva, to be godparents for
little Harald. No one else was invited to the christening ale,
except Karl Oskar's sister Lydia, who served as maid in
Krakesjo.

Nor was there much from which to prepare a feast this
winter. Kristina cooked the christening porridge from some
barley grains which she had hidden away in a small sack for
this very day, and she had also a little butter and sugar to put
into the porringer. Her three children stood around her as she
poured out the pot. It was a long time since the little ones had

seen such food in the house, food with such odor. Kristina poured the porridge into a large earthen bowl, not to be touched until the godparents returned from church with the newly christened one; she put the bowl in the cellar to cool off.

Karl Oskar and Kristina attended to the chores in the byre while Jonas Petter and Brita-Stafva were at church. The children were alone inside.

When the parents came in again they missed Anna. They started to look for her, inside and outside the house, but they were unable to find her. Nils and Marta did not know where she had gone; she was four years old, and able to go alone to the neighbors, but she never left the farm without permission.

Karl Oskar was greatly disturbed; what could have happened to the child? She was as dear to him as his own eyes, his constant comrade at work, keeping him company everywhere. Only today he had promised to take her to the shoemaker and have her feet measured for a pair of shoes; her old ones were entirely worn out. This she could not have forgotten; so much the stranger that she had disappeared shortly before they were to leave.

They looked in vain for the child in the wood lot, and the father was about to go to the neighbors to inquire when Kristina came running and said that Anna was in the cellar; she had passed by, had heard a faint crying, and had opened the door.

Anna lay stretched out on the floor of the cellar. She cried as if with pain. Next to her on the floor stood the earthen bowl which Kristina had put there a few hours earlier to cool off; at that time it was filled to the brim with barley porridge, now only a third was left.

The little girl was carried inside the house and put to bed. Tearfully, she asked her parents' forgiveness for what she had done. She had been unable to forget the bowl of porridge which she had seen and smelled in the kitchen; she was so hungry for the porridge. She had seen her mother put it away in the cellar; she could not resist her desire to steal down there and look at it. At first she had only wished to smell it, then she had wanted to taste it a little—so little that no one would notice. She found a spoon and began to eat. And once she had started eating, she was unable to stop. Never had she tasted anything so delicious; the more she ate, the more she wanted; each spoonful tasted better—she could not stop until most of the porridge was gone. Then she became afraid, she dared not go back into the house, she dared not show herself after her disobedience. She remained in the cellar, and after a while she was seized by fierce pain in her stomach.

Anna had eaten herself sick on the barley porridge; it was too strong a fare for her after the famine food of the winter. Her stomach swelled up like a drum, firm and expanded. She let out piercing shrieks as the pain increased.

Berta of Idemo was sent for. She was accustomed to relieve stomachache with the heat from woolen clothes, and now she laid a thick bandage of warmed woolen stockings around the waist of the child. She also wished to administer mare's milk for internal relief, and Lydia ran to Krakesjo, where a mare had recently foaled; she returned with a quart of milk from the mare and Anna was made to drink this.

But nothing eased the suffering of the child. Berta said the barley grains had swelled in the bowels of the little girl to twice their original size, thus causing something to burst. She could not take responsibility for healing such damage.

Anna cried loudly and asked someone to help as the pain grew agonizing. Again and again she asked her parents' forgiveness for having disobeyed: she had known that no one should touch the porridge before evening when the guests returned.

During the night she became delirious at intervals. Berta said that if she didn't improve before morning, God might fetch the child home; she wanted to prepare the parents to the best of her ability.

Anna heard her words and said she did not wish God to fetch her home; she wanted to remain here. She was wise for her years, she used to ask many strange questions which the grownups couldn't answer. As her suffering increased she called her father to help her; she wanted to get up and go with him to the cobbler for the measurements of the shoes she had been promised. Her cries could be heard out into the byre, where the cows answered with their bellowing, thinking someone was on his way to feed them.

Early in the morning the child died in her agony.

Anyone who spoke to Karl Oskar during the next few days got no answer. Nor did a second or third attempt help much.

At length, he might answer with a question, showing that he had heard nothing at all.

Nils asked if he should go out and make a coffin for Anna. This time Karl Oskar heard, and answered at once: The coffin for his dead child he wished to make himself; nothing else could be thought of.

He went out to the work shed where he kept a pile of well-sawed spruce boards; there was more than enough lumber for a coffin. Nor would many boards be required for a coffin to enclose Anna's little shrunken body. The father began to examine the pile, he wanted to choose straight, fine, knot-free boards, clear and without bark. But he discarded every one his hands touched; all were either crooked or warped, or outside boards, or knotty. He picked up one plank after another, inspected it, and threw it aside; it was impossible to find a single one in the pile that he could use, that would make a coffin good enough for Anna.

After a while he tired of searching for good boards and remained sitting on the chopping block, doing nothing. He sat there and listened to the child who had only lately spoken to him: "It hurts to die, Father. I don't want God to fetch me if it is so painful; I want to stay home. Couldn't I stay home, even though I ate the porridge? I'll never again taste anything without permission—please, let me stay home! You're so big and strong, Father, can't you protect me so God won't take me? Oh, Father, if you only knew how it hurts! Why doesn't anyone help me? I am so little. Would you like to die, Father? Do you want God to come and get you?"

As long as the father could still hear calls for help from his dead child, the living ones around him would receive no answer; he did not hear them.

In the evening Nils asked his son how he was getting along with the coffin. Karl Oskar answered he was still choosing boards.

The following day, also, no sounds of hammer and plane were heard from the woodshed. Karl Oskar's only explanation was that he was looking for boards.

On the third day, when it still remained silent in the shed, Nils hobbled out on his crutches and sat down at the work-bench. He then made the coffin for the dead one while Karl Oskar looked on.

When the work was finished the son said: "It's not good enough."

Now, Nils in his life had made more than one hundred coffins, and all who had ordered them had been satisfied—not one had ever been discarded. For the first time he had completed work that was not accepted, that was discarded by his own son: he had used one board with a big ugly knot, another was cut crookedly, and here a nail stuck out. Was Anna, his little girl, to rest on sharp nails? Karl Oskar found many faults with the coffin his father had made; he took an ax and smashed it to pieces.

Nils was hurt, his eldest son once and for all was an impossible person; nothing suited him. Now Karl Oskar must make the coffin himself. At last he found some straight, knot-free boards, which he accepted; he carried them to the workbench, where he remained through the night; in the morning the coffin was ready.

It was a father's labor, done during a lonely night of sorrow, in the dim light from the lantern out in the woodshed. Those who saw the coffin perhaps didn't understand. Perhaps, indeed, there was no difference between this coffin and the broken, discarded one. But this one was made by a father's careful hands, it was nailed together by fingers which still were reaching out for something lost.

God gave to two parents a child to love and care for, and when they had had time to grow attached to the little one, deeply, then He took her back. Had they committed some sin to deserve this? What evil had Karl Oskar done that he must make this coffin?

During the same week, christening and grave ale were held in Korpamoen. Karl Oskar carried his child's coffin in his arms to the grave, where the dean filled his shovel with earth and said that Anna would now be like the earth on that shovel, and would not live again until awakened on the last day.

The child had eaten of the barley porridge.

Of the wretched barley which grew last summer they had garnered only a few bushels, and of this a small portion had been ground to grits. From the last grits Kristina had cooked porridge for the christening. But when the barley field stood green, no one had said to the child: If you eat of this you shall surely die!

Anna had died because the earth here was cursed. It must be so; this field where the deadly barley had grown must be stricken by the Lord's word to Adam.

Karl Oskar beheld the pale beggar children wandering about, searching for sustenance in the refuse piles, and he thought: My child found good food, her bowels burst from sugared and buttered barley porridge. Yet she too was a pawn to hunger.

For many weeks after the funeral Kristina was crushed; most of what she did she did wrongly, and other chores stayed undone. A thousand times she reproached herself, asking: Why didn't I hide the bowl of christening porridge where no one could find it? Why didn't I let the children taste it before putting it away? If I had done this, Anna would be alive.

A long time elapsed, and the parents had not mentioned the name of their dead child. They never spoke of the little girl they had lost; their sorrow would have become doubly heavy if it had been brought out into clear daylight, and its power acknowledged. Now they tried to push it away, not let it penetrate beyond thought. As long as words didn't help, why use them? Exchanged between two mourning people, they were only a dissonant sound, disturbing the bitter consolation of silence.

A month had passed since Anna's funeral when Kristina one evening said to Karl Oskar: After what had happened, she had now changed her mind; she was not averse to their emigration to North America. Before, she had thought she would be lacking in responsibility if she endangered her children's lives on the ocean. Now she had learned that God could take her little ones even on dry land, in spite of her great care. She had come to believe that her children would be equally safe on the stormy sea, if she entrusted them to the Highest. Moreover, she would never feel the same in this place again. And so—if he thought it would be best for them and their children to emigrate, she would comply. They could know nothing of what was in store for them in so doing, but she wanted to take part in the emigration, she wished to go away with Karl Oskar.

The couple agreed: they would look for passage in the spring of next year.

So the decision had been reached, a decision which determined the course of life for both of them, which determined the fate of their children, the result of which would stretch through time to come to unborn generations—the decision which was to determine the birthplace of their grandchildren, and their grandchildren's children.

VIII

WITH GOD'S HELP AND THROUGH THE ASSISTANCE OF THE AUTHORITIES

1

One day in February the churchwarden, Per Persson, came to Dean Brusander with grave tidings: behind locked doors in Karragarde Danjel Andreasson gathered his house folk and neighbors to nightly meetings and administered the Lord's Holy Supper.

At first the dean would not believe his warden: the news was too shocking. But Per Persson had the word of eyewitnesses; some young people happening by the other night had peeked in through the windows in Karragarde, and had seen people gathered inside around a Communion table. After hearing of this, he himself last night had gone to the farm and looked through the window to ascertain the truth. He had seen some ten people sitting around a table, while Danjel conducted confession and Communion among them; no person with eyesight could remain in doubt as to what was taking place. By reliable people in the neighborhood he had also been informed that Danjel, through one of the timber drivers, had sent to Karlshamn for several gallons of Communion wine.

Dean Brusander sat for a long while with bent head after hearing the warden's report.

He had tried to bring Danjel Andreasson back into the church through peaceful and gentle means. He had warned, and thought he had enlightened him with kind admonitions. He had sought with mild measures to correct his false opin-

ions of God and spiritual freedom. He had avoided
commotion in the parish, and had treated the poor man with
caution and consideration. Only when Andreasson had inocu-
lated simple, spineless people with his poison, and had continued to gather them to meetings in his house, had Dean
Brusander excluded him from the Lord's altar. But through
all his kindness, patience, and tolerance with the strayed one,
he had apprently only given freer scope for the Evil Spriit:
the miserable people in Karragarde were now led so far by
the devil that they confessed and held Communion among
themselves.

The sacred sacraments, Christ's body and blood, the
church's most holy jewel and exclusive prerogative, these sacraments were desecrated by an ignorant peasant, they were
soiled by the hands of a coarse and criminal person. Andreasson was inflated with spiritual vanity; he had commenced with
Bible explanations and thereby encroached upon the ministry,
later his presumption had gone so far that in his house he or-
ganized his own congregation and held his own church.

Thus Danjel Andreasson in Karragarde set himself above
temporal and spiritual ordinances. If God still hesitated and
did not defend His holy and catholic church, then secular authorities must enter in, must discipline the strayed ones,
rebuke the leader and agitator.

Per Persson said: What now took place in Karragarde
would stir and upset parish people profoundly.

Deeply grieved, Brusander looked at his warden. "I fear
the same. We must immediately avert these excesses."

He now wished to ask the advice of Per Persson, his most
trusted churchwarden. Brusander had been unlucky in his
choice of wardens: one used to steal into the sacristy during
weekdays and drink from the Communion wine, so that one
Sunday when Brusander had announced a Communion he had
been forced to call it off; another had appeared drunk in
church and placed the numbers of the hymns upside down; a
third had, on the holy Christmas morning, repaired to a corner of the organ loft and there let his water, in the presence
of several women. But always the dean had had full confidence in Per Persson. Because he consumed only a fifth of
brannvin per day he was, in sobriety, a worthy example for
other parishioners. It was true that ugly rumors had
circulated concerning his moral life, but these were, fortu-

nately, unverified. When he had been accused of causing the pregnancy of a fifteen-year-old girl boarding in his house, as a parish pauper, the dean had questioned him privately, and Per Persson had repudiated the false accusation, saying it was spread by the malicious and jealous. And it was a fact that the warden's great success in worldly affairs had made him the object of much jealousy in the parish.

"Speak freely, Per Persson! What means shall we use against these Akians?"

The warden answered: Old parishioners remembered how much trouble Ake Svensson had caused in his day. This time they must prevent the dissenters from disturbing the parish tranquillity. There were already hot-tempered persons who wished forcibly to chastise Danjel and his followers: a few sturdy men intended to go one evening to Karragarde and with suitable weapons drive out the devil. This Per Persson had heard; but he thought it would be ill-advised and cause an unhealthy stir in the parish.

The dean agreed; he could easily understand the noble zeal which called for forcible discipline against the Akians; if a few good men were to go to Andreasson's house on such an errand, then this in itself would be commendable, proving an ardent devotion to the purity of evangelical teachings. But he must disapprove; they could use legal means only against the sectarians.

The churchwarden wished also to report that there were people who spoke well of Danjel and lauded his generosity toward the poor and homeless. As yet they weren't many, but their numbers might increase, and it would menace community peace and order if two parties were to arise, one for and one against the Akians.

"May God prevent such a calamity!" exclaimed the dean with emphasis.

The peasant of Karragarde showed an exaggerated and harmful zeal for things in themselves good, thereby misleading credulous people. No tempter was more dangerous than he who twisted the tools of deceptive goodness into the service of transgression. Brusander realized that he ought to have used stronger means against Danjel Andreasson's activities from the very beginning.

"The ministry must call on the secular authorities for help," advised the warden. "This malpractice of dissenters cannot be handled in any other way."

The dean nodded eagerly. He, also, could see no other way. And a conviction began to take shape within him: an overpowering certitude that God's patience with the heretics in Karragarde was now drained to the last drop.

He asked the churchwarden to keep him posted when the Akians next prepared to gather round their unlawful Communion table in Karragarde. This Per Persson promised before he left; a couple of boys would help him and watch near Danjel's to keep him informed.

Dean Brusander had been working on his next Sunday's sermon when the warden arrived, and his thoughts returned to his work when he was again alone. It was the first Sunday after Septuagesima, and the Bible text was the story in St. Matthew, Chapter 8—of Christ driving the devil from two possessed men into a herd of swine which charged down a steepness into the sea, to perish in its waters. Now, with the churchwarden's news fresh in his mind, he realized how profound this text was, a text that called for explanation and application. And to those listeners familiar with the appalling happenings in Karragarde, little explanation was necessary: "And when He was come to the other side into the country of the Gergesenes, there met him two possessed with devils, coming out of the tombs, exceeding fierce, so that no man might pass by that way. . . ." In like manner today, any man within this parish, on any road or at any moment, might meet a man in plain peasant dress who was possessed by the devil and tempted with the Evil One's words and promises. Never before during his time in office had he so felt the urgency of his message as he did about next Sunday's sermon.

Dean Brusander looked out through the window; snow had fallen the whole day, it was still snowing, and drifts were beginning to form on the road outside the parsonage. With an expression of concern his eyes followed the wafting flakes: perhaps the heavy snowfall might keep distant parishioners from church on Sunday, and they would miss a sermon of the utmost importance to their spiritual welfare.

Brusander was the son of a peasant who had fed and brought up eighteen children in a little cottage with two windows. He thus sprang from the peasantry which made up his congregation. He was the eighteenth child, and his mother had died at his birth. Even in early childhood he felt a strong call to the ministry; he had studied under great hardship, with no financial aid from his poor father, who was barely able to provide him with food during his school years in Vaxio. But the peasantry in these parts were flesh of his flesh and bone of his bone; he felt for these people as for his own children, and embraced them in fatherly love and devotion. He grieved over their vices and errors, their ignorance and drunkenness, their violence and whoring. But most of the parishioners were peace-loving, pious and devout, and hitherto subservient to their spiritual teachers and others who had fatherly power over them. *Hitherto*—he stopped short at that word; in these latter days, he had observed a dangerous sign of change.

At this time a great unrest was visiting all nations. The people were revolting, using force against their legal authorities, and many heretical teachings were spread and believed. The old and approved order was being thrown aside, the customs of forebears disregarded. The evil had its roots in disobedience to God's Fourth Commandment, in the disintegration of the bonds between children and parents, between servants and masters, subjects and authority. Those holy bonds which, according to God's ordinance, kept society united, and preserved order and security, had been attacked by gnawing, corroding evil.

Even in Ljuder Parish there had been signs of contempt for authority, and disobedience toward masters. Maids and farmhands left their employers in the middle of the service year, and had to be returned to their duty by the sheriff. In a few cases the authorities had been so lenient that the escaped servants were not returned to their service but had been allowed to go their way. Such happenings were spots of shame on a Christian church; such examples were dangerous. If the servant law were not obeyed by servants, society might sink into lawlessness, wildest disorder might ensue. Regard for laws and ordinances in force was based on the Fourth Commandment, tranquillity and security depended on that very commandment. God's world order rested primarily on adherence to His Ten Commandments, and the servant law—being part of God's world order—could not be set aside without setting aside the whole order; it was the covenant between masters and servants.

It became more and more apparent that literacy was, in the main, harmful to the common man who couldn't use it wisely. As knowledge of reading spread, so also spread heresy, dissension, and insubordination. Simple folk made wrong use of their reading knowledge. Here the authorities ought to keep stricter supervision and inspection; if you gave to the people a new knowledge—useful in itself—then you must also see to it that this knowledge was not abused. This was the holy duty of the authorities; the people must feel the guiding paternal hand. And the first duty of a spiritual teacher was to impress upon the common man the enduring order, created after God's will and not to be changed without His permission.

But the fundamental cornerstone of the community's existence was unity in religion. One God, one church, one congregation which strove to be one soul—only when humanity reached this perfection would the kingdom of God be established on earth, for eternity.

The Akians broke religious unity and tried to overthrow God's church. And who was the Enemy insinuating himself with fair words and promises—to cause strife and dissension among them? Hotheaded but righteous men in the parish wanted forcibly to throw out the devil from Karragarde. It was a method of simple folk, but their intent was Christian. God had been patient, and had waited, but now the time had come to defend the sanctity of the ministry and the purity of religion.

And the dean lost himself in new thoughts while preparing his sermon. He had much to say to his congregation next Sunday, deriving from Matthew 8:28.

He had also something to attend to today, something which could not wait. He sent for his servant and told him to pull out the sleigh and harness the fastest parsonage horse—he wished to drive to Sheriff Lonnegren in Aleback on an urgent matter.

Dean Brusander remained genial throughout. He was convinced he could take care of the Akian heresy—with God's help and through the assistance of the secular authorities.

2

In the middle of the big room in Danjel Andreasson's house stood a long table which Inga-Lena had put in order this evening. She had pulled out the extra leaves, she had polished two tall brass candlesticks until they shone, she had lit the candles and placed one candlestick on each end of the table. She had brought forth the tallest candles which they had made at Christmas. She had covered the large table with a newly woven cloth of whole linen, which she was using now for the first time; it was washed and ironed and white as the snow without. From her linen chest she brought forth her finest and most precious possessions, for tonight they expected the most important visitor a human being could receive in his house. Tonight their old table was the Lord's table, their tallow candles were God's altar candles, and Inga-Lena's new linen cloth was God's altar cloth: the Lord Jesus Christ would be their guest tonight.

In the center of the table, between the candlesticks, she had placed the earthen jug with wine, sweet wine from Karlshamn, and the cake plate with newly baked rye cookies; Inga-Lena had made the Communion breads in the shape of a cross.

The gathering around the Lord's altar in Karragarde was to take place one hour before midnight. The people from the neighboring farms, two married couples, had just arrived. They were stamping off the snow in the entrance hall, where they were met by Danjel, who bade them step inside and join the brethren in Christ's body. Those already congregated consisted of the house folk and the lodgers. No more visitors were expected, and Danjel locked the door and bolted it. The only time he allowed locked doors in his house was when the Lord Himself made a call. From the storm and snow outside the neighbors stepped into the pleasant, intimate stillness which reigned in Danjel's house. He asked his guests to find their places at the table. With his *psalmodikon*—a musical instrument with one string, resembling a violin—he himself took the seat at the upper end.

Danjel Andreasson was shorter than average, narrow-shouldered, and slenderly built. His face was covered by a light-brown, unkempt beard, and his thick, round-cut hair fell down to the collar of his jacket. The little peasant was gentle in manner, slow in movement, thoughtful and mild in speech. Under a broad protruding forehead his brown eyes had a look of peace in them. His lips parted often, as if about to smile.

At the table's long side, to the right of the master, sat the house folk: dishonorably discharged soldier Severius Pihl, a tall man with a disfigured face, sunken and devastated by smallpox and brannvin; invalided servant maid Sissa Svensdotter, lame in her right arm and crippled in her left foot; and unmarried Ulrika of Vastergohl and her daughter Elin. This daughter was the only one surviving of the four children of unknown fathers whom Ulrika had borne. Elin was barely fifteen years of age and would tonight receive Holy Communion for the first time. Because of her immoral life, Ulrika of Vastergohl herself had for many years been denied the holy sacraments by the church. It seemed remarkable to all that her life in adultery had not left noticeable signs of curruption, but her face retained the innocent features of a pure maiden, showing hardly a wrinkle; her well-shaped body, with its full bosom, was still supple and well preserved. Elin resembled her mother when young. She was a delicate maiden with a fair face.

At the opposite side of the table, to the left of Danjel, sat the people from neighboring farms, two men and two women. Inga-Lena had her place at the lower end of the table. There were ten guests in all at the devotional supper about to begin.

Danjel asked his wife to close the kitchen door, then he knelt beside his chair and prayed a silent prayer. All sat immobile, still and waiting. Outside, the snowstorm increased, and some loose boards at the corner of the house slapped as the gusts of wind pulled and shook them.

Danjel arose and said that Jesus had now arrived.

"We'll meet our Saviour with the hymn about Gethsemane: 'The Sacrifice Is Near. Bleed, My Heart!'"

The farmer of Karragarde picked up his psalmodikon; he tuned the instrument and began to hum the hymn while he listened to the howling snowstorm outside as if he were trying to imitate the sound of the blizzard in the tune of the psalm. Then he drew the wooden bow across the strings, he played and sang:

> "Wake, O Christian, while thy Saviour
> Bids thee share His cup of woe!
> Leave the haunts of sin forever—
> He alone can peace bestow.
> 'Watch and pray,' He pleadeth ever,
> 'Darkness seeks thy overthrow.' "

All joined in the singing, each according to his ability, and the hymn rose strong and powerful under the low ceiling with its cracked and sooty beams. The Akians sang while the wind whirled round the cottage and filtered through cracks in walls and windows, causing the candle flames to flicker in the draft. The tallow candles lit up only part of the room, a small circle around the table, leaving the rest in semidarkness.

The people gathered here tonight had come to tarry with their Saviour, not to deny Him, like Peter, not to betray Him, like Judas. All those sitting here around Danjel's table, waiting for him to give them the bread and wine, had experienced redemption through *their own faith*, the faith that Christ had suffered and died on the cross for their sins. In embracing this belief they felt that the body of Christ had taken possession of their own bodies, that they had sloughed off their old, sinful ones. Thus they were reborn, untainted, righteous, cleansed of all sins. The Lord's new apostle, sitting here at table with them, had said to them: "Your sins are tied up in the linen napkin which was about Christ's head when He was buried, and which He left in His grave." And they all believed this.

Tonight again Christ bade them eat His body and drink His blood. This was the covenant between the Saviour and the saved, which must be resealed. It was simple for everyone to understand. Christ's body was inside their bodies, while theirs were inside His, as His own words in Danjel's Bible on the table verified: "He that eateth My flesh, and drinketh My blood, dwelleth in Me, and I in him."

They were sundered from the church, no longer received at its altar ring. But the Lord was omnipresent and they could find Him everywhere, in all places under the roof of the heavens. Jesus had allowed Himself to be born in a stable, He could place His Communion table wherever He pleased, be it a byre, a woodshed, or a barn. He was with them wherever they sought Him, the Lord's table stood wherever He was present.

And tonight He was with them again; they were sitting around His altar table. The ceiling of sooty beams above their heads was the vaulted ceiling of the Lord's shining temple. This was a holy place.

> "The hours pass, keep praying, sinners,
> Follow Christ in happy mood."

The hymn rang out to its close. Danjel moved his Bible close to the tallow candle, so that its light fell on the leaves, and he began to read in a clear and even voice the sacred words of the institution of the Lord's Supper: "Our Lord Jesus Christ, in the night when He was betrayed, took the bread, gave thanks and brake it and gave unto His disciples, and said: 'This is My body, which is given for you' . . ."

The males had precedence in receiving the sacrament. With slow movements Danjel took from the plate a rye biscuit, broke it, and held a small piece to the mouth of soldier Pihl. "Jesus Christ, Whose body you receive, keep you in eternal life."

The old soldier sat with his hands folded and his eyes closed. He bent forward while his lips received the crust of the rye cookie from the peasant's hand. Severius Pihl was toothless; slowly his gums ground the bread to pieces. From the earthen jug Danjel now poured wine into a tin mug, and when the old man had swallowed his bread, Danjel held the mug to his mouth. The soldier drank the wine eagerly in one swallow, then gave thanks to the Saviour in a deep sigh.

> "Jesus Christ, Whose blood you receive . . ."

The other Communion guests had folded their hands and, deeply aware of Christ's presence, made not a single motion. A gust of wind shook the loose boards, which squeaked and banged. The candle flames flickered in a sudden draft from the window, the shadows moved quickly back and forth over the white tablecloth. The blizzard raged without, but the people locked in here were in a peaceful room, sanctified to the God Who had redeemed them, Who had gathered all their sins in His bloody napkin cloth.

Danjel Andreasson had administered bread and wine to the men; he continued with the women, and was about to give the bread to Ulrika of Vastergohl when a new sound from outside was heard above the storm: a man spoke with a coarse voice. The little peasant's hand, holding Christ's body, stopped in mid-air as for a moment he listened. Then he went on with the Communion as if nothing had been heard. He gave Ulrika a piece of the broken bread, and was about to hand her the wine when he was interrupted by another noise: someone knocked, then banged on the outside door.

All turned their heads and listened. Danjel put down the mug with Christ's blood on the table. The blows on the door came in even intervals. But Danjel said nothing and his expression did not change.

Apprehension came over the others; they began to whisper. Inga-Lena said: "Please, Danjel, do not open!"

His neighbors looked at Danjel, fear in their eyes, but he reassured them: they need not be afraid, they must remain fearless, sitting quietly on their chairs. The Lord Jesus was with them in this room tonight, no one need fear harm. Whosoever stood outside and tried to break in had no power against the will of the Almighty. This they must know.

The master of Karragarde went with sure steps out into the entrance hall. Before touching the door lock he asked gently: "Who is disturbing the stillness of our house this night?"

"Sheriff Lonnegren! Open!"

"Whom do you search for at this late hour, Mr. Sheriff?"

"You, Danjel Andreasson! I order you in the name of the law, open your door!"

Other voices were heard, several men were on the porch.

"I do not obey the laws of man."

"My official duty compels me to break down the door if you don't open!"

"Then I must help you, Mr. Sheriff. I cannot allow you to commit a great outrage and increase your sins against God."

Danjel opened the door. He saw horses and sleighs outside in the yard, but the horses had no bells, the visitors had driven without sleighbells so as not to announce their arrival.

Sheriff Lonnegren stepped inside, followed by Dean Brusander. After them came the assistant pastor, Krusell, and the churchwarden, Per Persson of Akerby, and lastly the village bailiff, and Sheriff Lonnegren's hired man. Danjel followed the callers inside; six men entered the room where Danjel's little flock waited in trepidation—three from the spiritual authorities and three from the temporal. Dean Brusander and Pastor Krusell were dressed in the official garb of the clergy. Both ministers were pale and serious, and their black garments inspired awe.

Sheriff Lonnegren removed his uniform cap but was still unable to stand erect under the low ceiling of the peasant cottage; he hit his forehead against a beam and half exploded in an oath before he remembered the clerical company. He turned to the owner of the farm. "What are these people doing here in the middle of the night?"

"We are gathered in a devotional repast," answered Danjel calmly.

The sheriff looked sharply at the neighbors. "I recognize people who do not belong to your house, Danjel Andreasson. It seems to me an unlawful meeting is taking place here."

The two neighboring wives whispered anxiously to their husbands as the sheriff requested their names and place of residence. Danjel again called on his guests to remain calm and unafraid.

Ulrika of Vastergohl did not seem alarmed, rather angry. She glared with disgust at the peacebreakers.

The dean still remained silent while he studied the parishioners gathered around the old table: Pihl, the old soldier, reveler and gambler, often reproved but never improving until at last dishonorable discharge ended his crown service; Sissa Svensdotter, a poor creature, crippled, lame, and committed twice for thievery; and Ulrika of Vastergohl, repulsive harlot to whom the devil had given a fair body to entice men for whoring, and who had been mainly responsible for adultery within the parish. Indeed, the new Åkian master had gathered the dregs of the community around him.

Brusander caught sight of the wine jug on the table, he looked at the cake plate with cookies in the form of crosses, and his face paled still more. He drew in his breath deeply, his voice vibrated with indignation, rising to despair: "Your poor confused creatures! You defile the holy sacrament!"

"We enjoy the dear sacraments," answered Danjel, humble yet inflexible.

"Which you have denied us, Mr. Dean!" injected Soldier Pihl.

"Because we no longer crawl under the priest cape!" added Ulrika.

Without paying attention to these remarks the dean turned to Sheriff Lonnegren, pointing at the table. "What more is needed? Danjel Andreasson administers the holy sacrament to these people! We have caught him in the act in his own house. We are all your witnesses to this offense."

The sheriff regarded Danjel's Communion table with a thoughtful and somewhat annoyed expression: he had set out tonight on this business most unwillingly, at Brusander's request. People gathering for devotion within four walls did not distress him as they did the dean. He liked to leave people alone as long as they were quiet within doors, didn't disturb the peace in public places, and didn't harm their fellow men. These here did not harm other people, they were poor, wretched creatures, in rags, with defects and ugliness, poor devils, but no nuisance here. And when others were allowed to gather in peace for gambling and drinking, why shouldn't these poor drones in religion be left undisturbed, as long as they in their turn left others undisturbed? The sheriff had advised the dean to attempt a reconciliation between the dissenters and the church.

However, the reconciliation had not taken place; and their meeting *was* forbidden by law. Law was law, and duty was duty, and it behooved a crown sheriff to do his official duty in this place.

Lonnegren spoke to Danjel sternly: "Do you admit that you hold meetings and administer the holy sacrament?"

"Yes, Mr. Sheriff."

"Have you tonight administered the sacrament to these people?"

"Not to all of them as yet. I was interrupted by you, Mr. Sheriff."

"But you must know that no one is allowed to hold Communion without being ordained?"

"That I do not know."

"But the dean here has told you so."

"I do not obey the dean, but Holy Writ. The Bible says nowhere that our Lord Jesus was ordained."

"Don't get yourself into an argument with this hair-splitter," advised the dean. "These things are too deep for the simple and ignorant."

"You hear what your pastor says!" said Lonnegren. "Aren't you going to obey him, you scoun—scou—" The sheriff's usual term of address froze on his lips this time. He met the calm, fearless look of the little peasant, and swallowed the other half of the word. There was something strange in that man's unchangeable meekness and unswerving politeness. In some way, through his gentleness and calm, he was beyond reach. It seemed to the sheriff that he couldn't touch Danjel with his reprimands.

Lonnegren continued: "It has been proved that you have broken the law pertaining to the sacraments, Danjel Andreasson."

"There is no law over those who live in Christ."

"There, you hear for yourself!" interrupted Brusander. "He sets himself above the authorities and public ordinances."

Danjel could only make matters worse through his fearless answers, and Lonnegren did not wish him to worsen his case. He might have a tedious investigation on his hands if this meeting came under the sedition paragraph; he wanted to finish the business as quickly as possible.

"I'll call you in for questioning, Danjel," he said. "After that you will be sued in civil court, as well as all others gathered here."

Danjel listened unmoved to the sheriff. Of late he had felt the time of persecution nearing.

Lonnegren ordered the bailiff to take down the names of all present at the meeting. The neighbors, on hearing that their names would be taken, immediately rose from the table, slowly easing themselves in the general direction of the door.

The dean held a whispered consultation with his assistant, then he stepped forward and demanded attention. "I have once forbidden you, Danjel Andreasson, to meddle in anything pertaining to the ministry. You persist in your excesses and it is therefore necessary now to treat you according to the letter of the law. The same holds true for the others who have broken the sacramental law here tonight.

"But I beg you to think of your eternal salvation. Each one of you who regrets his transgressions, and recalls them, will

be again received by me into the fold of the church. I cannot
be responsible to my God unless I do all I can to save you
from eternal fire."

He now had tears in his eyes.

Ulrika of Vastergohl threw looks of hatred toward the spiritual guide of the parish. "We have our Redeemer here
among us. We don't have to hang on to the coat tails of a
priest. To hell with you!" She spat.

"You blaspheme, woman!" Pastor Krusell exclaimed excitedly.

"This is our temple. Get out of the light, priests! You
darken this room. You stand there black and evil like the
devil himself!"

"This woman reviles the ministry!" said Pastor Krusell to
the dean.

Dean Brusander turned to Ulrika of Vastergohl, in all his
dignity. "I see that you have not mended your ways." He
looked at the wine mug in front of her, and repugnance and
loathing crept into his voice: "You harlot, how dare you take
Christ's blood into your foul mouth!"

"I do as I damn well please, you God-damned priest!"

Brusander recoiled. He took a step backward and sucked in
his breath; he mustn't lose his head.

The churchwarden, Per Persson, stepped forward to help
the parish pastor. He shouted to Ulrika: "How dare you insult
the dean!"

"Watch out! I might insult the warden, too!"

"Before you speak to our clergy you should wash out your
mouth!"

"How? With parsonage brannvin or priest piss?"

"Shut up, you old whore!"

"Whore? Did you call me a whore?"

Ulrika jumped up so abruptly her chair overturned with a
great clatter. Her whole body shook, her eyes flashed with
rage, and she screamed at the warden: "A whore? To you,
Per Persson? *You* call *me* a whore, you old son of a bitch?"

"What are you talking about, woman?"

"A whore to you, Warden? What was it you used to say in
the old days, when you came with a daler in one hand and
your cock in the other?"

"Shut up! Insane creature!" roared Per Persson with the
full strength of his lungs.

"What was it you said then? When you wanted me to lie on my back for you—for just a little while? Then you came crawling, then you asked, and begged, and fawned! Then I was good enough for you! Then the whore was good enough!"

By now words stuck in the throat of the churchwarden, and he could no longer answer Ulrika. But she drew breath to gather new strength.

Complete silence ensued after this exchange of words. The soldier Pihl and Sissa Svensdotter looked at the dean in malicious joy. The dean and assistant pastor looked at each other in bewilderment, and the sheriff stood open-mouthed and looked from the Akerby warden to the fuming woman.

Danjel remained quiet and stared at the floor, waiting for the foul weather to pass.

Someone began to weep—it was Ulrika's daughter; Inga-Lena moved her chair closer and comforted Elin.

Ulrika's shrill voice was heard again: "That whoring son of a bitch Per Persson is not denied the sacrament in church. Why? Because he is a good friend of the God-damned priests —those black devils who darken the light for us! Those lazy potbellies who live in their fat flesh!"

The dean and his assistant were still silent and irresolute, shocked by Ulrika's explosion. Per Persson shook his fisted hands as though he would grab her throat.

Sheriff Lonnegren did not interfere in the exchange of words between Ulrika and the churchwarden; experience gained from many hard years in office had taught him not to argue with whores; it led nowhere. And he felt no sympathy for Per Persson, whose lust for power made him difficult. He did not begrudge the warden this humiliation. And he experienced a great relief as he stood here and recalled a happening of many years ago, in his youth. One evening while drunk and reckless he had been on his way to Ulrika's cottage—on the same errand as Per Persson and many other men; the devil must have guided his steps. But Ulrika had not been at home; she had accompanied some caller a bit on his way, and he had had to return without having effected his purpose. An act of providence had averted his undertaking and sent the woman away at the right moment. Now he could bless this act of providence, he could thank God he didn't have to suffer disgrace from the mouth of the harlot here this evening.

The dean felt Ulrika had spoken the truth about his warden. He knew already that she had misled many honest and upright men, and with her body enticed them into her nest of sin, but this was not the right time or place to divulge the truth and lay bare Per Persson's debaucheries, his much-to-be-regretted youthful dissipations. Here the truth was not used in its right place; it became a raw insult to a trusted and well-thought-of man. But nothing could excuse or forgive the rude words (to say the least) which the sinful woman had used.

Brusander went over to the sheriff. "You must put a stop to this painful and shameful scene." By the strength of his office Lonnegren must disperse the gathering and send those present on their way.

The sheriff did not ask for anything better than to conclude his unpleasant mission here tonight. Danjel Andreasson had admitted his offense, the names of his accessories were inscribed, and he had nothing more to do in this house.

"In the name of the law I now order this meeting to disperse. Each go quietly to his own house!"

The bailiff said the neighbors had already left after giving their names and places of residence. Those remaining here belonged to the farm. In the words of the law the meeting was already dispersed.

But before Brusander left he had something to say still to the master of the house: "I strictly forbid you to continue Communions at this table."

"You cannot forbid the Lord Jesus my house, Mr. Dean," said Danjel.

"Who has told you that the Lord is here?"

"He has shown Himself to me in my heart."

"You think all your whims are inspirations from God. I assure you they are from the devil!"

The warden Per Persson interrupted, still red-faced from anger: "We'll throw out the Karragarde devil, we'll get rid of him when you, Danjel, are in prison on bread and water!"

Danjel had spoken to Ulrika in a fatherly way, silencing her. His words had power over her. But now the fiery woman could contain herself no longer. "Get out, you God-damned priests!"

And Soldier Pihl added in a rasping voice: "Leave the

house of the righteous and repair yourselves to the sinners' den!"

Pastor Krusell had a more easily disturbed temper than the dean, and he now exclaimed: "This is enough! Are we to accept such insults?"

It looked as if a new row were to ensue. Danjel admonished his people to keep quiet. To make sure, he reached for the psalmodikon and began singing a hymn:

> "Let me live in peace and stillness
> Giving to no soul offense;
> Pain or pleasure, health or illness
> Take I from Thy providence.
> Never wounding, ever healing,
> Thus a Christly life revealing."

And all the Akians joined in:

> "Here my cross with patience bearing,
> I will go where Jesus leads,
> All enduring, all forbearing . . ."

Danjel and his flock continued the hymn, verse after verse, as if no outsider were present in the room. Dean Brusander several times attempted unsuccessfully to make himself heard above the singing. He said to his assistant, for these hardened people nothing could be done. Lonnegren had performed his duty and was ready to leave with his men, who, he thought, might as well have stayed at home; vaguely it seemed to him that Danjel in his unshakable belief was in some way beyond the reach of the secular authorities.

All the intruders had left before the psalm was ended.

Danjel went outside on the porch: both the dean's and the sheriff's sleighs were gone. He locked his door for the second time this night; then he went back to his place at the upper end of the table. With sadness he gazed on the four empty chairs at the Communion table, lately vacated by his neighbors. Fear of worldly authority had been too much for them; they had not been steadfast in their faith; they had deserted their Lord and Master. As Peter once denied Jesus to the servant of the High Priest, in like manner Danjel's neighbors had denied him to Sheriff Lonnegren.

Danjel Andreasson comforted the devoted followers who still remained with him: the time of persecution was upon them; they should thank the Lord Jesus that they were chosen, thank Him for the joy of suffering for His sake.

So the farmer of Karragarde once more reached for the tin mug which served as chalice, and which had remained in front of Ulrika of Vastergohl; he held it to her mouth: "Jesus Christ, Whose blood you drink . . ."

Christ was still there, they felt His presence, and this was a holy place.

3

At Konga County spring court, 1849, homeowner Danjel Andreasson of Karragarde was fined two hundred daler in silver for transgressing the sacrament law and the ordinance pertaining to unlawful meetings Those who had received the Holy Communion in his house were fined one hundred daler silver each. As most of the offenders were without funds and unable to pay, the fines were changed to prison sentences and each one served twenty-eight days on bread and water.

Six of the condemned—former soldier Pihl, maid Sissa Svensdotter, and four neighbors—returned to the fold of the church after serving their sentences. They expressed to Dean Brusander their deep repentance over their errors. Since they again confessed the only true and right religion, they were admitted to Communion with the rest of the congregation.

Only Ulrika of Vastergohl and her daughter remained in Karragarde to follow the teachings of their master. Through the sentence of the county court Danjel's little flock had been scattered. No new followers came to him. The danger of Akianism in the parish was averted—with God's help, and through the assistance of the secular authorities.

IX

THE AMERICA CHEST

1

A whole year passed during which Karl Oskar and Kristina made preparations for their emigration, feeling as if they were already on the move. There was so much to do and to think about they could not sink too deeply into sorrow over their dead child.

Karl Oskar let it be announced from the church pulpit that his farm was for sale. News soon spread through the parish that the farmer of Korpamoen intended to move away from the country, intended to emigrate to North America, taking with him wife, children, and his only brother. There was much talk in the village about this strange projected undertaking. Whence had he got the amazing notion? Serious-minded older peasants shook their heads and came up to Karl Oskar on the church green on Sundays. To one who was younger they could speak as father to son, and they wished now—with the best of intentions—to dissuade him; how could he relinquish his farm, the parental home whose deed he had, and reach out for land in faraway North America, a country which neither he nor anyone else had seen? Wasn't it like trying to catch the will-o'-the-wisp on a misty morning? The project seemed rash to them; he would enter into a dangerous game in which he might win a little, but lose all; this they must tell him as older and more experienced farmers. It was not that he was forced to give up his farm. The sheriff had been to many farms this last year but he had not yet come to take anything in pawn from Korpamoen. Many were harder pressed on their farms than he, yet they remained at home.

Karl Oskar answered proudly that he acted according to his own good judgment, and after much thought. He understood well enough that a peasant who had tilled his farm some fifty years might think himself ten times wiser and more experienced than he, who had worked Korpamoen only five years. But did anyone gain in wisdom from living on the same place and tramping in the same furrows all his life? If a man's wisdom increased because he remained all his life on the patch where he was born, then the oldest farmers in the parish should by now possess more wisdom than King Solomon himself. But the fact was that most of them were square-heads.

Karl Oskar was considered arrogant and proud when he rejected his neighbors' kind advice. His emigration was taken as a reproach, an insult even, to the parish as a whole and to each individual: the community and the people here were not good enough for him. The old story of the Nilsa-nose was remembered; Karl Oskar's big nose protruded so far that he was unable to turn about in the parish. The whole of Sweden was not large enough to house his nose—he must travel to a bigger country, far away in the world, in order to be comfortable. And some wit started a saying which spread through the village: when Karl Oskar came to North America, his face too would be long.

Perhaps he thought himself such a bigwig that he could look down on his home community? Others surmised something wrong in his head; he was seized by a delusion of grandeur. Such ideas didn't suit a one-sixteenth homestead peasant.

Karl Oskar knew that people poked fun at him and spoke ill behind his back. But he didn't bother to get angry; after all, he tried to please himself, not others. If you spent your time worrying about what other people thought and said, you wouldn't get much done in your life. Outside his home everyone was against his proposed undertaking; even within his home, only his wife was for him; but she was the only one he needed on his side. His parents were against him, though they kept silent. Their reserved rights would now have to be met by an outsider, and this was not to their liking.

Once only did Nils quietly reproach his son: "You take many along with you."

"There will be six of us."

"You take many more. Your descendants are more numerous than you know."

Karl Oskar did not answer. He felt the grief he caused in taking the family from their own country to a foreign land.

"You have not asked the opinion of children and grandchildren," continued the father.

"I must be the one to assume responsibility. I do think of my children."

Nils sat on his chair, his fingers twisting the well-worn crutch handles; he answered softly: "I too think of my children."

He had but two sons.

Karl Oskar understood his father, who now asked himself of what use it had been for him to clear the ground here in Korpamoen, when this ground was now no longer good enough for his own son. Those twenty-five years of fighting the stones must now seem to him a futile strife, as it did not benefit either of his sons.

His mother thought Karl Oskar showed a sinful ingratitude by discounting his gain here at home. He had done nothing wrong, he was not driven by the whip to flee the country. But neither she nor Nils wasted much time in persuasion—they knew Karl Oskar. They turned to the Almighty in prayers that He might change their son's mind and make him give up the American journey.

Time passed—a summer sped by, and an autumn, and winter came again. But their prayers brought no apparent sign of change in Karl Oskar. Nils and Marta concluded at length that God had some secret purpose in their son's and daughter-in-law's emigration to the United States of North America.

2

Robert returned home for his "free week" after a year's service with Kristina's parents in Duvemala, where he had been treated well and given no chastisement. No one thought the sheriff would look for him any further and he remained in the parental home; Karl Oskar would need his brother's help this last year on the farm.

With Robert the United States also moved into the peasant cottage. From his "description book" he knew everything about the new land. Long ago he had landed on the other side of the ocean and made himself at home on distant shores. On the map which he had made up in his mind were marked the lakes, rivers, plains, and mountains of North America, all roads, on land and on water. He insisted he would not get lost

in the New World once he arrived there, and now he must
help his brother and sister-in-law to find their way. Karl
Oskar, too, had begun to read in his brother's book, and every
day he obtained new information from Robert.

In America the kine fed on a grass that stood belly-high.

In America wild horses and oxen existed by the thousands,
the fields were overrun with them and one could easily catch
a hundred in a day.

In America it would have been impossible for David to kill
Goliath; if he had searched forever he would have been unable to find a stone for his sling.

In America one could say "thou" to the President himself,
and one need never remove one's cap for him, if one didn't
wish to.

In America any capable and honest man could step directly from the manure wagon to the presidential throne.

In America there was only one class, the people's class, and
only one nobility—the nobility of honest work.

In America there were no taxes and no examinations in the
catechism.

In America you need not pay the minister's salary if you
did not like his sermons.

All sounded too good to be true, and during the long winter evenings Robert read to his brother and sister-in-law
about the strange roads of iron which existed throughout the
United States:

"In America one travels a great deal with the help of
steam and steam wagons, but for this are required roads
which are built in a peculiar way and which are called
iron roads or railroads. Such a road must be almost even
and practically level. On the road are placed crossbars of
wood and to these are tied strong iron rails which serve
to guide the wagons. The wagon wheels have on their inside a rim all the way around which forces them to follow the rail on the road.

"On such roads one travels with great speed, twelve to
eighteen miles an hour, nay, even faster. Several big
wagons are tied together and pulled by a steam wagon,
or that wagon on which the steam engine is placed. At
the end of each wagon is a small bridge which enables

the traveler to pass from one wagon to another during the journey, should he desire to speak to an acquaintance. Every wagon has a comfort room which makes it unnecessary to leave the wagon even on a long journey.

"These railroads, where with the help of steam one can enjoy a comfortable and inspiring journey, have now in America a length of 8,000 miles. . . ."

Kristina said: "It will be fun to ride with no beast pulling the wagon!"

She enjoyed riding in all kinds of vehicles, and in spite of her years she most of all, still, enjoyed swinging on a rope. Only a few days ago Karl Oskar had surprised her in the threshing barn, where she had again fastened the ox-thong to the beams and sat riding the swing.

There was now something she wondered about: "How can they steer the wagons when the railroad is snowed under in wintertime?"

"I don't know," said Robert, "perhaps they stable the wagons during the winter."

The book also said that no steam wagons were in use on Sundays. The drivers were at church, of course; and maybe the steam also needed rest to gather strength.

"I wonder about those iron rails," said Karl Oskar. "They lie without guards in the wilderness, night and day. Isn't the iron stolen?"

Robert told him with a superior smile, there was such an abundance of iron in America that no one cared to steal as much as the filings of a saw. And it was the same with gold and silver. Why should people steal and go to jail when they had more than they needed of everything? In America it was so easy to earn one's living in an honest way that no one was tempted to dishonesty. A thief was immediately strung up, often before he even had time to confess his crime. Therefore all thieves in that country were now exterminated. The gentry here at home lied in saying that North America was full of robbers and murderers and wickedness, when in truth it was populated by the most honest and upright people in the whole world.

"They must have an occasional scoundrel there, too," Karl Oskar said.

Robert admitted that this might be so but insisted that evil people were exterminated much more quickly than here at home.

Karl Oskar wished to settle in that part of the country where soil was the most fertile. Robert had read that the best regions for farmers were around the upper end of the great river Mississippi and its tributaries. This neighborhood was fertile, healthy, and rich in forests and beautiful mountains, in valleys and spring waters. The grass thereabouts was so abundant that in two days a man could cut and harvest sufficient winter fodder for a cow, and in three days enough for a horse. One farmer who had cultivated land on the Mississippi shores had in five years earned a bushel of gold.

Kristina did not wish to live in a place where there were crocodiles. Recently she had read in a paper a horrible tale about a settler family in America who had happened to spend a night in a cave where crocodiles were nesting. Early in the morning the man went out to hunt, and when he returned his wife and three children had been eaten by the crocodiles. The old crocodile had just swallowed the wife: only the head of the poor woman was still visible in the mouth of the beast, who had choked and lay there dead; the ground was drenched in human blood. Kristina could not forget the poor mother watching the crocodile feast on her small children while she was waiting her turn. But of course the woman had taken revenge by choking the beast with her own head.

Robert had never read about man-eating crocodiles in America; the piece in the paper must have been a lie; some duke or count must have had it printed to discourage simple folk from emigration.

Arvid, whom Robert had met again, had also been afraid of wild beasts in America. He had had to leave his service in Nybacken; Aron did not wish to keep a servant called the Bull. The old mistress was dead and Arvid was sure she came back to him in the stable room, accusing him of having tried to kill her—which indeed was true—so he had moved without regret. But he had asked at many farms before he found work; he was known everywhere as the Bull from Nybacken. At last he was hired by Danjel in Karragarde, who was unable to find another hand this winter. All servants were afraid of the place now that the devil had moved in there. People had actually seen the Evil One hanging to the back of Danjel's wagon as he drove along the roads; sometimes he even occupied the seat next to the driver, laughing and pleased. The devil was now the real master on that farm.

Arvid was saving every penny of his wages for his transportation to America. For a whole month he had bought no brannvin. Long before his confirmation he had learned to chew snuff (although children weren't supposed to use it before they had participated in the Lord's Supper); he would save three daler a year if he stopped, and this would help him a bit on the road to America. He realized he must give up some things in the Old World to make possible his move to the New; so he had thrown his snuffbox on the dunghill.

But giving up the box was difficult for Arvid. It had been good company for him, he had carried it in his pocket and enjoyed its contents. It had been a loyal companion in work and loneliness. The snuffbox had been his only friend after Robert moved. And now he had thrown it away—into the depths of the dunghill. He felt his pain keenly when others brought forth their boxes and used them without offering him a pinch: then he had to turn away to escape the sight of the refreshing mixture.

He admitted to Robert that after three weeks of suffering he had bought a new snuffbox. And again he bought half a gallon of brannvin each Saturday night. For at last he had clearly understood that a person had no right to treat his God-given body according to his own will; he had no right to torture and plague it and deny it all its pleasures; one could not treat one's body like a dog, denying it even the comfort of snuff.

Would Arvid ever follow him on the road to America? Robert did not believe so; apparently, in one year and a half, he had not saved a single daler; in his whole life he would be unable to save two hundred daler.

But in Korpamoen everything was now being put in order. One day the Nilsa family's old clothes chest—of solid oak painted black—was pulled forward from its place in a cobweb-infested corner of the attic, and carried down into the kitchen for inspection and dusting. No one knew how old this chest was—the hands which made it were mixed with the earth of the churchyard many hundreds of years ago. It had passed from father to son through numerous generations. More than one young bridegroom had entrusted his finery to it after the wedding feast, more than once had the farm's women fetched winding sheets from it when there was a corpse in the house to shroud. Under the lid of the chest valuable things had been secreted; this lid had been lifted by the shaking hands of old women, and by young, strong, maiden fingers. It had been approached mostly at life's great happenings: baptisms, weddings, and funerals. This enduring piece of furniture had through centuries followed the family, and at last been pushed away into a dark attic corner where it had long remained undisturbed. Now it was pulled out into the daylight once more; it was the roomiest and strongest packing case they could find—five feet long and three feet high, wrought with strong iron bands three fingers wide.

In its old age the Nilsa family clothes chest must go out into the world and travel.

It was tested in its joints, and the still-sound oak boards passed the inspection. It was scrubbed clean inside, and old rust scraped from hinges and escutcheons. After timeless obscurity the heavy, clumsy thing was unexpectedly honored again. From its exile in attic darkness it was now honored with the foremost place in the house. The chest had been half forgotten, years had passed without its lid being lifted; now it became the family's most treasured piece of furniture, the only one to accompany them on the journey.

The four oak walls of this chest were for thousands of miles to enclose and protect their essentials; to these planks would be entrusted most of their belongings. Again the old adage, "Old is reliable and best," was proved. And the ancient clothes chest which was about to pass into an altogether new and eventful epoch of its history was even given a new name in its old age. Through its new name it was set apart from all its equals and from all other belongings. It was called the "America chest," the first so named in this whole region.

3

One night Karl Oskar was awakened by a noise from without. Kristina also woke up and asked: "What can it be?"

He listened. "Someone at the door."

Now they both heard knocking.

"Who can it be at this time of night?"

"I'll go and see."

Karl Oskar pulled on his trousers and lit a stick of pitch wood to light his way in the entrance hall. Robert too had awakened, and came from the kitchen where he slept. He asked in trepidation if it mightn't be the sheriff . . . ? Rumor had it that Aron of Nybacken was still urging the sheriff to catch his runaway farmhand.

"I'll warn you before I open," assured the brother.

But there was no fierce, threatening sheriff to answer his question when Karl Oskar inquired as to who was knocking; it was a kind and friendly voice—Danjel of Karragarde stood on the stoop.

"God give you peace on your house, Karl Oskar."

Robert felt relieved; but he was curious.

Karl Oskar, surprised at this late visit, let his wife's relative into the house. In the light of his firestick he looked at the grandfather's clock in the corner: it showed half-past twelve. Something serious must have happened.

Kristina was both pleased and alarmed; she hurried out of bed and put on her skirt and night jacket; she took her uncle's hand and curtsied. Karl Oskar pulled up a chair for him and he sat down. His errand must be urgent, and they waited for him to communicate it at once, but he acted as if there were no hurry. As usual, he was slow and calm in his movements.

Kristina remembered that Inga-Lena only lately had given birth to a child, and had been seriously ill at the time.

"Is something wrong at home? With my aunt perhaps?"

"No. All is well with wife and child."

Inga-Lena had borne him a daughter since the couple's marriage had again become a true marriage.

Their curiosity increased. Why did Danjel disturb them at this late hour if nothing serious had happened?

"Has something . . . ?"

"I have a message for you, Karl Oskar."

"A message?"

"Yes."

"From whom?"

"From God."

"From God?"

Karl Oskar and Kristina exchanged quick glances.

"The Lord awakened me tonight and said: 'Go at once to

Karl Oskar in Korpamoen, the husband of your sister's beloved daughter.' "

Karl Oskar looked closer at Danjel but could see no sign of
agitation or trouble in his face; his eyes were not bloodshot
like a madman's.

"Now you must listen, Karl Oskar. I come with an order
from God."

Robert crept into the room and sat in a corner near the
hearth, listening to the strange message brought by the peasant of Karragarde.

Danjel continued, and it seemed as if he took his words directly from the Bible.

"Last night the Lord said unto me, Danjel Andreasson, as
He once said unto Abraham: 'Get thee out of thy country,
and from thy kindred, and from thy father's house, unto a
land that I will show thee!'

"The Spirit exhorted me to look up Genesis, Chapter
Twelve, verse one, and obey the words written therein. I
arose from my bed and lit a candle and read. Then I asked:
'How shall this come about?' Tonight the Spirit gave me the
answer: 'Go to Karl Oskar in Korpamoen. He will show you
and help you.' "

Had Danjel entirely lost his mind? Karl Oskar and Kristina
wondered. His actions were calm and his eyes peaceful and
mild. His words were strange, but not confused, and gradually
it all fitted together and took on meaning; soon they could
guess his errand.

The dean had reconciled many of the Akians with the
church again but had been unable to bring Danjel back to the
right religion. At the fall session of the county court last year
he had been cited for a second offense, and again fined for
preaching his heresy. But disregarding the court's judgments
at two hearings, he had continued fearlessly to hold Bible
meetings and administer the holy sacrament in his home.
Again this spring he had been summoned to appear in court
for the third offense, and people were sure that this time
Danjel would be exiled.

Kristina clapped her hands in delight. "Uncle, are you
coming with us to America?"

Danjel rose and went up to his niece, laying both hands
upon her shoulders, as if in blessing. "I live in a time of persecution in the land of my fathers. I am prevented from con-

fessing my God. But the Lord shall open for me a new land."

"You mean America, Uncle?"

"Yes. God has so ordered it: we shall move there together.
And none shall have fear; He is with us. I bring my God with
me."

Kristina forgot that a moment ago she had feared their
tardy visitor was mad. Now he was just her dear Uncle Danjel, whom she knew well. When she was a little girl and he
had visited her home he had always had lumps of sugar in his
pockets for her; he was still so kind to her, twice he had
helped them with the mortgage interest. Without his aid they
might not now be in possession of the farm. No one could
make her believe her uncle was an evil, dangerous man who
should be exiled. His peculiar ideas in religion should be left
undisturbed—he hurt no one but himself with them.

It gave her a feeling of security to know that Danjel would
accompany them on the long journey to America, a
journey which secretly still worried her. She felt almost as
though her own father were to go with them.

Now she must prepare coffee for her uncle, from the few
ounces left of the pound she had bought for Christmas. She
stirred up the fire on the hearth, washed out the old coffee
grounds from the kettle, and placed it on the tripod over the
fire.

Karl Oskar was not as well pleased as his wife at the prospect of Danjel and his Akians' company; their religious pecu-
liarities would cause inconveniences and trouble, he thought.
And when Kristina learned that Danjel was to take along Ulrika of Vastergohl and her daughter—now his only followers
outside the family—she too lost some of her enthusiasm. She
could not believe that the old whore had become a new person, and decent people ought to be spared the companionship
of Ulrika's ilk. She hoped to dissuade her uncle from paying
that creature's passage.

Danjel had fulfilled his errand: Karl Oskar would—according to God's command—help him find a passage to the
land the Lord would open to His exiled apostle.

Whether God ordered it or not, Karl Oskar was anxious to
help Danjel find his way. Besides, he was indebted to him for
help with the loan, and was prepared to assist him in return.

Harald, the year-old baby, awakened and began to cry.
Kristina had to sit down and take him in her arms to quiet

him; Karl Oskar tended the coffee while he talked with Danjel about the crossing to North America.

Spring was the most favorable time to emigrate: partly because the winter storms were over and it was less cold at sea, partly because they would arrive at their place of settlement early enough in summer to till and sow; they must have a fall harvest to meet winter needs. They ought to start their voyage in early April. Karl Oskar and Robert had already written to a firm in Karlshamn and been promised passage on a ship called the *Charlotta*. A down payment of one hundred daler for the transportation of six people had been required, and he had sent them this sum. Their ship was a merchant vessel sailing with cargo and emigrants. They were to embark in Karlshamn about the second week in April. They would sail to the town of New York in North America, without docking at any harbor on the way—it was best to sail direct. The *Charlotta* was said to be a good strong ship, commanded by an honest, upright captain who did not cheat his passengers.

Robert would write for Danjel and obtain contract for his passage, too, if the ship had space for more.

"How many of you will there be from Karragarde?"

Danjel thought a moment. "Nine—including children and house folk."

"Is your hired hand to be shipped too?"

"Arvid? Yes, I've promised him."

"Well, he might be of help to you, in America."

Robert listened and smiled to himself; he had anticipated Danjel's errand, had not been so much surprised by it as Karl Oskar. Yesterday he had met Arvid, who, in exchange for promises of secrecy, had related his master's offer; he had shed tears of joy.

As the patriarch Abraham when he was seventy-five years old departed with all his household out of Haran to the land of Canaan, so now the homeowner Danjel Andreasson at the age of forty-five was to depart with all his house folk from Sweden to North America. Robert knew his Biblical history: the patriarch Abraham had no children because his wife Sarah was as barren as the mistress of Nybacken, and he took along many souls whom he fed in his house, the same as Danjel. Abraham was afraid of being killed in the foreign land because of his beautiful wife; therefore he passed her off as his sister. He was a coward; Danjel would never behave like that. Of course, Inga-Lena was not a fair woman; it was hardly to be supposed that some American would murder Danjel in order to marry his widow.

In some ways God's order concerning the emigration remained foggy; He could hardly have referred to the United States when He spoke of the land in the Bible verse, because Columbus had not yet discovered America in the days of Abraham. Danjel must have misunderstood, but there would be no use in correcting him, thought Robert. Danjel had heard that Karl Oskar was to emigrate, and he wanted to emigrate with him as long as he was to be exiled anyway. Now he believed the idea was God's command. But no doubt he was honest in his false belief.

"I'll write about passage tomorrow," Robert promised him.

As they talked further he was amazed to learn how little Danjel knew about America; the farmer from Karragarde was only familiar with the word "America," he knew only that it was the name of another continent, he had not heard of the United States, did not even know where the continent was situated. He knew nothing of its people, government, climate, agriculture, or means of livelihood. Danjel needed enlightenment, and as they sat around the table and drank their coffee Robert tried to share with him his own knowledge of the country where they would settle.

The United States was located southwest of Sweden. To reach it one must sail across a sea that was about four thousand miles wide. With good wind and a speedy ship one might cross in five weeks. But unfortunately the wind on the ocean was mostly westerly, blowing straight against the ship, thus requiring eight or nine weeks for the crossing. At times contrary winds might be so persistent that three months would pass before reaching America.

Danjel listened patiently and with a benevolent smile to the seventeen-year-old boy; the lad sat like a schoolmaster and taught a pupil of ripe age. The peasant stroked his beard, brushing away the crumbs that clung there, and said with conviction: They need not fear contrary winds for the crossing; the All-High ordering him to depart would see to it that they were not delayed by the weather. No winds except favorable ones would blow in their sails; their ship would require only a month of sailing to North America. The Almighty would surely shorten their voyage as much as He could.

Karl Oskar remembered that the Konga spring court convened toward the end of April; Danjel would be out of the country when the sentence of exile was pronounced.

The farmer of Karragärde had paid huge sums of money in fines for his Bible meetings, and Karl Oskar could not help saying: "It's none of my business, Danjel, but why don't you stop holding meetings when they are unlawful?"

Danjel looked up in surprise. "Stop holding them? I?"

"Well . . . yes. No one else can do it."

"But you must know that I myself do not live any more?"

"What do you mean?"

"Hm . . . I thought you knew."

"No. I don't understand a bit any more."

"I don't live in myself any longer—Christ lives in me."

"But you do the Bible explaining?"

"No-o." Danjel smiled kindly and said in his meek way: "I myself do nothing more here in the flesh. Because I do not exist now as before. Christ has taken my place; He does all through me, and is responsible for me. He holds Bible explanations through my mouth. I need not be afraid of anything; what do I care about worldly courts and judges? They cannot hurt me; nothing can hurt me here in the flesh where I no longer live."

Again Karl Oskar and Kristina were confused, wondering how it was with Danjel's mind. Kristina poured some more coffee for him; for a moment there was silence around the table.

Danjel turned to Karl Oskar. "Where do you intend to spend eternity?"

That was a peculiar question, nor did Karl Oskar bother to answer it. He thought Danjel spoke clearly enough of worldly doings, but when he dealt with spiritual things he turned queer; there was no object in arguing with him.

The peasant of Karragärde continued: All of them sitting here around the table tonight, all their sin-bodies, that is, had died on the cross with Christ. He himself had carried his dead and rotten body for many years, until one night two years ago, when it fell off like a dirty rag, and Christ moved in in its place. His dear relatives should understand that the Saviour would not move into them as long as they carried their sin-bodies, their old rotten remains. They must understand that Christ would not dwell in them before they were reborn, before they had laid off their sour old bodies. Who would wish to live in a house that stank of cadavers, of corpses?

No one answered this amazing speech. Danjel rose abruptly from the table, saying he now would leave.

Robert had wished to teach him something about the New World; as an emigrant he needed knowledge of the United States. But Danjel said before he left that, about those things in America which were useful for him to know, the Lord would no doubt enlighten him before he set out on his voyage.

Karl Oskar reflected, as he returned to bed, that he was now no longer alone in his strongly criticized venture. There were now two homeowners. And Danjel was giving up a farm many times larger and better than Korpamoen. That thought was comforting.

Of course, he must admit, he must sadly admit, that he considered his companion a little unbalanced.

4

And so it happened in those days that another old chest, in another attic, on another farm, was dragged forth, inspected, dusted, scrubbed, and put in order—another America chest, the second.

Only a month before their scheduled departure Jonas Petter of Hasteback came to Korpamoen one evening to warn Robert: his neighbor had met Sheriff Lonnegren, who asked whether the hired hand had come home. Aron of Nybacken insisted that his servant be returned; the boy might try escaping to America when his brother left.

This message did not surprise Karl Oskar, who knew that Aron harbored an intense hatred toward him. For a few minutes once he had inflicted the greatest fear possible on Aron; now his hatred sought revenge on Robert: the farmer of Nybacken would try to prevent the boy's emigration.

Karl Oskar said it would be safest for Robert to keep out of the sheriff's reach during the remaining weeks.

Tears came into Robert's eyes. He had been afraid to appear in public since he returned home; together with other deserters in the parish recently he had been rebuked from the pulpit. The dean had preached a sermon about "unfaithful servants" who deserted their masters and set themselves up against God's ordinances; he had said that disobedient farmhands were spots of shame on a Christian community. Robert had felt so much disgraced that he never went out in public, and spoke to no one except Arvid, who also was disgraced although in another way.

Now he said that rather than return to Nybacken he would go to the mill brook, and this time it wouldn't be his jacket and shoes only. Perhaps that really was the fate awaiting him: a farmhand drowned in the mill brook.

Jonas Petter spoke comfortingly: Lonnegren didn't wish to harm any poor devil; he was sure to look for Robert in his home only. The sheriff never bothered more than was necessary about deserters. Robert should come with him to Hasteback. There he would be safe till it was time to leave. "And I promise to hide you if the sheriff comes," the neighbor assured Robert.

Karl Oskar advised his brother to accept the offer: "Dry your tears and go with Jonas Petter!"

Robert felt ashamed of having cried, grown-up as he was, but his heart ached at this thought: "Suppose . . . suppose I couldn't get away."

He obeyed his brother and departed with the obliging neighbor.

Jonas Petter sat down to supper in the kitchen at Hasteback, and asked Robert to join him. He took out the brannvin jug and poured two equally tall drinks for them: the boy was a man now. And Robert was eager to take a drink, perhaps two or three, for brannvin seemed to silence the humming sound in his left ear, which still bothered him. He had lost his hearing almost entirely in that ear, yet he heard a sound which no one else could hear. Perhaps it would never leave him, perhaps this echo from Aron's box would hum as long as he lived.

Brita-Stafva, the farm wife, came in from the byre carrying her wooden milk pails. She was a knotty woman, with hard, manly features. Dark shadows of an unmistakable beard covered her lips, and there was also a tuft of hair on the tip of her chin. A woman with a beard aroused fear in some way. Jonas Petter had a bushy, black beard, yet Robert did not fear him. But those thin hairs on the wife's chin made him uncomfortable; they were outside the norm. All children were afraid of Brita-Stafva.

She put down her pails and eyed the boy sullenly. But the look she then turned on her husband was hardly sullen: it was more—evil, full of hatred. Jonas Petter never tried to hide the fact that he and his wife lived on bad terms.

The men at the table drank their brannvin. Brita-Stafva said sharply, looking at Robert: "The sheriff's carriage just passed."

"Oh yes, my boy, he went to Korpamoen. Now you see, lad, we were lucky not to meet him!"

Robert lost interest in the food but he drank the brannvin. The roar in his ear was violent tonight, almost frightening him.

"Eat, lad. Don't be afraid," Jonas Petter encouraged him. "I've a safe hiding place if the sheriff comes here and asks for you."

Brita-Stafva was busy straining the evening milk; when she heard that the sheriff's passing might concern Robert, she became curious and looked questioningly at him. He felt ill at ease under her gaze, he could not help looking at the beard-tuft on her chin.

Jonas Petter poured himself more drinks; his eyes were taking on a blank look.

"Lonnegren is a decent sheriff," he said. "Sharp in his words but he's a hell of a nice fellow. I've known him since he was a boy—he's the son of the 'Stump of Orranas.' "

"I've heard about that farmer," said Robert, mostly to say something. "Why was he called the Stump?"

"How did he get the nickname? I'll tell you, my boy!"

Jonas Petter glanced in the direction of his wife, busy with the milk pans; he was by now quite lively from all the brannvin.

"It's an amazing story. It's a story of a woman who sharpened a knife."

At these last words a rattle from the milk strainer was heard. The farm wife had made a quick movement. It was almost dark where she stood in the hearth corner, but Robert noticed that her head jerked at her husband's words.

He also had noticed that the couple had exchanged no
words.

Jonas Petter knew of all unusual happenings which had
taken place in Konga County within the last hundred years;
he was about to tell Robert how it came to be that Sheriff
Lonnegren's father was called the Stump.

A Story About a Wife Who Sharpened a Knife

The farmer of Orranas was christened Isak, Jonas Petter
began. He was known far and wide because he was crazy
about women, and often led astray by them. He couldn't keep
his hands off a woman who was shaped well enough to be
used by a man. It didn't matter what her face was like,
whether she was spotted and marred by smallpox, harelipped,
warp-mouthed, or with any other defect; Isak would try to se-
duce her. He was married and in his own conjugal bed he had
a plump, good-looking wife to play with. But this didn't diminish his desire to visit other marital beds; neither married
nor unmarried women were safe from him. He had a strange
power over women, perhaps from the devil, perhaps from
somewhere else. His visits to married women often had got
him into trouble with offended husbands; once his arm was
broken and another time his nose smashed in. But still he persisted, he still had the same power even after his nose was
flattened.

His wife was exceedingly jealous of other women, and
many times she threatened to leave him; but each time he
promised and swore he would mend his ways and stick to his
own bed. She tried to find a cure for his sinful lust through
many concoctions which she mixed and gave to him—juices
from roots, bitter herb porridges to cool his blood. But no
matter what he ate or drank, strong as ever the whoring desire still possessed him.

There was, however, one successful cure for him, a cruel
and horrible cure, and his wife finally administered it.

One day she told their hired man that she wanted a cutting
knife sharpened: she needed it to cut old rags. He believed
her, of course, and sharpened the knife as she herself pulled
the grindstone.

In bed that evening Isak as usual sought his wife; he attended to her as often as she could wish, and never neglected her for other women. And it seemed now as ever that she was willing; he had no suspicions, poor man. He did not know that his wife had sharpened a knife and hidden it under the mattress.

As the husband now was ready she took out her knife and cut off his implement, root and branch.

Isak fainted and bled in streams. His wife had in advance sent for a blood stancher, who arrived at the house immediately after the occurrence. He now did what he could for the injured one, and the wife, also in advance, had made concoctions from *skvattram* and bloodroot, which herbs were used to stop bleeding from injuries. Together they stanched the wound of her husband before he became conscious.

The wife then nursed Isak with much love and care till his recovery.

Nor was it known that the couple became unfriendly toward each other because of her action; they lived together until their dying days.

But Isak of Orranas was never the same man after his operation; he grew slack and dull in his mind, and showed no interest in what he was doing. He neglected his farm more and more. After a few years he sold Orranas, which consisted of half a homestead, and set himself down on reserved rights.

Ever after he kept his hands and other limbs away from women. Indifferent as a gelded steer, he had no more interest in them. From now on he lived a harmonious and pious life with his wife, to whom he was greatly devoted in his old days.

The limb which the wife had cut from her husband she dried and put away. She wanted to keep it as a souvenir. She only brought it out once in a while, when visitors came, or at some celebration or other when relatives and friends were gathered. While Isak listened in silence, she would tell how she went about it that time when she cured her husband of his sinful lust. She would also take out the Bible and refer to that place where it says a man must cut off that limb that is an offense to him in order to save his soul from eternal suffering; she had done for her husband what ought to be done, because all must agree that the limb she had relieved him of had been a great offense.

It was rumored, however, that Isak of Orranas still had a

small part left, and this led to his nickname, the Stump, concluded Jonas Petter.

5

In the silence ensuing after the story's end Robert heard his ear roar more clearly. The wife had by now finished straining the milk, and was removing the dishes from the table. Her mouth was closed in a narrow line. She had looked at her husband a few times while he was telling the story, but remained mute. Robert had not yet heard them speak to each other this evening.

Jonas Petter many times before had told him tales of women's evil deeds, and Robert could guess why the farmer spoke so. But this, as far as Robert knew, was the first time his own wife had been listening.

It was a cruel fate that had overtaken Isak of Orranas, and Robert thought he must be careful before he lay down with a woman—he must always feel under the mattress to be on the safe side.

"The son who became sheriff was born many years before this," added Jonas Petter, as if this explanation were necessary.

In hearing the sheriff mentioned, Robert's fears returned: the sheriff was on the roads, looking for him. Wouldn't it be wise to run away and hide in the woods? His ear kept on throbbing, the brannvin could not silence that sound tonight.

Suddenly he rose: he could hear wagon wheels on the road; it must be the sheriff on his way back. Brita-Stafva, too, heard the sound of the carriage and went out on the stoop.

Jonas Petter said: "Sit down, lad! Don't be afraid!"

Robert did sit down but he was afraid. A desperate fear filled his breast; it felt too small, it was overfull, he could not ease the pressure. It didn't help to exhale, it was still full, it was strained and squeezed.

And a storm raged in his injured ear: Here, my little hand, here is a big box! This one you'll remember!

If . . . if he were left behind? If he weren't allowed to go with Karl Oskar? Then the gates on the America road would never open for him.

The wagon noise from without was heard more distinctly,

it came from light wheels, rolling speedily; it was a light carriage. It could be no one else but the returning sheriff.

The wife had gone outside and did not return. She had hard eyes and a beard on her chin. And she looked queerly at him. Why did she slip out as soon as she heard the carriage? What was she doing outside?

Robert moistened his dry lips with the tip of his tongue: "Jonas Petter . . . She went out. . . . She won't say anything?"

"Brita-Stafva?"

"Yes."

Robert was convinced the farm wife would betray him if in doing so she could vex her husband.

"She won't hail him?" the youth whispered; he was short of breath.

"She should dare!"

Jonas Petter's voice rose. He bent forward across the table toward the boy whom he had promised to protect against the sheriff. "If she dares, *then I'll sharpen the knife tonight!*"

Robert stared at him, forgetting his own fear at the words of the peasant. What did he mean? Sharpen the knife? What knife?

"Sharpen the knife . . . ?"

"Yes. *Otherwise I'd thought of doing it tomorrow.*"

What did Jonas Petter intend to do? He had lived in deep discord with his wife for many years—did he intend to harm her now? Would he cut her up? What kind of knife did he want to sharpen? He was getting drunk—it could be heard and seen.

The sound of the carriage had died down, and Brita-Stafva came inside.

She said it was the churchwarden, Per Persson of Akerby, driving by. He had been in Korpamoen to speak to Karl Oskar about the impending auction of the farm chattels.

At last Robert's chest felt free, he could breathe easier. He poured himself another drink.

As yet this evening he had not heard the couple of Hasteback speak to each other. Brita-Stafva now opened her tight lips, but only to eat of the potato porridge she had prepared for herself. Jonas Petter's eyes were brannvin-bleary, he repeated in a mumble, again and again: *A man, too, could sharpen a knife.*

There was really no meaning to what he said: it was always the menfolk who sharpened tools, knives and such. So Robert could not understand what the farmer sitting there meant with his insinuating remarks. He could not know what was to take place the following day between the husband and wife of Hasteback. There were to be no witnesses to these happenings—it was after Robert had gone out.

Story of a Man Who Sharpened a Knife

When they had finished their breakfast the following morning the farmer rose slowly from the table and turned to his wife, who was washing the dishes near the fire. He wanted to do some sharpening; she was to go with him and crank the grindstone; no one else was available at that moment; Robert was already in the fields.

Brita-Stafva did not answer. To answer would have been to use unnecessary words between them. After their latest great quarrel, three days of silence had passed. Today was the morning of the fourth day.

The wife dried her hands on her apron and followed her husband outside.

The grindstone stood under the large mountain ash near the barn gable. It was cool there in the shadow of the tree during hot summer days; now—in early spring—the wind howled around the corner of the house. Brita-Stafva wiped a drop from her nose-tip, while she leaned against the grindstone bench, waiting for her husband who had gone to the well.

Jonas Petter returned and poured well water into the grindstone trough. His wife took hold of the crank handle to begin.

But where was the ax? Brita-Stafva looked around; she had thought they were to sharpen an ax. A scythe wasn't used this time of year, and she knew of nothing else that needed sharpening. She almost asked: Have you forgotten the ax? But she remembered in time, she must not use unnecessary words. She would show her husband that she could keep silent as long as —nay, longer than—he.

Jonas Petter was not going to sharpen his ax today; he took out a knife.

His wife pulled on the handle, the grindstone turned, and the water in the trough rippled smoothly as water in a gutter. The crutch was dry, ungreased, and squeaked and whined; the peasant splashed a handful of water from the trough in its direction; the crutch, satisfied, was silent.

The wife gazed at the knife in her husband's hand. It was a sticking knife, used in cattle slaughter. Jonas Petter had had it for years, and many pigs, sheep, and calves had given up their lives to it. It was a good knife; she had borrowed it herself at times when she needed a sharp cutting tool. Jonas Petter used to say that it was sharp-edged as a razor when newly honed.

But no slaughter was impending on the farm. They had no animal to kill. Not before October would they have slaughter again, and this was only March. If one is going to use a sticking knife in October, one doesn't sharpen it in March. So much was sure and true.

Brita-Stafva was apprehensive; indeed, she had reason to be. And fear crept over her as she recalled the words her husband had repeated last night after telling the story of the Stump of Orranas. Why was he sharpening this slaughter knife today?

Jonas Petter stood bent over the grindstone, his countenance dark, his lips tightly pressed together. He looked sharply in front of him, eyes focusing stubbornly on the knife edge. He was sharpening his knife and it seemed that nothing in the world existed for him except his current occupation: the sharpening of this knife.

He turned the knife and sharpened the other side of the edge, moving it back and forth across the stone, from handle to point. But his eyes did not leave the edge. His face wore an expression of determination; there was determination in his immobile position, in his bent back, in his tightly closed lips. Every part of him radiated determination. He acted like a man who had made a decision which nothing could persuade him to change in the smallest detail.

And his wife at the grindstone handle asked herself: What was he going to do with the sticking knife?

She turned the crank. The stone was not heavy. It had been large and heavy once, when it came to the farm, but after all the scythes, axes, and knives whose edges had been sharpened against it, it was now no bigger than a Christmas cheese. A child could crank it. And when the wife let out a sigh, this was not because of the heavy stone or the hard work; it was caused by something entirely different: her husband's preoccupation.

During their marriage she had always been quick to correct
him when he made mistakes. If his actions lacked common
sense, or were willfully wrong, she used to tell him so; this
was a wifely duty. But now he accepted her corrections no
longer. She continued to point out to him all his foolish and
unreasonable actions, great or small. But no more did he listen to her. He called it criticism and scolding, and he didn't
like being blamed and censured. Yet he persisted in such behavior that she was forced to show him right from wrong.
Then he grew angry. At the least word from her he grew
angry. She, in her turn, both upset and sad, told him the
truth: he was an evil husband who cared not what she thought
or felt.

Owing to his difficult nature quarrels between them occurred at shorter and shorter intervals, increased in bitterness,
and began to last longer. After each quarrel the words between them seemed to dry up entirely; they went about in silence, without a syllable's crossing their lips for days at a
stretch. Even the time of silence was extended, sometimes
into weeks.

How she had worried lately over his unreasonable
behavior! No one knew what the devil might put into a person's head and make him do.

It was some time ago—after an intense and long-drawn-out
quarrel—that he had said: Rather than let you torture me to
death, rather than be nagged to death, I'll do it myself, I'll kill
myself with a knife! *I would rather cut myself to death!*

And what a look he had in his eyes that time, Jonas Petter!
Since then she had been in constant anxiety. What mightn't
the devil tempt a weak human being to do? Since then she
had hidden away all cutting tools—all but this slaughter knife,
which she had not found. But this was not sufficient to reas-
sure her; he might get hold of a thong, or a strap, and go to
the nearest tree or beam; he might jump into the well. There
was always something handy if you wished to take your own
life, always One ready to help you, always and everywhere.

For a while she had tried to keep back words that might irritate him. She would correct him only about small chores
and such, not worth mentioning. Nonetheless, he still became upset and angry. What could she do with so difficult a
husband?

And what was he planning now, with this knife? He wanted

it so sharp, it seemed he would never get it sharp enough! Never before had he needed so fine an edge, not even at cattle slaughter. What was she to think of all this sharpening?

Jonas Petter stretched his back for a moment, took the knife in his left hand and felt the edge with his right thumb, testing the bite. Brita-Stafva stopped cranking and the stone rested.

Still he was not satisfied with the edge on his knife; she must crank some more. Again the stone turned, the water in the trough purled and swirled. And he kept on sharpening the knife, morose, relentless, mute.

Perspiration was breaking out at the back of Brita-Stafva's neck, drops ran down her spine. It was not caused by the weight of the grindstone, but by the questions she asked herself. A knife could be well sharpened in five minutes; he had kept on for fifteen. What did it mean? It didn't make sense. He would never be satisfied with the edge—he seemed to want a razor edge today. *Was he sharpening the knife for his own neck? If not, for what?*

The peasant kept on sharpening, now and then testing the bite against his thumb, carefully, deliberately, then putting the knife back to the stone.

And the wife cranked on. This was not sane. What was it he had said last night?—A man, too, can sharpen a knife. And the way his eyes had looked of late, showing whites under the pupils; he no longer had the eyes of a sane person. It was plain he contemplated some madness.

She could ask: Why do you sharpen the sticking knife? No slaughter is imminent. But she had hardly spoken to him for three days, wanting to show him that she could hold her tongue. Moreover, she would receive no clear information, perhaps he might say something like: A sharp knife is always needed in a house.

Peace, also, was needed in the house; but that they would never have, except in the dull silences between their squabbles.

Now she had cranked the grindstone almost half an hour. No sane man acted thus, sharpening the same knife hours on end. She couldn't stand it any longer, her forehead was wet with perspiration, her body limp, her legs shook, unable to hold her up.

And when her husband tried the knife edge against his

thumb for the tenth or eleventh time, she burst out: "Won't you ever get it sharp? Are we to stand here the whole day? Are we to keep on for eternity? Get someone else to crank!"

She let go the handle and went over and collapsed like an old empty sack on a stone near the barn.

Jonas Petter did not look in her direction; it was as if he hadn't heard her. He felt with his thumb along the edge of the knife, slowly, unhurried. Then he dried the knife against his trouser leg, mumbling to himself: "I believe it'll do now."

He picked up the empty water pail in one hand and the newly sharpened knife in the other and went toward the house.

The wife followed his steps with vigilant eyes; when she saw him enter the kitchen she rose to follow. She didn't run, but she hurried. Did he intend to commit the crime inside the house? Perhaps he had gone up in the attic to be alone. There was no one in the house now, the people were at their work, the boy from Korpamoen with them; she and her husband were alone. And alone she could not get the knife away from him, she did not have sufficient strength. Should she run to a neighbor for help?

Brita-Stafva went after her husband into the kitchen. He was not there. He must have gone up into the attic; she thought she heard steps up here. Looking about, she seemed to remember something; she stretched herself on tiptoe and looked on the shelf above the fireplace: there lay the newly sharpened knife, glistening; her husband had put it back in its usual place. She let out a long, long sigh of deep relief.

Grabbing the sticking knife, she hid it under her apron and went out. She walked to the wagon shed and found her way into the darkest corner. There she stuck the sharp knife behind a beam against the roof. She pushed it so far in that no one could even see the handle. A more secret hiding place she could not find on the whole farm, she thought, as she climbed down again.

Meanwhile Jonas Petter had returned from the attic where he had walked about for no particular reason. On entering the kitchen he too went over to the shelf above the fireplace and looked. He nodded in confirmation, and satisfaction radiated from his eyes: exactly as he had hoped. The knife was gone; the threat had worked; he was safe from her now. It had gone so far that he had been forced to sharpen a knife for half an hour in order to get her where he wanted her.

He was pleased now; he knew that he would get the rest and peace he needed in the home during the time that was left—during the three remaining weeks before he was to break free from his wife, before he left her forever. He needed peace and quiet during this time of preparation. To gain this had surely been worth half an hour at the grindstone.

6

Robert remained at Hasteback for three weeks, and no sheriff came to search for him.

One evening Jonas Petter called him aside and said: "We'll keep company to America, you and I. I sail on the same ship as the others."

In secrecy, one more America chest was readied in this region—the third.

X

A PEASANT BOWS FOR THE LAST TIME

1

This was the dawn of a great era in the lives of the old clothes chests throughout the peasant communities. After centuries of neglect in dark loft corners they were now being scrubbed and polished and prepared for their voyage across the great sea. These chests were to be in the vanguard of history's greatest migration. To them would be entrusted the emigrants' most cherished belongings.

What must be brought along, what must be left behind? What was obtainable in the new land, and what was unobtainable? No one could advise, no one had traveled ahead to ascertain. It was not a move where wagon after wagon could be loaded; one small cartload must take care of all. Only the least bulky and most indispensable things were chosen.

In the bottom of the Korpamoen America chest were placed the heaviest items—iron and steel, all the timberman's and the carpenter's tools: adz, hatchet, chisel, drawknife, plane, hammer, horseshoer's tongs, auger, sticking knife, skinning knife, rule and yardstick. Also the hunter's gear: gun, powder horn, and the skin pouch for small shot. Karl Oskar took apart his muzzle-loader to facilitate its packing. There was said to be as much game in America as there was shortage of guns. A gun was said to cost fifty daler. Robert thought of all the streams and waters abounding in fish, and he packed trolling gear for pike, and hooks, angling twine, wire for fish snares. Nils brought out an old bleeding iron which might be of use to his sons; he advised the emigrants to bleed themselves often; the most reliable cure for all ills was to let one's blood.

Kristina packed her wool cards, her knitting needles, sheep shears, and her swingle, a betrothal gift from Karl Oskar, who had painted red flowers on it. A great deal she left because it would take up too much ship space, things she knew she would need later. She could not take her loom or her flax brake, her spinning-wheel or her yarn winder, her spooling wheel or her flax comb. She had been accustomed to working with all these implements; they were intimate and familiar to her hands; she knew that she would miss them in the foreign land.

Marta had helped her weave a piece of wadmal from which the village tailor had sewn them fine, warm clothing for the journey. And she packed warm woolen garments for both big and little, underwear and outer wear, working clothes and Sunday best. Woolen garments were scarce in America, she had heard somewhere, as they had not yet had time over there to make as many looms as they needed. She must take along woolen and linen yarns, and needles and thread of all kinds, so that they could patch and mend their clothing and stockings, for it would surely be a long time before they would again have new things on their bodies; the old must last. Between the clothes Kristina placed camphor and lavender to prevent mildew and bad odors; no one knew how long these things must remain in the chest.

Their bridal quilt they must take, and all bedclothes, sheets, mattresses, and bolsters were packed in two great four-bushel sacks which were then sewn up at both ends with heavy twine. All small gear to be used on the crossing was packed in the knapsack: drinking vessels, eating tools, mugs, wooden plates, spoons, knives, and forks. Kristina must also prepare a food basket for six people. The ship was to provide their food on the voyage, but no one knew if they could eat the ship's fare, and they had a long way to travel before they embarked, and after landing, too. The basket must contain dried, smoked, and salted foods which would keep well and not spoil on the ocean. A roomy willow basket with a wooden lid would serve as their food chest, and into this Kristina packed eight rye-meal loaves and twenty of barley, a wooden tub of strongly salted butter, two quarts of honey, one cheese, half a dozen smoked sausages, a quarter of smoked lamb, a piece of salt pork, and some twenty salted herrings. This filled the basket to the top. They must also find space for a pound of coffee, a pound of sugar, a bag of dried apples, a few small bags of salt, pepper, stick cinnamon, wormwood seed, and cumin.

They must keep clean and tidy during the voyage: they must not forget the pot of soft soap, and the phosphor salve for lice. Kristina had bought two excellent fine-tooth combs of brass to keep the children's heads free of vermin.

But even more important were the medicinal needs of the emigrants: camphor, and the tiny bottles of medicine containing Hoffman's Heart-Aiding Drops, The Prince's Drops, The Four Kinds of Drops. As a cure against seasickness Karl Oskar prepared half a gallon of wormwood-seed brannvin; a drink of this every morning at sea on empty stomachs would keep bodies in working order; wormwood-seed brannvin was also good for ship's fever, and protected the body against cholera and other contagious ship maladies.

Berta of Idemo called to warn Kristina about the seasickness; married women were badly attacked by it, worse than men or unmarried women, for unknown reasons. Perhaps the bodily juices in a woman changed when she entered into holy matrimony, so that afterward she became sensitive to the sea. Berta's father had been to sea and he had taught her the way seamen cared for their health and cured their ills. She had sewn camphor into a small skin pouch which she gave to

Kristina; this she must hang around her stomach while on board ship; it would ease seasickness. This was not a mortal disease, yet it was one of the most painful God had sent as punishment to man. Kristina must also eat a few spoonfuls of oat porridge every day, and take along a quart of vinegar to mix in the drinking water to freshen it up before drinking, because often water turned stale and poisonous on long voyages.

Kristina had confidence in Berta of Idemo, who in her youth had cured her gangrene-infected knee, and she listened to all the good advice: she must use pepper brannvin for diarrhea; indeed, she must guard well against diarrhea and constipation. She must keep a vigilant eye on her stool, to see that it had the right firmness—there was nothing more important for seafarers than to keep the stool firm; this the old seamen knew. And Berta had heard that people after landing in North America often suffered from intense diarrhea; even the intestines would run out, if they were not looked after. People became so wasted that they could hardly stand or walk; nothing helped except a drink of brannvin into which had been mixed a pinch of ground pepper.

The earth in America was said to crawl and creep with poisonous vipers and insects, and this might not be healthy for children running barefooted. Kristina was to put dry camphor into the wounds of snake bites. In all other fresh wounds warm urine, of course, was the best ointment; it cleaned and healed and had for thousands of years been their forebears' washing water for wounds. And if someone had an injury which didn't seem to heal, but might turn into gangrene, then Kristina must scrape the wound twice daily with a clean, sharp cutting knife—this perhaps she remembered? Broken arms and legs must be put into splints as soon as possible, and the firmer she got the splint the sooner the break would heal.

A question stole into Kristina's heart long before Berta had finished giving advice about injuries, accidents, diseases, and sicknesses which the emigrants might encounter on land or sea—the old, anxious question: Was it absolutely necessary that they carry out this dangerous foreign venture? *Must* they walk into all these dangers?

2

Karl Oskar sold Korpamoen to a farmer from Linneryd. His asking price had to be cut down; after all, the one emigrating was forced to sell, while the prospective buyer was certainly not forced to buy. Karl Oskar had to be satisfied with one hundred and fifty daler less than he himself had paid. On the other hand, his cattle—which were sold at auction—brought good prices because there was a great shortage of animals after the enforced slaughter during the famine year. But the auctioneer, Per Persson, the churchwarden, kept a quarter of all proceeds as he was to advance the money. Those were hard terms, but Karl Oskar could not stay home half a year to collect from all the bidders.

After the auction of the farmstead belongings the house seemed almost empty to Karl Oskar and Kristina. All objects sold were carried off except the beds, which they were to use until the day of departure so as not to have to sleep on the floor.

The emigrating farmer could now take stock of his position. One thousand two hundred daler remained from the sale of the farm and from the auction, after deduction of the mortgage and other debts. Their passage to America would cost six hundred and seventy-five daler for the whole family, three adults and three children. Karl Oskar would arrive in the New World with about five hundred daler. Then they must pay the entrance fee to America, and the transportation to their place of settling—an unknown way of unknown distance. Karl Oskar hoped to obtain land practically free of charge, but not much remained for the purchase of farm implements and cattle. Nils and Marta were dismayed when they heard how much the passage cost: almost half the amount necessary to buy a farm—their son threw half a farm into the sea!

Karl Oskar asked Kristina to find some safe hiding place for their five hundred daler; their only remaining security must not be lost or stolen during the long journey. She sewed the money into a sheepskin bag which he could fasten to a belt and carry next to his body.

Any person of good character was permitted to leave the country nowadays without having to petition the King. You could even leave without the extract from the parish register. So had Fredrik of Kvarntorpet done, and others who were listed under "End of the Parish." Robert, having escaped from service, dared not go near the dean to ask for his papers. But Karl Oskar did not wish to leave as if he had done wrong. He wanted to separate openly from his parish. He went to Dean Brusander and asked for his papers, as he and his household intended to emigrate to North America.

The dean looked quizzically at this first parishioner to come on such an errand.

"I've heard about your intentions. Why do you wish to emigrate, Karl Oskar Nilsson?"

"I have debts and hardships and cannot improve my situation here at home."

"It has pleased God to send us a year of famine. But a devout Christian does not complain in time of tribulation. You know your catechism, Karl Oskar Nilsson, that I remember. You must therefore know that trials and tribulations are sent for your soul's betterment?"

Karl Oskar stood there, three steps from the high-backed, leather-covered chair where his spiritual adviser sat before a desk. He held his old cap in his hands but did not answer; how could he argue on tenets of faith with the dean, who was schooled to understand and explain?

"You are known as a capable, industrious farmer. Can't you find sustenance in your home community?"

"It doesn't seem so, Mr. Dean."

"But you have adequate sustenance for your household. A person ought to be satisfied with adequate sustenance!"

Karl Oskar twisted his worn skin cap. He could mention Anna, his child, whom he had lost because of hunger. But he knew the dean would answer that this was a trial sent for his betterment. He could not argue with his pastor in spiritual matters.

"You'll make an unfortunate example for my other parishioners, Karl Oskar Nilsson."

And the dean rose from his chair and walked across the floor.

He had heard nothing but good about the people from Korpamoen; they were related to Danjel in Karragarde, but they had not been tainted by his heresy. Karl Oskar and his wife were among the most trusted, most devout people in the parish. Ill-willed persons would say that conditions in the parish must be beggarly when this industrious, diligent couple were unable to earn their living at home, and were forced to emigrate to another continent.

"The demented farmer of Karragärde has forfeited his right to live in this kingdom," continued Brusander. "He still goes free, thanks to our enlightened times. But I wish to keep an honest man like you in my parish."

The dean laid his hand on Karl Oskar's broad peasant shoulder. "Have you thoroughly thought over the adventure you throw yourself into, with wife and children? Do you know the truth about this land that tempts you?"

Brusander did not give the farmer time to answer; he himself began to explain conditions in the New World. North America had been from the very beginning populated by rebels and troublemakers who had tried to overthrow legal order in their own lands. From the time of its discovery America had been settled primarily by disloyal and refractory individuals, insubordinate to authority at home, people who had broken laws and wanted to escape just punishment. It had been overrun early by dissenters, sunderers of religion, exiled from home when spreading heresies. So it had been through many hundreds of years, so it was today. Those who incited others against spiritual and temporal authorities in their homelands in Europe escaped to the United States. To the United States fled murderers from the block, thieves from jail, swindlers from their victims, dishonest people from their debts, seducers from seduced and pregnant women, all those who feared something in their homeland, all those who did not like the order of a sound and pious community. In North America they had nothing to fear, they were safe there, all those rebels and criminals from the Old World.

Among the emigrants there were also, of course, honest people who had not broken the laws of their own country. But what drove these into adventure? Nothing but the desire for worldly gain, for enjoyment of the flesh, for vain and transient things. It was the evil desire in their minds that drove them away; they were too lazy to earn a living through honest work; they wanted to gain riches without work; the emigrants wished for quick riches so they might afterwards live in gluttony, drunkenness, idleness, and adultery. The greatest part of them were arrogant, foolhardy, reckless people who spoke ill of their fatherland, who spit at the mother who had borne them.

It was true that the soil was fertile in North America, so the inhabitants could find their living easily. But a Christian must also consider the spiritual situation of the American people. In that country there were still wild, red-skinned tribes who lived almost like animals; and even among the white-skinned people there were many who were unfamiliar with the true God and the pure evangelical teachings. True Christians ought not to be haughty toward them, ought rather to feel sorry for them; but all people living in Swedish communities should thank God that He had let them be born in a land where true Christianity was taught. It might be true that Swedes had to work a little harder for their food than Americans, nay, at times even eat their bread in the sweat of their brow. But their forebears in Sweden had for long ages had to eat bread from the bark of trees, and endure hunger, yet they had done great things, much greater things than the Swedes of today. Bark bread gave spiritual strength to men. They also found strength in their contentment, and in their obedience to God and authority.

Great confusion and chaos existed in the United States. Dissenters and preachers of unsound doctrines went about on the loose, allowed to do what they wanted. The authorities stupidly let them alone. There were no less than eighty-seven false religious sects. The Americans were building a new tower of Babel to reach into the heavens. But the Lord soon would destroy and crush this confused land called the United States. For a sound, enduring order could be built only on unity in religion, on the only true and right teaching—the holy tenets of the Augsburg Confession.

The Lord God was a strong avenger. Within fifty years those United States would exist no more; within fifty years they would be obliterated from the face of the earth, like the empires of Rome and Babylon.

"Within fifty years! Remember my words! Remember my words!"

The dean stopped short; he had intended to say only a few words, and now he had preached a whole little sermon, to a congregation of one parishioner. But he must tell Karl Oskar

Nilsson that America was a land for false prophets such as Danjel Andreasson, for adventurers and rogues such as Fredrik Thron—not a place of settlement for an honest, able farmer like himself.

And he pleaded: "Karl Oskar Nilsson! Remain in your home community and earn your living decently, as before!"

During the dean's speech Karl Oskar had stood quietly, twisting the cap in his hand, in right turns; now he started twisting it in the other direction, toward the left, while his eyes wandered along the walls of the big room in the parsonage, where hung many portraits of Brusander's predecessors in office. Perhaps a dozen deans and vicars and curates looked down on him from the four walls, some kindly admonishing, others urging more strongly, but all definitely dissuading—all agreeing in their successor's appeal: "Stay at home and earn your living honorably!"

"Aren't you misled? Aren't you seeing illusions and mirages?" the dean went on.

Karl Oskar stopped twisting his cap—then he began again, this time to the right. It was like an examination in the catechism, and, when he left home, he had not been prepared for an examination in order to obtain his papers. He could have answered these questions; but some of the awe for his confirmation teacher remained within him; he knew the dean did not like to be contradicted, and whatever he said the dean would twist so that he, Brusander, would be in the right.

The dean's brow wrinkled: a peasant leaving his farm to emigrate to North America—a new sign of that spiritual decay which had set in among the country people, tearing asunder holy ties. The outermost cause of this evil was disobedience of the Fourth Commandment; as a result of this primary disobedience, even the last tie might be broken, the tie holding people to the beloved fatherland.

"Your venture might be the ruination of you and yours; therefore I advise against it. And you must be aware I speak only for your good."

"I think you mean well, Mr. Dean."

Karl Oskar had always felt that his pastor was sincere in the fatherly care of his parishioners' spiritual and temporal needs, even though at times he assumed too great authority.

The dean went on: Because the emigrants were driven by selfishness and lust of the flesh—man's base, carnal desires—

emigration to the United States was contrary to God's commandments and the true evangelical Lutheran church.
Emigrants from Sweden had already been made aware of this
in a frightful way. A group of people from the northern provinces—from Helsingland and Dalecarlia—had been led astray
by an apostle of the devil, an instrument of falsehood, a peasant named Erik Janson, and in their blindness had emigrated
to North America. On their journey they were stricken by
cholera, that scourge from God. Hundreds of the poor people
had died before they reached their destination. The Lord God
was a powerful avenger, and cholera His instrument. The horrible punishment had calmed restlessness at home in the last
year, quenched desire to emigrate.

After the experience of these sectarians one could comprehend God's opinion of emigration.

"Answer me honestly, Karl Oskar: Is it not the desire for
high living that drives you to emigrate?"

Karl Oskar was still twisting his cap with both hands as before. He did not contemplate the voyage to North America in
order to abandon himself to those vices enumerated in the
catechism: debauchery, gluttony, adultery, and others, which
tended to shorten one's life. He had not had high living in
mind, of that he was sure.

"No. It isn't because of that. Do not think so, Mr. Dean. It
isn't because I desire high living."

"I believe your word," said the dean. "But you are seized
by the spirit of dissatisfaction. Otherwise you would remain in
the land of your fathers. And have you thought of your parents, whom you abandon? And your father a cripple!"

"Their reserved rights go with the property, as usual. The
old ones will manage."

"But if all young people and those fit for work should emigrate, and leave the old and decrepit behind, who would then
take care of the helpless?"

Karl Oskar kept silent, twisting his cap with fumbling,
clumsy fingers. If only he were quick-witted; whatever he
might say, the dean would surely put him in the wrong. And
it seemed to him that he must tell his pastor it was time to
stop his dissuasion. If the bishop himself were to come to the
dean's aid, he, Karl Oskar, still would not change his mind;
nay, not even if the King tried to persuade him. Moreover, it
was too late.

He now said, somewhat tartly: "I've already sold out. I'm free and without obligations. Perhaps I could have my errand attended to . . . ?"

Dean Brusander sat down and leaned his head against the high back of his chair. He set his lips, and his mouth took on a sterner look.

This peasant from Korpamoen seemed on the surface tractable and decent; but apparently he had a bullish nature. Through all the dean's kindness and repeated advice he had not been able to move Karl Oskar one iota. Occasionally he had answered a few words, but for the most part he had persisted in a silence that was deaf to God's words and his pastor's admonitions. No human power could remove the man's emigration notions. And now he sounded almost importunate, as he referred to his errand. It might well be that he lacked respect for the office of the ministry. Perhaps after all he was a horse of a different color.

At any rate, the dean had done his duty as teacher and pastor. And he was pretty sure this farmer would be alone in his America ideas. This desire for emigration among the peasantry, which had broken out here and there throughout the kingdom, would probably die down as quickly as it had flared up. Twenty years from now there would be no one in the land with a mind to emigrate.

"You shall have your papers!"

A silence ensued. Only the quill's scratching against the paper was heard from the desk. Karl Oskar took a step backward, as if wishing to leave the dean undisturbed with his writing.

Dean Brusander turned and handed the farmer the extract from the parish register.

"Once I gave you Christian baptism. Once I prepared you for the Lord's Supper. I've baptized your children. Now I pray God to bless you and yours during your voyage to a faraway land. May you never regret your bold decision!"

Karl Oskar bowed. "Thank you, Mr. Dean."

Brusander extended his hand. "May you be within God's protection! Such was the blessing of our forebears at times of parting."

"Thank you most kindly, Mr. Dean."

And Karl Oskar bowed once more, this time perhaps

deeper than he had ever bowed to the dean before. After all, it was the last time he would bow to his parish pastor.

Dean Brusander wrote a few words in the parish register, words which he never before had written about any one of his parishioners: he noted that homeowner Karl Oskar Nilsson of Korpamoen, on the twenty-eighth of March, 1850, had requested extracts from the records for himself and his household for emigration to N. America.

And the remaining blank pages in the parish register were in time to be filled with the repeated notation: "Moved to N. America." Through years and decades they were to be filled, page after page, with the names of Karl Oskar Nilsson's followers.

XI

ONE EMIGRANT PAYS NO FARE

1

In the newspaper *Barometern,* to which some of the farmers in the village subscribed, there appeared early in spring a news item about a lost emigrant ship: "Owing to absence of communications of any kind, one is now forced to admit the sad foundering and total loss of the small schooner *Betty Catharina,* built in 1835, measuring 80 lasts, on voyage from Soderhamn to New York. The schooner had taken on a load of pig iron in Soderhamn. On board the vessel were 70 emigrants who had left their fatherland to seek a precarious living in a foreign country. The *Betty Catharina* sailed through the straits of Ore Sund on April the 15th of last year but since that date her owner, the firm P. C. Rettig et Cie., has had no word from her. Since now almost a year has passed without the slightest information as to the ship's whereabouts, notice of the deaths of the crew—nine men—has been published in their respective home communities. The ship's Master was Captain Anders Otto Ronning. The emigrants came from different parishes in Helsingland; among them were 25 women and 20 children."

This copy of the paper was widely read in the village, and

no wonder, in those days; it was even lent to families who did not subscribe. Berta of Idemo brought it to Korpamoen, and Kristina read about the ship whose sailing time was supposed to be about five weeks yet after fifty weeks had not reached her destination. The *Betty Catharina*'s passengers had not arrived in a new land; they had emigrated to the bottom of the ocean.

A stab of pain went through Kristina's heart as she tucked in her three little ones that evening—". . . among them were 25 women and 20 children." All her earlier anxiety returned and pressed upon her. The children were left in her care by God—wasn't she an irresponsible mother to take her helpless little ones out in a fragile ship to cross the forbidding ocean? She did not fear for her own life; but had she the right to endanger her children? If they went down with the ship, then it was she who drowned them, and God would ask accounting for them on the Day of Judgment: How did you look after your children? What did you do with them? Who forced you out on the ocean? Weren't you warned of the danger?

Wasn't the notice of the lost ship a last warning from God, arriving as it did on the eve of their departure?

Karl Oskar said that most people on land died in their beds, yet people went to bed every evening. Only fools were frightened by stories of wrecks. Robert wasn't afraid either. He wasn't old enough, he didn't have his mature senses as yet. As if it were a pleasure to him, he now read a horrible piece to Kristina from his *History of Nature,* about "The Billows of the Sea."

"Because water is a liquid which can be stirred up, so it is also moved by wind and storm. This causes billows which are great or small depending on the wind's intensity and the size and depths of the sea. In heavy storms on the great seas the billows rise above each other to a height of thirty or forty feet; then they fall down with unbelievable power and crush all in their way. When such a huge billow falls over a ship it may break away large pieces of the vessel, splinter yard-thick masts, yea, even fill the whole ship with water, making it sink immediately."

"Think of it, Kristina!" exclaimed Robert excitedly. "Waves three times as high as this house!"

"Are you trying to make me feel better about the voyage?" And she couldn't help smiling at the boy. He didn't care

what might happen as long as he became free and got out
into the world. But he had only his own life to account for.

Kristina did not wish to approach Karl Oskar with her
worries. She had once agreed that all should be as he decided,
and she couldn't take back her words. He had once and for
all assumed responsibility for their emigration. She liked to
lean on him and have confidence in him. He was headstrong
and stubborn, but she liked a husband who could order and
decide for her at times; what woman would be satisfied with
a weakling, a shillyshallying husband? All the men in the
Nilsa family, born with the big nose, were said to have been
like Karl Oskar; unafraid, perhaps even a little refractory, not
to be swayed, never yielding. Of all the men she knew, Karl
Oskar was the one who most definitely knew what he wanted,
and because of this she liked him.

Kristina had not felt well lately; she was weak and had lost
her appetite. At first she thought this might be caused by her
worrying about the America journey. But when—on getting
out of bed one morning—she had to run outside behind the
gable and throw up, she knew how things stood with her. She
had had this ailment before, four times. It always followed
the same course: her monthly bleeding was delayed beyond its
time, then came weakness, loss of appetite, worry and mental
depression; and at last the vomiting, as a final confirmation.
Everything fitted in, there was no longer any doubt, she was
pregnant again.

She had feared a new pregnancy. She still gave the breast
to the little one and intended to continue to suckle him—
Berta of Idemo had said that women would not become pregnant while still suckling a baby. Berta herself had suckled each
of her children three years, and within a month after stopping
each time she had become pregnant again. It had never
failed. Occasionally there might be a wife in the neighborhood who suckled her children until they started school; when
the children had to eat from food baskets they must stop suckling and eat the food of grownups. Rarely did it happen that
a mother went with her child to school in order to feed it
from her breast in between lessons; children who didn't stop
suckling at school age were usually dull-witted; they hung on
to their mother's apron-strings, always hungry, always pulling
up a chair for her to sit on.

Berta's advice had not helped Kristina, but, indeed, the old woman had been careful to add: if she should become pregnant while still suckling her baby, then that might be the fault of Karl Oskar. Some men had seeds so vital that no prevention ever helped.

A few times during the past year Kristina had been seized by an evil temptation. She had wanted to pray to God that He would not make her pregnant any more. This thought had come over her for the first time when she laid Anna in the coffin after only four years on earth; she did not wish to bear children who were to die. But she had been able to withstand the temptation, she had not prayed this sinful prayer. How very sinful it would have been she realized now, when a new life was being created within her.

She must resign herself to the decision of the Highest One. As yet she had said nothing to Karl Oskar.

2

One thought constantly hammered within Kristina's head during the evening before their departure: Do not forget anything. Up to the last moment she kept finding indispensable objects, things which must be taken along but which she had not thought of earlier. She had forgotten tapers, and pitch splinters—they would no doubt need light sometimes while traveling. The children would want playthings on the ship—for Johan she took a clay cuckoo, and Lill-Marta must have her rag doll—neither one was bulky. The baby Harald, who during the last days had taken his first stumbling steps across the floor, and who handled toys only in a destructive way, could be without anything. She was annoyed with herself when she came across the tripod copper kettle, a wedding gift from her parents; why hadn't she thought of it before!

Now the only space she could find for the kettle was among the bedclothes in one of the sacks that had not yet been sewn up. As she put her hand into the sack to make room for the kettle she got hold of a pair of children's shoes, ragged and worn out. They were Anna's shoes! It was her first pair of shoes—and her last.

Kristina stood, deeply moved, with the tiny shoes in her hand. None of the other children could use them, they were too far gone, they barely held together in the seams; she remembered she had thrown them away. Karl Oskar must have picked them up and put them in the sack that was to go with them to America.

As soon as the girl had learned to walk she had followed her father, in these shoes she had often walked with him, in them she had gone long distances at his side. And as Kristina now found them in the sack they conveyed something new to her about her husband.

For a moment she fought back her tears; carefully she put the shoes back into the sack.

Then she pushed down the coffee kettle, which made the sack look out of form: it stood there on the floor like a hunchback.

The America chest was locked and tied with the thickest ropes they could find; it had already been carried out into the entrance hall in readiness. On its front Karl Oskar had printed in red chalk the owner's name and destination—there it stood in flaming red letters: *Homeowner Karl Oskar Nilsson, N. America.* Now the chest would not be lost or mixed up with another.

The Bible, the hymnbook, and the almanac were still on the table; these were the books to be taken along; their place was in the knapsack, they were to be used on the journey.

Karl Oskar came in. He had been to the village to fetch the new high boots which the shoemaker had made for him and which had not been ready until the last moment. No one knew what kind of slipshod footgear they were using in America, and to be on the safe side he had ordered a pair of high boots, to be made of oak-bark-tanned ox leather, the best to be had. The uppers came all the way up to his knees, they could be used in all weathers and on all types of roads. On the boggy roads in the wilds of America one had better be well shod if one wished to get through.

He pulled on the new boots and took a few steps across the floor so Kristina could admire and praise them. They were polished shining black and reinforced at the heels with irons, like small horseshoes. In these boots he could step on shore in America without having to feel ashamed. These boots he could show to the Americans with pride.

But the irresponsible cobbler had almost not finished them in time.

Kristina was brushing his Sunday-best clothes, which he was to put on tomorrow morning. She had put the children to bed and they were already asleep, newly washed and newly combed, in new clean night clothes. Johan and Lill-Marta knew that they were to get out and ride on a wagon tomorrow, that they were to go on a long journey, but the mother felt a sting in her heart as she reflected that otherwise they knew nothing. They had no idea of the long road they were to travel with their parents; it would be long before they were to sleep again in the peace of a home's protection.

Now, this evening, she ought to speak to Karl Oskar; before they began their journey he must know that still another life was on the way.

"I had better tell you. I am that way again."

He looked at her, confounded. Before he had time to ask questions she assured him she was not fooled by false signs: they were to have a little one again, he could rely on it.

"Hmm."

Karl Oskar looked around at the bare, empty walls of the home they were to leave forever tomorrow. At last they were ready, at last all the long, tiresome preparations were over, and when finally this evening he had fetched his boots, which he had worried about, he had felt satisfied with practically everything. Then he was given this piece of news, for which he was unprepared.

A sentence escaped him: "It could not be more ill-timed or awkward."

"What are you saying?"

"I mean, it is ill-timed just now."

She flared up. Her voice rose: "I cannot be pregnant to suit you!"

"Now, dear, don't take it so . . ."

"What exactly do you mean, then? Is it only I? Is it only *my* fault that I get to be with child?"

"I haven't said that."

"You have said it's ill-timed. Can you deny that? But is it not your fault also? Have you not had part in it, perhaps? Even more than I? Is it not you who have put me in this condition? Isn't it you also who come ill-timed?"

"Kristina! What has come over you? Father and Mother in there can hear you!"

But his wife's flare-up convinced him of her pregnancy

more than anything else; at those times she was always short-tempered and irritable and caught fire at every little word that could be interpreted as an insult.

"Must you take it so hard?"

Her eyes were flaming, her cheeks had turned red. "It sounds as if you accuse me! As if I alone were responsible! I'm to blame less than you! You should feel it yourself! If you for one day, for one hour, had to feel so ill as I . . ."

She threw herself face down over the kitchen table, her arms folded in front of her, and burst out crying.

Karl Oskar stood there helpless. He couldn't understand his wife's acting thus. He almost flared up himself. But he must keep his head, for he had no indisposition to excuse him. Kristina, besides, must be worn out with all the preparations for the journey.

He put his hand on her shoulder, patting her clumsily: he had used ill-advised words, which she had interpreted wrongly. He regretted them, but he had meant no harm. He had not tried to shun his responsibility in the pregnancy. How could she think anything as foolish as that? He had not accused her of anything. He had only meant that it was bad luck she happened to be pregnant just now, when they were starting out on their journey—which in this way would be harder for her. And perhaps they would barely have arrived in their new home when she would have to go to bed in childbirth; that also wasn't so good.

"You're afraid I'll be trouble," she sobbed.

"I've never said that. But I'm afraid it will be harder on you when we have one more."

It was during the first months of her pregnancy that she always felt indisposed and irritated. This difficult time, during which it was impossible to please her, would now fall during the actual crossing. But he would have acted more wisely if he had never voiced his apprehensions.

He took hold of her hand, which was limp and without response. But he kept it in his own and continued.

Things had to be as they were; no one could change them. And as long as they had nothing to accuse each other of, they might as well forget their quarrel. Now, when they were to travel so far away and build their home anew, they must stick together. Otherwise they would never succeed. They would ruin things for themselves if they quarreled and lived at odds with each other. They would hurt only themselves and their children if they pulled in different directions; they would ruin their good natures and their joy in work, now when they more than ever needed to be hardy and fearless. Shouldn't they, this last evening at home, agree to be friends and peaceful at all times? She wanted to be his friend, as before, didn't she?

"Of course I want to, but . . ."

She sobbed dryly and was seized with hiccoughs after crying.

"Why but? As long as you want to."

"Karl Oskar . . . You understand . . . I don't feel well."

"I know it."

"You must speak kindly to me."

"I won't speak unkindly to you, Kristina."

"Will you promise?"

Kristina was becoming more calm; she realized that she too had been unjust. She had lost her temper. But he had used such irritating words: "It could not be more ill-timed." Those words had escaped him and he must have meant something by them. Didn't he mean that she would ruin the journey for him through her pregnancy? It had sounded as if she had done all she could in order to be with child again. When, on the contrary, it always was he who was ready in bed! Perhaps she had misunderstood him; however, it was difficult to forget such ugly words.

But she remembered also how kind he mostly was toward her. Like that first time she was with child: her complexion had changed, her face had been covered with ugly brown spots. She used to be shocked when she looked in the mirror, she had looked like an old woman although she had been barely nineteen. She had felt she must run away and hide from people, particularly from Karl Oskar. She had never dreamt that wedded life would distort her. She had complained to her mother, who only laughed and said her brown complexion would soon disappear. The one to comfort her had been Karl Oskar, who had said that the brown spots were becoming to her. He was happy over them! She had the spots because she was to bear a child, she was to bear a child because she had been with him, and she had been with him because she loved him. The ugly brown complexion was to Karl

Oskar a proof of her love for him. How could he be anything but happy over it?

She would never forget the time he said this. And now she was again expecting the brown spots which would ruin her skin. She knew that she otherwise had a fairly nice face, perhaps even handsome, with evenly rounded, fair cheeks. But her face remained pretty such short times—only in between pregnancies.

Kristina's hand grasped her husband's fingers more firmly. "Karl Oskar, we must be friends . . . for all times!"

"We agree, then."

"Yes. It's true, as you say; we must hold together. Nothing else will help us."

And she rose hastily and busied herself; how could she have time to sit here and shed tears an evening like this when she had a hundred chores to do, chores which could not be delayed till tomorrow—not one of them. Now she must hurry as if it were butter to be raked from a fire; the buttons must go on Johan's new jacket, Lill-Marta's newly washed nightshirt must be mended and ironed, and her own nightshirt, and Karl Oskar's shirt for tomorrow, and then—then—She was a foolish woman, causing trouble this last evening.

Karl Oskar was soon adjusted to the thought that in seven or eight months his family would increase.

He said this was really good luck for them because now the captain would be cheated out of the passage for one person; their fourth child would accompany them without a penny's expense! What mightn't one day become of this emigrant who already was so clever that he managed to get a free passage to America?

Then Kristina burst out in joyful laughter. Shortly before she had wept; now she attended laughingly to the last chores for the journey to the land where she and Karl Oskar were to build their second home.

THE FIRST EMIGRANTS

from Ljuder Parish, who left their homes April 4, 1850

KARL OSKAR NILSSON, homeowner, 27 years.
KRISTINA JOHANSDOTTER, his wife, 25 years.

Their children:
JOHAN, 4 years.
MÄRTA, 3 years.
HARALD, 1 year.
ROBERT NILSSON, farmhand, 17 years.
DANJEL ANDREASSON, homeowner, 46 years.
INGA-LENA, his wife, 40 years.
Their children:
SVEN, 14 years.
OLOF, 11 years.
FINA, 7 years.
EVA, 5 months.
ARVID PETTERSON, their servant, 25 years.
UNMARRIED ULRIKA OF VÄSTERGÖHL, status unknown, 37 years.
ELIN, her daughter, 16 years.
JONAS PETTER ALBREKTSSON, homeowner, 48 years.

WHY THEY EMIGRATED

KARL OSKAR NILSSON: I seek a land where through my work I can help myself and mine.

KRISTINA: I go with my husband, but I do so with hesitation and half in regret.

ROBERT NILSSON: I do not like masters.

DANJEL ANDREASSON: I wish to freely confess the God of the twelve apostles in the land He shall show me.

INGA-LENA: "Whither thou goest, I will go; where thou diest will I die, and there will I be buried."

ARVID: I want to get away from the "Bull of Nybacken."

ULRIKA OF VÄSTERGÖHL: Sweden—this hellhole!

ELIN: My mother has told me . . .

JONAS PETTER OF HÄSTEBÄCK: I can no longer endure cohabitation with my wife Brita-Stafva; from now on let happen to me what may.

XII

ALL GATES OPEN ON THE ROAD TO AMERICA

1

They set out on a Thursday, and the day was well chosen. The heathen god with the hammer—Thor—had been a mighty god in whom their forebears had put their trust, and still far into Christian times his weekday was considered an auspicious day for the beginning of a new venture. Besides, there was a new moon, a good omen for the emigrants.

Nearly a thousand years had passed since people of this region had gathered into groups to sail the sea toward the west. At that time women and children had remained at home. But then as now the departing men had taken edged tools on their journey; the forefathers had armed themselves with weapons, this time the weapons were implements of peace, packed in the bottoms of the chests—broadaxes, augers, hammers, planes. This time the people traveled on a different errand.

Karl Oskar had hired a team of horses and a flat-wagon from the churchwarden in Akerby, and the team and its driver arrived shortly before sunup. He, Robert, and the driver loaded the wagon; the America chest was so heavy that the three of them had to use their combined strength to get it onto the wagon.

The leave-taking from the relatives took little time. Lydia had a day off to say farewell to her brothers. Karl Oskar called his sister aside and begged her to look after their parents, particularly later as they grew older and couldn't manage for themselves: he would pay her for this. Marta took each of her grandchildren into her arms and said: "May God protect and keep you, you helpless little creature!" The sons shook hands with their parents, a bit awkwardly, perhaps shamefacedly, almost like little boys who had been disobedient but were embarrassed to ask forgiveness. Neither one of them had ever said that he intended to return. Now Karl Oskar remarked, with an attempt at a smile, that when he had earned enough money in America he would come home and buy the manor at Krakesjo, and for his sister Lydia he would buy back Korpamoen. All knew he was joking, but no one smiled. Nils and Marta felt they were seeing their sons for the last time this bleak April morning.

Kristina had already said goodby to her parents, a few days earlier in Duvemala. She had not cried while there, but returning home she had been unable to hold back the tears any longer as she thought of her mother's parting words: "Remember, my dear daughter, I wish to meet you with God."

All that they owned in this world was now on the wagon. The load was high and wide, with the two large sacks on top; yet Karl Oskar thought there was room for more—it still didn't reach the sky!

Nils and Marta stood on the stoop.

"Drive carefully through the gate," said Nils to the boy who drove. Those were the last words his departing sons heard him utter. And the admonition was pertinent: the gate was narrow for such a broad wagon, the steering shaft caught one of the posts, and the team with the load could barely make it through the gate.

"Everything is narrow, here at home!" said Robert.

Karl Oskar was sitting next to the driver with Johan on his knee. Kristina sat behind with the smaller children, who in spite of the early hour were fully awake, looking about them with their clear eyes. Robert sat on the horses' hay sack on top of the load.

As they reached the village road Karl Oskar turned a last time and looked toward the house: his father and mother were still on the porch, watching the departing ones—his father gnarled and stooped and hanging on his crutches, his mother close by her husband's side, tall, her back straight. Here on the wagon sat the young ones, departing—there stood the old ones, left behind.

Karl Oskar could not see either of his parents make the slightest movement. As they stood there on the stoop, looking after the wagon, they seemed to him as still and immobile as dead, earth-bound things, as a pair of high stones in the field or a couple of tree trunks in the forest, deeply rooted in the ground. It was as if they had assumed that position once and for all, and intended to hold it forever. And as he saw them in the half-mist, this early morning, so they were forever to return to his mind: Father and Mother, standing quietly together on the stoop, looking after a cart driving through the gate and onto the road and after a minute disappearing among the junipers at the bend. In that place and in that position his parents would always remain in his mind. After many years he would still see them standing there, close together, looking out on the road, immobile objects, two human sculptures in stone.

Kristina did not mention to Karl Oskar that she had happened to hear a remark by Nils as the wagon was ready to depart: "I must go outside and behold my sons' funeral procession."

2

The spring was late this year; the ground lay frozen still. There had been a freeze during the night, and the April morning was chilly; the sky was overcast and it was not yet full daylight. The load was heavy but the wheels rolled lightly on the frozen road.

From his high seat on the hay sack Robert could see the horses' manes waving below him like young birches in the wind. Their strong-muscled necks rose and sank at regular intervals, their hairy flanks moved in soft billows, and the sharp horseshoes cut sparks from the stones in the road. Anticipation without measure filled his breast: this was no ordinary mill-wagon, this was not a slow timber load, nor was it a depressing Sunday church carriage. At last he was riding the chariot of adventure.

He would reach the sea tomorrow.

They passed Nybacken, and as the wagon gained speed downhill on the other side of the farm, Robert began to whistle. He could not hold back any longer, and his brother and sister-in-law said nothing about it.

He whistled a piece again as they passed the parsonage: he wondered if it could be considered sacrilegious. He had not asked for his papers, and he could hear the dean call his name at all the yearly examinations: Farmhand Robert Nilsson, not heard from since 1850. And the dean would write: Whereabouts unknown. After ten or twenty years it would still be written about him: Whereabouts unknown.

Every time they came to a gate on the road Robert jumped down to open it. Before they reached Akerby Junction he had opened five. He counted them carefully, he was to be gate-boy, he must count all the gates on the road to America.

The road also went through pasturelands, where the gates had been removed for the winter; but Robert still counted the openings as gates on the America road—if their emigration had been delayed a month, these gates too would have been closed.

Lill-Marta and Harald had gone to sleep in their mother's arms, rocked to sleep by the movement of the wagon. Johan played driver, holding on to one rein and shouting at the horses. Karl Oskar and Kristina sat silent and serious, their eyes tarrying on well-known places: this is the brook with the swimming hole, we are passing it for the last time; in this meadow we will never see the lilies of the valley in spring again. We want to remember what these places are like, we are anxious to remember them—they were once part of our youth. . . .

The emigrants had agreed to meet at Akerby Junction, and the other wagons awaited them there. Danjel of Karragarde had hired a team from Krakesjo. He too had a heavy load—his wife, his four children, and Ulrika of Vastergohl. Jonas Petter of Hasteback drove his own single-horse wagon and was accompanied by his hired man, who was to drive the horse back from Karlshamn. Two of the people from Karra-garde, unable to find room on Danjel's wagon, rode with Jonas Petter—the farmhand Arvid, and Ulrika's daughter Elin.

The wagon from Korpamoen had, besides its load, four full-grown persons, and Jonas Petter thought it should be made lighter; Robert therefore moved over to him and found a seat between the driver and Elin. Behind him, next to Jonas Petter's hired man, sat Arvid, who now welcomed Robert with a broad grin; the two farmhands from Nybacken were journeying together to the New World after all. Otherwise things weren't going as they had planned during their nightly combats with the bedbugs in Aron's stable room: they didn't sneak away in secrecy on a load of timber, nor were they alone on their journey.

There were nineteen of them at the meeting at Akerby Junction this morning. Three drivers were to return from Karlshamn. The emigrants were sixteen, nine grownups and seven children. Together they made a suitably large family, said Jonas Petter as he counted them. But who was to be head of the family?

All looked at Karl Oskar. He said he could hardly be head of them all, he was the youngest of the three farmers.

"You are the oldest one, Jonas Petter."

"But you were the first one to decide on this journey, Karl Oskar. I was the last one."

The loaded wagons started moving again, toward the province of Blekinge. Jonas Petter drove first, he knew the roads, and Robert continued to jump off and open gates. They drove a wagon length apart and mostly at a slow trot, or letting the horses walk to save their strength, as it was fifty long miles to Karlshamn. On steep downgrades they kept still farther apart, to give the horses more room.

As Kristina eyed the three wagons she thought of her father-in-law's words about his departing sons; it was true, their company looked like a funeral cortege. A small one. But there had been no more than three carriages when Anna was buried.

Now she would rather forget what Nils had said in the bitter moment of leave-taking—he had not thought anyone would hear him. Somewhere, some place, a grave awaited every mortal, somewhere there was a patch of earth which one day would open for one's body. So it might be said that every moment man was on his way to that place; all people's journeys were one long funeral procession.

Some one, or perhaps several, of this company might return home again—no one knew. Kristina supposed that most of them—though not Karl Oskar—nourished in secret the hope of returning. Of course, they wished to come back rich and well-to-do, not poor, impoverished wretches. Yet it was most likely that none in their group would ever travel this road again.

Robert was now opening gates which he had never before seen. They had left the roads he was familiar with, they were in strange country. They passed farm after farm, and he asked Jonas Petter the name of this place, and that. They passed a church with a much higher steeple than the one at home. They met completely unknown people who greeted them sharply and morosely and who stood for long moments looking after the three wagons—with open mouths, impolitely. But they were something to look at: three flat-wagons full of people and loaded high with chests, boxes, sacks, baskets, and bundles. One might indeed wonder what kind of travelers these were.

"They must think we are gypsies," said Jonas Petter. "These loads look like gypsy carts."

But they themselves did not resemble gypsies, thought Robert. Nearly all the grownups of the company, women as well as men, were tall with blond hair and light complexions. Gypsies were short and dark. And all of this company were well dressed, washed and clean; gypsies were ragged and dirty. And they traveled their way quietly and peacefully and soberly, while gypsies lived ill, shouted, and were drunk and evil-natured. It irritated Robert that they might be mistaken for such rabble. He wanted to call to all staring people whom they met: We are not gypsies! We are honest, decent people! We're emigrants! We're going to a country where there are no bad people, where we never will meet any rabble! Don't stand there and stare at us—go home and harness your horses and come with us to the sea, to the ship waiting for us!

But after a while he thought that if he told the people they met about about the members of his own group, then perhaps the strangers wouldn't join them. Those sitting here on the wagons were not too well thought of at home. How about Arvid, sitting there behind him? He was so much looked down on that no one except Danjel was willing to hire him. And how about Danjel himself? Nearly all at home were pleased and grateful that he left the parish. The dean was most happy; the sheriff, too, was pleased. And Ulrika of Vastergohl? All decent women thanked God that she was leaving the district. And, not to forget himself. Sheriff Lonnegren no doubt was thankful that he had left the village for ever, he had caused him so much trouble; the sheriff hated to chase "servant-scoundrels." No, outside of his parents, and his sister Lydia, no one at home would miss him.

And perhaps no one missed the others in the group either. At some time in the future, maybe fifty years hence, they might hold a celebration at home in memory of the day when they got rid of the rabble that was taken for gypsies on their America road.

3

Robert cast glances at the girl sitting next to him on the driver's seat. He had never seen Ulrika's daughter at close hand before. Elin was little and spindly, but her small-girl limbs had begun to fill out; she would soon be a woman. She had long hair falling to her shoulders, and it had a sheen of golden ripe barley. Her big eyes were dark blue, and gleamed like sloeberries. She was pleasant to look at. What a pity that her mother was the Glad One, the foremost whore in the parish.

Jonas Petter was broad through the hips, and the three of them were crowded in the driver's seat. It was lucky that Elin was so slender, said Robert, otherwise he would have been forced to walk beside the wagon. After he had said this he noticed that the girl kept moving away from him, but each time the wheels hit a stone in the road her body was moved closer to his and he could feel her thigh against his own, soft and tender as the supple flesh of a calf or a lamb. Never before had Robert had a girl so close to his body.

Elin kept silent; she was shy and bashful. Perhaps she was afraid of Jonas Petter, perhaps of Arvid sitting close behind her; perhaps she had heard of the Bull of Nybacken. She was only sixteen and her mind wasn't as yet developed, but she must have sense enough not to be afraid of *him*.

Robert tried again: "No one would ever take *you* for a gypsy."

The girl didn't answer this time either, and Jonas Petter nudged Robert in the side to silence him. After a while the driver stopped, and the men went off to let their water. As they stood together on the road's edge Jonas Petter explained the prod in the ribs: no one knew for sure who Elin's father was, perhaps not even the mother herself. But rumors had it that a gypsy was just what he was.

Robert felt embarrassed and had nothing more to say.

Elin wore a dark dress which had belonged to Inga-Lena, and which was too large for her. On her knees she held a basket. Her narrow blue-veined hands held tightly on to its handle, as if she were afraid someone might try to snatch it from her. It was a small basket for so long a journey, thought Robert, too small for emigration to the New World. It was only a berry basket, large enough for picking blueberries or wild strawberries—not much to go out into the world with. But probably the poor girl didn't need a larger packing box; all she owned must be contained in that little basket.

Elin belonged to the Akians; Ulrika had permitted Danjel to confirm her. The mother had been in prison on bread and water for participating in the illegal Communion in Karragarde, but Elin was under age and had therefore escaped punishment.

Suppose her father was a gypsy? The girl couldn't help who he was, she had not shown the way to her mother's bed; and she couldn't help who her mother was, either. Robert felt sorry for her, and thought he would be kind to her. They were to journey in close company for some time, perhaps several months. They couldn't sit together and not speak to each other, like this, the whole way to America. They must talk, she too must talk. He had no experience with girls, he had hardly shaken hands with a girl before. What ought he to say to make her answer?

They drove by a fine gray manor house on top of a knoll, and Jonas Petter pointed with the whip, saying that this was Galtakullen. Lotta Andersdotter had lived there, she who had become infamous through a horrible deed done to her first husband.

Robert thought probably the farmer would tell one of his stories again, and his supposition proved to be correct.

Yes, continued Jonas Petter, it was said that the farmer of Galtakullen could never satisfy his wife in bed, she was that kind of woman whom no man could please however much he worked and tried. Now she wanted to exchange her husband for the enlisted man of the village, a strong, bed-worthy man. And the soldier was tempted by the promise that he was to be farmer of Galtakullen. One night when her husband was sleeping soundly Lotta Andersdotter got out of bed and went to the toolbox for a hammer and a five-inch spike. With the hammer she drove the spike full length into the skull of her sleeping husband. He never awakened—unless it were in heaven or hell. Some blood splurted out of the hole in his head, but the murderess dried it off and left the nailhead well covered by her husband's hair.

Then she announced that her husband had died from a stroke; as people knew, he had been somewhat ailing lately. A grand funeral was held. The widow wanted to show that she mourned her husband deeply, and she cried profusely and bitterly at the graveside. No one suspected her of a crime.

As soon as her widow year was up she married the soldier. He in his turn died, after ten years of wedded life, from somewhat more natural causes than the first husband: people said from overwork in bed. The housewife of Galtakullen remained the same craving woman; she was about to take a third husband, but he became frightened of her, and changed his mind before it was too late. He is supposed to have said that the widow of Galtakullen was almost as much man as woman, that she had the organs of both sexes—though no one could be sure of this.

After two marriages she sat, a widow, on her farm for the rest of her life.

Then thirty years after her first husband's sudden death the gravedigger was one day opening a new grave in the churchyard. While digging he got hold of a skull on his spade. He usually paid no attention to a skull, big or small, any more than a potato picker looks at his potatoes; for human skulls grow in a churchyard as profusely as tubers in a field. But this skull was different: a long rusty-red spike hung rattling inside it. The gravedigger carried his find to the dean, and pointed out to him where he had found the skull. The dean looked up his records and made sure of who had once been buried in that place. Then he tied the skull up in a piece of black cloth, took it under his arm, and went directly to Galtakullen. The widow was at home and he handed her the parcel, saying: Here comes your first husband to visit you; he wishes to speak about the nail in his head. Later you can come to me and speak about your wretched soul.

With this the dean went home. The following day the widow Lotta Andersdotter went to the parsonage and confessed her crime, and in the evening that same day she hanged herself in the milk cellar of her farm.

"Right in there, in that gray house up there," concluded Jonas Petter.

Everyone looked toward the farm. Jonas Petter knew of all

the crimes and evil deeds perpetrated by wives against their husbands in Konga County during the last hundred years, but Robert thought he shouldn't tell them in the presence of a girl. Elin had looked straight ahead and acted as if she had heard nothing. Perhaps Jonas Petter had thought that the daughter of the Glad One was hardened.

Robert could see her eyes under the kerchief she had drawn forward over her brow, but she always looked away if he tried to meet her gaze. She did not appear sociable. So he turned his back to her and began speaking to Arvid behind him. He intended to buy a book in Karlshamn to learn the American language, he said; he would no doubt have time for study while crossing the ocean.

This was said for Elin's benefit, and for the first time the eyes under the kerchief turned to the youth beside her.

He met her gaze. "You can borrow the book—if you wish."

"I don't need it," she answered.

"You mean you speak English?"

"Not yet. Not before we land in America."

"Do you think you can speak fluently as soon as we land?"

"Yes, of course."

"Really?"

"I don't need to learn the language because I'll know it when we arrive," repeated the girl with assurance.

"Who has told you that?"

"Uncle Danjel."

And her eyes now looked into his, clear and trusting: Danjel had told them that all who were reborn in Christ would be able to speak the English tongue fluently as soon as they stepped on shore in America.

Robert was stupefied; he could hear and see that she believed this promise to the very letter.

Elin continued: Danjel had told them not to worry about the foreign language, for at their landing all believers would be filled with the Holy Ghost as once had happened to the apostles on the first Whitsuntide. Thus they would be able to understand and speak freely the language used in that land.

"*You* must learn the language, you yourself, of course," she added, "because you don't live in the spirit. But we who are reborn need not learn it."

"Can that be true?"

"Do you think Uncle Danjel would tell a lie?" She sounded hurt. "Or do you think I lie?"

"No, no! Indeed not—but . . ."

He didn't like to contradict Elin now that she had begun to talk; he wanted to agree with everything she said. But faced with Danjel's promise, he was unable to hide his doubts completely.

"I've never heard that story about the Holy Ghost," he excused himself. "That's why I was a little surprised."

"Have you never read the Acts?" she asked, a little puzzled.

"Yes. Yes, of course I have."

"You can read about Whitsuntide in the second chapter, if you don't believe Danjel. But he has never lied to us."

"I understand now. You won't need a book to learn English."

"That's so."

"Well—I didn't know. That's why I was confused a moment ago."

Arvid too had listened in amazement. He had not been received among Danjel's followers, but the master had high hopes that his servant would "awaken" one day. What Arvid now heard about the great advantage of the Akians, with the American language, made him thoughtful.

They were driving up a steep hill and the men stepped down to spare the horse. Arvid asked Robert: What were they to think of the girl's statement? Was the new language to come running from the mouths of the Akians as soon as they landed?

"I won't believe it until I hear it myself," said Robert flatly. "The girl seems cocksure."

What she said might be true, admitted Robert. It was written in the Bible that the Holy Ghost once filled the apostles so they could speak new languages. But it said nothing about their speaking English on that first Whitsuntide—the language was not yet invented in the days of the apostles, that much he was sure of. So no one knew if the Holy Ghost could teach people to speak English.

The air was colder; the north wind had begun to blow. It felt like a steel brush on their faces. The old frostbites on Arvid's nose, developed when he was hauling timber during severe winters, took on a red color, cracking a little and bleeding. On the horses the sweat foamed, remaining as white crust on their necks. Sparse, hard snowflakes fell and lay on the road like scattered rice. The emigrants sat silently on the wagons, hour after hour, mile after mile, a chill creeping into their bodies.

They had passed the border of a new province, Blekinge, once part of another kingdom—Denmark. There was still hatred between the inhabitants dwelling along the border, said Jonas Petter. When the Smålanders came driving their loads they were often attacked by Blekinge men, who were evil-tempered and used knives; they were another type of people. And their women, it was said, were hotter under their shifts than women farther north.

The emigrants now drove through wild, uninhabited regions. They rode through a forest of high pines where everything seemed deserted and dead. This was known as the snake forest, said Jonas Petter, for the stone-covered ground was filled with poisonous snakes—more poisonous here than the vipers in the north. Here it was that the Blekinge men used to lie hidden when the Smålanders came with their wagonloads, and here the two peoples often had fought bitterly. If one looked carefully on the stones along the roadside one might still see spots of blood from the old fights; the ground here was in a way sanctified.

Jonas Petter himself had once participated in a fight in the snake forest; a swarm of Blekinge men had surrounded him, buzzing and hissing like wasps on a hot summer day, cutting and hitting at any part of his body they could reach. When he returned home after that journey his body was cut up, open as a sieve. For many months he could keep no fluids in him because they ran out through the holes which the Blekinge men had cut through his body. It was half a year before he could drink brännvin again.

Robert's eyes shifted from side to side in the semidark underbrush of the forest, looking for men armed with knives, ready to waylay the travelers. But Jonas Petter assured him that it was much more peaceful on the Blekinge road nowadays, and they might feel especially safe from the evil-tempered people since there were so many in their company.

Jonas Petter continued to shorten the fifty long miles by his talk. Robert was busy opening gates; he had by now counted thirty of them. The gates had lately been closer together—the travelers were nearing inhabited places.

The forest came to an end and they drove into a large village. They were in Eringsboda, almost halfway to Karlshamn. This was their first resting place. The wagons came to a stop in front of an impressive-looking building with iron rings in the wall for the horses' halter straps; this was the inn. The travelers came down from their seats, and the horses were unharnessed.

Big as well as little ones felt frozen, and their faces were blue from the biting wind. The children's noses were running, making tapers, as it was called.

"We must get inside and thaw out our young ones," said Kristina anxiously.

Her own children had on warm woolen mittens which she had knitted for them especially for the journey, but the children from Karragarde were barehanded. Inga-Lena's last-born, a girl only a few months old, began to cry. She was hidden somewhere in a huge bundle of woolen shawls. Through an opening in the coverings her mother spoke comfortingly to the baby. Danjel came by and nodded and smiled at the little one, the child conceived in the couple's true, God-inspired marriage, after they were living in the spirit. But not even the father could silence the crying baby. Then the youngest boy from Korpamoen joined in the crying, and the two children tried to outdo each other.

The company of emigrants entered the barroom of the inn with their two loudly crying children.

Nearly every day the maids in the inn saw peasants from Smaland with their loaded wagons stopping in on their way to Karlshamn, but never before had they brought along wives and children. Now a question could easily be read in the maids' staring eyes: What was the idea of dragging suckling children along the roads in this bitterly cold spring weather? But it was warm in here in the barroom, a tremendous fire was roaring on the hearth. The maids busied themselves heating milk for the children and preparing coffee for the grownups.

The emigrants found benches and chairs, sat down, and opened their food baskets. They cut long slices from their rye breads, and brought out their dried lamb quarters. Jonas Pet-

ter and the Korpamoen brothers shared a quart of brannvin.
Kristina had baked a potato pancake which she divided
among husband, children, and brother-in-law; as yet she would
not open the butter tub.

The fire sparkled and all enjoyed the coziness of the inn
after the cold road. Their senses as well as their limbs thawed.
There was an odor of food and brannvin, snuff and chewing
tobacco, greased leather and warm, wet wadmal, there was a
fragrance of mothers' milk as the women suckled the children.

The people from Korpamoen and those from Karragarde
were gathered around their respective food baskets, but Jonas
Petter sat alone with his. He had left wife and children behind. It was said he had left without forethought: one evening
he quarreled with his wife and next morning packed his
America chest. But no one knew how long this had been in
his mind. He willingly told what he knew of other people, but
about himself he never said a word.

Kristina sat and thought of how some in the company still
were strangers to each other; as yet she had not exchanged a
word with Ulrika of Vastergohl, nor shaken her hand. Before
their departure she had told her Uncle Danjel the truth: she
could not stand that woman. Must she endure her as a traveling companion? Danjel had opened the Bible and read to
her about the meeting of Christ and the harlot. What the Redeemer had said to her, he, Danjel, had said to Ulrika: Sin no
more! And Ulrika had obeyed him, she had discarded her old
sin-body. Now it was Christ's body that lived in her, and anyone saying unkind words to Ulrika said them also to Christ.
But Kristina could not help herself—she still could not endure
that woman.

Nor did she notice any difference in Ulrika. She was good
to her daughter; when the two spoke to each other she was
sweet and careful in her words. Otherwise she was as foul-
mouthed as ever. And one could never misunderstand her
manner of looking at men; there was always something of a
come-and-let's-get-to-bed look in her eyes. Hadn't she today
looked at Karl Oskar in that way? She had long taken advantage of Uncle Danjel, who fed and clothed her and her
daughter and now paid their passage to America. Uncle Danjel was credulous and easy to take advantage of. Perhaps
Ulrika still carried on her whoring in secret, whenever she

had the opportunity. At least she *acted* like a sow in heat.

Good-looking she was, the bitch, no one could deny that. Now she was sitting in front of the fire, combing her daughter's hair and tying a red ribbon in it. The whore was as haughty as a queen, with her bastard a princess being decked to wed a prince. One could wonder what kind of virtues that woman had instilled in her child, poor girl who had to wear old women's cast-off clothing.

Sven was the eldest boy from Karragarde, and he had already torn his jacket on a nail—now his mother was mending the hole with linen thread and a darning needle. Inga-Lena and Kristina got along well together. But Danjel's wife was easily led, quite without a will of her own; she let her husband decide and rule in all matters. Kristina felt a little ashamed of her when among women.

Inga-Lena had suckled her baby, which was quiet now, after being freed from its bundle of shawls. But presently it began to cry again. The mother opened her blouse and offered the breast to the child once more. But the little one threw up what she had already eaten.

Kristina's thoughts turned to the impending sea voyages as she watched the child vomit.

"I wonder if we will be seasick on the ship," she said.

"Seasickness is no real ailment," said Karl Oskar.

"Nevertheless, one has to throw up."

Ulrika gave Kristina a meaning glance: "I guess it feels like being in the family way."

Kristina's cheeks flushed a flaming red. Ulrika apparently knew how things were with her. They had both gone to the outhouse when they had arrived, she must have noticed. And now Kristina was provoked by the color in her face. Why must she blush? She was married, and no man except Karl Oskar had touched her. She had a right to be with child a thousand times if she wished. Was she to blush because of that woman who had borne four bastards and given her body to hundreds of men?

The baby stopped suckling, and as Inga-Lena buttoned her blouse over her breasts, she said: "They say seasickness is painful."

"Are you afraid, Inga-Lena?" asked Danjel.

"No, no, of course not!" Her worried voice contradicted her. "But when one never has been to sea before . . ."

Danjel went up to his wife and laid his hand on her shoulder. "Don't you remember my words? Have you forgotten what I've told you?"

"No, I haven't, dear Danjel."

"A person who has Christ within him need not fear seasickness. He can endure the sea even the first time."

"Yes, I will have faith, dear husband."

And Danjel emphasized again to his wife that one reborn could sail on all the seas in the world without being seasick. One living in Christ's faith could endure the sea at any time; whether he traveled over narrow rivers or broad oceans, he would remain as sound and well as ever.

"Yes, dear Danjel, I believe it. I'm not afraid any more."

Inga-Lena patted her husband's hand affectionately.

"Don't you think you might get seasick, as well as we others?" asked Karl Oskar, who had listened in astonishment.

The farmer from Karragarde smiled kindly. "No! Because I believe Christ has died on the cross for my sins."

"You are a doubter, Karl Oskar," said Ulrika of Vastergohl, but there was no reproach in her voice.

"God will convince him when we are on the ship," said Danjel.

Ulrika wanted to help Danjel explain. "You know, Karl Oskar, it says in the Bible that Jesus had gone in a boat with His disciples and there was a horrible storm but no one was seasick. If Jesus or some one of His disciples had needed to throw up then, it would say so. But there isn't one word about it in the gospel. So you may understand, Karl Oskar, when a person has Christ's body within his own, he can never more feel rotten."

Karl Oskar snorted but said nothing. What use was there in arguing with the Akians?

To Kristina it sounded like blasphemy when the name of the Saviour was mentioned by Ulrika in this way; as if one were to think of Him lying in a ship, seasick and throwing up. He was God's Son, He could have no ills. But even if He had a toothache, or was footsore, or had other human ailments, He could heal Himself as He healed so many others. Ulrika used such vulgar words in spiritual things that no one in his full senses could believe in her conversion. Who could imagine Christ living in her worn-out old harlot-body?

Kristina turned to Danjel. "Berta of Idemo said the married women will get more seasick than the unmarried."

"Not if they live in the spirit."

"But most women do live in the flesh," interrupted Ulrika. "Bastards can be made in wedded beds, too."

She was hurt by the disrespect Kristina showed her, and now at the first opportunity retaliated. But Kristina decided not to answer the nasty words Ulrika threw at her.

Robert was disappointed because no one had asked him about seasickness. He had knowledge from books, and now he was able to get in a word: "Ship's fever and cholera are much more dangerous than seasickness."

He wanted to give a description of these ills, but his brother gave him a look that could not be misunderstood; he stopped short at the very beginning.

They were to rest a few hours. When all had eaten and were satisfied, Danjel kneeled on the floor and thanked God in a loud voice for the food. His prayer was so vociferous that it was heard out in the kitchen. The maids stared in surprise through the door: one of the peasants from Smaland was crying on his knees to God—indeed, a strange rabble that passed by today!

Kristina put the lid on her food basket. She was content that she hadn't opened the butter tub. It was supposed to be thousands of miles to North America, and as yet they had traveled only twenty of them; the butter would be needed.

4

Later in the evening the emigrants resumed their journey. The next road post was Moljeryd, where they intended to rest. From there the road went over Bredakra to Karlshamn.

Now the weather grew milder. The snow had melted, the air was moist, and soon a light rain began to fall. They could see that the spring was earlier in Blekinge than at home; the grass was high along the roadsides, the coltsfoot had opened in the ditches, and the buds on the trees were thick and swollen; the spring work could soon begin hereabouts.

Their horses were growing tired from the heavy loads, and

moved at a slow pace; even on small hills the men stepped off and walked; on Jonas Petter's wagon only the girl remained in her seat.

Robert could not help thinking of Elin. She thought she needn't learn English from his book. The language would pour forth from her mouth as once the languages of the Parthians, the Phrygians, and the Elamites had come from the tongues of the apostles, so that people thought they were drunk from new wine. Why did people think they were drunk? The more drunk a person was, the thicker his speech became, stammering, slurring, spluttering. But the girl must be given information about the land she was emigrating to. What did she know about the North American Republic? Its government, laws, religion, and railroads? Surely she needed more knowledge about the New World.

It would not hurt to show Elin what he knew about the United States—but before he had a chance to begin his discourse she said, almost confidentially: "You know—I'm afraid of America."

"Afraid? Why?"

"Because it's unknown—perhaps people are unkind to newcomers."

"Oh, no! I'm sure you need not be afraid. There are so few women in America that they treat them like gold and jewels. You'll be taken care of like a baby; you can have anything you want, you needn't worry about a thing."

Elin apparently did not know how well things were arranged for the women in the United States. He must cheer her up a little by telling her.

The Americans treated all women—were they old or young, ugly or beautiful—as if they were queens and princesses. They waited on them and guarded them as if they were costly pearls and diamonds. The women never need do heavy or foul chores, as here at home; they could go clean and white and with washed hands all day long; a maid in America was as well dressed as her mistress, because *all* women were allowed to dress in fine clothes. It wasn't a bit like here—all women had the right to wear hats, that right was written into the laws of the republic. It was strongly forbidden to mock or poke fun at a simple woman because she wore a hat like a gentlewoman. Moreover, there were no simple women, and no noble ladies—all were equals.

In the North American Republic it was the menfolk who
served the women, not the opposite, as here. If a man were
attacked and beaten by a woman, he had no right to defend
himself. Because the law was not like here. Outside a house a
man could go no closer to a woman than three steps, if she
herself didn't allow closer proximity, or perhaps order him to
come nearer. Inside a house the distance between the sexes
was two steps, according to law. Any man who wished to be
closer than two steps to an American woman must first marry
her. The law was not like the Swedish law.

So Elin need not be afraid of America. If a man spoke to a
woman in public, then she had the right to call for the police
and request protection. Even if, in all friendliness, he only
asked his way, she could have him arrested, or sue him for
breach of promise if she was in need of cash, whichever
suited her best. Women always had their own way in the
United States, so she need not worry.

If a man in the United States betrayed a woman, then he
was first decapitated and afterwards hanged; he would never
repeat his deed. Nowadays there were no unfaithful, untruth-
ful, or deceitful menfolk left there. They were exterminated
and destroyed. She need not be afraid of America.

Thus while the wagon rolled along one of the future inhabitants of the United States was informed of the position of
women in the new land. And Elin did feel more comfortable
and happy and expectant. She relied on his words, she felt she
would like her new country.

Robert and Elin sat as close as possible in the driver's seat.
The wagon shook and rocked, the girl pulled her clothes
tightly around her, she yawned and shivered from cold. And
while Robert was busy describing the railroads of America,
her head fell suddenly on his shoulder. He stopped short in
surprise while her head sank down on his chest. What did it
mean? What did she want? What was he supposed to do? He
held his body stiff as a steering shaft, yet her head remained
in the same position. Then he discovered that she had fallen
asleep. She slept, her tender girl-body resting against his.

She had gone to sleep at a moment when he himself was
carried away by his description of the United States—for her
benefit. He was disappointed in her. But here she lay, practically in his arms; for the first time a girl's head rested against
his breast. This could happen only on the chariot of adventure

—after just thirty miles on the road! How many miles were left? Many, many! This adventure would last a long time!

Little by little he too was rocked to sleep by the movement of the wagon. Jonas Petter did not have the heart to awaken him at the next gate, he opened it himself. Robert slept on, unmindful of the gates on the road to America, unable to count them any longer.

5

Early the next morning the three wagons drove into Karlshamn and came to a stop near the harbor. From the steeple of the town church they were greeted by a clock striking seven, slowly and solemnly. The harbor town was just coming to life for the day. The fishermen, returned from the sea with the night's catch, were busy mooring their boats at the pier where the town maids awaited the fresh herring with their baskets. A shop clerk with a long birch broom was sweeping the steps in front of a house with the sign *Sunesons Skeppshandel*. In the air was the odor of fish, tar, hemp, herring, salt, and sea.

The emigrants climbed down from their wagons, sleepy and frozen, stiff and aching in their bones after the long ride. The menfolk stepped aside and flapped their arms against their bodies to warm up. The women attended to the children who were whimpering and whining from lack of sleep. They were all rather depressed and dullish after the long night; no one felt morning-cheerful.

A sharp, cold, penetrating wind blew from over the harbor and bade the emigrants welcome to the sea.

For the first time in their lives they looked across water without seeing land on the other side.

They had reached the sea they were to cross—this sea now greeted them with its wind; it sent as its messenger this cold, severe wind as if to frighten them, to challenge them: Come out here! I'll teach you! The men turned up their coat collars and the women pulled their woolen shawls closer around their children and themselves. What an unmerciful wind they had in the coast towns! It cut through skin and bones, it penetrated their very marrow. Never did it blow so fiendishly at

home, not in fall or in spring, not in summer or in winter.
Even the heavy peasant wadmal seemed to give no protection.

The people of the earth met the sea, and they hardly had
time to behold it before the wind brought tears to their eyes.

The men in the fishing boats looked curiously at the group
of strangers who had stopped near the harbor with their high
loads and their crying children. Some men, gentry by their
dress, walked by in leisurely fashion and looked at the little
company in amusement: apparently honest-to-goodness gray
wadmal peasants with their simple shawl-wrapped wives and
their pale-faced, runny-nose children; a couple of farmhands
in new suits which were too large and puffed out in bags
front and back—jacket and trousers carelessly basted together by some village tailor. And whole loads of ancient
chests, flowery knapsacks, homemade baskets and boxes and
bundles—they must be backwoods people going on a long
journey across the sea. What kind of restless itch had got into
the poor devils?

Karl Oskar had arranged passage for them all, and it
seemed as if he was to be their head, also, during the whole
trip. No one undertook anything of importance without first
asking him.

He now went over to a herring fisher and asked about ships
in the harbor. He had paid passage to America—where might
their ship be anchored?

The fisherman peered at the peasant and sized up his solid
new boots. Yes, and America-sailer had arrived the night before last, she was a brig, the *Charlotta*. She was lying at anchor in the outer harbor—perhaps it was that old hull over
there.

The name was the right one. Karl Oskar looked toward the
outer harbor in the direction where the fisherman had
pointed.

"Is *that* the *Charlotta*? Our ship?"

All eyes were turned toward the ship indicated. They stood
silent, and gazed. It was a silence of disappointment, wonder,
anxiety, and bafflment. Could this really be their ship?

It was Kristina who expressed in five words what all were
thinking: "Is our ship so little?"

None among them had seen a sailing ship except in pictures. They had thought of ships as being much bigger than

this. And the ship that was to carry them across the enormous ocean they had pictured as *much* larger. In front of them was the wide expanse of the sea; and on this sea their ship seemed so minutely small. Compared with the water she was to cross she looked pitiful and puny.

"The boat is larger than you think. It just looks small at this distance," said Robert.

He attempted to choke his own feeling of disappointment at seeing the *Charlotta,* and wanted to encourage the rest of his company.

He pointed. "Look at the masts! Has anyone ever seen such tall masts?"

None had seen other masts on ships to make comparison. The small ship anchored landwards from the little island, in the entrance of the harbor, had two masts stretching toward the sky and seeming higher than the tallest tree in the forest. The masts were as tall as the ship was long. Robert thought that perhaps he himself had helped fell the trees which he now saw as naked, slender stems: perhaps he had cut the firs, helped remove them from their place of immobility in the forest to the sea, replanting them, as it were—these mast-trees which for the rest of their lives were to sail the seas, were to be supported by water instead of earth.

Karl Oskar wondered when they might be allowed to go on board. The fisherman said that the *Charlotta* was to take on freight, and as the vessel had barely arrived in harbor nothing had been loaded yet. It might be several days before passengers could board the America-sailer.

They could not remain here in the wind with their freezing, whimpering children. They must find quarters while waiting for embarkation. The kind fisherman showed them to the Maja's Inn, located in an alley near the harbor. It was the house behind the Hope Tavern, right there, as they could see; they were sure to get accommodations.

The emigrant wagons pushed on to the indicated place. Only Robert remained standing at the harbor.

He stood there alone and looked out across the sea.

The others called him several times, but he did not answer.

PART TWO

Peasants at Sea

XIII

THE CHARLOTTA OF KARLSHAMN

1

The Ship

The brig *Charlotta*, Captain Lorentz, sailed from Karlshamn April 14, 1850, with New York as her destination. The ship's capacity was 160 lasts, her length 124 feet, and her width 20 feet. She had a crew of fifteen: 2 mates, 1 bosun, 1 carpenter, 1 sailmaker, 1 cook, 4 able-bodied seamen, 2 ordinary seamen, and 3 deckhands. She was loaded with pig iron and sundries.

She carried 78 passengers, all emigrants to North America, making the total number of people on board 94.

It was the brig *Charlotta*'s seventh voyage as an emigrant ship.

The Passengers

Through its very nature the globe offers two kinds of life to human beings: life on land and life at sea; life on one-quarter of the earth's surface—the solid ground—and life on three-quarters, the water; life on the firm land, life on the ever-moving sea.

The emigrants were people of the soil; their whole lives had been lived on solid ground. On the day when they boarded the brig *Charlotta* they first encountered the sea. For an indefinite period they were to be settled on a ship, exchanging their accustomed existence for one new and alien to them.

Their feet stepped for the first time on a ship's deck, having hitherto always tramped solid ground. With awkward, fumbling movements and clumsy, unsure steps they walked the deck. They found themselves on a plank floor, yet it was not the safe, solid floor of the peasant cottage; these planks were laid lower at the rail, higher toward the center of the deck. And the water under them moved constantly—a wave fell, a wave rose. No longer could they control their movements independently, they must obey the sea.

The emigrants had the earth's heaviness in their bodies,

215

clay from the field clung to their feet. And their heavy footgear—their shoes of rough leather, their impressive high
boots—were only a hindrance to them on the surface of a
slippery deck. They had stood broad-legged and sure on firm
land; there they ordered their own motions. But here on the
vessel they stood on insecure and treacherous footing.

They were accustomed to walk freely in the fields, unham-
pered. Now they were on a small crowded ship, fenced in like
prisoners behind the rail. For months to come earth's people
must live at sea.

The emigrants came from a kingdom of stones and junipers, their muscles and sinews hardened and strengthened
from breaking stones and twisting the juniper branches to wattles. But their strong arms and powerful backs were of little
use on the sea. Here all of them stood equally helpless, the
most capable farmers and the handiest farm wives. The earth
was known to them, intimate, reliable, but they mistrusted the
sea; it was unknown and dangerous, and their mistrust was in-
grown and inherited through generations.

The passengers embarking on the brig *Charlotta* in Karlshamn this April day wandered about her deck uncertain, insecure, lost, bewildered. They felt they had surrendered
unconditionally to the unknown, were irrevocably in the
hands of a power whose presence left them impotent, a lord
whom they could not entreat—the Sea. This unfathomable
antagonist had taken them on its world-encircling back to
carry them to another continent.

It was a day of calm weather, haze and mist, when the
Charlotta sailed from Karlshamn. A light rain began to drive
in from the Baltic Sea. The ship's movement was only a weak,
slow roll.

A small group of emigrants had gathered in the stern. A
few peasants in their gray wadmal jackets and robust high
boots stood there on the ship's rocking deck and watched the
cliffs of Kastellholmen—that little isle in the harbor entrance
—gradually disappear into the April fog.

What they saw was the last outpost of the land they had rejected.

The travelers spoke in low voices while they cast their farewell looks on their homeland. Some spoke as if to themselves,
others stood silent, eyes peering landwards. Talking emigrants

and silent ones stood side by side; there were open words and hidden thoughts at this, their last glimpse of Sweden.

"I had a farm, foreclosed last fall; a homey place. It hurt me to see it go. But a farmer once fallen here at home can never rise again. I could never have got out of debt, not in a thousand years. Let the sheriff keep the place. Taxes were too heavy; when taxes are collected, that's the time we are good enough, we in wooden shoes and patched pants: then they come to see us. Other times we're peasant rabble. But I'll miss the old place. I'll miss relatives and friends, too; but never the country—no, never, never the country!"

Or—"I had nothing to lose. What could there have been? I slaved on the manor until I spit blood. Is that something to lose? I tired of the drudgery. I've stuffed the gullets of sluggards too long; I am through. The masters can be their own servants; that would only be fair. Perhaps one day they must be. The gentry's arrogance is the bitterest thing. They despise honest work, they despise us in our poverty. Let them do the dirty work themselves; it would serve them right. No one can stand it in the long run, to do the dirtiest and heaviest work, and be treated like a dog, looked down on. All poor people should emigrate to America; that's what they should do. So help me, all devils. That would serve the gentry right! Then they could do their own dirty chores! If only this ocean weren't so broad and big. . . ."

Or—"I couldn't stand the minister. We became enemies. I couldn't stay at home. Might as well go far away when you have to move anyway. Now the minister can sit and watch his sheep running off; he won't be able to shear them any more; he'll get less income, and a good thing, too. There are too many giving orders and commands—everyone must have some devil to torture. There are too many lords and masters to inspect and guard us; too many of the gentry for us to feed; too many useless lords. In the end it's unendurable. The gentry have smothered me long enough! It's over! I'm away from that country at last! But there's an ache somewhere. Why? I don't know. Perhaps I'll miss them, a little, the rest of them—only never the priest! I hated that priest. . . ."

Or—"I'll never regret it. I couldn't advance. It was hopeless: however I slaved, I stood in the same place. Labor brought nothing—I had to get out. But now land disappears,

I remember. Perhaps—perhaps . . . in the long run I'll miss
—I don't know. One is born there: father and mother remain;
I couldn't bring them, but I'll remember. It wasn't always sorrow. There was happiness too. I've been young in that country, been with girls on summer evenings, when it was warm
and pleasant. I've danced at road crossings and dance halls.
No, it wasn't always sad. I'll remember. And I'll never forget
the old ones, toiling still. Much comes to my mind as I stand
here, looking backward—things I haven't thought of before.
But regret? Never!"

So thought those emigrants in the stern, as the rock islet
melted into the April haze.

The Captain:

Back aft on the poop deck next the helmsman Captain Lorentz stood, near the wheel, where he would watch the easing
of his ship out of the harbor. The wind was southeast and
light, giving the vessel little speed, barely sufficient for steering.

"Starboard a bit. Steady. Steady as she goes."

His voice, trained in long service as ship's master, was far-
reaching and powerful. The *Charlotta's* captain was about
sixty, and of stocky build. He had an ugly face with thick,
blunt nose, protruding eyes, and weather-beaten red skin. His
broad, sunken mouth with the outjutting lower jaw was strik-
ingly like the snout of a large pike. He looked capable of biting as sharply as those beastly fish, too. From the pike-snout
hung a pipe. Captain Lorentz had spent almost fifty years of
his life at sea, and for the last ten years he had commanded
this old sailing vessel that was his home.

At last, anchor had been weighed, and his ship liberated
from her shackle to the bottom. The time in harbor always
gave Captain Lorentz a feeling of discomfort and disgust. At
sea was the decent place for a grown man; to the *Charlotta's*
captain, riding at anchor was almost degrading, to step on
land a disgrace. The only occupation worthy of a human
being in this world was to sail a ship. To this occupation, unfortunately, one repulsive duty belonged, one painful necessity
he could not shirk: at certain intervals he must steer his ship
into harbor.

But now this humiliating time was over again. Captain Lorentz had lain eight days in Karlshamn, and it had been a

week of annoying tasks, trying the patience of the *Charlotta*'s master. More cargo had had to be taken on, provisions stored, new crew members signed on. But the biggest nuisance were these damned peasants. In her old age the *Charlotta* had been turned into an emigrant ship instead of a merchantman, and her most important cargoes nowadays were these people emigrating to North America: peasants—peasants from Blekinge, Smaland and Oland. Each time he had shipped such passengers across the ocean they had filled and overrun Catain Lorentz's ship. This time they had even chased the rats from their holes before they all found room. This time they had come dragging still larger chests, still heavier boxes, still bulkier sacks, more baskets, bags, and belongings. Not even God the Almighty knew what junk they contained. This voyage they also had brought along more women and children than ever before. Never were so many brats aboard the *Charlotta* before—whole families, from old white-bearded grandfathers to suckling cradle-infants; cradles, yes, the number that were dragged on board this time! Devil take the captain if his ship wasn't a nursery this trip!

And all these people his old ship must transport to the other side of the globe. The *Charlotta* was getting somewhat squeaky and ancient and sour in her hull, but was still seaworthy. Captain Lorentz loved watching her ride the sea, taking rough weather, curtsying to the waves like a court lady to a queen. She had only one fault, the old ship: she sweated. Perhaps she hadn't been quite dry when launched—and such ships remained moist in their hulls as long as they lasted; only usually they didn't last long.

Skipper Lorentz thought back in regret to the years when the *Charlotta* had been a simon-pure merchantman. The captain on an emigrant ship had many heavy new duties, and much greater responsibility. Nor did Lorentz like the idea of taking so many people out of the country. With each voyage he asked himself: Why did these peasants with their wives and children cross the sea? What did they expect to find in North America? In the captain's mind all countries were equally good or bad. Dry land was dry land the whole world over, in North America as in Sweden. The sea was the part of the globe where sane people lived. He could never understand these peasants who undertook a long and costly voyage to the other side of the earth just in order to find another patch of soil to till! They might as well keep turning their patches in Sweden as in America; to poke and dig in the earth was the same degrading prison-chore everywhere. These peasants traveled from one field to another, from one dunghill to another—for what?

A seaman ought to spend his time at sea, a farmer on the farm. But strangely enough, it was actually the farmers, the homestead people in Sweden, who crossed the seas to change their country. Why? They were of course crowded in their bunk-beds over the fireplaces. There were too many around the potato pot. But it was their own fault: they begot too many children. If these peasants had been as busy in their fields as in their beds they would never need to emigrate. Apparently they used their wives every night of the year—except Christmas night; that night they abstained for fear of getting thistles and weeds in their fields next summer, for these peasants were as superstitious as they had been a thousand years ago.

Oh, well, some of them came from good stock in Sweden, and they might find a better lot in North America, where they would at least have elbowroom. He himself had never been farther inland than the harbor town of New York. And no decent soul could enjoy that dirty hole. When for the first time, some ten years ago, he had touched at that port, he had seen pigs poking in the stinking filth of the town streets. Some quarters were veritable pigpens. Cholera raged then, with hundreds dying daily, and most of the inhabitants had moved inland to uncontaminated regions. The town of New York had looked dead, stinking of corpses. Now it was lively again, and noisy, and beautiful women in white silk dresses drove in stately carriages through the streets. But it wasn't a town where a seaman felt at home, not even for a few days. On Broadway there were some taverns, but none could offer a traveler the comforts he was accustomed to in the harbor towns of Europe. New York, after all, was a town for peasants.

The brig *Charlotta* had at last cleared the harbor and was in the open sea. The captain sniffed the wind—it seemed even calmer than before; all sails were set but hung limp and dead; they were depressed and wrinkled, waiting for the wind.

The second mate, a Finn, approached the captain. He was responsible for the passengers in the hold, and in his Finnishaccented Swedish he reported that they all had found their allotted bunks and turned in; all was well. There had of course been the usual complaints that it was too crowded and too uncomfortable down below. It was always so at first. They kept on jostling each other in the hold, until they realized that they couldn't make the ship roomier or gain more space by pushing with their hands and elbows. As soon as they understood this they tired of their noise and settled down. And it looked as if they had fairly decent folk on this voyage; only one of the peasants appeared refractory, a man with the biggest nose he had ever seen. He and one other married man had been unable to find sleeping room within the partition set aside for families. Perhaps new bunks could be built for them near the family bunks, but for the time being they had been put up with the unmarried men, and this made the big-nosed man furious and hard to handle; he insisted on staying with his wife and children. He—the mate—had told him to pull in his big nose if he wished to remain on board with his huge elephant feet. My God, the boots these peasants wore! That man had such big underpinnings he no doubt could sail dry-shod across the Atlantic in his boots.

Captain Lorentz chewed his pipe while he listened to his mate. The peasants crawled over his ship this time like grasshoppers in the fields of North America. Hell and damnation! Perhaps he had allowed too many of them aboard. He hoped they would be manageable, as his mate predicted. The first few days of the voyage, while they were still on inland seas and had calm waters, the emigrants usually kept quiet enough and busied themselves in their curious way inspecting the ship. But when they reached open waters and began to feel the sea, even the most tractable of men sometimes went berserk. A peasant who on land was the most docile of creatures could, in a storm at sea, become the most ferocious beast, impossible to handle.

The *Charlotta*'s captain felt sorry for the pathetic earth rats who had been lured from their safe holes to spend weeks at sea. Perhaps these poor devils had never been in even a flat-bottomed skiff, or seen a larger body of water than a wash pan; and now suddenly they were off on an ocean voyage. The poor creatures could never take to the sea, and were as much afraid for their lives as old maids. But after all, what business of his was that? It was not his fault. He hadn't ad-

vised these farmers to leave their peaceful cottages in their
home parishes, he hadn't persuaded them to exchange the
sturdy fold-bed of the farm for the rolling bunk of a ship
under sail. They could blame only themselves.

The drizzling rain thickened, the southeast wind died down.
This time of year the winds shifted suddenly in the Baltic Sea,
and even an old skipper would not predict the weather; but it
seemed at the moment that the night would be calm. Captain
Lorentz might as well turn in and rest for the remainder of
the evening watch.

On the way to his cabin the captain almost fell over one of
the passengers, who was down on his knees near the rail. Lorentz grabbed the man by the shoulder and raised him up. He
was a rather short peasant, his face covered by a bushy,
brown beard; his long, round-cut hair fell on his jacket collar.

"Keep your eyes open," warned the captain. "Don't fall
overboard!"

The little peasant kept his hands folded across his chest, as
if he were protecting something under them.

"I did not fall. I was kneeling and praying to God."

"Why do you pray your prayers up here?"

"It's noisy down in the ship. I wish to thank the Lord in
peace."

"Oh—so that's it, my good man." Lorentz looked at him
and added: "You'd better wait awhile to thank God for a safe
voyage."

The farmer looked up and met the captain's gaze with two
mild, frank eyes. He wished to thank the Lord already—he
had been permitted to board a good ship, sailing under an
honest, conscientious captain, manned by a capable, orderly
crew. Now he could leave all to God. He knew the Almighty
would do what He could to help them cross the dangerous
sea.

"Hm—hm," mumbled the captain. "Be careful you don't
fall. The deck is awash and slippery."

Lorentz continued toward his cabin, musing over his discovery. So he had religious cranks aboard. He knew that
sort and didn't like them. A few years ago he had sailed to
North America with fifty of the creatures. They had embarked at Gavle; some of them had been so sorely taken by
the religious bug that they had tramped on foot from their
homes to the harbor town, walking many miles, day and night.

to board ship and escape the country. Their feet were bleeding when they arrived, and they had compared this to the blood in Christ's wounds.

Immediately he had recognized them as fanatics, and these sectarians had, indeed, been the most difficult passengers he ever had had on board. They did not consider him master of the ship, but insisted that the Lord God was in command. What is more, as soon as they reached the open sea they insisted that God ordered them to steer; the crew were hired by the devil, they said, and steered the ship to destruction. Many of the peasants, from Helsingland and Dalecarlia, had never seen the sea before, much less been near a helm. If God had meant passengers to steer, He no doubt would have chosen someone accustomed to the sea—even Captain Lorentz relied on the Lord to that extent. But when the sectarians had interfered to the extent of wanting to change the ship's course, he had at last been forced to read the law of the sea to them. To be on the safe side, he also had had to tell them he had guns on board. They were full of crazy notions. It had been a hellish trip with them aboard.

But he had done his fatherland a great service that time, when he shipped out fifty crazy Swedes and deposited them in North America. There were so many madmen there before them that this new load would be lost in the mob.

This brown-bearded fellow he had just encountered praying on deck seemed, however, a decent soul. He had thanked God for the capable captain; and as long as his religious nonsense took such expression, he might be considered harmless.

In his small cabin below the poop deck Captain Lorentz now brought out a jug of Bavarian ale which he kept wedged beside his table. He poured the foaming drink into a tremendous earthen stoup which held almost half a gallon. The handle of the stoup was in the shape of a female figure, the naked body of a young girl. She hung over the edge of the mug and dipped her hands and arms into the ale, bending her head as though she were drinking. Her back, a slender young girl-body, formed the handle.

This drinking stoup had been the gift of a ship's chandler in Barcelona to his good friend, the *Charlotta*'s captain. Many times the friend had helped Lorentz find girls with softer bodies than burnt clay; but that was long ago, that was when this old bachelor was younger and livelier. Now the siesta in a woman's arms—if one called it siesta—belonged to needs which Captain Lorentz had gradually left behind him. He led a quiet life, these days, where women played no part. But the big earthen mug with the girl's body he used daily in his cabin. Many a time he had satisfied his thirst with ale from this vessel, his hand holding the young, well-shaped woman. At regular intervals during the day he would caress her waist with his old, rough, seaman's hands. Nowadays she was his only girl, and she remained his constant and devoted mistress whether the brig *Charlotta* sailed inland seas or the open oceans.

The captain took a firm hold of the girl's body and raised the ale stoup to his mouth. When he had drunk he stretched his legs out under the cabin table and sighed deeply with pleasure: good thirst and good ale, two exceedingly fine things when one had both at the same time!

The captain was mellow this evening—he had the keel in clear water. Long days of open sea lay ahead; the entire spring would be spent at sea. He would not give the slimy Hudson—the entrance to New York Harbor—a single thought until the day he was actually there. He had set his ale stoup on a piece of paper, and the foam had wet it. He now picked it up, holding it close to his eyes. He recognized a comic prescription, written in a neat hand and given to him last night by the Karlshamn apothecary, at their farewell drinking party in the Hope Tavern.

"For Cholera
"(To my friend Captain Lorentz of the *Charlotta*)
"Temperately you must live.
Not be afraid, nor worries give.
Cheerful be, and every day
Throw all your medicines away.
Downhearted you must never be
Nor let your tempers disagree.
Eat a little, drink the more,
Forget the girls and let them snore,
Sleep every night and work each day.
This is the rule that keeps you gay."

The apothecary had wanted to cheer him with these verses, which he had copied from some paper. But Lorentz was not cheered by them tonight—quite the contrary. And this because twice during his long voyages across the ocean he had been visited by the disease for which the verses suggested advice. Now, sitting in his cabin with his evening ale in front of him, these lines reminded him of all the troubles and difficulties he had encountered as captain of this ship during earlier voyages with emigrants to North America.

In front of him on the table lay the ship's *Medical Adviser for Seafarers,* printed in Danish; as yet there was no good Swedish handbook for captains sailing without a doctor. This *Medical Adviser* was a most useful book. On one of the very first pages he had underlined in red pencil a few sentences: "If so many passengers are aboard that they must be treated as cargo, this is of course the most unhealthy cargo possible. A great deal of attention is then required of the captain. . . ."

Attention—in that one word was included all the responsibility resting on the captain of an emigrant ship like the brig *Charlotta.*

Captain Lorentz sighed again, this time not from the satisfaction which came from good ale. What did a captain's attention avail? Lorentz was sure he could sail his ship to her destination in North America. This time, as always before, he would sail her undamaged into port. But he was equally sure that not all of the passengers who had embarked today would still be aboard when he tied up at the pier in New York. Before the voyage was over he would have to read funeral prayers for one or more of the emigrants; one or more would have to be lowered into the sea.

What was printed in the book was true: he was ship's master to the unhealthiest cargo imaginable—human beings.

He had reason to regret that the *Charlotta* no longer sailed as freighter only. He preferred dead cargo in the hull to this unpleasant, living cargo; there was never need to read funeral prayers for ordinary freight. Of all his duties as captain, the one of minister was most repulsive—burying those who died. A freighter captain need seldom perform this duty, which the master of an emigrant ship on an unfortunate voyage might find almost a daily task. How many days had he been on deck and acted the priest that time when they had the cholera aboard! How often during that voyage had he thrown the three shovelfuls of earth over the canvas-shrouded bodies— only he had had no earth in the hold, not a handful, even. At first he had been at a loss what to use for the funerals, but finally had taken ashes from the galley—there was, after all, little difference between ashes and earth.

That was the time the idea had come to him to take along Swedish earth to be used at funerals: a bushel of Swedish earth. It was little enough.

The *Charlotta*'s captain had thought: I will take along earth for these emigrating peasants. They are covetous of earth, they are bound to the earth, they love the earth above all in this world. And when they die they will want their mouths full of earth. Let them have it. Their mouths are filled with earth when they rot in the churchyard. To die on the ocean is different—then they are lowered into water—so why begrudge the poor devils three shovels of earth over their bodies when they have to be buried at sea, far from home—just three shovelfuls of their own earth?

After that voyage Captain Lorentz did not use ashes from the galey for his sea burials. He had a bushel of Swedish earth ready on his ship. One provision for the passengers of which they had no knowledge—a bushel of earth to be used when needed at sea.

And he knew that bushel would be used on the brig *Charlotta*'s seventh voyage to North America.

XIV

FORTY PACES LONG AND EIGHT PACES WIDE

1

In the hold enormous pieces of canvas had been hung to separate the space into three compartments: one for married couples and children, one for unmarried men, and one for unmarried women. The family bunks were toward the stern, partitioned off by bulkheads of rough boards nailed together. The small cells looked like cattle pens or horses' stalls. Beds were made on the deck of the hold with mattresses and loose straw. Unmarried passengers slept in bunks, strung longships between the stanchions. There were one-man and two-man bunks, "upper and lower berths."

Dust rose from unaired mattresses, blankets, and skins as the emigrants spread their bedding and made up their bunks in the hold of the *Charlotta*—berths for seventy-eight people. Each passenger kept his belongings at the foot of his bunk. The overhead was low, and the air thick and choking. The three small compartments with canvas bulkheads seemed even smaller than they were, with this cargo of knapsacks, food baskets, bedding, and bundles. Here and there stood crude little tables or food boards, where people could sit and eat. These also were crowded with baskets and tubs, which must be put somewhere. At last there was hardly a spot left for the people to step on.

Only through the main hatch did light filter into the hold. After dark a few weak, smoking, kerosene lanterns were lit and hung along the sides of the ship.

As there was no room for Karl Oskar in the family pen, he must share a two-man bunk with his brother Robert, in the unmarried men's compartment. Above the two brothers slept Jonas Petter, and Arvid had his bunk next, on the same side. The men here had about as much space as pieces of kindling stacked in a woodpile: there was hardly a foot's width per person.

"They must have meant us to sleep on our sides," said Karl Oskar. "There isn't room for a man to sleep on his back."

Jonas Petter held his nose: "It smells of piss!"

Robert too thought the hold smelled of night-old urine. "The air is so foul," he said to Arvid, "let's go above."

The hold was dark as a cellar. He felt as if he were in a sack.

By using their elbows the two boys were able to force a way between fellow passengers and their mattresses and sacks and bundles, through the narrow passageway along the ship's side, to where they could struggle out through the hatch. Robert looked more closely at the hatch covering, which was pierced through by a number of small holes, like a milk strainer. The only entry for fresh air was through these pitifully small openings. No wonder the atmosphere below was thick and stifling.

"Why don't they make bigger air holes in this ship?" wondered Arvid.

On deck they breathed clear, fresh, spring-cool Baltic air. It was calm at sea, and the ship rocked with a slow roll which they hardly noticed. The water purled softly against the hull, like water from a slow-running spring.

Robert wanted to walk about and inspect this ship which was to be his home for a long time. At the embarkation yesterday there had been such hurry and disorder he had been unable to see anything of it. Their sleeping places had had to be found, chests and knapsacks, boxes and kegs, tubs and baskets carried into the hold. Wherever he had turned he had been in the way of someone. Today he was more at home.

Only he was a little afraid to get too close to the captain. In Suneson's chandlery in Karlshamn one of the clerks had shown him the newspaper *Karlshamns Allehanda*; there was a notice about their ship under "Arrived Ship Masters." At first he had thought it must be a misprint in the paper; it actually said "Ship Masters," not "Ships." It was the ship masters who arrived in harbor, not the ships themselves. Then the little man whom he saw yesterday, back aft among the crew, was more important than the whole ship. It would not do to get in his way.

The boys looked cautiously around. Arvid inspected the ropes, thick as a man's arms, coiled here and there on deck like giant snakes. He had seen the same kind of ropes at the ship chandler's in Karlshamn. When he had asked if these ropes were meant for huge ferocious bulls, the clerk had laughed and said they were to hold something much wilder and much more difficult to handle than all the bulls in the world. Robert had then nudged Arvid in the side and explained that the ropes were used on ships to tie something with.

Robert had tried to learn all he could about ships and sea life, and already he was instructing his fellow traveler: Their ship was called a brig; a brig could easily be distinguished from other ships because she had a gaff sail on the aftermast.

"A gaff sail? What in the world is that?" asked Arvid.

Robert couldn't answer this as yet; but he thought it must be a sail put up with gaff (whatever that was). The aftermast, anyway, was the one farthest back on the ship.

"Someone talked about a yard sail today," said Arvid. "What might that be?"

This Robert thought he could answer accurately: a yard sail, no doubt, was one made right in the shipyard.

The boys looked up toward the ceiling of sails; they counted eleven of them, breeze-tightened: three on the bowsprit, four on the foremast, three on the after- or mainmast, and one small square sail on the stern. The masts were many rods high: they seemed taller than a church steeple. The mainmast was a few feet higher than the foremast—hence its name.

Robert noticed the masts were of pine; he thought again, as he had on first seeing the ship, that perhaps he had helped cut down the very trees which made them.

"Is it all one tree?" asked Arvid. "They are equally thick all the way to the top."

Robert thought several trees had been joined to make up a mast; one pine could never be that tall.

Thus the two farmhands contemplated the riddles of sea life, staring at the mast-tops until their necks ached. Those pines from the deep forests had traveled far across the ocean. Trees which had been next neighbors to them were still rooted in the woods. They might never get out to sea. Fate dealt unequally, even among the trees of a forest.

Up in the masts hung strange nets of heavy rope; they must be intended for huge fishes, such large meshes they had. A few of the sea folk were climbing up there, shouting to each other. The farm boys went dizzy watching them suspended above. The seamen had nothing to hold on to, as far as the boys could see, and they feared that any moment the men would lose their foothold so Robert and Arvid would have to witness the bodies of these daredevils fallen to the deck, crushed into bloody pulp.

The boys continued their inspection of the brig *Charlotta*, and were astonished at the small space the passengers had in which to move about. They paced off the length of the ship and her width, and even though they shortened their steps somewhat, they found her length to be no more than forty paces, and her width eight. The floor in some farmhouses was as large as this deck. Their ship was small—not only at a distance. Forty paces long and eight wide—for almost a hundred people, for them to live, to sleep and eat and perform all the necessary functions of life. If everyone came on deck at once it would be so crowded they would almost push each other overboard. Overboard—and suppose something should happen to their small ship, out on the great ocean: what would they do? There were a few rowboat-like rafts, here on deck, but by no means enough for the passengers. Well, perhaps such gear was not considered a necessity by sailors.

As far as immediate necessities were concerned, Robert had asked a seaman today where the outhouse was located. He was told it was the roundhouse forward, just aft of the port bow. Robert didn't know where the port bow was, but he had found the house anyway—though it wasn't round, but square. He didn't understand why it was called the roundhouse. It was true, the hole one used was round, of course, but so were all such holes. Who could solve the riddles of the sea?

The America-bound boys looked at the anchor winch and felt the heavy chain. What gear! But naturally heavy chains were required to tether a ship to the bottom of the sea.

"Look at the man in the fore end!" said Arvid, and pointed to the bow. The "man" was a wooden figurehead. They went closer and saw it represented the head and neck of a huge bird: an eagle stretching out over the ship's bow. The long beak of the bird was open, and pointed over the water like a spearhead, as though he would guide the helmsman across the seas with his beak. The eagle looked ravenous and ferocious, his black, immobile wooden eyes scanning the waters of the Baltic Sea.

A bent old man with a long beard sat leaning against the foremast, busy with pieces of rope and such. He grinned in a friendly way at Robert, who asked him what he was doing.

"Can't you see, boy? I'm splicing."

Robert had picked up a new word—"splicing." The bearded old man was the ship's sailmaker. In his younger days he had been a bosun. Robert asked him about the *Charlotta's* figurehead, and the old man explained it served no purpose except decoration.

At the railing the boys looked down into the water rolling softly a few feet below them. Robert thought it might be a couple of miles to the bottom. Arvid shuddered—he had thought it would be a hundred rods at most.

The sea lay perilously near, and he was seized with terror. "If the sea should rise only half a yard, it would drown us!"

The possibility loomed before Robert for a fleeting moment, then he said there would be no danger: should the sea rise, it would only lift the ship higher. Arvid shook his head, unable to follow this.

A fellow passenger came up to the boys. He wore a broad-brimmed hat, a light brown, loud-checked coat, and trousers that fitted his legs as tightly as skin. From his hip pocket dangled a white handkerchief, swishing his thighs like a horse's tail; his shoes were of the finest patent leather. Robert had noticed this man earlier, on account of his colorful clothing. He seemed a gentleman among all these farmers.

The stranger looked down the side of the *Charlotta's* worn hull and waterlogged planking, which had begun to soften and splinter. He grinned contemptuously and spat on the old hulk.

"God-damn her! Damn this sour old washtub!"

He spat a second time for emphasis.

"This is a rotten, stinking ship! Do you understand, peasants?"

In some resentment, Robert answered that he had felt the same when he boarded the ship. She was damp and unhealthy.

"Her bilge water stinks like the devil," said the man in the checked jacket. "I've sailed on many ships, and I must say this old hulk is unwholesome."

"Are you a seaman, sir?" asked Robert with new respect.

"I should say so! Was for ten years."

Arvid was bending over the rail, and now he made a discovery. He pointed and said: "Look! There's a hole! Our ship is leaking!"

He pointed to a hole at the water's edge through which a stream ran in and out continuously. The man in the checked coat laughed.

"That's the scupper hole, my boy! But the ship *is* leaky, anyway."

Robert caught the word "scupper." Of course, it was the hole through which the passengers scupped, or vomited; Arvid ought to have known this. He noticed now the hole was lined with iron, no doubt to prevent waste from clinging to the wood and smelling. The presence of the iron convinced him that the hole had been made with a purpose, was not caused by rot.

"Yes," resumed the stranger, "now I sail to the North

American Republic again, if this old tub keeps afloat that
far."

"Have you visited America before?" asked Robert.

"Many times, my friend, many times. I have lived in America for years."

Robert viewed his fellow passenger with new interest. For
the first time in his life he was face to face with a person who
had been to the New World. What he beheld was a red,
flushed face, swollen as if the owner had the mumps; a flat
nose; and bloodshot, thick-lidded eyes. It was difficult to discover any redeeming features in this countenance, but the
owner had been to America, and spoke of this without bragging, as if he merely mentioned that he'd been to the outhouse.

"What did you do in America, sir?"

"Various things."

The stranger's eyes scanned the water as if his memories of
America were floating on the wave crests.

"This last year I helped a Mormon priest with odd jobs."

The man in the loud coat and the snakeskin-tight pants spat
again, this time straight out to sea. Robert need not urge him
further, he continued now of his own volition.

The Mormons were the Latter-Day Saints in the United
States, and he had been allowed to assist one of their greatest
and most saintly prophets—or so he had thought when he accepted the job. Later, he might as well admit it now, it turned
out that the priest was no Mormon at all! Things were not always what they seemed. But he would tell the story as it happened to him.

The Mormon priest (it was easier to refer to him so) had
journeyed on the railroad from town to town, and he had
gone with him to help with various things. It had not been a
heavy or arduous task. When the supposed priest held a
meeting in a town, then he, the assistant, had mixed in the
crowd as one of the listeners. When the priest's sermon was
over, then it was his duty to step forward and ask leave to say
a few words: that this evening, in this room, the spirit of reve-
lation had filled him. It had been granted him to see with his
own eyes the returned Lord's prophet. And deep in his heart
suddenly he had realized that he himself belonged to the lost
tribe of Israel. His memory of long-gone-by times had returned to him so that it spanned even the days of Father

Abraham. He wanted now to be a member of the Holy Sons of Zion.

He would be received immediately, the bogus priest would open his arms to him, hold him to his heart, and in the presence of the whole congregation call him his long-lost brother. And then many of those sitting in the audience, till now somewhat doubting and undecided, would come up to the priest and testify to the same thing: they too belonged to the lost tribes of Israel, and they too had this evening seen the prophet. All would be received into the church, and a collection would be taken up.

Evening after evening this was his sole occupation; he acted again and again the son of Zion, a brother of the Lord's prophet, and for his services he received a dollar a day in cash, two free meals, free journeys on the railroad, and beautiful clothes lent him by his boss.

Almost every evening some woman in the audience would remember that she had been a daughter of Zion. The priest would take the most tender care of the prodigal sister, and marry her immediately, as, he said, the Lord commanded him to do. This was the one and only salvation of a woman's soul: she must be taken to wife. There was no other road along which a woman might reach the glories of heaven. She must be sealed by a man who fulfilled his duties as bridegroom.

Sometimes it happened that more than one of Zion's lost daughters were granted their memory, and returned to the church. Then the boss was not able to marry all of them. Neither his time nor strength was sufficient for such a task; moreover, he was a little ailing at times—especially on Saturday evenings—and then he wished to have a little time off. On those days he seldom married more than once or twice. Sometimes he actually needed a little peace, particularly as his health was not rugged. Then he would order the speaker, his paid assistant, to help: he too, at the priest's order, would marry one or two of the lost daughters of Israel. He was not one to bar the road to heavenly glory for good sisters in Zion. Furthermore, he had been engaged to help in all matters.

The boss himself chose his brides from among the youngest sisters. Tender, helpless women were, of course, most in need of a skilled helper who could guide them to the Lord, who could lead them with experienced hands. It was the assistant's duty to marry older, riper women, many of whom had never

before known a man. But the more advanced in years the
bride, the more shy she appeared—sometimes dressed in innumerable undergarments for the marriage consummation.
Then the bridegroom's first occupation might be likened to
the patient, reverent turning of the leaves in the old family
Bible—one of those really old ones, with big pages. So there
was, after all, an air of religion in the wedding night.

But this job had lasted only half a year. The boss had had a
most unpleasant accident one dark evening in the fall. The
two of them had come traveling on the steam wagon to an
out-of-the-way little town far in the West, in which place little
was known about God and His Ten Commandments. The
people in the town were heathenish and wild, sometimes attacking strangers—before they had said a single evil word, or
even had time to fire a shot at the inhabitants. And as the
fake priest and his assistant stepped off the railroad car in this
town they were attacked without warning by a group of god-
forsaken hoodlums. They were infuriated by the idea of Mormons, it seemed, because in the past so many of the town's
women had become daughters of Zion. There were scarcely
any women left for wives and cooks among the settlers of the
district. Now of course he, as a hired assistant, had little to do
with this, he had only done what he was told to do. And luck
was with him, too: he was able to get away from his boss as
the mob surrounded him. As it happened, he had just that day
received his weekly pay, so there was no reason to speak further to the priest. He had left the town as fast as his legs
could carry him, and reached another village where people
were more humane and refined.

Meanwhile the infuriated mob took charge of his boss, and
the following day the assistant read in a paper, with great sorrow, that the poor man had been found dead, dangling from
a tree. He had really had bad luck, encountering such uncivil
people. He had been a just employer, too, and deserved more
friends—or someone, at least, to help him in his hour of need.

It had also said in the paper that many were anxious to locate the supposed priest's assistant. This he couldn't understand, as he himself had nothing to do with the Mormon religion, real or pretended: he was a Lutheran engaged merely as
servant to the priest—simply employed to help him with various things. And if the priest was not a priest anyway, and not
a Mormon—well, it was not in any sense reasonable.

The passenger in the loud-checked suit finished his tale. He spat once more over the rail, pulled out the large handkerchief from his hip pocket, and dried his eyes. Robert and Arvid silently stared at him, thinking he was shedding tears over the fate of his employer. But it appeared he was only drying spray from his face. Then he nodded to the boys, left them, and resumed his leisurely walk, his big handkerchief dangling behind like the tail of a skulking dog.

Arvid was unable to solve the stranger's mystifying occupation in North America.

"Was he an assistant pastor, do you think?"

"Something of the sort, I suppose," said Robert.

"Are they allowed to hang ministers from trees in America?"

"Perhaps—if it is absolutely necessary. Otherwise I don't think it's permitted."

The two America-bound farmhands continued inspecting the ship from stem to stern—forty paces long and eight paces wide. They would prefer to stay on deck both night and day. They did not look forward to going back into the huddle below, to the dark space under the deck, the moist, smelly hold filled with dust from mattresses and straw, stinking of urine and vomit.

When on land Robert had always imagined a sailing ship as something immaculate and shining. He had thought of sails as being like white angels' wings. But the *Charlotta* of Karlshamn had dark gray sails, dirty from wind and weather, gray as potato sacks in a muddy field in autumn. The brig *Charlotta* had no angels' wings. She was no yacht with white sails, flying lightly over the sea. She was a lumbering cargo ship, deep in the water, her lower holds loaded with pig iron, plowing her way heavily along. She wasn't Robert's dream ship, she wasn't the ship he had seen for days and nights in his expectant longing. Yet he felt pleased, nevertheless, as he walked about on deck, looking up at the rigging where seagulls swarmed with their wings white and clean against the gray sails.

He was participating in a great adventure. If only he didn't have to go below. . . .

2

The passengers had been called on deck and gathered around the unbattened main hatch, where the second mate announced in his sing-song Finnish-Swedish: "The first week's provisions!"

Two of the seamen were busy rolling barrels and tubs from the storage hold. Lids were removed from the provision vessels, and the smell of food, combined with the sea air, made the emigrants hungry.

During the passage they were to receive their food and water at the ship's expense. Curiosity about the fare was great, and all passengers—men and women, children and adults—assembled to watch as the provisions were handed out. But the mate told them it would not be necessary for every passenger to come up and crowd around him; one person from each family should fetch the food, the head of each family only.

He further said that definite portions of unprepared provisions would be allotted to each and every one weekly. They must manage so that their provisions lasted the intended time. They could not return after a few days, said the mate, to tell him they were hungry, and demand larger allotments. He wanted them to understand, once and for all, that this was a whole week's supply. Each in turn could prepare his food in the galley on deck, and use the ship's utensils if he didn't have his own. The passengers must agree among themselves on time, and take turns at the galley so that everyone's right was respected. Refuse, bones, dishwater, and sweepings must be thrown overboard—leeward, not windward. It was strictly forbidden to throw anything windward.

They could obtain fresh water from the ship's supply once a day, half a gallon each for drinking and washing; they must economize on water. They themselves must keep the hold clean, and every morning remove vomit and other dirt. Water would not be issued before the hold was cleaned; that would help them to remember this chore. Sick people could obtain medicine: drops, pills, balsam, and such from the ship's medicine chest. And if they needed to buy something during the voyage, goods were sold from the slop chest which the captain had charge of. Among supplies available at a fair price were soft soap, combs, brushes, Bibles, hymnbooks, snuff, chewing tobacco, knives, games, playing cards.

The passengers were admonished to handle fire with the strictest care. Below deck it was forbidden to smoke, or to carry or use unprotected lights. In general, it was the duty of everyone to obey the rules and orders of the ship's command. All must realize the necessity for order on shipboard during a long voyage, for their own protection and safety. The law of the sea was in effect, and the captain would punish those who did not obey instructions.

The emigrants listened in silence and awe to the second mate. Some wondered what sort of punishment was to be meted out according to the sea law—was there an altogether different law at sea?

Near the foremast stood Inga-Lena and Danjel Andreasson. The wife held her husband's hand and looked inquiringly around the deck. "Danjel—where might it be, that which he spoke of—windward?"

"I don't know, beloved wife."

"The place—where one is not allowed to throw anything? One must know where it is. I don't wish to do anything that is forbidden."

The old sailmaker standing near by explained to the peasants: "The mate meant that nothing must be thrown into the sea against the wind. Then it would blow right back onto the deck again."

"Goodness gracious!" exclaimed Inga-Lena. "That much sense anyone must have, without orders. I thought windward was a special place on the ship."

The second mate took out his wooden *betsman* and weighed the provisions, dividing them among the emigrants waiting around him.

Danjel Andreasson folded his hands. "God is feeding us for the first time on board ship."

There were many kinds of provisions which the Lord God now offered through the mate: ship's bread and ship's biscuits, salt pork, salt beef, butter, rice, barley grains, peas, salt herring, flour, sugar, syrup, mustard, salt and pepper. The emigrants crowded around the mate, they brought crocks and pans and vessels of all kinds in which to store their portions.

Some couldn't find containers, and tied their herrings, or peas, or salt pork, in towels or aprons. Others received their allotment with their bare hands.

The mate repeated: "Remember, now—economize, good people!"

His was a chore which required patience and skill. The smaller portions caused him endless figuring. Only pork and bread were allotted in sufficient quantity to enable him to figure in whole pounds; for the rest he had to count in ounces on his *betsman*: six ounces of butter, six ounces of sugar, thirteen of flour, four of salt, four of coffee, half an ounce of mustard, and a tenth of an ounce of pepper. And the vinegar too was measured, two ounces for each passenger. It was degrading work for a mate, to stand here and weigh and count and divide; and the second mate on the ocean-sailer *Charlotta* thought, as he stood arguing and weighing and measuring and counting ounces: This is a job for a shop clerk, not for a deep-sea sailor.

It took several hours before the provisions were distributed and the second mate could throw aside his *betsman* and measuring vessels. He sighed in relief: now it was done for a week. All had received their week's rations; but of course, as always with these peasants, they didn't have enough containers. A couple of women had received their flour in shawls, and the barley grains and peas in turned-up petticoats. However, they were never finicky, these passengers to North America.

Soon the smell of frying pork and boiling peas in the galley permeated the whole ship, but it would be long before each had his turn at the galley stove, and while waiting for the prepared meal the herrings and bread and such were taken out and eaten.

Arvid and Robert stood in the stern, each chewing on a ship's biscuit, hard as a stone chip. Arvid broke one of his front teeth on the very first bite; after that he was more careful, crushing the biscuit with his hands and eating the small pieces. He had often eaten month-old bread in Nybacken, but never had he broken a tooth on it. He thought if it was to continue this way, he would be toothless before reaching America.

It was growing dusk. The water around them darkened, rigging and sails were shrouded in mist as if the clouds had descended upon the ship. Their world seemed to shrink, no other ships were in sight, and their little sailing vessel seemed alone and lost on the darkening sea, with land no longer visible.

Robert shivered. It was a horrible depth there under the ship's bottom—and here he stood on a pile of old, half-rotten planks. He was inside a sour old wooden bucket which was intended to carry him across these depths; he felt infinitely helpless. Into the youth from firm land crept fear that bit and tortured him like a multitude of ants: the seafarers' life was precarious, it was not like life on land.

Perhaps it would be best after all to crawl down below and hide himself tonight in the dark bowels of the ship.

3

Kristina stood by the place where she and the children were to sleep, this bunk or bed-pen nailed together of roughly hewn odds and ends of boards. She had placed her mattress on the floor of the hold and spread her quilt, her bridal cover, over it. On top of the bunk stood the big willow basket, their food box—they had found no other place for it. And in this bunk tumbled and tussled the children; there was no other place for them, either. The bunk was their only room, and in it was gathered everything.

Kristina had slept the first night in the family bunk. The compartment was too small for her and the children—even without Karl Oskar. Almost every time she had been about to go to sleep, a child's knee or foot had poked her in the stomach or face and awakened her anew. She had lain there like a setting hen, unable to find space under her wings for her brood. In between she was kept awake by noise from the other passengers, and by the many sounds of the ship. So she had dozed uneasily and started awake through the whole night, and when she arose in the morning she was more tired than she had been the night before.

In the family compartment more than thirty people lived, men, women, and children, jammed together in one room that was no larger than Kristina's own room in Korpamoen. As soon as she stepped out of her bed she bumped into someone. And Kristina was shy in the presence of all these strangers crowding around her. All she did must be done in full view of these people. How was she to suckle little Harald? She felt uncomfortable opening her blouse to expose her breasts in the presence of strangers; she did not like to suckle her baby while other wives' husbands looked on. She was shy even in the presence of Karl Oskar, her own husband. It was dreadful that she had to dress and undress among all these unknown folk.

Lill-Marta had caught a cold in the windy harbor town, and was now in bed with a fever, perspiring, an alarming flush in her cheeks. Kristina wished she could obtain a mug of hot milk for her. But there was no milk on the ship. She must now mix honey in water and warm it for the child. And what was she to do with Johan? He was well enough, but he wet his bed nearly every night; that dripper ought to have had his own mattress. And the amount of clothing which the children already had dirtied—how was she ever to wash and dry it here on the ship?

She was now enclosed in a small pen, among all these strangers, with three children, one of them sick—never in her life had she felt so lost and helpless.

The children had no place down here to play and entertain themselves, and they hung on their mother. Johan kept pulling at her skirts.

"I want to go out, Mother!"

"We cannot go out here, little one."

"But I want to go out and go home."

"We are on the sea now."

"I don't want to be on the sea. I'll go home. I want milk and cookies."

"But we cannot get off. I've told you."

"Mother—I don't like it here!"

"Keep quiet now! Be a good boy!"

Thank God, she had some sugar. She opened the knapsack at the foot of the bunk, found her bag of sugar, and gave the boy a lump. He kept quiet awhile—this was her only way to silence him. Lill-Marta ought to have had a piece, too, but she slept in her fever. Kristina felt the child's forehead tenderly; she was still burning hot.

Karl Oskar came down from deck with a jar of water in his hand. Now they had obtained their weekly rations, but had not received potatoes; he missed potatoes, he was used to potatoes every day. Instead he had been given sour cabbage —but this he liked. Kristina thought that perhaps potatoes wouldn't keep on the ship, they would sprout and spoil, though she was not sure if this was the reason for their absence. Karl Oskar said they would eat just so many more when they planted their own in the rich soil of North America.

Soon it was their turn to use the ship's galley. But Karl Oskar said there was little room up there—it was as crowded in the galley as it was in church pews on a Christmas morning; the women stood and sat on top of each other. This did not cheer Kristina: was she now to elbow her way among strange women while she prepared their food, also?

Each time Karl Oskar came down from the fresh sea air on deck he would grin and sniff the air in the hold. "One needs a nose clip down here! The air stinks!"

Kristina had almost collapsed the first time she came into the hold. All evil smells that used to make her sick streamed toward her: rancid pork, old herring brine, dirty socks, sweaty feet, dried vomiting. In one corner she had espied some wooden buckets, and she could guess their use. She had felt as if she had been pushed into the bottom of a smelly old herring barrel. She had felt nausea, had wanted to turn and run up on deck—had wanted to get off the ship at once.

Little by little she was accustoming herself to the evil odors. But she still went about taking short breaths, trying not to inhale the bad air.

Karl Oskar explained that the bad air was caused by poor ventilation. The people took the air from each other's mouths down here. But as long as calm weather lasted they might go on deck and breathe fresh air during the daytime.

He was dissatisfied with their ship; he felt he had been cheated in his contract for the passage. And yesterday—when he had been denied sleeping place with his wife, and been put with unmarried men—he had spoken plainly to the mate: he did not ask to sleep like a king on silken sheets under eider-down in a gold-plated chamber; but neither had he imagined they were to live crowded and jammed together like wretched sheep in a pen. At least twenty people too many had been packed in down here. The shipowner had only been interested in getting their money. Each grown person paid one hundred and fifty riksdaler for his passage—forty-three and a half dollars, he was told it was, in currency of the new country they were bound for. Yet they had to lie here and suffer in a dark unhealthy hole so the owner might grow fat on their money. That was what Karl Oskar had said to the mate, and the most outspoken among the emigrants had agreed with him. The mate had threatened to call the captain, Kristina had become frightened and prayed him to keep quiet—but Karl Oskar was like that; he could not keep his mouth shut when he felt an injustice.

Moreover, they had had to lie and wait in Karlshamn a whole week, and their quarters in the harbor town had cost many daler which he had had to pay unnecessarily; they should have been notified in advance about the exact date of the ship's sailing.

One of the seamen, who looked decent and wasn't quite so haughty, had admitted that the ship was overloaded with people. But he had added that it usually thinned out in the hold as they got out to sea.

If that hint was meant as a comfort, then it was indeed a cruel comfort; as a joke, Karl Oskar liked it even less.

This much he knew by now: that their life on board ship would be neither comfortable nor healthy.

There were already sick fellow passengers. In one family compartment, on the other side, lay a young girl who had been ailing when she embarked. She had fallen ill with a throat abscess while they were staying in Karlshamn. Her parents boiled porridge in the galley and tied this as a warm compress around her infected throat. But it had been of no help as yet. The girl lay there breathing heavily, with an unpleasant rattle. Karl Oskar had suggested to the father that the abscess in the throat be opened. He himself had once in his youth had such trouble in his throat, and porridge compresses had been useless—only the knife had helped.

The enclosure next to Kristina was occupied by an old peasant couple from Oland. The husband's name was Mans Jakob, and the wife was called Fina-Kajsa. They had told Karl Oskar that they were emigrating to their son, who had been living in North America for many years. Karl Oskar had noticed the old Oland peasant when they embarked: he had brought a huge grindstone with him, and the mate had objected, wondering if it were necessary to drag that thing

with him. Couldn't they just as well heave it overboard? He
would no doubt get along without the grindstone in America.
But Mans Jakob thought a great deal of his stone: he would
take it with him on the ship, or demand the return of his
money. He was so insistent that the mate finally gave in; and
the grindstone was now in the hold. Mans Jakob had heard
from his son that good grindstones were expensive in America. They were cheap on Oland, and he wished to bring this
one as a present to his boy.

Karl Oskar recalled that he had practically given away a
new, even grindstone at his auction, because he had considered it too cumbersome for the voyage. Perhaps it would be
difficult to find an equally good stone—he would surely need
one to sharpen the scythes that were to cut the fat, rich, tall
grasses in America; a sharp scythe did half the haymaker's
work.

There were also other implements they should have taken
along.

"Did you see, there are those who drag along spinning and
spooling wheels and such?"

"Yes," admitted Kristina. "I regret leaving my spinning
wheel."

Seeing what others had taken with them, she regretted having left behind so many necessary household articles.

But they must reconcile themselves to the thought of what
they should have taken and what they would miss in America.
Kristina was much more upset by the fact that they must
travel in the company of one person who ought *not* to have
been taken along.

She pointed to the canvas bulkhead at the foot of her bunk:
in there slept one who ought not to have been in their company on this voyage.

She whispered: "She sleeps right there—the whore!"

That disgusting woman was as close to her as that; Ulrika
of Vastergohl had her bunk right next to Kristina's—only a
thin piece of sailcloth separated the beds. Kristina could hear
every move of the Glad One, every word she uttered—and
those were words she would rather close her ears to.

Kristina pointed, and Karl Oskar looked. There was a small
hole in the hanging, through which he caught a glimpse of Ulrika of Vastergohl; she was busy undressing, and he noticed
something white: her bare, full breasts. He turned quickly

away, embarrassed and a little irritated, and he became even
more irritated as he saw Kristina's vexed look: did she think
he was in the habit of staring at undressed women? She herself had pointed out Ulrika's place. But Ulrika ought to hang
a cover over that hole before undressing. Still, among all
these people on the crowded ship one must apparently grow
accustomed to incidents never before experienced.

"Why do they call her the Glad One?" asked Kristina.

"I suppose because she is never sad."

"If ever a woman needed to be sad, she is the one. She
should weep tears of blood, that woman."

"Don't pay any attention to her," said Karl Oskar.

"Attention! Certainly not! I have other things to do."

Kristina wondered if he could find her a bucket of water.
She must wash their dirty clothes. She intended to keep herself and her children as clean as if they were on land, both
underclothes and outer garments.

But Karl Oskar thought they could not obtain more water
today—not before tomorrow morning, after the hold was
cleaned.

"Too bad you can't ask the mate for an extra portion; he is
angry at you."

Karl Oskar did not answer. He was a little hesitant and
lost here on the ship. He always knew what to do when on
land, and if he needed anything usually managed to get it.
But here at sea he didn't know where to obtain anything, he
was not allowed to go where he wanted, he could not do as
he wished. And if he complained, he was threatened and
talked down to by the ship's command. He felt that these
seafaring people looked down on peasants as some order of
lower beings. They treated them almost like cattle. Here he
went about like an animal tethered to its stake; he could go
as far as the chain permitted him, around and around, but
not an inch farther. It was the sea that tied him. The sea outside the ship's rail closed him in. The sea was not for anyone
who wanted space in which to move freely.

He was disappointed mostly for Kristina's sake that their
ship was so crowded and their quarters so dark and moist and
unhealthy. It was he who had persuaded her to emigrate, he
was responsible for their being here. And from her countenance he knew what she thought—he had avoided looking her
directly in the face since they came on board, but he knew

what her expression was. Still, she was not one to complain and blame him, even when she had cause; that was one reason he had wanted her as his wife.

He would try to cheer and comfort her: "We have fine weather at sea! We can be happy for that!"

He had hardly finished speaking when the ship lurched heavily, the result of tacking. The movement came so unexpectedly that Kristina lost her footing and fell on her side, luckily on the made-up bunk.

"Our ship is leaping ahead!"

Karl Oskar gave Kristina a broad smile. "You should feel at home here at sea—you have always liked swinging!"

The ship had lurched and knocked over Kristina from Korpamoen. She did not smile. The young wife looked about her in the dark, dusty, smelly hold of the *Charlotta*, overfilled with people: these were to be their quarters during the long voyage to North America; here she was to live for weeks, maybe months, with her children. Here they must eat and drink and sleep, here they must live and breathe and be awake. Here they must remain in their bed-stall, like imprisoned animals in a byre during the long, dark winter.

And as she looked at her home at sea, the thought returned to her—a thought she had had the first moment she had put foot in the hold: I will never get away from here alive. This looks exactly like a grave.

XV

A CARGO OF DREAMS

Sometimes during the nights the emigrants lay awake and turned in their bunks, listening to each other's movements and to all the sounds of the ship.

Karl Oskar:

We are on the voyage and very little is actually the way I had thought it would be. But whether it goes well or ill, I'll never regret my step. The stupidest thing a man can do is regret something that's already done, something that cannot be changed. Perhaps I have brought unhappiness upon us—we may have to suffer a great deal; and all is on my shoulders. I insisted on the emigration—if it turns out badly, I can blame only myself.

If only we can get across this ocean, and land with our health.

Everything I own is in this venture. With bad luck all can be lost. At home they ridiculed me. They thought I had a crazy notion. This irritates me, but I won't let it get under my skin. Why should other people necessarily like what I do? Only cowardly dogs hang about lapping up praise, waiting to have their backs scratched. I'll have to scratch my own back. And I'll never return with my wife and children to become a burden to my parish—whether our venture turns out happily or not. That pleasure I won't give anyone. No; however it goes, no one at home shall suffer because of us. There are many back there who wish me bad luck, so I must watch my step. The home folk are envious and begrudge each other success, wish hardship on each other; they would be pleased if things went wrong for me.

I don't think things will begin easily for us in America. It's hard to start anew. But my health is good, and if it stays with me I can work enough to feed us. Hardship is not going to bend me; with adversity I shall work even harder, from pure anger. I'll work, all right, as soon as I have my land. And no one is going to cheat me—I won't put trust in the first soft-spoken stranger I meet.

As I lie here with my money belt around my waist I like to touch it now and then. It gives me a sense of security to touch it when I want to. It holds all I have left of worldly possessions, changed into silver coin. It's all we have to lay our new foundation; I carry that belt night and day—no one can steal it without first killing me. Of course, all the folk here in the hold are simple farmers, and perhaps as honest and decent as I; but I never did trust strangers. I suppose the other farmers are also lying here with their money belts around their bellies. But who can know for sure that there isn't a thief on board? He wouldn't go around saying: I'm the one who steals! And in the jostle down here we are so close to each other we can look under each other's shirts. The way we lie packed together one couldn't hide even a needle from the other fellow.

I have never relied on any person, except myself—and on her, of course. God be praised I have such a fine woman, industrious, thrifty, and careful of our young ones. A farmer with a wasteful, lazy, slovenly wife never can get ahead. And she came along with me, she did as I wished. But I'm afraid she will regret it, although she will say nothing. Perhaps she would rather see the whole thing undone; at times I think so. If she should begin to look back, and wish to return, what might I do then?

No. She has agreed, once and for all. She is a woman of her word, she'll stick to her promise.

It's bad luck she got with child at this time—it looks as though it had been planned—the very moment we left. Now she is sensitive—and I'm afraid the sea will aggravate her further. But I shall take care of her, and help her with the children where I can. Luckily, she too is in good health.

We can't expect much joy on this ship. Not in any way. It may be long before things go well for us again—for her and me. I don't even know how soon I can move over to her bunk. Lying here this way, separated at night, I can never touch her. Here I lie with the unmarried men—like a castrated steer. Here I lie in "the ox pen." I can't get what I need, what I long for. This can't go on too long. Why should one suffer just because one travels on a ship? They say one gets horny at sea; but of course, one gets that way on land too. Perhaps it's worse here because I see so many women. There are those who are young and shapely too. Oh, well, I don't care for any others as long as I have her. Nor have I ever had another one. But Ulrika of Vastergohl strolls about and shows what she has—to the men. That woman couldn't think that I—Oh, no. Not even if I were single. Not any more. Too many men have used her. But she is tempting; that I cannot deny. She is nicely shaped, and I believe there are men here who wouldn't hesitate. And she herself would no doubt be agreeable. Even though she is said to be "reformed," and Danjel thinks she won't sin any more.

Life at sea is dreary and monotonous. I must cheer her, my wife. I must tell her what we are going to do, once we are settled over there—a few years from now. When the earth in America has given us abundant crops. When I have built a big house. When the children are grown and can help us. When Johan can go with me out into the fields. When Lill-

Marta can help her in the house. When we have a farm without a mortgage. When we won't have to worry about the mortgage interest when we go to sleep and when we awaken. When we are independent in our own home. When we have begun our new life. When we live cleanly and comfortably in a house where it doesn't smell so damn bad as it does in this stinking hole. Yes, I'll tell her everything, as I have imagined it.

If only I could get near her; only once, at least. There ought to be a change soon.

One has such foolish thoughts. No one knows what we may have to go through. The old ones think that all is arranged before one is born. Then it doesn't matter what one does— what use would there be in labor and struggle? But I don't agree with the old ones. I think one must put one's strength into everything, and use one's head as well as one can. Always I have done it at home—I'll do the same over there. And I intend never to regret it.

But our welfare and maybe our lives depend on this emigration. If only we were safely across the sea. . . .

Kristina:

I should never have given in; I should have talked him out of it; I feel it can never go well. Something has warned me all the time: this venture will turn out badly.

And yet—if there were a bridge back to land, and I could take my children and walk back, I would not do it. Even if I knew for sure that it would turn out ill for us, I could never return. I have told him: I want to follow you! And this cannot be revoked. He is my husband and the father of my children; what else can I do but follow him?

I wonder if he is thinking it over, perhaps regretting it, now that we are on the sea. He is much more serious. He seemed concerned as long ago as when we lay at Karlshamn and waited. I wonder if it has dawned on him what we face. This notion came to him, he had to carry it through, he is so stubborn. But how far had he thought it through in advance?

We must stick together, even so. I've promised to stick to him as long as I live.

What a pity we can't sleep together here on board, and be more cozy. I must always be so careful when I'm not pregnant, I never dare give in—as I want to. I don't wish to be with child every year if I can help it. We must skip a year now and then. But now there would be no danger—I can't become pregnant when I am already with child. That's one reason why it's so disappointing and annoying, this sleeping arrangement.

I can see he wants me all the time. He has a strong nature and he can't help it. Sometimes I've blamed him when I myself was equally weak; it's not easy to admit your own weakness. When he wants me it's almost impossible to resist—he can always have me. Because deep within me I want just what he does—even though I've never actually admitted it to him. I'm ashamed to appear weak; my mother said a woman must not let her husband know how weak she is. She must be master of her desires—she mustn't be like the menfolk. That's why I never admit the truth. He must believe that I'm willing only for his sake, for his satisfaction. It may not be quite honest of me, but it is right.

Perhaps sometimes—inadvertently—I may have shown him how much I like it. Perhaps once or twice, when it was at its best, I've let out sounds. But nearly always I've been filled with anxiety and the thought: Now—in this moment—now it's happening, now I am becoming pregnant again. Then it has never been the same.

He pats me sometimes. I think he pats me more often since we left home. That last evening at home—how foolish of me. I regret it. I feel ashamed to remember the way I acted. But I've never misbehaved since then—nor has he used an ugly word since then.

I wish he could come to me tonight, now, when we don't need to worry. Now I could give in completely; then everything would be so much better. It's not right, and I feel ashamed of it, but my desire is much greater when I am with child than otherwise. A pregnant woman ought not to feel that way. I wonder if it is that way for sinful human beings only, not for animals. It must be the original sin within me.

But when you are a married woman, then it is permitted by God. And when you have your husband so near you—

It couldn't be done, of course. People are lying so close all around, listening in the night. It would be difficult here on the ship, probably impossible. No eyes can see in the darkness, but all ears can hear. Some people seem to lie awake all night long. And if one did try, one would have to forget all shame. There are those who do it—that young couple in the corner last night. They could be heard, I must say. They did not even try to keep quiet. I wanted to keep my fingers in my ears, but I didn't.

It is much worse when one has to lie here and listen to all sounds on the ship. One is aroused. And I dream so much. Last night I dreamed he was here with me. I'll go to sleep and dream that again. I've lost all shame here.

It will be a long, long voyage. And we don't know where we are headed. I'm afraid we may drown in the sea. And I'm afraid of the new country. All the little ones crawling about me. Those three creatures know nothing. Every time I feel fear, I take all three of them into my arms. But then I still miss him.

Karl Oskar—what a pity we didn't—that we didn't—I wanted—I should not have let you—I should have been against this venture—

Robert:

I wonder if the captain has any drops for earache in his medicine chest.

My left ear aches again tonight. At times I'm almost deaf in it. Inside, it feels like a weight. My hearing is much worse. I've become hard of hearing because I didn't listen to my master, and obey him. But when I get to North America the ache will disappear. There is another air there, healthy for sick ears. Those hard of hearing in the Old World will get their hearing back in the New World.

The roar in my ear is stronger at sea. Perhaps it is the wind that causes this. It feels like a sea closed up inside my head—boiling, hissing, booming. The sea is bursting, pressing, trying to get out. This causes me pain, great pain. I awaken from the ache and find my ear is wet—my pillow too: a few drops of the sea have escaped.

I am afraid of the sea—outside there—but I try not to show my fear. I am particularly afraid in the evenings, while I lie here in my bunk. Outside the wall—on the other side of the hull—I can hear the sea with my good ear. It is not very far away. The side of the ship is only five or six inches thick, perhaps a little more, perhaps a little less. There is no great distance between me and eternity. The ship might sink tonight —the sea has only five or six inches to travel. The sea can break in and reach me, fill my ears, nose, mouth—penetrate my throat and fill up my stomach. It can fill me and pull me down to the bottom. I would hardly have time to cry out—I would sink like a stone. I can't swim—hardly anyone here can swim. I'm afraid of the sea late at night.

Once I wanted to drown an old cat in the brook; I put her into a sack, not realizing that I should have put a stone in, too, before I threw it into the water. It didn't sink, the cat was alive inside and swam about with the sack. It floated there like a horrible hairy water-animal. The sack kicked and moved but would not sink. I threw stones at it to make it go down, I must have thrown ten before it sank. It was gruesome, I was afraid, and I remember I cried. I was about ten, I had no better sense then. I have many times regretted it. I have never drowned a cat since.

Why is it that I always think of that cat, every evening after going to bed? It frightens me. My brother is not afraid or worried. I have never seen him afraid of anything, on land or sea.

I wonder if Elin is afraid when she lies like this, and listens to the sea outside. I was often alone with her in Karlshamn, but here on the ship I have hardly a chance to speak to her. Yesterday when we sat together on deck her mother called to her: Come here, girl; hurry up! She sounded angry. She couldn't be angry at me.

I said to Elin once, I feel sorry for your mother. Then she seemed hurt—I can't understand why. Feel sorry for yourself, you, living in the flesh, she said. What did she mean? I did not say a word against her mother, I only said I felt sorry for her. But Elin got angry, and I was embarrassed. I must have said something foolish, though I don't know what it was.

I wonder if Elin sleeps with her mother behind the sail-cloth. If she sleeps alone, I might crawl across to her. No, I would never dare to. One only thinks about those things—I would never dare. But it is not forbidden to wish, no one can stop you from wishing. I can wish to crawl into bed with a princess. No dean or sheriff can do a thing about it. In the catechism it is forbidden even to wish for things, to covet—to covet a woman to whom you are not married is the same as to commit adultery with her in your heart.

But one has to desire a woman before one can get her, before one can marry her.

I don't wish to touch Elin in that forbidden way. I don't

wish to commit adultery with her. If I crawled into her bunk, here on the ship, I would just lie quietly and hold her, hold her in my two arms—as I did when we sat and slept together on Jonas Petter's wagon. What a wonderful ride! If I were near her now I could comfort her when she is afraid, when the storms come and our ship might sink.

Today she told me she is afraid of wild Indians in America. I have told her before that the Indians might at times be a little treacherous and evil and unreliable—they are known to have attacked white people who have tried to kill them. But otherwise they are docile and peaceloving.

My ear aches as though it would burst tonight. It will soon be two years since I got that box on the ear from Aron in Nybacken, and I still feel it. The ache tonight is from that box. It must have been a "big" box—I have nearly lost my hearing in that ear. This is not so good. One cannot know what people are saying if one doesn't hear. But I know my ear will mend as soon as we arrive in America.

For every wave I hear break against the ship, I am coming nearer to the United States. I am participating in an adventure. I will learn how big the sea is. There are few boys from our neighborhood who can sail the sea and find out how big it is. And when I arrive and step on shore I will be free for all time. On America's shore no old farmers will be waiting, calling me their "little hand." Never more will I be a servant to anybody. I shall be my own master.

It hurts awfully in my ear tonight. If only we could move a little faster, if only the ship could sail with higher speed, then we would soon arrive in the land where my earache will disappear.

Arvid:

A hell of a good thing that I could come along. I must thank the pious farmer for that. I think there never was such a kind couple as Danjel and his wife.

I am a passenger now. I've chewed that word over and over. Robert thinks I can read, and he tries to make me spell it. He says it has a che-sound in it. What the devil is a che-sound? I went to school a while but I never heard of a che-sound. No other sounds either, as I recall. I never let on to Robert, of course—he thinks I can spell and read. It is the same sound as in a chunk of dirt, he said. But I didn't understand it. You must mean shit, I said. I think they call that a piece of dirt in school.

Robert is a very learned man who has read much. I would like to have his eyes to read with and his head to think with. He is a clever devil in thinking, finished before I even get started.

Anyhow, now the Bull of Nybacken is a passenger and walks the ship and lives a lazy life. Sundays and weekdays the same. I don't earn my food, but I get it anyway—three meals a day. I can hardly believe it. Never in all my born life have I had it so easy and comfortable. Ever since I was a small child I have slaved every day—Sundays too. Even when I had my free-week, and came home, I had to help with chores. If I sat down and rested my mother used to say: "Go get some wood! Get a bucket of water!" Or my father said: "Come and crank the grindstone! Help me make this broom!" Never in hell did I have a free week. No, never. But here on ship no one says: "What are you doing, lazy dog? Give me a hand!" I haven't done a damned thing since we left home. I have been fed just the same, eaten three meals every day—and how good I feel!

I haven't been seasick either. A couple of times I have felt like spewing a little, but it went away. I think I have too much food in my stomach. I haven't missed a single meal yet, and I'll eat all I can get.

Christ, yes, what a good life! No damn farmer gets me up in the middle of the night to feed the horses. No devil gives me hell because I work too little. No one says a word because I take it easy. It's a hell of a fine thing. I am a passenger with a che-sound like in shit!

Our boat holds together—not a drop of water has come in through ceiling or walls. That hole on the side—that was made, it's good with water running through it. But the boat does wobble at times, and I feel it might turn over. It looks warped, up on one side and down at the other. Happily, it gets back in position. But if it did fall over, and sink in the sea, one would never get up again.

When I think that the boat actually can drown, I feel a kind of sickness in my breast. Mother gave me the prayer-book and she knows I can't read. "You must take God's word

with you to America, in any case," she said. "You can read
those prayers by heart which I taught you when you were a
little tyke." Oh, yes, I do know prayers by heart. The book
has one prayer for each morning and each night, the whole
week. I try to read as best I can remember—I am out at sea
and the ship is rickety and totters at times, and I don't know
how to swim. I know neither cat-swim nor dog-swim, and it
may be useful with God's word: ". . . help me sweetly to go
to sleep this night . . . help me this night that my soul does
not go to sleep in sin, and no calamity befalls my body . . .
if I live on land or sea . . . receive me at last in the safe
harbor, my dear Father. . . ."

Perhaps I mix the evening prayers. But God wouldn't care
if I said a few words from the Tuesday prayer on Monday
evening. He couldn't be that persnickety, not with me who
only read by heart. But it feels safer and easier in my chest
when I have said my prayer and put myself in the hands of
God. What luck that I can leave myself to the Lord on this
wild, un-Christian sea.

We must have been traveling very long on this boat. Today
I asked one of the seamen how much was left to sail. He said
it was nearly as far from here to North America as it is from
North America to here, perhaps only fifty miles' difference. I
thought a lot about that, it seemed so far. Then he laughed,
the devil, and the others around him too, and I got so mad I
wanted to give him one in the snout so his shit would run out.
I told him it was the same to me how far it was. If a seaman
who had traveled that way before couldn't give information,
then he needn't poke fun at honest people. "You must not
think, you sheep-coint," I said, "that we who come from the
farm country are any dumber than you who fare around on
the sea. We understand when anyone tries to make a specta-
cle of us."

However far it is, I think we'll get there, for the boat sails
every day, Sundays and weekdays, and Danjel says that God's
breath blows on the sails. And when I get to America I shall
ask all those old, tight peasant shits at home to kiss my ass.
No one has ever had such luck as I on my America journey—
a free-week in April, a free-week in May, free-weeks
throughout the whole damn spring! And three meals on every
one of God's days!

I am damn lucky to be here.

Danjel Andreasson:

The Almighty has so far given us fine weather at sea, and He helps us all He can.

Our ship sails with the Lord's chosen ones to a land which He has designated. She is a little, fragile ship, the work of faulty human hands, but she is the Lord's vessel. One night I saw two of God's angels standing at the helm. They helped the seamen steer the ship on the right course.

I was dubious at first, I worried about the great undertaking: to leave my land and all my kinfolk and voyage with my wife and children over the sea—when I am no longer in the days of my youth. But I drove fear away from my heart, and followed the call of God: His word is the lantern of my feet and a light on my path.

But I observe that doubt and fear assail my little flock: Inga-Lena, my beloved wife, our four dear children, and Ulrika of Vastergohl, and her tender daughter. The Evil One whispers tempting words in their ears to test their faith. My beloved wife fears the language of North America. She is afraid she will have to go about like a deaf-mute among the people of the foreign land. But I assure you, Inga-Lena, as I have done so many times, as soon as we arrive in the land the Holy Ghost will fill us so that we may speak the unknown tongue at once, as if we were born children of the American hamlets. We have the Lord's promise and the Bible's words about the miracle on the first Whitsuntide. I have read it many times for you, Inga-Lena: "And there appeared unto them cloven tongues like as of fire, and it sat upon each of them. And they were all filled with the Holy Ghost, and began to speak with other tongues, as the Spirit gave them utterance."

You must remember what I have so often told you, my dear wife: the Galileans, too, were simple unlearned men and women; yet they were able at once to speak Greek and Arabic, and the languages of the Medes and Elamites, Egyptians and Parthians and Libyans. They arose and spoke these tongues and praised the wonderful works of God. And according to God's promise, the same miracle will happen to all who are reborn in Christ. As soon as we land on the North American shore, the words of the Holy Ghost will shine over us and our tongues will leap as if we were drunk and the American language will be as accustomed to our lips as if we were children of that land. Sinners and nonrepenters may suffer hardship with the strange language. But we shall be able to stand up at once and praise our new land in our new tongue. And however far we may travel among other races—black, red, or mixed—the Spirit shall have power over our tongues so that we can use their languages.

Yes, no one in my flock need doubt that over us—the Lord's chosen—the prophecy will be fulfilled about the Spirit filling all flesh: ". . . and your sons and daughters shall prophesy, and your youth shall see visions and your elders shall dream dreams. . . ." And mockers and deriders will say of us that we are drunk from sweet wine.

The Lord has taken us away from evil spiritual powers at home. The church, that wicked harlot, snatched at us, wanted to swallow us in her sour, stinking mouth. But now we sail on the Lord's ship, and the ministers in their black capes cannot reach us with their talons here at sea. Evil has passed, my heart is joyous, and my tongue is glad.

All lands in North America will open up to me and be given to me and my seed. There we shall build our new church, which will be like the one of the first Christians. We shall gather together and break bread and drink wine, as the apostles used to do. And we shall have everything in common, as it is written: "They sold their chattels and divided, each what he needed." And no sheriff will bother us—we shall live in peace.

In the land of North America I shall build an altar of thanks for you, my Lord! And I will sing and play and praise Thee with my tongue and my strings, as once King David did. I am a simple man, I have no gilded harp, but I know You will listen to me when I string my old *psalmodikon*.

You give us good weather, Lord, and us old ones, all your chosen ones, you have protected from the evils of seasickness —for the sake of our faith. The unbelievers and the lost ones you have punished with this plague.

Last night I beheld one of your angels at the mainmast, and two at the helm. The angel at the mast greeted me before he vanished—I do not fear. You are carrying us in this night over the dark depths! The Lord is our captain, no want shall we know.

Blow, Lord's wind, fill the sails of the Lord's ship!—"And your elders shall dream dreams. . . ."

Inga-Lena:

Tomorrow I must darn his socks. He wears out so many socks; he always has—during our whole marriage. I don't know why. He doesn't walk heavily on earth. Perhaps it is because he has foot-sweat. Yes, that has always been a nuisance to him—and he doesn't bother to wash his feet. I always have to tell him to. He had three pairs of newly mended whole socks when we left home—besides the pair he had on. All his socks now have holes in them, and I haven't had time to mend them; and today I noticed he had a hole in the ones he wears with his high boots. Children must be chastised and holes must be darned while they are small; a hole should never be larger than the width of the little finger.

I must see to it that he has socks on his feet in North America—they say there is a scarcity of woolen things there.

They say that the Saviour always went about barefooted when He preached here on earth. But I suppose the ground is warm in the Holy Land. Figs and vines and sweet fruits grow there, they say. I can understand that the Saviour and His apostles didn't need socks. But my dear husband always gets an ache in his throat when his feet are cold. And he doesn't attend to his bowels the way he ought to. He says he doesn't have openings every day. "Empty your guts, keep your feet warm!" That's a wise saying.

Today when I was sitting on deck with my darning needle and my woolen yarns, trying to mend my black jacket, he came to me and said: "Come with me downstairs—we must pray together." "I'll only fasten the lining," I said, "there are but a few stitches left." Then he looked at me the longest while, without saying a word, and his eyes were so sad I suspected I had done something wrong. I had preferred worldly duties to the Lord's service, I was thinking of darning and mending. I could feel his sadness, and I did not want him to speak to me while in that mood, so I went down with him at once.

I am a poor creature when it comes to faith. I only understand a little. When I think and muse on spiritual things I must quickly stop. I get so astray and involved, and I mix the spiritual and the worldly.

I am afraid we will be poverty-stricken if this continues. He gives away what we have, to feed and clothe and take care of so many. I am afraid in the end he may give away everything

we own, and we will be left there, with our four children, in
dire need, without food or clothing. When I think of this—
that's when the doubt assails me. Yet I know that doubt is the
bloodiest of sins.

Once I made him very happy. It was when he told me he
would go to a new land which God had shown him—after the
court had exiled him. He said nothing about his wife and children, but when he looked at me his eyes were as sweet as
those of Christ in the altar picture. He asked me with his
eyes, and I answered him. I answered and said, with Ruth in
the Bible: "Whither thou goest, I will go; where thou diest, I
will die, and there will I be buried." Then his face lit up and
he said: "My beloved wife, we will stand together in Christ's
presence on the day of judgment!" And then I cried, and the
children cried, because they thought their father was unkind
to me and made me sad. But it was the opposite, and I told
the children that Father had promised to keep Mother company on the day of resurrection and lead her to God the Father's right side. And I told them they must never think ill of
their father.

And I try to believe that however he acts and whatever he
does, he is carrying out the Lord's errands.

I get so depressed at times, worldly worries take hold of
me, I cannot help it. As I count and count I discover we have
hardly anything left to begin life with in America. If only I
could rely on the Almighty helping us, then I wouldn't worry.
But I do worry, I can't help it. There are so many things I
must look after—I and no one else. If I don't attend to them,
no one else will.

I asked him today how we were to get a house and home in
America. "Before I put nail in wall," he said, "I shall build an
altar for the Lord. Before I lay a plank for our floor, God
must have His altar." And then he looked at me as if to reproach me for being so worldly; and I left him for a while. I
won't talk to him when he is in that mood.

I am such a wretched, forgetful creature—I know that. I
forget that my beloved husband is the Lord's new apostle on
earth.

Now he has worn out the last pair of socks—I saw it when
he pulled off his boots this evening. I must get up before him
in the morning, and darn them. The holes must not get too
big. Oh, oh, oh, he wears out so many socks!

In the old days, when the apostles went barefooted, there was much less to worry about and attend to.

Ulrika of Vastergohl:

I felt at once that this is a devil's ship. I could smell the stink of the Evil One in my nose. The devil is on board. Round about my bed are females who do not have the Spirit. Round about me crawl the brood of Satan. And among the menfolk—it stinks billy goat! I know that odor. But no one shall bite my rump, for I am under the Lord's protection. The mockery of sinners can't harm Christ's body. But I shall pray the Lord to remove the smell of billy goat from my nose—I cannot stand it.

Christ is in me and I am in Him. I've eaten His flesh and drunk His blood. That's why I was punished with bread and water in jail. A priest came and wished to preach to me in prison, but I spat on his black cape—I know those who come in black garments. I ate my bread and drank my water, and I wanted to be left in peace. The priest didn't come back, either. The last day the jailer brought me a bowl of barley porridge, but I pissed in the bowl while he looked on, and then he had to take it away. I said I was sentenced to water and bread. I did not want to receive favors from the children of the world; I accept no porridge from the devil's viper-brood, I said. They have no grace to give us, that's what our apostle says.

Now I have got away from Sweden, that hellhole, where anyone who receives Christ's body and blood is put in jail on bread and water.

With my old body, my sin-body, I practiced much whoring in my days of error. But I was taught to do it as a child, by my foster father, the peasant in Alarum. I never forget anything. I remember everything, and have since I was four years old, when I was sold at auction. After my parents died, the brat had to be farmed out to someone who was willing to clothe and feed her. A peasant couple in Alarum got me— they offered to take me for the lowest charge, eight daler a year. The farmer regretted afterwards that he had bid so low: I ate too much, and wore out clothes worth more than eight daler a year. So my foster father made me pay for his mistake. When I was fourteen years old he told me I should pay for myself. My body had developed so I could, he said. And

what a fourteen-year-old girl, sold at auction, to pay with?
I should spread my legs and lie still, he said. I didn't want to,
I cried and begged him to let me go, but I was only a slight
child and he was a big strong man. He knew how to make me
mete out pay. The first time—I can never forget it. He caught
me in the calf pen in the byre one morning when I was there
milking. The farm wife was in childbed, and the farmer himself had been lying in "the ox pen" for so long—Then he
reckoned up the pay: I owed him for food and clothes, therefore I must spread myself to him, and lie still. It was like
being cut with a slaughter knife, and I cried and prayed to
him to let me go. But he said that was out of the question.
Afterward, the peasant of Alarum stood there on the stable
floor and buttoned his pants, as if he had only been pissing,
and mumbled and said: "That's that, well, now that's over."
Then he picked up his bucket with the slops for the pigs and
went on with his chores.

In his way he requested payment many times, and I grew
accustomed to it. But as soon as I could I ran away from my
foster home, and soon I met menfolk and found company. I
received food to eat, and other things I needed, and when I
had to pay I gave the only thing I had—I understood no better. I had been trained by the farmer in Alarum. Since he had
insisted on payments so many times, there was little left to
save. At last I became Ulrika of Vastergohl; I whored, as
they called it. I was excluded from the Lord's table, and those
who had taught me, and used me, passed judgment on me and
thought it right that I was under the ban of the church.

But the rich farmer of Alarum, my foster father, was a
great friend of the dean, and went to parties with him. And
when the devil at last fetched him home, the dean gave a
pretty oration at his funeral and praised his good deeds on
earth. You may be sure nothing was mentioned about the
time in the calf pen when he had raped a fourteen-year-old
orphan girl whom he had bought at auction. Perhaps that
deed was considered a part of all the others he had performed
to get into heaven. But there is one who knows where he
landed! And when his coffin had been lowered into the grave,
and all the people left the churchyard, there was one who
stepped up to the graveside and spat on his coffin. It felt
good; damned good.

So I kept up my whoring, and in time I bore four bastards.

Three were taken home while they were little—the Lord was good to them. And my Elin is no longer a bastard, she is received among those reborn, she has been confirmed by the Lord's apostle.

A leprous person can be hated no more than I was in that old peasant village. The women shoveled most of the dirt on me; women never have been able to tolerate me. They cannot forgive me, that I have had more men than they themselves, that I have felt the rod of more men than any other woman in the parish. Go to Ulrika of Vastergohl! they would say; she will grind your seed! And it was true—in my mill everyone could grind. It was true that many women had to share their husbands with me. But why should I turn away those who came? They needed to come to me, it was good for them. It is dry and barebitten in the meadow for married men, when their wives get on in years. Some women grow fat as filled grain sacks, so no man can reach them; others grow skinny and bony and sharp as a swingletree, so the men cut themselves on them; and all become as large and bottomless as a peat mine. So one can easily understand why the men are not satisfied in their wedded beds.

I have heard men talk of their wives' shortcomings. That's one reason why the women hated me. But I have only pitied the menfolk, and let them in—as one opens a gate for hungry, thirsty cattle, and lets them into the clover field. God has given me a shapely body, and no male has complained. Many men who were forced to chew dry old hay at home have been given juicy clover with me. And I enjoyed it myself, many times. Excuse me, dear Jesus, but I did! My dear little Saviour, forgive me the joys I had while living in the flesh. Because one sins mostly when one has most joy from sin.

But if the sins of Ulrika of Vastergohl were blood-red before, they are snow-white now. I live now in Christ's body, and He lives in mine. And this body of mine is still white and soft as a snowdrift on Christmas night. I am not afraid to show it to anyone who wants to come and stare at it—it is a wondrous work of the Lord.

Tonight as I lie here in my bunk I smell billy goat worse than ever. My old body is nudging me, it wants to crawl back into me again. There are so many men around—I can't endure men so close; then my old body wants to come back. There are men who walk around here so hot their pants nearly burst. They can't get their seed ground here on the ship, they walk about and squeeze and suffer. I recognize them, I know how they act when that itch gets them. Who should know better than Ulrika of Vastergohl?

I can't stand Kristina of Korpamoen, that proud piece. She goes around staring at me as if I were an old whore, when in fact she is the one living in the flesh. She has no respect for Christ's body—the bitch! She thinks she is pure because she was married by the dean. But the Lord's apostle says that whoring goes on inside a marriage as well as out. Her husband is young and husky, and no doubt he can use his rod. But now he can't get what he wants because he has to sleep with the unmarried men. I can still please any man, if I wish. If I lived in my old body, I would try to help him.

I have no use for his brother, the young fool. He hangs about and sniffs at my girl the minute I turn my back. If he thinks he can pluck that little chicken, he has another think coming. What has such a whelp to offer? All he owns he carries in his servant bundle. And what little he has in his pants had better be left growing. Yet here he snoops around and fishes for my Elin. He wants to taste the brew, taste it and leave it, like all men. Oh, no—I know you wolves! Oh, no— you little snot-Joe! You walk about here like a wolf, stalking God's pure lamb. But you won't get to her! You shall never enter that door, you wretched farmhand. It is saved for someone more important than you.

My child is my only joy in this world. Elin was allowed to remain with me when the others went home to God, so I know she is meant to have a beautiful life here on earth. North America is teeming with rich men greatly in need of wives. Capable, beautiful girls have proposals before they can step on shore in America. Over there my girl shall marry a man of high station, prominent, and kind to boot. It will be her portion to eat eggs in a silver bowl, and sleep every night in a silken nightgown. She will not forget her old mother then, who once upon a time, among the peasants at home, had to whore in order to feed her.

Yes, but I can't get the smell out of my nose tonight—billy goat. Young and old bucks jostling. My old body is hard on God's chosen one. Dear Jesus, give me strength to withstand it! Because at times I don't know what I might do. But You must know of this Yourself—You Who live in my body. You must not let me be tempted too strongly. I am a wretched creature at times, You must have noticed that. And it is not always easy to be reborn. Yes—my dear little Jesus, You are so very good and kind to me.

But this is a devil's ship—I knew that at once.

Elin:

One has to think of something when one cannot sleep.

He shouldn't have said what he did about my mother. I haven't forgiven him for that yet. He didn't know how much he hurt me. He can pity himself. He knows nothing about this world. But he should learn. He need not have said anything. I know I am Ulrika of Vastergohl's bastard; I have been reminded of it every day since I was very little. I have known everything since I was very little.

Only men came to visit my mother at home, never women. And when visitors came I was sent outside, and my mother locked the door. In wintertime I had to sit in the woodshed and wait till she let me in again. She always tied me up in a warm sheepskin, so I wouldn't get cold out there—she has always been a good mother. Most of the time we had little to eat, sometimes nothing. When we were short of food, and a man came to visit, then I was very glad, for I knew it wouldn't be long before we had food again. And I liked many of the men. They were never unkind to me. Some were unkind to my mother. One of them hit her with an ox-whip once. I threw the pressing iron at his head—then I helped Mother push him outside. He fainted and lay outside for a long time.

I wondered at times why no women came to visit us—only once in a great while some very old hag. But as I grew older Mother let me know why only men visitors came—I was told their errand. I never thought Mother had done anything wrong.

One time I wakened in the middle of the night when Mother had a visitor. I had a kitten which one of the men had given to me, and I thought it was the kitten who cried and made sounds. But it wasn't. I think that was the only time I had bad thoughts about my mother. I spoke to her about it, and she forgave me. Then she cried, the only time I ever saw her cry. I'll tell you, she said, what people have done to me. And she told me everything. Since then I have never thought ill of my mother.

That poor, childish boy—he thinks I don't know anything. He speaks to me as if I were a little child, needing milk and swaddling clothes.

Mother thinks my father was a tramp who once stayed overnight in our cottage, and never came back. He was a happy soul, she says, and he could play the violin. I'd like him to be my father, as long as some man must be my father. Mother says it could also be the churchwarden, Per Persson of Akerby. She doesn't want him to be my father—nor do I. He is an evil man, and has called mother a whore—even though both she and I are reborn in Christ and washed pure in His blood.

Last night I dreamt that Mother made a little hole with her fingers in the flower bed in our garden outside the cottage. Then she put a plant in the hole. She pressed down the earth around it to make it stand up straight. Then she patted the earth around the roots as she pats me. The plant began to grow, and before I knew it it had grown taller than I. I stood there and stared at the flower as it grew and became taller and taller. It grew all the way up into the sky. At last it reached heaven, and then the crown opened up. The flower was white, and I noticed it was a China lily. And when it was in full blossom, a window in heaven was let open, and God peeked out. He was old and had a large head, white flowing beard, and a serious and wrinkled forehead. He looked thoughtful. God broke off the flower and took it—then He closed the window again.

The stalk began to wither, it turned black, like potato stalks in fall after a few nights' frost—they get black and slimy and stick to the fingers when one picks the potatoes. The stalk withered and I could see it lying in the flower bed where my mother had planted the flower shortly before. As I stood there and looked at the hole Mother had made I could see the black stalk lie there, rotten, smelly, and coiled like a horrible, slimy worm. I became terribly frightened, because the hole in the flower bed became deeper and deeper and more frightening. It looked like a grave in the churchyard. I began to cry aloud, for suddenly I knew where I was: in the churchyard when my little brother died. And a voice said: "She lies down there, her body is in the grave."

And as I awakened I understood that I myself was dead, and that it was I who lay there in the churchyard.

Mother had awakened when I cried, and I was so frightened that I told her my dream. She explained it to me: I was the flower she had planted. But the stalk that blackened and withered and rotted and was eaten by worms—that was my sin-body. The grave where my body rested was our home parish in Sweden, that hellhole, said Mother. But the crown of the flower that God picked and saved, that was my soul.

When Mother comforted me I lost my fright.

And now she and I are traveling to the promised land. There we shall live forever. And the way Mother explained my dream, I shall now grow up and blossom and open like a flower in that land.

Mother has told me that. . . .

Jonas Petter:

Sometimes I don't rightly know why I am lying here on this ship. I must be traveling somewhere, I think; I am after something, I believe.

Anyway—I have freed myself of her. She never thought I would do it, but there are already many miles between us. There will still be many more—so many that I can never travel them again.

I woke up one morning and made my decision. We had quarreled the night before. It began with the grain shovel. I wanted to get some oats from the attic bin for the mare, but I couldn't find the shovel. I asked her if she had seen it. Must I keep track of your shovel? she said; am I your maid? That's not what I said, I answered; but I need the shovel to get at the oats for the mare. For that gluttonous creature! she said. Your mare stands there with her fat belly like a barrel, and eats all our oats. My mare? I said. Yes, she said, you have most use of her, for you drive around the roads on your own errands. Then I began to get angry. I said, I want the shovel! Have you used it? Have you shoveled oatmeal for the cows? Never, she said. My wretched cows never get oatmeal. Your cows? I said. They are mine as much as yours. Have you forgotten that I brought two cows in my dowry when I moved to this farm? she said. No, I said—and now I was really angry—that I have never forgotten. How could I forget something you have reminded me of every day for twenty years?

It had started with the shovel. The quarrel lasted the night through, and the next morning I had made up my mind.

We have been married for twenty years, and during those years we have had about two small quarrels every week and a big fight every month. All together there must have been several thousand quarrels, over the years. But the shovel one was the last. I couldn't stand it any longer. I prepared to leave. And in order to have peace and quiet while I got ready, I sharpened the knife and let her crank the stone. That was the only way.

I found the shovel next day. It had slid so deep in the bin I couldn't see it. And I was grateful to the shovel that it had hidden itself—it helped me get started on my way to North America. I pressed the handle, as though I shook hands with the shovel: Thanks for the help!

I have quarreled away one whole year of my life. Now I am so old that I cannot afford to give up any more years in quarrels. I will be careful with the days I have left. I wish to live in peace with all. And I have lived in peace with everyone but her. Why should I live with the only person with whom I can't get along? Why should I dwell under the same roof with someone who only criticizes and irritates me? Why should I live in a house where I never can have peace?

We should never have married. But our parents thought we were suited for each other—we were equals as far as possessions were concerned. And God tells us in His Fourth Commandment that we must obey and honor our parents so that things may go well and we may live long on earth. I obeyed my parents, and she hers, and we were married. Her outward appearance was shapely enough, she was young and healthy, but otherwise I knew nothing about her. Not what she was like inside, not her disposition. That I got to know by and by.

The first years I had some pleasure in bed with her. But it became less and less, I couldn't understand why. I became indifferent and lost my desire for her—I couldn't help it. Now when it was too late I realized that I had never really liked her and would never do so in the future, either. Nor did she care for me or for what I thought. She was more married to the farm than to me. But as my desire for bed play lessened, then hers increased, and she mocked me and wondered if already I was impotent, young man as I was. Then of course I had to show her. I preferred not to touch her, it became merely a sort of habit; I could take it or leave it, without enjoyment. I never dared tell her this, of course. It was the only thing I couldn't tell her. I was a coward, I know, but I suppose she guessed my thoughts: I take part in this because I dare not refuse. Yes, I think she knew I had lost my desire for her, so she began to hate me. And she acted in such a way that I began to hate her, too. Perhaps I hated most that which could not be changed: the fact that I was married and tied to her.

It should never be between married couples as it was between us.

Our quarrels came more often and lasted longer. There was no peace in the house. And as the children grew up they took her side. They turned against me, because she spoke to them and said: Such is your father! Such has he always been to me, your mother! And then she told the children all I had said and done when I was angry and upset. At such times a person often does things he later regrets, he should not be condemned for what he does or says in those moments.

She turned my children against me, and I had to quarrel with them also. They lost respect for me, they obeyed their mother and believed her but they never obeyed their father or believed in him.

These last years we were seldom together in bed. Once in a while I pleased her when I realized I couldn't get out of it. I dared not refuse, I was too cowardly. I have been a coward many times in my life, and I would agree to do it for the sake of peace—when I satisfied her in bed she was milder in her mouth for a few days and it was more bearable at home. Sometimes I thought I would tell her: This is the last time! But I was afraid of her, afraid that she would take revenge in some way if I said no to her. Then she would have plagued me worse. Many times I had to swallow a few drinks before I could make myself go near her. Yes, the brannvin helped many a time, without the brannvin I would not always have been able to. But afterward I felt sick with myself; I felt more wretched than any creature in the whole world, worse than the animals. They don't drink brannvin in order to be able to—they do it only when they have desire. I lay with the one I hated, the one who hated me. Animals don't do that.

We were a married couple, joined together in Christian and holy bond—matrimony—wedded together as God has ordained. But it should not be so between married mates, not as it was with us.

One time during a big fight I said I would go and cut my throat. It would take more of a man to do that, she said. She mocked me, she didn't believe me, but that time I did mean it. I went after the sticking knife, I wanted to kill myself. I stood there and felt the edge of the knife, to see if it was sharp enough. I felt the bite with my thumb. And I set the knife against my throat. But then I couldn't do more. When I felt the cold edge against my skin, I couldn't. The knife cooled me so that I felt chilled through my whole body; I had no more strength left in my hands, I couldn't press, I couldn't cut. I have stuck and killed many hundreds of animals in my day, I have seen the blood gush from their throats, and I knew where to put the knife to myself, I know where the big blood artery is. But I could not make my hand perform the thrust, I couldn't force it to cut my own flesh, make my own blood gush.

I had a wish to do it, but my hand did not obey—I was too cowardly.

Then I discovered something—she had lied, because she *did* believe me, she thought I was going to kill myself. I noticed that she hid away cutting tools from me. She was afraid, after all. And for a long time she was quite bearable and kind to me, and we had no quarrels.

I had thus discovered one way to get peace, and I used it a couple of times—I sharpened my knife and let her crank the grindstone.

But it shouldn't be that way between mates in a union which God has ordained—one shouldn't need to sharpen knives to get peace.

Perhaps she did see through the knife trick in the end; because when the day came that I told her I intended to emigrate to North America, she didn't believe me. You are too much of a coward, she said. You are afraid of getting out on the sea. You dare not, you poor coward! You have never dared anything. You dare not sail on the sea!

But that time she was mistaken.

When at last she realized that I wasn't the coward she had thought—when she saw my America chest packed on the wagon—then she began to cry. She cried very often from anger, but this time she cried in another way: she almost moaned, slowly and softly, as some animals do when they are in great pain. Perhaps one should feel sorry for her; she is as

God created her, she can't help it. She can't change herself. Yes, one should feel sorry for her; but I know it has given her pleasure to torture me, and *that* I haven't as yet forgiven her.

Now I lie here out at sea, and I am free of her. I lie here and muse over what I have missed in life. It is bitter to think of this. There are men who are good to their wives, and wives who are good to their husbands. How would it be to have a wife who was kind and thoughtful and wanted only to do good, who could understand that one can mean well even when one does wrong, a wife who may criticize and scold, yet interprets all for the best—not for the worst, as my wife did? Well, how would it be? I turn here in my misery when I realize what I have missed in this world.

I feel ashamed of myself. But old as I am, there is still something left inside resembling hope, a very small hope. There is something that whispers: Perhaps good luck awaits you somewhere in the world. Perhaps you need not die before you have tasted some of that which you so sorely missed. You have lived like a dog on your farm, a dog without a master, a wretched creature who doesn't belong to the house—so have you lived, Jonas Petter. You have sneaked about, searching, silent, hungry in your own home. It is true—who can be more hungry than you for that which a woman can give to a man?

Yes, I am ashamed, a little—but mustn't a wretched human being have at least this left—a little poor and puny hope?

One can seldom sleep well here on the ship; I lie and fret too much. I am on a voyage to another continent. I am going somewhere, I don't know where, but one thing I do know: I search for peace.

XVI

HAPPENINGS ON BOARD THE SHIP

1

The brig *Charlotta* sails through night and day in the mist and drizzle of the April spring.

The sails in her two full-rigged masts hang limp and lifeless
—the wind is still light. The ship's heavy body lies deep in the
sea. The sea's beast of burden, a camel in the water desert,
she plows her way slowly through the soft, blue-green billows.
The figurehead on her prow—the eagle—incessantly scans the
sea with his piercing eyes. At times foam sprays his neck and
washes his open mouth; it drips from his beak, ever ready to
taste the salt water; it runs from his eyes, ever washed clean
by the sea. The neck of the bird rises proudly: the eagle's eye
searches the width of the ocean as though trying to find the
path of those who sailed this way before. Here ships have
sailed for thousands of years, but on this path wanderers
leave no footprints.

The last time the emigrants saw land it was the outermost
point of Denmark, appearing at a great distance. But sometimes they saw other ships, larger and smaller than their own;
they saw faster sails, and slower ones. Either way, the *Charlotta* soon was alone again on the sea.

For several days the weather had been so cloudy that Captain Lorentz had been unable to take their position by the
sun. He measured distances and figured his course by dead
reckoning. The speed was slow, the ship moved at a snail's
pace across Kattegat.

The little peasant with the wild brown beard came up to
the skipper near the helm and smiled in his quiet way: God
was giving them fine, calm weather on their voyage. Lorentz
replied that if God wished them well, He ought to give them
stronger wind.

If this damned peasant only knew how long he would have
to stay on board if this weather lasted the whole crossing!
Then he would no doubt throw himself down on his knees
and pray for wind.

But these poor farmers had no idea about anything at sea.
They acted as if their ears and eyes were full of earth. They
had only traveled on manure wagons, never before been carried by the waves. And they had one reason to be satisfied
with the calm weather—up to now they had practically escaped seasickness. Nor was there any hurry, apparently, for
these earth rats to reach North America. They were only
traveling from one piece of land to another, from one field to

another. They would reach their destination soon enough, and begin to poke in the turf on the other side.

Day after day, for days on end, the first mate wrote in the *Charlotta*'s log: Wind light southeast. Cloudy. At times rain and fog.

2

In the daytime the emigrants were on deck. It was bitter cold and they wore all their garments—coats, shawls, blankets, sheepskins. It was more comfortable on deck for those who stood the sea poorly and were afraid of nights in the hold. Here there was fresh air—in the hold the air was fetid. In their bunks at night seasickness stole over them, as though the illness kept itself hidden somewhere down there and crawled out at night. Then it might happen that there were too few wooden buckets, or that someone couldn't find a bucket in time in the darkness; lights were not allowed after ten in the evening. Then, when daylight began to creep in, it revealed the long night's happenings.

The emigrants began their day with a cleaning of their quarters. Men carried water in big buckets, and women scrubbed and scoured and washed and hung wet clothing to dry on deck. This chore must be completed before the thirsty were allowed to drink, before the dirty could wash themselves. Now they understood why the day's portion of drinking water was withheld until they had cleaned up after the night.

There were complaints among the passengers that half a gallon of sweet water a day per person was too little. This half gallon must last for preparation of food, for drinking water, for washing themselves and their babies. And they were accustomed to draw water from full wells. The second mate tried to explain to them that this amount had been decided, once and for all, that the ship's total supply of fresh water did not allow greater rations: they were on a long voyage, it might take three months if they were unlucky with weather. There might even come a day when they would have to manage with less. They must learn now to save the drops.

The women tried washing their woolen things in sea water,

but the soap gave no suds. One morning a heavy rain fell. Then the seamen stretched a sail on deck to gather rain water. The sailors washed themselves and their clothes in this, and the passengers stood by looking on, some following their example. Danjel Andreasson said that the Lord had remembered them with good washing water from His heaven.

The emigrants talked among themselves about sending someone to the captain to ask for more water. But who? No one volunteered. There was respect for the captain among them. Whenever it was mentioned that someone should go to him, invariably the reply was: The captain is asleep now, or, The captain is taking his siesta, he cannot be disturbed. It seemed as if the commander of the ship slept in his cabin the clock around. Yet they all knew he took his siesta only in the afternoons.

As early as on the first day, Karl Oskar had told the second mate the truth about the crowded situation on the ship, and since that time he had been considered a particularly fearless person by his fellow passengers. Several of them now urged him to see the captain about the water. But Karl Oskar flatly refused; he was not going to be used as a shield for others.

Neither Karl Oskar nor Kristina made friends easily. Of all the people in their quarters they were most friendly with Mans Jakob and Fina-Kajsa, the old peasant couple from Oland. Those two were kind and helpful people. Only, thought Kristina, they seemed somewhat dirty—perhaps because she herself was trying so hard to keep clean. She had never seen Mans Jakob wash himself, he always had some water left from his half gallon, and she asked to use this. Yet she thought that more than anyone else, he needed it. His clothes and everything around him he dirtied with snuff spittle and dribble which ran in two horrible rills from the sides of his mouth. And Fina-Kajsa had black cakes of dirt in her ears, and the furrows on her neck were like black ribbons. She must be afraid of losing them, as she didn't wash them away! Mans Jakob and his wife each carried more Swedish dirt to America than any other passengers on the *Charlotta*.

Soiled and worn, too, were all the things they carried in their homemade knapsack, made from old, gray sailcloth, fastened at both ends to pieces of one-inch boards. Narrow wood en laths kept the end-pieces apart. The Smaland farmers sewed their knapsacks; the Oland farmers apparently hammered theirs together. But all were on the same long journey and in time would become equally experienced travelers.

Mans Jokob kept worrying about the grindstone he was bringing to his son. He was afraid that it might be damaged in he hold, that it might be broken on this long voyage. And how was he to transport it to his son when they landed? Perhaps it might cost too much money in freight to send it on in America. The grindstone weighed heavy on the old Oland peasant as he lay in his bunk and suffered from the sea. He didn't seem to care so much whether or not he himself arrived in America, if only the grindstone reached its destination whole and sound. The grindstones over there were expensive and poor; his son had written he was unable to sharpen his axes well enough on the American stones.

Since their embarkation Karl Oskar had more often mused over the question: Where would they go once they landed in the town of New York? No one in their company had any idea, not one of those from Ljuder Parish. And he must plan for himself and his family, think about it in advance, arrive ahead of the ship, so to speak. Now he heard the Oland farmer talk about his son, who had taken a homestead in a place called Minnesota.

He asked Mans Jakob: "Is there good farming land in that place?"

"First-class, according to my son. The topsoil is much deeper than at home. My boy has taken one hundred acres."

"Our boy is able, that's what he is!" said Fina-Kajsa, with a questioning look at Karl Oskar, as much as to say: Would he be able to clear land?

And while the two narrow rills continued their peaceful course down the chin of the old peasant, he went on: His son had written him that there were such extensive, fertile plains that all the farmers in Smaland and on Oland could have their own farms there if they wished to emigrate. The ground only needed to be turned. And the place was healthy: in the summers the air was somewhat humid, but at other seasons it was neither too cold nor too warm—about the same as at home. A likable place for simple folk. In other places in America the emigrants died like flies, they couldn't stand the foul climate—yes, the climate was evil in some places, wrote his son. He himself was a little afraid of this, he was ailing somewhat in his old age, he had a wicked pain in his heart—that was

why he used so much snuff; snuff was supposed to comfort his
ailment. The heart—inside him—wanted to stop at times, but
it always started again as soon as he took a couple of pinches
of snuff. It might stop for long times when he had no snuff at
hand. This was very inconvenient. Because of his advanced
age he had hesitated about the emigration. He had never
moved before in all his days, he was born on his farm at
home. But his son had paid for his voyage, and he was anxious to see the broad fields his son owned in North America.

Karl Oskar wondered if that place, Minnesota, might not
be the right one for his family to settle in. He asked Robert
about the type of soil there, but his brother could not find the
name in his description book. There was no such state in the
Union, of that he was sure, but he thought maybe the great
wilderness around the upper end of the river Mississippi was
named thus. This was the biggest and most useful river in the
whole world. It had more water than any other river. Its
shores were fertile and healthy, covered with forests and
meadows, abounding in fish and game and Indians and all
that people could need for their existence. On the fair shores
of the Mississippi it had happened that a settler in five years
had earned a bushel of gold.

"I'm not interested in bushels of gold," said Karl Oskar. "I
asked about the soil."

But the information sounded favorable. And Karl Oskar
kept the name, Minnesota, in the back of his mind. It was
easier to remember than any other word because the first half
was *Minne* itself, memory.

                              3

Kristina was in the galley and had just finished preparing dinner for her family. The women stood in a long row near the
door, awaiting their turns to use the stove. As soon as one pot
was taken off the fire another was put on. Kristina was looking forward to the day when she could cook and fry over her
own fire again, when she could leave a pot standing as long as
she pleased. No one could prepare food aright in the rocking
cookhouse on the ship, which had to be used by so many.

When her peas didn't get soft fast enough, there was always some woman at her elbow impatiently wondering if she weren't soon going to remove her kettle. As if she could help it that the old ship's peas became harder the longer they boiled! And oftentimes the water splashed over and killed the fire. She hadn't known how well things went for her in those days when she prepared food on a stove where the kettles didn't dance.

After the meal Kristina picked up her knitting and went on deck, as was her habit in calm weather. Little Harald was asleep in the bunkpen, and Johan and Lill-Marta were playing up here with other children. Karl Oskar watched to see that they didn't climb the rail. Lill-Marta had—God be praised—thrown off her cold, and the other two children were hale and hearty.

It was a blessing she had taken along her knitting needles and some balls of woolen yarn—now she had something with which to while away the time on the ship; her hands were not happy when still.

Now, as Kristina sat there knitting, she discovered a small speck on the sock, a grayish yellow something on the white wool. She picked it up between her thumb and forefinger, and placed it in the flat of her hand and looked at it. She sat there and stared at it. She could not be mistaken—the speck moved, the speck moved about in the palm of her hand.

There was no doubt about it: she had in her hand a big fat, proud, body louse.

While her eyes followed the little animal that moved so valiantly across her hand her anger rose within her. Lice! Big, fat, body lice! And now she recalled that she had felt a peculiar itch the last few days.

With the thumb of her other hand she quickly killed the creeping creature. Then she rushed down into the hold, to her bunk, where she stripped to the skin.

All her garments were filled with lice. They were in her vest and in her petticoat, she discovered them in every seam and hiding place of her woolen clothing—the living, gray-yellow little specks were crawling all over the warm, soft, woolly cloth. And the pleats and creases were filled with nits. In the armholes of her vest there were veritable nests of them. And as she stood there naked she could see in the poor light that her body was covered with small red spots—her shoulders, stomach, and chest were dotted with louse-bites. She had felt some pricking and itching, but in the dim light when she dressed and undressed mornings and evenings she had not seen the disgusting marks.

Kristina sank down on her mattress and broke out crying. Karl Oskar wondered why his wife had left the deck so suddenly. He went after her and found her lying there naked. Was she sick?

She turned away her face and sobbed: "I'm full of lice! Body lice! Oh, Lord my God in heaven!"

He stood there, awkwardly, and stared at her.

"Don't look at me! It's horrible!" She pulled the bedcover over her. "Such a disgrace!"

"But, Kristina dear, we have never had vermin."

"No—I've always kept us clean. The children and all of us —you know that. And then I come here—to sea, to get filled with lice!"

"But, dear sweet, don't cry!"

He had not seen her cry since the night before they left their home, she had been in good and even temper until now.

She cried out between her sobs: she had never in her life had a louse on her body. Once only, when very little and going to school, she had picked up a head louse from one of the children, but her mother had immediately cleaned her with a fine-tooth comb. And her own children had always been kept clean, she had taken pride in it—even though head lice in children weren't actually considered vermin.

"It's an eternal disgrace!"

In her parents' home it had been instilled in her that it was disgraceful for people to have vermin. Only bad people— tramps and whores—bred vermin on their bodies. Vermin on the body were the outward sign of a person's soul and disposition: lice made their nests on lazy, indolent, and dishonest people. Vermin did not feel at home with industrious, honest, decent people, and the absence of them was their mark of honor. Kristina felt dishonored and debased.

Karl Oskar tried to comfort her: she mustn't take it so hard, she herself had not bred lice on her body, she had received them from somebody on board. The vermin were not her disgrace, they were the disgrace of some fellow passenger. There must be someone here in the family compartment who had brought the lice along with him. And the unpleasant creatures spawned and multiplied very fast. A night-old louse was already a grandmother.

Karl Oskar looked at the bed-pen next to them, where the old couple from Oland slept, Mans Jakob and Fina-Kajsa—perhaps Kristina's next neighbors were the guilty ones. He had definitely heard that the people on Oland had more lice than those living on the mainland.

As he was about to confide his suspicions to Kristina, Inga-Lena and Ulrika of Vastergohl came down from the galley with their noon meal in their baskets and crocks. Inga-Lena noticed that Kristina had bloodshot eyes, and she approached helpfully to ask how things were.

But Kristina's eyes fell on Ulrika: there—on the other side of the hanging, at the foot of her own bunk—there that woman and her daughter had their sleeping place. It was not a foot's distance between Ulrika's mattress and her own, and the opening between the hanging and the wall was an inch wide—that was the easiest way for the vermin to get through, there they could march through unhindered and carry each other on their backs.

Without hesitation, Kristina shouted to Ulrika: "It's you! No one but you, you old whore! You have infested us all with lice!"

"Kirstina!" Karl Oskar cried out in warning. But it was too late.

His young wife went on: "It's you, you slut! You always had your louse-nest in Vastergohl. All men running after you spread your vermin over the parish. Now you have infested the ship with lice! And you are on your way to infest all of America, too."

Kristina's eyes were flaming. But the accusation she threw at Ulrika was only part of what she felt. She had long endured biting words from that woman, now she shook with suppressed hatred—the decent woman's hatred for the harlot.

Ulrika winced and narrowed her eyes till they seemed like small, white, gleaming slits. Those who knew her would have understood: she would not be easy to deal with now.

But she did not answer Kristina directly, she turned first to Karl Oskar: "So that's it—your wife brought along her lice from her home? I guess they didn't want to part from so fine a woman!"

"Be quiet now, Ulrika!" he said harshly.

"You would do better to admonish your wife!" And Ulrika's eyes narrowed still further, and her mouth twisted in a grimace as was its habit when it spat fury.

"She must take back her accusation! This moment! I'll go up and get Danjel!"

She ran up on deck.

"Now you have started something," said Karl Oskar with concern.

Kristina had stopped crying. A sudden fearlessness came over her, as if she had made a decision. "I called her whore and slut. Those are her right names. I take back nothing!"

"But here we must let bygones be bygones. We must be friends as long as we share our journey to America."

"I have not asked to be in the company of that woman!"

Ulrika returned with Danjel Andreasson at her side.

"Now we will hold our reckoning, Kristina of Korpamoen!"

And as she went on her voice rose to a shout: "Kristina accuses me of having infested the ship with lice! She accuses me of having vermin! She has derided Christ's body and His pure, innocent lamb!"

Most of the passengers were on deck, but those in their bunks came near to listen to the commotion. Karl Oskar looked at Danjel, appealing for his intercession.

"Let there be peace among you, women!" said Danjel beseechingly.

"She accuses me when she herself is full of lice!" cried Ulrika. "I want her to ask my pardon on her bare knees!"

"Bend my knees to you?" exclaimed Kristina in uttermost contempt.

"You must ask Christ's body for forgiveness!"

"I would rather kneel to the devil himself!"

"Do you hear, Danjel? She blasphemes!"

"Be calm, dear sweet ones! Keep quiet, both of you," entreated Danjel persuasively. "We all wander together on the same road and the Holy Writ says: 'Quarrel not on the road.'"

The peasant from Karragarde looked on the two enraged women with compassion, his eyes wandered from his sister's daughter to his sister in Christ, and his eyes were even more entreating than his words.

"She must take it back!" shouted Ulrika furiously.

And she turned to Danjel and went on. She, Ulrika, was innocent. As sure as the Lord lived on high, she had never seen a louse on her body since she could remember. In the old days while she still lived in her old, sinful body, she might at times have found something crawling that had lost its way in her underwear, for lice did feel at home in woolen underwear. But since she had been reborn through her faith in Christ she had been clean and free of lice. And he, Danjel, must know this better than anyone else, he must know that no vermin would cling to Christ's body. He must know that neither Christ nor any of His disciples had lice while they walked here on earth—possibly with the exception of Judas, the betrayer, she could not answer for him, he was no doubt a vermin-infested shit-heel. But lice could live and thrive only on an old, sinful, rotten body—not on God's pure, innocent lamb.

And Ulrika began to unbutton her blouse. "I shall strip to the skin! No one will find a single louse on *me!*"

"Have you no decency?" Kirstina's face flushed red. "You disgrace all womanhood!"

"You have accused me! Anyone who wants to can look for himself!"

Her bare, full breasts were uncovered as she unbuttoned her bodice. Karl Oskar turned away, a little irritated that the sight of the white breasts somewhat disturbed him.

Ulrika would have undressed and bared her whole body if Danjel had not taken her by the arm and dissuaded her. He now spoke to her about a Christian's true behavior in the presence of worldly people. He warned her of the dangerous temptation of vanity which might entice her to show her body, a wonder of God's handiwork, which she must not use for the purpose of arousing sinful desires in menfolk.

"But I must clear myself!" insisted Ulrika. "Inga-Lena must examine my clothes—she must be an unbiased witness for me. Come and look, Inga-Lena!"

Ulrika and Inga-Lena withdrew behind the hanging to the unmarried women's compartment. In there, on the other side of the sailcloth, Ulrika completed her undressing.

After a short moment the two women returned. In Ulrika's gleaming face one could immediately read the result of the inspection.

"Speak up, Inga-Lena! Did you find any lice on me?"

"No-o."

"Did you find as much as one single nit?"

"No-o."

"There, you can hear, all of you! I am innocent! Kristina must get down on her knees to me! She must ask my forgiveness!"

"Never while I am alive!" exclaimed Kristina in disgust. "I would rather jump into the sea!"

"You and your man can undress each other! You two can pick the lice off each other! But now you hear that I am free of vermin, and you must ask my pardon! You have blasphemed God's pure, innocent lamb!"

"Shall I ask *your* pardon, you old, inveterate sinner?"

Down on your knees with you!" Ulrika's eyes spat fire. "If you don't, I'll tear your eyes out!"

She was ready to spring at Kristina, as Danjel and Karl Oskar grabbed hold of her arms and held her back.

Kristina did not ask her forgiveness. But another woman stood by, ready to bend her knees: Inga-Lena was sad and ashamed and almost ready to cry. All turned to her. She held something between her thumb and forefinger, she held it up to her husband's eyes. It was something that moved, something gray-yellow—a big, fat, body louse.

"Danjel—dear—look, I too—I have—"

Ulrika was innocent, but Inga-Lena had found a louse in her own undergarments. And now she stood there and fumbled for her husband's hand, as if she wished to ask his forgiveness.

Danjel Andreasson examined the louse which his wife held up to his eyes. He said softly: This animal, too, was the created work of the Lord. They must therefore not hate and detest the creature, but accept it in quiet submission. It must remind them that they should wash themselves and keep clean here on the ship. The vermin were sent as a trial for them— for everyone's betterment.

Karl Oskar could now feel a crawling along his spine. He went to his bunk, among the unmarried men, and began to undress; he soon found what he was looking for.

It turned out, by and by, that all the passengers in the hold were infested with lice, all except one. The only one to escape the vermin was Ulrika of Vastergohl, the old harlot.

4

Kristina at once began the extermination of the small crawling creatures. She saw other women sit around and pick lice
from their clothes and kill them one at a time with their
thumbnail against a wooden plate. But this required too much
time and was, besides, not a reliable extermination. The soft
soap she had taken along now came in good stead. In the galley she boiled all their underwear in a strong, seething soap-
lye which no louse could survive. Then she took a quicksilver
salve and rubbed it over the whole bodies of herself, her husband, and her children. With her splendid fine-tooth comb she
went after the children's hair so thoroughly that their scalps
bled from the brass teeth.

It irritated her deeply that Ulrika of Vastergohl could walk
around in malicious joy and feel superior to everyone on the
ship. But Kristina did not believe that Ulrika had escaped the
vermin because Christ lived in her. Uncle Danjel, no doubt,
was more pious and Christian-spirited than Ulrika—yet the
lice had not spared him.

She had accused Ulrika wrongfully, and she regretted it,
but she could never force herself to ask forgiveness of that
woman; that would be to admit that she was lower than the
Glad One, the infamous whore. The one to ask forgiveness
was Ulrika—she ought to ask forgiveness of all those women
at home whom she had insulted when she gave herself to their
husbands.

And Kristina half admitted to herself what had driven her
to the accusation: she had watched Ulrika strut about in front
of Karl Oskar; one could easily imagine how she would act if
she were alone with him in a dark corner. Of course, he
would never let himself be tempted, but Ulrika had a strange
power over men. Karl Oskar had a strong nature, and he had
slept alone here on the ship for many nights. So one could not
be sure, not absolutely sure . . . The look which crept into
Ulrika's eyes when she turned them on the men, on both Karl
Oskar and others, those disgusting eyes, radiating seething lust
—in those eyes whoring gleamed.

And Kristina sought comfort in the thought that as soon as

they landed in America, they would be rid of Ulrika of Vastergohl.

It turned out that the number of "free passengers" on the
brig *Charlotta* was infinite—the greatest number of which
probably were created on board. There was a great demand
for quicksilver salve for their extinction, from the captain's
medicine chest—so much so that after a few days the second
mate reported the ship's supply was dangerously low, so many
jars had been distributed.

It was never determined who had brought the disgusting
vermin on board, but Captain Lorentz said to his second mate
that he wondered how things actually were in old Sweden
when even the lice emigrated to North America.

5

Robert went everywhere on the ship, and was a keen ob-
server. He listened to the orders of the ship's officers, and he
watched the seamen execute them. He learned what it meant
to "sheet home" and "hoist sail"; he learned to distinguish between tackle, boom, and stay; he knew what a block was, and
he could point out to Arvid the spar, the hawse, the bollard,
the shrouds, the bolt, and the winch. He knew that luff meant
the ship went more against the wind, and fall away was to
have the wind more to the side. He had made friends with the
old sailmaker, who gave him all the information he might
want. He was told that the ship's earth-gray sails were never
washed—except when God the Father Himself cleansed them
with His rain and dried them in His sun and wind. He was informed that the strongest sails in the world were made in Jonsered in Sweden, and were known on all seas as "Jonsered
sails"; he was told that the *Charlotta* carried her cargo of pig
iron in her bottom, to make her lie deep in the sea; he was
advised to eat all the peas and sauerkraut he could get—then
he would not become sick of scurvy; scurvy was the most
dangerous disease for emigrants—many succumbed to it during ocean voyages. But he must be careful and eat meat in
small quantities—though salt pork was probably least dangerous.

Robert also kept close to the man in the broad-checked

jacket and narrow pants—the one who was referred to on the
ship as "the American." Robert questioned him endlessly
about things in the United States. To some inquiries he received an answer; others were ignored. The man said that the
American President had forbidden him to tell all he knew
about the country. He had held such posts over there that he
was in possession of important secrets concerning the country's government, and if he divulged them to outsiders he
would never be allowed to enter the republic again. Robert
wondered about this statement.

So far he knew only that the American's name was Fredrik
Mattsson. And now he thought of another man with the same
first name—Fredrik of Kvarntorpet, who had made the famous America journey to Gothenburg and had afterwards
disappeared. Robert thought that the stranger on board might
be Fredrik Thron—it was rumored that he had gone to sea.
Robert confided his suspicions to Jonas Petter, who had
know the Kvarntorpet boy while he was growing up. Jonas
Petter looked carefully over his fellow passenger when unob-
served, and finally said that this man could be Fredrik Thron,
the escaped farmhand. He was about the same height, and his
face was similar. But he hadn't seen the rascal in twenty years,
and a person can change much from youth to manhood. He
could not say for sure. Now, the American had said that his
home parish was in Blekinge, and that might prove that he
came from Samland, for Fredrik Thron lied at all times, except when he told the truth in momentary forgetfulness. But
at such moments he always used to blush, he was so ashamed
of it, said Jonas Petter.

Robert recalled that he had read somewhere about a President of North America—George Washington—who always
told the truth and even confessed that he had cut down an
apple tree; they now celebrated that day in the United States.

He decided to try to find out the truth about Fredrik
Mattsson, the American.

After one week at sea, Robert was convinced that his place
was on land. Nearly every chore of a seaman was dangerous.
The farm service on land was hard, but it was never dangerous. How could the ship's officers make the seamen climb up
there in the mast-tops? The seamen worked their regular
watches and were free in between, but real peace they never

had; neither day nor night could they rest completely. One who served as seaman on board a ship was no more free than a farmhand. The farmhand must look after the horses night and day, Sundays and weekdays, without letup. And the seamen must lie there in their bunks in the forecastle, as closely packed as salted herrings. He and Arvid had had better quarters in the stable room in Nybacken, even though there was an abundance of bedbugs there.

A farmhand must eat salt herring all the time, but a seaman must eat rancid pork at every meal. And the seamen must live here year in and year out, imprisoned inside the rail; they couldn't take a step outside—only forty steps lengthwise, and eight sidewise.

A farmhand on land had more freedom than a seaman at sea.

There were also moments when the farmhand Robert Nilsson from Korpamoen was filled by other thoughts than those of the dangerous, chained life on three-fourths of the earth's surface, the sea: ". . . but he who learns to understand why the water takes so much space shall therein see a proof of the Creator's omnipotence and kindness." For hours on end he would stand and gaze toward the mast-tops. Up there—in dizzy heights above the deck—the forest pines stretched their heads: those widely traveled trees, those debarked stems of the large, prolific family of evergreens. These pines had lost their branches and crowns, and instead had been decked in clothes of sail. Dressed in these, they rose here at sea higher and more proudly than ever in the forest. From their fenced-in wood lot they had been let out on the world ocean, there to sail for life. But for each fir cut for a mast, one hundred remained rooted, sentenced for all time to the drab and dreary life at home. There they stood—fifty, sixty years—then they were cut down for rafters or used as timbers in a house, byre, or barn. Then there they lay, in their deep disgrace for a hundred years or more, growing hairy with moss and green with mold, brown-spotted from cow dung, hollow and filled with cockroach nests. Slowly, very slowly, they would rot down in the unromantic stable wall, and when the old building at last had served its time and was torn down, they would be thrown away with odds and ends on the woodpile, to end their lives in the fire—to succumb at last under a peasant pot in which potatoes for the pigs were boiling.

Such is the fate of pine trees which remain at home.

But the chosen mast trees fly the sails which carry ships across the oceans. They help people emigrate from continent to continent, in search of new homes. Their graceful heads carry the winged sails, they are the wingbones of the sailing ships. They may be broken in their youth by storm and shipwreck, or they may sink with their ships in old age, but they will never end in smoke and ashes under a pot filled with potatoes for swine. And when the ship goes down, the masts follow her to the bottom of the sea and proudly lay themselves to rest in the roomiest, deepest grave in the world.

Such is the fate of seagoing pines.

One hundred remain rooted while one is let free to sail on the sea that covers three-quarters of the earth.

And for each farmhand who emigrates across the sea to the New World, hundreds remain at home. There they sit, in their dark stable rooms in the Old World, and gaze through the small fly-specked windows during dreary Sunday afternoons, rooted in their home communities, in their service, until one day they die an ignominious death in bed in a corner of some moss-grown cottage, or as a pauper in the home of some charitable soul.

Such is the lot of home-staying farmhands.

XVII

"... THE SHIP WAS COVERED WITH WAVES ..."

On the North Sea the emigrants encountered their first rough weather.

It began to blow in the evening—at midnight the captain judged the wind to be the ninth grade, according to Beaufort's Scale. The *Charlotta*'s topsails were now bottom-reeved, and in the log the first mate wrote: "Storm."

Robert:

He awakened. Something heavy had rolled on him—his brother's body.

He had gone to sleep as usual in his bunk next to Karl Oskar. He had already had time to dream. His dream had been about a word, "Dead sea."

He had stood on the afterdeck at dusk when one of the seamen had said, they were almost in a dead sea. It had sounded horrible—as if they were sailing over a sea where they were to die. The sailmaker had told him what it meant: waves that were remnants of an old storm—afterwaves, so to speak. They were the ghosts of the sea, threatening billows that came from some place where a ship shortly before had gone down. They came with a message from the drowned ones—the dead ones told about their shipwreck.

Someone had said: Dead sea is a foreboding of storm; the wind has shifted to northwest.

Round the ship rose steep, high knolls—white-topped—swelling like rising bread in the oven. Suddenly a wave had broken over the deck where Robert stood, soaking his trousers to above the knees. He had become frightened, and had wanted to run away, when he heard one of the seamen—a young boy of his own age—laughing at him and his wet pants. Then Robert had pretended that it didn't matter, and had remained there.

Until now he had known the sea as a pleasant splash against the hull at night. But the kind, friendly sea was changing: a beast with thousands of high, seething humps coiled around the ship. He heard the first mate's command: Batten down the main hatch!

He had been about to wring the water from his wet trouser legs when suddenly the whole deck became a steep, slippery downhill. The brig *Charlotta* listed to one side. He grabbed the rail with both hands so as not to slide away, and there he hung, waiting anxiously for the *Charlotta* to get back on an even keel—which she did, only to roll over on the other side: downhill became uphill.

Robert wanted to remain on deck, he didn't want to appear cowardly. But a feeling of dizziness took hold of him, and he had a sensation as though his stomach were rolling about loose inside him. What was this? What was the matter with him? Hadn't he read in his *History of Nature* about that which overcame him: "This rolling movement of ships at sea causes inexperienced people who voyage on them . . ."? And now he noticed that only a couple of passengers were left on deck; he was not the most cowardly. Then he had gone below and lain down in his bunk.

A great hue and cry was heard from the other side of the sailcloth, where the women were. One of them had been badly burned by scalding water while she was preparing her evening meal in the galley. A pot with boiling water had fallen over her foot as the rolling began. The woman had cried out loudly: "I shall complain to the captain! The captain shall hear about this!" But from the men's side was heard a rough voice: "Damned hens, those women! Must the captain hold their pots? Why in hell can't they be more careful?"

The young girl who was ill with an abscess in her throat often moaned softly—tonight Robert could not hear her.

Then he had gone to sleep, but the word had penetrated his brain like an auger, working away inside: dead sea—*dead sea —dead sea!*

It was night, and the darkness impenetrable. He lay on the inside of the bunk, and his brother's heavy body had rolled over him so he could not move. Karl Oskar slept. Robert could hear men turn in their bunks—snore, groan, puff, vomit, fart, talk in their sleep, pray, swear and curse.

Karl Oskar rolled back to his place, their mattress seemed to sink. Robert grabbed hold of his brother's shoulder—their bunk was sinking! Nothing stopped it—now he was lying on top of his brother and they sank together, toward the bottom of the sea!

He clung to his brother's shoulders and was able to whisper: "Karl Oskar—"

Then their bunk stopped sinking—it rose. And again his brother's body rolled over onto his. Now it was his turn to sink, with his brother on top of him. No bottom hindered— they sank and sank. Now they must be deep under the water —*they must be going down!*

He heard himself cry out: "We are sinking!"

Karl Oskar seemed to waken—he mumbled, half asleep: "It's only storming. Keep quiet!"

It stormed. An uninterrupted roar was heard from the sea on the other side of the hull, like thunder after a bolt of lightning. The mass of water outside, which until this evening had carried their ship on its back calmly and patiently as a docile beast of burden, had now become a wild beast with frothing, foamy jaws, and it heaved with all its pliant humps as if to throw off its burden. Already it had snapped at Robert—his wet trousers hung near the bunk: the sea had licked him with its wet tongue.

And now he lay there and sank: the sea had swallowed him. It had licked his legs in the evening, tonight it had swallowed him.

He wanted to throw up. There seemed to be no air around him, he could not breathe.

"Karl Oskar! Have we sunk? Has the ship gone down?"

The water had not yet come in to them. But as soon as the hull broke, when the planks splintered, when there were holes in the bulkhead—then the sea would rush in and drown them.

"Karl Oskar! Can't you feel we are sinking?"

"It's only seasickness."

The two brothers kept rolling over each other. Their bunk went up and down. The older one explained: in a storm a ship rocked like a cradle.

"But it is stifling in here tonight," panted Karl Oskar, and turned over on his other side.

One could hear that he, too, suffered. He had not yet been seasick, every morning regularly he drank his wormwood-seed brannvin on an empty stomach; he was sure this kept his body in good order.

Now the crew had battened down the hatch, as the waves were constantly washing over the deck. In so doing they had also closed all the small holes which let air in to the hold. That's why it's so stiflingly thick in here tonight, Robert thought. The air he inhaled had already been used. His fellow passengers had used it, men and women had sucked it in through their throats, old men and hags had held it in their filthy mouths. It was not air any more, there was no air. Robert inhaled—this is the last, is no more air—it does not suffice for all, there isn't air for one more breath, this is my last one in life. Perhaps one more—if I use very little only. This is my last breath—next time I cannot . . .

The air dried in his throat, and he became faint from fear: he was dying.

He gasped for breath in short, weak jerks: "Karl Oskar—I'm choking to death—"

"You have as much air as I. Keep quiet!"

A light fluttered above them; Jonas Petter had lit a tallow candle.

An angry voice was heard through the darkness: "Don't start a fire, you bastards!"

"I can't see to puke," panted Jonas Petter. "It runs beside the bucket."

But he blew out the light before he was through vomiting.

Robert kept on breathing; the air seemed to give out at each breath he took, but there was always enough for one more. People around him puffed, groaned, swore, vomited, prayed, moaned, and cried.

The brig *Charlotta* sailed on with them all, through the night, over a sea with hissing, wet tongues licking the vessel on all her sides. The night was dark and starless with low sweeping clouds. Two lanterns were burning on deck: the green on starboard and the red on port. But they gave out poor light, these kerosene burners, hemmed in by darkness and the storm. Two fragile little lanterns on a black, raging sea, two lights in a little world that moved above the depths of a great tempestuous water.

Yet in this little world lived nearly a hundred people, cramped and crowded.

Robert listened to the sounds of the breaking waves: they roared, splashed, and flowed as they broke over the deck above him. Mighty masses of water came rushing, crashing tumultuously, and falling. When a wave broke against the deck the sound increased to a thunder-roar, deafening as a big box on his ear. Surging and splashing, the water ran in small runnels over the deck planks, flowing like a swollen spring back to its home. A wave rose, broke itself against the ship, and fell back into the sea. The next one followed—a hard thud, the water threw itself over the deck, then followed the roar, the soughing, the purl of running water. He lay there and listened to wave after wave, and each time he could hear how the ship freed herself from the lashing tongue of the sea, and escaped the yawn of the wild beast. The brig *Charlotta* was still afloat.

A baby cried incessantly on the other side of the hanging. It sounded like the mewing of a tortured cat. A cat—it wasn't a child he heard cry, it was a cat! It was the old cat which he once had drowned in the mill brook, the cat in the sack that wouldn't sink. The cat was in here and she was being choked slowly, she mewed pitifully, the sack would not sink before he had thrown many stones at it. And the cat mewed, she mewed incessantly, she had mewed for many years, ever since she was drowned. And now she mewed here, behind the hanging, while he himself lay here and was being choked, tied in a sack, sinking—

His punishment was inescapable: *he must die in the same manner as the cat.*

Perspiration clung to his whole body, like a cold, wet cloth against the skin. He folded his hands, he had not said his evening prayers last night. When he had finished he took hold of his brother's shoulder again. "Karl Oskar—please. I'm afraid."

"Keep quiet! It'll blow over."

"But I'm afraid I'm going to die—"

"No one can do anything for you—you understand that much."

No. No one could do anything. All the hundred people inside the hulk of the ship were forced to lie and wait, they could do nothing else. The ship might sink with them all, and no trace would be left on the water's surface, no one in the whole world would know how they had died, no one would be able to find their grave. In the space of a few minutes they would all disappear from the world, remain lost for eternity; and soon it would be as if they had never existed. And not a soul could do a thing about it. No one could bend a finger to help them. Here they would lie, inside the sack when the sea broke in, filling their mouths with water, filling their eyes, their ears and throats, choking them as the cat was choked in the mill-brook sack.

There was no one but God to turn to.

"Karl Oskar—"

"What do you want?"

"I drowned a cat in the brook when I was little. She suffered terribly before she died. Do you think I can—can be forgiven?"

"What nonsense is that?"

"I can hear the cat mewing—in here."

"You are out of your head!"

But Robert prayed God's forgiveness for what he had done to the cat in the mill brook. After that he felt as if his fear had eased.

His breathing came in short gasps. But suddenly his nose and mouth felt clogged: a slimy, sticky fluid was covering his face; something from the bunk above him dripped onto him. In the dark he could not see what it was, nor need he see it— the smell told him all.

The stench of the vomit overwhelmed him. He rose, and tumbling over his brother's body he got out of his bunk. Out . . . Out! He would die, this very minute, if he didn't get out at once. He felt his way through the darkness, between the close bunks of his fellow passengers. The floor beneath him fell away—the floor rose, and he crawled uphill. He reached the narrow passage longships as if walking on stilts. He skidded in the vomit, it splashed in his face, he spat, he dried himself with his hands, he groaned. Out—out in the open! Here he would die. The filthy stench forced itself into him, it went deeper into his throat, it filled and choked him. Up—up on deck!

He reached the ladder in the hatchway, he tried to crawl up on hands and feet. But the hatch was fastened solidly, he pulled and pushed, he could not move it, he could get no farther. The sack was well sewn together, he could not get out, he must choke to death down here. He could hear the seamen on deck shout to each other: A hell of a gale! Batten down and secure! What a bastard!

We are in a dead sea—*dead sea—dead sea.*

Robert remained clinging to the ladder, vomiting. He clung there until he felt a pair of strong arms around his body, a pair of arms that dragged him back to his bunk.

"It's only seasickness," said Karl Oskar.

But during the horrors of this first stormy night Robert felt, for the first time in his life, that he was participating in death.

Kristina:

The swing here in the barn was ready. Both ends of the ox-thong were fastened high up in the roof beams. The swing was so high she felt dizzy when she looked up. They used to sit, two of them—two girls together—and hold on to each other. It felt safer that way; but they cried out each time the swing went high. If you were afraid, you jumped off. Now she would ride the swing alone, and that was dangerous.

She crawled up and sat down in the swing, grabbed hold of the ox-thong with both hands, and held on. Then she kicked against the barn floor and started.

You have always liked to ride on a swing, said Karl Oskar.

But once she fell off the swing and broke her knee, and gangrene had set in and she was sent to Berta in Idemo. Karl Oskar came into the kitchen; he was a tall man with a big nose. She remained in her chair the whole time he was there, because she limped when she walked—and for some reason she didn't want him to see her limp. But now we shall get married, he said, and then she sewed her blue bridal quilt.

If she hadn't fallen from the swing she wouldn't have been sent to Berta in Idemo, where she met Karl Oskar, nor would she have been with him in the ship on their way to North America. The happenings of her whole life were decided that day when she made a swing of the old ox-thong in the barn.

Nothing must spot our bridal cover here; our quilt must be kept clean—we must use it in America, when we build anew.

She was riding her swing—at last she could ride as much as she wished, and no one said a word about it. But she must hold on with both hands, she rode higher and higher, she rode backwards up against the roof, and the ground was so far under her that she felt dizzy—she rode forward again, down to the floor. If she fell out she would surely kill herself. She held on harder to the ropes, they cut into her hands, it hurt.

It was dangerous to swing as fast as this—it hummed at her ears, she must slow down. But that was impossible. What should she do? She could not get hold with her feet; she might easily fall out. It was much safer to sit two in the swing, then they could hold on to each other. Why didn't Karl Oskar come? She wanted to hold on to Karl Oskar.

Here she sat in the clouds—and there, deep below her, was the barn floor.

She cried out; she must stop the swing.

She was awakened by her cry. Lill-Marta lay on her arm and moaned in her sleep, like a little whelp. Her small hands and cheeks felt warm and soft. Children were always warm, they warmed their mother's hands. Her babies were healthy, God be praised. And they were all on their way to America, where they would settle and build a new home.

She must be careful not to let anything drip on her quilt. But she had nothing more to vomit—the last time it had been green, like the cows' cuds, pure gall. Now it was finished, some time it must come to an end—though as long as she still had something to throw up, she felt better. Now she would not feel better.

Children were crying, but they were not her children. It's probably Eva, Inga-Lena's little one. Poor Inga-Lena, her little one is so sick. She is not six months yet, it is difficult at sea with such a little one. Poor Inga-Lena—she has much to look after, and no help from Danjel. She is killing herself for his sake.

Now Kristina was riding the swing again. She flies up through the air, she falls down, back and forth she rides. She is thrown through space, back and forth. She holds on with both hands, in panic. She wants to jump off, she wants to get back on the floor again.

How far was it to the floor? She looked down. *The floor was gone!*

Horror seized her, her hands grabbed hold of the rough boards of the bunk-pen, desperately—while the ship rolled and she sank, sank. There was no longer any floor to receive her feet—she fell, and nothing stopped her.

For there was no bottom.

Oh—she must get down, she must rest, she must lie down and rest against something, something onto which she could jump, something soft and warm—arms that would embrace her. She must get to the floor.

How thirsty she was! Her throat burned, in her mouth she chewed embers and ashes. But she was unable to reach out her hand for the water jar which stood near the bunk. She had no power to move her hands, to move her feet or her head. She would never be able to move again.

"Seasickness is harder on married women . . . and when a pregnant woman goes to sea, inexperienced with sea and sailing . . ."

But it didn't matter, nothing mattered any more, nothing could happen to her any more. And whatever happened, she would never attempt to raise her head, or her hand even. She had only one wish: to lie here, still, still, still. Never to move any more, never move in all her life, just lie here, until it was all over at last.

Wives who were with child suffered doubly because they were with child. He shall travel free of charge, the little tyke, Karl Oskar had said; he will cheat the skipper. But she paid the fare in her suffering. Three children around her, one inside her—that unborn one—what sort might he be?

But it didn't matter. Now she only wanted to reach the bottom. She must stop the swing, she wanted to sit on solid ground, she wanted to rest on something soft. But there was no bottom.

Except the bottom of the sea.

The sea was deep, the water was soft, the bottom of the sea was soft. Oh, how she would rest there!

The one who was afraid when the swing went too high could jump off. Other girls jumped off. But she had always liked to ride high. She never used to be afraid.

Kristina of Korpamoen rode on a swing. She was thrown into the clouds, she traveled through space without end or beginning, she sank into depths without bottom.

And from this swing she could not jump off.

Inga-Lena:

It had happened when she stood in the galley and fried pork. She had cut up a side piece, and laid the slices in the frying pan. Then the devil came to her and whispered: You mustn't rely on that, don't think for a moment it is true. You mustn't think that you more than anyone else . . . and suddenly she had become dizzy and exhausted and weak. She had rushed to the corner where the buckets were, and thrown up.

Perhaps it was the smell of the pork, sizzling there in the pan. The fat was yellow and had a rancid odor when it was placed over the fire.

She had been forced to go below and rest her head for a moment. All around her people were sick. Men and women vomited like cats. But they were children of the world—the believers were saved from seasickness. Yet now she had been seized by the same illness as the unbelievers. She prayed God for help in her bodily weakness, then she put some more camphor in the pouch she carried against her stomach—a remedy for seasickness—and took a spoonful of medicine—The Four Kinds of Drops.

At supper she was unable to eat a single bite. The rancid fried pork grew and became larger in her mouth. The ship's pork had never tasted good, today it was inedible. But she dared not tell her husband how things stood with her, he must not notice her bodily ailments, she must keep her seasickness a secret.

Danjel asked why she put her food aside. She answered

that she had eaten some in the afternoon when she prepared
a bite for the children.

She thought that it must soon pass. She must be well for
the sake of her husband and children. And her littlest one so
ill—no one knew how it might go with her.

But when she wanted to rise from her bunk, to take the
utensils back to the galley, her legs refused to carry her. She
lay down on her bunk again.

Ulrika of Vastergohl came up to her and looked at her
questioningly.

"You are green in the face! Are you ailing, Inga-Lena?"

The wife from Karragarde kept her silence. How could she
tell the truth?

Ulrika felt perfectly well; she enjoyed the sea as much as
solid land. Now she was practically the only woman in the
hold feeling completely well. There lay Kristina of Korpamoen and suffered sorely, there she lay and grunted in her
bunk like a farrowing sow. All who lived in the flesh became
sick, the Lord had no mercy on sinners. But she, Ulrika,
went free. One who lived in the true faith could stand the sea
in any weather. One with Christ's body in him could never
feel sick.

Only how was it with Inga-Lena? Was not she one of the
Lord's chosen?

"Have you fallen seasick?"

"I'm afraid so," whispered Inga-Lena.

"Can this be true?"

"Yes—and what will Danjel say if I cannot get up? What
shall I do?"

Ulrika was well and full of health and happiness. She could
comfort an unhappy one, and now she told Inga-Lena to keep
up her spirits. Perhaps there were some remnants of the old
body left within her, and these she must give up. They were
sinful parts anyway, good to get rid of; it would be well for
her to vomit a little. She would feel cleaner and lighter and
happier afterwards. When not the slightest piece of the old
body was left in her, then Christ would feel much more at
home inside her.

Ulrika left Inga-Lena to view the devastation of the seasickness among the children of the world. Inga-Lena remained
in her bunk and cried—cried from sorrow that she had been

unable to withstand the seasickness and thereby please her
husband.

Soon Danjel could see with his own eyes what had happened to her. As he approached their bunk a few moments
later, the illness overpowered her and she had to make quick
use of the bucket.

"My dear wife!" he exclaimed in consternation.

"Yes, dear Danjel—"

"Was that why you put your food aside?"

"Yes, that's why, dear Danjel."

"You have gone to bed? Is your faith weak?"

"Dear, sweet husband, forgive me."

"Have you listened to the Enemy? Have you
doubted . . . ?"

But the reproach in Danjel Andreasson's voice was only a
mild, kind reproach.

Inga-Lena lay on her bunk and groped for her husband's
hand, crying in despair. She sobbed out: yes, it was true, she
had doubted.

Danjel bent his head as after a hard blow: in every unguarded moment the devil was near, trying to entice and
tempt and cheat a poor sinner, making him doubt that God
could help in trouble and tribulation.

His wife now admitted the whole truth: in her simple mind
she had sometimes wondered if it were really true that those
who adhered to Ake Svensson's teachings would escape seasickness on the American voyage. She had thought it sounded
a little strange, and she had not believed it a sin to wonder.
And today when she stood in the ship's cookhouse, and saw
the tremendous waves, and heard the storm carry on so that
their vessel jumped like a cork on the water, then she had become afraid. She had felt sick at her stomach. She was
standing at the stove, turning the slices of pork, when doubt
at its worst assailed her. Again she had wondered if it could
be true—that about the seasickness. She didn't know what to
believe any longer, she couldn't rely on not getting sick, for
she felt in her body that she was about to vomit. That was
why she had started to doubt.

Now Danjel understood that it was the devil who had come
to her when she was frying pork. But she had not at first recognized him.

"He is always difficult to recognize," said Danjel. "But

don't you rely on our God, Inga-Lena? Don't you think He has power to save you from the seasickness, if He wishes?"

Yes, that she believed fully. She had only wondered a little, in her simple mind, only a very little. She had not thought that this could make any difference—if she wondered and questioned, just a little. . . .

"But you must know that man should not wonder and question! Why didn't you close your ears to the soul-fiend?"

Danjel's voice grew more severe; but his sorrow was still deeper, and he gave his wife devout admonitions: she must never never let go of her hold to faith, she must always cling to it. A little carelessness, and she might fall and be lost; and she had been careless while she prepared the meal in the storm. But he could understand this.

Inga-Lena needed to vomit again, and her husband held the bucket for her.

When she was through she said, as if to excuse herself: "The sickness may have started because my bowels are so hard. I have not had an opening for several days."

"Isn't that a sinner's defense, Inga-Lena?"

"No, dear Danjel, I know I would feel better if I could cleanse my bowels."

"If it were God's will, you would have openings," answered her husband.

"Yes, that I believe, of course."

"But you do not rely on the Lord your God!"

She wanted to. But she wished, so much, that she had a quart of buttermilk to drink here on the ship. Buttermilk had always helped her when she had hard bowels on land. By drinking half a quart a day she could always keep her bowels in good order.

"Do not worry and think of worldly things now, my dear wife," admonished Danjel, and softly patted the hand of his seasick wife. "Now you must reconcile yourself with Jesus. Do as Ulrika does. She feels hale and well. She believes that the Lord helps His devoted ones on the sea. She holds on to her faith."

And Inga-Lena felt a deep repentance, and prayed her husband to forgive her for having wondered and questioned and doubted: she hadn't known any better. But when she got well again, and free of the seasickness, then she would never doubt again. She knew very well that Christ had calmed the storm and walked on the sea and turned water to wine when He lived here on earth. She knew He could save her from any ailment He chose.

Danjel Andreasson kneeled at his seasick wife's bunk and prayed to God that He might give her more strength to adhere to faith in her Saviour.

Meanwhile Inga-Lena's head was filled with anxiety: she must improve, she must be able to get up on her feet again. Who, otherwise, would prepare the food for her husband, who could neither boil nor fry? Who would look after his clothes, and keep them clean? He was so sloppy, and dirtied himself so, he wouldn't care if he finally went about in rags. If she were to lie here—who would feed her children? And the baby who was ill, with something in her chest: who would take care of her? The milk in Inga-Lena's breasts had gone dry here at sea and she had been forced to stop suckling little Eva; someone had to feed her now by chewing her food. Who would chew for the toothless child, if her mother lay here abed? And who would see to it that the other children were washed and combed and dressed in the mornings? Her husband couldn't handle children, he was too clumsy with them. And who would watch the children when they played on deck? They might run too close to the rail and fall into the depths of the sea. There was no one to look after the poor little ones. Her dear family required her health and strength; if she were sick day after day, her poor husband and their poor children would be helpless and lost.

And while Danjel prayed for stronger faith for his wife, she herself prayed for strength so that she could do her daily chores and help her loved ones—she prayed for strength to get up the following morning.

Danjel Andreasson:

His feet sought a hold on a fragile little ship—a few brittle planks tossed about like shavings by the storm on these terrifyingly high waves. But each plank he stepped toward seemed to escape his foot and sink away. Darkness reigned over the great water, and darkness ruled the depths. And he could hear the cries and complaints of his fellow men, when the claws of pain tore their stomachs and bowels and emptied from their insides all they had consumed for their bodily sustenance. And they were all afraid they might drown on this ship, in this storm at sea. The sinner's fear of death penetrated to his ears, the unconverted's anguish at the thought of the resurrection and the Day of Judgment, when the King should sit on His throne of glory and separate them, one from the other, as a shepherd separates the sheep from the goats, saying unto those He did not recognize: Depart from me, ye cursed, into the everlasting fire prepared for the devil and his wicked angels! Danjel looked for the Lord's angels, but saw no sign of them. No white wingfeather gleamed through the darkness; and he feared there was no angel at the rudder guiding the hand of the helmsman.

Fright was about to overtake him, the weakness which shortly before had seized his wife. He knew the danger of doubt was lurking for him too. Where are you, my God? Are you near by? But the fright came closer. Why need he ask? Why must he question? There was no need for him to ask; he must know, he, who believed. It was not allowed for man to question and doubt. He must not let himself be overtaken by questions and doubts; they must be suppressed. God was surely here on the ship. Danjel could seek Him out, he could go to Him and throw himself on His bosom.

And Danjel now fled in this late moment to his God—he opened his Bible, the Almighty led his hand to the ninety-third Psalm: "The floods have lifted up, O Lord, the floods have lifted up their voice; the floods lift up their waves. The Lord on high is mightier than the noise of many waters, yea, then the mighty waves of the sea."

From the words of the Bible, confidence was restored to his heart: ". . . *the Lord on high is mightier* . . ."

What harm will you do to me, you high, horrible billows out there? The Lord is greater than you. And you noisy, roaring wind, blowing at us tonight—I fear you not! The Lord is stronger than you! And what evil can you bring, you great, wide, dark sea, embracing our ship? The Lord is mightier than you!

God had shown His presence to Danjel Andreasson in the words of the Psalmist: they were not alone on the brig *Charlotta* in this terrible storm. God sailed with them. God was as close to Danjel here on the ocean as He was on dry land at home in Karragarde. They could walk as safely on this little rocking ship as they did in solid, timbered houses set on rock and earth-fast stones.

And while this knowledge filled his breast he hurried to tell suffering, frightened people in the bunks around him that God was here among them on the ship—they had brought God with them, He was sailing with them to North America. And the storm He had let loose was a storm of trial—He wanted to try their faith and their belief in Him.

As a comfort and help for his fellow passengers he read for them from the Gospel of St. Matthew: "And when He was entered into a ship, His disciples followed Him. And, behold, there arose a great tempest in the sea, insomuch that *the ship was covered with the waves*: but He was asleep. And His disciples came to Him, and awoke Him, saying, Lord, save us: we perish. And He saith unto them, Why are ye fearful, O ye of little faith? Then He arose, and rebuked the winds and the sea; and there was a great calm. But the men marveled, saying, What manner of man is this, that even the winds and the sea obey Him!"

The Bible reader's voice rose so as to be heard above the roar of the waves that broke against the ship. But the Gospel word could not penetrate the indifference of the seasick ones: they were too deeply involved in their own pain and discomfort. They heard the story of a tempest at sea once upon a time, a storm in the time of Christ, blown out and dead many hundreds of years ago. What had that storm to do with them? They were seafarers on another sea, in another time, on another ship. Another storm had arisen, but Christ had not boarded their ship to still this storm. He let them lie there in their suffering. Ye of little faith, He reproached them. But He lived no longer on earth, He did not now come to help them —how could He accuse them of little faith? And their sickness in itself protected them against fear: those very sick had neither great nor little faith, they were neither afraid nor brave: they lay there in their vomit, unable to believe or to doubt. They were in a sort of beyond—coiled up in their indifference, completely insensible.

Danjel Andreasson, who, for the sake of his belief, had been exiled from his home, could now hold his Bible explanations wherever he wanted—in houses or in the open, on land or at sea. No sheriff would close his mouth, no minister would accuse him of being possessed by the devil. So he explained the Bible story to his fellow passengers: Keep quiet and be calm, Christ had said to the sea. And the waves subsided and the sea became calm, as an obedient dog crouches on the floor at his master's command. All these horrible waves on the sea, all roaring waters and noisy winds, all could be compared to God's creatures, who were allowed to bark and low and roar and bellow, but would instantly keep silence at their Master's command. How then could a person who believed in the Saviour be frightened by a storm? Even in this little fragile, rocking ship, he could rest safely and sweetly in his Creator's hand. The whole world rested in that hand, like a bird in its nest.

In a bunk near Danjel lay Mans Jakob and his wife Fina-Kajsa, the old peasant couple from Oland, and they were suffering much from seasickness. They lay on a worn old mattress with the straws pricking them like spears. The husband was the sicker, he shook as in fever and did not answer when spoken to, but only moaned. In his delirium he talked of the grindstone he was taking to his son in America. He thought it had been broken and was now useless. The grindstone worried him even now, in his delirious seasick dreams. The old man's face was drenched with perspiration and lined with black runnels from the escaping snuff in his mouth, which Fina-Kajsa tried to dry off now and again with a piece of cloth. She was still clear in her mind, and waited on her husband, although she was weak and suffered much from seasickness.

Fina-Kajsa listened to Danjel's explanations about Jesus on the ship in the tempest, and now she wished to talk to him. They should never have attempted the voyage, she and her husband, old and ailing as they were. When people had walked safely on land for more than sixty years, they ought to remain there for the rest of their days. She herself had wanted to remain on their farm, but something had got into the old man—he wanted to go; and their son in North America had written them persuasively. Now no one could tell if there would be enough left of their lives to last them to America. Mans Jakob's condition was bad, hers was not much better. Hers was a worn-out rickety old body, she could feel she would soon lie there dead with her nose in the air and smell cadaver. What was the meaning of her going off to sea, old woman that she was, now to lie here and suffer? Was this God's will?

If she were to face God the next moment, she would not be

afraid: she could look God in the eyes, she had long ago confessed her sins to Him.

She listened for a while to the uneven breathing of her husband. A few words escaped him: "I wonder if the—grindstone—will hold together—all the way—"

In the old woman's unwashed face dirt had gathered like
seed corn in her wrinkles—from her sour eyes a yellow fluid
ran. She lifted her head from her pillow, and turned to Danjel, who was sitting near the bunk with his Bible on his knees.

She wondered about that sea in Palestine, the one he had
read of, the Galilean Sea on which the Saviour had sailed—it
couldn't be nearly as big as this sea, could it? Was it possible
that the billows on Gennesaret were as high as these? Perhaps
it was easy for Christ to perform a miracle on that sea, it
would be nothing to still the storm on such a little sea. She
wanted to know what Danjel thought: perhaps the waves on
this North Sea were too strong, too overpowering for Christ,
so that He would be unable to handle them. Otherwise she
couldn't understand why He hadn't stopped the storm—so
many had prayed to Him, it had been raging for hours. . . .

"God have mercy on you!" exclaimed Danjel in terror.
"Are you prepared to die? If you don't think God is almighty—"

"I am only wondering why He doesn't help us—when we
lie here and suffer so."

"He has let loose the tempest for the sake of the unbelievers, because of the doubting ones."

From Mans Jakob came a groan of anguish: "Fina-Kajsa."

"Yes, my little man?"

"Some water—"

Fina-Kajsa picked up the water jug and held it to her husband's mouth. She straightened the pillow under his tousled
head, removed her kerchief and dried off the perspiration and
snuff from his face—she had nothing but her headcloth
handy. The snuff had mixed with the sweat into a slimy mass,
her kerchief became wet and soiled, but she used it to dry her
own face as well, as she turned to the Bible explainer. "Those
who doubt?"

Danjel Andreasson was sitting close to the old people's
bunk, his Bible lay open on his knees, and he wanted to admonish the sick old woman who lay here suffering because of
her disbelief. But before he could get another word across his

lips the Bible fell from his knees onto the floor of the hold—
he let go of Holy Writ in order to grab the bunkboards with
both hands, and a swaying sensation of dizziness cut through
his whole body, from the top of his head to the heel of his
foot. Danjel was suddenly lifted into the sky, and the whole
hold rose with him.

What is happening to me, O Lord? The ship is losing her
grip on the water, and with all her sails like wings is taking
flight toward heaven! Dear Lord—is my hour near? Has it already arrived? Shall I, like Elijah, travel to Thee fully alive as
I sit here at this bunkside and explain Thy word to this old
woman? Dear Lord, is this ship the chariot Thou offerest me
for my ascension? Yes, Thou art lifting me on high, I feel it—
I am blessed—but I dropped Thy Word—Thy Bible. Forgive
me, O Lord. I flee to Thee—I come!

But the ship quickly sank down again, and with her Danjel,
and his soul and body. His heavenly flight led him back down
to earth, he was not to follow Elijah. And on the journey
downward he was suddenly seized with a cruel pain; at first it
seemed as if his intestines were being strangulated, then as if
they were all swelling up inside, as if they did not have sufficient space in their allotted place in his body. They were all
crying to get out, to force themselves out. They craved new
space, were relentlessly finding their way out.

He was at once overpowered: he fell, face down, on the
floor, vomiting violently.

The ship was again sailing on water—the earth journey was
resumed.

And next morning Danjel Andreasson lay in his bunk wri-
thing in the unrelenting embrace of seasickness. When his
agony left him for a moment, and his thoughts became clear,
doubt and prostration assailed him. Then he stammered again
and again, the same prayer. He prayed with trembling lips,
prayed God for forgiveness for the greatest of all transgressions, the greatest of sins. With the remnants of the night's
vomit still in his beard—like many-colored roses and red blossoms—he prayed his prayer of mercy: O Lord, Thou didst
push me down again, from Thy Heaven—O Lord, who can
endure Thy presence?

A seasick man prayed, and the prayer came from one
stricken by God.

The brig *Charlotta* sails through the great tempest which the Lord has let loose over the North Sea, in the path of the emigrants, this April of the year 1850. In the ship's hold, in her narrow stomach, lies her living cargo, closely packed human beings strangled by the sickness that is caused by a ship's swaying motions at sea—emitting all the sounds that witness the disease. The ship has only one stomach, but inside this one are many stomachs—healthy and sick, old and young, children's and old people's; stomachs belonging to converted and unconverted, sinners and repenters, good and evil. In all of them the pain digs deeply with her multitudinous talons—in all these wretched bodies are nausea and loathing.

The brig *Charlotta* sails through the storm with Indisposition as guest and passenger, with Wretchedness in her bowels.

XVIII

A BUSHEL OF EARTH FROM SWEDEN

1

Karl Oskar Nilsson was one of the passengers in the ship's hold who could best stand the sea. He felt as well here on the ocean as he did on firm land. As yet he had not missed a single meal. The food was supplied by the ship, and he liked to get his due; many of the seasick peasants lay and fretted because they couldn't swallow a bite, although they had paid for the fare, and no money was refunded.

During the storm most of the emigrants remained in their bunks, day and night, without consuming anything except the half gallon of water which was their portion. Of all the grownups from Ljuder Parish, only Karl Oskar and Ulrika of Vastergohl were able to be up and about. While Kristina remained in bed, the father alone looked after the children. They were well and lively and did not suffer from the sea. Karl Oskar prepared food for himself and the children up in the galley, as best he could over a fire that rocked like a cradle with the ship's rolling and pitching. He had to stand and hold the handles of pots and pans to be on the safe side; once when he left them unguarded for a moment he had to get down on his knees and gather the food from the galley deck.

He had long ago given up trying to make Kristina eat; she had asked him not to speak of food, as this made her still more uncomfortable. Butter and pork he was particularly forbidden to mention: one was as rancid as the other, and if she heard either referred to she was immediately seized by convulsions.

The storm was still raging on the morning of the third day, when Karl Oskar stood at Kristina's bunk and asked the usual question.

She tried to move her head enough to meet his eyes. How did she feel?

Did he have to ask? She didn't have enough strength to answer.

He held the tin cup to her mouth, water he had saved from his own portion. The ship's water had become old, it was murky, as if it had been taken from some swamp or peat bog —slimy, and full of sediment. It stank, and had the taste of old laundry tubs; all edibles on board now had an old taste— of chests, cupboards, and barrels. But the water could be somewhat refreshed by a few drops of vinegar, which the emigrants were accustomed to add before they used it.

Kristina drank, and some water ran down her chin and neck. Karl Oskar dried her with his handkerchief.

"The storm will soon be over."

But Kristina did not care about the storm—it could do what it pleased, die down or rage on. She had only one wish: to lie here, still, still.

When her indifference left her for a moment, her first concern was for her children. Harald crawled about in her bunk-pen and could not get outside its fence—she need not worry about him. But when she didn't see Johan and Lill-Marta, she wondered where they were. Sometimes they stood at the edge of her bunk and prayed and entreated her, pulled at her arms and clothing, persistently, stubbornly: "Mother, get up! Why don't you get up, Mother? You can't stay in bed any longer!"

And now she asked her husband, as she had asked him twenty times a day: "Are you able to find some food for the little ones?"

"They get enough to manage."

"I'm glad they are well—glad you are well."

Suddenly she broke off: "Karl Oskar—the bucket!"

The water she had just drunk came up, mixed with greenish slime.

"Do you want a spoon of The Prince's Drops?"

"No. I want nothing—nothing."

Neither Hoffman's nor The Prince's nor The Four Kinds of Drops seemed to relieve her. She had tried all the kinds that were obtainable from the medicine chest. And why should she take medicines, only to be tortured in throwing them up again?

Karl Oskar bent anxiously over Kristina: her face was green-white, pale and wan in the meager daylight down here. She could keep down neither food nor water, and these vomitings night and day were weakening her. Her pregnancy added to her discomfort. He had become seriously concerned about his wife—she could not stand this for very much longer.

The voyage across the sea to North America was more unhealthy and perilous than he himself had imagined. But no one could know in advance what a crossing would be like. Of one thing he was sure, however: since people so often became sick on the sea, they were meant to live on land. Only because God had created water between the continents were they forced to go on the sea at times. It would feel good with solid ground underfoot again.

"Is there nothing you wish, Kristina?"

"Ye-es, Karl Oskar—I would like to—I wish—"

She broke off again, and was silent. He never knew what she wished him to do. The fact was, she had suddenly felt dizzy when her swing almost touched the stable roof, and she had wanted to ask Karl Oskar to help her down from the swing.

2

The second mate unexpectedly came down to the family compartment in the hold. The bedridden emigrants gazed at him; some were even able to gather enough energy from this visit to emerge from their apathy and ask themselves: What errand could the mate have down here? Something must be out of order.

The mate carried a piece of canvas in his hands. What was the canvas to be used for? The emigrants wondered, yet they were fairly indifferent in their wonder. So much they understood, that something was out of order here in their quarters; but they had not the strength to guess what it might be. Something had happened, however, and they were soon to know. It could not be kept a secret.

The first death had occurred on board the ship.

A corpse was to be shrouded in the canvas. The young girl with the throat abscess had died. All the warm porridge which her parents had boiled and applied had been prepared in vain, all the salves from the medicine chest had been of no avail. The captain had been down to look at the girl's throat, and he had said the abscess ought to be lanced. But neither he nor anyone else had dared use the knife. In the end the boil broke, and a few minutes later the girl breathed her last.

It was said that the dead girl was seventeen years old, but she was small of growth, hardly bigger than a twelve-year-old. Now it turned out that the mate had brought a piece of canvas far too large; there was enough to wrap it twice around her body before she was carried away through the main hatch.

A dead person had been lying among the living down here. But now she was gone, and everything was in order again in the hold.

That day the northwest storm spent its force and began to die down. The waves sank and the surface of the sea became smoother; toward evening the weather was almost calm. The lull that came after a great upheaval on the little brig at first seemed strange to the passengers.

Karl Oskar had not mentioned the death in the compartment to Kristina; it had passed her by unnoticed. Now he said: "You'll soon get well when the weather is calm."

"I wonder."

But at the same moment she raised her head from the pillow, and her eyes opened wide. She listened. She could hear something going on on deck; the main hatch was open and she could hear singing from above. "Am I delirious, Karl Oskar, or—"

Did she dream or was she awake? Were they no longer on

board the ship? Had they landed? Was she in church, or in the churchyard? People were singing! If she still was alive, she could hear them singing a hymn.

"Yes—they are singing a psalm up there."

Kristina was listening to a funeral hymn. A funeral was taking place on the afterdeck.

Karl Oskar now told her: the girl with the abscess had died this morning. But it was not from seasickness; she had been ill when they sailed from Karlshamn, she had lain abed ever since she came on board.

Kristina lay silent and listened to the hymn from on deck. It could be heard only faintly down here. Presently she said: "I wonder—"

"What?"

"The dead. Are the dead ones sunk into the sea?"

"Yes. They can't have corpses lying about on the ship."

"I suppose not."

"They lower them. They have to."

"I suppose so. Then the dead sink to the bottom of the sea."

Kristina was lying and staring at the ship's timbers above her, but she saw nothing.

"On the bottom of the sea—one can rest in comfort. Don't you think so, Karl Oskar?"

"Don't think of that! You must only think about getting well."

Karl Oskar wet a rag and tried to remove a few spots from the bedcover. Kristina had always been cleanly and particular, and she must be far gone when she didn't mind her bridal quilt's being soiled with vomit. But she had hardly been interested in anything these last days.

In the bunks around them lay the sick ones, listening to the singing which came down to them through the open hatch. It seemed clearer now, they could distinguish the words—the hymn went slowly and somberly:

> "You wicked world, farewell!
> To heaven fares my soul,
> To reach her harbor goal. . . ."

There was one word Karl Oskar particularly noticed, and it seemed as if his wife had marked it too. She turned her face toward him. "I must tell you something: I'll never reach the harbor."

"Kristina!"

"No, Karl Oskar. I'll never put foot on American soil."

"Don't talk such nonsense! Seasickness is not fatal!"

"I have known it the whole time."

"Crazy notions!"

"Ever since I stepped on board the ship I've felt it: I'll never get away from here alive."

"You only imagine it!"

"No. My forebodings never fail."

"Forget it! Get it out of your mind! Kristina, dear—"

He took hold of her hand and patted it. Her hand lay limp and unresponsive in his.

She must know that the seasick always become depressed and downhearted and afraid they won't survive; but as soon as they near land they are perfectly well and full of life again.

"Do you remember, Karl Oskar? I was afraid before we—"

Yes, he remembered. He was sorry to say he did remember: she had been afraid and dubious—he had persuaded her to come. He remembered that he was responsible.

No more singing was heard from on deck. The funeral hymn had been sung to its end. The funeral up there was over, the *Charlotta*'s captain had once more fulfilled his duty as clergyman. There was one human body less on board. And from the bushel of earth which the ship brought from her homeland there were now three shovels less.

"Oh, yes, Kristina," Karl Oskar broke the silence. "We will reach land, you and I—we will reach the harbor in America."

She did not answer. She lay there as before, and looked upward with still eyes; every fiber of her body was still.

And Karl Oskar thought, perhaps he had been too persuasive; perhaps he shouldn't have tried so forcibly to convince her—perhaps he had assumed too great a responsibility.

3

A few days later, in the morning, the second death occurred in the family compartment: Mans Jakob, the old Oland peasant, was found dead in his bunk-pen.

The discovery was made by his wife, who would not believe that he was dead. When she awakened in the morning she shook her husband by the shoulder, as she always used to do. She shook him harder when he didn't respond—the old one wouldn't open his eyes. Finally Fina-Kajsa called Danjel Andreasson, who came to her help. He said that her husband was lying there dead, but Fina-Kajsa refused to believe it. She said he had lain like that many times before in the mornings, and she had had to shake him thoroughly before he awakened; it was caused by his heart, which stopped at times and didn't start as quickly as it ought. Moreover, Mans Jakob had during his whole life been a heavy sleeper—she knew, she had been married to him for more than forty years. Now she was convinced he would awaken if, together, they shook him sufficiently.

But all who looked at Mans Jakob agreed with Danjel: no one could shake life into that body again. Mans Jakob was not to be awakened until Doomsday.

No one could tell what had caused his death, but his fellow passengers guessed it must have been his heart which had missed some of its regular beats and stopped so long that it couldn't get started again. Karl Oskar thought he might have choked to death from his vomit; he had been found lying on his stomach with his face downward, and in this position it must have been difficult for him to get rid of his slime. Perhaps he hadn't got the attention he needed during the night, even though his wife was lying close to him. No one had heard him call for help, but a dying man might be too weak.

The second mate came down again. When the Finn appeared in the hold at unexpected times they now knew his errand. Something was wrong again. The piece of canvas he brought now was not too large; this time it must cover the body of a grown man.

The mate began to remove the dead man from his bunk, but Mans Jakob's wife attempted to stop him: "Wait a little! My man might still awaken!"

The Finn lifted the eyelids of Mans Jakob, and looked carefully into his eyes. "Your man is as dead as he can be. I know what dead people look like."

"Wait a little, be kind! Only an hour."

"You want him to lie here till he begins to stink?"

"Only a little while!"

But he did not heed the entreating old woman; he pulled the corpse from the bunk. Then she let out loud cries, at the same time grabbing hold of one leg of her dead husband, trying to keep the body by her in the bunk. Only after much trouble could the mate break her hold.

Danjel and Inga-Lena attended to Mans Jakob's widow while Karl Oskar helped the Finn with the corpse. After death the old peasant seemed even more black and dirty than he had been in life. The snuff runnels over his cheeks and chin seemed wider than ever. This was not attractive on a living person—it was still more disgusting on a dead one. Karl Oskar felt they should wash the corpse's face before placing the body in the canvas.

"He'll get clean in the sea," said the Finn.

"But that won't be till after the funeral," said Karl Oskar. He had heard from old people that one ought not to read the funeral service over an unwashed corpse. And Danjel was talking about people's responsibilities when they awoke on the Day of Resurrection; he agreed with Karl Oskar: as Christians, they owed the dead one this last service. His dirty old body had, after all, been the shell for a human soul, created by God. So, as there were no women to give them a hand, the two men helped each other, soaking old scrub rags in sea water, with which they washed the face of Mans Jakob. It was not a thorough cleaning, but at least they were able to remove the black streaks from the face before the corpse was enclosed in its shroud.

Then the mate laid a weight in the canvas, as was his custom. Karl Oskar thought they should have used Mans Jakob's grindstone, which was in the storeroom. This fine grindstone, which he had talked about constantly, which he was so much worried about, which he must get to America—what would happen to it now? Who in America would take care of this grindstone without an owner? Perhaps Mans Jakob would have liked to have the stone with him at the bottom of the sea; there he need not worry over its fate, there it could lie at his side, in safekeeping until the Day of Doom.

The new death in the hold caused some changes in the accommodations for a few passengers. Fina-Kajsa, who one morning had awakened as a widow, must now move to the other side of the sailcloth hanging, among the unmarried women. Two married men, Karl Oskar and another farmer,

who until now had slept with the unmarried men, were allowed to move in with their families and occupy the bunk
vacated by the old peasant couple.

From the bushel of earth from Sweden three shovelfuls
were taken again. And the deathbed of one became the sleeping place of another. Karl Oskar slept from now on in the
bunk vacated by Mans Jakob, who himself rested on the bottom of the sea, his face washed, cleaner than he had been in
many a day. And the young farmer remembered what he had
heard the very first day on board the brig *Charlotta*: "There's
more room in the hold the farther out we get."

XIX

AT HOME AND AWAY

1

> ". . . To the storm he said: Be calm!
> To the billow: Lay thee down!
> And the billow down she lay
> And the roaring storm he died away.
> The sun so glorious and dear
> Looks down upon the water clear.
> Our sails we hoist!
> Our Lord we praise,
> He heard our prayers' qualm!"

> (Morning hymn sung on the brig *Char-
> lotta*'s deck, chosen by homeowner
> Danjel Andreasson from Ljuder Par-
> ish, and sung when the great storm
> had abated.)

The weather improved, the air was warmer. They had clear
days when the sun remained long on deck. And for several
days the brig *Charlotta* of Karlshamn enjoyed an even stern
wind which gave her good speed.

When the sea had come to rest the disquiet and upheaval in

the passengers' intestines disappeared. When the weather grew calm, calmness also entered into the people. The seasick ones improved little by little; one after another, they returned to the deck. And in the galley, which had been practically deserted during the storm, the women thronged again with their cooking utensils, and the smell of boiling peas and rancid pork again spread over the deck and was diffused by the wind over the sea.

The course of the emigrant vessel was now southwest: the *Charlotta* was sailing into the English Channel.

The land people somewhat wonderingly beheld this water, which was not as they had thought it would be. The English Channel—a channel to them was a broad ditch, dug in order to drain low-lying ground—bogs and swamps. They had hoped they were to sail through a narrow trough; they had harbored a wish to sail a small water, where they had solid ground near on both sides, so they would feel safer than on the open sea. And now they discovered that the English Channel was no ditch. Its water was not moss-brown, its waves came and went as they did on the sea. They discovered that this channel was also a sea.

And they soon learned that this water was an important crossroad of the sea, used by many vessels. Every day they saw other ships—they met them, they were in their company, they passed them, they were overtaken by them; they saw vessels both smaller and bigger than their own, with people from foreign lands on board, vessels flying flags in all colors.

Then one morning they discovered land on the starboard side—a glittering white shore rose before them, like a high, steep bank. It was the coast of England, said the seamen. There were knolls and cliffs of chalk, shining white in the sun. Beyond the shore—farther inland—high towers and steeples rose up; those were forts, castles, and churches. And the emigrants stood there and looked over the bank into the foreign land; they beheld England, a land they sailed by, the soil of which they were never to tread on. This was the first foreign country they had seen so close—when they passed Denmark, land had been a long way off—and the vision was strange to them. But strangest of all was this white wall, this beautiful, high-chested shore which rose up in front of them. It looked like a tremendous whitewashed fireplace, a giant stove wall which the sea's surging waves had been unable to demolish.

They thought, this must be a strong kingdom, with such fortifications.

The white wall was to be their abiding memory of England.

In the Channel the ships thickened, masts from many
lands were gathered here; here was the meeting place of the
seafaring pines. Here rose masts much taller and thicker
than the two from Swedish ground which had been trans-
planted to the *Charlotta;* but perhaps these foreign masts
came from other trees than the family of evergreens.

After one day the white cliffs of England disappeared from
their view and sank slowly into the choppy sea astern. And
with this the emigrants said another farewell: this stretch of
shore was the last they were to see of the Old World. Many
days would pass before they saw land again. Now the *big* sea
opened its expanse to them, now there remained only the
ocean.

And when next they espied a shore, it would rise at the
prow, it would be the New World.

2

The emigrant ship met new storms and bad weather, but her
passengers were growing accustomed to them as something
inescapably belonging to their new existence.

In their early days on board they had willingly talked about
Sweden, and bitter, angry words passed, for the most part, as
they compared each other's lot at home. But as the days after
their departure increased, they spoke ill less often of the land
they had left. They had left it, once and for all, and that
seemed sufficient. Their homeland lay behind them and it was
already far away—already a foreign place. And it seemed
wrong to them to speak ill of someone or something that was
so far away, and couldn't hear them. Now they did not wish
to revile their homeland. They had their relatives there—indeed, the whole country seemed to them a relative. They had
left this relative—that was enough; they might never again
see what they had left; they had closed their accounts with
the kingdom that had borne them—there was no reproach.

But one day they met a ship flying a flag which they recognized: from the stern flew the flag of their homeland. The em-

igrants stared in amazement, and watched. The time they had
been at sea could be measured in weeks only, as yet, but they
had already experienced storm and suffered seasickness and
endured all the inconveniences of seafarers, and it seemed to
them that they had sailed for months. They felt they were immeasurably far out in the world: they had sailed over the unfathomable expanse of sea, their homes seemed to lie in a
faraway land behind them. And now, suddenly, that land was
close to them—they had encountered it out here on the
ocean. Over there, only a few hundred yards away from
them, must be people from the same sort of hamlets as their
own, people who spoke the same language they did. There
might even be someone on that ship whom they knew.

The eyes of the *Charlotta*'s passengers followed the vessel
with the known flag waving to them so near. Her course was
exactly opposite to their own; she sailed their own route back.
Those people sailed home; their own ship sailed away.

Home—they surprised themselves by still thinking of Sweden as their home. Yet none of them had a home left in the
land that they had turned their backs on. They had all deserted their old homes—to seek new ones. And yet—Sweden
was *home*. It was inexplicable, and they mused over it.

The brig *Charlotta* was loaded with seekers of new homes.
Her passengers were people who had left their old homes but
as yet had no new ones. The emigrants were a flock of homeless people, roaming the sea. This ship—forty paces long and
eight wide—was their refuge on earth.

They were the tramps of the ocean—the ocean was their
path, and this little brig was their lodging. And in the evenings before they crept into their bunks they looked out over
the sea which expanded round their shelter. The sea darkened
at night, and in the darkness rose the roaring, belligerent
wave crests, which became downhill and uphill, which became
the depths of the valleys and the heights of the mountains
around their ship. Then they felt the great depths under them
open up, and over them stole the shiver of insecurity: only
this fragile little ship, floating like a feather on the water, was
their home and protection. Now they must go to sleep in this
restless, tossed-about home—down in this ship they must
close their eyes. How dared they? How dared they go to sleep
down there, and entrust their lives and their belongings to the
brittle planks which surrounded them?

The emigrants no longer felt a bond with the earth, they had been thrown out to sea, pulled away from all footholds; they were lost in the world.

A home to these people of the earth meant a peaceful, stable place on the ground, an unmoving room, a house with sturdy walls and closed doors, with secure bolts and locks—a peaceful cottage on land where in the evening they could seek their beds in security and comfort.

Such a home they had left behind. And now they met a ship which sailed in the direction of this home. They stood and looked long after this home-going vessel. It shrank and grew smaller. Soon it was only a gray speck on the horizon. A home-going Swedish ship disappeared in the direction from which they had come.

The emigrants had met a ship sailing *home*. After this they understood and felt still more strongly that they were sailing *away*.

XX

STORIES ON THE AFTERDECK

1

Robert and Elin sat on the leeward side of the afterdeck, close together, their backs against a coil of rope. They were reading a textbook in English which Robert had bought in Karlshamn.

It was a pleasant afternoon on the *Charlotta*; she was sailing in a leisurely way with a moderate quartering wind. The emigrants sat in small groups on deck and whiled away the time; the May sun shone over the Atlantic Ocean, and a continuous penetrating odor of fried rancid pork exuded from the galley, as was its wont this time of day. And two young emigrants sat by themselves and read. *About tongue- and lip-position in the use of the English language.*

Robert's narrow textbook was hardly larger than the Little Catechism. It was designed for the average reader among the peasantry: *Guidance for Immigrants Who Wish to Gather Necessary Knowledge in the English Language in Order to*

Get Along. It was exactly what Robert wanted. He did not wish to become a linguist—at least not at once. And the bookseller in Karlshamn had said that it was written for simple folk. Simplicity and easy comprehension were emphasized, rather than a scholarly approach. But to Robert this *Guidance* was very difficult to understand: after several weeks at sea he had read only three of the simple and easy pages.

Today he began on the fourth page. Today he and Elin read together for the first time. Fortunately, Elin had no need of learning English, as the Holy Ghost was to visit her and all the Akians as soon as they landed in America; they would be able to speak the new language without difficulty at the moment of stepping ashore. But she was curious as she heard Robert use words from the foreign language. Even now she did not wish to seem less learned than he; she must participate. He also was of the opinion that it could hardly hurt her if she learned a little in advance about the difficult pronunciation. When she landed she would then have cleared away a little work for the Holy Ghost, and this could not be a sin.

English was a complicated and tricky language for unlearned people. The most difficult thing of all was that the words were spelled in two entirely different ways: first they were printed as words usually are, then the same words appeared in brackets, spelled entirely differently: "Yes, I am a stranger here. (aj am a strehndjer hihr.) What are you looking for? (hoat ahr joh loking far?) What do you wish? (hoat doh joh oisch?)"—Robert could not understand this arrangement; what use was there in writing and spelling the same word in two ways? It caused only unnecessary time and trouble. It was strange that the Americans, who were considered so clever, couldn't agree on one way of spelling their language. It could hardly have anything to do with the different classes, as all people were equally good in America and no one was above anyone else.

The youth and the girl started with "Conversational Exercises." They sat with their heads very close together, which they must do as they were reading the same book. And they read aloud about the position of the tongue and the lips in the correct use of English: "When English and American people speak, their tongues are usually pulled back in their mouths a great deal farther than is the case when we Swedes speak our mother tongue. The lips are moved less than in Swedish. They

are neither rounded nor pursed as much as with us, nor are
they opened as much. It is very important that no protruding
of the lips takes place, especially in making the difficult
ch-sound."

"Do you understand?" he asked.

"Yes, I do. Every word of it," she lied.

"Otherwise I'll show you."

And then he pursed his lips: this she must not do when she
spoke English.

"I don't make such an ugly mouth when I speak Swedish!"
she said.

"Say the ch-sound!" continued Robert. "Say 'church'!"

"Church," repeated the girl slowly and seriously.

But he thought she pouted her lips too much.

"Pull in your lips! Say it again!"

She repeated the word "church" a few times while his face
was close to hers so he might see the movements of her lips.
She wanted to protrude them too far, he thought. She said the
word half a score times, but he was still not quite satisfied. At
last she succeeded: exactly so must the word be pronounced!
He gave her other words with the ch-sound, he continued his
instructions with the aid of his fingers, and he thought this
was a good way to teach English.

While busy with his lesson he suddenly discovered that Elin
had a small and sensitive mouth, and that her lips were
downy and a little moist from the spray of the ocean.

And then he must teach the girl to keep her tongue far
back in her mouth while using the English language. The
Holy Ghost might not remember to tell her all the details.
Especially when she used the letters *d, e, l,* and *n,* she must
keep her tongue as far back as she could; those were the most
important letters, used perhaps every day in America.

In order to administer his instruction more efficiently, he
now wanted to see how her tongue was shaped. He asked her
to stick it out.

The girl obeyed, and the young man carefully scrutinized
her extended tongue, which had the light red color of early
wild strawberries, and was narrow and pointed like a cat's.
He thought she would be able to speak English with it if she
had the necessary practice. He let her sit there with her
tongue extended toward him so long that she finally became
tired and pulled it in. Wasn't he through with his inspection?

He told her that the learning of English required great patience; she must not tire from holding her tongue out such a short while; she might have to endure greater hardships before she knew the new language.

Elin had hardly pulled her little tongue into her mouth again before Ulrika of Vastergohl called: Elin must help her mother with the evening meal. The girl obeyed and left Robert at once. And he sat on alone, annoyed and hurt; no sooner was he with Elin than her mother found something urgent for her to do. Ulrika could easily have prepared the food alone and given her daughter an opportunity to learn English, now that she had such a good teacher.

Fredrik Mattsson, the so-called American, strolled by in his loud-checked jacket. Robert showed him the textbook and asked him to read a piece aloud in English. But the American waved him away: Not today! Some other time. He had read in English books for many years, while in America; he was tired of the English language. He was now taking his afternoon stroll to rest himself. Some other day he would read in the book.

Robert had asked him about North America many times—its government, soil conditions, and climate. But the American only answered that he was not allowed to divulge anything; he had promised the President of the United States not to say a word. The President had become one of his close friends while he was over there, they had caroused together, drunk and played cards through many nights, they were the best of friends. And the President had told him in confidence many of the republic's great secrets—with Fredrik's assurance of secrecy, of course. That was why he couldn't say anything, at least not before the President of America released him from this promise of secrecy. For he, Fredrik Mattsson, was an honest man who stood by his word.

But there were some things in the American's tales which made Robert suspicious.

Now Fredrik went over and sat down among some youths who were sunning themselves on deck, and Robert joined their company. The American told about his various occupations in the United States. For one emigrating there, it was most instructive.

The far-traveled gentleman crossed his legs, pulled out his pipe and filled it; then he looked to the prow, toward the west, as if he wanted to recall his memories of America from that direction, and began.

The second year he spent in America he had taken a position on a ship which sailed the great Mississippi River with a cargo of whores. This river was as broad as all of Sweden, and the whore ship followed the shores; he had charge of the cargo—the women on board. There were more than a hundred of them, and a great sense of method and orderliness was required of the supervisor. Night and day he walked the ship with two loaded pistols in his belt. It was his duty to prevent and shorten all fights on board—between the women themselves as well as between the women and their men customers. If he was unable to stop the participants in any other way he was to shoot them in the legs. He began at the ankles, and if this didn't help he continued higher and higher. But the women he was not allowed to shoot higher than a little below the groin: their calling must not be impaired. The men he could shoot all the way up to the head to subdue them. It was a very responsible position he had held on that river vessel.

The ship sailed from town to town, and they remained a few days in each place while the men came on board and business was conducted. These were the most peaceful days, for the women were not belligerent when they plied their trade.

His work was well paid; his salary included food, clothes, and two women a day—if he wished to use them. Some of the girls were young and beautiful, but others had been at their trade so long that he lost all interest in women when he looked at them. And he never felt really at home in this job on the whore ship on the Mississippi. For if you have to supervise and keep order among one hundred whores, you have little time for rest and serious thinking. There was commotion and noise all through the days and nights. At that time he hadn't enjoyed good health, either, because of a most annoying diarrhea from the hot climate. And he was a serious-minded person, who had need of rest and time to gather his thoughts. The only rest he had the whole week was on Sunday mornings between ten and twelve, when the ship's minister held services and preached to the employees; so as not to disturb their devotion, no one was allowed to fire a pistol then except in extreme necessity.

Otherwise he had had to use his guns almost constantly. He

could do nothing else when the whores bit, scratched, and kicked. They were even inclined to attack him—the job had some undesirable points.

When they had sailed up and down the river a few times he decided to leave his post and go ashore. The captain had given him a fine letter of recommendation—he had this in his sea chest still, if it hadn't been lost during his long voyages over the world. The captain had written of him that he was reliable, and had a sense of order, and a good hand with the whores both during their working hours and in between. He did, indeed, have the best kind of recommendation if he wished to continue in that line of work. But in the long run such occupation would never satisfy a person of his caliber.

The story came to an end. The younger men among those who sat on deck around the American ogled each other. They had not been near a woman since leaving home. In the close quarters in the hold even the married men could hardly get their satisfaction. They might play with their wives, some nights, so quietly that no one heard them. But all those without wives, without anyone to crawl near to, they must pine and suffer. And this description of a whole ship filled with willing women, always ready, tickled the young men's fancy and stimulated secret desires.

Several other men passengers now joined the crowd around the American; a ring of listeners formed, and all sat there, around the man in the checked coat, in inspired silence. The silence could only be interpreted as a wish that the storyteller continue. He looked questioningly at his listeners, as if wishing to know what they thought of his experiences in America. Then he continued.

The Americans had many almost unbelievable institutions. In the United States there were luxurious places where women could seek pleasure with men. There was such a one in the great city of Chicago—a male whorehouse where men attended to women, where the whoring was practiced upside-down, so to speak. It was the same business as on the Mississippi ship—only just the opposite.

One spring in the month of April he and a friend had arrived in Chicago in search of work. In a saloon they had met the manager of this male whorehouse, who was out looking for men. And as both the American and his friend were hard up, they had, after thinking it over, accepted positions; the pay was high, and—of course—they were a little curious about their duties: they had never before heard of a place where one was paid for that which one usually did because one felt like it. They had worked as lumberjacks the whole winter and they needed some change. In the logging cabins they had lived for many months among men only, and some of their fellow workers had completely lost their minds because they were denied women—for this could, in the end, affect the brain; when the seed never is sown it forces its way to the head, where it may cause ugly growths on the skull; a doctor has to open these growths to save a man from insanity. So they were willing to take on any women who came along, after this winter.

Disappointingly enough, they never knew what kind of women they had to take care of, for all who came to this male whorehouse wore masks over their faces. It was mostly women with strong desires, unable to find men in the customary way. There came fine, prominent wives whose wedded husbands were on long journeys and who might not have had any amusement in bed for years; others might have some defect which made them unattractive to men and left them without a chance. But most of them were women who had been widowed while their youthful blood still was warm; they had accustomed themselves so strongly to men that they couldn't get along singly. In this house men were always ready for them, and what the women sought there they always obtained; no one could gainsay this.

In the beginning it had felt strange to lie with masked women. It seemed always to be the same woman, it felt like being married and sticking to one's wife. Of course, there was a great deal of difference in other parts of the body, but he had soon forgotten that. He hadn't looked at the differences; there had been other things to do. At first it had been like a fresh clover field, but this did not last long. Soon it was only a chore which he was employed to perform; soon he didn't care how the women were shaped. At times it happened that a bold woman showed her face, but only a good-looking one would do that. Perhaps they had thought that a beautiful face would make it easier for him, help him in his work, as it were. And this line of reasoning was correct, he thought.

This much he understood, after taking care of a few hundred women: not all of them were beautiful princesses. But he couldn't choose, all must be attended to equally well. The whorehouse manager had issued strong rules about that, and no one was allowed to dodge. Some never got satisfied; they were angry and complained afterwards that they hadn't received their money's worth, not by a long shot. Well, fretful and troublesome women did exist in this world; one couldn't satisfy all.

But soon he and his friend had had enough of their job in the male whorehouse; they tired of it, both of them. They were fed rich and sustaining food in the place, they ate eggs and juicy lamb chops and fat ham and soup at every meal— this was only what the body required in such a job. But even sustaining food was not sufficient in the long run; they grew wan and lost weight and fell off. After a few months their faces were unrecognizable when they looked at themselves in the mirror. Their strength waned; the weakness first attacked their knees, which felt like straws—their legs bent under them when they tried to walk. They were wasting away completely. Their fellow workers who had been longer in the house than they were bare skeletons. They hobbled about the rooms, their bones rattling. No man could remain in the place over three months. Those who stayed longer had never recovered, they had lost their strength of youth for all time, they were ruined for life.

But he and his friend had quit in time—after six weeks' employment they had returned to the forest. In the last analysis he liked it better among the men in the logging cabin than among the women in the house of luxury. But there was a certain satisfaction in this work among the women: he had done good deeds, he had sacrificed himself in an unselfish way. However, neither he nor his friend had been willing to waste their health and strength utterly, not even for a good cause, a sacrifice on the altar of charity, as it were.

For a man has responsibilities toward himself too, concluded Fredrik.

Complete silence ensued in the gathering of menfolk after he had finished his story. The circle of listeners sat and gazed at him. Not one among them could find fitting words to utter, after the story of the male whorehouse in Chicago.

Suddenly a young man let out a roar of laughter. The others looked at him. The laugher stopped short, reddening from embarrassment. The American, too, looked at him with

disapproval, with deep scorn, as much as to say: Have you no
manners? The man who had laughed met this look of the
American, and said not a word, but it could be seen that he
felt deeply ashamed. And the teller of the tale wanted him to
feel ashamed.

Fredrik rose quickly, nodded, and strutted away.

2

That same day Robert discovered the secret about the American. He happened to mention him to the sailmaker. The old
man said that Fredrik Mattsson and he had been born in the
same parish—Asarum—in Blekinge. He had known Fredrik
since the time he lay in his swaddling clothes. The man had
always been a rascal and liar and a ravenous preyer on
women. He had managed badly for himself at home: at one
and the same time three women were pregnant by him, he
owed money to God and everybody, and he had a beating
coming from more than one. That was why he was sneaking
away to America on the *Charlotta.* But he had never been at
sea before he set foot on this ship; he had been a seaman on
land only. He had never been to America, he had not even
been outside his home parish, Asarum, until now.

Soon Robert discovered that he was practically the last one
on board to find out the truth about Fredrik Mattsson: the
passengers had called him the American just because he had
never been to America.

For a few days Robert felt disappointed in his friend with
the loud-checked coat, who had not wished to divulge his secrets about the United States of America. From now on he
could not believe what Fredrik told him; one must admit that
he did not stick to the truth.

But Robert knew this about himself, also: when he wanted
to relate something he had read or experienced, truth alone
did not always suffice. He might come to a place in the story,
unable to go further, and then he must invent something to be
able to continue. Later on he might return to the truth again.
And the strange thing with a lie was that it was always there,
inside one's head, ready to be used when need be. It was easy
and convenient to mix in a lie. Then, afterwards, when he had

finished his tale, truth and lie were so intermixed that it was impossible to differentiate—all was truth.

Perhaps this was the case with the American when he described all the various positions he had held in America. That he had never been to that country mattered little, after all. He believed he had been there, and therefore, in reality, he did not lie.

If God had meant people to use truth only, He need not have allowed untruth in the world. Perhaps He had created the lie because He knew people couldn't get along without it.

XXI

IT WAS CALLED SHIP-SICKNESS

1

As the weeks went by most of the emigrants accustomed themselves to the rolling of the ship.

Kristina recuperated from her seasickness; she was up and about and able to eat almost regularly. But she did not feel as well as she used to on land. A certain weakness remained in her limbs, and a weight, as it were, pressed down her whole body—she moved about sluggishly and unwillingly. Something pressed on her chest too, so that her breath became short. Other passengers—men and women—complained about the same feeling; perhaps it was some ailment caused by their long stay on board.

Kristina had also started worrying about her children: they grew pale and their eyes looked yellow. They were no longer lively in their play, and they had lost their appetites; they refused to eat the ship's fare because it was too salty—they complained and wanted fresh milk. And Kristina, too, missed more than anything the sweet milk they used to drink every day. But she understood—they could not bring milch cows with them on the sea. If only she had had a quart a day for her children! They had not tasted one drop of milk for a whole month. The sugar pouch was long ago emptied, her cakes were gone, the honey was eaten, the dried pieces of apple finished. When the children fell and hurt themselves and came to her, crying, or when they wanted to "step off" the ship, then it had been a blessing to have a lump of sugar or a cookie to comfort them with. Now she had nothing to give them when they came and begged.

The weaning of Harald had taken care of itself because her milk dried up after a short time at sea. She had hoped it would remain in her breasts, as she had no other milk for the child. He was otherwise fine for his sixteen months; he had entirely quit creeping about, and had begun to walk upright between the bunks in their crowded quarters. But a ship rolling on the waves, seldom still, was hardly a place for a child to learn to walk. Little Harald had to sit down on his rump many more times than had his brother and sisters at home on the firm floor of their house.

Johan and Lill-Marta were still babbling about "stepping off" the ship and going home. They had not forgotten what they used to eat and drink on land—they wanted to go back and eat cakes and drink milk.

Kristina promised them sweet milk and wheat cookies, as much as they could manage, as soon as they arrived in America. But she soon regretted this promise; now she was beset constantly by the children: When would they arrive in America? Tonight? Or tomorrow morning? They would arrive soon. How far away was soon? It wasn't far, if they were good and kept quiet, said the mother. If they kept quiet the whole day and didn't say one word, would they then reach America by tomorrow?

Lill-Marta was satisfied at times, and kept silent, but never Johan: "Shall we always live on the ship, Mother?"

"No, not after we get there."

"Shall we never live in a house any more?"

"We shall live in a house in America."

"Is it true, Mother?"

"It is true."

"I want to live in a house soon."

"So you shall, if you keep quiet."

"In a house like the one we slept in at home?"

"In such a one."

"Where is that house, Mother?"

"We shall see, when we arrive."

"Is it sure we are to live there?"

"It is sure. Father will build one. Now, keep quiet, boy, otherwise you'll always have to stay on this ship."

At times Kristina thought that maybe it wasn't right to silence the children with promises. What did she know about their new home in North America? Exactly as much as the children! What she knew for sure was that they owned not the smallest patch of ground over there, had not the smallest corner of their own, not the poorest earth but they could call home. Not the most humble shed awaited them, not the most wretched shelter could they move into. When Karl Oskar and she had set up housekeeping last time they had been able to begin in a well-established home where furniture and household gear awaited them. The second time they were to set up housekeeping they must do so in a foreign country, and they must begin from the very ground, with nothing. She dared not think of the settling that awaited them: they had not a single nail for their walls, not a board for flooring, not a shingle for their roof. When they landed in North America, nothing would be ready for them—no table set, no bed made. They had no bench to sit on, nothing on which to rest their heads. This was the only thing she knew. And as she understood it, they were to travel far away into the wilderness to seek their new home. There, she assumed, they must sit on one stone in the woods and eat from another (if they had any food), and they must sleep on a bolster of moss with spruce bows for a covering.

She did not wish to speak with Karl Oskar about this their second setting up of housekeeping; he would only be annoyed by it. He had promised her nothing. What could he promise? But she could think herself, she could imagine how it would be.

They were to begin from the very beginning—as people at home had begun thousands of years ago; they must live with the earth the way the very first tiller and his wife had done.

2

There had been nineteen children on board the brig *Charlotta* when she left Karlshamn. But two small canvas bundles had been lowered into the ocean from her deck: one one-year-old

boy had died with the whooping cough, one five-year-old girl
in ship's fever. The seventeen children, surviving now were
considered in good health.

Danjel's and Inga-Lena's last-born, little Eva, had been so
ill that everyone thought she was going to die. But God let
the parents keep their child, she had now gained strength and
was completely well. Danjel thought a miracle had taken
place, as their daughter had been suffering a much more severe illness than the two who had died.

But the girl was hardly well before the mother sickened.
When the seasickness had left Inga-Lena she was often seized
by a great dizziness and headache. While she was cooking or
attending to heavy chores she would have spells of fainting;
then she must go and lie down for a time. Early in the voyage
she had suffered from hard bowels—now things had changed
and she must run to the roundhouse on the foredeck at all
hours of the day and night. This went on week after week,
and no one could have loose bowels such a long time without
becoming exceedingly weak and worn out. Now there was
blood in her stool, too, and this worried her a great deal.

Inga-Lena did not like to complain, but now she confided
in Kristina: maybe she wasn't quite well. She had prayed God
particularly for help against the bloody stool, which frightened her, but she had as yet received no answer to her prayers. Perhaps she had caught the ship-sickness, or what did
Kristina think?

During the whole voyage Kristina had felt sorry for her
Uncle Danjel's wife: Inga-Lena never gave herself any rest,
but always waited on her husband and children, seeing to it
that they had their food regularly and that their clothes were
in order. Always she busied herself with something. Inga-
Lena was like a ship at sail on the sea, she was in motion
every moment. This must not go on, she had become gaunt,
worn to the bone. Sometimes she could scarcely walk, she
staggered as if every step were her last.

Kristina said that she should go to bed; Danjel must take
over her chores.

Inga-Lena looked confounded. "Danjel musn't know! He
musn't know that I am ailing."

"Why not?"

"He has enough troubles of his own, poor man!"

"But he is well."

"No-o." Inga-Lena lowered her voice: "He has sufferings of his own. He must make peace with God."

"Oh. But he could be useful all the same," said Kristina. "He doesn't need to pray every minute."

"He won't suffer worldly things. And now he must make all right for himself with the Lord."

And Inga-Lena spoke almost in a whisper: Kristina must not repeat it to anyone, but her husband had confessed to her that he had committed a great sin, the greatest one of all: he had fallen into the temptation of spiritual vanity by thinking himself free of sin, that he had once and for all been forgiven by Christ, that he could sin no more because he believed in the Saviour. He had held himself righteous, and felt above the law. But then one day God had undressed him, unto his naked soul, and shown him what it looked like; he had been dragged down in seasickness among sinners and the unredeemed. Since then he was much changed.

Danjel had said that he had received a severe box on the ear from the Lord because of his vanity and self-righteousness; now he walked about dazed from that box. He had reproached others because they were doubters; now he asked forgiveness from all of them. He had asked Inga-Lena's forgiveness although he had done nothing but good to her.

Her dear husband had previously held himself better than other sinners, now he considered himself lower. He had told Inga-Lena that there was only one righteous person on the whole ship, and that was Ulrika of Vastergohl. She had gone free of the vermin, and she had escaped seasickness. She was chosen. A hundred times was she guilty of whoredom—yet she was chosen by the Lord.

And for the sake of this one righteous person, for Ulrika's sake, said Danjel, the Lord had buoyed up their ship in the horrible tempest and saved them all from drowning; all of them had the Glad One to thank for their lives.

"That's a lie!" exclaimed Kristina excitedly. "I'll never believe it! That woman isn't a bit holier than the rest of us!"

"Don't repeat what I have said," begged Inga-Lena. "Say nothing to Danjel. And don't tell him I'm ailing. Please, promise me!"

Kristina found she must give this promise. But how much she would have liked to tell the truth to her uncle. Don't you realize your wife is killing herself here at sea? God can never have meant her to give up her health in order for you to escape worldly cares. Doesn't God, on the contrary, require a wedded huusband to be kind to his wife, and assist her when she is sick? And if you have your senses and your eyesight, you must understand that your wife is very ill!

But the strange thing was that she would have been unable to speak reproachfully to her Uncle Danjel. In the presence of this man with the kind eyes one could not use hard words. There was something in his look that calmed one's mind and created reverence. When he bent his knees and prayed, an illumination came over his face—even if he kneeled in vomit on the floor. He sometimes acted foolish, but all hesitated to make fun of him. Kristina could not understand why it was so difficult to reproach him. Perhaps he *was* nearer to God than other mortals—perhaps it was this she was aware of.

The fact remained, however, that his wife was killing herself, without his noticing it. Inga-Lena was like a domesticated animal that follows its master. According to the catechism a wife must be subject to her husband—but did God mean that she was *absolutely obliged and forced to follow him* when he dragged her out to sea?

Kristina was not sure of this.

3

Karl Oskar remained sound and healthy in his body, while at sea, but the prolonged stay in their narrow quarters was depressing to his mind. When he began life anew on another continent he would need an undaunted spirit, and now he was not as he used to be on land. He went about worrying over the future, and this he had never done before. Then, there was a certain something lacking physically: not once during their whole voyage had he been able to satisfy himself with his wife. This was due to bad luck. While Kristina still was well, he had had to sleep with the unmarried men; and when later he had moved to the other side of the sailcloth, she had been ill. As she still remained weak, he could not ask for her.

Ever since his marriage, his satisfaction with his wife had been a habit with him. When he could no longer follow this habit a restlessness and irritation crept into his body, his temper became uneven and his sleep was not restful. There was something missing, and his thoughts were drawn to it—to that missing something. When he could satisfy himself with Kristina he seldom thought of other women—they did not concern him. Now, during his continence, they aroused him so often that he felt annoyed and ashamed. But why must he feel ashamed over this? It was only as it should be: he missed what he couldn't get. It was only natural that a healthy man should enjoy a woman; the situation here on the ship was unnatural.

Nor did Karl Oskar have enough to do at sea. He had time to brood and to wonder. He went about and thought of that which he must be without. The times he and his wife had enjoyed themselves together came back easily to his mind, and this tortured him. It didn't happen to him by intention, he tried to shake off such thoughts; he had other things to think about, now, in the midst of the greatest move in his life. But there he went again, thinking of their bed-pleasure, and again he felt ashamed: what was the matter with him? He should be able to get along without it for a while. This must be something that happened often to many men. Why was it so painful to him? Was his lust stronger than other men's? Here he fought it now, it was his own particular ship-sickness. And he knew for sure—in the long run, he could not survive without a woman.

One night Karl Oskar dreamed that he went in to the unmarried women—to Ulrika of Vastergohl, and used her.

He awakened and felt ashamed of his dream; his thoughts had carried him as far as to the Glad One, the infamous whore, where more than a hundred men had been before! He had been asleep during the act, of course, but it still surprised and shocked him. Though a deed in his sleep, it was nevertheless a shameful one.

He wondered if, while awake, he ever would go in to Ulrika. If he must deny himself and go without long enough, perhaps he might. He wasn't quite sure. He *had* looked at her sometimes, and felt that something about her tempted him. Her body was unusually well preserved, and men were often aroused in her presence. But enough sense surely must remain in his head to keep him away from such a woman. And he began to agree with Kristina: as soon as they landed in America they must separate themselves from the Glad One. Kristina could never make friends with the old whore. If they remained in her company, sooner or later some misfortune was likely to happen.

There was no way of telling how soon he and his wife could live together again as a healthy, happy couple. Kristina complained of new ailments: her limbs and joints ached, she had pains in the small of her back. It was very strange that she, still so young, had joint- and limb-ache, like an old woman. At times she was seized by chills, she said they felt like ice-cold runnels of water over her whole body. This ailment could not be caused by the sea, because she had it both in stormy weather and when it was perfectly calm. She always felt cold—even when she sat on deck in the sun, chills would overtake her. She felt as if all the blood within her had cooled off and could warm her no more. And then there was the pressure in her chest, which interfered with her breathing, and the weakness and fatigue that never left her.

In all her life Kristina had never been sick in bed, except in childbed; but now she was sick.

Her illness was accompanied by "the great laziness," as the old people called it—one of the worst of vices. She did not wish to move, she did not wish to use her arms or legs, to walk or to stand; she didn't want to perform her duties and chores. It was a great effort for her to prepare a meal, it was an effort to undress herself and her children, every morning she had to force herself to arise and wash and dress. More and more of the chores she left for Karl Oskar. She began to feel wretched and useless on this voyage. So lazy she had never been before, so little she had never done in a day. It must be the sea that sucked strength from body and mind of land people.

Kristina had emptied two bottles of medicine which her husband had obtained for her from the captain's medicine chest. But she only felt weaker afterward.

"You bring a wretched wife with you to America, Karl Oskar," she said. "I'm afraid I'll only be a burden to you."

"You'll get well as soon as you are on land," he assured her. "It's just the rotten ship's fare you can't stand."

They received only old salted foods, tainted by the smells of kegs and wooden boxes, tasting of sour barrel bottoms and ancient tubs. They never obtained a drop of milk, never a fresh slice of bread, never a taste of newly churned butter, never a bite of unsalted meat; only food which had been stored away for a long time. Never were they able even to boil a pot of potatoes—potatoes, which more than any other food kept the body in order and gave it its daily and necessary opening. No, Karl Oskar wouldn't be surprised if every person on the ship were to get sick in the end from the fare they received. He, too, felt somewhat loose and limp in his limbs. And nearly everyone he spoke to complained of the same ailment as Kristina, only she was a little worse than the others. But none seemed to improve, they wouldn't until they landed and lived and ate as folk ought to live and eat. Life at sea was destructive and unsound for a human being; this, indeed, he had learned.

Within himself Karl Oskar added: This sea voyage he would never repeat; for the rest of his life he would live on land.

Kristina was convinced that a creeping, treacherous, dangerous disease had taken hold of her—though she kept her knowledge a secret from her husband. This time life itself within her was assailed—and the anxiety she had experienced the first day on the *Charlotta* came over her again: this is not seasickness, this illness attacks life itself. This time you cannot get well; but you were warned, you received a warning from God those last days at home: Do not go out to sea! Stay at home! You do not belong at sea! But you didn't obey, you left. And now you know. That's why you had the premonition, felt it the moment you came into the hold. It's like a grave down here, a musty, horrible grave. Something within you told you it would be *your* grave. One day they will come down with a piece of canvas for you; never, never will you get away from here with life—they will carry you out in a piece of canvas. . . .

Kristina might have heard the name of the sickness which she and several others suffered from down here: the *scurvy*. It was a repulsive name, it seemed like a name for something rotten, fallen apart, contaminated—something already dead.

The evil was also called ship-sickness.

XXII

STORY TOLD AT THE MAIN
HATCH

1

The passengers on the *Charlotta* were active people. Their lives had been passed in work; Sundays and weekdays they were accustomed to being occupied. Peasants and their wives always have something to do with their hands. On the ship which now carried them they encountered something new: idleness.

They cleaned their quarters in the hold daily, they prepared food three times a day in the galley, they mended their clothes, mattresses, bolsters, everything that broke, and the mothers attended to their children. But these chores were not sufficient to fill out their time at sea. Almost three-quarters of the day, most of them were inactive—left to themselves without a thing to do. And these toiling people had never learned what to do with spare time.

During their hours of inactivity the emigrants sat listlessly gazing out over the sea. What will we do now? And the endless water, the endless waves that carried their ship, gave them no answer to that question. There was nothing to do but sit and look across the sea. So the days passed, and the days became weeks and months during this long voyage.

The days seemed long and empty. Their lives on the brig *Charlotta* were monotonous. It had never occurred to them that time itself—life, which they had been given to live— would turn into something unpleasant to get rid of, something they must hasten when it passed too slowly. They were driven inward upon themseves, they were dissatisfied with their idleness; they could be alone but never idle. They began to seek each other's company.

When the weather at sea was pleasant they gathered around the main hatch. There they formed a thick cluster of bodies, standing, sitting, lying or half lying, occupying every inch of deck space. Wives might sit on their husbands' knees,

334

children nestled in mothers' or fathers' arms. Then they brought forth whatever might be left in their food baskets from home, and offered each other tidbits: one had a whole loaf of bread left, someone else had saved a smoked, dried quarter of lamb, a third had butter left in his tub, and a fourth proudly displayed a whole, uncut cheese. The bread, lamb, and cheese went the rounds; each one took his knife and carved himself a slice of each part of this trinity, then spread butter over the bread and ate. Sometimes it might happen that a gallon of brannvin was brought out, made in the still at home on the farm, from last year's crop in the barley field.

These were happy moments for the passengers on the *Charlotta*. They regained something of their old home in these gatherings.

Thus while the sea was smooth and the ship rolled moderately, the emigrants sat gathered around the main hatch and helped each other while away the time, so stubbornly slow in passing. Hymns were played on the *psalmodikkon*, and dance tunes on the violin; someone sang a song—well known at home—and someone told a true strange story.

The ocean was broad, the *Charlotta* had contrary winds, and so it was that many stories were told while the emigrants sat around on the deck. One day homeowner Jonas Petter Albrektsson related a strange and unusual happening which had taken place in his home parish in Sweden.

2

It had happened about a hundred years earlier, said Jonas Petter.

Dean Drysell, who for many years had been the pastor in Ljuder Parish, had a stroke in the sacristy one Sunday morning before the service, and died before they had time to carry him out of the church. He was nearly seventy years old, and had had two strokes before the last one. Drysell had been a conscientious, fearless pastor, good to the poor and suffering. He was particularly liked by the women in the parish. He had lived his whole life as a bachelor, but it was known far and wide that he had not led a chaste life. It was said that in his days of strength he had used his favor with women in a way which is forbidden in God's Sixth Commandment. Once in his younger days he had been reprimanded by the bishop, who had heard rumors that the young priest had visited a married woman in her bed. Later, when the bishop came to Ljuder and saw how beautiful the woman was, the minister had received absolution from his whoring-sin.

But now the Ljuder dean had left this earth, on a Sunday, in the midst of fulfilling his duties. The whole week passed—and the dead man was not yet buried! This caused great wonder in the parish, particularly as the death had happened during the dog days of the summer when maggots quickly get into meat, and a corpse soon exudes an evil stench. Eight days was a long time for a corpse to remain above ground at that time of year.

Eight days *more* passed, and Dean Drysell was still not buried! Through the whole parish people began to wonder, and ask what the trouble might be. Why wasn't their departed pastor buried within the usual reasonable time? Some complication must have arisen which was being kept secret. But what could hinder a servant of the Lord from going into the earth and receiving Christian burial?

Pastor Stenbeck from Langasjo, who temporarily held the dean's office, could have answered the question—but no one wished to ask him. On the other hand, many asked Magda, Drysell's maid, who had served her master faithfully for many years, ever since her youth, and who had been closer to him than anyone else. But when the funeral of her master was hinted at, her mouth closed so firmly that a chisel would have been needed to open it. All felt she must know the secret of the delay in the funeral.

Now there was one other person who knew the reason, and he was the carpenter in the church village who had made the coffin for the dead pastor. He had promised Pastor Stenbeck not to say anything, but in a moment of confidence had shared the secret with his wife, who promised to keep it to herself. The wife in her turn confided in two neighbor wives, with the same promise, and in this way the truth was spread over the whole parish within a few days.

For weeks and months nothing else was spoken of in Ljuder Parish than what had taken place with the corpse of Dean

Drysell—that inexplicable sign which after death had appeared on his body.

Magda, the old and faithful maid, had made the discovery in the mangle shed of the parsonage which was used as a corpse-house for the dean. She had gone out to wash her master's body, and had been filled with consternation at her discovery. She had washed the corpses of many men before, but such a sight she had never seen. Her master lay there dead and cold, but his body was ready for a man's action with a woman! Even with men in their best years, the power of that limb disappeared with the arrival of death; and Drysell had been an old man. At the sight of the sign the old woman became weak in her whole body. She was near fainting, and, unable to continue with the washing of the corpse, she left the mangle shed.

She went back the following day, but nothing had changed in the corpse. This time, however, she finished the washing, not mentioning to anyone what she had seen. She had served the dean faithfully while he lived, she wanted to remain equally faithful to him after his death. Nothing must be said that could tarnish his memory.

Magda returned to the corpse-house on the third day, but the amazing sign still remained in her master. That same day the carpenter came with the coffin, and now her discovery could not be kept secret any longer. The carpenter saw the same as she had seen, and he was as disturbed as she. And he agreed with the old maid that their parish pastor could not be buried in this horrible condition. The maid asked his advice: What should she do? The carpenter himself could do nothing; this was not a job for a man of his trade. Against the evil powers that were active here nothing could be done by carpenters' tools—neither hammer nor plane could be used. For he realized at once that the Evil One himself had taken up his abode in the dead corpse's limb—in the very limb with which most of men's sins are committed. By seizing this tool of sin the devil had taken possession of Dean Drysell's remains. Some spiritual man who had his power from God must step in here and save the dead one. The carpenter advised Magda to see the new pastor.

The maid went to Pastor Stenbeck and tried haltingly to explain the situation of her dead master. The minister followed her to the corpse-house. The body was now shrouded, but the faithful servant uncovered it sufficiently so that the pastor could see with his own eyes. He paled at what he saw. He told Magda to cover the corpse, and said: My colleague cannot be buried in this abominable condition. He said nothing more. He did not call by name the power which had seized Drysell, but Magda understood that the carpenter was right.

Dean Drysell's funeral was to take place on Friday—today was Tuesday.

Pastor Stenbeck was a clergyman with powers to exorcise Satan. He had once liberated a farmer in Langasjo, and another time the old wife of the captain in Grimsgol, who had been possessed by the devil for many years. Now he went back to the parsonage and put on his vestments. Armed with the Holy Writ and many pious church books, he returned to the corpse-house and locked the door behind him. He was always alone with Satan when he exorcised him.

The good parson remained in the mangle shed several hours. The following day he returned again: no change had taken place in the body of the dead dean. Pastor Stenbeck locked himself in the shed an hour on each of the two following days, and continued his efforts. But the sign of the devil's presence remained. Stenbeck had failed in his exorcism this time. The funeral must therefore be delayed—a funeral could not be performed with Satan holding on to the mortal remains of his brother in the ministry.

It was the month of sultry dog days, and the deceased dean had now stood above ground for a whole week. Strangely enough, no odor came from the corpse. It seemed as if the power which had taken up its abode in the dead one's limb preserved the body from decay.

Pastor Stenbeck was unable to defeat the old Enemy, he needed help. He saddled his horse and rode to his colleagues in Linneryd and Elmeboda. The ministers of these two parishes were both noted for extraordinary spiritual powers. Stenbeck described to them the calamity which had overtaken their old friend Drysell after his death. Wouldn't they return with him, and assist in forcing Satan to let go his prey?

The ministers in Linneryd and Elmeboda knew of their colleague's weakness for women—those creatures who are so often the ruination of a good man. And they understood that it was because of the dean's sins with women in his youth that the devil had taken possession of him now. They promised to help Pastor Stenbeck.

The following day three ministers in vestments and regalia met in the Ljuder parsonage at the bier of their deceased colleague. They prayed, they sang hymns, they made the sign of the cross, they performed the mass which is used in exorcising the devil. Three living priests prayed for a dead brother. They went on with their mass through half of the night.

The neighboring clergymen remained in Ljuder until the following day, when they went out to the corpse-house to view the results of the exorcism of yesterday. But nothing had changed. Satan still remained in the limb of the dead one, he still retained hold on his prey. By now Dean Drysell had remained above ground for eleven days.

The three ministers took counsel together in great consternation. What was to be done? Spiritual powers did not suffice here. They could not bury their brother and colleague—not commit him to the earth with the Enemy still in his body. Nor could the corpse remain unburied many more days. The secret of the delay had in some way leaked out, all people spoke about it, and this was not an edifying occurrence in a Christian community.

The clergymen spoke of traveling to the bishop in Vaxio, to ask his advice. The bishop was an experienced servant of God, thoroughly familiar with the devices of Satan.

Then old Magda approached Pastor Stenbeck, and asked leave to speak with him alone. She had a confession to make, a terrible secret to divulge. She told the following. When first she came to the employ of Pastor Drysell she had been seventeen. She had come to him a virgin, but after only a few weeks in service her master had enticed her into carnal connection. For a long time she had lived in sin with him. But at last she began to worry about it—she feared for her salvation. And she grew more and more averse to the master who had tempted her and led her astray. She began to hate her seducer. By this hate she had once been led into a cruel deed: she had prayed to God for revenge. She had prayed that her master might receive punishment—that after death he might be delivered to Satan.

Drysell had soon finished his satisfaction in her, and had then turned to another woman. But Magda had remained in

his service. She had had nothing more to complain about, he
was good to her. She remained year after year; at length she
became his faithful old servant; and now, when she no longer
lived in sin with him, her peace of mind had returned to her.

After many years she had even forgiven her master his
stealing of her maidenhead, and leading her to whoring-sin.
Not only had all hate been deleted from her mind, she had
become entirely devoted to the man who had led her astray.
She served him well, and looked after him in all ways. She
had come to depend on him, and he had depended on her.
They had both passed the age when men and women seek
each other for the sake of bodily lust, but they were in other
ways a help and comfort to each other. Magda had learned to
know her one-time seducer as a good man, generous, kind,
and helpful to the poor and destitute. And she had suffered
deeply from the memory that once in her youth she had
wanted to condemn this man to eternal suffering and deliverance to Satan. It had been a bloody sin.

And then one Sunday morning the Lord touched the
forehead of his servant: Drysell had a stroke in the sacristy
and died. And the moment had arrived when Magda made
her horrible discovery: the devil had indeed taken up abode in
her master's body. With her own eyes she had seen that the
Lord had answered the prayer she had uttered in her youth.

Many nights had already passed since her prayer was answered, yet not one wink of sleep had she enjoyed during a
single night. She had lain wakeful in agony; the master whom
she loved had through her instigation become the possession
of Satan.

This was old Magda's confession. And now she wished to
make her own attempt to liberate Dean Drysell. She intended
to remain through a whole night in the corpse-house, alone
with the dead one and the one who had taken possession of
him. How she was to save her master, she did not know, but
she wished to confess at his bier what she had done.

The pastor advised the maid eagerly: Go and do as you
say!

She went to the corpse-house that same evening, and people could see a light burning there throughout the night. What
she did to the seducer of her youth no one knew, but they all
guessed, and probably guessed aright: she protested to God
that she forgave Drysell the evil he had once done her; she as-

sured Him that she no longer hated her master but instead loved him and blessed his memory—she retracted her prayer of hate and substituted for it a prayer of love—she prayed for his soul.

And when Pastor Stenbeck came into the corpse-house the following morning, the body of his deceased colleague was the same as all dead men's bodies. Satan had at last let go his hold of Dean Drysell. What the three learned and experienced ministers, God's servants, had been incapable of doing, this simple, unlearned woman had performed. What three worthy parish pastors had been unable to effect, the poor maid had managed alone; her sincere love had conquered the sinister power in the corpse-house.

Two days later Dean Drysell was at last given Christian burial. All the people in the parish followed him to his resting place, and the joy was great that Satan finally had been driven from his limb. For he had been a good pastor; so said, in particular, the women of the parish, who now thronged about his grave in great numbers.

And this amazing happening, which had taken place a hundred years ago, was now told by an emigrant to emigrants, when, one day in fine weather, they gathered around the main hatch of the brig *Charlotta* as she sailed with her storytellers and her listeners to North America.

XXIII

PEASANTS AT SEA

1

The emigrants—the strayed ones in this world—brought with them a small book, *Almanac for the Year after the Saviour Christs Birth the 1850th*, which they consulted daily. In the empty space between the date and the sign of Taurus, Gemini, Cancer, they marked each passing day with a small cross. They wanted at least to know where they were in the calendar year, even though unable to fathom their whereabouts at sea. On the ship all days were the same, weekdays and holidays. The seamen performed their duties on Sundays and

weekdays alike. The emigrants would have become lost in
time, as they were in space, without the *Almanac*. The cross
marks on the days that had passed gave their lives consistency
and meaning. At home on land they had made these
crosses only when they took a cow to the bull, so as to
know when to expect the calf.

The *Almanac* also predicted the weather: Clear, Cloudy,
Occasional Clouds, Rain, Clear and Beautiful Days. Sometimes it was cloudy, or rained, on Clear and Beautiful Days,
and many times the sun shone from morning to night on
Rainy Days. It also sometimes happened that the weather and
the *Almanac* agreed.

The wind was mostly westerly; it was against them. And
the wind that hindered them, and delayed their landing, this
wind came from the land they were trying to reach. They did
not know how to interpret this.

                               2

The emigrants had now been at sea for five weeks. The year
had passed far into May—the month of flowers.

But now the people of the land lived on the sea, which
showed no signs of the seasons: from its depths no plants shot
forth to tell of spring or autumn, sowing or harvesting. The
sea had no verdure, did not blossom. When the cold north
wind swept down upon them, and the water turned as gray as
the skies themselves, then the sea was like old fields with rotting stubble, and then they might guess at winter. When the
sun shone and the sea lay there shimmering as blue and as
calm as the small tarns at home, then they could guess it was
summer. But the water did not divulge the seasons of the year
to the people of the land—not so they could be certain.

During the month of flowers, however, there were days
when a balmy air flowed over the deck; then they knew that
spring had come on land, and they eagerly inhaled this new
wind—perhaps (if it were not westerly) it had blown over
their fields and meadows at home. These peasants at sea, sailing from tilled fields in the one continent to an unbroken wilderness in the other, drew the air in through their nostrils,
wondering: How far advanced was the spring work at home?

Were the oats sown? Had the potato field been prepared as
yet? Had the sheep pens been cleaned? Did the fields reek of
dung after the showers? Were the cattle still in their stalls,
bellowing and longing, or had they been let loose in the pastures?

The emigrants came from land, and they were traveling to
land. To them, the sea was only a passage which they used, a
water which they must cross in order to reach land on the
other side—they could not understand the sea folk on board
who were traveling nowhere, who lived permanently on this
ship, who only voyaged back and forth across this sea. The
peasants traveled with a definite purpose in mind, the seamen
only traveled.

To the peasants the sea was the same everywhere: there
was no difference between the water in this ocean and the
water in the inland Baltic Sea. The expanse of sea which their
eyes beheld was no greater in one place than in another. And
what they saw today was the same as they saw yesterday.
Had they actually moved?

The wheels of a wagon never roll over the same stone
more than once on a journey. But here it seemed as if the
same wave lifted the ship on its shoulders day after day.
When they traveled on land they passed through varying landscapes—meadows and forests, hills and valleys, brooks and
lakes. But on the sea they were constantly surrounded by the
same water. They sat and gazed across a desert water-field
where nothing interfered with their vision: everything was
alike, everything the same. The sea was great and endless as
infinity, yet it was also small—it consisted of only *one* landscape, it was one region only. It was always the same landscape, it was the *sea*.

And this monotonous view aroused a longing within them:
they wanted to see a patch of green ground soon, if only a
tree or a bush—they would be satisfied with a juniper bush,
that weed of the forest; anything that grew green would gladden their hearts.

When, now, during "Clear and Beautiful Days," a balmy
wind blew into their nostrils, they recognized the spring. But
their eyes looked in vain for signs of the season. They sat on
the worn and splintery deck of a ship and the month of May
failed to bring them armfuls of blossoms. Round and about
rose the blue-green crests of the waves—the hills at home

would now be covered by the cuckoo's breeches, the butter-
cups, the rabbit-foot, the dog-ears, and the bumblebee-
blossoms. But the fragrance from these blossoms of spring
was not carried to them by the wind.

They were to lose this spring, for they were seekers of new
homes. They traveled away, and it was still difficult for them
to imagine that *away*, some time in the future, might mean
home. Yet they felt this must be so.

The passengers on the brig *Charlotta* looked out over an
empty, barren water-desert, as formidable and tiresome as the
one the children of Israel had passed through when they were
seeking the Promised Land. The emigrants were a sailing car-
avan: their ship was the rolling camel, carrying them across
this unyielding and empty desert known as the Atlantic
Ocean.

3

During some "Clear and Beautiful Days" the ship was enveloped in a thick fog which still further diminished the world of
the passengers.

The fog enwrapped the brig *Charlotta* like a thick gray
woolen shawl, so that the passengers' range of vision narrowed down to a few yards. Now they could see nothing outside the ship's world; no other world existed. The whole living
earth consisted of this old, worn deck. The outside world was
only something gray, penetrating, raw, fleeting, impenetrable
—it was fog. A sticky, soft wall had been built close to them.
They could not see the masts and the sails above them, the
wall moved in on deck, it crept into the ship. It increased
their irritation to the same degree as it narrowed their space.
The downy fog was soft and light, yet it weighed heavily on
their minds and caused them to become depressed and short
of temper. The world seemed ever more gray and more sad.
The emigrants were easily angered now, and quarreled about
inconsequentials. As the men talked among themselves all
gladness and friendly jesting disappeared, and in the galley the
women fought during the preparation of the meals, and used
pots and pans as weapons. The people could ill endure themselves, much less each other.

The gray soft wall enclosed them on all sides, enclosed the whole sea. They sailed through a wall hundreds of miles thick, and it seemed as if they sailed at random. Did their ship move at all? Might not the brig *Charlotta* lie still as an island on the water, tethered to the bottom with invisible chains? They could not see that she was arriving anywhere, she sailed, but sailed nowhere. Their ship lay here in the fog, swaddled in a woolen shawl which hid and wrapped up the whole earth.

And during these days of fog an anxiety began to spread from one to the other among the emigrants: hadn't they sailed astray?

They began to count: six weeks, seven weeks—soon their voyage was in the eighth week. The year had passed into the month of June. How great a distance was still left to America? They had oftentimes asked the seamen, and equally often they had received indecisive answers: almost halfway, about halfway, nearly halfway, a little over halfway. Now they were tired of this halfway, and wanted to pass it. They had been told it would require at the most eight weeks for the crossing to North America, and they ought soon to arrive. But week was still added to week, and the anxiety spread. No one could tell them how far they had sailed, or definitely tell them their location. Perhaps they were lost? Perhaps they had already passed the shores of America? Perhaps they would never arrive?

Could they rely on the captain who charted the course? Could they be sure he would find his way over this water without signs, where no marks were left by those who had sailed before? He might steer in one direction but the winds and currents of the sea drive the ship in another. He might sail by the sun in the daytime and the stars at night, but what could he do when neither sun nor stars were shining? Or when it was misty and foggy, as now? They were afraid that by this time not even the ship's commander knew where they were.

The patience of the passengers was almost at an end from the long sailing, and there were many things they would have liked to ask the captain. But the taciturn little man who was seen on deck only occasionally, spending most of his time in his cabin, encouraged no one to approach him. And there was talk of an answer which he had made to a bold and curious passenger who had asked the question which was in everyone's mind: When do we land in America? The captain had

answered: Which day do we arrive in the harbor of New
York? That he would willingly say, he was anxious to tell
them. Only, first he must have a little information—a little
information about the weather. He would like to know what
sort of weather they would have in the few weeks ahead, day
by day. Would it be cloudy or clear, calm or stormy, would
there be good wind or poor, rain or fog? Also, would they be
so kind as to tell him from which direction the wind would
blow in the near future, day after day? Would it blow from
the east or west, from the north or south? When they could
furnish him a little information about these things, then he
would immediately tell them on what date the brig *Charlotta*
would tie up at the pier in the harbor of New York.

It was a chagrined and disappointed interrogator who returned from the *Charlotta's* captain. After this, none was
willing to approach him again with the question. And Captain
Lorentz thought that he might perhaps have explained a little
about the continuous contrary wind. But why try to instruct
these ignorant peasants about the prevailing winds which in
these latitudes sweep the North Atlantic? He might as well try
to explain the compass to them. Of course, the emigrants
suffered, longing for land, but soon enough they would begin
their poking in their dunghills again, soon enough they would
dig themselves into their holes in the earth. What was their
hurry? He could well have forced his speed somewhat, but he
was afraid to strain the rigging further. The two full-tackled
masts of the *Charlotta* could develop a large spread of sails
that, in favorable wind, would give her great speed. The vessel was somewhat overrigged, however, and a moderate breeze
was therefore the wind her skipper liked best.

But had all the days of contrary winds been days of favorable winds, then the *Charlotta* would already have landed her
passengers in America.

The contrary winds had prolonged the emigrants' voyage so
that they had grown suspicious and wondered if they had
been misled as to the distance: it must be much farther to
North America than they had been told. They did not measure the distance in miles but in the lengthy days which they
had spent at sea. And it seemed to them as if they had traversed countless thousands of miles since that second week in
April when they had left their place of embarkation. Their

homeland was now incalculably remote—and remote, also, was the land where they were to seek their new homes.

The winds and the currents were against them. And the fog. The ocean constantly heaved new hindering waves into the path of the vessel, as if to force them to turn back. They grew bitter in their souls against the sea which delayed their arrival. And many thought: If I could only once more put my foot on firm land, then I would never again entrust myself to the sea.

4

But the sun was still in its place, and one morning it shone again. The west wind—the contrary wind—blew up again and swept over the sea like a giant broom tearing away the thick woolen shawl of the fog, which dissolved and disappeared, leaving behind a blue, cleanswept sea.

The embrace of the fog was loosened, indeed, but now they found themselves in the clutches of the contrary wind. The west wind—the American wind—continued to delay them on their voyage. It was like a greeting from the New World: Don't hurry! You have plenty of time! You'll arrive soon enough! Certain it was that the winds of the sea would not hasten their arrival in the New World.

They had now been sailing for two months. They had passed only a single ship—the one with the Swedish flag —since the English shore had disappeared and they had reached the open sea. During this whole time they had seen no human life beyond the rail of their own ship. It seemed to them as if they alone were traversing this ocean. All other people lived on land—they were vagabonds of the sea, the only human creatures on the ocean, forgotten by the world. And a foreboding burrowed into their souls: perhaps someone still missed them in the land they had left, but no one awaited them in the land ahead.

Then one day, on the afterdeck, it was seen that the brig *Charlotta* had a new passenger. Someone called aloud: Look, a bird! Then many shouted to each other: A bird!

Within a short moment the news had spread throughout the

ship: there was a bird on board! And the emigrants thronged
around this new fellow passenger and gaped at him.

It was a tiny bird, hardly bigger than a wagtail. Its head
and tail were blue-black, its wings and back were green, its
throat and breast white. The bird put up a long pointed beak
into the wind, and tripped along on a pair of legs as thin as
threads. When he ran about on deck his feet moved so
quickly that it seemed as if he used a single leg only, and
when he flew his wings fluttered like a yarn winder.

No one among the ship's passengers or crew recognized this
bird, no one knew the name of his kind. Some thought he was
a wader, because of his pointed beak and quick wingbeats.
Others guessed he was some breed of swallow, because his
neck and breast were like a swallow's. Others again maintained that the bird was only a fledgling: when he was grown
he might turn out to be a seagull, or a stork, or even a sea
eagle. But none among them knew much about birds.

His sudden appearance, however, seemed to the emigrants
a Bible miracle. They could scarcely remember when last they
had seen a bird. Early in the voyage a swarm of seagulls had
moved about the rigging of the ship, and daily perched on her
masts, but out here on the ocean even these flying companions had vanished. No wings fluttered now above the vessel,
and with the gulls, all living things seemed to have deserted
the emigrants' ship. But now came this small bird and made
himself at home on deck. He came to them a messenger from
land—it was a miracle.

How could the tiny flying creature find its way to their
lonely little ship? Birds lived on land—in trees or on the
ground, in the reeds along the shores, or in the mountain
crags. No bird could build his nest on the ocean waves. And it
was many hundreds of miles to the nearest land. How had
those delicate wings been able to carry the bird this great distance, through darkness and tempest, through rain and storm?
From where had the bird come? What was his errand?

It struck the emigrants at once that there was something
supernatural about the arrival of the bird; he was not one
bird among others. The long loneliness at sea was a fertile
breeding ground for thoughts of the supernatural and such
strange things as one spoke of in low tones around the hearth
in the evenings.

The eyes of the bird gleamed black and deep as riddles

which no one could solve. He made no sound, he never sang.
He was completely mute. And his silent beak was still another
riddle. They had heard about birds with cut-off tongues, birds
which could not sing; was he perhaps such a one?

The new passenger on board became the most cared for
among them. All wanted to feed him. The emigrants generously crumbled their bread and ship's biscuits. The bird was
treated to so much food that it would have sufficed to burst a
thousand stomachs like his. He had the privilege of eating his
sufficiency from the hands of human beings, and soon he became choosy, he didn't bother to pick up crumbs from the
deck. Unafraid, he wandered about among his feeders. When
a wave washed onto deck he fled away on his thread-thin legs
—he was so quick that a drop of water never wet his feet.
Now and then he went on a flying jaunt beyond the rail, as if
he wanted to inspect the sea a moment, but he always returned to deck. The brig *Charlotta* was his home.

A little bird had entered into the world of the people on
the emigrant ship, transforming their thoughts and dreams,
their very lives. He came with a message from the sprouting
ground, from the flowers, from the trees in the forest and the
seed in the fields. His wings were green as the newly opened
leaves of the birch, his neck was white as from cotton-grass in
the marshy bogs. The colors of his feathers came from the
earth and that which grew thereon. He came from that part
of the globe which God had destined to be home for men and
beasts, and because of this he belonged to them. In their loneliness and forsakenness at sea the emigrants were visited by
one of their own.

Many days had passed since they last stood on a firm and
steady spot. Now the bird reminded them that firm land still
existed.

Some among the emigrants had read fairy tales, and they
were convinced that this was an enchanted bird. How could
he have arrived here, so far out at sea, where no other flying
creatures lived, if it were not through magic? Perhaps it was
a princess walking here among them on a pair of bird legs.
Perhaps it was a king or a prince they fed with their hard
ship's biscuits. No one could know for sure. Perhaps the en-
chantment would end one day, so that he could lay off his
feather shroud and put on a golden mantle and a glittering
golden crown. Such things had been heard of, they happened

rather often. And even if the bird were not a royal person, he
was at least of great importance, maybe a duke or a count.
Because only people of high station were enchanted into
birds; ordinary, simple people became wolves and snakes and
similar beasts. Thus the little bird was held in superstitious
awe among certain of the passengers, and they felt some fear
in his presence. He might do them good, but he could also
bring them harm. Still, they wished to be friends with their
messenger from the earth, because deep within them they
could not help but feel that his arrival was meant as a blessing
to them.

The crew men, too, pointed out that the wind had been
with them ever since the day the bird first appeared on deck
—no one was more careful about his well-being than the seamen, no one took more care that harm should not come to
the little creature.

During the days the bird spent his time on deck; at night he
found protection behind the sail near the mainmast. The sailmaker had prepared a soft nest for him from sewn-together
pieces of wadmal. Each one did his bit to make the bird feel
at home on the ship, and every one of his movements was followed by someone's eyes—when he dodged the spray, when
he flew along the rail. To the peasants at sea he was a reminder of their mutual home. When they looked at him they
were cheered and remembered they were not to remain imprisoned on this ship forever. Another life existed. Tree
trunks existed, where birds built their nests, there were fields
covered with blossoms, there were forests where the wood-
cocks flew about in the spring evenings.

Never had a little creature brought so much joy to so many
mature human beings as this little bird did on the emigrant
ship *Charlotta* during a few days of her voyage to North
America. And everyone hoped and wished that the messenger
from land would remain with them for the rest of their crossing. But if he were—as many thought—an enchanted king or
prince, then he could not be held by anything. This they understood.

And one morning the bird was indeed gone. There was
much excitement on board—the whole ship was searched but
no sign was seen of the lost one, not a feather, not a dropping, nothing. The puzzling guest had left the ship as mysteri-

ously as he had arrived. If he had died his body would have been found; no, they knew he had deserted them.

Would he ever reach land? The emigrants did not worry about this. They felt that weather and wind and distance had no power over this bird. They were convinced now that he was no real bird.

He had flown away, and he never returned. For many days sorrow reigned on the ship. The people on board had lost a near relative, and they mourned him as one of their own. And they mused and wondered and asked: Why did he not wish to remain with them? Why did he not stay long enough to see the fulfillment of the miracle? He had been a messenger from land; what had he wished to tell them? This they would never know.

Old seamen who had sailed thirty or forty years were serious and said it was an evil omen that the little bird had left. It seemed they might be right: the day after his disappearance another storm broke.

And with the bird gone there was nothing on board to remind the peasants at sea of the green earth.

5

So the *Charlotta* of Karlshamn sailed on—a cargo ship loaded with sundries, an emigrant ship loaded with human beings. She sailed over the boundless Atlantic Ocean through all winds and weathers, through storm and fog, rain and sunshine. But for the most part the wind blew against her, bracing the ship's bow and rigging, hindering her progress. And to the impatient, earth-bound passengers it seemed as if the same billow lifted them up, again and again, the same eternal wave tossing them about.

The emigrants thought of the endless distance they must have traveled since they had left their place of embarkation. Their thoughts went back over the immense water they had sailed for a space of two months, and they were overawed by this sea without end which they were passing over. At home they had never fathomed the immensity of the sea.

And one conviction took still deeper root in their minds:

whatever was in store for them on the new continent, whatever awaited them in the new land they were seeking—a return voyage to their homeland was beyond conception. The
move they were now undertaking was to the end of time;
never could they sail this eternal distance back again, never
again would they cross this endless water.

Theirs was a voyage which people took only once.

XXIV

A LONG NIGHT

1

One night Karl Oskar was awakened by Johan. The child
stood at his bunk, pulling at his blanket.

"Father! Wake up!"

"What is it? What do you want?"

"Mother is bleeding!"

"What is Mother doing?"

"She is bleeding—I was to tell you."

Karl Oskar was not far from his wife's sleeping place, and
he was at her side in an instant. On the floor beside her bunk
stood a quart bottle with a piece of tallow candle in its neck.
He lit this, and in the flickering light could see Kristina's chin
and throat streaked with blood, her white nightshirt smeared
with blood. In her nostrils were stuck two cotton wads,
soaked through with blood and looking like a couple of dark-
red ripe cherries.

"My God, Kristina! What has happened?"

"I sent Johan—"

"Why didn't you call me before?"

"I thought it would stop."

Her lips were ash-white, her voice weak. She had been
about to go to sleep when the bleeding began. At first she had
thought she had caught cold, and had blown her nose. Then
she had seen that her kerchief was full of blood. She had been
lying like this for a long while, she didn't know how long, and
the blood was still flowing. She had lain still on her back with-

out a pillow, but it didn't stop. She had put cotton in her nostrils, but the blood ran right through. She didn't know what else might help.

"I'm so tired . . . I can't last this way."

The shining blood streaks on her thin neck made it look as if she had been stuck in the throat. Red cotton wads swam about in a pan by her bed like freshly drawn entrails. It seemed as if a slaughter had taken place in the bunk. Karl Oskar always suffered at seeing blood, and now he felt weak in his legs.

Kristina's eyes were large and glassy. The last few days she had been so weak she had stayed in bed all the time, eating hardly a bite. She did not have the resistance she needed when the hemorrhage began. She lay there stretched out like a dead body, her gray-white complexion the color of a corpse's. Karl Oskar understood what was taking place here: life was running away from his wife.

The number of passengers had decreased by three during this last week. All three were grown people, and all had died in this ship-sickness. It was actually growing roomy in the hold. Inga-Lena too had been very ill, but would not admit it, not wishing to disturb Danjel. And yesterday it was said that she had begun to mend. Tonight no sound was heard from the pen where the Karragarde people stayed—they were sleeping peacefully.

"Are you in pain?" asked Karl Oskar of his wife.

"No. No pain. I'm only tired—so tired."

"It's because of the blood you've lost. We must stop the bleeding."

Kristina moved her head slowly to look at Johan, who was sitting at the foot of her bunk. The red runnels from her nostrils increased from this little movement.

"Lie quiet—please. Still!"

A weak whisper came like a gentle stir of air from her mouth: "If it doesn't slow down I suppose I'll die."

"It must slow down."

"But if there is no help?"

"There must be help somewhere."

Johan listened attentively to his parents and gazed at them with large eyes. He was not old enough to understand everything, but he had a child's intuition. He began to cry: "I don't want Mother to bleed any more. I don't want her to."

"Keep quiet, boy!" said the father. "Lie down and go to sleep!"

Lill-Marta and Harald were sleeping peacefully on the inside of the bunk against the hull. Outside the sea wailed, the waves broke and crashed against the ship. There had been a storm again during the day, and tonight it blew harder than before. A child cried in its sleep, somewhere in its pen. A woman snored noisily. Between the woman's snorings the rolling masses of water could be heard breaking against the side of the ship.

The ship rolled heavily. Kristina lay there and rolled on her bunk, they all rolled—the sick and the healthy.

Someone shouted angrily because a light was lit: could one never sleep in peace? But Karl Oskar was oblivious to sounds, he heard neither the sea outside nor the people around him. He stood bent over his bleeding wife: this flow of blood could not go on for very long. If it didn't stop she would die; if it weren't stopped very soon, he would be a widower before the night was over.

He stood at the side of his fellow worker, his bedmate, his children's mother, and life was ebbing away from her—from her who was the most indispensable human being in the world. Was God going to take her from him—as He took Anna? What must he do? Must he stand by, completely at a loss, wretched and helpless? He must do something. One must always do what one could, use one's senses to the best of one's ability, never believe matters were hopeless. He had never given up, and he could not give up now when Kristina's life was at stake.

At home in the parish there had been many bloodstanchers; here on the ship he knew of none. But perhaps there was one human being here who could help.

"I'm going to call the captain."

"We dare not—" Kristina's voice was hardly audible. "It's the middle of the night."

"The captain must help us. He cannot refuse!"

Their captain had charge of the medicine chest on board, and was supposed to take a doctor's place. He was austere and brusque and the passengers were afraid of him; the seamen too held him in awe. He had never shown feelings or compassion for the sick or dying in the hold. The sick obtained medicines from his chest until they recuperated or died, and when they died he officiated at their funerals and lowered the corpses into the sea. The emigrants thought he was a hard, unfeeling person. But Karl Oskar decided to seek him out. He could not deny help when one of his passengers was in the throes of death.

"Don't go, Karl Oskar," entreated Kristina. "It's no use."

Yes, he knew that Kristina thought it preordained that she was to die here on the ship, that she was never to reach America. But he did not agree. His thought was always that nothing was so definite as to be unchangeable. If one tries, perhaps one can change things. One is forced to try.

"I'll be back at once."

Karl Oskar rushed away. After some trouble he was able to open the hatch, and reached deck, feeling his way in the darkness. The weather was rough tonight. Heavy waves washed over and broke against the deck. He immediately became drenched to his waist. But he hardly noticed it. He must get to the afterdeck. He skidded and fell on the slippery deck planks, he rose and fell again. Tonight the whole ship was in danger, but he did not care: the ship might go down, anything might happen, but they must stanch Kristina's blood.

He held on to ropes and lines and found his way to the hatch on the afterdeck through which a ladder led down to the captain's cabin.

He knocked heavily on the door. Only at his third knocking could he hear a powerful, penetrating voice: "What in hell do you want?"

Karl Oskar opened the door and stepped inside. Captain Lorentz had been asleep, and was now sitting upright in his bunk. He had been sleeping with his trousers on. His gray hair was tousled and stood straight out over his forehead like the horns of a ram. If any man ever looked ready to gore, it was the *Charlotta*'s captain at this moment.

"My wife is bleeding to death. I wanted to ask you to do something for it, Mr. Captain."

Captain Lorentz had thought that some one of the crew was calling him for urgent reasons of duty—for other reasons no one on the ship would dare to disturb him—but nevertheless he had given out an angry grunt. When he now discovered that the trespasser in his cabin in the middle of the night was one of the passengers, his astonishment was so great that he could only glare at the intruder.

"She's bleeding. We can't stanch it—I'm afraid she's giving out!"

The captain yawned, opening his ugly pike-mouth. He needed his sleep more than any other person on the ship. This God-damned weather—because of this weather he had been forced to stay awake more than anyone on board these last days. The damned peasants could take a snooze whenever they pleased, they were not responsible for anything on board. He ought to tell this big-nosed farmer to go to hell. He thought he would—but he didn't.

The man stood there and repeated that his wife was dying. To this the captain couldn't answer that he himself was sleeping. Lost sleep a person might regain, but once he had lost his life it was not easy to get it back.

Lorentz had recognized Karl Oskar by his big nose: the Finn had spoken of him, he was supposed to be one of the more smart-aleck peasants. Hadn't the mate been forced to tell him off?

Yet he might need help if his wife were lying at death's door. She couldn't be too old, the man himself was rather young.

"Has your wife been bleeding long?"

Karl Oskar gave a description of what had happened, and the captain listened.

"Hm, from the scurvy, no doubt. I recognize it."

"You see, she is with child also."

"Hm, that too. Well, it doesn't sound good."

The captain stepped down from his bunk. Then he pulled on boots and a slicker. Karl Oskar followed his movements with a grateful look.

"We'll see if we can't stanch the blood."

Lorentz searched for his *Medical Adviser for Seafarers*. He found it among the papers on his table and opened it:

"Bleeding from mouth or nose can in some cases be so strong and last so long that it becomes dangerous.

"Treatment: If the bleeding becomes strong enough to weaken the sick person, one may attempt to stanch the blood flow by bringing the patient out into fresh and cool air, then make packs from sea water and place over forehead, nose, back of the neck, and if this does not help, also around the sexual organs. In very severe cases

one may bind a towel around each of the four limbs,
above the elbows and the knees, so as to stop the blood
in these parts.

"If there is suspicion of scurvy . . ."

It had been a long time since the *Charlotta*'s captain had
last stanched blood—he had had to refreshen his knowledge.
From a chest he pulled out some clean rough linen towels
which he threw over his arm. Then he lit a small hand lantern
and followed the young farmer up the ladder.

While crossing the deck Karl Oskar nearly fell down twice
as the *Charlotta* dove into the waves; both times the captain
grabbed hold of his shoulder and steadied him. "Hell of a
choppy sea tonight."

The captain himself followed the movements of the ship as
if his feet had been nailed down with seven-inch spikes to the
planks of the deck.

Kristina lay with closed eyes as they approached her bunk.

"Here comes the captain—"

Slowly she opened her eyes.

Captain Lorentz took one look at her face, then at the pan
with the blood, and he thought to himself: This has gone too
far; anyone who has lost such a pool of blood must also lose
life. This woman had suffered from scurvy for a long time,
that he could see.

And now the end was near. He felt sorry for the bleeding
woman; she was still in her youth, no doubt she had been
good-looking in her healthy days. Her husband would need
her to get along in North America. And a pity about the
three brats, too, lying there curled up together in the family
pen; the lot of the motherless was doubly hard in life. And
this woman was supposed to have another child inside her—
they were regular rabbits, these peasants, dropping offspring
like that. This whole emigration to North America was
caused by crowded conditions, the result of constant spawning
and multiplying in their cottages and bed-pens.

How much better it would have been for this poor young
couple had they not attempted to cross the ocean. Then the
wife's young life might have been spared, the youthful husband would not have needed to become a widower, the three
children motherless.

The captain looked from the wife to the husband: poor devil!

To Karl Oskar the face of the captain was as hard as if carved from a piece of wood. He thought: that man can never have any sympathy for other creatures.

"We will try to stanch."

Lorentz was, after all, going to do what he could. He sent Karl Oskar after a bucket of fresh sea water, soaked his towels, and laid them as cold packs around the head of the sick woman. He had still a few towels left which he did not soak; he tied these around Kristina's limbs, near elbows and knees. He tied the knots as hard as he could; she groaned faintly, and he knew it hurt, but they must be tight if what blood was still left in these limbs was to remain.

When a patient bled so profusely a cold pack should be laid around the sexual organs as well. But Lorentz omitted this: the women of the peasantry had a deep-rooted shame for that part of the body, and Kristina might have become frightened and tried to defend herself if he had as much as uncovered her stomach. When he touched her body her eyes opened wide and full of fear, as if he were trying to kill her. He was sure that no man other than her husband had ever laid hands on or come near this young farm woman.

What he could do here was soon done—no doctor in the world could do more. Before he left he gave Karl Oskar his instructions: Kristina must remain absolutely still in this position on her back, and the wet towels about her head must be changed every hour so as to keep them cool.

It sounded brusque and final, it was an order from the commander of the ship. Karl Oskar would have liked to know how to manage in keeping his wife's body still in the bunk with the heavy rolling of the seas.

Captain Lorentz returned to his cabin. Now there would be no more sleep for him tonight. If this storm kept on increasing they must reef down to the very rigging. A skipper could never take his rest when he needed it, only when he could get it. But first he must sit for a moment and squeeze his girl on the ale-stoup, his most pleasant occupation while resting. Her muscles were hard, hard as stone, and she did not warm the hands of a man, but she was always there, always to be relied on. The girls with the soft flesh, the fickle ones, had belonged to his younger years; the girl on the stoup was a woman for a seaman's old age.

The young peasant and his dying wife lingered yet for a moment in the mind of the *Charlotta*'s captain. He wondered if the loss would break the man. But most of these greedy, earth-hungry peasants hardly cared about the human being in their wives: when they mourned them they mourned mostly their loss of labor. And the farmer with the big nose would soon find comfort and another female beast of burden in America. He seemed a capable man, and capable men went without women less than others. It was the men with strong natures who did most of the things in this world. What a pity this fellow was a peasant—had he been born near the coast, instead of inland, he would no doubt have made a very able seaman.

Now they were nearing the end of their voyage—the seventh for the *Charlotta* as emigrant ship. It had been a pleasant voyage with moderate storms. The mortality on board had also been moderate: seven deaths among seventy-eight passengers; there had been more among fewer on other crossings. Apparently the eighth death was to take place; for the eighth time this voyage he must fulfill the duties of minister.

It was indeed true—people were the most unhealthy cargo a vessel possibly could carry: ". . . a great deal of attention was then required from the captain . . ." Who knew this better than the captain on the brig *Charlotta?*

Happy those captains who carried other cargo across the seas! They might sometimes get a wink of sleep, even on a stormy night.

2

Karl Oskar had changed the cold pack once; but the bleeding from Kristina's nose was continuing as before.

Johan had at last gone to sleep. He lay across the bunk, over his mother's legs. Lill-Marta was dreaming and talking in her sleep about a cake which someone wanted to take away from her. From the neighboring bunks came groans and puffs. The woman who had already snored for hours snored still louder. And outside, against the side of the ship, the Atlantic Ocean heaved as it had heaved during all tempests since the day of creation. Kristina lay there and rocked on her bunk, as she had rocked many nights and days. The ship rolled, and Karl Oskar grabbed hold of the bunk planks now and then so as not to fall off the stool on which he was sitting.

Now and again he lit his piece of taper and looked at his wife. She lay mostly with her eyes closed, but at times they would open and then he tried to gain her recognition. But she was away from her eyes, he could not find her there. He sat by her but she was not with him. Another woman snored. Some people snored, while others lay at death's door. And from the pen of the Karragarde people an even, monotonous mumble was occasionally heard. It was prayer; Danjel was praying. He must, then, be awake now. Inga-Lena lay very sick, but she denied her illness and insisted she was well—who could fathom these Akians?

Another hour passed. When Karl Oskar again changed the cold pack, he thought he could notice that the flow of blood had stopped a little.

The watch was changing on deck, it was four o'clock, the dogwatch was over, the early-morning watch was going on. Karl Oskar continued his vigil, he was watching over Kristina, he had stood all the watches this night.

A heavy thunder was heard from above—a sound of splintering timbers, as if a wave had broken something on deck. Kristina awakened and opened her eyes. Karl Oskar looked into them and found his wife: she was awake and clear in her mind. From her mouth came a weak breath—he bent down to hear what she was saying: "Karl Oskar—"

"Yes?"

"I only wanted to ask—be kind to the children."

"Of course I will."

"You'll look after the little ones, won't you?"

"You may be sure of it."

"That's good to hear. You'll have to be father and mother, both."

"Don't think of that now, Kristina."

"No. We shan't mention it again."

"Is there anything you wish?"

"No. Not a thing."

From the pocket of his jacket Karl Oskar took out a few lumps of sugar, wrapped in a piece of old paper—they were from home, he had saved them a long time.

"Will you have a piece of sugar in your mouth?"

"No."

The sugar lumps had been in his pocket for weeks. They were no longer white; he blew off the dust to clean them. "I've saved these for you."

"You are kind, Karl Oskar—but—I can't chew."

"Isn't there anything I can give you?"

"No."

He took a firm hold of Kristina's hand on the quilt; it felt even colder than the sea water which had cooled her head.

Now it came over him, that which he always tried to evade, that which he never wished to feel or admit: he had persuaded her to follow him, he had taken wife and children with him on this voyage across the sea; he it was who had forced their emigration—someone had had to take the responsibility; I shall take it! That was what he had said—and now was the day of reckoning, now he must shoulder the responsibility. If he had known what it would be like—if he had known—if he had known the price. Now it came over him, overpoweringly it rushed forth. *Regret.*

Karl Oskar regretted what he had done.

"Kristina!"

"Ye-es."

"I want to ask you—ask your forgiveness."

"What must I forgive?"

"That I wanted to go—"

"I too wanted it."

"But I forced my will through."

"You didn't mean anything wrong with it."

"You know what I meant, Kristina."

"You wanted to improve things for us—for all of us."

"Yes. One might mean well—yet spoil it all—spoil it for all of us—"

"Don't regret it, Karl Oskar. You can't help it."

"I'm to blame most."

"You have only struggled for us. You mustn't be sad."

"You will forgive me, Kristina?"

"I have nothing to forgive you. Remember I said so."

"That is good to hear."

"I like you, Karl Oskar, always have. We are the best of friends."

"Yes. The best of friends—that's what we are!"

Thus Karl Oskar and Kristina spoke to each other as those people do who may have no more chance to speak to each other in this world.

Kristina was in her swing again. She closed her weak eyes. "I wish to sleep a little longer."

"Sleep! You need it."

"Only a short while."

"Of course you will sleep—only you must not—not—not—"

His tongue froze in his throat, he could utter no more words, he was unable to finish: *only you must not die and leave me!*

"I wish to rest now, quietly," it came from his wife. "I'm so tired."

"Yes, rest now. I'll change the packing."

"Let me down now!" she said. "Let me down from the swing, Karl Oskar! It's no fun any more."

Then he understood she was delirious.

3

The taper had burned out. He sat in the dark and listened to Kristina's breathing. Of course you will sleep! You may sleep as long as you wish—the rest of the night—the whole day tomorrow—many days. Day after day you may sleep—only, you must wake up again, you must promise to awaken—you must not die.

Be father and mother both, she had said. Shall I arrive alone—alone with the three little ones? And the fourth one? The fourth she takes with her—it follows her. The other three follow me—the other three—who no longer have a mother—no! They still have father and mother—I can hear her breathing. She is only asleep. But if she shouldn't—if it so should happen, then I can blame only myself. I myself have caused all this. I said: Someone must take the responsibility, I take the responsibility. She has been against it the whole time, she was against it from the very beginning. But I persuaded her. She came with me but I think she regretted it the whole time. But she said nothing. I was the one who insisted, I and no one else decided. And now she could blame me, but instead she says: I have nothing to forgive you; we are the best of friends. And I am causing her to lose her life—and she says—I like you—

This is your payment for being so stubborn and insistent. Now you feel what it's like! You wanted to push your will through—and now, see what has happened! If you had listened to her, if you had listened to your wife, and your parents and other people—those who wished to put a stop to it—then you would not have to sit here tonight, fumbling with a burnt-out taper, wondering if she is dead or alive. Do I look at my wife Kristina? Or at a corpse? Then I would not be sitting here, rocking back and forth, in this rolling ship—in this tempest tonight. Then I would never have set foot on this devil's ship, never been on this damned ocean—damned for time and eternity! That's what it is, if it takes her. If that damned Finn comes down with his canvas—comes up to this bunk—right here—and takes her—and says, as he usually does: We must—yes, now we must—If he comes—if HE comes—and I must blame myself. Stubborn and obstinate—the big-nosed are always stubborn. It's your big nose, Karl Oskar.

You didn't mean it wrongly—you didn't want to harm us—you mustn't feel downhearted—don't be sad! But if that Finn comes—at early dawn, he usually comes in the mornings—and tries to touch her—to find out—It must not be morning —not yet—not for a long while yet. It's better the night should last, better than that morning should come—morning, and a Finn, with a piece of canvas in his hand. You have yourself to blame. . . .

Thus Karl Oskar Nilsson stood watch at the bedside of his sick wife—the longest night watch of his life.

And with daylight and full morning he heard a child's voice —his little son Johan crawled up on his knee and took hold of his trousers and said: "Father—Mother isn't bleeding any more."

4

Night had passed and calm weather had come with morning.
The ocean had lowered its rough, roaring storm-voice—no
more waves were heard against the side of the ship, and the
rolling was negligible. In fact the rolling was all but gone
when the emigrants began to crawl out of their bunks and
waken to a new day in their old quarters in the hold.

Johan had crept down from his mother's bunk. "Mother
has stopped bleeding!"

Kristina lay quietly on her back as before, her eyes
gleamed open and bit in the meager daylight which came in
through the main hatch. Her lips moved slowly: "Karl Oskar.
Are you here?"

"Yes."

"I believe—I think I've slept."

"Yes. You've been sleeping a long time."

"I don't feel so tired any more."

"That's good."

"I think—I think—"

But that was all. She was too weak to say anything more.
Karl Oskar noticed that the blood no longer ran from her
nostrils; the flow of blood had stopped—perhaps many hours
ago. He had not been able to see in the dark, and he had been
afraid of striking a light, he might have awakened her. But
the blood was stanched. There was at least one blood-
stancher on board the ship—the captain himself. One must always do what one could, things might change if one tried.

While raptures of joy went through Karl Oskar, a man approached him and touched his shoulder, timidly and clumsily.
It was Danjel Andreasson. He was pale and his eyes were red
from the night wake—they seemed strangely glazed and distant when he looked at Karl Oskar and then at Kristina. His
voice, too, was foreign and distant, as if he were speaking
from another world: "She is dead."

"No! She lives!" said Karl Oskar. "I think she will survive
now!"

"She died just now," said Danjel.

"But can't you see for yourself—"

"You must believe me, Karl Oskar, she died a moment ago. She had never told me how ill she was."

"Don't you see she is alive?"

"She is dead—you can see for yourself, if you doubt me."

"Am I asleep? What are you talking about?"

Karl Oskar looked in consternation at Danjel.

Beside him stood a man in deep sorrow. Danjel did not speak of Kristina, he spoke of his own wife: Inga-Lena had died without admitting to her husband that she was ill.

Another man than Karl Oskar had become a widower this morning.

XXV

ANOTHER THREE SHOVELFULS OF EARTH FROM SWEDEN

1

Captain Lorentz sat in his cabin and mused over a piece of paper with a few lines written on it: "Wife Inga-Lena Andersdotter from Karragärde in Ljuder Parish, Konga County, born October 4, 1809; joined in marriage with homeowner Danjel Andreasson, June 23, 1833. . . ."

Name, sex, and age—that was all he required, all he needed to know to conduct the funeral. This was now the eighth funeral. But there was something about the information which did not check. Nothing checked, as he thought further about it. He had seen the woman's bleeding body, he had tied her arms and legs. She had been a young woman, barely thirty, but now it seemed that the dead one was forty years old. And he had been told that she left behind four children, all on board with their parents. Yet he remembered definitely having seen only three small ones in the bunk of the dying woman.

Apparently another death had occurred than the one he had expected.

Once more on this voyage must he stand on deck and from the prayerbook choose suitable prayers and thought-worthy

hymns, "as well as some sentence from Holy Writ," as it was
prescribed in "How to Bury a Corpse on Board."

"Teach us all to remember that we must die and thereby
gain understanding. . . ."

This potent prayer could have two meanings: either that we
gain understanding and use our lives well before we die—or,
the meaning which no doubt had been in the mind of the author, that we gain understanding to prepare ourselves for
death. But the person who used his intelligence well would not
concern himself in life with constant preparation for death.
There could be no meaning in thus wasting one's few allotted
days. Man must live in comfort and good cheer as long as life
lasted—soon enough death comes with joy to no one.

And the thought of his own death—probable within the
next few years—occupied the captain of the *Charlotta* for
some fleeting moments. While still young, his death-day had
often been in his mind; but the older he grew, the less often
did he think of it. Some wisdom he had gained with the years.
At sixty he was still sailing the seas in fairly good health.
Nearly all the comrades of his youth had been taken by the
sea, and their bodies had become part of the water that had
surged about their ships. Some had sailed five years, others
ten, still others thirty. He himself had already been allowed
forty-six. Why? Nothing could be more foolish than to brood
over this question. He might just as well ask why the wind
was southerly today and northerly yesterday, and not the opposite. Once one knew there was no answer to the question,
one ceased to ask. Only a simpleton would query the inexplicable.

It might be difficult to die, but it was rather common. All
people must die, people had done so throughout time, and he
too must face up to it when his time came. Since he couldn't
escape it, he might as well pretend that he would live forever.
For all eternity he would sail the seas, his ship would rot
down but the master remain. By thinking death nonexistent,
he could best use his life.

How had the wife Inga-Lena Andersdotter used her life—
the forty years that had been given to her? A funeral officiant
on a crowded emigrant ship could seldom know anything
about those over whom he read his prayers. His passengers
had been removed from their parish registers on leaving
home, and had not yet been recorded elsewhere. They were

registered nowhere—the emigrants on his ship were homeless, they had no plot in a churchyard. Only the sea opened its depths to them. The sea had room for all of them.

These peasants often feared death at sea, because of the final resting place—they wanted to be put in consecrated ground, and the ocean was not consecrated. But they were caught in deep superstition: this water where so many good seamen had found their graves ought to be a good enough resting place for the wretched land-rats.

Perhaps the wife Inga-Lena Andersdotter had died, too, in fear of the unconsecrated burial place of the ocean. Her forty years she had lived on solid ground, bending over the earth in her potato furrows and barley fields, poking in pens and manure piles, tramping between byre and barn. Yet she would find rest in the sea, in the most extended churchyard in the world, where nothing marked the graves. She would not be registered anywhere—she was an emigrant who had failed to reach her distination, a wanderer in the world.

But this peasant woman had still left her mark after her on earth: she had borne four new citizens for the North American republic.

With his stiff fingers, wasted and gray from the salt of the sea, Captain Lorentz picked up his pen to add a few lines on the small paper: "Died June 17, 1850, on board the brig *Charlotta* of Karlshamn, on voyage to New York. Certified, Christian Lorentz, Master."

2

It was a calm and beautiful June morning on the Atlantic Ocean. The emigrant vessel sailed with a feeble southerly breeze. The sun mirrored itself in the water, its rays reflected like burning flames. This morning at sea the emigrants had their first feeling of summer.

A group of passengers were gathered on the *Charlotta*'s afterdeck. The people stood in a semicircle around an improvised bier: a few planks had been laid upon two low sawhorses, and on these was placed an oblong bundle wrapped in canvas. The emigrants had donned their Sunday best—the men, gray or black wadmal jackets; the older women wore silk kerchiefs. Those of the crew who were free mingled with the passengers.

The men stood bareheaded, the women's covered heads were bowed. All faces reflected the gravity of the moment. They were an immobile, solidified group of people, gathered around the bundle on the improvised bier. A human body was wrapped in the white canvas; the bier leaned toward the water, the feet touching the rail.

The *Charlotta*'s flag was lowered to half-mast. The captain emerged from his cabin and issued a quick order: the mainsail was braced, reducing the slow speed of the ship to almost nothing, hardly enough for steering. The brig *Charlotta*'s voyage was delayed for the sake of a human corpse on the afterdeck this beautiful summer morning.

The captain had exchanged his oilskins for a black redingote; on his bare head his thick gray hair now lay smoothly combed. He went to the head of the bier, then looked for a moment into the rigging as if to see how his ship carried her sails. Under his arm he held a prayerbook. As he opened it the emigrants folded their hands and their faces took on—if possible—a still more serious mien.

Captain Lorentz turned a few pages in his prayerbook, turned them back again, made a jerky, impatient movement with his shoulders when he was unable immediately to locate the place: he must remember to turn the page at "How to Bury a Corpse." And what was the number of the hymn they were to sing?

While he was looking for the prayer he happened to notice the man standing beside him: a small peasant with a bushy brown beard. He remembered that man well. The first day out he had stumbled on him praying on deck. Now the little man held a baby in his arms; beside him stood three other children. Together they were four children and a father.

Lorentz quickly turned his eyes away from this group and looked about him on the deck. There was something he needed—there, at his feet, it stood, the wooden bushel measure half filled with earth. In it was stuck a small shovel, resembling a winnowing scoop.

He found the page in the prayerbook and began to read. His voice was clear and resonant, trained during many years at sea to rise above the roar of the waves and the storms:

"O Lord God! Thou Who for the sake of sin lettest people

die and return to earth again, teach us to remember that we must die, and thereby gain understanding. . . ."

Now all the people present held their hands folded, in reverence they bent their heads and listened to the words of the prayerbook. The ocean's water played softly against the side of the ship, a breath of air lifted a few tufts of hair on the captain's uncovered head. With the last words someone was heard sobbing, but the sound was quickly drowned in the captain's powerful voice.

The seagulls had returned, and they swarmed this morning in large flocks through the rigging. Life was again visible on the sea.

The funeral officiant took up a hymn. It began haltingly, and he had to sing half of the first stanza alone. But gradually the people joined in—slowly as the rolling of the ship the singing proceeded:

> "You wicked world, farewell!
> To heaven fares my soul,
> To reach her harbor goal . . ."

When the last notes of the hymn had rung out over the sea, the captain bent down and from the bushel at his feet picked up the little scoop. Three times he filled it with the earth his ship carried with her from the homeland, three times he emptied it over the dead body in front of him. With a soft thud the soil fell on the canvas. But heavy and terrifying fell the captain's words over the bent heads of the people: "Dust thou art, to dust thou shalt return. Jesus Christ shall awaken thee on the Day of Judgment! Let us pray."

Heavy was the truth, but the prayer was a mild comfort. Someone cried out at the words "Day of Judgment." It was not a cry of hope, it sounded rather like a bird's eerie and hopeless cry. It might be a sea bird calling, and some of the people turned their eyes toward the rigging—it might be a gull disturbing the solemnity of the funeral. But the cry did not come from a hungry seagull—it came from a child.

On the canvas-covered bundle there still remained the sprinkling of earth, three unshapely little mounds with a few pinches of mold in each, three ugly gray-black spots on the clean white cloth. But before the captain had finished reading the ritual, the lighter particles of earth separated from the mounds and trickled down the side. With the bier leaning toward the rail, toward the water beyond, some earth ran slowly across the rail, into the sea.

This was soil that had traveled a long way. It came from the land where the feet of the dead one had tramped the earth during her forty years, where she had struggled with her potato baskets and her barley sheaves, where she had carried milk pails and water buckets, where she—in concern for the food of her dear ones—had locked the larder every evening, where she had lived out her summers and her winters, all her autumns and springs—all except this single spring, when she had followed her mate out on the sea. It was a little earth from Sweden, a little of the three shovelfuls which accompany the words about creation, destruction, and the resurrection, which now trickled into the sea as if anxious to reach it before the human body which had just been consigned to its watery grave.

But no one noticed the movement on the canvas. As the grains of earth separated and rolled on their way the group now sang the second and last hymn of the ritual:

> "Let my body then be hidden
> In a humble, nameless tomb;
> When at last I shall be bidden
> To forsake that narrow room,
> Jesus knows where they are sleeping
> Who were given in His keeping. . . ."

The sun shone down on a peaceful sea which had calmed this morning and now lay quiet before the song about a patient and resigned human soul who sought his sleep with God until the end of time. Still a little more earth trickled down the canvas toward the water.

Captain Lorentz was ready to give his crew men the sign: Lower away.

At that moment someone stirred behind him—the little brown-bearded man with the baby on his arm stepped up to the captain. He looked at the ship's commander beseechingly, hesitatingly. Lorentz stepped aside, leaving his place at the head of the bier to the surviving husband.

Danjel Andreasson wanted to say something. His voice was not strong, he had never issued orders, he had no command-

er's voice. And few were the words he had to say to his mate
in the canvas: "The Lord said unto you as He said to Moses:
'You shall not get into that land.' You, my dear wife, were
not allowed to see the new land—yet you reached the harbor
before us.

"When I wanted to move over there, then you spoke to me
and said: 'Say not to me that I should separate from you;
where you go, there will I go, where you die there will I die
and be buried.' "

Only those closest to Danjel Andreasson could hear his
voice, his words were uttered in such low tones.

He took a step back from the bier, a long, hesitating step.
Then the captain gave the sign—two seamen stepped forward
and the oblong bundle glided into the sea. Almost as it disappeared over the rail a vague splash was heard from the side
of the ship. It sounded as if some of the sea's creatures had
moved in play on the surface, or perhaps it was a little billow
breaking.

The ship's flag was raised and lowered—three times this
was repeated.

Meanwhile the emigrants began to disperse. Soon the bare
rough bier stood alone. But two crew men came and took it
to pieces, carried away the planks and moved away the sawhorses, while the mainsail was spread to its full capacity, and
the brig *Charlotta* sailed on—with one passenger less.

It was a radiant morning on the Atlantic Ocean. The sun
had risen still higher and the beams glittered in the clear
water where a moment before the ship had left part of her
cargo from the hold. It was almost as if a fire glowed below
the surface, a flame burned down there.

XXVI

SAILING TOWARD MIDSUMMER

1

Robert and Elin stood leaning against the rail and watched
the porpoises play alongside the ship. The fat round fishes
looked like suckling pigs, and they tumbled about in the water

as a mill wheel turns in its channel. These were the largest
fishes the youth and girl had ever seen. But Robert had no
fishing gear handy. His fishpoles, lines, and hooks were in the
America chest, put away in the storeroom below the main
hold at the embarkation in Karlshamn—Robert had not seen
it since.

The eternal westerly wind was blowing; because they had
contrary winds the porpoises moved faster than the ship.
They swam and jumped and played around the bow as if
mocking the tardy vessel: Here we are! Where are you? How
far have you come? What kind of old pork barrel are you,
splashing about like that?

Elin pointed at the water where the porpoises played: right
there the water was green, she had seen similar spots before
on their voyage—how did it happen that the sea water was
green in some places? Had some ship spilled green paint
there? Robert thought a bit before he answered: perhaps God
at the Creation had intended to make the sea water green,
perhaps He had at first made a few sample lakes of that color
and later changed His mind and created all waters blue. Then
afterward He might have thrown the green lakes into the sea
here and there, just so as to make some use of them.

There was always something to observe at sea. Robert did
not agree with the other passengers, he did not think the sea
was a desolate landscape, depressing to watch day after day.
In storm the sea was a hilly landscape, each knoll mobile and
rolling about. In sunshine and calm weather the sea lay there
outstretched like a blue and golden cloth of silk or satin
which he would have liked to stroke with his hand. The sea in
moonlight at night was made up of broad, light paths, for the
angels of heaven to walk on. A hill or a knoll on land always
remained in the same spot, and looked exactly the same each
time one passed by it. But the sea was never the same.

During a few nights early in the voyage Robert had
thought he was going to die at sea. While the first storm raged
he had lain in his bunk, his forehead moistened by the cold
and sticky sweat of death-fear. This experience he had not
liked. To be enjoyable, an adventure must not involve fear for
life. But he had grown accustomed to the sea, and now he felt
ashamed when he thought of his fear during that first storm.
Now he could go to bed in the evenings without fear of
drowning during the night.

And as they approached the end of the long-drawn-out voyage he had even begun to like the sea. Soon he must part from it. It was said they might expect to see land almost any day now. Every day passengers gathered in the prow and looked for America, as if thinking that that land was such a small speck they might pass it by if they didn't keep a lookout for it. Those among them who possessed almanacs, and marked the passing days by crosses, said that it would be Midsummer in a few days. Perhaps they would reach the shores of America for the Midsummer holidays.

"Shall we read in the language book?" asked Elin.

"If you wish, let's."

She was now as eager as he to learn English words. He suspected she no longer relied on the Holy Ghost to give her power to use the new language immediately on landing. And he had several times reminded her that the descending of the Holy Ghost upon the apostles on the first Whitsuntide had taken place long before the discovery of America, long before the English language was invented. Therefore no one knew for sure if it could be taught in the same manner as the languages of the Greeks, the Elamites, the Syrians, and the Copts, which the apostles learned in one day—and this a holy day to boot.

In the textbook Robert and Elin had now reached the chapter about "Seeking Employment." It was an important chapter; the very first day when they arrived in America they both must earn their own living, and anyone who must earn his living must also know how to find employment.

Robert had finally decided that they must pronounce the English words as they were spelled in the first sentences and disregard the spelling within the parentheses which only confused and complicated the language for them.

Could you tell me where to get work?—What can you do?

Here the work-seeker must answer that he was a carpenter, a tailor, a cobbler, a harness maker, a tanner, a spinner, a weaver, a mason, a waiter, or whatever occupation he pursued. But Robert had skipped all this, he was not concerned about what a harness maker was called in English as he couldn't make harnesses anyway. He himself stuck to one single sentence: *I am used to farm work.*

He was a farmhand. The only work he had done was farm work, the only chores he had performed were those of the

farmer. And he had long struggled with this sentence, but he
knew it now—he repeated the words slowly and tried to pronounce them carefully as they were spelled.

I am used to farm work. He wished already the very first
day to astonish the Americans by being able to tell them what
he could do, and he wished to say it correctly in their own
language. He wished to inspire respect from the very first day.

At home in Ljuder Elin had only worked as nursemaid, but
now that she had passed sixteen she hoped to find a position
in America more worthy of a grown woman. She read the
chapter in the textbook entitled "Doing Ordinary Household
Chores." It dealt with every hour of a maid's workday in
America, and Robert urged her emphatically to learn this
chapter well before she landed: having done so she would inspire respect.

*I am the new servant girl. You must get up at six o'clock in
the morning. Make fire and put water to boil. Get the broom
and sweep the dining room. Clear off the table. Wash your
hands before you handle food.*

When Elin had gone so far she looked at her hands, which
were clean and white, with a fragrance of soap. It was early
in the morning and she had just washed them.

"In America they must think all maids have dirty hands,"
she said.

"The Americans hate all kinds of dirt," said Robert. "Everything is cleaner in the New World than in the Old. That's
why you'll fit in well there."

"Do you really believe it's true that a maid need not get up
before six in the morning?"

About that, Robert dared not offer anything definite. There
was the chance that she might accuse him of having told her
something untrue. He answered cautiously: "Perhaps she isn't
allowed to sleep so late in all places. But I've heard that farmhands can sleep till five o'clock."

Where Elin had served as nursemaid she had always been
awakened by her mistress at four o'clock or half past. She
liked to sleep late in the morning, and now she was a little
disappointed in Robert's answer. He had once said that all
women in America were waited on, and if this were true,
then it was only right that they be allowed to sleep later than
the men.

The deck rolled slowly under the youth and the girl, the

changing world of the sea surrounded them, the same eternal billows lifted them and carried them to a New World where they must find their way. And they sat there close together and with inexperienced, obstinate tongues tried to learn a new language—seriously and persistently they struggled through the English sentences, reading the words aloud as they were spelled.

I am used to farm work. I am the new servant girl.

In these two sentences the youthful emigrants must let the Americans know what kind of people they were, and they must pronounce them correctly, inspiring respect. This was of great importance for their future.

2

The brig *Charlotta* of Karlshamn was sailing toward Midsummer.

The eagle on her prow still looked incessantly toward the west, his eyes washed clean and clear by the spray. And the two tall masts—fir trees from the forests of the ship's homeland—bowed gracefully as the vessel glided down the billowy vales, rose proudly again as she encountered the crests of the waves. So they bowed while they carried the sails across all the sea, always rising to their full height again, proudly, defiantly. They had bent a little in hard gusts of wind, they had been pressed down by the storms, but they had always come back up again. They were slim and slender pine spires, in appearance so delicate at the top that they could be broken with the fingers—but these the ship's pinions had endured the tempests of all seasons on the sea. They were pines from a little land far away, they came from the same stony meadows and moors as the people on this ship—they were related to these voyagers, they were tough and indomitable as the people they helped carry across the sea.

And soon they will have conquered the ocean once more. The *Charlotta* now met other vessels daily, sailing ships and iron steamers, she was passing vessels, she was overtaken by vessels, she kept company with vessels. The swarm of sea birds was thickening in her rigging. In the water—up till now uncontaminated in its clear blueness—slime and flotsam began to appear, various discarded objects sailed about on the surface. All signs indicated that land was near. And soon the ship would no longer sail on the sea, she would enter a broad river mouth.

The sun was high in the heavens and bathed the deck in warmth. Sick passengers were carried up from the hold and lay the whole day through in the beneficial sunshine. Slowly mending, they felt they were enjoying a warmer sun than the one that shone on them at home. It was high-summer weather, Midsummer weather.

Kristina had improved slowly after her bleeding during the night of the storm. But as yet she was too weak to stand. Karl Oskar carried her out of the dark and stuffy quarters up on deck every day when the sun was out, and each day her sensation of returning strength increased. It worried her that she was lying here so useless; she could not help them now when they had so much to do: they were getting themselves in order for their landing.

The passengers had begun their great cleaning up and were busy preparing themselves for the landing. There was washing and scouring and scrubbing in the hold, garments were washed and rinsed and hung to dry. Clothing of all kinds, Sunday best and underwear and bedclothing, must be cleaned, mended, patched and brushed. This was not work for menfolk, but Karl Oskar must do it now, and he found it a tedious task. Many things had been ruined on the long voyage— worn out, torn, rotted, drenched with vomit. Mattresses and bolsters and garments were in shreds—these he could only throw into the sea. And nearly everything smelled musty and evil—like the quarters where they had spent more than two months. He gathered, sorted, and discarded a large pile.

"There should be a rag-and-bone man on the ship. He would have a thriving business!"

Now he, like the other passengers, must throw his rags into the sea. And he mused that little by little a whole mountain of ragged discarded belongings of emigrants must have accumulated near the shores of America, if each new arrival threw overboard as much as this.

Kristina thought that he threw away too much. Some of the things in his pile could have been cleaned and mended, could well have had more use. But Karl Oskar felt it a relief to get rid of the stinking rags, reminders of his anxiety during

the storms and the plague of seasickness—he wanted to free
himself of these witnesses to the troubles of the crossing. The
sight of them would only torment him on land when they
were to begin anew.

"I don't want to feel ashamed among the Americans," he
said. "If they were to see these rags, they would wonder what
kind of people we are."

Karl Oskar admitted no debt to the homeland where all his
struggle had repaid him so little, but he did not wish to shame
Sweden in the eyes of America: he wished to show that it was
a land with a cleanly, upright peasantry, that those who came
from there were decent and orderly, even if they brought
nothing more than their poverty in their knapsacks. He
wanted to be neat in his dress, and appear sensible and experienced as he passed through the portals of the New World.

He discarded the *old* with the rags that he heaved
overboard—now the *new* was to begin.

Of their bedding, Karl Oskar saved only one piece: their
blue bridal cover which Kristina herself had sewn. It too was
spotted, and several holes gaped in it. Tears came to Kristina's eyes as she now beheld it in full daylight, and saw how
badly it had fared. But maybe she could wash it, remove the
disgusting spots, mend the holes—once they had landed and
her health and strength had returned. Her bridal quilt was
dearer to her than any other possession they brought with
them from home. It had been part of her setting-up-of-home
in Sweden, she had made her bridal bed with it, Karl Oskar
and she had slept under it for six years—during their whole
lives as husband and wife. She could now hope that they
might rest together under it once more, and use it for many
years. Surely they would never be happy and prosperous unless the bridal cover was part of their new settling in America.

During their preparations for the landing Karl Oskar
showed himself so handy and efficient with the chores of
womenfolk that Kristina could not help but admire him. It
seemed he could do almost anything he wanted—if he only
wanted to. His old disposition had now returned, and he was
more cheerful with each day. Midsummer was imminent, he
said, he must have on his holiday disposition.

The closer they came to land, the more Karl Oskar became
himself.

3

One morning at daybreak Robert was awakened by Arvid,
who excitedly shook him by the shoulder. "They see
America!"

Still half asleep Robert jumped into his trousers, still half
asleep he emerged through the main hatch onto deck where
he continued to button himself up. Many passengers had already gathered up here, mostly menfolk, but also a few early
risers among the women. They all stood there silently in grave
expectation: they saw North America.

As yet there was not much for the eyes to behold. They
sailed up the mouth of a broad river, a broad bay of the sea.
It was not yet full daylight, and a mist hung over the land:
America was still sleeping this morning, had not yet shed her
blanket of night. Land rose over the stern and on the prow
and on either side of the ship, but in the mist of dawn it appeared fragmentary, visible in places, hidden in others. As yet
no one could discern if this land was barren or fertile, rich or
poor, beautiful or ugly. But they had reached the shores of
America, and this knowledge sufficed them.

Their speed up the bay was good—now, during the last
stage of this long voyage, the wind was with them, and their
sails were full as women's skirts in a breeze. Innumerable
ships filled the passage, sailing ships, sloops, steamers, vessels
of all sizes and kinds. The brig *Charlotta* had long traveled
alone on the ocean, now she was in great company.

Little by little the land threw off its morning shroud.
Slowly the naked shores arose. And soon a populated stretch
of land jutted out in the path of their ship, like a large penin-
sula. Here the clearing mist gradually uncovered a multitude
of clustered roofs, long rows of houses could be seen, and
high above the roofs stretched spires and steeples, exactly like
the church steeples at home. Before them lay a town, greater
than any they had ever seen before. When full daylight broke
through, they could see their harbor: New York.

Robert and Arvid stood in the prow, as immobile as people
can stand on a moving deck. Next to them stood the second
mate, the Finn, who had taken part in every one of the *Char-*

lotta's voyages to North America. He told them that the land they saw was only a large island. It was originally called *Manna-Hata*, which was an Indian word—the name of a favorable god among the Indians, he had heard. The god had lived on this pretty island of *Manna-Hata* for thousands of years, until it once was flooded by the river and he had been forced to move. Now it was mostly people who lived here, but the Finn had never been to any church while in port so he was not sure which god—if any—lived on *Manna-Hata* nowadays.

The *Charlotta* steered toward a shore which seemed to them made up of fortifications and piers. But above these rose also a large, round, yellow-gray building with a tremendous round tower. Robert wondered what this could be.

"That's called Castle Garden. It's a *kastell*."

Robert did not know what a *kastell* was, he had never heard the word before, but he didn't wish to ask. Instead, Arvid asked the mate.

"A *kastell* is the same as a prison," said the Finn.

Robert looked at him with wide-open eyes. That yellow-gray house with the large round tower was a prison? There were then imprisoned people in the house called Castle Garden. He had not imagined that the first house he saw in America would be a prison, a house where people were locked up when they lost their freedom. And he said that he had hardly expected to find any prisons in the United States of North America, where all evil and criminal people were exterminated.

The mate then explained that Castle Garden was no longer used as a prison. There were no prisoners there any more—it was instead a hell of a good place, a saloon. He knew, he had been there himself. The fare was good, and the ale of first quality. One could eat there to one's satisfaction, and get good and drunk too. On Sundays the saloon was crowded, people sitting on each other's knees while they ate and drank. Castle Garden was indeed a damned good saloon, a place where one was free to do as one pleased, use one's knife in a brawl and all other kinds of entertainment.

Then it was really as Robert had thought it would be: the prisons in America were actually not prisons with prisoners, as was the case in Sweden, but rather fine inns with guests who there could enjoy and entertain themselves as best they pleased. No doubt about it, America was a land with a kind government.

4

Only a short time elapsed before all of the *Charlotta*'s passengers were gathered on deck. Those unable to crawl up by themselves were carried: America was visible, and all wanted to see. They saw houses, churches, embankments, piers, streets and roads, people and carriages. But the eyes of the emigrants missed something—they looked in vain for something which the shores of America as yet had not shown. Their eyes had been searching for it during the whole passage up the bay—at last they found it, on the outjutting tongue of land over the prow: behind the big house with the round tower the morning mist was lifting, uncovering a grove of trees—large leaf-trees with thick foliage, and grass on the ground around the strees. The shore they had left at Karl-shamn had been a dark shore—here a light shore greeted them. Bushes and trees grew there, leaves and green boughs, herbs and grass: at last they could see the green earth.

The long-drawn-out voyage with all its storms, sufferings, ills and troubles—the confinement on the ship during endless days—all this had gnawed hard on the emigrants' lives and spirits. Scurvy and ship's fever had lowered their resistance. From the monotonous life on board they had grown depressed and downhearted, and many had ceased to care what life and fate would bring them. But now this new vision unfolded before them, a bit of living ground near them—and they knew they had safely crossed the sea, and were here with the earth lying before their eyes again.

They stood crowded together on deck like a herd of cattle —shackled in the narrow stalls of the byre during a whole long winter, and at last stretching their necks and turning toward the door when it began to smell of spring and fresh grass and meadows: soon they would be let out, soon their imprisonment would end. And in this moment a new energy and ambition seized the emigrants. They felt cheered, encouraged, born anew, as if a fresh spirit were blown into their breasts.

The scurvy-sick feel now that they will recover. The weakened ones come to life again, a new strength enters them. Fresh power comes to the tired ones, initiative returns to the depressed, boldness to the timid. The spirit of indifference flies away from their minds, as the mist and fog this morning had lifted from the earth.

It was *land-frenzy* that overtook the passengers on the *Charlotta*. The life at sea had undermined their bodies and souls. The land-frenzy was bringing them new strength. They had again seen the green earth. As seekers of new homes they had come sailing from the earth—now they were back on the earth, and felt life returning.

5

The little Swedish vessel had anchored at the pier. The gangplank was lowered, and the passengers had begun to disembark. A burning-hot summer day met them in the new land.

The family from Korpamoen had gathered in a group, waiting their turn. On one arm Karl Oskar held his youngest son, with the other he held his wife around the waist. Kristina wanted to walk down the gangplank on her own legs. Many passengers had come on deck for the first time in a long while today, and some were so weak that they must be carried ashore. But Kristina told Karl Oskar she did not wish it said that she had been unable to walk onto land in America on her own legs. It would not be a good omen if she were carried ashore. Her limbs were weak, however, and she leaned heavily on her husband. Robert looked after Johan and Lill-Marta, and stood there holding one child with each hand. The children were not yet quite awake, and were troublesome and complaining, frightened by all the noise and jostle at the landing. Little Harald wanted to get down from his father's arms. He, too, wanted to walk on his own legs.

The children were pale and agunt, and the flesh hung loosely on their limbs, but they would soon improve with fresh food on land. A fourth child was still slumbering in its unconsciousness within the protection of the mother. This unborn life would be the first one from among the *Charlotta*'s passengers to gain citizenship in the North American republic.

Of the sixteen people who had emigrated from Ljuder Parish and gathered at Akerby Junction a bleak morning in early April, fifteen had arrived at the threshold of a new continent. One was missing. Of the seventy-eight people who had embarked at Karlshamn, seventy had arrived. The *Charlotta* had given up eight of her passengers to the ocean.

But Karl Oskar Nilsson had his whole family around him, and he himself stood there, healthy and sound and filled with deep satisfaction that they had all traveled safely over the sea.

He did not worry about the journey over land, where all lay firm under his feet. For the landing he had polished his splendid high boots, tried on for the first time the last evening in their old home. With the fat from a large pork rind he had greased the leather until it was shining black. His boots were of the best leather, made from oak-tanned ox-hide. He was well shod—they knew how to make fine boots at home. In this footgear he was well prepared. If the roads of America were poor, he would get through with these boots on his feet.

Otherwise, he, along with his fellow passengers, was poorly equipped. When their ship at long last landed, the emigrants were shabby and worn in faces and clothing. They must now go ashore in the same garments they had worn during the long voyage, and these did not resemble the clothing one wears to festivals. Men and women alike looked like molting hens. And when they had gathered together their possessions —chests, bundles, baskets, and boxes thrown together in a pile on deck—then the ship looked like a large high-loaded gypsy wagon. When they had driven to the harbor town of Karlshamn, Jonas Petter had likened the emigrants from Ljuder to a pack of gypsies. At their disembarkation this comparison was even more appropriate than then.

But however shabby and weak they seemed, however wretched and poor they were—North America admitted them.

It was time to go over the gangplank. The pier was high and their small ship was low—the gangplank became a steep uphill. But Kristina used all her strength, and walked onto land by herself. And little Harald was let down from Karl Oskar's arms at last, and walked on the plank at his father's side. Even the youngest in the Korpamoen family walked on his own legs into America.

But at the very first steps on solid ground Karl Oskar

stopped still: his head swam—he felt dizzy. The ground under him rolled exactly as the deck had done. Giddiness made him stumble a bit. Never once at sea had he felt this way. Now when he stood on firm land dizziness overtook him and his legs were wobbly. He could not understand it. Perhaps he had forgotten how to walk on solid ground, perhaps he must begin anew, as he must with his whole life. But in this unknown new land, which he now entered, he must stand firmly on his legs. That much he knew.

It was on Midsummer Eve, in the year 1850, that the brig *Charlotta* of Karlshamn tied up at the pier in New York, after ten weeks' sailing from her home port. Precarious, insecure, and unstable were the first steps of the immigrants on American soil.

The Emigrants is the first volume in a planned trilogy.
Monterey, California, August 1949

V.M.

Unto a Good Land

"And I am come down to deliver them ... and to bring
them up out of that land unto a good land
and a large, unto a land flowing
with milk and honey."
Exodus III: 8

PART ONE

In Search of
Homes

I

A Ship Unloads Her Cargo

On the elongated island of Manhattan, in the Hudson River, the largest city in North America had sprung up, already inhabited by half a million people. Like an immense hippopotamus resting immobile in his element, Manhattan sprawled in the water, at the mouth of the Hudson. The hippopotamus turned his head toward the Atlantic, and back of his enormous snout lay the piers of the East River, where ships with emigrants from the Old World tied up.

On June 23, 1850, there arrived in the port of New York the brig *Charlotta* of Karlshamn—Christian Lorentz, Captain—carrying seventy passengers, emigrants from Sweden, nearly all of whom were farmers with their families. The *Charlotta* was several weeks overdue, delayed by contrary weather; this arrival completed her seventh voyage as an emigrant vessel. The brig tied up at the East River pier between a tall, coffin-shaped English bark and a low Norwegian schooner heavily loaded with iron. Besides the human cargo in her hold, the *Charlotta* also had pig iron and sundry items of freight.

One of Captain Lorentz's first errands on American soil was to change his passengers' money. During the last days of the voyage he had collected the emigrants' cash and, carrying a leather sack, he now went to a bank on Wall Street to exchange Swedish daler and shillings for Ameri-

7

can dollars and cents. He did not accept paper money, only gold and silver coin; he knew nothing for sure about American bills, except that their value never was the same as the amount printed on them.

Sweating and puffing in the intense heat, he returned to his ship. Captain Lorentz had been in New York port during every season of the year; he was familiar with all North American weathers and disliked them all; this summer heat he abhorred. Down here by the docks there was at least some breeze from the Atlantic, but in the *Charlotta*'s hold the air was unbearably oppressive. To be tied up near Manhattan this time of year was one of his most distasteful duties as ship's commander.

In his tiny cabin the captain pulled out the passenger list. After each name he had noted the sum entrusted to him, and now he must figure out how much each passenger was to receive in American money. It was an annoying chore, a chore for shop clerks. He was not a counting man, he was a seaman; but a captain on an emigrant vessel apparently must also be a scrivener and a moneychanger. Like a father with his children, he must look after his passengers and see to it that they weren't cheated or robbed.

And having sailed these Swedish peasants across the ocean from one continent to another, Captain Lorentz now felt so great a responsibility for them he wouldn't even leave them to shift for themselves after they had landed. Hardly had his ship tied up at the pier when all those who made their living from the simplicity and inexperience of immigrants flocked around the gangplank like rapacious dogs at slaughter time. These *runners* and *grafters* and *brokers,* and whatever they were called in the language of this new country, watched for every newly arrived ship. There were agents from freight companies which the captain knew were fraudulent; there were men from taverns and quarters of ill repute; well-fed and well-dressed men in funny little round caps with large visors; lazy men who avoided honest work and whose presence was repugnant to Captain Lorentz. He would always place an armed guard at the gangplank to keep such rascals off his ship, for once on board they would steal all they could lay hands on, down to a single nail or a piece of rope. The rogues came from all lands, but they pre-

8

ferred to rob their own countrymen. By talking the language of new arrivals they gained their confidence and made easy victims of them. All European nationalities, it seemed, plundered and defrauded each other here on American shores: English robbed the English, Irish swindled the Irish, Germans preyed on Germans—while Americans plundered the immigrants from all countries, regardless of nationality. In this respect at least, thought the captain, the Americans honored equality among men.

The authorities in New York were too lenient. Lost and unsuspicious immigrants enjoyed no protection against the scoundrels lurking at the landings.*

The passenger list stuck to Captain Lorentz's rough, sweaty hands. His brain worked sluggishly in the infernal heat, and he lost himself in numbers as he figured daler into dollars. He was looking forward to evening, when he hoped to enjoy his supper and cellar-cool ale at Castle Garden. This tavern was conveniently close by, and it was the best eating place he knew of in New York—though not up to his standard in other ports. Its fare might do for the rich New York swine breeders who usually gathered there, but a man who sailed to Marseille, Bordeaux, and Barcelona had his own standards of good food. The Americans had lived such a short time in their country they hadn't yet learned how to prepare their food properly. There were too many other things to attend to. For example, they were said to be particularly good at building churches; he had heard New York alone had a hundred and fifteen of them. And he recalled what he once had read in a book by a famous Frenchman: The French had one hundred different sauces, but only one religion, whereas the Americans had a hundred different religions, but only one sauce. Captain Lorentz had, unfortunately, not yet had the pleasure of tasting this sauce.

He could never reconcile himself to the strange customs and ideas he met in North America. Here people of many races mixed, and the classes were so turned about that one couldn't tell which were the upper and which the lower. Lowly people considered themselves changed when they landed on American shores; they thought themselves equal to those of high birth and position. Every farm hand and

* Not until 1855 was an official reception station for immigrants opened at Castle Garden.

servant wench assumed a conceited, disobedient, insolent attitude. Several times it had happened that able-bodied men of his crew had become so arrogant that they had boldly broken their contracts with him and had simply remained in America. Here, respect for authority and masters was disregarded, and consequently, the servant class was ruined. Here all felt at home, even those who smeared pork grease over their faces while eating, not yet having learned the use of a napkin.

The *Charlotta*'s captain counted and wrote numbers, and the sweat from his face dripped onto his paper. For each passenger he must deduct the landing fee—two dollars and a half—which must be paid to the city treasurer immediately on arrival; Captain Lorentz must rob each of these poor devils of six riksdaler and twelve shillings. The emigrants themselves certainly needed every penny, but the money went to the lean purse of New York—which no doubt also could use it. Here landed thousands of impoverished wretches, and when completely destitute, they were forced to remain in the harbor until provided for by that lean purse. Europe emptied her workhouses and literally shoveled the inmates over onto America; how long would the Americans meekly accept these discards from the Old World?

Including these passengers on his latest voyage, Captain Lorentz had sailed five hundred of Sweden's inhabitants to North America. A whole little town his brig had moved across the world ocean. Which one of the two countries ought to be more grateful to the *Charlotta* and her commander—the kingdom of Sweden or the North American Republic? Sweden got rid of her religious fanatics and other troublesome, law-breaking citizens, but at the same time she lost many useful and capable men. On every voyage, the *Charlotta*'s human cargo was nine-tenths thrifty peasants. The lazy and useless ones, the rogues and the deserters, came mostly from other countries, on other ships. Also, of course, many enterprising Europeans found their way to New York; the captain had heard of some who immediately on arrival bought trunkfuls of guns and continued westward to seek a new way of living.

The gentlemen from the Commissioners of Emigration who pried about his ship as soon as it docked used to say that the North American Republic wanted healthy, work-willing, moral immigrants. But no one prevented the sick, lazy, immoral ones from landing, as long as they could walk ashore. The captain was responsible only for the incurably sick and was required to put up a bond. This time, he had to confess, the *Charlotta*'s living cargo was badly damaged by seasickness, and scurvy too, after ten stormy weeks at sea. Some of his passengers, during their first weeks in America, would no doubt be unable either to work or to lead immoral lives.

And this time, on arrival in port, Captain Lorentz had been met by a new proclamation: Captains carrying passengers must keep them on board for three days after docking.

The *Charlotta*'s gangplank was already lowered, and some of her passengers had gone ashore when the health officer arrived with the new order and sent them back aboard. His question indicated how things stood: Had there been cholera on board the *Charlotta?*

New York again was seized by the fear of cholera. Last summer the epidemic had frightened the inhabitants out of town, and this year, with the intense heat, it had flared up again. The authorities thought cholera was brought by emigrant ships from the Old World, and now every ship from a foreign port must be carefully inspected by health officers before the passengers were allowed to step onto American soil.

Crossed-out names on the *Charlotta*'s passenger list indicated to the inspector that eight passengers had been buried at sea, but Captain Lorentz could assure him with a clear conscience that none had died of cholera. He once had had the Eastern pestilence on board his ship, and he knew well the signs of the sickness: severe diarrhea, violent vomiting, and a thirst which burned like fire. But his passengers on this voyage had been free from these symptoms. And the inspector himself looked at those still sick and ascertained that the Swedish brig was not bringing cholera to New York. But he warned about an English merchantman, the bark *Isaac Webb* of Liverpool, arriving the same day as the *Charlotta*; on this ship the Oriental pest had raged so horribly that seventy-seven of the passengers had died.

11

Yes, Captain Lorentz had always known it, human beings were the most annoying and unhealthy cargo in the world.

There were now many additional troubles and complications in getting rid of this cargo. He must keep the passengers on board for another three days, for which he would receive no thanks from those crowded into the hold in this heat. Fortunately, now as always, the sick got well as soon as it was time to land; even the weakest wanted to look their best. Only one passenger caused him real worry and concern, a sixty-five-year-old farm wife from Oland. He had expected her to die before they reached port, he had been so sure of it he had made a mark after her name —like a small cross. He noticed it now as he read the passenger list: Fina-Kajsa Andersdotter. She had become a widow on the North Sea, where he had read the funeral service over her husband. The old woman was so weak from scurvy he had not believed she could survive. If she now were to be taken from ship to hospital, the commander of the *Charlotta* must post a bond of three hundred dollars with the mayor of New York.

Why in hell would a farm woman go out to sea at such an age? Why should the shipping company be expected to pay three hundred dollars for an old, worn-out hag-body? One way to avoid the bond, perhaps, would be to keep her on board as long as the brig remained in port. While they unloaded the pig iron and other freight, the old woman would no doubt die, and then the health officer would come and fetch the corpse, and the captain wouldn't even have to think about the funeral.

It was always easier to get rid of dead cargo than living.

2

The passengers were now coming to the cabin to collect their money. A tall, husky man hit his forehead against the cabin ceiling as he came down the ladder. The captain said, "Look out for your skull! You might need it in America."

An unusually large nose protruded from the man's face; Captain Lorentz need not ask the name of this farmer, he remembered him well. One night during the voyage— while the worst tempest was raging—he had stanched a

12

hemorrhage for this man's wife. The peasant had thanked him and said that his wife owed her life to the *Charlotta*'s captain.

He consulted the passenger list: "Karl Oskar Nilsson. Paid 515 rdr. bko."

At the exchange rate of one dollar for each two and a half daler, the farmer had two hundred and six dollars coming to him. But from this sum the captain must deduct the exchange fee and the landing fees for man, wife, brother and three children.

He told the farmer, "You have to pay thirty-seven and a half daler for six people."

"Is that the entrance fee to America?"

"We might call it that. There is also the exchange fee. Four dollars—that is, ten daler."

Lorentz counted and deducted: Balance to pay—a hundred and eighty-seven dollars. He counted out this sum in twenty-, ten-, and one-dollar coins, gold and silver, which he gave to the young farmer, who himself counted the money slowly and carefully. Then he put the coins, one at a time, into a homemade sheepskin belt which he carried around his waist under his shirt. The captain gave the hiding place a nod of approval.

The big-nosed farmer, having received his money, still remained standing in the cabin.

"Do you think you've been cheated in the exchange?" the captain asked.

"No. No, it isn't that. But I would like to ask you about something, Mr. Captain."

"Yes?"

Karl Oskar Nilsson continued: There were fifteen of them, eight full grown and seven children, all from Ljuder Parish in Smaland, who had undertaken the voyage together to this new country. Now they had been delayed at sea, the summer was already far advanced, and they were anxious to reach their destination as soon as possible, so as to be able to find land and get something planted before winter set in. All of those from Ljuder Parish intended to go to Minnesota, where land was said to be reasonably priced for people with little money. Now they wanted to continue their journey without delay; would the captain be kind enough to advise them how to get started inland?

"Have you any defi ite place in mind?"

"Yes. Here is the name."

From his purse Karl Oskar took out a soiled, worn piece of paper, once part of an envelope:

Mister Anders Mansson
Taylors Falls Past Offis
Minnesota Territory
North-America.

"Who gave you this address?" asked the captain.

"An old woman on board the ship. Mansson is her son. She's going to him and we'll all be in the same company; they say there's good land where her son lives."

"You rely on the woman? What's her name?"

"Fina-Kajsa. She is from Oland; her husband died in the first storm."

Captain Lorentz suddenly straightened. "You mean the old woman who is so sick?"

"She is better now, she says; she feels so well in her body she'll be able to go with the rest of us."

"Then you'll take the old woman in your company and be responsible for her?"

"Yes. She has money for her journey. And we'll look after her as best we can. When we get there, perhaps her son will help us find land."

The captain's face had suddenly lightened; it was not the first time Providence had helped him out of a difficult dilemma. This time, apparently, Providence had chosen the farmer to get him out of his difficulty with Fina-Kajsa Andersdotter, and thus save his company three hundred dollars.

He handed the important piece of paper back to Karl Oskar.

"It's a long way to the territory of Minnesota. About fifteen hundred English miles, I believe."

"Is it so . . . so . . . far away?" Karl Oskar's face fell, and he scratched his head with its unkempt hair, yellow as barley straw, grown very long during the voyage from Sweden.

"Of course, it's only two hundred and fifty Swedish miles," the captain hastened to assure him. He did not wish to frighten the farmer by dwelling on the journey's length, but rather to encourage him to undertake it. He continued: Every time he had transported farmers in search of land he had advised them to go as deep as possible into America; the farther west they went, the richer the soil was, and the broader were the regions to choose from. Most of the distance they could travel on river steamboats.

"Two hundred and fifty miles! It isn't exactly next door."

The infinitely long road which had worried Karl Oskar at first had shrunk to one-sixth, but it was still two hundred and fifty times the distance from Korpamoen to Ljuder church. He thought to himself, he must be careful how he spoke of the distance to others in his company; it might dishearten them.

"I will arrange the contract for the journey," Captain Lorentz assured him. "Including the Widow Andersdotter, there will be sixteen in your company?"

Karl Oskar had never seen this taciturn, unobliging man so talkative and willing to help as he was today. The captain spoke almost as to an equal: Yes, he often arranged contracts with honest companies for transportation inland. His conscience bade him help immigrants leave New York as soon as possible; they couldn't stay here in the harbor, they couldn't settle in Battery Park. And he knew an honest Swedish man in New York whom he often asked to guide the immigrants and act as their interpreter. The man's name was Landberg, he had once been carpenter on this very ship, the best carpenter Lorentz had ever had. But several years ago, when the captain was transporting a group of religious fanatics from Helsingland, followers of the widely known prophet Erik Janson, Landberg had been so taken by their religion that he had left the ship in New York and joined the group. After half a year, Landberg had lost faith in the prophet, who had plundered him. The poor man had been forced to flee from Janson's tyranny penniless and practically naked. Landberg now earned his living by acting as interpreter and guide for Swedish immigrants. He spoke English fluently, and it was Captain Lorentz's custom to send for him as soon as the ship docked in New York. This time also he had notified the one-time carpenter, and Landberg had been given a pass by the health officer to come aboard the brig.

15

"How much would the interpreter cost?" Karl Oskar asked.

"It depends on the distance he must accompany you. I believe he charges three dollars for each grown person as far as Chicago."

"Hmm . . . Well, we can't manage by ourselves. None of us can speak this tongue."

The captain thought, to leave these poor, helpless peasants to shift for themselves would be almost like driving a flock of sheep into a forest full of wolves. He said, "If you would like speedy transport inland, you must take the steam wagon from Albany. Landberg will get contracts with all the companies concerned."

"Thank you, Captain, for your great help."

It had been reported to the captain during the voyage that this big-nosed peasant had been dissatisfied with his quarters, had complained of the small ration of water, and had been insubordinate to the ship's officers. But Lorentz no longer disliked the man: Karl Oskar undoubtedly had a good head; and then, he was the tool of Providence.

". . . And you think the old woman is strong enough to be moved?"

"She says she is. She was on her feet again today."

It was indeed strange; a few days ago the Widow Andersdotter had been shaking in every limb with the ague, fallen off to the very bones from diarrhea. But such miraculous recoveries had happened before, and even though Lorentz had little use for the customs of the North American Republic, he had to admit that the mere sight of the country worked like magic on people; one day they were lying in their bunks sighing and crying and ready to die, unable to lift head from pillow, and the next day they were on their feet again. When semi-corpses saw the shores of America, they returned to life.

3

As Karl Oskar felt the new money in his belt, it seemed to him that a hundred and eighty-seven dollars was a poor exchange for five hundred and fifteen daler. His property had somehow shrunk on his arrival in America. And what he now carried in his belt was all he and his family owned

16

in worldly possessions; it was all they could rely on for their future security.

He went to tell his fellow passengers that the captain would arrange for their continued journey; all were anxious to get away from the crowded ship's quarters and were disturbed over the delay on board.

On the deck he met Jonas Petter of Hasteback, the oldest one in their company; he should really have been the one to plan the journey, to act as leader for the group, rather than Karl Oskar.

"Ulrika is stirring up the women," Jonas Petter told him.

On the foredeck, next to the watchman whose duty it was to prevent anyone from going ashore, stood unmarried Ulrika of Vastergohl, the Glad One, talking to a group of women, gesticulating wildly, loud, upset.

"She insists our captain is a slave trader," Jonas Petter said.

What had the Glad One started now? Karl Oskar had long been afraid she might bring shame on their company.

He went to Ulrika; her cheeks were blossoming red and her voice was husky with anger.

"So it's you, Karl Oskar! Now I've found out the truth! Now I know why they won't let us land!"

"It's because of the cholera," said Karl Oskar.

"No, it's not! It's the captain! He keeps us confined here because he is going to hold an auction and sell us! He is going to sell us as slaves to the Americans!"

The women around Ulrika listened fearfully. They might have been listening to the auctioneer she predicted calling for bids on them; one woman had folded her hands as if praying God for help.

Karl Oskar seized Ulrika by the arm. "Come and let's talk alone." He pulled her away from the others and they walked over to the mainmast.

"Don't spread such lies," he warned her. "You might have to pay for it."

"It's the truth," insisted Ulrika. "We've been swindled! We are to be sold on arrival—that's why the captain keeps us penned in on the ship!"

"What fool has put such ideas into your head?"

"You don't have to believe me if you don't want to. But

17

I'm going to run away; I'm not going to stay here and be sold as a slave!"

Ulrika's eyes were flashing. As a little girl in Sweden she had been sold, she knew what it meant; she had been a four-year-old orphan when she was sold at auction, to the lowest bidder. The one who had offered to take her and bring her up for eight daler a year had been a peasant in Alarum, and he had raped her when she was fourteen. The only difference between Sweden and America was that in this new country you were sold to the highest bidder, instead of the lowest; perhaps it might be considered more flattering to be sold to a high bidder, but nevertheless she would have nothing to do with it; she had left the hellhole Sweden to get freedom in America. Now she was going to take her daughter with her and escape from the ship.

"But this is a lie!" exclaimed Karl Oskar. "The captain is not a slave trader."

"Ask your brother if you don't believe me! He is the one who told my daughter."

"Robert? What do you mean?"

"I'll fetch him. Then you can hear for yourself." And Ulrika of Vastergohl hastened to find her daughter Elin and Robert, Karl Oskar's younger brother, dragging them with her as she returned.

"Now tell Karl Oskar what you heard!" she demanded.

Elin looked trustingly from her mother to Karl Oskar. "Robert said the captain is keeping us on board until he gets permission to sell us to the Americans."

The youth looked reproachfully at Elin. "I only said one of the crew told me so."

Karl Oskar turned sternly toward his brother: "Now, tell the whole truth!"

Robert's jaw fell in embarrassment and he looked down at the worn and splintered deck: he had asked one of the seamen why they weren't allowed to land, and the man had said they must stay until the Americans came and got them; they were to be sold at auction. Last voyage, he said, the captain had sold all the passengers to the Turkish Infidel for ten thousand dollars; this time, he didn't wish to rush things, and that was why he kept them aboard. Last time he had sold everyone except two old, worn-out hags who couldn't be used for work or aught else. And no

18

complaints had been raised, for no one had had any relatives in America on whom he could call for help.

The seaman had said he was telling all this to Robert because the captain had refused to share his ten thousand dollars with the crew. The seaman was angry that he couldn't share in the profits from the slave trade in New York, and that was why he had warned Robert and other passengers to get away from the ship before the auction was advertised.

Robert admitted he had not believed the seaman; if the captain wanted to sell people to the Infidel, he would undoubtedly have sailed to Turkey, where the Infidel lived, and not to North America. There was no sense in shipping people back and forth across the Atlantic. Moreover, Robert knew from a book he owned—*Description of the United States of North America*—that it was forbidden to sell white-skinned people as slaves; a person had to have curly hair, and black skin to boot, before he was allowed to be sold.

Robert had told the seaman's story to Elin only because it struck him as funny.

"But you didn't say it was a lie," Elin protested.

"I thought you would know I wasn't serious," Robert explained in embarrassment.

Thus Karl Oskar killed the rumor. And he urged Ulrika to quiet the anxiety she had aroused in the other gullible women. Neither she nor anyone else on board need fear slave chains or sale at auction in North America. The captain was an honest man who was doing all he could to help them, he had even promised to help them get started on their way inland.

Ulrika now turned her anger on Robert: "You brat! You're responsible for this! Karl Oskar, better keep your brother in line from now on."

And Robert was severely reprimanded by Karl Oskar for sowing lies in the mind of a credulous girl. Suppose these stories reached the captain; then there would be trouble. Now they must go and find the man who had started the rumor.

"He isn't on the ship any longer," Robert said hastily.

"You just come and show me the liar!"

"I can't find him. They say he has run away."

Karl Oskar gave his brother a stern look; it had happened before that Robert had been caught in a lie, and it did seem strange that the man had vanished. But this time Karl Oskar let Robert off with a strong warning: If he didn't stick to the truth he might get himself and others into great danger. He was now seventeen years old and he must begin to have some sense of responsibility; he must remember that here in a foreign land unknown dangers awaited them.

Robert felt he had been betrayed by Elin. He had told her this story about the slave trade in strict confidence. The way it had happened was this: Not far from the ship stretched a park, a real manor-house park, with tall, green, thick trees, below which lay cool shadows. But Robert was not allowed to go there, he must remain here, on this rotten ship, in the burning sun. So he had just had to talk to someone to make the time pass more quickly. This he could not explain to his older brother, but he thought Elin might have understood. He certainly would tell her no more stories if she must run to her mother and repeat them.

4

The *Charlotta*'s ex-carpenter entered Captain Lorentz's cabin, stooping so as not to hit his head against the low ceiling. Long Landberg, as he was usually called, was the tallest man ever to sign on this vessel—almost seven feet. His lengthy arms hung loosely against his narrow body. A well-trimmed full beard half hid his healthy smile.

The captain greeted him with a warm handshake. "Any news since last time? This infernal heat is the same." He could easily see that the man he had sent for was eager to unburden himself, and even before Landberg sat down he began: "Yes, I have news this time. You haven't heard, then, Mr. Captain? Wheat-flour Jesus is dead!"

Lorentz stared at him.

"Yes, it's true. Wheat-flour Jesus was murdered. Last month."

"Whom are you talking about, Landberg?"

"Erik Janson, of course. A prophet even in the old country, where he traveled about and sold wheat flour. That's why they called him Wheat-flour Jesus."

"The prophet Janson? Murdered?"

20

"Yea. He was shot like a dog at Cambridge, in the court where he had brought suit. The defendant shot him."

The captain was not surprised by the news. He thought he had some knowledge of the handling of legal matters in this country. Perhaps, tacked to the wall of the courtroom, was the same notice he had seen in a saloon in New York: "Shoot first! Live longer!"

But he realized that the *Charlotta*'s old carpenter was much excited by the happening.

Long Landberg, the apostate, continued: Erik Janson was the worst scoundrel ever to tramp the ground of North America. Landberg had seen him daily during many months and he knew the prophet's creed. Janson called himself the new Christ and had chosen as his apostles twelve befuddled louts whom he kept in attendance, like a tyrant king. Indeed, he had been a cruel tyrant to his followers, plaguing them enough to make angels weep, if there were tears in heaven. No doctor was called for the sick; when one of the disciples lay at death's door, unable to move toe or finger, Janson ordered him to rise up and be healthy, and if the sick one could not, Jason condemned him for sin and lack of faith. Janson, of course, was free from sin and righteous in all ways.

Once, Landberg had defended some poor sick sectarians against this tyranny, with the result that Janson had seized everything he owned, including most of his clothes. Without means, he had been unable to bring suit against the prophet. Janson had said that he was equal with God. . . . Well, the fact was, humanity could thank the man who had shot Wheat-flour Jesus; through this splendid deed he had freed North America from a beast. Janson, a raw, presumptuous peasant boor! Yes, said Landberg, he even looked like the Evil One, his teeth were like tusks, no doubt he was possessed by an evil spirit and had been sent into the world by the devil.

Captain Lorentz, when he had transported some of Janson's followers, had heard them speak of their leader as a Heavenly Light, lit for them in the dark heathen land of Sweden. They had been honest in their faith; to them he had been the returned Christ. And now, after his murder, they would undoubtedly say that, like Christ, he had sealed his religion and faith with his blood.

Was Erik Janson sent by God or by the devil? Perhaps

by neither; who could tell? One had to be satisfied that God Himself knew.

Now Lorentz asked his former carpenter how things were with these sectarians; how were they getting along in that vast prairie land of Illinois where he had heard they were settled?

"Janson said he founded a new Jerusalem," Landberg retorted with derision. "But the fact is, he founded a new hell."

It was true that the community which Janson had built and named Bishop Hill, after his home parish Biskopskulla, had been called Bishop Hell by the Americans, and letters so addressed had reached their destination. But the Janson followers, Landberg admitted, were fine, industrious farmers; they had greatly improved their situation; no longer did they live like beasts in earth huts, but had built themselves houses of bricks, which they made. Nor were bricks the only things they made: though in Sweden they had been temperance people, in Bishop Hill they had built a still, operated by steam and capable of making three hundred gallons of brannvin a day. When they got drunk, they blamed this on the Holy Ghost "filling them," as they called it.

Last spring the sectarians had sent a group of their men to California to dig for gold in the name of God. Even two of their apostles had been sent. Could anyone imagine Saint Peter or Saint Paul digging for gold? But Janson did not seek first the kingdom of God and His righteousness; he was said to have grown so rich that he had the tusks pulled out of his evil mouth and replaced by pure gold. Could a mortal here on earth descend to lower depths of vanity and conceit?

Landberg continued: The people in Bishop Hill believed Erik Janson would rise from the dead in the same manner as his predecessor, Christ. They went about their chores now, making their brick, distilling their brannvin, while waiting for their master's return. Jesus arose on the third day, but six weeks had already elapsed since Janson was shot, and nothing had been heard from him so far as anyone knew.

And this much Landberg said he wished to add: Should Wheat-flour Jesus return to the American continent alive,

22

there were many who would be glad to shoot him a second time.

Captain Lorentz thought to himself, Janson had undoubtedly been in many ways a fine man. But he realized how important it was for Landberg to give vent to his feelings, so he had not interrupted him. Now he returned to their business at hand: "Now you must again help me unload my human cargo."

"Gladly, Captain. I am free at present."

Landberg was pleased to get a new commission; his income had been poor lately, since no emigrant ship had arrived from Sweden for some time. For a while he had helped English captains. But most immigrants this year were German or Irish. If only he had known German, then his income would have been better. It was hard this year to earn an honest living, he told the captain. The swindlers and the runners were as fast as ever, but an honest agent was recognized by all captains: a thin man!

"And tall as a mast," added Captain Lorentz.

"Precisely, Captain! And how large is the cargo this time?"

"Seventy. Most of them are going inland."

"Fine. The immigrant transfer, *Isaac Newton,* runs now every second day up the Hudson to Albany."

The two men began to go over the list of passengers and their destinations. While so occupied, Landberg remembered that he had a message to the captain from a well-known countryman: The Methodist pastor, Olof Hedstrom, on the Bethel Ship here in the harbor, sent his greeting and intended to pay a call the following morning.

"Hmm. So Pastor Hedstrom is still preaching on his old ship. Tell him he is welcome. A fine fellow; he might help the people a great deal."

Through fortunate circumstances, the Swedish Methodists in New York had been permitted to unrig an old ship and turn it into a church. Lorentz had been on board the Bethel Ship after she had been converted into a God's House and he had liked it there. Now that the *Charlotta* was beginning to rot, perhaps some other sect might buy his ship and make a church of her, here in New York Harbor. He mused that it might mark great progress for Christianity if all old, worn-out ships, those nests of sin, could be stripped of their rigging and turned into churches.

23

Pastor Hedstrom undoubtedly was coming to invite the immigrants to a sermon and Holy Communion aboard his Bethel Ship. And Lorentz thought he must ask the minister to make it clear to the passengers that he belonged to the Methodist religion before he gave them the Sacrament. After the *Charlotta*'s previous voyage, some of the Lutheran immigrants had received the Lord's Supper on the Bethel Ship, and only later had it been made fully clear to them that they had been given the Sacrament by a sectarian minister, a teacher of heresy. They had been thrown into great anguish and fear of eternal judgment; they had prayed to God that He might let them throw up the false tokens of grace, but their prayers had not been heard. Yes, even the souls of the emigrants were the responsibility of the captain of an emigrant ship.

"Yes, my old carpenter—three days from now you'll get another load of Swedish farmers for the North American Republic."

And on June 26, early in the morning, when the three-day quarantine was over, the brig *Charlotta* of Karlshamn could at last discharge her living cargo on the pier near Castle Garden in New York Harbor.

II

Battery Park

After seventy days at sea, the seekers of new homes were
again on solid ground—though the restlessness of the Atlantic Ocean remained a while within them. As they set
foot once more on the trustworthy, immovable earth, they
were well satisfied to part with those great masses of water
which the Creator on the Third Day had called Sea, and
they blessed in their hearts that dry part which He had
called Earth. They gave thanks to the Lord God Who in
His mercy had helped the brittle planks to carry them over
the terrifying depths to the longed-for harbor.

On an outjutting tongue of land in the East River stood
Castle Garden, the old fort, now transformed into an
amusement place, and near by, separated from the river
piers by a broad walk, Batttery Park spread its greenery.
This piece of wooded land so near the harbor resounded
daily with heavy peasant tramping and foreign tongues.
The Old World people, having passed through the portals
of the New World, found here their first resting place on
American soil. Battery Park was to the immigrants a cool
and shaded grove on their day of landing.

Here they sat down and refreshed themselves in the
comforting shade of spreading elms and linden trees, here
rested side by side men, women, children, and aged ones,
surrounded by their possessions—chests, baskets, bags,

and bundles, filled with essential belongings. As many knapsacks and bundles as they had been able to carry they had clutched in their hands when walking down the gangplank, holding them so tight that their knuckles whitened, and their cheeks reddened with fear lest hustling foreigners snatch their belongings from them. Never during the whole journey would they leave these important possessions out of sight, these inseparable bed companions during the transport across the ocean.

Rough, broad-shouldered peasants, their faces marked by all the seasons of the year, stood here with hands behind their backs, their eyes appraising the new land. On their bodies hung heavy wadmal clothes, wrinkled and baggy. (These woolen garments—such splendid protection against the bitter cold of the North Sea—were now drenched with sweat and a burden to their wearers on America's sunny shores.) There was a constrained lust for action in these men's hard muscles and sinews; their bodies were power restrained. Crowded in narrow ship's space for many weeks, their hands had had no chores to perform. They had arrived on a new continent anxious to resume accustomed duties, their hands eager to hold the familiar ox thongs and plow handles. Their hands possessed much knowledge, acquired from childhood, inherited through centuries. When now again they stood on solid ground, they felt the lust for work spring up after the painful time of inactivity. But yet a while must their forced rest last, yet a while must they carry their hands behind their backs.

Mothers sat leaning against tree trunks in the park, feeding their babies from the breast; the women emptied their scrawny breasts without filling the stomachs of their babies. The milk gave out long before the babies' hunger, and the little ones cried and fretted, irritated by the heat and discomfort of the heavy woolen garments in which they were bundled. And the mothers rocked their children on their knees—mother-love's cradle, the softest and most comfortable cradle on earth—and tried to lull them to sleep. But the babies whimpered, they wanted to stay awake; now that their eyes saw for the first time the land their parents had chosen for them, it seemed as if they wanted to take in everything; this was the land where they were to grow up, the land that was to be their home.

26

A five-year-old boy, wrapped in a coat that hung to his ankles, sat on his haunches in the grass, chewing a crust of rye bread, a coarse, dark loaf; spots of mildew testified to the fact that this bread had not been baked yesterday, nor on this continent; it came from an old oven in a hidden, stony part of Europe. The boy chewed ravenously and swallowed with determination; the bread in his hand disappeared until only a few crumbs were left; these he tossed into his mouth. The loaf was finished but his hunger remained, and the child looked questioningly at his empty hand: Why did food end before hunger? Mother said: "It is the last loaf I have, the last one from home; now you will never get any more bread from home." And the boy pondered this . . . Why no more bread from home?

In Battery Park the immigrants took stock of their food baskets; they counted their loaves of bread and scraped away the mildew; many were those who ate their last slice in confidence that the soil of the new country would feed them from now on.

An even stream of people moved along the river road which separated Battery Park from Castle Garden: these were the inhabitants of New York, the people who lived in the greatest city of North America. Here walked leisurely men in tall, black hats, dressed in tail coats and tight-fitting trousers which enclosed their legs almost like cloth skin. Here walked women in bonnets and tightly laced waists from which hung skirts of generous proportions, reaching the ground. Others had skirts spread out like birds' beautiful tail feathers, and of all colors: red, white, green, and gold; checkered skirts, polka-dotted and striped. Over their heads the women held parasols in bright colors, like small-paned canopies of heaven. The men carried Spanish canes.

The walkers paid no attention to the people camping in Battery Park. The appearance of immigrants under the trees in the park was neither new nor unusual—they saw immigrants almost every day when walking along the river. Shiploads of immigrants arrived daily and would continue to arrive; the people landed, waited in Battery Park for inland transportation, moved on and were gone. A new group arrived in their place—new people gathered here constantly, waiting under the trees. This was the endless train of aliens, outsiders; the immigrants were one of the permanent sights for promenading New Yorkers; they would always be there, they were part of the park, they belonged to it, like the leaves on the trees and the grass on the ground. The immigrants, it seemed, would always wait there, under the trees in Battery Park.

The immigrants came from places where they knew everyone and were known; they had seldom seen a stranger. Now they had arrived in a land where everyone was a stranger; the inhabitants of New York were a new and strange sight to the immigrants. The people in the park looked at the stream of people on the road: the newly arrived looked at those who were established here; these were the Americans, settled, comfortable, having found their place in the new land, able to move unhindered, walking in security, free of worries, and able to speak to any one they met. The immigrants were strayed wanderers, seeking a place to live and work; the others had found what they were seeking; the homeless observed those who had homes.

The home seekers stopped a moment in Battery Park, alien, confused, bewildered, insecure. They were overtaken by surprise at their first meeting with the unknown country. But they were to participate in the breaking of the land and the changing of the character of the country they had just entered, these waiting here in the cool grove on the East River.

III

Milk and White Bread

The day they left Sweden the emigrants from Ljuder Parish had counted sixteen in their group. For one of them a watery grave had opened during the voyage, but as Fina-Kajsa from Oland had joined their company, they were still sixteen when they gathered together on the American shore in Battery Park.

Danjel Andreasson of Karragarde sat by himself, a little to the side of the others, next to his America chest. He was reading in his psalmbook, his head was bent down, and his bushy, brown beard swept the book, open at Hymn 344—"At the Death of a Mate." A dried flower, a reseda, lay as bookmark between the leaves; it had grown in the flower bed at home, cared for and tended by his wife. The page with the psalm was badly worn from much use.

> O Death, why hast thou snatched away
> My bosom Love from me?
> In sorrow and despair I pray,
> But comfort flees from me. . . .

Danjel Andreasson had arrived in the new land to which the Lord had guided him with four motherless little children. He had lost Inga-Lena, his dear wife and earthly helpmate; the Lord had stricken him and trampled on him; he was now only a wretched human worm, wriggling under the heel of the Lord.

He had searched his inner self and arrived at a new understanding: he had sinned the sin of self-righteousness. In his presumption he had considered himself better than others and had believed that his sins once and for all had been washed away and tied up in Christ's napkin cloth that bound His head at burial. He had held himself righteous, unable to sin any more. But on the ship, as he had lain in all his wretchedness covered with his vomit, listening to the tempest and feeling the depths below him, he had learned that he had been found wanting in the eyes of the Lord.

In his vanity he had believed that when he reached the harbor he would be able to praise God in the foreign language; in his conceit he had considered himself an equal of Christ's apostles who were visited by the Holy Ghost on the first Whitsuntide, and he had thought that the outpouring of the Holy Spirit would take place in him so that he would be able to use the American tongue. His Creator had already given him a speaking tongue, and this in itself was so great a miracle that it was presumptuous to expect God to give him the ability to use the tongue for all languages.

Sitting here now, he heard the buzz of this foreign language which he had expected his ears to understand and his tongue to imitate. But his ears recognized no sounds and his tongue remained dumb. The words of the language he heard did not reach him, he could not use them in his mouth. No outpouring of the Spirit filled him, no cloven tongues appeared, no visions were seen. He could not prophesy in the new language; his ears were closed and his tongue lame.

Danjel Andreasson entered North America a mute and lost stranger among all other strangers in this multitude of people, races, and tribes here gathered. Once, in Babel, the Lord had confused human language so that men could not understand one another; because each was a sinner, his tongue was capable of his native language only. And because Danjel had thought himself righteous, the Holy Ghost had failed him in the new land; he was not worthy of spiritual outpouring.

Danjel was stricken to the earth, God had chastised him, left him naked in all his frailty and faults. He beheld one vision only, a terrifying one: Man was smaller than the worm, because he was the food for worms—he, Danjel Andreasson of Karragarde, was food for crawling creatures of the earth.

Once he had conceived this picture of himself, he ceased to explain God's word to his fellow travelers on the ship; how could he explain Holy Writ when he hadn't rightly understood it? How could he advise and admonish others when he himself had committed the grossest of sins? How could he be a spiritual guide for others if he were unable to guide his own soul?

"At the Death of a Mate"—Danjel knew this hymn by heart and he closed the book and laid it on the ground. Then he knelt down and folded his hands over the lid of his America chest: "In Thy presence, Father in Heaven, I crawl in the dust."

On the ship Danjel had given a promise to the Lord— he would build an altar of thanks in the new land. The old clothes chest from the loft of Karragarde became a Lord's altar on American soil, and next to it now knelt a crushed man, praising and thanking God; with a full heart he thanked Him for the trial which had been sent for his betterment; he thanked the Almighty Who had snatched away Inga-Lena, taken from him his earthly helpmate; he thanked the Lord Who had taken the mother from four little children; he blessed and praised the Lord God for the ills, sufferings, and persecutions he and his beloved ones had had to endure; he thanked his Creator with the warmth of his heart for all the evils which had been bestowed upon him.

God had sought out Danjel Andreasson who now bent like a worm under His foot. At his entrance into the new, young, and healthy world, he prayed for a rebirth, he prayed to be washed clean from that vanity and self-righteousness which clung to him from the Old World. And he felt that God had come close to him now, closer than He had ever come to him in the country he had left.

2

Kristina lay with her head on the bulging knapsack; it was

31

a hard and knotty pillow but to her it seemed the softest down; the knapsack had come with them from home—it was something intimate and friendly. She lay still; she was weak from her severe illness, every limb was weak and weary. If only she could rest, rest a long time; if only she could lie like this, quite still, stretched out on her back in the grass, without having to move even a little finger or a little toe. Such were the delights she desired. If she could remain still, perfectly still, then the tiredness would leave her body. But as yet she could only find momentary rest, soon they must move on again.

A few feet away from her another woman was sleeping, no doubt more tired than she—old Fina-Kajsa lay there with open and gaping mouth. She had pulled up her skirt in a roll around her waist, exposing a worn-out, mended, dirty petticoat which once must have been red. In her arms, tight against her chest, she held a wooden casket decorated with green and yellow dots. It contained her most treasured possessions. The casket had no lock but was tied with heavy string, and the sleeping old woman held it close to her breast the way a mother holds her little child. Through her pointed, toothless mouth, which opened like a black hole, Fina-Kajsa snored. At her feet stood her iron pot, now wing-broken and crippled, one leg lost during the voyage. No wonder people had ill endured the crossing when even iron vessels were broken.

Uncle Danjel's large white linen sack, once Inga-Lena's pride, was now frayed and dirty, having fared badly on the ship. Ulrika of Vastergohl, who was looking after Danjel's belongings now he was a widower, had just opened the sack and was searching for something in it. She was dressed today in Aunt Inga-Lena's best dress; she and her daughter had divided the dead one's clothes. Kristina never spoke to Ulrika more than was absolutely necessary; for her uncle's sake Kristina had endured Ulrika's company, but Karl Oskar had promised that they would separate themselves from the former parish whore as soon as possible. Kristina did not begrudge the Glad One her aunt's clothing; both she and her daughter must have something to cover themselves with, and they had earned the garments now that they were taking care of the poor children who had lost their mother.

The dress Elin was wearing had also belonged to Inga-

32

Lena, and it was too big for the sixteen-year-old girl. It flowed in large billows and bags about her lithe body. She sat with a small chip basket on her knees and it reminded Kristina of berry-picking time. What kind of berries might there be to pick in this country? Wild strawberries, so sweet to taste, and with such delicate white flowers in the spring? Blueberries which colored the fingers black in summer. Fiery red cranberries on the tussocks in autumn? Elin held the handle of her basket firmly, as if just about to go out into the berry lands—she held on to it as one holds to a single worldly possession.

And Kristina sat up, the better to keep an eye on her family belongings. There stood their chest—five feet long and three high—reinforced with broad iron bands which had held it together unharmed across the Atlantic; only one corner of the lid was scraped a little. On the front of the chest glowed the letters, still red, painted there before departure: *Home-owner Karl Oskar Nilsson, North America.*

And there stood their sacks and their food basket. The small bundle next to Kristina moved at times, it was alive —in it slept little Harald, the baby. Karl Oskar had gone back to the ship to pick up something forgotten and he had the two other children with him.

From where she sat among the trees Kristina could see the harbor and the long row of ships at the piers. Right in front of her was a tall, yellow-green house with a round tower which it carried like a crown. The house was built on an islet, and people went to it across a bridge. High up on the wall over the entrance there was something written in tall black letters, visible from where she sat: *Castle Garden.* It was, of course, the name of the house, whatever it might mean. In front of the round house on the same isle there was a smaller and lower house, one wall of which was almost covered by an inscription: *Labor Exchange;* the name of that house was painted in the largest letters she had ever seen.

They put names on the houses in America. And the incomprehensible writing she saw reminded her that she was now in a land where she understood not the smallest word of what people said; they might speak into her very ears, yet she wouldn't hear them; she might talk, and they would not hear her. From the first moment here in Amer-

33

ica she suffered from two defects—deafness and dumb-ness; she must go about among strangers a deaf-mute.

It was gentry she saw walking about there near the big house with the tower; the women had umbrellas like the ladies at home in Sweden. But it wasn't raining, it was en-tirely clear, the sun shone in a cloudless sky. Why did the women carry umbrellas today? Perhaps they had brought them along for show.

Yes, the sun was shining, there was an unmerciful heat in America. The air was oppressive and she breathed with difficulty; she had the sensation of inhaling pungent steam while bending over a pot of boiling water. But her happi-ness in being on the earth again was so great that it almost obliterated the discomfort of the American heat. On the ship she had believed that she never more would get out into God's clear daylight; she had felt she would end her life enclosed in the dark hold; she had thought she would never again see a patch of grass or a green leaf. But now she lay here on the green earth in the sun. She could just as easily, like poor Inga-Lena, have been lying on the bot-tom of the ocean, her body lowered for monsters of the deep to devour. But she had been saved from them, she and her loved ones—what else mattered?

To go out on the ocean in a fragile ship with three small children—she felt it had been to tempt the Lord God. In a long and fervent prayer she thanked her Father in Heaven Who in His mercy had let them reach solid ground in health.

She almost felt as if she had been dead and awakened to life again, as if a miracle had happened to her. How wonderfully still everything about her seemed! The joy of lying here on the peaceful, quiet earth could only be fully appreciated by one who had long lived in a constantly moving and heaving bed, one who had been tossed about on high, restless billows. At last she was liberated from the ship's swing which had thrown her up and down, she was free from the dizzy journeys to the top of the waves and into their valleys. She had always loved to play with a swing but never again would she be tempted by the swing of the sea; with this she was sated for life. Never again would she desire to see this terrifying ocean, never again would her feet leave solid ground.

She felt thirsty, her tongue was parched, and her appe-

34

tite was returning now that she was on land; she must eat well now that she had one more life to feed.

She put her hand against her abdomen: again she could feel the stirring within her. Many days had passed since the last time she felt the child move, and she had begun to wonder if it still could be alive. It would not have seemed strange to her had it died, so ill and weak she had been from seasickness and scurvy. A joy filled her as she now felt it stir: once having conceived a child, she wished to bear it alive; a stillborn child was a shame and God's chastisement—the woman was not worthy to carry into the world the life He had created within her.

When was it due? She counted the months on her fingers: she had conceived it sometime in the middle of February—March, April, May, June—she was already in her fifth month. July, August, September, October, November—her childbed would be sometime in the middle of November.

About half the time left until she was in childbed. Would they have a bed by then, a bed in which she could bear her child?

The child was alive. A life that had traveled free across the ocean had come into the land. It stirred and moved in its hidden nest, stronger than the mother had felt it before. Not only had she herself come to life again, the child within her seemed to have gained new life, now that she had carried it into the New World.

3

"Are you asleep, Kristina?"

She had dozed off. Karl Oskar stood by her side, wiping his sweaty face with his jacket sleeve.

"What a heat! They can fry bacon on the roofs here!" He took off his wadmal coat and threw it on the ground. Johan and Lill-Marta came rushing to their mother.

"Guess, Mother! Father has bought something!"

"Guess what Father bought!"

In one hand Karl Oskar carried a paper bag, in the other their own large pitcher. He held up the bag to Kristina's nose. "You want to smell something?"

"Look in the bag, Mother!" shouted Johan. "Father has bought sweet milk and wheat bread!"

35

"Sweet milk and wheat bread!" Lill-Marta repeated after him.

Kristina inhaled a pleasing odor which she had not smelled for a long time. She stuck her hand into the bag and got hold of something soft: fresh, white rolls, wheat rolls!

"Karl Oskar—it isn't true."

"Look in the pitcher!"

"Mother! It's sweet milk!" shouted Johan.

Karl Oskar held up the pitcher, so full of milk that it splashed over.

"Be careful. Don't lose any," she warned.

"Now you must eat and drink, Kristina."

"Karl Oskar, I don't believe my eyes. How could you buy it?"

"The Finn helped me. Eat and drink now. We have already had some."

Sweet milk! Fresh milk! When had she last tasted it? Not one drop had they been able to obtain on the ship. It was in their quarters in Karlshamn that she had tasted milk last time; long, long ago, in another world, in the Old World.

Kristina took hold of the pitcher with both hands, carefully; she mustn't let it splash over. Tears came to her eyes; she had to see what milk looked like, she had forgotten. This milk was yellow-white, thick and rich; no spoon had skimmed off the cream; and it smelled as fresh as if it had just been milked into this pitcher.

Karl Oskar opened the knapsack and took out a tin mug which he filled with milk from the pitcher. "Drink— as much as you are able to. You need it to get well."

Kristina held the mug. "But the children? Have they had enough?"

No mother could begin to eat and drink before her children had been given food and drink. But Karl Oskar told her that Johan and Lill-Marta had eaten themselves full and drunk until their thirst was quenched back there at the store where he had bought the food.

Kristina drank. She emptied the mug in a few swallows, and Karl Oskar filled it again; she drank until she felt satisfied; never before had she realized that milk could be so good. She herself had sat on the milking stool and pressed out hundreds of gallons of milk from cow udders, she had

36

strained milk for her children morning, noon, and night, she had fattened calves on milk, she had brought up piglets on milk—during her whole life she had never longed for milk until she started on this voyage. Now she accepted the pitcher of milk as a gift from God; she felt she would cry.

She said the milk was cream-rich and good. Then she took a roll from the bag and looked it over; this roll was almost as big as a small loaf at home.

They still had a little left in their food basket. The ship's fare had been rancid, bitter with salt, smelling of old chests and musty barrels; Kristina still had a taste in her mouth from the dried, hard rye loaves. Toward the end of the voyage there had been worms in the bread, and they had been forced to soak it in water and fry it in pork fat before they could eat it; much of the fare they had been given on the ship had been little better than pig food.

After those hard loaves, how delicious it was to bite into a soft, fresh wheat roll! The rolls looked a little puffy, but she soon saw that they were well filled under the crust. At the very first bite she felt that she was eating festival food.

"They bake mighty fine bread in America," said Kristina.

"Here they eat wheat bread on weekdays as well as on Sundays," said Karl Oskar.

"I've heard so. Can it be true?"

Kristina was a little skeptical. To her, wheat bread had always been a food for holidays and festival occasions. She used to buy a few pounds of wheat flour for a baking at Christmas, Easter, and Midsummer. Then she counted the loaves and locked them in the bread chest so the children couldn't eat them unless allowed; such food had to be carefully portioned out, each one getting his share.

"It's swarming with people here in New York," she said. "Is there enough wheat bread for all of them?"

Karl Oskar said, that, according to what he saw with his own eyes, there must be plenty of food in this country; in several stores he had seen quantities of wheat loaves, piled high like stacks of firewood at home, and he had seen whole tubs full of sweet milk. He was sure that both she and the children could eat and drink all they needed to regain their strength.

The bundle at Kristina's side began to move and a sound came from it; Harald had awakened and cried out. The mother picked him up and his cry died as soon as he felt the sweet milk in his mouth. The little one swallowed the unfamiliar drink in silence, he simply kept silent and swallowed: surprise overwhelmed him.

It hurt Kristina's heart to see how fallen off her children were, how pale their faces, how sunken their cheeks, how blue their lips, how tired and watery their eyes. When she took them in her arms their bodies were light, their arms and legs thin, the flesh on their limbs loose; it was as if muscles and bones had parted from each other. They had dwindled this way from having been kept so long in the dark unhealthy hold below decks. How often had she worried about them when she lay sick, unable to care for them, while all three of them crawled over her in her bed. How often had she reproached herself because of her inability to give them a single bite of fresh food, or a mouthful of sweet milk. How she had longed for the moment when she could walk on shore with Johan, Lill-Marta, and Harald. These poor, pale, skinny children certainly were in need of America's good sweet milk and fresh wheat rolls.

Johan had been told to guard his father's coat lying there in the grass, and he said impatiently: "Father, you forget the apple! The apple for Mother!"

From the pocket of his father's coat he took a shining red apple, amost as big as his own head. The boy handed it proudly to his mother.

"Have you ever seen such a big apple?" said Karl Oskar. "I got it for nothing!"

Near the pier, he told her, they had met a woman carrying a large basket filled with beautiful apples. Johan and Lill-Marta had stopped and looked longingly at the fruit. The woman had spoken to them, but they had not understood a word. Then she gave the children each an apple, which they immediately gulped down. He, too, had received an apple—which he had saved for her.

"Karl Oskar—you're good. . . ."

She weighed the large apple in her hand; it must weigh almost a pound, she thought; it was the largest one she had ever seen. The children's eyes were glued to the fruit in their mother's hand, and Kristina asked Karl Oskar to cut it in four equal pieces, so that all would get even portions. He pulled out his pocketknife and divided the apple carefully; each quarter was as big as a whole apple at home.

And the immigrant family ate and enjoyed their first American fruit, which was full of juice and cooled their mouths.

"Is it a new apple?" exclaimed Kristina when she tasted it.

"Yes, doesn't it taste like one?"

"I thought it was fruit from last summer."

"Here in America the apples ripen before Midsummer," said Karl Oskar.

Yes, the sour-fresh taste in her mouth convinced Kristina. It must be true what Karl Oskar said—she was eating a fruit of the new crop; yet it was only Midsummer.

Midsummer—the holidays had passed, a Midsummer no one had celebrated. Enclosed on the ship, they could not celebrate, they could only talk of the Midsummer holidays in the land they had left.

Just a little more than a stone's throw from where she sat Kristina could see the pier where the *Charlotta* was still tied up, discharging the rest of her cargo. She recognized the Swedish brig by its familiar flag. After unloading, it would sail back again. The ship would once more have to find her way across the restless, endless water. It had been a bleak and misty spring day when she left the Swedish harbor; perhaps it would be a bleak and misty autumn day before she returned to the same harbor. Then their ship would be at home. *At home*—the thought cut Kristina to the quick, and she chewed more slowly on her piece of apple.

Midsummer at home—Father putting young birches on either side of the door, Mother serving coffee at their finest table, which had been moved out into the yard and placed under the old family maple; Maria and Emma, her sisters, picking lilacs and decorating themselves for the village dance. The house would smell of newly scrubbed floors, smell clean, inside and out, smell of lilac blossoms and flowering birches. And when they gathered around the table under the family maple—the guardian tree of their home—they would all be dressed in their Sunday best, and there would be much fun and much laughter. At home it was always so for Midsummer.

Did they speak this year of one who had been among them before? Did they mention her name—Kristina, who had moved away with Karl Oskar to North America? Did they ask how it was with her this moment, this afternoon, this Midsummer Eve?

She knew how it was at home, but those at home did not know how it was here.

She had traveled a long road, almost endlessly long; she knew the sea that separated her from her homeland, that incomprehensibly wide water which separated *home* and *here*. She would never again travel that road, never again traverse the sea. So she would never again be with them at home.

Now for the first time she began to think deeply into this: *Never again to be with them at home.*

The thought suddenly disturbed her profoundly, not less because she could still see the ship, over there in the harbor, the ship that was to turn about, to sail home again. This ship on which she had suffered so horribly, what did it mean to her now? Did she want to go back with it again? Did she want to stay another ten weeks in a pen in the dark hold? No! No! Why was it then that her tears were breaking through? Why? She did not understand it.

Karl Oskar sat down and wiped the perspiration from his forehead with his sleeve; even in the shade the heat was melting.

"We are to board a ship and ride on the river this evening," he told her.

She was thinking of the road behind them—he was thinking of the way ahead.

"We are late getting started," he said.

He was afraid they might have arrived too late in the season. No one could have imagined they would sail the sea until Midsummer. He had expected them to reach their place of settling by now and have to time to hoe some land, sow some barley, plant some potatoes. What would happen to them next winter if they didn't get something into the earth before it was too late this year to grow and ripen?

Karl Oskar agreed with what Kristina had said, and it worried him: this town of New York swarmed with people; perhaps the whole country was already filled up. No

40

one in their group had ever seen so many human beings in one place. Great numbers must have come before them, this they could see with their own eyes, and every day new ships arrived, with great new flocks of people. Perhaps they had been deceived, perhaps it was too late, the best land already taken; perhaps America was entirely filled up with new settlers.

But he must not disturb Kristina with these thoughts on their very first day in the new land. He must, rather, try to cheer her up, she was so weak and depressed after her illness. He had just given her a foretaste of the delicacies offered them on entering an American store, and he must assure her that all he had seen and heard so far was promising.

"I think America is a good land. We need have no regrets; that I must write home."

Kristina swallowed hard and turned her head. Karl Oskar must not see her tears today, their day of landing. And why did she cry, after all? She was on solid ground, she had all her loved ones around her. They were drinking sweet milk and eating fresh white bread—what more did she want?

Karl Oskar continued: For the past three evenings he had been writing a letter to Sweden, and now while they were waiting here in the park he must finish it. He could write on the lid of the America chest, it made a good table, then he could send the letter back with the ship. It would be September before it reached home, it would take from spring until fall before the nearest ones at home would hear anything about their voyage.

Kristina had not spoken for a long while; she had not said a single word since he had told her that American apples ripened before Midsummer. Could that have surprised her so much? He turned and looked at her. Something must have made her sad. But he would not ask her —whatever it was, a question now would only increase her sadness.

He handed her the bag with the bread: "Eat some more, Kristina."

"It tasted awfully good. If you think there'll be enough for . . ."

She ate one more white roll. And her first day on American soil was ever after to be a memory of sweet milk and fresh bread—milk and wheat rolls.

41

IV

A Letter to Sweden

North America, 26 Day of June, 1850

Dearly Beloved Parents and Sister,

That you may Always be well are my Deep Wishes to you.

I will now let you know about the journey from our Fatherland. We completed it in 10 Weeks and arrived in the town of New York. The Swedish Ship reached the American strand safely on Midsummer Eve.

There was great Joy among us as we beheld the New Land, the Americans are noble folk, letting all foreigners through their Gates, none asked us One word about our Situation, no one is denied Entrance. We were not asked if we were Poor or Rich.

All in our family are with Life and Health. The Sea heaved considerably but we endured the Journey well. I must tell you that Danjel of Karragarde was stricken by the great Inconvenience that out at Sea He lost his wife Inga-Lena. Her time was up. But it would be too cumbersome to describe our Journey.

New York is a large town and the Houses are large and high. It swarms with People of all kinds of the known World, Black, Brown, and Colored in Skin.

But they are People. We are met with kindliness by all.

The Americans are Thin and Pale, they say it comes from the Heat. The air is warmer here than at home.

All strange Phenomena can be seen here—they can not be described in a Letter. They say the Time in North America differs six Hours with the Time in Sweden in such a Way that all Clocks and Watches have been turned back Six Hours. Swedish Paper Money is not allowed to be changed here, except with the Captain on the Ship, but Gold and Silver have their value here the same as at home. Our Swedish money is less in value than American money.

Carry no Sorrow for me, kind Parents. Here we are well taken care of. I left satisfied my Fatherland. If Health and Strength remain with me I shall fairly well take care of Myself and Mine here in North America. When I get something to work on with my Own Hands I shall look well after it, I think it will not be hard to get along here.

On our Arrival we met a Nobel Woman who gave us Apples from her basket. Apples in America are uncommonly large. Many fruits are offered here but not Planted in Sweden. The Americans eat wheat Bread at nearly every meal and use Good food.

Our dear Children are healthy and well, they talk much of you. Go with Our Greeting to Kristina's Beloved Parents and Family in Duvemala, say to them their Daughter has arrived in America with health and Satisfaction.

Our Ships Captain has bespoken a Boat which will freight us deeper into the land. On the enclosed piece of Paper I have written down a Place where we intend to Stop and settle. Will you, Sister Lydia write to your Brother, we wish next time to hear of the changes at home.

Be kind and let us know the date when this letter arrives in Sweden so that I may figure out how long Time it takes from North America. Do not Pay the Freight for the Letter, then it is more sure to Reach us.

I send my Greetings to all friends and relatives in Our Parish, we are alive and well bodily and Our Souls, Nothing in this world is Wanting Us.

Written down in great haste by your Devoted Son
Karl Oskar Nilsson

V

The Most Beautiful Street in the World

It had been generally understood on the brig *Charlotta*
that about half the inhabitants in the town of New York
were loose people—thieves, rogues, robbers, and criminals. Consequently, none of the immigrants dared go alone
on the streets of this town. But the second mate had promised Robert and Arvid, who was Danjel Andreasson's
servant, that he would go with the boys and show them
New York as soon as they arrived. And on the afternoon
of the day of landing he had to do some errands for the
captain and invited the boys to accompany him through
the city.

The second mate had been kind and helpful to them
during the voyage. They had never heard his real name
mentioned—when anyone spoke to him, he was called Mr.
Mate; when anyone spoke of him, he was referred to as
the Finn. He was a talkative man and the only one of the
ship's officers they had come to know.

The Finn now went with the two youths, walking by the
long row of ships tied up at the piers; on the East River
there were piers along the whole shore, it seemed. And the
Finn pointed and explained: In this port flew all the flags
of the world, side by side; over there lay a frigate with the
American flag, strewn with stars and stripes. They must
learn to recognize this flag, now that they were to settle

45

here. This vessel was an East Indiaman, as seafolk called it. It had a beautiful sail. American ships had nice hulls. The ship over there, the one like a barge, was a Dutchman; nothing fine about that one; it was called a smack. And that long ship loaded with planks was Norwegian, or half Swedish, for after all the two countries had the same king. But they had better not mention that to any Norwegians they met, they might get their heads knocked off.

On the broad river arm the ships were crowding each other, steamboats, sailing ships, sloops, rowboats, ferries, and barges in one great galaxy. In the middle of the river, boats moved with the aid of sails; nearer the shore, wheels under the water drove them. The tall narrow smokestacks of the steamers rose like a forest of black, burned tree trunks over the harbor. The Hudson and the East River, with their bays, estuaries, and canals, flowed around the city of New York, encircled it in their arms, and the city of New York pushed its piers and embankments into the rivers and broke them up. Smoke from house chimneys and steamer funnels flowed together into great clouds, floated by a weak westerly breeze toward the Atlantic.

A small vessel without sail, wheels, or oars moved with great speed across the water and aroused Robert's interest. He asked what made it move so speedily. The Finn said it was a steam ferry. Didn't they see the smoking funnel from a small house in the center of the ship?

The *Charlotta*'s second mate pointed out and explained things to the boys; he spoke of barks and smacks, schooners and galleases, but of this they understood little. From the deck of a large sailing vessel came song and loud, gay voices. A group of men in broad-brimmed hats, apparently passengers, were making merry on the ship. The boys wanted to stop and listen to them; they were quite curious.

The Finn said that this was a clipper ship from California, ready to sail for San Francisco. The ship was a new, fast sailer, sheathed in copper; the men on board were California bound, to dig for gold.

The ship's name was *Angelica,* and from her prow hung a red, flapping pennant with jolly words: *Ho! Ho! Ho! For California!* This pennant did not resemble the flags on other ships, nor did the passengers resemble other ships' passengers; these men were laughing, noisy, singing lusty

46

songs. It seemed to the boys as though the ship had no command.

The Finn further informed the boys that a shipload of women, both white and colored, was to sail from New York for the gold fields. There was a scarcity of women throughout America, in San Francisco there were only fifty, and the gold diggers were said to be languishing from lust. Cases of attacks on mules and mares had been reported—woman hunger could drive men insane.

But there was plenty of gold out there, it grew in the earth as potaotes grow in Sweden. In the rivers they could fish for gold lumps, big as eggs. The Finn himself had seen samples of twenty-three carat California gold right here in New York. Beggars in California, of course, went about in rags, as did beggars the world over, but California beggars were dressed in glittering golden rags. A hundred ships had arrived in the port of San Francisco, and every crew member had run away to the gold fields. The gold would soon be spread all over the world, and in a few years the whole world would be rich.

But very few men returned alive from the gold fields. The Finn had heard that the passengers on the *Angelica* had ordered their tombstones in New York and were taking them along—this to save money, since it was cheaper to have them engraved here.

Robert came to new life, seeing and hearing about this clipper ship; he looked wonderingly and longingly at the *Angelica*. She wasn't like the *Charlotta,* either in name or otherwise. She was a happy ship with happy passengers; as soon as the men finished one song they immediately started another:

> Blow, boys, blow for California!
> There's plenty of gold,
> So I've been told
> On the banks of the Sacramento. . . .

The men waved, hats in hand, to the crowd on the pier. The passengers on the Swedish *Charlotta* also had sung, but mostly hymns, funeral hymns, and seldom had any of her passengers laughed. And while Robert didn't understand the words of the songs from the *Angelica*, he didn't think her passengers were singing hymns. Yet these sing-

47

ing gold diggers were traveling with their own engraved tombstones. How could people be so boisterous and happy, sailing with their tombstones? Perhaps, thought Robert, they were happy and sang because they were doing the wisest thing people can do in this world: their course might be perilous, but anyone wanting to get rich in America must, danger or no, head for the place where gold could be picked from the earth itself.

"They have fun on that boat," said Arvid with a touch of envy.

"The men on the gold-rush ship are drunk," explained the Finn. "I wouldn't be surprised if they drink up their tombstones before they leave."

The *Angelica*—Robert looked at the clipper ship's stern where the name was painted. *Angelica* and *Charlotta* were two women's names. *Charlotta* was heavy, hard, dour, stern, harsh, and commanding; *Angelica* easy, soft, light, and gay. *Charlotta* sounded like the name of a fat farm mistress, authoritative, masterful; *Angelica* like a tender, delicate girl, like a bird's twitter in a flowering meadow early in spring; there was joy and freedom in that name.

The next ship he would travel on must have such a name.

Now the passengers on the clipper ship began jumping about in wild leaps.

"Those men must be dancing the polka," said the Finn.

"What kind of dance is that?" asked Robert.

"It's a new Hungarian war dance; in fact, an unchristian whore dance. Let's get on, we've lots to see today."

Reluctantly, Robert left the *Angelica* with her fluttering red banner; there were many hundreds of ships in the New York Harbor, but only one he wished to board.

They left the piers and turned off to the left, cut across the Battery, and went into town. If they wished to get a good view of Manhattan, the Finn said, they must go over to Weehawken; unfortunately, he didn't have time to go with them, but once up there they could see thousands of houses and hundreds of churches; up there they could feel they were really seeing the world.

In his description book Robert had read about New York, and he knew it was the New World's largest, most active town, that houses were six stories tall, and streets sometimes seventy-five feet wide. Now he wondered whether it were true that half of the inhabitants were murderers, robbers, and swindlers.

"It's a little exaggerated," said the Finn. "Only one-tenth are criminals." And he added: It might be better to put it this way: every fourth house they passed was a saloon, every fifth woman they met was a whore, and every fifty man a criminal. Perhaps it would be better not to say exactly, but rather thereabouts, as far as a visiting seafarer could judge.

Robert began to inspect the people they met on the street more closely, particularly the younger women.

"Every fifth woman a whore, Mr. Mate?"

"Yes, maybe thereabouts, yes, just about."

The Finn continued: There were in this town twenty thousand known and public sluts, besides all the private ones whom only God could count. There were two thousand whorehouses, open day and night, seven days of the week, except for the hours of service on Sundays. There were ten thousand saloons, and every saloon keeper had in his pay an undertaker, who came with his cart and dragged away the corpses of those who drank themselves to death. The American brannvin was the strongest in the world, and some saloon keepers even put a pinch of poison into the drink to make it smoother and more tasty; from childhood Americans had hardened themselves to spiced and poisoned drinks, but a foreigner might fall dead on the floor as he stood at the bar. In the most notorious nests, like the Old Brewery at Five Points, the saloon was on the first floor, the whorehouse on the second, and the morgue in the cellar. The guests got drunk in the saloon, then went upstairs to the girls, where they were robbed, murdered, undressed, and pushed through a chute to the morgue in the cellar. Yes, it was true, there were places here in New York where one was served speedily and efficiently. The police never dared go near such places. One den at Five Points had been demolished a few years ago when more than a thousand corpses were found.

Robert and Arvid felt their scalps tingle at the Finn's stories. But, fortunately, remembered Robert, he carried nothing of value with him, and if you didn't carry anything on a walk, you couldn't be robbed. His inheritance had been used for the voyage, and only a few Swedish coppers remained in his purse.

But Arvid clutched the watch chain which hung across his vest and whispered into Robert's ear: He had brought along his watch, perhaps it was risky, what should he do about it? Robert didn't even have a watch; no one could rob him even though each tenth person was a thief.

The boys from Ljuder knew very little about towns. Before coming to New York, they had passed through only one town, Karlshamn. (Arvid had not even read about towns, as he couldn't read; before Robert had shown him a geography schoolbook, he had thought the whole world consisted only of Sweden.) But the boys did not wish to appear ignorant, as though unused to people. Robert therefore asked the Finn, with an intonation reflecting familiarity with the subject: Were the women in the New York whorehouses born in this country or were they immigrants?

The Finn answered that nearly all such women were born in the Old World; some had fallen into sin while crossing on the ships; others, perhaps, ran out of traveling money when they reached New York, and when they couldn't get beyond the pier, they sold that which could be sold most easily and quickly. But a whore's life in North America lasted only four years at the most. Then came death. That is to say, if she were healthy and sound at the beginning. Most of them became venereal cases, their bodies covered with stinking sores, their limbs rotting away, falling off one after the other. The poison buried itself inside their bones, he had heard; there it reproduced itself, from generation to generation. In this way God's law was fulfilled, as it was written in the commandment of the catechism: the sins of the fathers were visited on the children, unto a third and fourth generation "of them that hate Me."

When they rounded a corner, their guide stopped and pointed to a stone pedestal near the street: "On that foundation stood the last king who reigned in America."

The mass of stone was at least twenty feet high. Robert asked: "What was the king's name?"

"I don't remember. He was an English king. He was made of lead!"

"Oh, I understand; it was a statue?"

"That's right, boys! It was a lead statue of a king!"

The Finn explained: The English king reigned so

poorly and so tyrannically that the Americans went to war to get rid of him. But they had a scarcity of bullets for their guns, so they melted down this leaden image of their king. When the English came to chastise the obstinate Americans, they were greeted by pieces of lead from their own king. The fine bullets hit them right between the eyes! So the Americans won the war and became a free people. That's what happened to the last king in America.

And who could tell—perhaps the European people one day would put their king statues in pots, and boil and melt them and make bullets of them. Then they too might be free.

Robert nodded; he understood: because kings were forbidden in America, one might speak as one would about them.

Now they turned right and entered a wide street. In great pride the Finn held both his hands out over the street as though to show something particularly his own, something his hands had made: this was Broadway, the most beautiful street in the world!

They had been sucked into a solid mass of people moving slowly about their errands, as it was impossible to hurry, giving way always to the right to avoid bumping against one another. So the boys did likewise. The walkers did not look each other in the face when meeting, no one stared in curiosity at anyone else. Robert and Arvid kept as close to the Finn as they could; they were jostled and pushed a little when they failed to give way fast enough, and they felt dizzy and bewildered in this multitude, faced with the endless horde passing on this street, said to be the world's broadest.

Robert tried to estimate the breadth of Broadway and he thought it must be more than seventy-five feet wide. The Broad Way, he knew the meaning of the name from his language book. Once he had seen a picture with the same name, and this picture had illustrated the road Man walked through life, crowded with people indulging in sin. That road had led to the Gates of Hell. On this street, also, wherever it led, was a jostling crowd. Most people he saw had white-skinned faces and were shaped like his own people. But the great difference in dress surprised Robert. Here walked men in elegant, well-brushed, expensive clothes, with clean, white-shining linen around their necks

51

and polished boots on their feet. He saw other men, too, in worn-out, ragged garments, dirty shirts, and with their feet wrapped in old rags; some even went barefoot; they must burn their feet on these hot stones. He thought those poorly dressed men must be new arrivals in this country; they had not yet had time to get rich.

He saw many Negroes, all going about free and unchained. He had thought that black people held as slaves were in chains and led by guards, like dogs on leashes. He noticed Negroes laughing so broadly that their teeth gleamed white against their dark lips; but others looked so sad, shy, and downtrodden that the sight of them hurt him deep inside. He guessed that those who laughed had kinder masters than the others.

The Finn said the houses on this street were the highest ever built in the world. Some were, indeed, as tall as six stories, and taller houses could not be built.

"Danjel says we have arrived at the Tower of Babel," volunteered Arvid.

"Babel's Tower fell long ago," Robert informed his friend.

They looked at the houses along Broadway; some were built of wood and stone, and painted in many colors—white, clear red, black, and yellow. Some houses even had walls with white stripes of plaster; this was a curious sight, striped houses.

In the middle of the street rode men in black coats and high hats, their horses well fed, newly curried, with flanks shining. Wagons rolled by, gilded spring wagons bearing women in fine clothes; there were plain carts loaded with ale barrels, carriages with white teams, cabs, gigs, clumsy wagons drawn by oxen, light vehicles drawn by horses small as colts, four-wheelers, two-wheelers, big and small wagons, light and heavy ones. Everything that could be put on wheels and pulled by animals rolled by on this street.

Arvid pointed in amazement at a small, gray, long-eared, long-haired animal which stood quite still between the shafts of a cart: "That thing is neither horse nor ox!"

"It's an ass," said the Finn.

Robert hurried to show what he knew: "One can ride on them too," he said. "It's told in the Bible that Jesus rode on an ass into Jerusalem."

52

"On an animal like that?" asked Arvid. "How could he sit straddle-legged on such a puny creature?"

They slowly continued their walk up Broadway. A great fat sow with a litter of pigs was poking about in the gutter on their side of the street. The mother sow was as long legged as a calf, but her teats hung so low they almost reached the ground; the little piglets were light brown, almost like whelps, and ran between the legs of the walkers so that Robert almost tripped. Arvid counted fourteen in the litter and observed that American swine were longer legged than Swedish.

Robert said the Americans didn't seem afraid to lose their pigs, letting them run around at will, but the Finn informed him that every owner marked his swine with an ear cut; moreover, there were so many swine in America, no one cared much if an occasional litter were lost. All garbage and sweepings were thrown into the streets, and the swine kept the town clean, he added. Here slops were lying in piles, and some of the houses they passed smelled as though more slops were being prepared inside.

But the street smell of pigsties was familiar to the two youths from Swedish peasant communities. In Sweden or North America, in Ljuder Parish or New York City, they could find no noticeable difference in the smell of swine dung.

From time to time the Finn stopped and peered into windows as though he were looking for some particular place. Arvid and Robert stopped also, but as far as they could judge, every house was a shop, and every entrance had something written over the door in large, gilded letters.

At last the Finn stopped in front of a small house, not much bigger than a shed; it could be a shop, but there were no shop articles in the window. The Finn pointed to a placard nailed to the door:

NOTICE!

This shop is closed in honor of the King of Kings,
Who will appear about the twentieth of October.
Get ready, friends, to crown Him Lord of All.

"Now we're near the place I'm looking for," said the

Finn. "This same notice was on the door last fall when I was here."

Robert, who had begun to learn English from his book during the voyage, tried to read the notice on the door. He recognized some of the words but could not understand their meaning; he wanted to ask the Finn, but Arvid took the question from him: "What do the words say?"

The Finn explained: It had been predicted that the Day of Doom would take place in New York during October last year, and the owner of the shop had closed in advance to honor Christ on His return. The King of Kings had not appeared, but the shop still remained closed; perhaps the owner had starved to death by now.

There was another notice a little lower on the door, and the Finn bent down to read it: *Muslin for Ascension Robes. Muslin to meet the King of Kings. 20 cents a yard.*

The boys wanted to know what this notice said.

"Oh, just that the storekeeper sold wedding gowns for Christ's brides," said the Finn.

And now the Finn must attend to the captain's errands. He told the boys to find their way back to the ship alone; it was not difficult, only turn right about and then to the left. And if they wanted to go to the end of the street, they could do so. Broadway was about three miles long and ran right through Manhattan. They would not lose their way if they stayed on Broadway.

The Finn nodded good-by and they saw him enter a saloon with the name *Joe's Tavern* on the window; it was next door to the little shop which had been closed for the arrival of the King of Kings.

2

Arvid and Robert continued alone up Broadway. It was only today that they had been released from their long imprisonment. A feeling of unaccustomed freedom filled them now that they were free to move unhindered on solid ground. Boldly they decided to walk to the street's very end, however far it stretched. Then they would turn straight about and walk back to the harbor and their fellow passengers.

And so they continued along the most beautiful street in the world; they stopped and looked at the tall houses, they examined inscriptions over doors: *Store, Steak House, Coffeehouse, Lodging House, Brown's Store, Drugstore.* They tried to interpret the inscriptions and guessed at their meaning. Could this be a tavern? Was that a hawker's shop? Or an apothecary? The word *store* in particular impressed them, it appeared on one building after another. At last Arvid espied a small house, which he thought must be an outhouse, and he pointed for Robert to look, and laughed: "Look at that one! They call that a store too!"

"They must be bragging," said Robert. But he did not mind this exaggeration; it was always true that the smaller you were the more you needed to seem bigger.

He tried to understand words and sentences he overheard, but every thing was unintelligible, senseless jabber; not even one word, not a single syllable, was he able to recognize from his language book. He felt discouraged and disappointed. When he had stepped ashore he had thought he knew enough English to understand what he heard, even if he couldn't answer properly; he began to think they had cheated him in Karlshamn by selling him an unreliable book.

The boys arrived at an open square where many booths had been erected, and they thought this must be a market day. Here they stood long and gazed; Robert had said they shouldn't stand and stare because they might be laughed at, but this market fascinated them.

Wooden barrels stood in long rows, running over with potatoes, turnips, cabbages, carrots, peas, beets, parsnips, and many other roots which they saw for the first time; barrels in great numbers were filled with fruit—yellow, red, green, striped—apples, cherries, plums, and other fruits and berries which they never before had seen and the names of which they did not know. Between the barrels were long rows of baskets full of eggs and tubs full of butter, so fat that it seemed to perspire; on poles hung yellow, round, fat cheeses, big as grindstones; carcasses of animals, legs of pork, steaks, shortribs, and sides of bacon were stacked like firewood in high piles. Sizable, well-stuffed sausages hung in lines over tables on which stood vessels of ground meat and salted hams. There were booths with fowl: chickens, ducks, game birds; other fowl were stacked in hills of feathers, of all earthly bird colors, with a sprinkle of blood here and there on heads, necks, and wings. Four-footed beasts of the wild hung here in great numbers, hairy bodies of stags and does, hares and rabbits, known and unknown animals. In other stands were large tables with fish, long and short, broad and narrow, fat and spindly, black and white, red and blue; fish with striped bodies, misshapen fish, all head and protruding eyes, fish with ravenous jaws and sharp teeth like dogs', fish with fins as sharp as spears, and fish with long tail fins by which they hung on hooks, swinging like pendulums as the shoppers brushed against them. On the ground stood wooden boxes in which crawled and crept shellfish, horrible-looking sea monsters, lizardlike creatures, frogs, crayfish, mussels, snails, animals in shells that opened up like caskets, and shellfish that crawled about and resembled who knew what; nothing they had ever heard of, seen, or known, now or ever in all their living days.

The barrels, baskets, tubs, tables, boxes, and buckets in this market place were filled to overflowing; the whole place seemed flooded with fruit and meat, pork and lamb, fins and feathers, shell and hides, flooded with food of endless variety. People shopping here tramped in food, hit their heads on food, were enveloped in food, tumbled about in food. Who would skin all these animals, pluck all these birds, scale all these fish? For strangers and new arrivals, there was a booth in the market offering samples of all the food products which the new land offered its inhabitants. Here they saw the Creator's many gifts, fruits and berries, roots, herbs, and plants; they saw crawling, flying, swimming creatures, and meat from the cattle and beasts which God had created on the Sixth Day, before He created Man.

The two youths beheld the earth's abundance in a market next to the most beautiful street in the world. This much they understood: there was food in sufficiency in North America; it would be enough for them too, and for the seventy immigrants who had arrived with them today; they knew, from what their own eyes told them, that they had entered a new world.

3

The day was nearing its warmest hour, the heat lay like a

heavy weight over the city, making breathing difficult for the crowds on the street. People sought the shade and sat with their backs against house walls, drowsy, resting with their eyes closed; little babies slept at their mothers' breasts, women sat leaning their heads against men's knees. A half-naked Negro boy with a shoebrush in one hand a jar of shoe blacking in the other strolled about, calling: "Black your boots! Black your boots!"

Robert and Arvid dragged their steps, burdened by their heavy wadmal clothes. Their hair, grown long during the voyage, felt sticky and uncomfortable. They pushed their way among brown pigs poking in the gutter, they squeezed themselves in between the carts of fruit sellers; now and again they were hailed by peddlers offering them wares; once a man stopped and spoke directly to them. Robert had learned what to say when accosted by an American: he had the sentence ready on his tongue, he was glad to use it now for the first time: "I am a stranger here."

But the man only stared at him. Robert repeated the words, carefully, clearly, he pronounced each syllable as directed in the language book. But the man only shook his head.

How could this be possible? He had practiced this sentence so many times. Yet the American failed to understand him. The book must be wrong.

A man in fiery red pants and a tall black hat kept following them. On a leash he led two sharp-nosed, starved-looking dogs. "You want to buy a dog?" Robert did not understand these words. He looked at the dogs whose long, red tongues were hanging out of their mouths; they seemed fierce and dangerous. Robert was afraid of the obtrusive man; now he had taken his arm. He did not know what the man wanted, but he wanted to get away. At last he managed to free himself from the man's grip, and he and Arvid hurried their steps until the stranger was lost in the crowd.

Now Robert began to contemplate their situation, and he became fearful: here they walked about, entirely alone, in a town where everyone was a stranger, every tenth man a criminal; they were unable to say anything to anybody, they understood nothing that was said to them. If danger should overtake them they could not even call for help.

Perhaps the Finn had exaggerated, probably only one man in twenty was a robber, but even so it was unpleasant. They did not know what robbers in America looked like but they had seen many faces behind which an evil and treacherous soul might be hidden. He suggested that they return to their company. He did not wish to scare Arvid, he only said the others might be apprehensive if they stayed away too long. He was not afraid for his own sake, nor did he think Arvid had anything to fear; still—

"I have my nickel watch," Arvid reminded him, and began nervously fingering the broad, yellow brass chain which hung on his vest.

When Arvid left home his father had given him this watch, his dearest and most expensive possession. The father had said that the watch must be considered his paternal inheritance, given to him at this time because of his emigration. It was of fine nickel and had cost twelve riksdaler with the chain. During the forty years Arvid's father had worked as cotter under the name of Krakesjo, it was all he had been able to save as inheritance for his son. The cotter would not have given Arvid his inheritance in cash, even if he had had any; he would have been afraid Arvid might spend it on snuff and brannvin. But a watch he would always keep with him: he had admonished his son never to sell or lose his Swedish inheritance.

Now Arvid was walking about in the dangerous town of New York, surrounded by robbers and swindlers, and he was carrying the watch with him.

"Put it in your pants pocket," advised Robert. For it occurred to him that the shining brass chain on Arvid's stomach might attract robbers. Arvid unhooked the chain and put the watch in his trousers pocket.

So they continued their walk up the street. Arvid wanted to go farther, he was happy today; Robert had never seen him so excited and gay. Arvid said that as long as he was back on land again, he wanted really to use his legs, he wanted to walk all the way to the end of the street. Now that they were in America and could go anywhere dry shod, he was willing to walk the whole way to where they would settle, however far it was. He was sure he could walk there, because he was one of those who could use their legs.

A blond girl in a red dress held out a basket of fruit to the boys—black-red, juicy cherries. Robert shook his head; in vain he tried to remember a suitable English word from his language book; he would have liked to tell the girl (even if it was not true) that he had just bought a bagful of cherries.

But the girl remained standing in front of them, smiling at them in a kind, friendly way, and they each took a handful from her basket, as though wishing to taste her cherries before deciding whether to buy. The girl said something that sounded rather kind and went on her way. The boys were a little ashamed of their daring, and Robert regretted that he hadn't at least said "Thank you." That much he knew in English.

The juicy cherries were a treat to their dry mouths, and they ate them eagerly and spit the stones about them. A fat woman offered big loaves of wheat bread for sale. The loaves had been made in the form of rings, and she carried them hanging around her arms; the boys thought this quite ingenious: to use one's arms for bread poles. The smell of the fresh bread aroused their appetites—they felt hungry.

A black-haired, ragged little man, carrying a hand organ on his back and holding a monkey on a leash, stopped them with a stream of words. But they understood not a single syllable issuing from his mouth. Neither one of them had ever seen a monkey before. The creature went on two legs like themselves, and it had a hairless behind, red and swollen like an open wound. Arvid, in great disbelief, stared the monkey in the face and said with great emotion: The creature looked impudent—it was inexcusable of an animal to resemble a human being so closely.

A cart loaded with fruit turned over in the gutter with much noise and commotion. Large, yellow, and bigger than apples, the fruit rolled into the horse and swine spillings of the street and was allowed to remain there. The driver turned his vehicle back on its wheels and drove on, his cart empty. None of the walkers paid any attention to the accident, none made the slightest move to pick up the fruit. Only Arvid and Robert remained standing there a few minutes, but they were afraid to gather any of the beautiful unknown fruit.

The sight of so many edibles increased their hunger.

But they had no money, they must wait to eat from their own food baskets—Robert would have to eat with Karl Oskar's family, Arvid with Danjel Andreasson's.

The boys would not admit to each other that their stomachs were calling loudly for food, nor would they disclose their astonishment during this walk. They had never imagined that all these things existed in the world, these tall houses, these shops with inscriptions over their entrances in glittering letters, all these valuable things that were hung or spread in the store windows: glittering jewelry, gold, silver, precious stones, watches, rings, chains of gold and silver; expensive materials, cloth of gold and of silver, linen, wool, silk, velvet in quantities that could have covered this whole, long street; the expensive, gilded carriages, the light-footed, agile horses in glittering harnesses; all the things with names and uses they did not know, which they could only look at, admire, and guess about.

Before they recovered from one surprise, another even more amazing met their eyes. Two tall men in striped green and white coats and trousers, each carrying an upright pole with a placard on its upper end: *See the Anaconda! See the Serpent Charmer! See the Great Boa Constrictor! Five Cents!* The men stopped at the corner, calling loudly, and Robert tried to interpret their message. From his book he recognized the word *boa constrictor*. And in an open place near by he espied a reddish tent with the same inscription; then he understood what it meant and explained to Arvid: Over there in the tent one could see the boa constrictor, the most dangerous snake in the world, it might be as long as forty feet; it cost only five cents to go in and see. . . .

The boa constrictor? ruminated Arvid. Hadn't Robert once read to him from his *History of Nature* about this peculiar crawling reptile? He seemed to remember: ". . . the boa constrictor can be dangerous because of its great size and strength; it has happened that it has crushed and swallowed people; it grows to be almost forty feet long. . . ."

"If only we each had five cents!"

It hurt Robert that they must miss this opportunity to look at the world's greatest snake; a snake forty feet long that swallowed people, to be seen for only five cents. . . .

"Is the beast bound?" asked Arvid.

He looked toward the tent where a crowd of people thronged; he was not as anxious as his comrade to see the man-eating snake. From the very beginning, he had been worried about American reptiles; in his nightmares, America had been filled with hungry, hissing snakes, a veritable snake nest. He now wondered if it could be healthy to look at a snake that big. For himself, a snake five, six feet long would satisfy him, he wasn't so interested in snakes. Perhaps they could see part of the snake, maybe its tail; that might be cheaper.

Robert said it didn't matter, since they had not even one cent. He suddenly felt depressed and disappointed. All day long he had seen beautiful things for sale, and it had bothered him that he was unable to buy anything; now he actually suffered from having to leave the tent with the large snake.

Truly, on this, the most beautiful street in the world, there was everything one might strive for in this world, all one's heart might desire was here. And Robert felt that the street would have been still more beautiful had he a purse full of American money.

But the very thing he lacked, he had come here to earn; he had come to America to be free—but in order to be free, he must first become rich.

4

The humming in Robert's left ear suddenly began again, so intensely that it drowned all the street sounds. It was an echo from that box on the ear received at home in Sweden many years ago; it was a reminder of the servant law— "suitable chastisement." This his master had given him for laziness in service. The windy weather at sea had worsened his ear injury, and again a yellow, malodorous fluid ran from it. The humming sound, which sometimes increased to a roar, was constantly and depressingly with him. It had followed him from Sweden to North America, he could not lose it. Something was hurt inside the ear.

The hum carried with it a memory from his farm-hand service, a memory which troubled him day and night, year after year. Because of this memory he did not wish to serve as farm hand ever again; he did not wish ever to have a master; he wanted to be free.

61

He had tried to reconcile himself to the throbbing, had tried to make friends with the sound; it was a voice in there, wishing him well, comforting him when something went wrong, warning him when danger lurked. He had noticed that the hum began when something was happening to him, or about to happen; perhaps his friend in the left ear now wanted to comfort him because he had been unable to see the forty-foot, man-eating snake. . . .

Suddenly the sound was drowned by a loud outcry from Arvid: "Look, Robert! Look over there!"

"What is it?"

"A corpse! Look!"

"What?"

"Can't you see—there's a man lying there dead!"

They crossed the street and saw a man lying stretched in the gutter on his back; he was half naked, dressed only in a pair of worn-out pants which hardly covered his legs. His upper body was black with dirt or paint, but the skin of his face was white; he was not a Negro. His eyes were closed and his mouth open, disclosing toothless gums.

Arvid bent down over the body, bustling and excited: "He's dead! The man is dead! Stone dead!"

Robert, too, looked closer. The man's chest did not heave, his mouth did not move, he did not seem to breathe. With his foot he lightly touched the foot of the man; he did not move. "I believe he *is* dead."

Here a corpse was lying in the street, and people went by without noticing. Living people passed by the dead man, stepped over his outstretched legs, but no one paid any attention, no one noticed he was dead. It was extraordinary. Robert thought this must be because of the great size of the population: there were so many living people jostling each other here in America that no one could pay attention to the dead ones, who were so silent and so still. He and Arvid noticed the body because they were new in the country and not accustomed to seeing corpses lying about.

They looked at each other in consternation: What should they do? Perhaps they should report their discovery, but how? They probably ought to call the police, but they did not know where the police were, and they could not talk, could not ask. Robert remembered there was a sentence in his language book to be used when calling the

62

police. But that was in case of attack on the street. . . . And he couldn't remember the sentence, anyway, either in Swedish or English. And the police might wonder about them, perhaps even suspect them of having murdered the man lying there in the gutter. It seemed he had only lately died, the corpse was still warm, and it didn't smell as might be expected in this heat. Perhaps the man had been murdered. Yes, Robert was sure they would be suspected. And they couldn't say a word, couldn't deny it, couldn't defend themselves. No doubt they would be put in prison for murder. It would be best to forget about calling the police. They might stop a passer-by and point to the corpse, and then let him fetch the police. But in that case they might be held as witnesses. It would be best just to walk on and let the dead one lie there.

"We'll pretend we haven't seen anything," advised Robert. "Come, let's go!"

But Arvid remained leaning over the man. He had made a new discovery: "He smells of brannvin!"

He poked the man carefully between his naked ribs: "Yes, I believe he is—"

Next moment Arvid jumped backward with an outcry: the man had suddenly risen from the ground like a Jack-in-the-box. In front of them stood a heavy-set giant, a living man, swiftly resurrected and roaring furiously.

At this threatening apparition Robert crouched in fright, and Arvid, in his backward jump, almost landed on top of him. They grasped each other's hands.

Arvid never had time to finish his sentence that he thought the man was alive. Nor did he need to: they could see it—they heard it; they saw and heard a furious, insulted giant standing on his feet, though a little shaky. He took a few steps toward them, and from his enormous, red throat flowed a stream of words which the boys did not think were of a friendly kind. A few words Robert thought he understood: *Damned—thieves—bastards.* Never in their lives had they heard such terrifying sounds come from a human throat.

The passers-by stopped in the street, people began to gather around them, attracted by the resurrected one's roaring. The boys held each other's hands as they backed away. The man so suddenly sprung from the ground spurted spit and fury, he bent forward as though ready to spring at them; something gleamed in his right hand, it flashed in the sun.

Arvid cried out at the top of his voice: "A knife! He'll stab us—Run, run!"

The boys took to their heels and ran. They ran into the middle of the street, still gripping each other's hands, down the street the same way they had come; they ran until they lost their breath and felt a burning in their lungs; they ran past riders and wagons, carts and carriages, horses and asses, they slid between animals and vehicles, they ran for their lives—to get away from the man who sprang at them with a flashing knife in his hand, from the dead man who had come back to life. They had no trouble finding their way, they knew it—all the way down the broad street, the whole length of Broadway, until it ended, then a turn to the left where they would see the harbor and the ships.

During their race they jostled people, and angry voices were heard from the crowd. At last Robert held Arvid back: they must slow their pace and be more careful or people would become suspicious of them.

As they reached the market place they stopped for a moment and looked back, puffing and breathless. No one was following them, they were saved. And they resumed their leisurely walk, protected and hidden by the crowd.

"He was a dangerous man," said Arvid, still shaking. "He might have killed us!"

In a flash Robert could see himself and Arvid lying there stretched out in the street, knife slashes through their throats, like pigs at slaughter time, their blood gushing like ale through a bunghole; their legs kicking a last, weak kick, a helpless kick against death; a feeble twitch of their limbs—then death overpowering them. And there they would be lying, dead in the street, people walking by, no one noticing or taking care of their corpses, nor shrouding them, nor burying them, nor grieving over them here in a foreign country. And when they began to rot and smell, they would at last become food for the swine in the street. So it might have happened.

Robert had seen something glitter in the man's hand but now, as he recovered his breath, he thought it might not have been a knife; it looked more like glass, perhaps a small bottle. But Arvid insisted he had seen the gruesome

64

man pull out a slaughter knife, a real sticking knife with a point as sharp as an awl.

Robert was still trembling a little, and now he felt ashamed of it and wondered if they hadn't run simply because of their own fear. He told Arvid they must agree never to let fear overtake them here in America.

"Silly to run away! If the man had touched us, we could have reported him to the police."

He had just remembered from his English instruction book how to call the police in case of robbers and murderers on the street: *Please listen to me, Mr. Policeman! I appeal for your protection against this unfriendly person who is annoying me.* This was a long sentence, requiring much time to say. . . . He thought one would have to be very quick if one were to finish the whole sentence before being murdered. He realized he must learn English as soon as possible; he must know the language in order to save his life in case of sudden attack, if for no other reason. He had forgotten, earlier, that he had something of value he might lose; now he remembered: his own life!

But what had happened was really Arvid's fault: "I told you to let the man alone!"

"I thought he was dead from drinking. He stank of brannvin."

"But why did you poke him in the ribs?"

"I like the smell of brannvin, and I thought a corpse couldn't be dangerous."

Robert lectured him. He had been foolish and curious, and as a result almost got them killed. Finally Arvid agreed that he had been careless; but he had felt happy and reckless today, walking along this broad, beautiful street. Now he became dejected and sad; he promised on oath, using God's holy name, that it would never happen again. If he found droves of corpses here in America, if people lay dead in piles on every street and road, he would never bother to stop. No, he wouldn't even cast a glance at a single one of the corpses, no one could ever persuade him to look at dead men, or poke at them—even if they smelled of brannvin ever so much. He and Robert shook hands on this.

They were a little disappointed not to have reached the farther end of the street, not to have seen where Broadway ran—either to the portals of Heaven or Hell. But now

65

they trailed dejectedly and cautiously back to its beginning, where they had started out, near the green grove, the manor park. They went back to join their families, both of them anxious to tell the others about their walk on the most beautiful street in the world, where they had almost been robbed of the only thing they owned—their lives.

Arvid soon consoled himself, and his happiness returned as he stuck his hand into his trousers pocket and felt his watch still there.

VI

Journey with the Steam Wagon

Contract for Transportation of Immigrants

The undersigned agrees to carry the immigrants, who have arrived on the Swedish brig Charlotta *of* Karlshamn, *from New York to Chicago, on the following conditions:*

1. From New York to Albany by steamer, from Albany to Buffalo by steam wagon, and from Buffalo to Chicago by steamer.

2. For every adult person the fare is 8 dollars, children under 3 years free, children between 3 years and 12 years half fare.

3. The same fare entitles the traveler to 100 lbs. baggage free, and 150 lbs. on the steam wagon.

4. The baggage of the passengers is transferred free of charge from the vessel in New York to the steamer, and likewise in Albany and Buffalo, the whole way through to Chicago.

New York, June 26, 1850

The immigrants traveled up the Hudson from New York to Albany on one of the largest steamboats plying the river, the *Isaac Newton.*

The steamer left New York at eight in the evening, loaded to capacity with passengers and baggage. The immigrants were crowded together on the lower deck, while their belongings were piled almost as high as the smokestacks of the steamer on the upper deck toward the bow.

This was a night without rest for the travelers; there were no sleeping accommodations, and the immigrants sat or stood on deck, so closely packed together that no one could lie down. Parents held their children in their arms, older children and grownups stood upright. When they were tired, they tried to find rest by leaning on each other. Fortunately, they were to travel on this boat for only one night.

And this night they might have been able to sleep without concern for their lives if only there had been room to stretch out; this was not a dangerous voyage over a heaving ocean, violently pitching and rolling; this was a steady, easy passage on a calm, protected river. The Hudson stretched serenely before them, dotted with islands and inlets, following its furrow in quiet power. Through the night, mist towered over the high, steep shores. They were like secret dark fortress walls or silent sentinels, which guarded their water passage on either side. The journey on this water, where they could see land on the right and on the left, was to these ocean travelers almost the same as a trip on solid ground.

The *Isaac Newton* was driven forward by its great stern wheel, which dug deep into the river, stirring up whirls of foam; the wheel twirled the water like a giant egg whisk. The Hudson's even current slowed the progress of the heavily laden, deep-lying vessel. The stern wheel cut a deep furrow through the white foam, a wheel track in the water, evened out, obliterated, and gone as soon as its wake had passed. Behind the vessel the river flowed as before, calm, slow, even, majestic, on its way to the Atlantic.

One hour after daybreak the *Isaac Newton* tied up at the pier in Albany. Tired, limp, worn-out by lack of sleep, the immigrants left the boat and were divided into groups by their guides and interpreters, who marched with them on a road along the river to the railway station. They were shown into a large hall in the station house, and here the different groups—the English, the Irish, the Germans, the Swedes—were told by their respective guides in their own languages to remain absolutely still; no one was allowed to move from his indicated place. They were not told why they must stand so still, but gradually they learned: two American inspectors went about among them, pointing their fingers at each one, counting them. The men came back, pointed and mumbled once more, and again the immigrants were told by their guides to remain absolutely still; a few had moved and confused the inspectors in their counting.

The immigrants were counted like sheep in a pen, their numbers must check with the numbers in the passenger contracts. Then they were let out of the station to board the steam wagon.

2

At home, the immigrants from Ljuder had heard stories about these newly invented wagons, which were driven by steam and rolled along on iron bars strung over the ground. But until now none of their group had seen or used the railroad. To them this newfangled method of transportation seemed dangerous, possibly disastrous. But Karl Oskar had said that the steam wagon was the fastest means of transportation inland, and as their interpreter had told them the same, they had agreed to try the new way of traveling.

They considered themselves lucky in obtaining so tall a Swede to be their interpreter and guide; the ex-carpenter Landberg was a whole head taller than anyone in this great multitude of travelers, and wherever he happened to be, they could easily see him, they would not be likely to lose him. And Landberg was careful not to lose any of them. He stayed close to the group from the *Charlotta,* explained things, and was helpful in all ways. Now he led them up to the steam wagon and told them to be careful when climbing on board, so as not to fall and hurt themselves.

Some twenty wagons, high and covered with roofs, were tied together in a long row, and the immigrants gaped at them wide eyed, half from fear and half from curiosity. Each wagon was built on eight iron wheels and had windows. They thought it might be strong and steady. The wagon at the forward end was unlike the others; as it was first, it must be the one that was to pull, the real steam wagon. It had only four wheels, but these were three times as large as the wheels on the other wagons. Then there were two small wheels, in the very front end. The steam wagon had a tall chimney, broad at the opening and narrowing downward; it sat there like a huge funnel stuck in the throat of a bottle. At the fore end this wagon had iron bars twisted together to form a large scoop or shovel.

Thick, black smoke belched from the chimney and sent red-glowing sparks whirling into the air. The steam wagon had fire inside, it burned there, and this worried the immigrants.

They had always been taught to be careful with fire, to carry burning candles cautiously, to handle lanterns and firesticks with utmost wariness; they harbored a fear, implanted in them from childhood, of fire on the loose. And now they must ride in a row of wagons drawn by one with fire burning inside it; it smoked, crackled, sputtered, and sparks flew from the wagon's bowels. How easily one spark could fall on the roof of a following wagon and ignite it! They realized that they were to be exposed to continuous fire hazard, at least while the fire burned inside the steam wagon. They had also heard that a steam wagon might easily explode and fly to pieces in the air.

Robert had read about steam engines in his *History of Nature* and tried to explain to the others: Inside the steam wagon they were boiling water in a great big kettle, and it was that kettle which pulled the whole row of wagons. But he did not know what purpose was served by the large iron scoop in front of the steam wagon, and he asked Long Landberg about this. Their guide said that this contraption shoveled away wild animals if they stood between the rails and threatened to overturn the train.

Ulrika of Vastergohl said she wanted to ride as far away from the burning wagon as possible. She expressed the desire of all in their group.

When they were ready to take their seats, the guide showed them into the fifth wagon from the engine; they were disappointed not to be farther away from the fire. They climbed a small ladder, slowly and cautiously. Their wagon was about fifteen feet long and half as wide. A bench had been built on either side with a narrow passage in the middle. The seats were made of carelessly nailed-together rough boards. Two more groups, somewhat smaller than their own, were to share this wagon with them. Their knapsacks, food baskets, boxes, and bundles took much room, and they had to crowd together in order to find space for all. Those unable to find room on the benches stood or lay down on the floor. The immigrants felt as though they had been packed into a good-sized calf coop.

On the end of one bench a place was made for old Fina-Kajsa, so that she might ride half-sitting; she was weaker than she would admit and could stand on her legs only a few minutes at a time. For the third or fourth time she inquired of the guide about her iron pot, and for the third or fourth time she was given the information that the pot rode with the chests and other heavier pieces in a special wagon.

"But where is the grindstone?" asked Fina-Kajsa. "Where is it?"

The grindstone, brought along by her husband who died on the voyage, had, through carelessness at the New York unloading, fallen into the harbor, and all said this was good luck for Fina-Kajsa, who need not now pay the expensive inland freight for it. But she thought they were telling her a lie. Her son Anders in Minnesota had written home that grindstones were scarce in America, and now she thought the Americans had stolen her stone as soon as they laid eyes on it.

And Fina-Kajsa kept on complaining: "Oh me, oh my! What an endless road! We'll never arrive!"

In great harmony the immigrants shared the wagon space with each other; no one tried to spread out, all made room; they had learned on this journey to live closely packed in narrow quarters, and they endured it good-naturedly. In the wagon, too, they had more space in which to move than they had had on the river steamer. But the air in the wagon seemed thick and stuffy after a score and a half people had pushed their way into it. At daybreak a heavy shower had fallen and cooled the earth, but now the sun already felt burning, in spite of the early hour, and they understood that the day was to bring intense heat, heard to endure.

As yet the wagon stood still, and the passengers were quiet in silent anticipation and wordless worry: What would happen when they began to ride? Unknown dangers lurked on this journey; what mightn't take place when the

71

wagon with fire inside it began to move? They had heard that some persons could not stand being freighted along on the railroad; it was said to be so hard on them that they fainted and lay unconscious for hours.

Kristina had heard the same as the others; she sat in a corner of the wagon with Lill-Marta and Harald on her knees. Johan had climbed up on the knapsack standing between the bench and her feet. The oldest boy had also wished to sit on her knees, and she would gladly have let him if she had had three knees. But Johan wouldn't understand that she had only two. The boy had grown impatient and troublesome since they landed.

He pulled his mother's arms: "Aren't we going to live in a house now, Mother?"

"Yes, soon—I've told you so."

"When is soon? When shall we live in a house?"

"When we arrive."

"But Father says we have arrived in America now."

"Yes, we have. Please keep quiet."

"It isn't true, Mother! You said we would live in a house when we got to America. Now we are in America—aren't we going to live in a house?"

"Yes, yes—please keep still, can't you, boy?"

Johan tired her beyond endurance, and she didn't know what to do with him, except to let him be until he tired himself. After the night on the river steamer without a moment's sleep, she was too exhausted to answer her children. All she wanted was to stretch herself out somewhere and rest; she wanted to lie still, still, and sleep, sleep. But there never seemed any rest on this journey, no real rest, no satisfying sleep; now that they were to travel on this dangerous steam wagon there would be no sleep tonight either.

Karl Oskar stood pressed against the wall near her and talked to Jonas Petter and Danjel about the new form of transportation. Danjel said that now the prophesy had been fulfilled which said that toward the end of the world wagons would move without horses.

Danjel had asked himself if it could be God's will that His children use the steam power as beast of burden; if this power were something good and useful, why had the Lord kept it secret from man ever since the creation of the

72

earth—nearly six thousand years? It might be that the steam power emanated from evil powers. But thus far the Lord had helped them on their journey. On the steam wagon they were still in His hands.

Kristina remembered Dean Brusander's words at a catechism examination, to the effect that the steam wagon was a wicked human device, tending to estrange the soul from its Creator, and, like all mechanical contraptions, leading to disaster for poor and rich alike. Steam power weakened and undermined soul and body, encouraging idleness, fornication, and immorality. The dean had therefore prayed God to spare them this curse and prevent steam wagons from ever being used in Sweden.

Kristina wondered if they sinned against any of God's commandments by riding the steam wagon; she thought, if she had understood the dean rightly, it must be the sixth commandment.

She knew nothing in advance of what might happen on this steam journey, but as she and her loved ones were in the clutches of the wagon it was too late to regret it. She felt as though she had stepped into a conveyance which had been harnessed to a wild, untamed horse in the shafts for the first time; a romping, ferocious beast capable of anything, which might run off the road, bolt, or roll over on the ground in play. She could not forget the belching sparks from the steam wagon's bowels; she felt that this was the most perilous part of their journey thus far. As yet nothing dangerous had happened to them in America, but they hadn't got far from the shore: anything might still happen.

Danjel had opened his psalmbook to the "Prayer before Starting a Journey," and when Kristina saw her uncle fold his hands, she did the same. She, her husband, and children already had risked their lives at sea, now they must do it on land as well; in silent prayer she invoked her Creator's protection.

3

In each end of the wagon was a narrow door, and over both doors were identical inscriptions in tall black letters:

DANGER!
WATCH YOUR STEP!

Karl Oskar had seen the same inscription near the pier in New York and as he now recognized it he asked their interpreter to tell him the meaning. Landberg said that these four words warned of dangerous places; when they saw the sign they must watch their steps and look carefully where they set their feet. Inexperienced travelers could easily take a false step when entering or leaving the wagon, and fall off.

Karl Oskar in his turn explained the words to Kristina, who said it was thoughtful to nail up placards in dangerous places in America; she too was going to keep in mind the four words signaling danger, they were so black and threatening she could never forget them.

Outside their window was a tall, white-painted signpost with several lines of foot-high letters:

SAFETY SIGNALS FOR TRAINS
A WHITE FLAG BY DAY
A WHITE LAMP BY NIGHT
SHOWS
ALL CLEAR

Karl Oskar wondered what this placard might mean; no doubt it concerned the travelers, therefore they ought to know. And it annoyed him that he understood not a single syllable of the new language, that he couldn't decipher a word. It was like the first day at school, when Schoolmaster Rinaldo had held the ABC book to his eyes for the first time. But now he was a full-grown man, twenty-seven years of age, with three children of his own; yet in this country he felt like a schoolboy once more; he must learn to spell all over again, he must learn to recognize words. His inability to read the language did not seem so bad, but it vexed him not to understand the spoken words; it hurt him to hear people speak in his presence without understanding them; he felt inclined to believe they were talking about him, and he was ashamed and annoyed to be talked about before his face, disregarded. Here in America one

74

could stand face to face with people who insulted one, yet one couldn't do a thing about it; only stand there and stare, awkward, helpless, dumb. Since stepping ashore in America not many hours ago, he had felt foolish more often than during his whole life in Sweden.

But he refused to believe his intelligence had suffered from the emigration.

Their guide Landberg was standing at the entrance, his tall head concealing the inscription; he was speaking English to a man in a blue coat with yellow buttons; the man had a yellow sign on his cap, he must be one of the American guards, or steam-wagon officials. Karl Oskar surmised they were talking about the travelers inside the wagon. He listened with his ears open, trying to understand something that at least *reminded* him of words he understood. But the language of the interpreter and the American did not sound like human speech, rather like the buzz of a bumblebee in his ear; the sounds were distorted, mixed up, crazy through and through. The men twisted their mouths and made knots of their tongues in order to emit strange sounds; it seemed they imitated each other, made faces at each other as children might in play. To Karl Oskar's ears the American language seemed an unaccountable mixture of senseless sounds, and he grew more depressed each time he listened to it; he would never be able to teach his mouth to use this tongue.

The official left the wagon after he had seen to it that both doors were closed, and now Landberg spoke in Swedish: "Hold on to your seats, good people! Our train is starting to move!"

The warning was followed by a long-drawn-out, piercing, evil yell from the first wagon. The immigrants had never heard the like of this horrible howl, produced by neither beasts' nor human beings' throats, but by a lifeless thing and consequently much more terrifying. When it stopped, there was silence in the wagon, a silence of fear and apprehension. Faces turned pale, hands grasped hands, the travelers clutched each other or sought support against benches and walls, against anything within reach.

The moment had arrived; the steam wagon was moving. They could hear the wheels thunder under them as they rolled along on the iron bars, they could see through the windows that they had started ahead.

Their wagon jolted and shook, it cracked and creaked. A minute passed, and two, it pulled still harder, and the wagon rolled and leaned over a little to one side. Some of the travelers crouched in terror to weigh down the other side with the weight of their bodies; Fina-Kajsa shrieked to heaven. It was like the shriek of a dying person; she said she was being choked. Ulrika of Vastergohl hurried to her and loosened her vest, and soon she grew quiet and breathed more easily.

"It's turning over!" Johan screamed and gripped his mother's legs. "It's tipping over, Mother!"

"Keep quiet, boy!"

"I'm afraid!"

"Don't be afraid! It isn't dangerous!" Karl Oskar reassured the boy. "Lill-Marta and Harald aren't crying. You're the biggest, you mustn't cry."

Johan wanted to crawl up onto his mother's knees, already occupied by the smaller children, but the closest he could get was to cling to her legs; he held on with all his strength while the wagon rolled on, and great tears rolled down his pale cheeks.

Kristina was as much afraid as the child holding on to her, but she forced herself not to cry out. As she looked through the window and saw houses, trees, and the very ground itself move backward, she felt nauseated, her eyes blurred, her throat closed, her head swam. She wanted to see nothing, feel nothing—she closed her eyes and clenched her teeth. She must drive away this dizziness. She held her children closer to her, she clenched her teeth still tighter, she mustn't faint. . . . Perhaps she might escape it by sitting quite still, eyes closed. . . .

And while the train increased its speed, faster and faster, Kristina sat with her eyes closed. The engine blew out smoke and sparks from its interior, it belched and sputtered, it drew its breath heavily, in and out. The wheels rolled, creaked, and thundered, the wagons rocked and jerked, pulled and shook. And the people closed up inside sat in tense turmoil, each moment anticipating calamity.

But their wagon did not leave the rails, nor did it turn over, nor catch fire; nothing happened.

After a long while Kristina opened her eyes. She saw through the window how trees, bushes, hills, fields rushed by her with dizzying, indescribable speed, and her feeling of faintness returned. They were traveling with frightful speed, she could not endure to see how fast they moved, her head could not stand it; she was forced to close her eyes again.

And the immigrant train continued inland. Pale, silent, serious, the travelers felt they were moving with the speed of the wind.

Karl Oskar said, perhaps they were the first from Sweden to ride on a steam wagon.

4

The passengers gradually grew calm, they began to talk to each other and move about. But they suffered sorely from the heat that pricked their skins with a thousand invisible pin points. As no air was admitted, it grew more and more oppressive inside the wagon, breathing became almost impossible; the children grew restless and irritable.

Karl Oskar turned to their guide: "Couldn't we open the windows ever so little?"

"The windows are nailed and cannot be opened."

"Couldn't we open the doors, then?"

"The doors are locked. They won't be opened until we stop."

And Landberg admonished the travelers to be calm and to rely on him; they were in his hands and he would look after them the way a shepherd watches his flock.

Landberg continued: It had happened that traveling immigrants had fallen off the wagons during the journey and been killed; it was in concern for their lives that the doors had been locked. But he would see to it that they got the air they needed during the journey. He knew that locked doors, too, could be dangerous. Last year a gruesome disaster had happened to an immigrant train. When it had arrived in Buffalo, and the doors of one windowless freight car had been opened, five travelers were dead of suffocation. Three of those stifled had come from Sweden. All the other passengers were far gone. They had cried and begged to have the doors opened, but no one had understood them as there was no interpreter in their company. So, Landberg pointed out, the travelers could readily see how useful a guide was to newcomers. Since that tragedy, the railroad companies had been instructed to open the doors every time the train stopped. Landberg would see to it that sufficient air was admitted to keep his flock alive; no one would suffocate on this journey.

And the ex-carpenter, their tall countryman, smiled encouragingly at them. He had a mouthful of teeth which glittered white and handsome, and his cheeks were covered with a black, well-kept beard. He was a man whom women looked at. When unmarried Ulrika of Vastergohl asked him a question, she stuck her finger in a buttonhole of his coat so as not to let him get away. Long Landberg was kept busy answering questions, as they had no one else to ask, no one else to hear complaints; but he was never impatient or short.

Hardly had the passengers got their promise of fresh air than they were disturbed again: the sound from the wheels had suddenly grown more intense and hollow. They looked out and saw water streaming on either side of the wagon. They were riding over a bridge that crossed a broad river. The Americans had laid the iron bars for the railroad right across the water! The guide said the Americans were very daring people; above all, they liked to risk their lives; they did it frequently, as a matter of course.

Robert and Arvid sat together on the wagon floor and spoke to each other in low voices. Arvid did not feel well, he had a toothache; he wished he had continued the journey on foot. The first day on land he had had the motion of the waves in his legs and had felt as though he were walking over a quagmire; now when all his limbs were in good order again he must sit locked up in this calf coop. He was sure the wagon had been used for cattle transport —under one bench he had found dry cow dung. Robert showed this to Landberg, who said yes, maybe the wagon had been used for freighting cattle before it had been turned into an immigrant wagon.

Arvid asked if they could trust the wheels to follow the iron bars all the way. Robert told him there were rims on the wheels which forced them to follow the bars. It might, of course, happen that a wagon would lose a wheel, particularly as they drove with this terrible speed; they must be going eighteen miles an hour, or three times as fast as an ordinary spring wagon. That was how fast and strong the steam was.

Arvid looked at him in disbelief: "They say steam is nothing but mist?"

"Ye-es. The kind of mist one sees when water is boiling."

And Robert explained the power of steam to his friend: Once he and some other boys had picked up an old, discarded gun pipe; they had plugged one end, filled the pipe with water, and then plugged the other end too; they had made a fire in the forest and laid the gun pipe over it; soon it became red hot and blew up; it made a terrific explosion, and the pipe burst into a thousand pieces. One of the boys had had three fingers torn off—so strong was steam power when loosed.

If they were unlucky, it might well happen that the steam in this train would break loose and tear all of them to pieces like a mash of meat so intermingled that flesh scraps and bone chips could hardly be separated.

Arvid chewed one of his knuckles, as was his custom when uneasy. "You think the steam will break loose?"

"No. I said, only if we are unlucky."

Robert meant to recount all he had read in his *History of Nature* about iron roads and steam power, so that his friend might feel comfortable and safe on this journey. But Arvid's face showed that his mind was in a turmoil. He whispered: "Do you remember what we promised each other? Always to stick together. Whatever happens, we must stick together."

"That we must, Arvid." Robert suddenly became very serious. "I do not forget a promise. Whatever happens to us in America, we must be friends."

Once, in their farm hands' stable quarters, back in Sweden, they had clasped hands and promised always to stand by each other. After their lives had been endangered on New York's broadest street, they had renewed this pledge.

Robert nodded toward his elder brother, he told Arvid he did not care for Karl Oskar's masterful ways, he did not like masters, he would rather be in Arvid's company. To be such friends as he and Arvid were counted more than blood relationships.

The train was slowing down, and soon their wagon stood quite still. Landberg kept his promise: the doors were opened at both ends of the wagon, and fresh air came in to ease their breathing. Through the windows they could see a few tall houses along a street and many small houses clustered near by, some no larger than woodsheds.

At last Kristina dared open her eyes and she gazed out as long as their wagon stood still. Karl Oskar asked how she felt after this first stretch.

"Not too bad. A little dizzy."

"It's because the wagon runs so fast, of course."

Across from Kristina sat Ulrika of Vastergohl, who had been looking out the window ever since they left Albany and did not seem to have suffered from dizziness. She was still as rosy cheeked and healthy as when she left Sweden, she had suffered no inconvenience during the long voyage, she had not missed a single meal at sea, she had never been seasick for one minute, nor had she thrown up one bite of all the food she had eaten. Scurvy did not attack her, lice did not come near her. No other passenger had remained as well as she. It had been given to her to step ashore in America in full health, with all her strength intact. And now she sat here, unruffled by the terrifying speed; it agreed with her to ride behind the steam wagon.

Kristina wondered how this woman was created, what she could be made of. Most remarkable of all was the fact that twenty years of whoring had left no visible marks on the Glad One. Since embracing Danjel's teaching she no longer followed her profession, and lately Kristina had begun to believe that Ulrika's nature had improved; she was kind to Danjel's motherless children and took good care of them; this everyone had remarked on. Perhaps she wanted to expiate her life of whoring. Surely, in God's redemption book much was written concerning Ulrika of Vastergohl; each time her body had been used for fornication was noted. (Ulrika, however, thought that Christ's blood had washed her clean and that her sins, like a bundle of soiled linen, were tied up in the Saviour's napkin cloth.)

It had always bothered Kristina that she was forced to use the same privy as Ulrika; she could never forget the great number of men the Glad One had consorted with. In one end of the wagon was a small booth serving as a call-of-nature room for the passengers. Someone was always waiting near the booth, as the immigrants suffered from a severe diarrhea, which had attacked them after landing.

But diarrhea was to be expected when they first arrived in America, said their interpreter; it was a special kind of immigrant diarrhea, caused by the change of country and different weather conditions; hardly one newcomer escaped it. Now all of them had been running to the privy this last day, at least once an hour—all except Ulrika of Vastergohl. She seemed to have normal, undisturbed bowels. She had escaped all ills and evils, even the diarrhea. God had verily shown her great patience, even though she was so deeply sunk in sin; yet He had severely tested Uncle Danjel, who always strove to live righteously. The ways of the Lord were inscrutable. But Kristina was grateful that Ulrika did not often use their privy here in the wagon.

For the third time since boarding the train Jonas Petter emerged from the little stall at the end of the wagon, fumbling with his trousers. He had lost weight during the crossing, and his face was pale and sunken. He complained to Karl Oskar: "This plagues one's bowels!"

"Diarrhea is not dangerous to life; it will pass as soon as the bowels are accustomed to the climate." And Karl Oskar pulled out his knapsack: "I heal myself with pepper-brannvin. Have a swallow, Jonas Petter."

He poured the brannvin from its earthen jug into a tin mug, and from a small bag added pepper until the brannvin looked as black as dung water.

"Pour it down fast!"

Jonas Petter emptied the mug of dark pepper-brannvin and made a wry face. "It's like swallowing burning coals."

"But it closes the hole. Take another drink in the morning—then you won't be forever running."

Jonas Petter said it was a strange invention to sit on a wagon and ride while attending to one's needs. What would the people at home say if they knew how comfortable they were, traveling with such a contraption! He admitted Americans were smart. This invention saved much time; should the train have to stop each time someone needed to cleanse his bowels, they would have traveled scarcely more than a stone's throw a day. But he wondered if anyone collected all this human dung so that the earth and the crops might benefit. Or perhaps American soil was so rich that no manure was needed.

Karl Oskar offered some of the pepper-brannvin to Kristina, but she refused it, thinking it too strong for her;

she had tried it on the ship but threw it up again. Perhaps this was because of her pregnancy, which also caused her to suffer more than the others from the heat. She had often wondered why God 'inflicted so many miseries on pregnant women when He Himself created the human lives inside them.

As half her time had passed now, it would soon begin to show that she was with child. No one in their company except Karl Oskar knew as yet how things stood with her. But it couldn't be kept secret much longer. It was the women who first made such discoveries in each other; they always noticed the signs. Indeed, probably Ulrika already knew—she had seen the shameless creature, from time to time, look searchingly at her body, and even before they left Sweden the Glad One had said to Kristina, in a meaningful tone, that seasickness was much like being in the family way. Kristina had no hiding garment to don; she had not found time to sew herself a forty-week apron before they started out on their journey, and she did not think she would have opportunity to sew one here in America; she had a needle and thread, but not the smallest piece of cloth.

At home it was the custom for a woman to hide her pregnancy as long as possible. But why should she need a forty-week apron far away in a foreign country where she didn't know a single person and no one knew her? And perhaps no one in this country was offended by women showing their pregnancy. Perhaps they had different customs in North America. She had heard that no one cared how other people lived here or what they did.

But there sat Ulrika staring at her again, as if wondering in which month she might now be. This look on Ulrika's face angered her; she had a full right to be with child. She lived with her husband in a Christian marriage, she had a known father for her child. But how had it been with Ulrika's own brats? Who was father to Elin, the girl next to her, now looking after Danjel's children, sitting this moment with little Eva on her knee? There had been rumors about tramps; the churchwarden in Akerby had also been mentioned. And who had been the fathers of those children she had lost? Their fathers were known only to God. Ulrika ought to remember this before she stared at honest women.

Kristina would have liked to sew a forty-week apron—
if for no other reason than to irritate Ulrika.

5

The immigrants from Ljuder rode on the steam wagon
through a green and fertile country. From their train they
saw vast fields covered with a thick fell of beautiful crops;
in other fields the crops already had gone to seed. They
saw meadows with tall fodder grass where cattle grazed in
great numbers; in places the grass was so tall that they saw
only the animals' backs. They thought the cattle here must
tramp down more grass than they ate; they counted as
many as fifty cows together and wondered if such large
herds might belong to one single owner. They passed
through forests of tall, lush leaf-trees and recognized oaks,
maples, elms, and birches. They saw groves of unknown,
low trees and wondered what the name of such beautiful
little trees might be. Danjel Andreasson thought they
might be fig trees, of which Jesus often had spoken in
parables and which grew also in the land of Canaan.

They passed through a smiling landscape—it was a fertile world they saw here. A verdant ground promised food
for both man and beast, ample crops, and security. Where
the earth grew green, there life throve; it marked a good
place for people to live.

They were looking for such green places with rich
growth in which to build their own homes—here they
would have liked to stop and settle, if others hadn't arrived before them.

Karl Oskar was pleased with what he saw: the earth
here seemed rich, and his eyes did not discover a single
hindering stone in the fields. As he looked out over the
cultivated land he remembered the picture of a wheat field
in North America which he had seen in a newspaper at
home; the picture had spoken the truth—the American
fields lay before his own eyes now, as vast and stone free,
as even and fertile, as they had been in the picture. And it
was said that still vaster fields existed farther inland.

At times they passed through poorer regions, they saw
hills and mountains, morasses, plateaus, and forests of
pine trees. But Karl Oskar had not expected the whole

American continent to look like the picture of the wheat field.

The journey on the steam wagon was long, hour after hour passed, and new landscapes came into view, new fields, new pastures, new forests, new crops, and new meadows with more large herds of grazing cattle. Karl Oskar noticed that the cows were larger than those in Sweden, they were white or light yellow in color, like milk and butter; at home they were red or sometimes black. The American horses too were taller than those in Sweden; he wondered if they might be wild horses that had been tamed. The sheep were black and white, fat and round, with bodies like barrels. He saw black and red-brown pigs in the pastures; but the hogs were lean and long legged, not at all resembling those at home. Thus he observed that cattle in the New World were not shaped like the kine at home: cows and horses were larger, sheep fatter, with shorter legs, hogs leaner with longer legs.

Seldom did he see workers out in the fields or forests. There seemed to be a scarcity of people but an abundance of cattle. Seeing the multitude of people in New York, Karl Oskar had begun to worry that America already was overcrowded, that they had arrived too late. He now discovered that his worry was groundless. This country was so vast that it still had room for many more; it wouldn't be filled up tomorrow, or next year. And he recalled how crowded it had been at home, people had even said there wasn't enough room for his big nose, and perhaps they had been right. But here there was room for all in his group, here he was sure he would find a place to settle, large enough to turn about in and do as he pleased, and where others would not be disturbed by him or his big nose.

Danjel Andreasson had long been silently watching the green fields on either side of the railroad. At last he said, "This land is fertile and fruitful. It is a good and broad land, a blessed land. We must humbly thank the Lord God for His grace in letting us enter it."

6

Landberg said that when all went well, about twenty-four hours were required for the journey on the steam wagon to Buffalo. But delays were likely to occur. Once, for instance, the steam wagon had been delayed six hours because the iron rails were covered with a thick layer of grasshoppers.

Ulrika was disappointed that their journey on the steam wagon would come to an end so soon. In her whole life she had never before experienced pleasure like this. The poor back home in Sweden were never treated to such entertainment. Most of them were not allowed to ride on any kind of wagon until they were picked up by the corpse cart. And the gentry in Sweden would have preferred to see them walk to the grave as well.

Their guide nodded to her with a broad smile: "You, my dear *Fru,* will ride on the steam wagon many times in America."

He had several times called her Mrs., and it sounded strange to those in her company. She had always been called Unmarried Ulrika of Vastergohl. Under that name she was registered in the church book, and everyone called her so. It was as if it ought particularly to be emphasized that she was unmarried, and it sounded as if she were more unmarried than any other woman. Now they could all see that Ulrika sat there, greatly enjoying it that the first man she met in America raised her to a married state, nay, even to the level of gentry, by calling her Mrs.

She guessed what the others were thinking and she said, half mockingly: "Perhaps I ought to change my name as well."

It happened often that Swedes changed their names when they came to America, Long Landberg replied. Many took entirely new names. Those named Andersson and Larsson at home had here assumed high-sounding names like Pantzarskiold, Silverkrona, or Lejonstjerna. But it was, of course, mostly rogues who felt in need of changing their names; it was of no use to an honest person, nor did it help a useless one, for here no one got along better because of a noble name, as people did in Sweden.

That was exceedingly just, Ulrika of Vastergohl remarked, although she wouldn't mind being called Mrs. Ulrika von Lejonstjerna. For a lonely, poor woman, a noble name would be a comfort. But she was sure menfolk would find nothing different in the body of a noble lady than in a simple woman: each was made in the same way.

85

Landberg laughed heartily, but the members of Ulrika's group who knew her past did not smile. They were familiar with her talk. And now she was making up to their guide, who couldn't know what she actually was.

From his bag the guide now took out a number of medicine jars which he was accustomed to sell to immigrants during his trips. *Painkiller* was the name on the jars, and he explained what it meant. These were pills which healed all ailments attacking newcomers during their first weeks in America. *Painkiller* healed fatal diseases as well as small wounds and scratches: cholera, red soot, diarrhea, fever, ague, yellow fever. A jar cost one dollar, leaving Landberg with a profit of only five cents. But he was not one to take advantage of his countrymen.

Danjel and Jonas Petter had bought a jar of the *Painkiller,* mostly to be agreeable to the seller. Karl Oskar declined; his family was in good health at the moment and not in need of medicines. Landberg kept urging him—it would be well to have a jar handy in case of sickness; there were many fatal diseases in America, neither young nor old could be sure of tomorrow. But Karl Oskar could not forget how the money in his skin pouch had shrunk; he had paid twenty-four dollars for their passage to Chicago; if they were to have any money at all left when they arrived in Minnesota, he must confine himself to buying the food his family needed on the journey.

Arvid complained of his toothache to Danjel, who bought another jar of *Painkiller* for his servant. Landberg told Arvid that in case the pills didn't help the toothache he could have all his teeth pulled painlessly with the aid of gas at only twenty-five cents a tooth. Then he could buy new teeth. A professor here in America had recently discovered how to make teeth of gutta-percha; they were comfortable and indestructible; they cost only ten dollars a row, or a dollar apiece. He advised Arvid to get a whole row, since this was cheaper.

Danjel again opened his purse with the broad brass lock and took from it a new silver dollar. He looked carefully at the strange American coin before he handed it to Landberg: on one side was an eagle with extended wings and searching eyes; the bird held some silver branches in one talon and some sharp arrows in the other; turning the coin, he saw a bare-armed woman dressed in flowing robes; she held bunches of flowers in her hands and sat there like a queen on her throne, surrounded by a wreath of beautiful silver stars.

"They have nice money in America," said Danjel. "It's decorated with the stars of heaven."

"The stars represent the first thirteen states," explained Landberg.

"What does the searching eagle represent?"

"I don't know. The Americans have no king to put on their money. Perhaps they find a bird of prey more suitable."

Karl Oskar also had taken out a silver dollar to inspect; it might be well to familiarize himself with the coin of the country.

"There is writing under the throne where the woman sits," he said. "Mr. Landberg, can you interpret it?"

"Yes, that I can. It says 'In God We Trust.' "

"What are you saying, man!" exclaimed Danjel. "Is our Creed printed on the money?"

"Yes, that's so. These words are printed on all money in this country."

A ray of happiness lit Danjel's eyes, and he began to examine his silver dollar with renewed interest and wonder: "Can that really be true? They have faith in God, those who make the money in this country. That's good to hear; no heathenism exists in this country."

And Danjel of Karragarde was pleased and satisfied as he sat there inspecting the shining coin in his hand; at home the coins carried only the picture of King Oskar I and his name; in Sweden they thought it sufficient to serve and worship an earthly ruler. But those in charge of money matters in America knew that no coin could be reliable and sound without God's name stamped on it; here they put their foremost trust in the heavenly king.

"In God we trust," he repeated to himself.

To Danjel Andreasson this silver dollar had gained a new and greater value through its four-word inscription; he had come into a land where the rulers had imprinted on the country's coins the uttermost tenet of their faith. Now he knew that North America had a God-fearing government, that it was a Christian land. He understood now that the Americans in a faithful, humble spirit remembered the Lord God each time they held a dollar in their hand. They were thus ever reminded that gold and silver were only dust, to be eaten by worms and corroded by rust, and that they themselves in the presence of their Creator were the like of worms. "In God we trust!" In a land where such coin passed, honesty and confidence between fellow men must rule, and no one could be tempted for sordid gain to cheat his fellow brethren.

Danjel held the coin up to the window so that it glittered in the bright sun: "Behold! God's silver dollar!"

Then he gave the interpreter the coin as payment for Arvid's medicine, and Landberg collected his jars of *Painkiller* and walked on to offer them to other passengers.

Arvid had become very curious about the American coin and he asked Karl Oskar if he might see it. He showed it to Robert and asked who the beautiful woman in the flowing robes might be: "Could it be the queen of America?"

"When they don't have a king, they couldn't have a queen," Robert instructed him.

"Hmm. That's so. They have a president instead."

"And the woman has no crown either."

Arvid looked once more at the picture; then he exclaimed in great excitement, "Now I know who she is— the president's wife, of course!"

Robert supposed his friend had made the right guess. The bare-armed woman in the flowing robes, sitting on her throne among the stars, with flowers in her hands—she couldn't be anyone except the wife to the president of the North American Republic.

7

The children whined for food, and for the third time since leaving Albany Kristina brought out the food basket. By now there was not much left of their provisions from Sweden—a couple of rye loaves, a dried sausage, the end of a cheese, and a piece of dried leg of lamb. But these were precious scraps and must be carefully rationed. They could buy no food in the railroad wagon; those without food baskets must starve.

From Karl Oskar's purchase in New York Kristina had saved two wheat rolls for the children, from one of the rye loaves she cut slices for her husband, brother-in-law, and herself, and among them she divided the sausage the best she could. The rye bread was dry and hard, and she had been unable to scrape away all the mildew. But they all ate as if partaking of fresh Christmas bread.

Jonas Petter also took out his food basket and began to eat. Danjel's two boys, Olov, fourteen, and Sven, eleven, sat next to him and looked longingly as he chewed and swallowed. And now Kristina remembered that she had not seen her uncle or anyone of his family eat a bite today.

"Aren't you going to eat, Uncle Danjel?"

Danjel looked shamefacedly at the wagon floor and said they had not the slightest crumb left in their food basket.

This was poor management, thought Kristina, as she remembered what an enormous food basket Inga-Lena had brought along—a score of big breads, many fat cheeses, half a side of pork. Yet, her family couldn't sit here and eat their meal and let Danjel's motherless, hungry children look on. She could see the boys following every bite with their eyes and she knew how starved they must be.

She cut the rest of the loaf in slices and divided them among Danjel and his four children. A piece of the cheese crust she gave to Arvid, to whom Robert already had given some of his portion. But because of his toothache Arvid wasn't very hungry and stuck mostly to his jar of pain-killing pills.

Kristina's hand, still holding the bread knife, fell on her knee: there were two hungry people in her company who had nothing to eat, Ulrika of Vastergohl and her daughter Elin. They belonged to Danjel's household and had shared his food throughout the journey. But now their food basket was empty, now Ulrika and her daughter must sit and look on while others ate their meal.

Kristina's hand, a moment before so busy cutting and dividing the bread, lay now quite still upon her knee. Not for one moment would she entertain the preposterous thought that she should divide her food with the Glad One —no, certainly not.

Ulrika was looking out the window, gazing at the landscape they were passing as if she weren't aware that the others were eating. Elin had picked up her little berry basket in which she found a dried bread crust; this she chewed with an expression of contentment, as if she were

89

sitting at an overloaded table. Neither mother nor daughter seemed aware that they were being left out of the meal.

Kristina reflected that Ulrika had taken charge of the family food basket at Inga-Lena's death. But she was not one to save or be stingy with the possessions of others; she had been so generous with the food that already it was gone; she had only herself to blame.

But it was true that the Glad One's healthy body required much food, and she never willingly missed a meal. As she had put nothing in her stomach the whole day, she must be thoroughly hungry, must ache with hunger, even more now that she saw the food the others were eating. Kristina could not help feeling sorry for her! as she now shared her food with all the others, could she pass by Ulrika and her brat? It said in the Bible to break one's bread with the hungry.

Kristina had only one bread loaf left, one single loaf. Must she cut this for the Glad One's sake? She had a hungry husband, brother-in-law with a heavy appetite, and three small children, lean and pale, who needed regular meals. She did not know when they might be able to buy more food. Could God mean that she ought to take the bread from her own poor children and give it to a person like Ulrika, a harlot, an evil creature? How she had insulted other women, this Ulrika of Vastergohl! How detested and looked down on she had been in the home parish! And how Kristina had suffered from being forced to travel in her company! If she now offered the infamous whore food from her own basket, then it would be as if she invited her as a guest to her own table. It would be accepting her as an honorable woman, and equal. Giving her food would be like taking her hand; it would be a humiliation to Kristina, a debasement, if at last she gave in to the Glad One, as though wanting her for a friend.

One could hand a piece of bread to a beggar. But Ulrika had never begged; she was proud, she was more than proud, she was haughty. When she was in prison for breach of the sacramental law, she had refused to eat; she had spit in the porridge, it was said. She would accept nothing unless it was offered to her as to an equal. And Kristina did not wish to consider her an equal.

Her hand with the bread knife was quiet on her knee.

Mixed with the rumbling of the rolling wheels she could hear the sound of eagerly chewing jaws; but she who had divided the food had not yet begun to eat.

Kristina's heart beat faster, so greatly was she perturbed. Should she cut the last loaf—or should she save it? She had a vague feeling that what she did now would be of great importance to all of them. She had a foreboding that fundamental changes awaited them in this new land, everything seemed different from home, they were forced to act in new and unaccustomed ways. And as they now were driven through strange country, with everything around them foreign and unknown, they were more closely united —it seemed more and more as if they were one single family. Then they must try to endure each other, at least not irritate each other. Otherwise, how would things work out for them?

Ulrika suffered hunger, and any one able to give her food but withholding it increased her suffering. Could Kristina be so cruel as to let another human being suffer when she could help her? She had many times asked herself why people plagued each other so mercilessly in this world; now she put the question to herself: Ulrika is hungry— why do you let her suffer? You say she is proud—what are you? Is it not from haughtiness that you pass her by?

Kristina's hand took a firmer hold of the knife handle —but this was the children's bread. They were weak and needed every bite. She thought, you cannot take it away from them! To cut that bread is like cutting your own flesh. The Glad One is big and strong, vulgar and forward, she will always manage, she'll never starve to death. It's different with your helpless little ones. If there were plenty of food, more than they needed, then . . . Now—never!

But it couldn't go on like this. They couldn't continue to hurt each other. They were all of them poor wretched creatures, lost in the New World; no one knew what awaited them in this new country, no one knew what they might have to suffer. One loaf would save no one's life in the long run. And if one could help another . . . Help thy neighbor! The Glad One too was her neighbor; she too had been given an immortal soul by her creator. He had from the beginning considered her as worthy as others; she too was made by God, Who must care for her as for others. Kristina felt He would see to the little children also, so they needn't starve. . . .

She took out the last loaf, cut generous slices, and handed them to Ulrika of Vastergohl and her daughter: Wouldn't they please share her bread? It was old and dry, but she had scraped off the mildew as best she could. . . .

Mother and daughter accepted gratefully. "Thank you very much," Ulrika said, and this sounded strange when all she got was hard, old bread. Nor did Ulrika seem surprised at the offer; she only looked grateful, truly grateful. And Kristina also handed them the knife and the smoked leg of lamb that they might cut themselves meat for the bread. They both chewed slowly, with restraint, but it was apparent they did so with effort, trying not to reveal their ravenous hunger.

Kristina herself began to eat and she wondered: What would the people at home think of this? What would they say, if they could see her cut her last loaf from home in order to share with Ulrika of Vastergohl, the parish whore?

8

In the evening the twilight was short, and soon it was dark as a potato cellar outside the windows of their railroad wagon. Everything went faster in this country, even the twilight passed more quickly than at home. And the thick darkness which now fell over them on a night so near Midsummer surprised the travelers. At this hour it would still be full daylight at home. But it seemed as if everything American was opposite to Swedish: here they had dark summer nights instead of light, white cows instead of black.

Their train stopped and remained standing a long time. At least an hour passed, and still they did not move. They could no longer see the landscape outside the windows; perhaps this was one of the towns where the interpreter had said the train stopped for a long rest: Schenectady, Utica, or Syracuse. Those were difficult and unusual names for towns, almost like Biblical names, towns in Canaan. Then some of the company with good eyes reported that they were in the middle of a wild forest—there were huge, thick tree trunks on either side. Their guide had gone

92

to another wagon, and they had no one to ask about this.

Perhaps the train couldn't go on during the night when it was so dark; perhaps they had to stay here until daybreak.

No light was lit inside the wagon, and the passengers couldn't see each other's faces, but they sat close to one another and each knew where his own family and his belongings were. They were not in need of light and they were thankful to have air; those in charge of the train had opened the doors at both ends of their wagon as soon as it stopped; the cool night air refreshed them. But none of the travelers dared step outside.

One more hour passed, and the immigrant train still stood there. They began to grow restless, they wondered and worried. Outside the windows they could see sparks from the steam wagon, whirling about in the dark like a swarm of fireflies, and this increased their anxiety. They began to fear that some accident had befallen their vehicle, or was about to happen. Why hadn't their guide returned? Someone suggested that perhaps Landberg had deserted them.

They could hear the wheezing and hissing from the steam wagon in front, and they saw the flying sparks; they were in the depths of a dark forest, and here they sat clustered together, blind, like chickens perched in darkness, and could not even ask anyone if they were in danger. They knew nothing, therefore they feared everything.

At last they began to confer with each other: shouldn't they elect someone to step out onto the ground and try to discover what was the matter with their unmoving train? Even if he couldn't talk, he might learn something with his ears and eyes.

They were talking this over when the doors suddenly slammed shut, and the train started up with such a jerk that the passengers tumbled against each other. And suddenly the man they had missed stood among them; Long Landberg had returned, friendly and calm, and he explained: There was a steep, difficult hill ahead of them on the railroad, and one more steam wagon was required to pull them uphill. Their train had been waiting for the extra steam wagon, and now it was added to the back of their train, and would help push the wagons up the steep hill.

So their journey continued; the immigrant train pushed on through the night, seeking its way into North America. As yet nothing dangerous had developed, but anything could happen, they did not even know what to fear.

VII

Voyage on the Lake Steamer

In the forenoon of the next day the immigrants arrived at Buffalo. That evening they started across Lake Erie on the steamer *Sultana*. The whole remaining part of their journey was to be on water—across lakes, up rivers, and through canals. Just ahead of them lay three great lakes over which they must pass. They had embarked on a vast, restless, inland water, but on this voyage they at least could see land on one side of the ship. At intervals, the *Sultana* touched shore to discharge or take aboard passengers, cargo, and firewood for her engines.

The *Sultana* was a fairly large steamer with one water wheel on either side; she was overloaded with people and cargo. The immigrants were given quarters below, on the middle deck, and when they were sent to their quarters, they learned another English word, *steerage*. Cabins were built in three rows in the hold, each one four feet wide, and each one accommodating two full-grown persons of the same sex, or a married couple. Two children under eight years of age were counted as one grown person; children under three years of age were transported free of charge, but no one asked the little ones' ages, and all children carried aboard by the parents were allowed free passage, however old they were.

Kristina took charge of Harald while Karl Oskar carried Johan on one arm and Lill-Marta on the other. Johan was four, but tall as a six-year-old. Other parents carried children even larger, never before had such big two-year-old babies been seen. But it seemed as if all Americans loved children; they brightened and smiled as soon as a child came near them, and no one spoke harshly when the youngsters were noisy or caused trouble; children were the most welcome of all immigrants, it seemed.

Kristina was uneasy each time she boarded a new means of transportation—she was afraid her family might be separated during the journey; she wanted them to hold on to each other all the time.

The American steamer was new and the middle deck roomier, lighter, and drier than the immigrants' living quarters on the old Swedish ship; nor did this vessel smell musty. But when all had gone aboard and packed themselves in down there, it was just as crowded and uncomfortable as it had been on the *Charlotta*. The passengers' belongings were stacked together helter-skelter on the lower deck, and the owners had to look after them and watch that nothing fell overboard. On the *Charlotta* they had been allowed the unrestricted use of the upper deck in fine weather, but here they were confined to the lower deck. Yet they could see there was plenty of space on the upper deck, where only a few passengers walked about. The immigrants enviously watched these fellow travelers who had their individual cabins and more room than they needed: why was that deck up there in the fresh air and daylight reserved for only a few, while such a great number of people must stay below, packed together?

Long Landberg explained that the upper deck was first class, which cost much more than a berth in steerage, and the ladies and gentlemen up there were wealthy travelers on a pleasure excursion.

Kristina noticed that the passengers on the upper deck were dressed like the people she had seen walking about near the harbor in New York: the women in silk skirts and velvet shoes, the men in tall hats and long coats of costly cloth. And here, too, the women went about with open umbrellas even though it wasn't raining. Those passengers up there were not, like themselves, traveling to find homes; they already had homes. Why did they travel when not forced to? How could anyone, of his own free will, roam about on lakes and seas? If Kristina ever found another home in this life, she would certainly stay there.

And these passengers who traveled just for fun were allowed to keep the whole upper deck to themselves, while the immigrants, forced to find new homes, were crowded and jostled down here. Kristina thought that the passengers in first class were like the gentry at home in Sweden, and she asked her brother-in-law Robert, who had learned so much from all kinds of books, to explain this: Hadn't he said that the inhabitants of North America were all alike and not divided into gentry and ordinary people?

Robert tried to make himself clear: He had only said that different classes did not exist in the New World, no one was born into a class. But there was, of course, a difference between people, in that some were rich and others poor; some could afford to spend more, others less; some could afford first class, others could not. There were only two kinds of people in North America: those who had lived here long enough to grow rich, and those lately arrived and still poor.

There was no other difference between people, Robert insisted. Kristina could observe for herself—did she see anyone who took off his hat or cap to another? Did she see any man bow or any woman curtsy? Here one didn't stand on ceremony, the poor didn't kowtow to the rich as they did at home in Sweden.

The ship's fare was ample, even abundant, but to the Swedish peasants it seemed oddly prepared and peculiarly flavored. American food consisted mainly of things mixed together, and one's tongue was unable to distinguish one kind of food from another; the immigrants did not always know what they were eating. But still more foreign than the food were their fellow passengers in the hold. They were lodged with other immigrants, people who, like themselves, came from countries of the Old World, each speaking his own language. Their fellow passengers were dressed in outlandish clothes, they laughed and sang and behaved in the strangest ways, and they were loaded down with an amazing variety of things: axes, hoes, spades, harnesses, saws, tubs, barrels, cradles, clocks, pots, yarn winders, ale kegs. The Swedish immigrants began to feel that they had arrived empty handed in North America when they saw what these others carried along. Many of those who crowded the ship with their belongings were Germans, the guide told them; a German was wedded to his possessions and would not part with them when emigrating. But when they saw a spade with a six-foot handle, said Landberg, they might be sure the owner was Irish: the Irish were too lazy to bend their backs while digging; at work they stood upright.

He pointed out some tall men in skin jackets who carried guns and hunting sacks and had knives in their belts. They were fur hunters on their way to the forests of the West for autumn game.

But strangest of all the steerage passengers were two Indians. The immigrants studied them with timid wonder. The two men were draped in pieces of red-striped woolen cloth which covered them from head to knees and which they usually held closely around themselves; they wore trousers reaching the middle of their thighs and held in place by strings to a belt around their waists; on their feet they wore skin shoes but no socks. From the Indians' ears hung beautiful glittering silk bands; the color of their faces was sooty brown, and their sloe-black eyes lay deep in their skulls, lurkingly under their brows.

Most of the time the Indians sat immobile, staring moodily before them, each holding his blanket tight around his body as if this garment were his only possession. No one addressed the brown-hued men, and they themselves seemed inclined to silence. When they spoke to each other they used a language which sounded like a series of short grunts. These Indians could not be wild, as they were allowed to travel unhindered among white, Christian people. But they sat apart from the other passengers, who walked by them in silence and with some uneasiness; perhaps they were heathens after all; one couldn't know for sure; there was something dark, threatening, and cruel in their looks, something inspiring fear. The immigrants did not know what to think of or expect from these curiously draped figures.

The steamer had a large crew—bosuns, engineers, stokers, and deckhands. Negroes served in many capacities; those black men with hair like wood shavings prepared the food and served it, loaded the ship, cleaned it, and busied themselves everywhere. The black crewmen were free, but among the passengers in steerage were two

98

Negro slaves shackled in foot chains, because they were said to have wild tempers.

Kristina felt pity for the two black-skinned men sitting there chained together, unable to move. Why were people put in chains and foot irons when they had done no wrong? The slaves' owner was among the pleasure travelers on the upper deck: Kristina would have liked to ask him to unshackle the poor Negroes, had she been able to speak his language.

Little Johan watched the Negroes for a long time in silence. Then he asked his mother: How long had their faces been so terribly black?

"They have always been that way."

"Are they black both morning and evening?"

"Yes. Negroes are always black."

"But, Mother—how can they know when they need to wash themselves?"

"I don't know. . . . Quiet, now."

But the boy insisted: "Tell me, Mother, how do the Negroes know when they are dirty?"

Kristina was unable to give Johan this information. She herself was deeply disturbed by the dirty white passengers in steerage. No Negro could help it that the Lord God had made him black, but when God had given people white skin, then they owed it to their Creator to keep it white. Children and menfolk seemed to crave a little dirt for comfort's sake, but Kristina demanded more from women. Here she saw womenfolk who were sorely in need of a thorough scrubbing in boiled lye-soap, and their children appeared never to have touched water since they were baptized. Fina-Kajsa, to be sure, wasn't very clean, and washed herself unwillingly, but compared to these foreign women she stood out as clean as an angel. They were probably too lazy to keep dirt from them; slothfulness bred uncleanliness and uncleanliness bred vermin; among these people they must be careful or they might again become lice infested.

In the hold there were no spittoons, which seemed strange; one would expect to find them in nice places, among cleanly people. The deck soon was awash from the tobacco-chewing menfolk's spittle, and Kristina had to hold up her skirts as she walked over it; she was horrified to see little children crawling and creeping about on their hands and knees on this bemired floor; only with great effort was she able to keep little Harold away from it.

Washing buckets were set up for the steerage passengers, but the water was never changed. After a score of people had dipped their hands and rinsed their faces in the tubs, the water became as thick and black as though blood sausage had been boiled in it. And the same towel passed from one hand to another—there was only one for this multitude. Perhaps the ship's command felt: If fifty people have dried themselves on the towel before you, then it's good enough for you too! But Kristina washed neither herself nor her children in water used by dirty fellow passengers. The very first morning on board she asked their guide for help, and as soon as the steamer touched shore he managed to get her a tub of clean water. Then she used her own towels, which she had brought along and laundered during the voyage.

But in spite of her annoyance at this lack of external cleanliness, Kristina was unable to dislike her fellow passengers. These foreign people—poor, dirty, and badly dressed—appeared so friendly; only kind eyes and smiling faces were turned on her and her children. When strangers spoke to her, Kristina realized they spoke no evil, but rather something kind and cheering, wishing her only well. She felt ashamed that she could not answer them with the same kindness, that she could not make herself understood by them. All she could do was to smile back as broad a friendliness as she could and shake her head for the rest. She longed to enter into conversation with them; she suffered from being unable to do so and felt as though she were doing the strangers a rudeness. Besides, here she could have found honest friends, and these friends she turned away, again and again, through her silence.

Kristina suffered and worried over the lot awaiting her in the new land: to walk like a deaf-mute among other people.

2

It had been agreed that the interpreter Landberg was to accompany the immigrants to Chicago and from there return to New York.

While he still was with his countrymen he tried to advise and inform them about the things they needed to know. Landberg said he had traveled all the great seas, he had seen much of the world, on land and water, but he had found himself most at home in North America. Nowhere had he been less disturbed by the authorities, nowhere had he been so free to make his own decisions, nowhere were people so helpful to each other as here. His deepest needs—freedom to move as he pleased, and sufficient food—he had found in North America. Yes, more freedom and cheaper food than anywhere else on the globe. Just as an example—pork could be bought for three Swedish shillings per pound, pork so tasty and fat that the grease spurted between the jaws while one was eating it. Long Landberg called the North American Republic the Land of Liberty and Fat Pork.

But, he reminded them, they must remember that here, as elsewhere in the world, people were good and evil, industrious and lazy, generous and greedy, honest and crooked. They must be particularly on their guard against two types: the runners, who wanted to rob them, and sectarians, who wished to snare them into their fold. Among the latter he warned them against the Jansonites, who had come earlier from Sweden. Their prophet, Erik Janson, had been a plague to humanity, a torturer of his followers. First he had forbidden marriage in his sect, as childbearing interfered with the women's work, but when his adherents grumbled at this, he was forced to allow it, and prepared a wedding for fifty couples at one time. But the sectarians were allowed no will of their own; when a married man wished to sleep with his wife, he must announce his wish to the prophet far in advance and obtain his permission. And when the tyrant gave his assent to the bedding, he insisted also that husband and wife must perform it in full view of all the other sectarians. Many hesitated at this. Landberg himself had for a while been a member of this sect, but he had soon left it, with many others, who, like himself were unable to put up with Janson's demands.

They must also be on the lookout for the Shakers, who served God by making their bodies shake and shiver, nay, even danced and hopped about, singing and howling until, exhausted, they would fall to the ground and faint. The dancing and the shaking themselves into insensibility were supposed to illustrate the ascent into Heaven by the saved

101

ones. These sectarians maintained that the praising and blessing of the Lord should not be confined to the tongue only—the whole body, head, and limbs had the same right to share this joy. (To this point Landberg was inclined to feel there was some reason.)

Another dangerous sect was the Whippers, who exorcised evil spirits by beating each other with scourges until their bodies were a bloody mass. Sometimes the evil spirits might resist the mistreatment and remain in the body until the soul had left it. Yes, these sectarians actually whipped each other to death.

Landberg himself had by now returned to the church of his forebears, the Evangelical-Lutheran religion, and he earnestly begged the Swedish immigrants to remain in the faith of their fathers, to stick to the only right God here in America; they must not allow themselves to be led astray by irreligious and false prophets. He was pleased to see that they had brought along their Bibles and psalmbooks, so that they could hold their own services.

Kristina asked how it would be possible for Swedish Lutherans to partake of the Sacrament out here. Their last Sunday in Sweden, before they started out on their fateful journey, she and her husband had received the Lord's Supper. At that time she had felt as if she were undertaking a death journey. Now again she was in great need of the Sacrament. At home they went to the Lord's Supper table every month; three months had already elapsed since they had enjoyed the Sacrament, and man sinned in many matters daily. How much time they'd had to sin in the last ninety days! Idleness breeds sin, according to the old saying, and they had long been idle. Kristina had lately felt the burden weighing on her, disturbing her mind and soul. Original sin clung to her like an invisible, loathsome mange; it was a degradation. She longed to be cleansed in Christ's pure blood, and no doubt there were many in their company who were in need of forgiveness for their sins, and absolution; how long would it be before they might again enjoy the Sacrament? The Swedish pastor who had come aboard their ship in New York had promised them communion, but when they heard he was a Methodist, not one among them had dared follow him to his altar.

Long Landberg answered: In Chicago there was a

Swedish Lutheran minister by the name of Unonius; he was an upright man and a true Christian. Landberg said that a few ministers of the right religion were to be found also in Andover and in Moline, both places in the state of Illinois. When they arrived in Chicago, he would himself look up Pastor Unonius, who surely would be happy to give the Sacrament to all wishing to partake.

Landberg said that he intended to leave Chicago as soon as he had performed his duties there. This town was the only place in North America he detested. But it was the gateway to the West, which all travelers must pass through, although most thanked the Lord they could journey farther. Chicago was a swamp hole and a blowhole, built on the low shores of a lake and a river. On one side was the lake and on the other the prairie, with no protection against the winds, which blew so intensely that eyebrows and hair were pulled off people's heads. The town had only three decent streets: Chicago Avenue, Kinzie, and Clark Streets. Yard-high stumps still stood in the other streets, and almost all the surrounding country was desolate wasteland where cows grazed. The houses were newly built, yet gray, dirty, and unpainted, for the hurricanes blew the paint off the walls. And the whole town stank from the mud and ooze of the swampy shores. Pools of water abounded, filled with crawling snakes and lizards and other horrible creatures. Thirty thousand people lived in Chicago, and of these, several thousand earned their living as runners, robbing immigrants passing through. Grazing was fine in Chicago, and cattle lived well in that town. But honest people, non-runners, could ill endure an extended visit in the place. Landberg thought Chicago would within twenty years become entirely depopulated and obliterated from the face of the earth.

Pastor Unonius worked zealously advising all his countrymen to settle in Chicago, but the guide thought that on this point the minister had wrongly interpreted God's will.

Landberg was indeed like a father to the immigrants, and all agreed he had well earned the three dollars each person was to pay him.

"He is an upright man and an honest guide," was the way Karl Oskar summed up their feeling. And he worried a little about their future when they would no longer have an interpreter to help in their dealings with the Americans.

Landberg had given Robert a new English textbook: *A Short Guide to the English Language*. This book had a chapter entitled "Instruction in Pronounciation for the Swedes." Here were enumerated those English words in common use, as well as advice in general for immigrants. Landberg's gift was quite a small book, hardly bigger than the almanac; Robert could carry it in his pocket and take it out when he needed it. Landberg had explained Robert's difficulty with his first language book. The Swedish youth had been unable to comprehend why the sentences in English were spelled in two entirely different ways, one sentence always within parentheses. Now he was informed that the words were to be pronounced according to the spelling within the parentheses. Robert had learned English altogether wrong from the very beginning.

The first thing he had tried to say to the Americans was: "I am a stranger here," and he pronounced the words carefully, according to their spelling and Swedish pronounciation. But people had only stared at him, he had been unable to make a single soul understand that he was a stranger. From this new book, he learned how the words were supposed to sound: *Aj am a strehn' djer hihr.*

And Robert began at once to practice the pronounciation of the twenty-six letters of the English alphabet. He hurried his study of the language, in order to help himself and to lend his mouth to others of his group when their interpreter left them. He must show the others what he could do, and they would then value him the more and show him the respect due to learning. From now on he read in his language books every free moment, and always without Elin's company. He told her, somewhat sarcastically, she was supposed to know English already; hadn't the Holy Ghost filled all the reborn ones?

After her disclosure in New York of his secret concerning the captain's "slave trade," there was no longer the same intimacy between them. Moreover, Elin had difficulties with the foreign language, she moved her lips too much and pushed out her tongue too far while speaking English. How many times he'd told her to keep her mouth still and pull her tongue back; but she did not obey him. Not all people were so fortunately born as to be able to learn a new language; not even the rebirth seemed of any help to Elin.

Robert had been in danger of his life and he knew the importance of learning English. Moreover, Landberg now told him of a terrible thing that had befallen a newly arrived farm hand from Sweden: the boy had been one month in America when he met a cruel, heartless, cunning woman who inveigled him into going with her to a priest, who married them. The farm hand understood what was happening but he didn't know one word of English, he couldn't even say "No" at the wedding, and this the wicked woman knew. And now her victim had been ordered by the court to support her for the rest of his life. So Robert understood that there were many reasons why it was necessary to learn the language—in order to escape the many dangers that lurked in this land.

3

Karl Oskar and Kristina were standing at the starboard rail where they could keep an eye on their belongings—their bulky linen sacks and the great America chest—stacked with other movables against the ship's wheelhouse. The lake heaved moderately, the breeze was cooling, the heat did not seem a plague when the steamer was in motion. Karl Oskar complained of the slow speed: he was constantly worrying lest they arrive at their place of settling too late for sowing and planting. If they were unable to gather any crop this summer, they would be in ill circumstances. Now he was a restless man, he would not be at peace till the day when he could start to work.

Kristina watched the purring drive wheel, whipping the water like a dasher in a churn full of cream. When she used to make butter, the cream would splash up in her face, and now, as the wheel threw water against the side of the ship, the spray splashed on her face and into her eyes; it felt refreshing.

Ulrika of Vastergohl came up to them hurriedly. She addressed Karl Oskar in agitation: "Now I know the truth! Just try to explain this away!"

He turned slowly toward her: "What is it this time?"

"You have deceived us! You've swindled and cheated us and made us travel this long way!"

105

"What in hell are you accusing me of?"

"You said it was only two hundred and fifty miles!"

"That's what the captain of the *Charlotta* said."

"But our guide says it's fifteen hundred miles! Six times as far as you said! Landberg doesn't lie, but you've lied to lure us along! Now comes your day of reckoning, Karl Oskar!"

Ulrika's lips quivered, her eyes flamed, her whole body shook with anger: "Because of your notions the rest of us have to travel many hundreds of miles unnecessarily! Because you lied to us, Karl Oskar! Why have you deceived us? Answer me, you—you—lying—" She called him an obscene name.

His cheeks paled at this insult, and Kristina grew frightened lest he lose his head.

Ulrika did not give him time to reply. She continued to rant: How could he be so low, such a scoundrel, as to cheat his own countrymen in a foreign land, so shabby as to lure them all this way, so deep into America? Not one of them would have followed him had they known what an eternal distance it was. He was certainly the most selfish and cruel and false of all the menfolk she had met. They must sail sea after sea, only because of him! They were all tired to death of this endless traveling! They wanted to settle down somewhere, they wanted to arrive! But now he couldn't deceive them any longer, now it was over! Now his true colors were discovered! Now he was at an end with his smirking, his lying, his cheating! Now was the time of reckoning, now he must answer!

His anger seethed within him so he could hardly speak. He burst out: "You accuse me? You insult me? You—you —you dirty old sl——"

He stopped short. But Ulrika egged him on: "Yes, say it right out! Say what you started—'You old slut'! That's what you meant—say the whole word! Say it quickly!"

By now both of them were shouting at the top of their lungs. Long Landberg hurried to them. Danjel Andreasson and Jonas Petter suddenly appeared.

"Ulrika accuses me of deceiving you about the distance!" Karl Oskar shouted.

Landberg explained soothingly: When Karl Oskar had said it was two hundred and fifty miles from New York to Minnesota, he had spoke the truth, because such was the distance measured in Swedish miles. And when he, Landberg, had told Ulrika that the distance was fifteen hundred miles, then he too had spoken the truth, for he had meant American miles. An American mile was only one sixth of a Swedish mile.

Both Karl Oskar and Ulrika were in the right; they might as well end their quarrel.

But the words uttered on both sides had been too insulting. Karl Oskar was deeply offended: "If anyone thinks I have lied and cheated our group—step up!"

Kristina held on to his elbow: "Be calm, Karl Oskar! It was only a misunderstanding."

"No! Now *I* want to tell the truth!"

And Karl Oskar continued angrily: It concerned no one but his family that he had decided to settle in Minnesota. He had never asked anyone to accompany him; the others had followed of their own will. Why? Why did they ape him? They could go and settle wherever in hell they wanted—it didn't concern him. He had never asked to be the leader of their group. But when they had come to him, he had done their errands gladly. And now he got his reward. Ulrika and the others need only say the word if they wanted to leave him and travel alone. He would not cry over their departure; he wouldn't shed one single tear for those outside his family. It would be less trouble for him to travel alone with his wife and children. He wanted to hear one word only, if the distance was too great!

"Ulrika was excited, pay no attention to her," advised Jonas Petter. "We rely on you, we're grateful to you, all of us."

Then Danjel Andreasson attempted a reconciliation: "There is no quarrel between the two of you. Shake hands, now!"

"Shake his hand!" sputtered Ulrika. "Did you hear what he called me?"

"You called me a lying—" Karl Oskar could not make himself repeat the obscenity in his wife's presence.

"Take back your words, both of you," urged Jonas Petter.

"Be Christian and forgiving," admonished Danjel. "Forgive each other as our Lord Jesus forgives all of us."

"If a group of immigrants want to succeed, they must live in harmony," Landberg said.

107

Karl Oskar and Ulrika, surrounded by curious fellow travelers, stared fixedly into each other's eyes, silent, immobile, neither one yielding an inch.

Robert and Arvid had heard the commotion too and approached the group as Long Landberg left, shaking his head and muttering that Swedish peasants found a peculiar enjoyment in personal quarrels, at home and abroad.

"Be at peace, good people," Danjel entreated once more, deeply concerned. "Won't you shake hands?"

Karl Oskar and Ulrika remained silent. Both had calmed down and each would have taken a proffered hand. Ulrika knew that Karl Oskar had acted in good faith, and that she had unjustly accused him of skulduggery. Karl Oskar regretted the words he had uttered; there was reason enough to call Ulrika of Vastergohl an old slut, but it was unnecessary and foolish to dig up dirt from home to throw at her in a foreign land. Both admitted inwardly that it would be right to retract; both were ready to shake hands in forgiveness. But neither one offered his hand, each feared the humiliation of refusal from the other.

And so no hand was offered. Danjel bowed his head in sorrow, his shaggy, unkempt beard sweeping his chest.

Elin called her mother from their cabin, and Ulrika departed with long strides, proudly.

Jonas Petter looked after her and said in a low voice to Robert and Arvid: Ulrika of Vastergohl was getting illtempered because of lack of close male company; what she needed most of all for a few nights ahead was a man.

Karl Oskar and Kristina walked over to the wheelhouse.

"I can't stand the Glad One any longer!" he said. "We must part from her."

"But she is part of Danjel's family," protested Kristina. "She is like a foster mother to the children. You don't want to take her away from the poor motherless children?"

Karl Oskar kept silence gloomily, wondering what to do.

"And how can you get rid of Ulrika?" continued Kristina. "You can't throw her into the lake."

"You've always disliked Ulrika before. Now you defend the old whore!"

108

"I didn't defend the way she acted just now. But I can stand her better in this country."

Kristina pointed out that Ulrika had softened a little since sharing their food on the train the other day. She was more friendly and talkative, and the two women had these last days talked with each other as if no unfriendly feelings had ever existed between them. Ulrika had spoken many words both true and wise, and Kristina had enjoyed her company. Earlier, she had avoided the Glad One as one avoided vermin, she had thought her full of hatred and ill will, always trying to hurt others. But Ulrika wasn't entirely wicked and evil; there must be something good in a woman who was so kind to Danjel's offspring, poor little ones. And perhaps injustice had been done her at home in Sweden, ever since her childhood when they sold her at auction. That was why she always thought the worst of people. If they mistreated her and scorned her, then she acted the same way in return; and she could give ten for two; she could act like a viper if tramped on, biting, spurting out venom. If now they were to be considerate of her, if they made her feel one of them, perhaps . . .

"There will be no peace in our group until we get rid of her," Karl Oskar insisted. But what Kristina had said seemed to him worthy of thought, although he wouldn't admit it now.

Kristina also harbored an opinion of her own, well hidden from Karl Oskar: she felt the same way as Ulrika about this long journey inland.

They had barely started; the guide said several weeks would elapse before they reached their destination. Why must they travel such an unfathomable distance? Why hadn't they settled on a nearer place? It was Karl Oskar who wanted it that way, the responsibility was his, his will was being carried out. He had decided that they were to travel with the old woman, Fina-Kajsa, to her son in Minnesota. The others were willing to follow along: they thought what he did was best. He gave advice, and the others listened. But who could tell if he were right? Need they traverse so many lakes and rivers to find a home? Couldn't they have found one nearer?

This was Karl Oskar's great shortcoming: he never let well enough alone. All other men were satisfied at last, satisfied some time—never he. Many would have thought a move to another country quite sufficient—he wasn't satisfied until they moved to another continent. To others it would have been enough to travel two, three hundred miles inland—he must travel fifteen hundred miles, five times as far; he must get as far inland as he possibly could, before he would be satisfied. He said he wanted to find the best soil. But was it so sure (he acted as though God had said so) that the best land lay farthest away? Such was Karl Oskar's nature: things far away were better than those near by; what he couldn't reach was better than what he had, and the best of all lay farthest away in the world.

And now they were on a ship again, even though it didn't move by sail, but by steam and wheels. And she who had made up her mind never again to travel on water! The others too had come along. Ulrika alone had murmured, she was not afraid to speak her mind. Her unfair accusations against Karl Oskar were inexcusable, but what she had said about this eternal traveling could just as well have come from Kristina's own mouth. It was well for him to hear it! He should know that there were those among them who were tired to death of this journey. Kristina was. Three long months had elapsed since that morning when she stepped onto the wagon in Korpamoen for a ride to the sea; she was still riding! And deep within her she marveled that her little children had survived this dangerous, unending journey; it would not have surprised her had it killed them all.

How intensely she longed for a place where she could stay. Where she could be by herself and make her own decisions, where she wouldn't have strangers with her always, where she could rest in her own bed, under her own roof, where she could make a home for her husband and her offspring! How fervently her heart longed for a home again, how desperately she prayed that she might see the place where she was to live.

4

The steamer *Sultana* entered a sound which soon turned out to be a river mouth; shortly they tied up at the pier in Detroit.

The immigrants were now approaching the northernmost boundaries of the United States. In this harbor the *Sultana* was to remain long enough so that anyone who wished to go ashore was allowed to do so.

Detroit was an old town, well built and of pleasing aspect. It was not a settlement village with streets crowded with cattle and tall tree stumps; it had well-ordered streets, almost like a town in Sweden, as Landberg said. From the boat it seemed that Detroit stood on a high bank along the river; they could see rows of well-built and well-looked-after houses, topped by church towers and steeples; next to the pier there was an extensive market place. Coming up the river they had seen vast orchards on either shore, filled with apple and cherry trees, their branches overloaded with delicious-looking fruit. The country around the town was fertile and good as far as their eyes could see.

Nearly all the *Sultana*'s passengers went ashore. Of the group from Ljuder, the two smallest children were left behind, Karl Oskar's son Harald and Danjel's little daughter Eva, and Fina-Kajsa also remained on the shop to take care of the babies.

The older children were much excited by the prospect of walking on solid ground again; they asked if they might go back to where they had seen the cherry trees, but the parents told them there would not be time. Kristina took Johan by the hand and Karl Oskar held on to Lill-Marta, so as not to lose them in the crowd. They walked about the town for a few hours, looking at many strange things, but it was surprising how soon both children and grownups tired from walking: they had been freighted about for so long that they had no strength to walk any distance. The heat was more infernal on land, too, and they were almost glad to return to the ship.

By the time the passengers were back on the pier, the *Sultana* had finished unloading her freight. A wide barge loaded with cattle was tied to the steamer's side. Half a dozen sturdy men, their upper bodies bare and their heads covered with broad straw hats, were bringing the cattle from the barge onto the pier. Then an accident befell one of the animals: a large bull refused obstinately to walk onto the landing plank: he skidded and fell into the water. The river was quite deep near the pier, and only the head and back of the bull could be seen above the water. A curious crowd gathered immediately to see the beast rescued. The bull struggled in the water like a sea monster, snorting, bellowing, and squirting quantities of water through his nostrils, until the men finally succeeded in getting a rope around his horns and pulling him on shore.

While the others of their group went aboard, Karl Oskar and Jonas Petter had remained behind to watch the rescue of the bull. As Karl Oskar turned to climb the gangplank he was met by Kristina.

"Are you alone?" she asked.

"Yes. Is anyone missing?"

She stared at him, fear in her eyes: "Isn't Lill-Marta with you?"

"No. I thought she was aboard."

"She was with you. Only Johan came with me."

"The girl is not on the ship?" Karl Oskar asked breathlessly.

"No."

"Are you sure?"

"Yes—I told you, the girl was with you. Where is she?"

"She was on the pier when you went . . ."

"You let her out of your sight?"

"I thought she went with you."

"Lord Jesus! Where is Lill-Marta?" Kristina shrieked. "Lord in Heaven! The child is left behind somewhere!"

She rushed down the gangplank, followed by Karl Oskar. They ran back and forth on the pier, looking for their missing child. The men, a moment before busy with the drowning bull, turned their attention from the now safe beast to the man and woman who ran about on the pier, calling out their child's name. No one answered. They looked everywhere for the little one, on the pier and near it, among the unloaded freight, behind barrels and boxes and sacks and coils of rope; they searched behind cords of wood and stacks of boards, they examined every place imaginable that might be a hiding place, every nook and corner where a three-year-old might have crawled. On the pier were only grownups, there was no child in the crowd. They looked up toward the market place and along the shores, as far as their eyes could reach. But there was no sign of Lill-Marta. Their child had simply disappeared.

She had been on the pier a short time ago, when Karl

Oskar stopped to watch the bull in the water; he had thought she followed her mother aboard. But the child had been in his charge, he felt the blame was his.

The *Sultana*'s bell rang piercingly, it was time for the boat to leave. The bull responded with a long-drawn-out, angry bellow, as if wishing to chase the boat off, and Karl Oskar glared at him fiercely: if that damned beast hadn't fallen into the river—if he hadn't stopped to watch it . . .

Kristina turned to the man who had done the unloading: "Have you seen a little girl, about three years old?" She grabbed hold of the arm of a bearded giant, wailing in despair: "A very little girl . . . in a blue dress . . . red ribbons in her braids?"

The man stared at her helplessly, mumbling some words in his own language. Kristina ran to the next man, she ran from one to another, and asked, and asked; she had forgotten that none of them understood a word: "A girl . . . haven't you seen her . . . our little girl?"

Karl Oskar searched in silent anguish; he remembered that he was among strangers, that here he was no better than a mute.

Their child had disappeared, and they couldn't tell a single soul that she was lost. No one could tell them if Lill-Marta had been seen, no one could tell them where she had gone, no one could help them, because they couldn't ask anyone for help—no one could help them search for a little girl in a blue dress and red ribbons.

"Maybe she has fallen off the pier . . . into the water," he said to Kristina.

"It was you! You let her get away from you!" Kristina broke out accusingly.

"Yes . . . it's my fault . . . I forgot . . . for only a moment. . . ." Remorse swept over him.

"Lill-Marta! Lill-Marta! Lill-Marta!" Hysterically, the mother called her child's name, and no one answered. She broke into tears. "We've lost our child! She was with you!"

"Yes, Kristina. She was with me."

"Our first girl. Anna. You remember?"

As Kristina mentioned Anna, their dead child, memories of the past flashed through Karl Oskar's mind: He carried a small coffin in his arms, he was on his way to a grave, he walked with heavy steps carrying the coffin he himself had made, had hammered together of fine boards,

113

the finest, knot-free boards he had been able to find. That was Anna, that was the other time, the other child whom they had lost.

The *Sultana*'s side wheels were beginning to churn, foam whirled about, the bell rang again, and a man on deck shouted, "All aboard!"

Some of the crewmen made ready to pull in the gangplank—no one was aware that two passengers had gone back on shore.

Karl Oskar stood on the pier as if paralyzed. But suddenly, at the sound of the bell, he came back to life: "The ship is leaving us!"

"We cannot leave Lill-Marta!"

"The boys are on the ship! All we own is on the ship!"

"I stay here on land. I must find our child." Kristina sank down on a packing box among the freight, unable to move.

Karl Oskar looked wildly in all directions, searching for the lost child; he looked at the ship, ready to depart; he looked at his wife, sitting on the box, forlorn and shaking with sobs. In that moment he was a thoroughly bewildered, helpless human being, not knowing what to do next. Yet within the minute he must know, his decision must be made.

Two of their children were on board, one was here on land. If they went on board without the girl, they would never see her again. If they remained on shore, their sons would be left to themselves on the ship. What must they do?

He would never give up in despair, never consider all lost; he must do the best he knew how, he had always done so in critical moments, he must do so now.

He would rush on board and find Landberg; their interpreter might persuade the captain to delay the ship until they found . . .

But now the gangplank was hauled in.

Karl Oskar made two jumps to the edge of the pier, waved both arms and shouted as loudly as he could: "Wait! Wait a little! Have mercy, people!"

A crewman came to the rail and shouted something back, something he didn't understand. But suddenly he heard another voice, a voice he understood, a voice shouting in his own language, louder than all the noises of the ship, louder than any human sound around him: from somewhere on shore came a woman's voice, a coarse voice, a penetrating, fierce, furious voice, rising above all the din and bustle on the pier: "Wait, you sons of bitches! I'm still on shore!"

A woman came running along a footpath that followed the shore, and she called, short of breath and angrily, while running, yet louder even than the bellowing bull: "Put down the gangplank, you bastards! I'm coming as fast as I can!"

Karl Oskar recognized the voice; it belonged to Ulrika of Vastergohl, who, it seemed, was also in danger of being left behind. But Ulrika was not alone as she came running to the pier, she carried a burden, she carried in her arms a kicking, obstreperous child, and because of this burden, and the fear of being left behind, Ulrika was short of breath and angry. In her arms the Glad One carried a little girl in a blue dress with red ribbons on her hair. Panting, she put the child down next to Karl Oskar and yelled once more toward the ship: "Those sons of bitches! Trying to get away!"

While Karl Oskar and Kristina fell upon their child, the gangplank was once more lowered.

"The girl was back there under the trees," said Ulrika. "She was eating cherries."

Near the shore, Ulrika told them as they hurried to the gangplank, she had seen a grove of cherry trees, and thinking their boat would remain a while longer, she had gone there to pick some fruit—her throat was dry in this awful heat. The child was already there, reaching for the cherries. But Lill-Marta had been unable to reach the branches, she was too short, so Ulrika had picked her a handful. The child had wanted to remain and eat cherries, and that was why she had kicked and fought so hard when Ulrika carried her back.

Lill-Marta was still restive; when Kristina pressed her hard to her breast, the girl began to cry: the mother had squashed one of the cherries which she still held in her hand.

The crewmen greeted Ulrika with happy smiles and gestures as the four belated passengers walked up the gang-

115

plank. Who knows, perhaps they would have been equally friendly had they understood the words she shouted at them a few minutes earlier.

Slowly the steamer *Sultana* glided out of the Detroit harbor, with none of her passengers missing.

As soon as they were inside the rail Karl Oskar held out his hand to Ulrika; he shook hers violently, he pressed it in his own, he would not let go of it for a long while: this was the hand that had brought back their child, had saved the little girl and—the parents. But he was unable to speak, not a syllable would cross his lips, not a sound. He felt something in his throat, something he couldn't swallow. Only a few times before had he had this feeling, it came over him instead of tears.

Karl Oskar wept, wept inwardly like a man, with invisible tears.

5

After six days' sailing across the Great Lakes and the rivers and sounds which separated them, the steamer *Sultana* reached Chicago. Waiting for a river steamer, the immigrants remained three days in this town, lodged in quarters Landberg had found them. Meanwhile, their guide was busy making arrangements for their continued journey. Pastor Unonius, the Swedish Lutheran minister, unfortunately had gone to visit a new settlement outside the town; consequently, the immigrants were unable to participate in Holy Communion while in Chicago.

On July 6, early in the morning, Landberg escorted the group on board a steamer in the Chicago River which plied a canal to the Illinois River and which was to carry them to the upper Mississippi. With this last service the guide finished his obligations. Landberg bade his countrymen farewell, wishing them health and success in their new homeland. They were now entirely dependent on themselves, but he commended them all to the hands of Almighty God.

The immigrants had passed through the portals of the West. They were on a new ship, and on the new ship they met a new sea, a sea unlike any they had ever seen or traversed: the prairies' own Sea of Grass.

116

VIII

Peasants on a Sea of Grass

Through the vast flat land the Creator's finger had carved a crooked furrow and in this furrow flowed the river, carrying the vessel of the immigrants. The shores of the waterway lay close to them, just beyond the boat's rail. The solid earth on either side gave the travelers a feeling of security. Fear for their lives, their constant companion on the ocean voyage, was no longer with them; they traveled on water, yet they were near land.

But their sense of being lost, astray in the world, remained with them on this river journey as it had during the ocean voyage.

They were passing through a vast level country, an endless emptiness of open, grassy, flat land. No more here than on the ocean could their eyes find a point of focus: no trees, no groves, no hills, no glades, no mountains. They saw one sight only—stretches of wild grass, herbs, and flowers, fields of tussocks, hollows of grass, billows of grass, springing from the ground on all sides, rolling forth in infinity; the same green billows extended all the way to that narrow edge where the flat land flowed into the globe of heaven, all the way to where the eye could see no farther. Like the Atlantic Ocean, this treeless expanse seemed to them one region only; nothing under the sun

117

separated one landscape from another. The grassy tussocks swayed and sank and came up again from the hollows; the tussocks were like billows, always the same, everywhere; when they had seen one, they had seen them all. This unchanging, monotonous expanse was called the prairie.

For seventy days they had traversed the Atlantic Ocean —a sea of water. Now they traveled across the North American prairie—a sea of grass.

Here blossomed a hay meadow, vast as a kingdom, yet here no cattle grazed. Here was hay to harvest in such abundance that all the barns in the world would not suffice to hold it; here a haymaker could go forth with his scythe and cut one straight swath, day after day, mile after mile; he could continue his straight swath the whole summer long, the meadow was so vast he need never turn. Here were blossoming fields and grazing lands, here abounded flowers and fodder. Here, spreading before them, the travelers saw a verdant ocean which they might have walked through dry-shod, which they might have traversed without a ship.

This was not the sterile sea with darkness in its depths, existing below the firmament before dry land was seen: this was a growing and yielding sea where crops had as yet never been harvested.

Over this sea, too, the winds wailed, sweeping through the grass, stirring waves that rolled on endlessly. The fierce wind fell upon the grass, flattened it with all its power, rolled over it, pressed it down, so that it lay there as slick as if it had been combed with a comb. But when the wind lost its force and the pressure slackened, the soft grass rose again, straightening its blades. The sea of grass lay there again—living, irrepressible, billowing back and forth in its eternal way, unchanged since the creation of the earth.

The immigrants had lived in woodland regions in Sweden, they were at home in forests, they were familiar with trees, bushes, and thicket paths, they were intimate with valleys, glades, ridges, and hills. In the woodlands at home they had easily recognized familiar landmarks to guide them. But in this sea of grass they could find nothing to notice and remember: no roads, no wheel tracks, no paths, no cairns. In whichever direction they looked, from the deck of the river steamer they could see only a wild, untrampled expanse, where nothing indicated that man had passed. Without a guide, a wanderer over these flat lands would be lost, swallowed up; how could he find his way when one mile was forever like another?

The peasants from the forest regions passed over the prairie and shrank from the land opening before their eyes in all its incomprehensible vastness. They desired nothing more than to till smooth, level ground, but this prairie was not what they wanted. There was something missing in this flat land: God had not finished His creation. He had made the ground and planted the grass and all the other growing herbage, but the trees were missing, the bushes, the hills, the valleys, the swales. Moreover, this grass sea was too immense; it frightened them. Anything stretching farther than their eyes could see aroused fear, loneliness, a feeling of desolation. They feared the sea of grass because they were unable to see its end, they feared it in the same way that they feared eternity.

The prairie stung their hearts with its might and emptiness. The grassland lay on this side of the horizon and it lay beyond, continuing into the invisible, encircling them on all sides; they wanted to shrink and hide within themselves in their helplessness; the farther the earth stretched, the smaller man seemed.

Here was fertile soil, offering itself to the plow, a ground of potent growth. Where the earth is green, there people can live and feed themselves. And the rivers and brooks had cut into the land and watered it with their flow. What more could a tiller wish? Yet, here they would not like to settle, not under the best conditions; this land was not what they were seeking.

Born in the forest, they would never feel at home on the prairie. They wanted *all* of God's creation around their homes; they wanted trees which gave shade and coolness in summer, warmth and protection against winds in winter. Here was not a single tree to fell for house timber, hardly a shrub to cut for firewood. They wanted to live within timbered walls, to gather high piles of wood for fires in their stoves. Settlers on the prairie must dig holes in the earth and live the life of gophers, and when above ground they must bend their backs because of the unmerciful winds. The woodland peasants would languish from

119

the monotony of the unvarying, desolate, empty endlessness which would surround their homes if they lived here. They would wither away from loneliness and the sense of loss. Delivered into the infinity of this sea of grass, they would perish, soul and body.

No, the prairie was not a suitable place for permanent settlement. From the deck of their moving steamer they looked out over this flat land, satisfied to pass through it; they thought of the prairie as a thoroughfare, another sea they must cross.

Their journey continued in the river furrow, and more great stretches of prairie opened up. The new country was showing its size to them, and the more they saw of its vastness and immensity, the smaller they felt themselves; more than ever before during this long journey they felt lost and strayed in the world.

2

At night, darkness was upon the face of the deep, and on this sea of grass. The wind held its breath and died down. From the ground rose a surge like dying billows on a calm water. Grass and wild flowers were veiled by the cloak of darkness, the verdant ocean was hidden by night. In the firmament—stretched over the earth by the Creator on the Second Day, and called by Him Heaven—the stars shone with clear brilliance. The world down here was great, but the heavenly firmament and the lights up there were greater still—so it seemed when night descended with darkness over the land, comforting those who felt too small for the great earth.

One evening at dusk, they saw a bright light in the sky ahead of the steamer. Somewhere far away a fire was burning, reflecting its gold-red flames in the heavens. On the earth a fire was throwing its flames so high that it wove red stripes into the gray clouds all the way to the top of heaven: the sea of grass was afire.

Far into the night the immigrants stood and gazed at this fire, so brilliantly reflected in the firmament ahead of the steamer. A wall of fire and flames rose into the sky, and they could discern thick clouds of smoke spreading above their heads like the wings of a black bird of prey. The stars faded away behind this red-glowing heavenly

120

wall. A fire was sweeping the prairie, devouring the grass, feeding on a sea of fuel.

To the immigrants, watching from a distance, it seemed as if God's heaven were burning this night, and a burning heaven is an awesome sight to see. Even the children noticed the fire in the heavens above them, and asked about the angels and wondered if they could fly away before their wings got burned.

The immigrants were reminded of the altar picture in their village church. It showed the Last Judgment and Christ's return to earth. In the picture, too, fiery clouds and smoke belched forth, heavy and dark and so real one could almost smell the smoke. And from on high Jesus came riding down on a burning cloud, in snow-white mantle, surrounded by a host of white angels. The people who were to be judged stood in fear on trembling legs, while the earth was lighted by pale rays from a darkened sun. It was daylight, yet it was dark as night, because it was the Last Day, the Day of Doom.

And now they were seeing the heavens burn in a fire which spread a fearsome light over the earth: their village altar picture was now hanging before them in the firmament, immensely enlarged and brought into living reality.

As yet that part of the picture which gave meaning to it remained undivulged: as yet Christ remained invisible in the fire-wreathed clouds. Christ and His angels had not yet made their appearance.

But many among them would not have been surprised if during this night He had descended from on high, in the glare of the heavenly flames, to judge living and dead.

They recognized the signs, they saw them in the very skies: like this it must be on the last day of the world. The seas and the winds would make much noise, and the heavens would tremble. Any moment now the world's Judge might descend from His heavenly throne, the burning skies lighting His way to the earth.

But even if this were only an earthly fire—the prairie turned into a burning sea—they were nevertheless drawing closer to this fire each moment. The steamer followed the river, and the river flowed right into the red wall of flames and smoke. They would have liked to ask the captain why their ship didn't moor, why he continued to steer right into the fire. Did he with intention bring his boat into the

121

flames, to destroy it with passengers and crew? But unable to speak the language, they could not ask. All they knew was that the fire appeared closer and closer, and the boat approached the fire: the boat and the fire must meet.

Would it be possible to pass through a burning wall and yet remain alive? The alarmed and anxious immigrants sought comfort in their Bibles, where the prophet Isaiah had written the Lord's words: "When thou passest through the waters, I will be with thee; and through the rivers, they shall not overflow thee: when thou walkest through fire, thou shalt not be burned; neither shall the flame kindle upon thee."

All stayed awake through this night; those who went to bed rose at short intervals to look at the burning skies; many prayed in anguish and despair; if it were so that their last day was upon them, hadn't it come too suddenly? Would the heavenly King recognize them as His own, or would He say to them: "Depart from Me, ye cursed!"

Toward morning they could see the fire and the smoke far to the right of the steamer; during the night they had passed a turn of the river, to the left, and were drawing away from the fire.

In clear daylight, it paled and diminished, losing its terrifying effect on those who had taken it as a sign of approaching Doomsday. During the day, the flames gradually disappeared, and at dusk could no longer be seen from the deck of the steamer.

Far, far away they had seen a fire on the prairie. But all around them, all the way to the horizon, the flat land remained green and untouched by flames.

Earlier the immigrants had crossed the *stormy* sea and had safely reached shore. Now again they thanked their God Who had helped them: He had saved them from the *burning* sea.

3

The river steamer brought them farther West, following the deep furrow which the Creator had cut through the land of grass, where the billows rose and fell under the wind's persistent comb. Down in the river the drive wheel churned its circular way, hurling the glittering drops into the sunlight.

Since leaving their homes, the immigrants had traveled by flat-wagon and sailing ship, by river boat and steam wagon, by canal boat and steamer. They had been pulled by horses and transported by winds, they had moved by the power of steam. They were still traveling through night and day, traveling across this country which seemed to have no limit. And every moment drew them farther from the land that had borne them. Their native village was now so far behind them that their thoughts could scarcely traverse the distance from the point on the earth where their journey began, to the place where they now were. They shuddered when they tried to comprehend the whole distance they had traveled across land and water. Trying to remember, they were unable to reach back—not even their imagination could undertake a return journey. The distance was too overwhelming; the earth which God had created was too large and too wide to fathom.

A realization which their minds had long resisted became fixed in their hearts and souls: this road they could never travel again; they could never return. They would never see their homeland again.

IX

Danger Signs Are Not Always Posted

A bell rang on the upper deck, the steering wheel turned, and the prow of the river steamer headed shoreward. The boat moored to a lonely bank deep in the forest; there were no signs of people or human habitation. The gangplank was thrown out, and two of the crewmen went on shore, carrying an oblong bundle between them. Two other men with shovels followed them. All four disappeared behind the thick wall of trees and bushes which grew to the water's edge.

After a short while the men returned to the ship. But now they carried nothing except the shovels dangling in their hands. The bell rang again, the gangplank was pulled in, and the steamer backed into the river, resuming its course after this short, unscheduled delay.

These stops at wild and lonely shores took place every day, some days many times. Except for the ringing of the bell, the stops made not a sound, indeed, they happened so quietly and unexpectedly and were of such short duration that at first the passengers hardly noticed them. Otherwise they might have asked why the steamer made shore; no passenger disembarked, they saw no freight unloaded, no firewood or timber was taken aboard. And at the mooring places not the smallest shed could be seen, there were no piles of wood, no stacks of lumber;

untouched wilderness was all that could be seen. Why was time wasted for these stops?

Only the most observant travelers had noticed that a bundle was carried ashore, they had seen the men with shovels, and on closer inspection had seen earth clinging to the shovels when the men returned to the boat. And so they had figured out that the men remained ashore long enough to dig a shallow grave.

Soon all had guessed the riddle of the frequent stops in the wilderness, so quickly and silently undertaken. Something—wrapped in a piece of gray cloth—was carried ashore. Some one of the passengers was taken on land, not alive, but dead. A corpse was removed from the boat, a funeral was performed during the brief interval while the steamer was moored to the bank.

Some passenger died every day; and there were days when several died. Soon all on board were aware of this and counted the number of times the bell rang and the men with shovels went ashore.

No one on board had died by act of violence or by accident, no one had starved to death, no one had frozen to death in this summer heat. A disease was killing the passengers, a disease which in a few short days transformed the healthiest person into a corpse. And the sickness which had stolen aboard the river steamer was so greatly feared that it could not be called by its name, it was the *disease*, nothing else. To call it by name would have been to challenge the dreaded scourge, make it appear sooner. People became sick from fear. In terror they watched for the signs: when the bodily juices dried up, when the skin turned blue-red and coarse, when the nose grew sharp, when thirst burned the tongue and the membranes of the throat, when the body could retain nothing, neither fluids nor solid matter, when the limbs felt cold and cramped, when the eyes sank into their sockets, when nasal slime and saliva stopped, when all tears dried up— then it had entered the body! And if the miracle didn't happen—perspiration breaking out over the whole body within two hours of the seizure—then death had prepared his work well and would finish it within twenty-four hours.

It was a painful sickness. Yet it could be called merciful because it killed within a fairly short time: in a day—perhaps two—it forced the warmth of life from a body, leaving the chill of death in its place. The strongest and healthiest suffered the worst agonies, because the stronger and more capable of resistance life was, the more painful the death struggle.

The murderous disease was the Asiatic epidemic, the cholera.

For the past two years this disease from the East had been sweeping over North America. The Old World had given the New World its most deadly epidemic. It was a gift out of Bengal, from the Holy Ganges, the river of swampy death lands and poisonous waters. The emigrants from Europe had brought this pestilence with them, they carried it with them inland as their journey continued, it was spread from place to place, from boat to boat, from river to river: the pestilence of the East had come to the West.

No one had announced to the passengers that cholera was with them on the steamer: it was not registered in the passenger list, it was not entered on the list of cargo. Inconspicuously, hurriedly, the bodies of the victims were removed. There was need for haste—in this heat.

When the mysterious visits on shore had continued for some days, the name of the horrible disease began to be whispered among the passengers. Then not only the unrelenting pestilence but also the fear of it paralyzed all on board: here, in the midst of them, it had stolen in, invisible, yet it was everywhere; death was close upon them.

2

Karl Oskar remembered the sign he had seen on the steam wagon, which their guide had translated for him, that sign which cautioned about places to be avoided, places where one must be careful: *danger! watch your step!* He kept his eyes open wherever he went, he was always on the lookout for these English words of warning. But this sign was not posted in all dangerous places in America: he had not seen it on their boat. The passengers had boarded the steamer in confidence, unaware that it was tainted.

At home they had heard of the cholera as a scourge. But the pestilence had little power in Sweden, where the climate was cold. In the heat of this country, Karl Oskar realized that the pestilence might flourish and spread; the very air seemed to burn, it was the worst heat he had experienced since landing in America. He did not know how to combat it. Against cold weather he knew what to do; when the cold grew intense, one could put on heavy clothing. In hot weather one must remove one's clothes, and here he went about as much undressed as he could without feeling ashamed. But it did not help. Even stark naked he would have suffered; it wouldn't have helped to remove his skin!

Against cold one could light fires, one could crawl all the way into the fireplace, if necessary. But where could one flee to get away from the heat? There was no place to crawl into, nowhere to hide from it.

And in this melting heat the steamer fare seemed foul and dangerous. Sometimes the food smelled bad: the nose performed its duty and warned the mouth to refuse it. No fresh food would keep; the blowflies buzzed everywhere and laid their eggs, which hatched almost immediately. Worms crawled in newly slaughtered meat, and soon no one dared touch even the fat pork, swimming in its thick grease, and until now eaten greedily by all.

The cholera must be something living, something that entered one's body through food or drink, some little worm or creeping thing. It might be a tiny creature floating about in the drinking water, perhaps a worm so small that the eye couldn't see it. The cholera might hide in every bite they swallowed, in every drop of water they drank. The murderous pestilence might lurk in their eating vessels or drinking mugs—how could they avoid it when they couldn't even see it? Never before had Karl Oskar felt death so close upon him; it was here everywhere, yet invisible to all.

Not all passengers ate the steamer fare; those who had money bought their own food. Karl Oskar noticed the travelers on the upper deck: each time the steamer stopped at an inhabited place, the first-class passengers went on shore and bought fresh food; they returned with heavy loads of bread, butter, milk, eggs, pancakes; even hens and chickens, which their Negro cooks prepared for them. The passengers up there could eat special, healthy food. And Karl Oskar recalled he had not yet seen a

127

corpse carried ashore from the upper deck. But in steerage, a room for the sick had been prepared with beds all over the floor.

One day when the steamer sought shore three times to accomplish its hurried errand, Karl Oskar said to Kristina: "Those who leave the food alone keep healthy. From now on, we starve."

Kristina agreed, and they let the meals go by; they could starve many days without endangering life. Their appetites had greatly diminished due to the heat, and in a few days they would leave the contaminated steamer. But thirst plagued them sorely, and they had to use the drinking water on the ship. They mixed some vinegar into it; vinegar killed all poisons in water, according to Berta, the Idemo woman who had healing knowledge.

But the best remedy against cholera was said to be a handful of coarse salt, taken a few times daily and washed down with brannvin. Karl Oskar had brought along some wormwood-seed brannvin, which had so far kept his body in good order. Now it was all gone. Fortunately, they had some camphor-brannvin left, and they drank this; Kristina gave the children spoonfuls of "The Prince's Drops" and "The Four Kinds of Drops." Fresh milk was also said to be good against the pestilence, but there was no milk on the boat, neither fresh nor sour. "All gone," they were told, and Robert explained that this meant the milk had been drunk to the last drop.

Jonas Petter borrowed Karl Oskar's bleeding iron and let his blood several times. He said he must get rid of his bad blood to be on the safe side. He also used the iron on Fina-Kajsa, who had long been asking for it. She, being the oldest in their group, was more afraid of the sickness than any of the others, and having lately been near death from another illness, she thought it would be unfair were she again to be laid down on a deathbed. She also tied one of her woolen hose around her throat and after this she felt comparatively safe. Arvid ate conscientiously from his box of *Painkiller,* and he shared the pills with Robert until not a single one was left. Ulrika of Vastergohl prepared plasters of mustard, which she placed across her stomach and Elin's; these plasters would draw the pestilence poison from the entrails where its home was.

The only one of their group who used no remedy

against the cholera was Danjel Andreasson; he did not
fear the pestilence. He refused to believe that the epidemic
was contagious. Who had contaminated the first person to
die of cholera? Could anyone tell him? To Danjel, no contagion existed; the cholera was sent directly to each one by
the Lord God. God was now visiting His people, already
He had decided which ones among the passengers were to
die. How could anyone believe this decision might be
changed? Danjel saw his fellow immigrants, each one
using his medicines and plasters, and he asked: Why not
leave the healing to their Creator? Were they so weak in
their faith as to doubt God's omnipotence? And he asked
his relatives Kristina and Karl Oskar: Did they actually
believe they could escape if God had chosen one or both
of them to die? Did they think they could hide from the
face of the Almighty?

Kristina answered: Man should not sit with crossed
arms and shovel everything onto the Lord. She believed
God might be more inclined to look after her if she tried
to help herself a little.

Danjel was more sad than ever when he learned that
Ulrika, his obedient disciple, tried to protect herself
against the pestilence with a mustard plaster. He reproached her for this and said she committed the heavy
sin of doubt when she relied more on a plaster made by
herself than on her God. Did she think, while preparing
this plaster with her own sinful hands, that she could do
more than the Almighty? She provoked the Lord with the
mustard plaster on her stomach, and he entreated her earnestly to remove it.

After Inga-Lena's death, Danjel had admitted to Ulrika
that he himself had been mistaken in his belief that one reborn was rid of sin forever: no human being on earth
could be free from sin as long as he remained in a mortal
body; neither he, Danjel, nor anyone else. All were
wretched sinners, burdened by fallen man's body as long
as they lived. There was no hope except through God's
grace and mercy.

When Ulrika heard this, she was deeply upset and perplexed; how could Danjel fail her thus? Weren't all her
sins washed away, once and for all? Did Jesus no longer
live in her body? She had believed what Danjel had told
her, and now he retracted what he had said. But she didn't

want her sin-body back, under no conditions did she wish her old corpse back. Nor had she sinned with any man since coming into Danjel's house and eating his bread. She had been cleansed—why then did not Jesus wish to remain in her? Ulrika felt cheated and insulted: she had confidently relied on Danjel's word, and she demanded that he, as the Lord's prophet, stand by his word. She had long obeyed him and been subordinate to him in all things, but now doubt stole over her: Was Danjel too weak a man to be the Lord's messenger? Yet he looked so much like a prophet, with his long, wild-grown beard.

Now Danjel tried to frighten her with God's wrath because of the mustard plaster she had prepared. She felt irresolute, wondering what to do. But she was not convinced within herself that she had angered God because of such a little thing. She left the mustard plaster in its place.

3

Every unfortunate victim chosen by the cholera sickened so suddenly that one moment he stood erect and strong, and the next, he almost fell to the floor. In the sickbed he immediately grew so weak that he was unable to lift his head, he shook in convulsions and moaned pitifully; some screamed in agony before they sank into the merciful depths of unconsciousness. After this the shrouding cloth was soon brought forth.

On the *Charlotta*, Kristina had not been conscious when anyone died; at the time of the deaths around her she herself had been desperately ill. But now she remembered the night on the ship when she nearly bled to death: a few times she had heard a woman's weak voice: "The poor little ones! I don't want to die!" It had been a low, moaning cry, and she had wondered whence it came. She had learned afterward that Inga-Lena had died that same night; it was Inga-Lena who had cried.

And as she now sat with her children about her, Kristina thought: "I do not wish to die and leave them!"

She had seen other creatures die: she had seen the animals at the slaughter bench. She had always had a feeling of compassion for them and had tried to avoid being present at the slaughter. But sometimes, when the men had no other help, she had been forced to hold the bucket for the blood. She had seen the dying animals suffer, she had heard their moaning and bellowing as they lay there, chained down, feet tied, and had seen their helpless kicking and struggling as long as they could move. She had often cried over people's cruelty to innocent creatures who had never done them harm, and she was often aware of her own share in this as she stood at the slaughter trough and received the butchered animal's blood in her bucket.

As she now heard the victims of cholera she was reminded of the times when she had helped with the slaughter. Now it was human creatures who suffered, and when their agony was over, they were hastily buried in unconsecrated ground in the same way as carcasses of diseased cattle were flung into shallow graves in the wastelands.

God must help her; He was the only one she could turn to. She herself would do all she was able to, and then God must help her.

The youngest one of their group, Danjel's daughter Eva, who had not yet learned to walk, was suddenly seized by the pestilence one morning.

The child's face turned blue, her small limbs were contorted with convulsions, her body twisted itself into a round bundle. It seemed as if the arms and legs of the little one had been pulled out of their joints. She cried pitifully, and at times lay still and moaned; she could not describe her pains, but if anyone touched her she screamed. Ulrika gave her all the medicines and pills at hand, but she refused to swallow anything, either dry or fluid. She lay in the vise of cramp, and no one could help her.

After a few hours the child's moaning died down. She was still, now, as if in deep slumber. Her breathing could still be heard, her heart still beat in her little body, but her breast fluttered up and down so quickly the eye could not follow its movements. Her last sounds were like a little bird's peep in a bush. In the late afternoon she grew entirely silent.

Eva Maria Emilia, not yet a year old, died in Ulrika's arms. And Ulrika would not give up the little one after her breathing had stopped. She sat with the dead child in her arms, her weeping shook her whole body. Danjel sat next to her, immobile, his hands folded. He did not weep, he prayed. God had again touched him and he uttered his

131

prayers of thanks for this: he had been too deeply devoted to this his youngest child, and because of this God had taken her away from him. He could not belong to the Lord soul and body while he loved a living creature here on earth. He had idolized little Eva, now the idol was removed, and he thanked his God that He had taken her.

Danjel was beyond human compassion, nor did he seek mortal comfort. It was Ulrika of Vastergohl who was in need of comfort at this moment, she who had been a good foster mother to Danjel's tender daughter, this daughter who had left the earth before she had learned to walk on it. And Ulrika remained sitting with the dead child in her arms until one of the crewmen came and took the little body away from her, and wrapped it in a piece of gray cloth.

At sunset the bell rang on deck, the prow turned shoreward, the steamer moored at an outjutting cliff. Two men with shovels in their hands went on land, one man carrying a small bundle. A flock of half-grown wild ducklings were disturbed and lifted from among the reeds; they flew noisily in circles over the cliff; they were mallard ducks, with beautiful feathers in changing colors. While dusk fell the men dug a hole behind the cliff. Soon they returned on board with their shovels; only a small grave had been needed this time.

Little Eva's funeral was over. And while the steamer put out again and darkness quickly fell over land and water, the flock of ducklings, still disturbed, kept crying plaintively as they flew about over the promontory behind which was the newly dug baby grave.

4

Their group had now lost one of its members. When, after this, they spoke to each other about the terrible pestilence, there was always in the mind of each: Who will be next?

Ulrika, up till now free from all pains and ailments, began to complain of diarrhea and aches in her legs; she hoped it was only the usual immigrant diarrhea that bothered her; and so it seemed. Karl Oskar suggested that she use the bleeding iron and get rid of some of her blood. Kristina had lost so much blood during her sickness on the *Charlotta* that she did not consider it necessary to be bled, nor did she think they should bleed their children; the little

132

ones were so pale, they probably had no more blood in their bodies than they needed.

Kristina interpreted the smallest discomfort in herself or her children as a sign of the pestilence. All except Danjel kept away from the unhealthy ship's fare and starved themselves. The grownups went about starving in silence, but the children begged for food. Children could not starve day after day; yet they mustn't eat the food either. Kristina said they must get fresh food, at least milk, for their offspring; they still had the means with which to buy it.

The silver in Karl Oskar's skin pouch had melted away during their journey inland, and he had less than a hundred dollars left. Their transportation from Chicago to Minnesota had cost more than he had figured, and they had spent more for food than they had expected. How much would be left on arrival?

One night little Johan was seized with intense vomiting. It continued until green bile came up. Except for pain in his stomach he did not suffer, but Kristina watched in anxiety for the usual sign: the thin limbs twisting in convulsion.

Next morning the steamer made shore at a settlement where firewood for the engine was to be loaded. This stretch of the river flowed through a forest region, and groves of evergreens and leaf-trees grew on either side. A group of bearded, long-haired men met the boat at the pier; they were woodcutters, waiting to load the steamer. These men of the forest had revolvers and knives in their belts and did not look very kind.

A narrow strip of land had been cleared along the river, and behind tall stacks of firewood and piles of lumber a row of houses could be seen. People lived here, so it should be possible to buy food. Kristina entreated Karl Oskar: "Go on shore! Try to get some milk for the little ones."

Karl Oskar picked up their large tin pitcher and went on shore. Robert had seen a map and he said that this was a town, but to Karl Oskar it seemed no more than an out-of-the-way farm village. Not much building had taken place; there were a few houses on the cleared strip, recently built of green lumber, and a little farther away, near the edge of the forest, he could see some primitive huts,

133

not larger than woodsheds; probably the woodcutters lived there. All the houses seemed to have been hammered together in a hurry. A road had been staked out through the village, and work on it begun, but it looked more like a timber road; it was uneven and full of ruts, winding its course between piles of logs and stumps many feet high. Karl Oskar had noticed these tall stumps in many places: apparently the timbermen in America did not bend their backs but felled the trees while standing upright. This left ugly stumps and wasted lumber.

He looked at the row of houses, trying to find a store where food could be bought. He had made up his mind not to return to his children with an empty pitcher.

The biggest house had a sign painted in yard-high letters on the wall toward the river: BANK. Karl Oskar spelled the word twice to be sure, b, a, n, k. A word from his own language was painted on a house far away in the American wilderness! How could this be? Was it done to help arriving Swedes, unable to understand English? Or was the owner a Swede? Robert was not there to inform him that bank was spelled the same in both languages. Karl Oskar decided to go in and ask the bank master where he could buy some milk and wheat bread.

The door below the sign was locked. Karl Oskar knocked, but no one answered. Not a single person was in sight, neither inside the house nor near it. He walked farther, and through a window noticed some men standing at a counter of packing boxes. Behind the counter were shelves, and he thought perhaps this was a store.

Upon entering he immediately realized his mistake: on the counter stood a keg with a tap in it; a man in a white apron behind the counter was pouring a dark-brown drink from the keg. Karl Oskar recognized it as the American brannvin. The men at the counter were drinking, the shelves were filled with bottles, but there was no sign of food. He had entered a saloon.

He did not want to buy brannvin, he wanted milk. He turned in the door, mumbling something about being in the wrong place. It vexed him that he couldn't ask where to buy fresh food and milk for his children. It was pitiful the way he had to act—like a suckling, not yet able to speak, unable to ask for food when he was hungry.

But the few words Karl Oskar mumbled as he left the

saloon had an unexpected result. One of the men at the counter followed him through the door and called after him: "Hallo! Are you Swedish?"

Karl Oskar turned quickly. At first he only stared, the Swedish words surprised him so much.

Many Swedes had moved to North America before him, but it was the first time in this country a stranger had spoken to him in his own language.

"You are Swedish, aren't you?" the man repeated.

The stranger was about his own age and size, somewhat thin, with large hands and feet. He was dressed in a red-striped woolen shirt and well-worn skin trousers, held up by a broad, richly ornamented belt. A wide-brimmed straw hat hung on the back of his head; his cheeks were puffed out as if swollen with a toothache or mumps, but his tobacco-spotted chin and lips divulged the secret of the swollen cheeks: they were filled with tobacco quids. Karl Oskar had seen many Americans dressed similarly and equally tall, gangly, and swollen cheeked; the stranger did not look like a Swede.

"I'm a countryman of yours!" the man said.

"Did you come from Sweden?" Karl Oskar was still dubious.

"Yes! Can't you hear me speaking Swedish?"

The stranger wasn't speaking exactly the way Karl Oskar did, but perhaps he had forgotten some of his Swedish. And Karl Oskar was well pleased to have met someone he could converse with.

He pointed to the sign on the building near by: "Are you the Swede who owns the bank?"

The man laughed: "No, I'm sorry. Mr. Stone owns the bank. My name is Larsson. I came from Sweden five years ago."

Karl Oskar listened carefully—yes, the man must be Swedish.

The stranger smiled, he had dancing brown eyes, lying deep under his forehead, and his grin exposed a row of long, grayish-yellow, pointed teeth, spaced far apart.

"What can I help you with, countryman?" he asked. "I guess you came with the steamboat?"

Karl Oskar told him there was a group of Swedish immigrants on board. He was careful not to mention the cholera, he only stated his errand on shore: "I want to buy

135

some food for our children. They can't stand the ship's fare."

"Oh, yes, I understand. I'll show you a store."

"Have they milk and bread?"

"As much as you and your children can eat. Come along, I'll show you. If you have no money, I'll pay for it."

"I can pay for myself," said Karl Oskar. He wanted to make it clear to the stranger that he could pay for anything he got. He was no beggar, he told Larsson; he had been a farmer at home, all his life he had been able to meet his obligations and he intended to do the same in America.

"But it's hard here for a new settler," Larsson said kindly. "We immigrants must stick together, we must help each other."

Karl Oskar was in need of aid; he needed someone to show him the way to a store; and for once luck seemed to be with him.

"I have a wagon over here. Come along!" said Larsson.

They turned a corner and found Larsson's horse, harnessed to a kind of gig, a two-wheeler with a double seat and the driver's seat behind. The vehicle reminded Karl Oskar of similar contraptions in Smaland, called "coffee roasters." Larsson untied the horse and asked Karl Oskar to climb in while he himself mounted the driver's seat.

"Is it a long way?"

"Only five minutes."

"I don't want to miss the boat."

"The steamer loads here for several hours," Larsson told him. "You'll have plenty of time."

His new acquaintance kept addressing Karl Oskar with the intimate Swedish *thou,* something a stranger in Sweden never would have done, and Karl Oskar found it difficult to be equally familiar.

The gig turned onto the rutty road. The horse was a black, powerful, ragged animal, with dried-up dung clinging to his flanks and legs and a long, uncombed tail. Karl Oskar asked if he were young, and the driver confirmed it: "He's just been broken in; hard to handle."

The two-wheeler hopped about and shook on the rough road, though they drove quite slowly. They left the row of houses and, as the road turned away from the river, passed the small huts so much resembling woodsheds.

136

Heavy logs were piled high on either side of the road, the ruts became deeper, the stumps more numerous, and as they passed the last shed, the thick forest lay only a few hundred yards ahead of them.

"Is the store in the wood?" asked Karl Oskar, puzzled.

"Just inside; only three minutes more."

Then Karl Oskar began to be suspicious. Why would they build a shop in a wild forest, far away from the other houses? How much did he know about the stranger who had offered to take him to the store? Landberg, their honest guide, had warned the immigrants particularly to beware of their own countrymen, who could cheat and rob them the more easily because they spoke the same language. "Never confide in the first stranger you meet just because he speaks your language!" Landberg had said that more than once. Yet Karl Oskar had confided in this man he had just met and had climbed into his carriage. He had been careless enough to say that he had money; in the sheepskin belt next to his body he carried all he had left in cash.

A robber wouldn't commit his crime near houses. He would wait until they were in the forest where no one could see them; in the forest Karl Oskar would be alone with the stranger.

He glanced back at the unknown man sitting behind him on the driver's seat. In America he had seen many men with guns, pistols, or knives, but Larsson had no weapon in sight. Karl Oskar would have felt more comfortable had a wapon been carried openly. As it was, he didn't know what kind of arms the man might have hidden on him. He himself had only an old pocketknife in his hip pocket.

He looked about—perhaps it would be best to jump off the gig while he still could see the houses back there by the river.

The vehicle rolled along, the driver tightened the reins and squirted tobacco juice quite calmly into the wheel tracks: "Where do you intend to settle, countryman of mine?"

"In Minnesota, we had thought."

"Don't know that country. Why don't you stay here— you can make two dollars a day in the forest."

Larsson went on: He had helped many Swedes find

137

good jobs. But not all of them had been reliable, he had been cheated and robbed by Swedish crooks when he himself had first arrived in America. As a good friend he wanted to warn Karl Oskar: he must never rely on or confide in anyone; he must be careful.

Karl Oskar felt slightly embarrassed: his new acquaintance seemed to guess his thoughts.

But Larsson seemed as friendly as before, he laughed and talked with the same geniality that he had shown earlier. Judging by his looks and speech, he must be an honest man. And why should Karl Oskar think he was a bandit? Nothing indicated he had evil intentions. One shouldn't think ill of a stranger only because he seemed anxious to help. He felt a little ashamed of his suspicions; he was here for his children's sake, to get them food which might save their lives. Yet he was full of fear and suspicion when he met a helpful countryman. It wasn't like him to be so timid. His father used to say, if you weren't afraid within yourself there was nothing to be afraid of in the whole world. Of course he dared drive a short distance into the forest with this man!

They had reached a stream and were about to cross it over a newly laid bridge of wooden planks, when the driver reined in his horse; on the bridge stood a man holding up one hand and saying something in English. The driver greeted him with a broad grin and a stream of English words. It seemed that the man wanted to ride along with them, and he climbed in and sat next to Karl Oskar.

"Max is an American friend of mine; he is coming to pay me a visit. I have not seen him for a long time," Larsson said and again showed his thin, sharp teeth in a broad grin.

The two-wheeler drove on across the bridge, and now three men were riding in it, two in the low seat and one on the driver's box.

The newcomer was a thickset man with a round face and curly, black hair. He spoke English rapidly and smiled broadly at his neighbor on the seat, as though in Karl Oskar he had met a close relative after long separation.

And the fact was that Karl Oskar did recognize the man who had just jumped up beside him. He had noticed him in the saloon, in the company of Larsson.

138

Larsson had said that he had not seen Max for a long time, and the two now acted like long-lost friends. Karl Oskar did not need to know English to understand that this play was put on for his benefit. After all, it was not more than minutes since he had seen them stand side by side in the saloon.

Apparently they considered him more simple than he was; now he knew for sure that two robbers were driving him into the forest. Larsson had followed him outside in order to get him into the gig, and meanwhile Max had sneaked away to meet them at the bridge. Now Karl Oskar had two men to handle, one beside him and one behind. The gig kept rolling closer to the edge of the forest; ahead of them the road swung in among the heavy close-standing trees; within two or three minutes he would be alone with two robbers in a thick forest.

He carried his money next to his body when asleep or awake; without it, he and his family would be destitute in this country. No one was going to take it away from him, without first killing him.

He had fallen into a trap. He had been led to believe there would be a store in the wilderness where he could buy milk and bread; he had ridden along like a meek beast to slaughter. But he was not going to ride another step with these robbers.

They had left habitations behind, and not a soul was in sight. He must use cunning, he must pretend he had to get off on an urgent matter, "to call on the sheriff," as the authority-hating farmers at home used to say, when they had to go behind a bush.

But it wouldn't be wise to mention the sheriff now, it might arouse suspicion. With forced calm, he turned to the man on the driver's seat: "Would you mind stopping for a minute, Larsson? I've got to relieve myself."

"All right. Whoa! Whoa!"

The Swede calling himself Larsson spit on the road and reined in his horse. The gig came to a stop. On the right were some bushes, on the left a tall pile of logs. Karl Oskar had been sitting on the left side of the gig, and he jumped off in that direction.

The driver had believed Karl Oskar's excuse valid and had not objected when he wanted to get off; now he became suspicious. Karl Oskar had been in too much of a hurry to get off the gig, he had lost his feigned calmness; and he could see the two men exchange quick glances. They saw through his ruse.

Larsson rose from the driver's seat, and his genial look disappeared; his pointed yellow-gray teeth showed in a sarcastic, malicious grin: "You almost dirtied your pants, I believe. Perhaps I'd better help you unbutton them."

For a fraction of a second Karl Oskar stood paralyzed, his tin pitcher in his hand. Now he could not sneak away from behind the bushes as he had intended to do; now they would not let him go, and there would not be a single person to witness what they might do to him in the forest.

He glanced at the pile of logs beside the road; one log was sticking out toward the hindquarters of the horse. This gave him an inspiration: the logs and the horse must save him. The horse was young, barely broken in; the horse must run away with the robbers, since Karl Oskar couldn't run away from them.

Larsson said something in English to his fellow bandit and handed him the reins. A sarcastic grin was still on his face as he said to Karl Oskar: "You can stay right there and use your pitcher! Don't move, countryman, I'll be right down to help you."

But in the split second before the man jumped from the wagon, Karl Oskar gave the outjutting log a kick with his iron-shod heel; he kicked with all the strength in his body, and the added strength of a man fighting for his life.

The pile of logs started rolling onto the road. The young horse tossed his head, his whole body trembled, he snorted excitedly, jumped sidewise, and then bolted off in a wild gallop, pulling the light vehicle with the two men behind him, barely missing being crushed by the rolling logs.

Karl Oskar saw the gig disappearing with the two men clinging to the seats for their very lives; they were still hanging on as the vehicle disappeared among the trees. Karl Oskar felt pleased—the kick had been sufficiently hard, they made good boots in Smaland.

But in his excitement he forgot all about the rolling logs behind him. Suddenly one of them hit his left leg with such force that he fell face forward over a small stump. He had the sensation of a sharp knife blade being stuck into his

140

chest, and he heard himself cry out. He was in such intense pain that a wreath of red-hot sparks flashed before his eyes.

He ground his teeth together and managed to rise. He had fallen over the stump of a small tree which had been felled by an ax, leaving large sharp splinters sticking up, and these had cut him like knife points. He pulled out one splinter sticking through his shirt: blood oozed out. He was aware of pain in his left leg, it felt stiff and useless. A shudder of terror ran down his spine—suppose his leg were broken?

But he was able to stand on it. Slowly he moved the leg; he was able to walk. He noticed the milk pitcher which he had dropped in the fall, and he stooped to pick it up; then he limped along the rutty road, back toward the village; every step was painful.

He did not look back for the bolting horse, the gig, and the two strangers. He had no further interest in his countryman who had promised to show him the way to a store where he could buy as much milk and bread as his children could eat; he was in a hurry to get back, back to the houses and the steamer, and to his own family. Slowly he hobbled along; the return took him a long time. He could still see sparks before his eyes, but his head was clear, and his injured leg was good enough to help carry him back.

The steamer was still at the pier loading firewood. One passenger—gone ashore to buy milk and bread—returned, limping on his left leg.

5

Karl Oskar made his way toward the steerage. He walked slowly to hide his limp. Lill-Marta came running toward him, crying out jubilantly: "Here comes Father with milk!" For he still carried the tin pitcher in his hand. Kristina and Johan also ran to him expectantly. "Father has brought us milk! Come!"

Silent and embarrassed, Karl Oskar stood with the empty pitcher in his hand.

"You took your time," said Kristina.

He dropped his hand with the pitcher so they could see for themselves; it was empty.

141

"We've been waiting for you," Kristina was saying; then she broke off as she looked into the pitcher. "You haven't any milk?"

"Not a drop."

"Not a single drop?"

"No. No bread, either."

Kristina's lower lip quivered in disappointment. "No luck?"

"No, this time I had—no luck."

Johan pointed to his father's chest: "There's blood on Father!"

"What are you saying, boy?" Kristina exclaimed.

Karl Oskar's shirt was of a reddish color, and the blood didn't show much. But she touched his chest, and her fingers became sticky with blood. "God in Heaven! You're bleeding! What happened?"

"I fell over a tree stump, got a small splinter in my chest. Nothing to bother about."

"Mother, I was right!" Johan cried triumphantly. "There's blood on Father!"

"Only a very little blood," corrected Karl Oskar. "Just a scratch from a splinter."

"I must bandage it! Go to your bed and lie down," Kristina ordered Karl Oskar.

Karl Oskar went over to their bunk and removed his shirt. Lill-Marta ran after him: "I want milk. Mother promised!"

"Be quiet, child," admonished Kristina. "I must bandage Father."

"But you promised us milk, Mother!" the child insisted.

"Father fell down. Go away, children."

"Did you lose the milk when you fell?" Johan asked.

"Did you lose every drop?" Lill-Marta echoed.

Kristina took the children by the hand, led them to Robert, and asked him to look after them while she took care of Karl Oskar. She was relieved about Johan, who had improved during the day, having vomited up all the poison of the pestilence—if the sickness had been that. But now that her son was better her husband was hurt.

Karl Oskar had a deep wound just below his right nipple, blood had coagulated around the hole. The left side of his chest hurt when he breathed; he thought perhaps a rib was cracked.

142

"How did it happen?" Kristina asked.

"I told you, I fell on a stump. Accidents will happen."

Karl Oskar had not told a lie; that was how he had hurt himself. But how much more he should tell her, he didn't as yet know.

After her long sickness at sea Kristina had gradually regained her strength, but at the sight of coagulated blood like a wreath of fat leeches on her husband's chest, she felt wobbly in the knees. Nevertheless, she had learned as a girl to look after wounds, when she had stayed with Berta, the Idemo woman, to have a gangrenous knee treated, and now she soaked a piece of linen cloth in camphor-brannvin and washed the wound clean. Then she applied a healing plaster which Jonas Petter had brought along. She tore up one of her old linen shifts into bandages which she tied around her husband's chest. Berta had said that bandages must be tied as hard as though horses had helped pull them, in order to stanch the blood. Kristina tied the bandage as hard as her fingers were able to, but she thought regretfully she had not the strength of even half a horse.

"I'll change the rags if it bleeds through," she said.

Resting on his bunk, Karl Oskar reflected that he now had two bandages around his body, one of sheepskin and one of linen, one for his money and one for his wound. He had got the second because he must defend the first; the security belt for himself and his loved ones was still intact around his waist. But how near he had been to losing it— he had gone in a cart with a stranger, and this alone had been sufficient to endanger the lives of himself and his family. Yet who would have refused to go with the friendly Swede who offered to find as much healthy food as he and his family could eat?

Sitting close by him, Kristina was still wondering: "How could you fall so awfully hard, Karl Oskar? You're usually steady on your legs."

"When ill luck wills it, one might fall on an even floor."

"You must look where you step in America. They have signs in dangerous places."

"There was no sign in this place."

Those danger signs they had seen so often should be painted not only on posts and walls in this country, they should be written in flaming letters across the sky of all

143

North America; from above they would shine as a warning to immigrants in every part of the country.

"Your luck has left you," mourned Kristina. "In spite of your big nose."

For this "Nilsa-nose" which Karl Oskar had inherited was said to be lucky.

Yes, he, the father, was bleeding, and his children were without milk and bread. Another day and another night they must remain in this pest house with its unhealthy fare. But a little blood and a hurt leg could not be counted among the irreparable disasters of life. A whole family need not be destroyed by these misfortunes. He had merely fallen and hurt his leg, and a splinter had pierced his chest. Later, when all traveling dangers were behind them, he would tell the whole truth to Kristina. Then he would let her know how close she had come to continuing the journey without him, staking out and building the new home alone, a defenseless and penniless widow with three children.

It was not long before the bandages around his chest were saturated with blood.

"You won't bleed to death?" Kristina's voice quavered.

"Nonsense!" He smiled at her. "Only a little blood keeps dripping."

"It goes right through the rags!"

"It drips a little from my nipple, like milk from a woman. It will soon stop."

He reassured Kristina: His superficial scratch would soon heal, his flesh was of the healing kind; he was in good health and could well afford to lose a quart of blood; it was good against the cholera; he had thought of bleeding himself anyway, now he needn't use the bleeding iron. It had been different when a woman called Kristina had bled streams from her nostrils one night at sea; she must have lost many quarts that night. Then, indeed, it was a question of her life. It had been the most horrible night he had ever lived through.

A warmth came into Kristina's eyes: "You were good to me that night, Karl Oskar. If you hadn't gone for the captain, I would not be alive today."

Then he had taken care of her, now she bandaged and cared for him. Then he had tried to stanch her blood, now she tried to stanch his. Blood was the very life inside one;

144

when the blood ran away, life also ran away. Karl Oskar and Kristina were concerned for each other's lives. It was between them as it ought to be between husband and wife: they were joined together to ease each other's burdens, heal each other's wounds. They were two people who in God's presence had given the promise to love each other through shifting fortunes as long as they both should live.

X

Their Last Vessel

The boatman is a lucky man.
No one can do as the boatman can.
The boatmen dance and the boatmen sing,
The boatmen are up to everything. . . .
      (Old Mississippi River Boat Song)

The Boat

The *Red Wing* of St. Louis, B. Berger, Captain, Stuart Green, clerk, was an almost new side-wheeler, having started its runs on the Mississippi only two years earlier. It measured 147 feet in length, 24 in width, had one engine for each wheel, and a capacity of 190 tons. Toward the prow two tall funnels rose close together, like a pair of proud twin pillars. The *Red Wing* lay in the water like a floating house, long and narrow, well cared for and newly painted white. On either side of its prow a great wing had been painted, spreading its blood-red feathers. The steamer was named after a famous Indian chief, and its wheels plowed the same waters on which warriors of his tribe still paddled their primitive canoes.

New steamers, new sounds: on the *Red Wing*'s deck no bell rang, instead the booming of a steam whistle reverberated through the river valley, drowning the sounds of Indian powwows. The steam whistle was new and alien in this region where until lately only the sounds of the elements and of living creatures had been heard on land and water.

The rivers were the immigrants' roads inland, and the Mississippi was the largest and most important of them all. No less than eight hundred steamers churned its waters, a fleet of eight hundred steamboats moved the hordes of travelers northward to a virgin wilderness. The *Red Wing* of St. Louis was one of the vessels in this river fleet, proudly displaying on its prow the Indian chief's red feathers, as it plowed its way upstream, loaded with passengers.

The River

Broad and mighty, the Father of Waters filled his soft bed, like a mobile running lake with two shores, a lake now rising, now falling, yet never draining. From the lakelets of Minnesota in the north to the levees of Louisiana in the south the river flooded its shores and let them dry again; low, swampy shores, tall, rocky cliffs, grassy meadows, sand banks, and sandy bluffs, shores of tropical lianas, cotton fields, giant trees shadowing the water with their umbrageous crowns. Vast and varying was the river's domain: now choppy as a sea whose mighty waves have been arrested after storm, now flowing smoothly, and overgrown with twisted brushwood, tangled masses of thorns, willows, sycamores, alders, vines, brambles, and cedars; here flowering blossoms stood high as altar candles in the swamplands, the nesting place of wading birds, here mountains and cliffs rose on either side, like tall, dark, triumphal arches through which the river roared like the procession of a proud ruler passing with much fanfare.

Trees and bushes grew not only along the shores but also in the water. The river bed itself was a mass of root wreaths; when the trees fell, they fell into the water, and there they lay, their branches stripped of bark, naked, like fingers feeling the stream, like drowning human hands grasping for something to hold. The waves from the steamers' wake washed the wooden skeletons along the shores, hastening their disintegration. Trees lost their foothold on shore and floated into the current; whirling, spinning in circles, the trees floated about, twisted together, caught in each other's branches, as though seeking protection on their uncertain, thousand-mile voyage to the sea.

Veritable islets of trunks, roots, branches, bushes, brush, bark, and leaves swam about on the surface. And down deep, in the river bottom, was the grave of dead forests.

The Father of Waters embraced in his bosom other rivers, streams, brooks, becks, creeks; went on shore and stole plants, pulled trees out of the earth to make islands, seized all that was not anchored to the very rocks; the Mississippi, since the beginning of time the earth's mightiest concourse of running waters—going onward for all eternity, onward to the sea.

The Captain of the Steamer

The travelers from Ljuder had seen many ships and boats since they left Sweden, but the steamer *Red Wing* of St. Louis was the most beautiful of them all.

When they stepped on board and showed their tickets, the captain himself came up to them and spoke in a mixture of Swedish and Norwegian which they could understand: "Ah, *Svensker!* Welcome aboard! I'm a Norseman —we have the same king."

Captain Berger of the *Red Wing* was well past middle age, with gray hair, and a beard that grew thick, covering his face to the eye sockets, except for his red nose tip. The immigrants had observed many bearded men, both at home and during their journey, but Captain Berger was the most richly bearded man they had ever seen. He was also the first Norwegian they had met.

"We *Norsker* arrived before you," continued the captain. "We were wondering how soon you Swedes would come along."

They couldn't understand all the Norwegian he spoke through his beard, but by and by he and his passengers were able to carry on a conversation. At last on this journey they seemed to have come upon good luck; after the cholera-infested steamer, they were now on a clean boat where the pestilence had not made its appearance, and where the captain himself welcomed them warmly as if he had long known them. The *Red Wing* was their sixth vessel, and here they felt more secure than on any of the other five, even though Captain Berger warned them that the river was so crooked a steamer sometimes met itself on the curves.

The Passengers

The travelers were now on the last stretch of their journey; the Mississippi was their last river, the *Red Wing* their last vessel.

The Father of Waters was emigrating to the sea, the steerage passengers on the side-wheeler were immigrating against the current to the northwest country. Yet both the river and the travelers were on the same errand—seeking new homes. Captain Berger said that all types of people were aboard his ship: settlers, traders, fur hunters, lazy rich men, restless farmers, high government officials, card-sharps, honest working people, happy-go-lucky adventurers. But the greatest number of his passengers were immigrants on the last lap of their journey.

There were German peasants who said *Bayern* at every second word—was it the name of their home parish? They were blond and wore blue linen shirts over their clothes, shirts with outside pockets like coats. Their women had thick legs covered with blue woolen hose; both men and women wore small, funny-looking caps. Among all the immigrants, the Germans alone still had something left in their food baskets. A sausage was always discovered in some bundle; the Germans were always eating sausage.

The Irish immigrants spoke loudly among themselves, seeming to be in a constant quarrel. About half of them were dark haired, the rest red haired. They drank whisky from large wooden stoups, as calves would gulp down sweet milk. Captain Berger said an Irishman would not work unless someone stood with a club over his head: he would no longer use them as crewmen, he preferred Negroes. But a German must be threatened with a club before he would quit work. The two races differed in another way: an Irishman could never get enough to drink, a German never enough to eat.

Then there was the large Jewish family which the bearded captain pointed out to the Swedes: a father bringing his ten sons, four daughters, five daughters-in-law, four sons-in-law, twenty-two grandchildren, and three great-grandchildren; all together forty-nine people. The old father, the head of the family, was a little man; he had a longish face with a black beard and a long crooked nose; he didn't seem over fifty or fifty-five years of age. He always wore a small round cap without a visor, and when the family gathered together, he was always in the center. The little family father sat there, calm, silent, sure, smoking his long pipe, surrounded by his many descendants. Captain Berger guessed that this Jewish family was the largest one that had ever emigrated to North America, which to the children of Israel was the New Canaan; Jacob and all his sons were well represented here.

Karl Oskar asked himself how he could be so filled with concern for his own family of six, when he saw this little Jew with eight times as many.

The crewmen on the *Red Wing* were both colored and white; there were also men with yellow-brown skin, offspring of white fathers and black mothers. All seemed dirty, as if rolled in mud. All were half-naked. Deep down in the steamer's bowels they stoked the engines; in the evenings they gathered on their own separate deck, sitting in clusters, singing their songs—or song, for it seemed they sang the same tune over and over again. In the evenings, when the heavy darkness fell over the river, their song rang out over the black, wandering Mississippi:

We will be free, we will be free,
As the wind of the earth and the waves of the sea. . . .

2

On a small deck near the prow, set aside for steerage passengers, the immigrants from Ljuder were gathered in a group. The deck was roofed but open at the sides, and in the melting heat the passengers sought their way up here to find coolness; some even slept here at night. They had lived so long on the water that a deck now felt like home to them.

A heavy thunderstorm had passed over the valley in the early morning, and fiery swords of lightning had crossed each other over the blue mountains; but the relief it brought had been of short duration. They could feel in the air that the thunderstorm was still near. The travelers from cooler regions sat listless and lazy in the stifling heat and gazed apathetically at the green countryside with its immense fertility, plants and herbs in great numbers spreading far on either side of the river. They pointed out to each other an occasional tree, a bush, or some clinging vine with unusual leaves; or their eyes might follow the flight of some unknown bird, whose name they would ask.

From time to time the river narrowed or broadened; at its greatest width they thought the distance must be about two American miles. At times the strong current slowed down their speed. But the steamer kept to the center of the stream and met the oncoming current with such force that water splashed over the forecastle. Behind them the smoke from the funnels hung in the air like serpentine tufts of hair behind a fast runner.

Time dragged for the immigrants; at sea the wind had delayed them, here on the river the stream hindered them. It was already the last week in July.

Fina-Kajsa lay outstretched full length on the dirty old blanket which she had shared with her mate before he was buried in the North Sea.

"Oh me, oh my! We'll never get there, never! Oh me, oh my!"

From the lips of the old woman two questions constantly issued forth: Had anyone seen her iron pot? Would they never arrive?

With each day since landing in New York her health had improved, and by now she was as well as anyone in their company. She liked the heat; her old backache, a constant plague in the wet climate of Oland, had entirely disappeared. If they could put Fina-Kajsa into a well-fired oven and keep her there for a while, Jonas Petter had remarked, she might come out with new life and hop about like a young girl.

"Oh me, oh my! We'll never get there! Oh me, oh my!"

If they ever arrived, they would meet Anders, her only son, who had emigrated five years before. And now as they were nearing their destination her fellow travelers began questioning Fina-Kajsa about him. She told them: As long as he had stayed at home he had been an obstinate and unmanageable scoundrel; she and her husband had beaten him harder than an unbroken steer to make him tractable. He was lazy, evil-tempered, drunken, and ready to fight anyone; he had spent his time in the company of loose women, obeying neither father nor mother. When he was only ten years old, they had realized his nature: at one time they had refused to let him go with

151

them to a Christmas party, they had locked him up. When they returned, the boy had broken out and given vent to his unchristen nature by smashing nearly all the furniture, from their fine chiffonier to the porcelain chamber pot. But after he had gone out into the world he had regretted his behavior; a few years ago he had written from America, asking his parents' forgiveness. Out here he had become a different person, he worked hard, and he was capable. And he had written and told them about his fine home and the extensive fields he owned in Minnesota. She was sure she would find security and comfort with her son Anders as soon as they reached his beautiful farm. And he would help them all get settled, for whatever else she might have said of her son, he was capable, he knew what to do. According to his letters, there would be farms for all of them where he lived; as soon as they reached Anders all their worries would be over.

"But America has no end. We'll never get there! Oh me, oh my!"

Karl Oskar still kept the piece of paper with Anders Mansson's address. "Have patience a little longer, Mother Fina-Kajsa. We'll get there," he comforted the old woman.

Robert and Arvid were looking down into the water, trying to figure out how fast they were traveling. Robert had read in his book about the Mississippi that it drained a greater area than any other river in the world, and that it flowed with a speed of four miles an hour. And their bearded Norwegian captain had said that the boat could move with a speed of two miles an hour. This didn't seem to make sense; if the river flowed faster than the steamer moved, they wouldn't get forward at all, rather backward.

Robert deducted the speed of the steamer from the speed of the current—two minus four—then he said: "Now I've figured it out. We go two miles backward an hour! We'll soon get back to the ocean again."

"Christ in heaven!" Arvid exclaimed in terror. "Not back on the ocean again! I told you we should have walked once we were on dry land!"

But Robert's figures did not give the truth of the matter. By watching the shores they could see for themselves that their boat was moving upstream. Luckily, Robert had been mistaken.

He asked his brother how the boat could move faster

than the river even though the river moved faster than the boat? Karl Oskar said, perhaps Captain Berger had counted in Norwegian miles. But he did not wish to be drawn into arguments about miles and distances, he had already had enough trouble with the difference between Swedish and American miles.

Ever since Ulrika had found Lill-Marta in Detroit, harmony had reigned among the group; there was no longer talk of anyone's leaving it. They realized that in their sitation they could be of help to each other. After reaching these distant regions where their language separated them from other travelers, their group had become more unified than before: they owned one thing in common—their language. Since Landberg's departure in Chicago, they had been left to rely on themselves, and a greater intimacy had sprung up among them. Kristina said if they all stuck together, they would get along; she told them the secret of success was that none must be proud. No one must feel above anyone else. They mustn't act the way they used to at home in Sweden.

And they all agreed not to dig up old quarrels and scandals from their homeland; the past must be dead and buried forever. Ulrika had been the parish whore and spent time in prison; Danjel had many times been punished with heavy fines for breach of religious laws and had been threatened with exile by the authorities; both were now banned by the church in Sweden; but who cared about that out here? The deeds for which they had been punished in Sweden were not considered crimes in America. Moreover, no one here cared what they had done in Sweden. Why then bring it up among themselves? More and more they began to realize that Sweden was an antiquated country, behind the times, her unjust laws written by the masters that they might dominate the simple people. Here in America they could tell both the bishop and the sheriff to go to hell. As Jonas Petter put it, they could tell all of them—the bishop, the dean, the warden, and the sheriff—to kiss their bottoms.

The health of the travelers was improving. At little Eva's death, on their previous boat, nearly all had felt pains and aches, but they had escaped the cholera. Ulrika had become perfectly well the moment she stepped aboard the *Red Wing* though at first sight of the steamer she had

153

refused to go near it: one wheelhouse had an inscription in tall letters—PACKET. In Swedish *packet* meant rabble, mob, loose people. If they were to be lodged in the part of the ship called packet, she refused to go near it. Here in America all were supposed to be equal, and no one group ought to be called packet. She calmed down only after the Norwegian captain's explanation that packet meant his steamer carried mail.

The captain had risen in unmarried Ulrika's estimation since he addressed her as *Min Fru*. Apparently all men in America raised her to married status. Now, too, she was well again and without pain. She believed the mustard plaster had saved her from the cholera. In spite of Danjel's friendly remonstrance, she had used it, but for a few days she had worried lest God punish this disobedience to His apostle. Never before had she disobeyed Danjel. However, the Lord God had not taken revenge because of her plaster, and now she wondered if she should always follow Danjel's advice and warnings. She had noticed he was not as stern as before; it seemed as if he sometimes doubted that he had been chosen to guide their souls.

Kristina looked after Karl Oskar's wound, which was healing well, but his chest was sore and blue all over and it hurt when he breathed. In his left leg some stiffness remained, and he still limped a little. His Swedish good luck had deserted him in America, Kristina insisted.

Since they had now been a whole month on their journey from New York, Karl Oskar was thinking of writing another letter to Sweden; but he decided to wait until they arrived at their place of settling. There was nothing new to tell his parents; nothing had happened that was worth mentioning in a letter.

As they sat together on deck they spoke for the first time in a long while about their old homeland, and now it appeared Karl Oskar was the only one who had written home to Sweden. Danjel had no one to write to there; after the church had pronounced its ban, none of his relatives would have anything to do with him, no one expected a letter from one who was exiled, no one cared what happened to him after his departure. His servant Arvid could not write. Jonas Petter could write, and he had his wife Brita-Stafva to write to, but after twenty years of daily quarrels they had at last reached complete disagreement,

154

so he had left her; he was in no hurry to write to the cause of his emigration; nor would he have anything to say to his wife, except that he was glad to be rid of her, and that she already knew.

When she heard them speak of letters home, Ulrika of Vastergohl exclaimed: "Write to Sweden? But that country doesn't exist any more! That hellhole is obliterated from the face of the earth!"

Jonas Petter asked what she meant by this, and Ulrika explained: When leaving Karlshamn, Danjel had said that their old homeland would immediately perish. The Lord's vengeance would smite the land which had put His faithful in prison on bread and water. The Lord God had long intended to destroy Sweden, but He had to wait until Danjel and his followers had left. Soon four months would have passed since their ship had sailed away, and undoubtedly divine judgment had by now been meted out; the Almighty had surely stricken Sweden and erased her from the earth. If they wanted to send letters home, Ulrika suggested they address them to Hell Below, if mail were delivered there.

Danjel admitted in a low voice that at the departure he had made a prophecy concerning the homeland's imminent destruction. But he did not know whether the Lord had as yet carried it out. Perhaps the Lord in patience held back His avenging hand.

Kristina looked at her uncle and shook her head: Surely the Last Judgment could not have taken place in Sweden without having been noticed here in America? Or what did he think?

Danjel turned his kind eyes toward his sister's daughter: He would never again prophesy the Day of Doom; he had now learned that this happening was not postponed until the end of the world but that every day, for every mortal, old or young, was a day of doom. For the Last Judgment was the judgment of conscience within one's soul, it was meted out in the heart of every pious Christian each time he committed a sin.

Robert had this to add: They must all realize that when the world was destroyed, then the whole globe would be destroyed in one moment. That little part of the earth's surface called Sweden could not fall out by itself and disintegrate.

155

Ulrika said: "I wouldn't send a letter to that hellhole, whether it has sunk below or not!"

She continued in bitterness as her memories rose within her: To whom would she write? To the dean in Ljuder who had chased her away from the Lord's altar and forbidden her the Sacrament, and who many times had called her a child of Satan? She had always answered him: "Yes, dear Father, I hear you calling me!"—Or should she write the sheriff and thank him for putting her in prison? Or the judge of the county court who sentenced her to bread and water? Or should she send a letter to the prison guard who gave her this fine fare, who brought her the dirty water and the mildewed bread? Should he receive an epistle of love from her, was he worth it? And all those in the home parish who had spit at her and thrown filth after her—should she remember them with a letter? Was any single creature among that damned *packet* worth a letter? All they did was to serve the devil every moment of their lives.

Only one person in Sweden would Ulrika like to honor with a letter—the King himself. She would like to thank His Majesty for the feast she had enjoyed in the royal prison, and she would like to tell him that she daily thanked her Creator for having liberated her from being a subject of His Majesty. She would also like to ask the royal person on his high throne how his conscience could let him rule a kingdom where little children were sold at auction, their whole childhood through to be mistreated by greedy, cruel peasants. She would like to tell the King how happy she now was to have escaped from his kingdom, to have arrived in a country where neither he nor any of the lordships at home had any power, a country where she was considered one of God's own creatures.

Yes, indeed, next time she got hold of paper and writing tools she would send the King of Sweden a farewell letter from one of his former subjects. And before she put this letter into an envelope addressed to the "King by God's Grace" at Stockholm Castle, they could guess what she would do with it!

They all laughed at the Glad One's letter to the King—they all knew she couldn't write.

Karl Oskar said: "Forget the old! It's over."

What purpose could be served by harboring grudges

against Sweden? Now that they had arrived in a new, young country, it was better to forget all that old stuff, throw it away as they threw away old rags. They must not keep their homeland so much in their minds that it depressed and irritated them; this would only hinder their success in America.

Ulrika agreed on this point, as did Danjel and Jonas Petter. But Kristina sat silent the whole time and let no one know how she felt about the danger of thinking too much of her homeland.

3

Every day Robert read in his language book, every day he practiced the new forms and positions indicated for his lips and tongue. The most useful sentences he learned by heart: how to ask one's way to inns and lodging places, to food stores and eating places; how to ask the price of food and quarters; how to find work, and above all—the salary paid for work: *How much wages do you pay?* He must be sure to ask the right question in each instance. He also learned the numbers in English, as he considered these of the greatest importance to avoid being cheated when receiving change or pay.

Not only was it important to ask rightly; it was equally important to answer correctly when the Americans asked questions. He studied the exercises on getting a job: *What can you do?* In Sweden he had been a farm hand. But he didn't like the English word farm hand. *Farm hand!* It sounded too lowly an occupation, as if he were one hand of the farmer, a piece of his master's body, another farm tool used by the master. In Sweden he had actually felt that he was nothing more than a tool, a most insignificant and helpless tool, used by the masters as they saw fit. But here the servant was as good as the master, and he had emigrated to America because he didn't wish to be a tool used by masters; he didn't want to have any masters, he wanted to be free.

No, he wanted to tell the Americans what he could do: *I can plow and tend cattle!* It sounded more like a *man* talking, inspiring more confidence than to say, *I am a farm hand;* it sounded more capable and grown-up, as if he worked with his own hands and not with the master's.

The Americans were polite and considerate and always asked a stranger how he was. Robert wanted to be equally polite and he had learned by heart the reply: *Thank you! I am feeling very well!* True enough, he wasn't quite well, his ear still bothered him, but he wasn't going to admit that, not even if he were worse than he was. He didn't want to cause the friendly Americans anxiety in any way. He didn't want them to go about worrying over his health; they had so many other things to worry about, and so much to do.

If he were offered some food that was spoiled or tasted bad (for in America, too, he had discovered such dishes), then he would be courteous, like a man of the world; he would say that he didn't have time to eat and drink just now, he had *a few things to attend to.* The Americans, themselves so industrious and thrifty, would hardly blame him for attending to his business.

The language book gave advice about conversations with people of different trades and positions: *Conversation with an Innkeeper, Conversation with a Watchmaker, Conversation with a Hatmaker, Conversation with a Shoemaker, Conversation with a Laundress, Conversation When Purchasing a Country Place, Conversation When Building a Log House.* Each conversation listed a dozen questions and answers, and as soon as one knew the person concerned, it was merely a matter of opening the book and starting off. Under different headings were lists of words most frequently used: *Time, Nature and the World, Man, Mental Qualities, Bodily Attributes, Plants and Flowers, Metals and Stones, Animals—Wild and Tame.* If Robert wanted to report to the police that he had found a corpse in the street, he would only have to look under *Man.* And if he wanted to compliment someone on his great intelligence, he would look under *Mental Qualities;* if he wished to tell a girl how beautiful she was, he must turn to the heading *Bodily Attributes.* And when he had become rich and wanted to buy a riding horse, a thoroughbred stallion, he must choose the words for this transaction under *Animals—Wild and Tame.* Having bought the stallion, he might also wish to buy a golden watch, and instruction for this purchase might be obtained under

Stones and Metals, or perhaps under *Conversation with a Watchmaker.*

Robert had written down on a list the names of all the dishes he liked: veal, mutton, pork sausage, rice porridge, pancakes. He had learned to name forty-three different dishes and twelve kinds of drinks. He wanted to have everything in order for the day when his riches were accumulated so that he could order anything he liked and finish up the order with this sentence from his book: *Put all the dishes on the table!*

He had heard stories of immigrants who in a short time had accumulated immense fortunes but had been unable to handle their riches. Greed had eaten them up or dried them up, or gluttony had made their stomachs swell to abnormal proportions. Some rotted away in unmentionable vices. Money was their destruction. Robert felt a warning in this for himself. Ever since entering the portals of the New World in New York, he had pondered his ambition in America and how best to effectuate it. He would neither become puffed-up and haughty in prosperity, nor would he worry in adversity, like a weakling. He would not wish for everything he saw, he would be satisfied with sufficient possessions, a small fortune, easy to handle; moderate riches would not be dangerous, would not tempt him to destroy himself.

But all the steerage passengers on the *Red Wing,* whatever their language, were as poor as he, and all wanted to get rich.

Robert's purpose in coming to America was perhaps best expressed in a song which he had heard from the crew's quarters many evenings. Their voices could be heard from their place of gathering on their own deck, where he could see their half-naked bodies in the semidarkness. At first he had only been able to understand one word of their song—*free.* But after listening for a few days he could interpret the whole meaning:

We will be free, we will be free,
As the wind of the earth and the waves of the sea. . . .

This was the crew's song in the evening, it was the song of the wandering river, it was the song of Robert's aim in America.

From the deck of the *Red Wing* Robert and Arvid saw a constant change of scenery: the shores, the river itself, the many passing steamers with strange names, logs floating along on the current, pieces of lumber, bushes, trees, boxes, barrels, dead birds. Once they saw a corpse sail by, only part of the head sticking out of the water, a gray-white face and black hair entangled in a mass of green grass and branches; they thought it was the corpse of a woman, floating along with this unusual bridal wreath on her head.

They watched for new trees and plants along the shores, for Arvid had heard that shirts and pants grew on trees in America, and he wanted to see these trees. Robert said he must have in mind the cotton bush which grew only in the Southern states; they would not see it here.

Robert was looking for crocodiles; he had read in his book that these monsters inhabited the Mississippi. And one day Arvid pointed out an animal, swimming near the shore, so ugly that the like of it he had never seen before; it must be a crocodile. But the captain assured them that crocodiles didn't swim this far north, and the ones in the swamplands near the river mouth weren't really crocodiles, they were alligators.

One night an immigrant from Scotland, sleeping on the deck, fell into the river. No one missed him until morning. He left a wife and six small children on the boat. A collection was taken up among the passengers for the destitute family, and each one contributed something. In all, more than thirty dollars was collected as comfort and aid to the fatherless family; but the widow and her six children continued to weep just the same.

Arvid was horrified at the thought of the Scotsman; not only did the poor man lose his life, if his body floated toward the sea, he might be eaten by the gruesome crocodiles. How could he, on the Day of Doom, rise up from the stomach of a crocodile?

One morning Arvid called to Robert in consternation: "Look over there! The wild critters have come!"

On a cliff overlooking the river stood a group of strangely immobile figures, all facing the steamer, which passed them at a distance not above a gunshot. Feathers on their heads indicated they were Indians; some had bows in their hands. All watched the steamer intently, its funnels spewing smoke, its wheels rolling along through the water, splashing like large fins. The Indians stood like trees grown out of the rock, petrified by the sight of the steamer.

Undoubtedly these were wild Indians, Robert said.

Several times during their journey inland they had seen Indians, but they had been civilized. Now, for the first time, they saw wild Indians, Indians in the bush. And Robert understood that the immigrants were now approaching the vast, unknown, dangerous wilderness, a much larger and much more dangerous wilderness than they had traveled through before.

"They might shoot arrows at us!" Arvid said, looking for a place to hide.

But the Indians remained like statues, straight and silent, intently watching the puffing, pushing steamer on the river.

Suddenly the stillness was broken by the *Red Wing*'s steam whistle; a piercing sound reverberated across the water, echoing back from the cliffs on shore. The sound cut like a lance in Robert's ear.

The Indians answered the whistle with a shriek of terror and disappeared from their cliff as quickly as if swept away by the wind; quicker almost than the eye could see, they had run and hidden behind bushes at the foot of the cliff. The two boys had never seen human beings so swift of foot. The highly entertained passengers on the upper deck laughed heartily.

Arvid was much surprised: he had heard that the Indians were cruel and horrible as wolves. How could they be dangerous when that little boat whistle could scare them away? And now he knew what he would do if encountering wild Indians in the forest: he would whistle; then they would scatter like chickens from a hawk.

Robert thought that perhaps these Indians had never before seen a steamer. At home people said steamers were Satan himself traveling about on water in these latter days, spurting fire and smoke. The heathens out here could hardly be expected to have more sense than Christians in

161

Sweden. Perhaps they thought the steamer was an evil monster risen from the depths of the river. They might be familiar with crocodiles, sea serpents, and other river creatures, but had they ever seen an animal spewing smoke, sparks, and fire? Were they accustomed to roaring river creatures, paddling along with wheel-feet, shrieking like a thousand pigs simultaneously stuck with sharp knives? Robert's own ears could not stand the sound of the whistle, and Arvid had said that his heart had stopped inside his breast for many minutes when he heard the whistle for the first time. Robert was sure that a sound like the steam whistle had never before been heard on God's earth.

And he thought it was an evil deed to let loose the whistle in order to frighten the Indians and entertain the passengers. It was true that the Indians were heathen and unchristian, but there was no need to plague them unnecessarily.

Robert had read about the Indians shooting with poisoned arrows and killing people with dull wooden spears. He had even heard that they scalped people without sharpening their knives, a thought which made him shudder so that his hair stood on end. Such were the deeds of unchristian people who were neither baptized nor confirmed; heathens knew no better. This would change as soon as they became civilized and Christian. When the missionaries arrived among the Indians and baptized them and gave them the Lord's Supper, the one-time wild Indians would learn to use their enemies' breech-loading guns and scalp their victims with sharp knives.

The captain said: "The Indians are horrible people; they tie their captives to poles and burn them to death; they fry them the way Christian people fry pork."

And Robert appreciated this warning. He had now actually glimpsed the natives of this unknown wilderness where he and his group were about to build their homes. They would soon reach their destination; a new, strange life would soon begin. And the life awaiting them began to take shape in his imagination.

Each day Robert carefully observed the new country, its natives, plants, animals, general appearance. Sometime in the future, when he had leisure and writing implements, he intended to write a description of his surroundings according to his own observations. He possessed a small writing book, once given to him by Schoolmaster Rinaldo, in which he had put down the most unusual happenings so far.

With the arrival of evening, both river and shores flowed together in that impenetrable darkness of North America, the densest and thickest darkness of all the darknesses God had created. Then Robert could observe neither land nor water. But sometimes in the evenings or during the nights, flames could be seen from the invisible shores of the Mississippi. They looked like moving torches or tongues of fire; they were fires from Indian camps, glowing, flaming somewhere on land. The Indians were there— they weren't visible, but they were there, they lurked somewhere in the forest, somewhere in the bottomless darkness—the most horrible people the old Mississippi captain had ever seen.

And Robert watched these fires with deep apprehension; they indicated to him the presence of the cruel redskins; they were all around him here, they were close. And this very country was to be his home, in the midst of these heathens he would have to live, among Indians he would pass the rest of his life.

He felt a great fear, and a still greater foreboding.

5

On the last day of July, 1850, the immigrants from Ljuder stepped ashore in the town of Stillwater, on the St. Croix River, a tributary of the Mississippi, in Washington County, Territory of Minnesota.

They arrived at a time of year most inconvenient for farmers: the summer was by now so far advanced that it was too late to sow or plant anything. They were peasants who had lost a year's crops, and they knew what this meant.

PART TWO

The Settling

XI

"Will No One Help Me?"

The place smelled of the forest products and forest debris
—green, lately milled lumber, pitch, sawdust, boards at
seasoning. Along the river ran a fairly broad street covered with pine needles, bark, sawdust, sand—truly a
lumber-town street. The riverbank was piled high with
boards and logs for blocks, and on the river floated logs in
such numbers that the surface seemed one vast, cobbled
floor. Both earth and water smelled of pitch and pine. The
travelers had arrived in a forest region.

Karl Oskar and Robert wandered up the street, to
where the newly built houses clustered; they walked leisurely, trying to read the shop signs and other inscriptions: *Oxen for Sale Cheap for Cash; William Simpson,
Druggist; Shoemaker and Watch Repairing; The House
That Jack Built*. They passed a number of stores where
tools and implements of many kinds were displayed in the
windows. The largest inscription was painted on the side
of a house: *Stillwater Lumber Company*. They had seen
the same sign near the pier as they landed.

It had been late afternoon when they disembarked from
the *Red Wing;* they must find lodging before nightfall. For
two weeks Robert had practiced this one important sentence from his language book: *Please show me to a lodging house*. He was now completely familiar with every part

of this sentence, even though he had not as yet used it. But now two more important and urgent questions confronted the immigrants: How were they to manage with all their belongings? How would they find their way to their place of destination?

Captain Berger had informed them a few days earlier that the *Red Wing* would be unable to carry them all the way up river to Taylors Falls. The Mississippi steamers turned back at Stillwater as the St. Croix was not navigable beyond this point for larger craft; the current was too strong and there were several rapids. Consequently, he was forced to land them some distance short of their destination. At the same time Captain Berger had warned them not to remain in this region, which was ravaged by cholera; he had pointed out many places along the river where houses and huts stood empty. Immigrants from his homeland had built them but had already been forced to move —not away from the district, but six feet down into it, to final decay. The survivors in these Norwegian settlements were impoverished, almost starved to death, existing in utmost misery. It was so bad, Captain Berger wasn't sure which immigrants were better off, those in the ground or those above it.

Such information was not encouraging to the newcomers, and they had felt downhearted and filled with concern as they left the steamer. Captain Berger had promised to ask someone to help them find their way after landing, but he had fallen ill that morning, and when they landed, he lay in high fever in his cabin; they had not seen him again. And as the *Red Wing* departed they were left alone on the pier, completely dependent upon themselves in this unknown place. There they sat down among their chests, sacks, bundles, and baskets, without knowing in which direction to go, or how to transport their possessions.

While the rest of the group remained at the pier to watch over their belongings, Karl Oskar and Robert went to seek information. Besides the question concerning lodgings, Robert had learned two sentences from the chapter entitled "The Journey": *Respected Sir, how can we reach Taylors Falls? Who will take care of our baggage?* The name Taylors Falls he had added himself, but he did not know how to pronounce it. He meant to put these questions to someone in the street who looked kind and helpful and seemed to have plenty of time; he was particularly on the lookout for older persons.

But they met only young people on the street of this new lumber town. And all were in a great hurry, passing them by quickly. Robert hoped to address someone who was walking slowly. But they met no limping old men or women. Few women were in sight on the street. Three times, Robert spoke to older men; each one stopped, shook his head at the questions, and muttered some incomprehensible answer. He spoke to a couple of middle-aged women sitting on the steps in front of a house, but they, too, shook their heads.

Karl Oskar was growing impatient: "I don't think they understand you!"

Robert had asserted that by now his English was so good he could lend his mouth for the use of all, and Karl Oskar was reminded again that he could not always rely on his brother.

Robert had followed the instructions in his book: *Practice the Speech Exercises! Become familiar with the words and phrases most frequently used!* He replied to Karl Oskar: The Americans undoubtedly understood what he said. But they spoke their own language so rapidly that he couldn't understand their answers.

He tried his questions on a few more passers-by but without success, and then Karl Oskar said they had better go back to the pier.

Their fellow travelers were still sitting among their possessions, all together, but helpless and at a loss as to what to do next.

Jonas Petter said it looked as though the inhabitants might be afraid of them; they had been left entirely alone on the pier; did people think a gang of robbers had arrived on the steamer?

Fina-Kajsa sat with her skirt tucked up, her broken iron pot on her knees. She sighed: "Oh me, oh my! We'll never get there! Oh me, oh my!"

All were hungry, and someone suggested opening the food baskets. But Karl Oskar said it would soon be dark, they must find quarters before they did anything else; they couldn't remain on the pier all night.

Ulrika spoke up: "That was supposed to be your job, as I recall."

"*You* go and try!" Karl Oskar retorted tartly.

He was in low spirits and this affected the others. Even the Glad One, who usually encountered trouble with indifference, was now upset and irritable, and as it suddenly began to rain, she poured forth bad language on this new misfortune.

It was a cloudburst—apparently, all rains in America were cloudbursts. It splashed and thundered over the river, the heavy rain soaked the immigrants' clothing, it struck like knives, penetrating to their very marrow. After a few minutes they were all as wet as if they had been dipped in the river. The children yelled and refused to be comforted.

Everyone in the group was hungry, tired, and wet through and through; night was upon them, and they did not know where to find shelter. One after the other they felt despair overtake them. The company from Ljuder had never before during their whole journey felt so helpless, lost, and forsaken.

Robert went over and over his recent attempt to find his way with the new language—his hopelessly miscarried attempt! It was easy enough to remember and repeat the sentences to himself. But when he wanted to say them to strangers he grew nervous and confused, then he began to stutter, he hemmed and hawed. He couldn't understand it: not one of the three sentences he had learned had been of any use today. And he began to practice a fourth, which he would repeat until he was successful: *Will no one help me?*

2

Henry O. Jackson, Baptist minister in Stillwater, was busy sawing firewood outside his cabin near the river. Only a few steps separated the sawhorse from the water, and he kept his foothold precariously on the sloping ground. Pastor Jackson was a short, rather fat man of about forty, dressed in well-worn brown cotton trousers and a not-too-clean flannel shirt. He worked bareheaded, and tufts of thin hair fluttered in rhythm with the movement of the saw as it dug its way through the dry pine bough on the sawhorse. The handle of his saw, cut from a crooked limb, chafed his hands after a while; the pine log was tough and

170

resistant, the saw teeth, dull from lack of sharpening, rasped slowly through the wood. The work was hard, and after cutting each piece, the minister rested a moment, drying the sweat from his forehead with a great linen handkerchief that hung on a peg of the sawhorse and flapped in the wind like a flag.

The St. Croix River, separating the new state of Wisconsin from the Minnesota Territory, made a large bend as it flowed by Stillwater. Right here near the town the current was slow, almost imperceptible, and the river expanded into a small lake, on which all the timber floated down from above had been gathered; here on the west bank it would be hauled up and milled. A little farther to the west the ground rose in high hills, and the town of Stillwater had been built between these hills and the river. The community had an advantageous position, protected from winds by the forested hills at its back, and with the river flowing at its feet. Within a short space its population had grown to more than five hundred inhabitants; next to St. Paul, it was at this time the largest settlement in the territory. A year before, Stillwater had been made the county seat of the newly formed Washington County.

On the east shore of the St. Croix, directly across from Pastor Jackson's cabin, steep cliffs of red-brown sandstone obstructed the view of the countryside: there lay Wisconsin, which two years ago had become a state of the Union.

Jackson had been pastor in Stillwater ever since the Lord had founded his parish in the town. Up till now he had lived in a log cabin belonging to a fur trapper who spent most of his time in the forests, but a more comfortable abode was being built by his parishioners near his church and would be ready this fall. Most of the members of his congregation were generous, helpful people. Practically all gained their living from the lumber activities in the region or from farming. Many of the timbermen in the logging camps and the laborers at the mills in Stillwater were worldly and unregenerate, but the farmers moving into the district were nearly all good Christians. Some fifty homesteaders had moved into Washington County in recent years and these new settlers often had errands in Stillwater: Sundays they came to hear Pastor Jackson preach; weekdays they came to sell their grain, potatoes, pork, or mutton.

171

The minister's cabin stood only a few hundred yards from the pier where the *Red Wing* of St. Louis—well known in Stillwater—was unloading her cargo of beef, pork, and flour barrels. Soon the sound of her steam whistle drowned the saw's screeching and announced to Pastor Jackson that the side-wheeler had returned down the river toward the Mississippi. But before he had time to lay a new log on his sawhorse, a dark cloud suddenly came up from the Wisconsin side. During the heavy downpour he sought shelter in his cabin. The street outside quickly became empty of people, everyone running inside. But through his window he now noticed on the steamship pier a small group of people who had not sought shelter from the violent shower. They must be newcomers, passengers from the *Red Wing*. The minister guessed they were immigrants. And no one had been there to help them—all were afraid of the cholera which new arrivals might bring with them.

Last spring German immigrants had brought the cholera to Minnesota, and during the whole summer the pestilence had raged in the settlements farther south. Along the St. Croix, enormous graves had been dug and filled with the bodies of immigrants. In Stillwater a score of deaths had taken place, and the inhabitants were stricken by fear of this pestilence. Careful watch was kept over newcomers, and the city council had removed a great number of them and placed them on an island in a forest lake some ten miles to the west. Here they had been left to live, separated from other people, until free from contagion.

But Pastor Jackson never avoided strangers, he felt no fear of the dreadful disease: Whither in this world may man flee, that death shall not o'ertake him?

As soon as he saw the group on the pier, he made his way toward them. The violent rain was barely over. Huddled among the bundles and chests sat grownups and children. Shawls and coats had been tucked around the children to protect them from the rain; babies cried in the women's arms.

He saw at once he had come to people who needed him. He recognized that they had come from far away, they were immigrants from Europe. Both men and women were light complexioned, tall and sturdy, and he guessed

172

they were from Germany, like so many other recent immigrants. He spoke German passably and made an attempt to address the strangers in that language: He was a Baptist minister. Wouldn't they come with him to his cabin?

He repeated his question but received no answer; all stared at him without comprehension. Then German was not their mother tongue.

As Pastor Jackson looked at the group more carefully he saw that nearly all were pale and starved-looking. Immigrant Germans, both men and women, usually arrived well fed, their cheeks blooming. He concluded these immigrants might be Irish—though why did they not know English?

A tall, gangly youth with a light down on his upper lip spoke a few sentences in a language Pastor Jackson recognized: immigrant English. Pastor Jackson was familiar with newcomers' first attempts to use the language of their new land, and he smiled encouragingly at the speaker, listened carefully, and did not interrupt him. And at last he understood. The yough wanted to tell him that he was a stranger in America and wondered if anyone here would help him.

The American asked where the immigrants came from, and in the answer he seemed to recognize the name *Sweden*.

Pastor Jackson had gathered much information about the various countries of the immigrants, and he knew that Sweden was a county of Norway. A Norwegian family in Marine belonged to his congregation. The newcomers on the pier must be countrymen of the Norwegian people in Marine, who were good, religious people. A Norwegian also lived here in Stillwater—Mr. Thomassen, a shoemaker who had resoled his shoes and made a good job of it. Thomassen lived some distance away, on the other side of the church. He would send a message to him to come and meet a group of his newly arrived countrymen.

And the minister turned again to the youth and spoke to him in English; he spoke as slowly and clearly as he could and tried to extend his message to the whole group. The people here were friendly and good people, but afraid of strangers who might bring the cholera. The newcomers need have no fears, he was a minister here in town; now they must come with him to his cabin and he would take care of their belongings and have them brought inside for the night.

The pale, gangly youth did not try to explain to the rest of them what Pastor Jackson had said. But he pulled from his pocket a small book, the leaves of which he turned eagerly as if searching for something. The minister turned to a young woman with a whimpering child on either knee and took the smallest child in his arms. It was a baby boy, and he held him as carefully as though baptizing him. The child was wrapped in a soaking-wet shawl, and water dripped from the shawl and wet the minister's clothing quite through.

Then Pastor Henry Jackson walked away with the child in his arms, and the whole group followed him. Last in the row came the youth he had spoken to, still searching in his book. He continued to turn the pages all the way until they reached the cabin, unable to find what he was looking for: *Conversation with a Minister*.

3

Before Karl Oskar stepped across the threshold of Pastor Jackson's cabin, he turned to Jonas Petter to seek his counsel: Was it advisable to believe this peculiar, bare-headed man? How could they know what he intended to do with them? Perhaps he was leading them to a lair of robbers and thieves? How could they know what kind of den they were stepping into?

"But he looks kind and helpful," Jonas Petter said.

"That's just it," Karl Oskar insisted. Didn't he know! The kinder and more helpful a stranger seemed in America, the more dangerous it was to go with him. He still carried on his body marks he could feel and see: a great scar on his chest and his left leg still aching. He did not believe in any stranger in North America.

"We need not be afraid. He is the minister in this town," Robert said, with respect in his voice.

"Minister? He? No! He lies!"

Karl Oskar's suspicions increased: this helper of theirs, going bareheaded outside, poorly dressed in worn trousers and a shirt that wasn't too clean—this man a minister? If

174

this man was a minister then he, Karl Oskar, could stand in a pulpit!

Robert insisted that the man had said he was a *minister,* and that meant a preacher. They could see for themselves in his book. But Karl Oskar thought Robert must have heard wrong. He had no confidence in his brother's knowledge of the English language. And he suspected that the stranger was luring them away from the pier so that he might steal their belongings.

But as the bareheaded man wasn't taking them so far away that they couldn't keep an eye on their movables, his suspicions were somewhat allayed, and he went inside the cabin. He whispered, however, to Kristina: They must not forget, the most seemingly helpful persons might be the most deceitful.

Pastor Jackson busied himself making a great fire in the stove so that his guests might dry their wet clothing. The women undressed to their petticoats and hung their skirts to dry in front of the fire; the children's wet garments were removed. The men weren't much concerned over their wet clothing as long as they felt warmth; they elbowed each other around the stove. Their host attended to all their needs: he acted as though they were his nearest relatives come to visit him. They weren't allowed to do a single chore—neither fetch water nor wood—he did everything himself, attended to them as if he were their servant.

He put a kettle on the stove and placed a sizable chunk of venison in it; fortunately, one of his church members had brought the gift to him this very day. He split some of his newly sawed logs and carried in dry pine wood and fed the stove until it was red hot. He put on a white apron and set his broad table with bread, milk, butter, sausage, cheese; he set out knives, forks, plates, and spoons as capably as a woman. He fussed over the children, warmed milk for them, found playthings for them. And during this whole time his guests sat wide-eyed and stared at him, struck dumb by all the work an unknown man in an unknown place was doing for them, and all the things offered them. He made his house their home.

And when they sat down to table, they discovered he was a cook worthy of a noble family; the venison was tender and juicy, melting in the mouth like butter. None

175

among them had ever eaten such fare. Even Fina-Kajsa, with her single tooth, was able to chew this meat. And when they had eaten to their satisfaction, there was still a great deal of food left. As they sat there, sated and comfortable, they entirely forgot their miserable situation of a few hours earlier.

The women were still in their petticoats, but after the meal Ulrika took down her skirt, which had dried in front of the fire: "When I get my rump wet, I lose my good temper." So saying, she gave Pastor Jackson her broadest smile of honest appreciation.

He smiled back, full of understanding, not of her words, but of her need for dry clothing. And he behaved toward her and all of them as if concerned with only one thought: Did they have all the food they wanted and were they comfortable?

As they were dry again, they had indeed all they could wish for. And all were satisfied; since landing in America they had never eaten so well and enjoyed food so much as this evening, and yet all of it was a gift.

Now they knew the bareheaded man who had met them on the pier; now all realized who he was. They didn't understand what he said, but they understood what he did, and this was sufficient for them. Robert had asked if no one would help them, and this man was the answer: he helped them all.

After enjoying the food, the immigrants were also to enjoy rest. Pastor Jackson made up beds for his visitors. For his fifteen guests, big and little, he made beds over the entire floor of his cabin. He brought out sacks and filled them with hay for mattresses, he produced animal skins for covers; he made such roomy and comfortable beds that he himself could find no place to sleep in his own house—he said good night to his guests and went to sleep with a neighbor.

And they were barely awake the following morning when he was back, busying himself at the stove, preparing the morning meal for them. He boiled a pot of potatoes and beans, he warmed yesterday's leftover venison.

Their benefactor told Robert he had sent for one of their countrymen as interpreter. And while they were still at their breakfast a small, tousle-haired man with a broad nose entered the cabin; he had on a black cobbler's apron

176

of skin which smelled of leather and wax. He greeted them all as if knowing them in advance: "I am Sigurd Thomassen. I am a *Nordman*."

He spoke to the Swedes as if expecting them to know who he was: shoemaker in Stillwater, the only Norwegian in town.

The man was not exactly a countryman of theirs; Robert had been mistaken. But the Swedish immigrants understood his language as well as they had understood Captain Berger on the *Red Wing,* and they learned from him that Robert had been right in saying their host was a minister.

Karl Oskar felt ashamed of his suspicions yesterday; and all beheld in deep wonder the man whose guests they were, this kind American, now busying himself with women's chores. A man of the clergy, called and ordained for the holy office of preaching the Gospel—yet here he was making beds, washing dishes, tidying up the house, sweeping, performing the chores of an ordinary maid. They could not comprehend it. They could not imagine this man in the white kitchen apron, standing in the pulpit in frock and collar, they couldn't understand this man who scoured pots and pans on weekdays and would stand at the altar Sundays, administering the Holy Sacraments. Why should a minister, able to preach, stoop so low as to perform menial kitchen chores?

"I have never seen a man so handy in the kitchen," Kristina said to Ulrika.

"He is the kindest man with the biggest heart I've ever met," replied the Glad One. "Who could ever have guessed he was a priest?"

"Is he married?" Kristina asked.

"He is a bachelor." Thomassen used the English word.

"I mean—does he have a wife?"

"No. He lives single." He used the English word *single,* which Kristina didn't understand. She thought, however, the minister in Stillwater must not yet have married.

The Norwegian told them that women were scarce in the Territory. Here in Stillwater there was hardly one woman to ten men, and in the countryside maybe one to twenty men. So the men went about as eager as Adam in Paradise before God created Eve.

"You are most welcome! The settlers have been waiting for you!" he told Kristina.

177

And he looked from one to the other of the three Swedish women. Kristina did not like his eyes; there was lust in them. When he looked at her. she felt as though he were in some way touching her intimately. This she was sure of —she needn't ask if shoemaker Thomassen was unmarried

Karl Oskar questioned him concerning the road to Taylors Falls, and he showed the Norwegian the piece of paper he had carefully saved, the address of Fina-Kajsa's son:

Mister Anders Mansson
Taylors Falls Past Offis
Minnesota Territory
North-America.

From Thomassen he now learned that Taylors Falls was a small settlement deep in the wilderness to the north. There were only a few settlers there and they would find Manson without difficulty. Taylors Falls was on the banks of the St. Croix, but no passenger boats went there. The lumber company in Stillwater had cut a road for timber hauling with their ox teams some distance along the river —after that there were trails. They would have to go by foot to reach their destination. He was sure the lumber company could be persuaded to freight their belongings up the river in one of their barges. It was almost thirty miles to Taylors Falls, and if they were good walkers, they might manage it in two days, but the paths were overgrown, and as they had children with them they ought to figure on three days. But they would have no trouble finding their way: if they stayed close to the river, they couldn't miss it, for Taylors Falls lay right on the bank.

The weather now was pleasantly cool, and as they had already been much delayed it was decided that they should continue on their way immediately. Thirty miles sounded a formidable distance to walk on foot, but counting in Swedish miles it was only five. Often on a Sunday they had walked the distance to Ljuder church and back, which made two Swedish miles. Having sat inactive so long on ships and steamboats, they felt they ought to have rested themselves sufficiently to walk the distance.

They asked the Norwegian if there might be any danger

of wild Indians during the walk, but he did not think that the Redskins they might encounter on the road to Taylors Falls would be dangerous, if left alone. There were only Chippewa Indians living in the wilds to the north, and they were a docile and peace-loving tribe. The Sioux, who had their hunting ground to the south and who roamed in great packs through the forest this time of year, were much more fierce and warlike, and the settlers were afraid of them. But he was sure they would not meet any members of that tribe in the region they were to pass through.

The Swedes wondered if shoemaker Thomassen didn't minimize the dangers. Perhaps he only wanted to allay their fears.

"You may meet Chippewas, but they are friendly to the settlers," he insisted.

The youngest and the oldest in their group would cause most concern during a long walk—Fina-Kajsa and the babies. Karl Oskar asked Fina-Kajsa if she would be able to go with them; perhaps she had better stay here with the kind minister for the time being.

The old woman flared up in anger: "Who says I'm not able to walk? Who will recognize my son Anders if I don't come along?"

And she assured them with many oaths that they would never get there if she didn't go with them to find her son for them; they would never arrive without her aid. They would lose their way in the wilderness, and no one would help them, unless she was with them and brought them to Anders.

So they prepared to get under way. They brought along as much food as they thought would be needed, and clothing and bedding for sleeping in the open; they took their knapsacks and their bundles, as much as they thought they could carry. Pastor Jackson had taken charge of their heavy goods, and he was to send it on the lumber company's flat barges to Mister Anders Mansson at Taylors Falls.

As the immigrants parted from the goodhearted man who had made his cabin their home for a night and half a day, they were all very sad at not being able to say a single word of thanks in his tongue. None of their honest words of gratitude were comprehensible to him. But all shook him by the hand in such a way that they felt he must understand. And Robert tried to express in English how grateful they were: Pastor Jackson could rely on them to do him a favor in return as soon as they could. This sentence he had not taken from the language book and he was not sure the pastor understood him. Robert was particularly grateful to the Stillwater minister: he was the first American able to understand his English. Pastor Jackson had understood more of his sentences from the language book than anyone else, and of the English words Pastor Jackson spoke, Robert had understood many more than any other American's. Robert had used a sentence which he had long practiced: *Please speak a little more slowly, sir!* and after this the minister had spoken more slowly and clearly. Their conversation had progressed almost to his full satisfaction, even though he had been unable to find a chapter, *Conversation with a Minister*. This American had understood him from the very beginning, ever since his question: *Will no one help me?*

And they were still all fifteen together as, toward noon, they started northward from the logging camp where the Stillwater Lumber Company dominated everything with its great signs. Thomassen, anxious to talk to the women, accompanied them part of the way, admonishing them to keep close to the river on their right hand; then they could not miss Taylors Falls: "You couldn't miss it even if you tried to."

During their long journey, the group from Ljuder had traveled on wheels and keels, they had ridden on flat-wagons and steam wagons, on sailing ships and steamships, on side-wheelers and stern-wheelers. They thought they had used all the vehicles in existence to transport a person from one place to another in this world. But for the last stretch of their long journey they must resort to the means of the old Apostles—the last part of their thousand-mile road they had to walk.

XII

At Home in a Foreign Forest

The immigrants had now seen a part of the new continent in its immense expanse; its size was inconceivable to them. Yet during their journey through this vast land they had lacked space in which to move about; in crowded railway wagons and ships' holds they had been penned up in coops or shut in stalls. The country was large, but the space it had offered for their use had until now been very small. At last they were liberated from the shackles of conveyances: here they had great space around them and nothing but God's high heaven above them.

They had felt lost in the towns through which they had passed, fumbling, awkward, irresolute. Mingling with great crowds of unknown people, unable to communicate with them, they had felt downhearted, worried, completely bewildered. But here they had at last come back to the earth and its trees, bushes, and grass. The immigrants now walked into a great and foreign forest, into untilled wilderness. But something marvelous happened to them here: For the first time in North America they felt at home in their surroundings.

They walked through a wilderness, and here they had elbowroom, a feeling of space in which to move freely. The path they followed resembled the cattle paths at home, but this path was not made by domestic animals, it

181

was trodden by wild animals and wild people. They followed the paths of Indians and deer, of hunters and beasts. They were on the hunting trails which had been followed for thousands and thousands of years. But they were homeless wanderers without weapons, not looking for game or following animals' footprints. They only followed a trail that would, they hoped, lead them to new homes.

Their path was along a winding ridge of sandstone, and this ridge followed the river. On their left extended a valley, on their right flowed the river that was to guide them. At the beginning of their walk, the forest near the river had been cut down in great sections and these seemed to them like graveyards, with their high, carelessly cut stumps resembling tombstones. But after a few hours they reached sandy plains with tall, straight, branchless trees, topped with lush dark-green crowns. Here each tree was a mast tree, capable of carrying sails across the world's greatest oceans. On the foothills to their left were groves of leaf-trees, like a woof through which broke the darker warp of the pine forest. Here they discovered all the trees which each spring budded anew in Sweden: oaks and birches side by side, trembling aspens, elms, and lindens intertwined their branches with maples and ash trees; here and there they also espied the hazel bush. Of smaller trees, crouching under the tall ones, they recognized willow branches stretching above bushes of sloeberries, blackberries, and wild roses. Here lay fertile ground overgrown with underbrush of innumerable varieties whose branches, leaves, and clinging vines were intertwined, making one heavy impenetrable thicket, a living wall of greenery.

In these extensive thickets they discovered many thorny bushes that were new to them. They stopped now and then to inspect more closely some tree or bush which they didn't recognize. They would scratch the bark, or break off a small branch, or gather a handful of leaves, and try to guess the kind of tree or bush to which these might be related.

As far as they could judge, here grew everything in God's creation: trees for all their needs: for house timbers, floor planks and roof, for benches and tables, for implements of all kinds, and for firewood. The dead trees rotted in the places where they had fallen, never had a

182

stump been removed, never had a dead tree been cut. All old bare trees remained standing, an unattractive sight with their naked, bark-shedding limbs in this healthy, living forest. Indeed, there were enough dead pines here for firewood for a thousand fireplaces for a thousand winters through. The forest was uncared-for, neglected, but it had cared for itself while living and covering the ground: it had died and lived again, completing its cycle: undisturbed and unmarked by man's edged tools, it had fallen with its loosened roots decaying on the ground and disintegrating among grass and moss, returning again to the earth from which it had sprung.

The farther into the wilderness the immigrants pushed their way the denser grew the oaks. In one day they had seen more oaks on root than in their whole lives before. At home the oak was the royal tree—King and Crown had from old claimed the first right to it, while the peasants had to be satisfied with poorer and less sturdy trees. At home the noble oak tree was nursed like a thoroughbred colt. Here they walked through an oak forest that stretched for miles. And when their trail brought them atop a knoll, they saw across the western valley a whole sea of oak crowns, wreathed together until they appeared like one many-miles-wide crown of rich foliage. Here was a whole region—wide as a county at home—entirely filled with royal trees. In their fertile valley the oaks had for countless centuries grown straight and proud through their youth and maturity and quietly rotted in their old age. No Crown-sheriffs had disturbed them with marking axes, no despotic king had exacted timber for his fortifications and men-of-war. In this heathen land the royal tree had remained untouched and unviolated, here it displayed its mane of thick foliage, the lion among trees.

The landscape changed often and quickly, with hills and dales on both sides. They came to an open glade with still more fertile ground: here herbs and grass prevailed rather than trees and bushes. Here grew crab apple and wild plum, the heavy fruit bending the overladen boughs. Between thickets of berry bushes the ground was covered with wild roses, honeysuckle, sweet fern and many flowers. Here throve in abundance a lower growth of fruit and berry plants: blueberries, raspberries, currant bushes, black as well as red. And the berry vine did not crawl re-

183

tarded along the ground in thread-thin runners' as in the forests at home; here it rose on thick stems covered with healthy leaves, thriving as though planted in a well-fertilized cabbage bed. The blueberry bushes were flourishing with berries as large as the end of one's thumb, as easy to pick as gooseberries.

They would cross a meadow with fodder-rich grass reaching to their waists. Here the ground lay as smooth and even as a floor in a royal palace. No stone was visible, no scythe had ever cut this grass; since the time of creation this hay meadow had been waiting for the harvesters.

They climbed over brooks and streams where fallen trunks lay like bridges, they saw a tarn into which branches and other debris had fallen in such great quantity that it filled the lake completely, rising above the surface, a picture of death-haunted desolation. They walked by small lakes with tall grass all around the edges, the water bubbling and boiling with wriggling fins. They stopped and looked at the fish playing. The water was so clear they could see to the bottom where the sand glittered in the sun like gold. And they mused over this clear blue lake water, seemingly taking its color from the skies above.

In one opening they came upon a herd of grazing deer, sleek-antlered animals with light-red fur and short white tails. Fleet-footed, the deer fled softly, their tails tipping up and down. The immigrants had already tasted their meat, they knew how tender and delicious it was. Now and again a long-eared rabbit disappeared into the grass directly at their feet. Known and unknown forest birds took flight along their path, on the lakes swam flocks of ducks, undisturbed by their passing, and several times they heard the potent, whizzing sound of many wings in flight: flocks of bluish doves flew over their heads.

In this wilderness there was plenty of game; in the water, on the ground, and in the air there was meat, fowl, and fish. Many a meal had run past them into the forest, swum away into the depths of the lakes, flown away into the air.

The immigrants had reached a lush country, fertile and rich earth, a land well suited for settling. Here people could find their sustenance if anywhere on earth. Yet nowhere did they see tilled fields, nowhere a furrow turned, nowhere a prepared building site. No trees had been blazed to mark a settler's claim. This was a country for people to settle in, but as yet few settlers had come.

The group from Sweden walked along an unknown path in an unknown region, with no guide except the river; but they felt less insecure and put down their feet with more confidence than at any time before in the new country. They were walking in accustomed ways through old-country landscapes. They walked through a forest, they tramped on tree roots, moss, and grass, they moved among pungent foliage, soft leaves, herbs, among growing things on earth, its running and flying game, and they began to feel at home.

The travelers from Ljuder were in a foreign forest, yet they had arrived home: No longer were they the lost ones of this world.

2

At first the group of immigrants walked with good speed along the path on the ridge, but as the day wore on their burdens grew heavier and their steps slowed. All grown-ups had something to carry: of the children, only Danjel's two sons were able to walk the whole distance; he had to carry his four-year-old daughter Fina. Karl Oskar held Lill-Marta on one arm, extra clothing over his shoulder, and the knapsack in one hand. Kristina carried Harald, and this was considered sufficient, as she also carried another child within her. The food basket was entrusted to Robert. Johan could walk short distances, but his little legs soon tired and he too wanted to be carried. Karl Oskar stooped down and let the boy climb onto his back with his arms around the father's neck. Karl Oskar was no longer a fast walker.

Jonas Petter walked ahead of the others to locate the trail, which sometimes seemed to disappear in dense thickets filled with mosquitoes. It was his duty to see that they never lost sight of the river. As they progressed the thickets became more prevalent, and those with heavy burdens had to walk with care through the thorny bushes.

They had feared Fina-Kajsa would delay their progress but the old woman had a surprisingly tough body, and in spite of her emaciated condition, she kept well ahead of the younger walkers. She trotted along quite briskly, holding onto her iron pot, which she dared not leave behind with the minister in Stillwater, fearing it might be lost, as the grindstone was in New York. She had walked many miles during her lifetime, going to church at home on Öland every Sunday for fifty years, a distance of fifteen miles back and forth. Altogether, this would make enough miles to cover the distance from Sweden to Minnesota many times; indeed, she would easily manage the short distance left to reach her son's home, if it were true that they were now so close to him. And she described again the fine house he had built himself in the wilderness. He had written many letters to his parents about it—there was no place on Öland that compared with his home, his extensive fields, and possessions. He had asked his parents to come and see it, then they would be well pleased with their son. And Fina-Kajsa was convinced her son had changed into an industrious, capable man here in America, or he wouldn't have been able to acquire such a home. It had been well for him to get out in the world.

A west wind was blowing, cooling their perspiring brows; the air no longer felt oppressive.

By midafternoon they sat down to rest under a great oak that stood all by itself in an open, pleasing meadow. Now their communal food basket was brought out; during the last weeks of their journey they had become one big household; it seemed unnecessary to divide themselves into two families at meals, leaving Jonas Petter to sit alone. It was easier to keep all the food together; what one missed someone else had, one had bread but no meat, someone else meat but no bread.

After the meal, the immigrants stretched out on the ground under the giant oak; it was comfortable in the shade, and they all felt well and rested contentedly. But the children played in the tall grass of the meadow; they had already eaten their fill of raspberries, blueberries, currants, and wild plums. Many unfamiliar berries also grew hereabouts but parents forbade the children to taste these, fearing they might be poisonous. On little trees almost like bushes grew clusters of berries resembling over-large blueberries, and Robert insisted these were wild grapes. From them wine could be pressed, the drink of noble people at home, which ordinary people got a taste of once a month at communion. They tasted the grapes cautiously,

186

they seemed sweet and good, but they dared not eat more than a handful lest they get drunk from these sweet berries that made wine: it was written in the Bible that one could get drunk from sweet wine.

Elin filled her little basket with great, juicy dark-red raspberries, which she showed proudly to her mother. The girl's fingers were stained blood red from the overripe berries.

"Here in America we can have beautiful rosy cheeks," Ulrika said. "We can wash our faces in raspberry juice."

Kristina's eyes never left her children. They mustn't go too far away, no one knew where snakes might lie hidden in the thick grass which was indeed a good hiding place for all kinds of dangerous creeping things. Jonas Petter had already killed two green-striped snakes, but they were no larger than the snakes at home. Danger was by now such a persistent companion that Kristina considered it omnipresent: its shape might alter but it was always at hand in some guise. She had once and for all accepted danger, and consequently she met it with less worry than before.

Here in the forest only the venomous mosquitoes annoyed her and all of them; they swarmed about constantly and bit every exposed part of the body. The delicate skin of the children was attacked most fiercely, and their faces showed welts from the bites. They had never encountered such disgusting gnats before. Everything was different in America, day and night, weather and animals: the warmth was warmer, the darkness darker, the rain wetter than at home—and the mosquitoes were a thousand times worse.

Kristina's eyes had come to rest on the men sprawling in the grass, and suddenly she burst out laughing: "Ulrika —look at those shaggy-bearded, long-haired men! Don't they look worse than scarecrows?"

Unmarried Ulrika of Vastergohl joined in the laughter. None of the men had had scissors or razors near their heads since leaving Sweden, and now their hair hung down on their shoulders. Danjel had always worn a beard, but Karl Oskar and Jonas Petter, accustomed to shave at home, had left their beards unattended—it had been difficult to use razors on the journey. Arvid had a thin growth of beard and seldom needed a shave, and Robert had not yet begun to shave, but their hair had grown long.

187

Gathered together in a group, all the men seemed equally shaggy and rough. On the journey, Kristina had not paid much attention to their appearance, but alone here in the forest she was suddenly conscious of their uncombed hair and beards: they seemed like a group of wild highway robbers. And she said, if this had been the first time she had laid eyes on Karl Oskar, meeting him like this in the forest, she would have been scared to death of the man and would have run away to hide as fast as her legs would carry her.

"Hmm," said Jonas Petter. "The worst part is, my beard itches like a louse nest."

"Our poor men are pale and skinny," Ulrika said. "That's what makes them look so frightful."

Yes, Jonas Petter thought he had lost about fifty pounds from heat and diarrhea, his trousers hung loose around his waist as though fastened to a fence post. Their bodies were only skeletons covered by sun-parched skin. But all American men were thin; they were Americans now—and by and by they would also be rich.

Ulrika admitted that the men in America were skinny. But she insisted they were courteous and well behaved and kind and considerate toward women. She had never before seen a man like that priest they lodged with last night—he had even grabbed the pail out of her hand when she wanted to fetch water and had gone to the well himself. A minister in America fetching water for Ulrika of Vaster-gohl—what would people in Ljuder say if they had seen that!

Ulrika kept an eye on her daughter, who was now busy picking flowers.

Elin called to Robert: "Come and see! Such beautiful cowslips!"

Robert hurried to her side; he looked on the ground between the lush bushes but could see neither cowslips nor any other flowers. "Where are they?"

"They flew away!" the girl exclaimed in surprise.

"The flowers flew away?"

"Yes! Look, they are flying up there!" Elin was staring wide-eyed at a great many butterflies, beautiful yellow ones, sailing about above their heads. "I thought at first they were flowers."

She had mistaken butterflies for flowers. And Robert

188

thought perhaps she hadn't been so much mistaken. After all the strange animals and plants they had seen in this country, he would not have been in the least surprised had he suddenly found flying flowers. Hadn't they seen a flying squirrel today—a squirrel that flew between two trees and used his tail for a rudder! If squirrels in North America could fly, why not flowers also? "Anything might take flight!" Robert said.

They sat down near a raspberry bush and ate the juicy red berries.

Robert and Elin had made peace again, they had agreed they had nothing to quarrel about. She ought not to have been so talkative in New York, she ought to have kept to herself what he had confided about the captain's slave trade. She had not asked Robert to forgive her for this treachery, but he had forgiven her in his heart. Besides, she had admitted to him that he had spoken the truth when, before leaving the ship, he had insisted that the Akians would be unable to speak English when they stepped ashore, even though they were convinced they had been given the tongues of apostles. The only English words Elin knew, she had learned from Robert and not from the Holy Ghost.

And after she had promised not to divulge to a living soul what he was about to tell her, he related what had happened to Arvid and himself on Broadway Street in New York: He had saved Arvid's life. An enormous, sinister-looking man had rushed toward them with a long knife in his hand, ready to stick it into Arvid and steal his nickel watch. He had been one of the fifty thousand murderers who lived in New York and who every day except Sunday commit at least one murder. The murderer had managed to get the watch away from Arvid and was aiming the knife at his heart, already piercing the cloth of his vest, when Robert had rushed up and given the man such a hard blow with his fist, right on the man's temple, that he had immediately fallen backward and fainted. Then Robert had pulled the knife from the murderer's hand and recovered Arvid's watch. Police had arrived and had jailed the fallen bandit, and Robert had understood enough of their English to realize that they had lauded him profoundly: Thanks to his coolheaded interference, one crime less than usual had been committed that day. If he had wanted to, he could easily have stayed in New York and joined the police force.

But Elin must promise not to whisper a word to anyone about his saving Arvid's life: he was not one to brag about his deeds; if he were able to do a favor for a friend, he liked to keep it to himself. Nor must she mention it to Arvid, who might feel embarrassed about the incident.

Elin listened to Robert in great admiration and gave him her promise of silence. In turn, she wanted to confide something to him: She was not going to remain with Danjel when they arrived in Taylors Falls, she intended to find employment with some upper-class American family. And he promised to help her with this, now that he could speak English with ministers and other learned Americans. As a matter of fact, he himself had no intention of working for Karl Oskar. He had other prospects of getting rich.

"What are you going to do?" the girl asked.

"I'm not going to work as a farm servant all my life. I remember *Angelica*."

"What does that mean?" she asked curiously.

"It is the name of a woman, but it means much more than a woman ever could mean."

And he was about to tell her of the clipper ship with the gold diggers and the red pennant which he had seen in the New York Harbor, when he suddenly lowered his voice and then stopped speaking: someone was approaching them from the other side of the bush. It was Arvid, picking raspberries. He did not notice them, although they could see him through the bush. Elin whispered: Arvid still had the hole in his vest, right over his heart. Yes, Robert said, that was the tear slashed by a murderer's knife, on the most beautiful street in the world. Now she could see for herself that Robert always spoke the truth.

The others were ready to resume their walk, and the youth and the girl, their hunger lessened by forest raspberries, rose to join them. Arvid caught up with them and complained to Robert that he had just torn his vest on these darned big thorns on the bushes here; he must have it mended at once or he might lose his watch. Robert glanced around rather nervously to make sure Elin had not heard.

The travelers now felt rested and well pleased. Evil and good fortune shifted quickly for them: yesterday they had

190

been lost, hungry, and wet; today the weather was pleasant and they rested in fresh grass under a shady oak and ate fresh fruit. They were pleased with the land they saw about them; it gave good promise: this was the land where they would settle. They felt almost repaid for the arduous journey and its great inconveniences.

"Fair is the country hereabouts," Danjel Andreasson said. "The Lord has led us to a blessed land."

All agreed with these sentiments. Danjel had just finished his table prayer and now he took out his Bible: before he rose from his first meal-rest on the ground of the new land he would like to bend his knees and thank the Lord God who so far had led and aided them.

He knelt near the great oak and read from the Bible the Lord's words to his servant Joshua, who, with the tribes of Israel, was ready to ford the river Jordan to dwell in the promised land after the many years of wandering in the wilderness: "Be strong and of good courage: for unto this people shalt thou divide for an inheritance the land which I sware unto their fathers to give them."

The playing children were silenced and all the grownups rose and stood in a circle around Danjel; the men removed their hats, and men as well as women folded their hands and bent their heads. The little group of wanderers stood immobile and silent under the great tree. Danjel Andreasson knelt and bowed his head toward the sturdy trunk of the oak, now his altar, folded his hands over his breast, and uttered his prayer of thanks:

"A strange land has kindly opened its portals to us, and we have come to live here peacefully and seek our sustenance. But we would have been like newborn lambs, let out to perish among the heathens in this wilderness, hadst not Thou, Lord, sustained us. Hunger would have ravaged us, pestilence stricken us, wild animals devoured us, if Thy fingers of mercy were not upon us. We have journeyed thousands of miles, over land and water, and Thou hast saved our lives and all our limbs. Be strong and of good courage! So Thou spakest to Thy good servant and to his folk. Thou hast promised to give us this land and we want to be Thy servants. Aid us in this foreign and wild land, as Thou hast helped us until now. We have here eaten our meager fare in Thy forest, and we call on Thee from this ground which Thou created on the First Day. We are

191

gathered in this church which Thou Thyself builded and whose roof is raised taller than any other church—Thy heaven is its roof. O Lord, here in Thy creation, in Thy tall temple, we wish to praise Thee and sing to Thy glory as well as we may with our singing tongues! Turn Thine ear to us and listen, O Lord!"

Then slowly and haltingly Danjel Andreasson, still kneeling under the oak, began to sing a psalm. He sang in a weak and trembling voice. The group around him joined in, one after another, as they recognized the hymn:

> Eternal Father in Whose hand,
> From age to age, from land to land,
> All mortals comfort seek,
> Ere mountains were, or man, or field,
> Ere pastures gave their season's yield,
> You were, and are forever. . . .

The wind had died down and the voices echoed through the forest—weak voices and strong, rough voices and sweet, husky and clear, trembling and steady, men's and women's voices. And the chorus rose for each verse higher and higher under the lush ceiling of branches and leaves of the wide tree; a hymn in a foreign language, by a little group from far away, a song never before heard in this wilderness:

> The lilies bloom with morning's breath,
> Yet eventide beholds their death,
> So Man must also meet his doom,
> A flower, a mere withering bloom. . . .

When the song to the Creator's glory had rung out to an end, the immigrants again loaded their burdens on their backs and resumed their walk with increased confidence. And over their resting place with its down-trodden grass stillness and silence again reigned, disturbed only by a faint whispering in the thick foliage of the oak.

3

They knew how quickly dusk could fall in this country, and a good while before sunset they began to look for a

192

place to camp. They chose a pine grove where the ground was covered with thick moss. They collected fallen branches in a great pile, and so dry was this excellent fuel that the very first match ignited it. Karl Oskar, Danjel, and Jonas Petter each had a box of matches brought from Sweden, which they used sparingly, each box being used in turn for fairness. The women cooked their evening meal in Fina-Kajsa's limping iron pot; they fetched water from a running brook and to the water they added various leftovers to make a stew: Kristina donated a piece of pork, a few bread heels, and a pinch of salt, Ulrika scraped together a few spoonfuls of flour from the bottom of Danjel's food basket, and Jonas Petter contributed a dozen large potatoes, which he had got from one of the cooks on the *Red Wing* in exchange for some snuff.

This stew was eaten by all in the company with such great appetite that none noticed how it tasted. Then Kristina offered as dessert one of the last things she had left in her Swedish food basket: a small jar of honey, which they spread on their bread. Each of the grownups got a small slice, each child a large slice.

After supper they gathered more faggots for the fire, which they had to keep burning, less for the sake of warmth than to keep off the swarms of mosquitoes. Nothing except smoke seemed to drive them away. Jonas Petter expressed the opinion that the North American mosquitoes were far more dangerous than the Indians, whom they hadn't seen a sign of today; no heathens or cannibals could be so thirsty for Christian blood as were these bloodsucking insects, flying about everywhere with stingers sharp as needles. All complained about this new plague, and Fina-Kajsa most of all: she had been able to escape the scurvy and the tempests at sea, the fire in the steam wagon, the cholera on the steamboat—was she now to be eaten by these hellish gnats before she reached her son and had a chance to see his beautiful home? No, God wouldn't allow this to come to pass. He ought to give her credit for the thousands of miles she had walked in her life to hear His word every Sunday. If God had any sense of justice He undoubtedly had written down in His book the many miles she had walked to church.

They gathered moss to sleep on and covered themselves with warm clothing and a few blankets. The children went to sleep the minute they lay down. All were tired from the day's walk and their heavy burdens; they would sleep soundly in this camp during the night. But they didn't forget that evil people and dangerous beasts might be in their neighborhood. The four men each in turn kept a two-hour watch; they must tend the fire, guard the sleepers, and rouse them in case of danger.

Robert was too young to keep watch, but he couldn't go to sleep. He lay under a pine tree with his head toward the trunk. He had gathered enough moss to make a soft bed, but he felt as though his body were broken to pieces. Every muscle ached. And the forest had so many sounds to keep him awake. The leaves rustled, bushes and grass stirred, he wondered what kind of reptiles might lurk in the thickets. Buzzing insects swarmed in the air, the mosquitoes hovered over him with their eternal plaintive humming. There were sounds everywhere—hissing, whizzing, chirping. But the most persistent sound of all came from some small animal in the grass, it screeched and squeaked like an ungreased wagon wheel. It reminded him of a cricket, but it was louder and more intense, and it hurt his ears. He looked for the animal but could not find it; how was it possible that an animal could be so small and yet make such an infernal noise?

From his *Description of the United States of North America* Robert remembered all the wild beasts of the American forests; all of them might now lurk quite close to him in the dark, waiting their moment: the bear and the wolf to bite his throat, the rattlesnake to wreathe its body around him, the crocodile . . . But Captain Berger had said there were no crocodiles in the northern part of the country. Wild Indians, however, were here in the forest, even though they hadn't yet encountered them, and Indians could move without the slightest sound: before he knew it, without the least warning, he might lie here with his scalp cut off, wounded and bleeding to death. An Indian could cut off a scalp as easily as a white, Christian person could cut a slice of bread.

As herdboy at home Robert had never been afraid, but here he lay on his bed of moss and scared himself until he felt clammy with perspiration. Arvid slept only a few feet away from him, snoring loudly; he did not hear any sounds, not even the ones he made himself. And Robert could see Karl Oskar, who had taken the first watch—he moved like a big shadow near the campfire, now and then poking the embers with a branch, making the sparks fly into the air until they died high up among the treetops. His brother was not afraid: Karl Oskar and the others didn't know enough to be afraid, they didn't realize how dangerous it was to lie here and sleep. Had they possessed all the knowledge Robert had concerning lurking dangers during the night in Minnesota Territorial forests—if they only knew what he knew about the unbelievably sharp knives the Indians carried, and with what complete silence they could sneak up—then they wouldn't enjoy a moment's sleep.

Each time Robert was about ready to go to sleep he was disturbed by the screeching noise like an ungreased wheel from the small animal in the grass. And his injured ear began to hum and throb as it often did when he lay still. What kind of a sound could it be in his ear, never ceasing? Sometimes he wondered if some buzzing insect hadn't managed to get in there. And as this noise had continued he had grown to hear less and less with his left ear. For two years now the sound had pursued him; it had followed him from the Old World to the new one. Perhaps it would stay with him and annoy him for the rest of his life, perhaps he would suffer from it until he died, and by then there would be small joy in losing it. And all because of that hard box on the ear which his master, Aron of Nybacken, had given him when he served as hired hand in Sweden; all this a hired hand suffered undeservedly because of the master. He had secretly shed many tears at the memory: How had God allowed this injustice to befall him?

Now he lay listening to his ear until the noise sounded like a warning: Don't go to sleep! You may never awaken again! Or you may wake up with a knife cutting through your scalp! You will cry out and feel with your fingers and find warm, dripping blood. . . . Better not to go to sleep! Listen to what your ear says!

But Robert slept at last, and slept soundly, awakening only when Karl Oskar shook him by the shoulders: It was full daylight, they must resume their walk while it still was cool—they would rest again later in the day when the sun was high.

195

The pot was on the fire again, the food baskets open. Blinking, still with sleep in their eyes, the immigrants sat down to their morning meal and scratched their mosquito bites. The men keeping watch had not once had to warn the sleepers. Several times during the night Karl Oskar had heard a howl in the distance—it might have been wolves but it could also have come from human throats, for it had sounded almost like singing, and he didn't think wolves could sing. During Jonas Petter's watch a sly, hairy animal had sneaked to the food basket and attempted to scratch it open. It looked like a young fox, it had a sharp nose, a long bushy tail, and was yellow-gray in color. He had shooed away the creature with a stake and hung the basket in a tree, to be on the safe side. But the beast had scared the devil out of Jonas Petter later—it had come back and climbed the tree to get to the food basket! He had had to throw a fire brand at the animal before he could get rid of it. He hoped he had burned the beast good and well—in fact, he was sure he had—he had smelled the singed hair for quite a while afterward.

It couldn't have been a fox or a wolf since those beasts didn't climb trees. Jonas Petter thought perhaps their night visitor had been an ape or large wildcat: the animal was long but short legged, and moved as quickly as a monkey.

Fina-Kajsa had her own opinion: "You say he was hairy? Then it must have been Satan himself. He must have tried to fetch you when you were awake alone!"

"If that was the devil, then I'm not afraid of him any longer," retorted Jonas Petter. "If he is so badly off that he must snoop about nights and try to steal our poor fare, he must be near his end."

But Fina-Kajsa knew that the devil was afraid of fire only, and if the brand hadn't been thrown after him, Jonas Petter would have been missing for sure when they awoke.

"Did you hear the screech hoppers?" Ulrika asked. "I thought at first it must be ghosts or goblins. I couldn't see a sign of them."

All had heard the continuous screeching noise, but no one had seen the animal producing it. Kristina said that crickets and grasshoppers were, of course, also different in North America—perhaps they were invisible here.

Their walk was continued, but today the immigrants

196

moved at a slower pace than yesterday, their legs weren't so limber. Karl Oskar was footsore from his heavy boots, and his left leg gave him trouble intermittently. Johan, riding on his shoulders, grew heavier and heavier and he tried to persuade the boy to walk on his own legs. But after a few steps he wanted to ride on his father's back again: "You carried me before, Father."

"But don't you understand, dear child, your father is worn out," said Kristina.

"He wasn't worn out before. . . ."

Arvid had a strong back and could carry more than his allotted burden—he relieved Karl Oskar and carried the boy now and again. Karl Oskar was more heavily laden than the others, and Kristina felt sorry for him; she could hear him puff and pant as their trail led uphill, and she knew that his left leg wasn't quite well yet. He didn't complain, not one single word, but she wondered where his thoughts might be: Hadn't their troubles and inconveniences been greater than he had anticipated when deciding to emigrate? Here he lumbered along like a beast of burden—had he ever expected to haul his children on his back miles and miles through wilderness in America? She was sure he hadn't. Yet he would never admit this, he would never admit anything was more difficult than he had thought it would be.

"It's too much for you to carry two children," she said.

"You also carry two," he reminded her.

They kept up their walk during the morning hours when the weather was cool, rested for a while during the noon heat, and continued in the afternoon as the sun grew lower. During the second day they did not meet a single person, either red or white. This did not surprise them. The forests were vast, yet sparsely settled. But as long as they were able to manage by themselves, they were just as pleased to find the forest empty of people—strangers weren't always trustworthy.

The ridge with the trail wound its way through ravines and clefts in the rocks. The terrain was hilly, the soil poor, and for long distances the ground was bare, with no signs of the trail. Then they walked where the going was easiest and kept close to the river that was to show them the way to Taylors Falls.

The second night they made camp in a cleavage of the ridge. This night no furry animals came to sniff their food boxes, and they were disturbed by no living creature except the mosquitoes.

They had been told they would arrive about evening of the third day. During the afternoon they began to look for the village in the forest where Anders Mansson, Fina-Kajsa's son, had his home. As yet they had seen no sign of human habitation, no sign of people.

According to her son's letters, insisted Fina-Kajsa, his home was situated near a river with great cliffs along its shores and many falls and rapids. One place was called The Devil's Kettle because it was the entrance to Hell. Now they could see how steep the cliffs were along the shore of the St. Croix River. All stopped to look at the rapid current as it came rushing along down the cliffs with a terrific roar. This could well be the region Anders Mansson had described in his letters. But there wasn't the slightest sign of people living near by.

They walked on a little farther, and Fina-Kajsa was now sure they had lost their way. A farm like the one he had described could not possibly be located in this region —her son couldn't live near here. She suspected that the little Norwegian who directed their way from Stillwater had been false and unreliable: he had undoubtedly led them astray on purpose. By now the old woman was completely exhausted, dragging her feet, stumbling and falling into holes in the trail, she had to be helped up several times.

"Oh my, oh me! We'll never get there! Oh my, oh me!" said Fina-Kajsa.

They had only a few hours until darkness would fall and their third day would come to an end. They must again prepare to sleep in the open. And their food was running low, they would hardly have enough for the evening meal. They had eaten a lot of berries during their walk, but berries did not satisfy hunger.

The men were talking about what to do, and all walked with slower, wearier steps as the sun sank lower. Should they make camp or go a little farther? Then they came into an opening in the forest and suddenly discovered a clearing where every pine had been cut down. They stopped short in surprise.

"These trees were only recently cut down!" Karl Oskar exclaimed.

The stumps were new, and branches and logs were strewn about. The stumps were three feet high—yes, those lazy bastards had stood straight backed while felling the trees.

"And there they have left the ax," said Arvid, and pointed to a tall stump. Karl Oskar quickly stepped up to the ax and loosened it, not only because he wanted to inspect an American tool but for a much more important reason: If a pregnant woman let her eyes fall on an ax stuck in a stump of chopping block, then her child would be born with a harelip, and this was an incurable defect. Karl Oskar hoped that Kristina had not noticed the broad-bladed ax.

Jonas Petter, who was a bit ahead of them, now called out in great happiness: "Folks live back there!"

A few gunshots to the left of their trail, the clearing ended in a green meadow where a cabin could be seen against a stand of leaf trees.

It took only a few minutes to reach the newly built shake-roofed log cabin. A small field near by had growing crops, and two cows grazed in the meadow, fine, fat animals with full udders.

This was a settler's farm, here they could buy milk; cows with such splendid udders must give many gallons at each milking. They all sat down in the grass outside the cabin, and Karl Oskar brought out his stoup from the knapsack; then he went up to the door and knocked.

A middle-aged, scrawny woman with heavy men's boots on her feet opened the door. She looked curiously at the group outside. There was fear in her eyes as she turned them on Karl Oskar. Seeing her look of fright, he remembered what Kristina had said about his unkempt beard and hair. Not wishing to be mistaken for a robber he tried to look as friendly as possible and greeted her pleasantly in Swedish. The few English words he had learned he could never remember at such a time, but he talked with his hands and held out his stoup, then he moved it to his lips as if drinking. He tried in this way to tell her that he wanted to buy milk. The woman in the doorway said something incomprehensible and then she just stared at him. He opened his mouth still wider and acted as if gulp-

199

ing gallons from his vessel, at the same time pointing to the cows—the woman must understand what he wanted.

But she looked still more frightened and stared at him as if he might be insane. Perhaps she thought he was making fun of her. He was unable to make himself understood and he had little confidence in Robert after their experience on the street in Stillwater.

However, just as the woman prepared to shut the door, Robert stepped up and said clearly in English: "We want to buy milk."

She looked searchingly at the English-speaking youth who was beardless, but long haired, and they realized she understood him. He repeated his request a second and a third time, and each time she nodded in comprehension. Then she left them and disappeared into the house, returning in a few moments with a large wooden pail filled almost to the brim with milk.

Both Kristina and Ulrika spoke heartfelt Swedish words of thanks to the woman, and all gathered with their mugs around the milk pail.

Kristina turned to Robert and said: "We have you to thank for this milk!"

At last Robert had shown that he could lend his mouth as a help to all, explain in the foreign language what they wished, and obtain what they needed. This time he had prepared himself well: he had repeated the words to himself many times before he used them: *We want to buy milk*. This was the way we must do it—chew the words many times, as he chewed his food.

Robert grew courageous from his success, and as the kind woman was returning to the cabin he followed her and said: "Respected Sir, how can we reach Taylors Falls?"

He asked Karl Oskar to show her the piece of paper with Anders Mansson's address. But she did not look at it or answer him—instead she hurried inside and closed the door. When Robert tried to open it he found it bolted. The woman had given them a pail of milk and then she had locked herself in the cabin, without even waiting to be paid! That was peculiar.

The immigrants eagerly emptied the milk pail; the children were given as much milk as they could drink, and there was still plenty for the grownups. The milk was cream-thick, the cows hereabouts must get good grass; all felt refreshed by this unexpected refreshment.

But the American woman had not waited to be paid. She had locked herself in the cabin. She was afraid to let them come inside, this much they understood.

They put the empty pail at the door and waited for her to reappear. Robert was still determined to find out where Anders Mansson lived. And he began to practice a new sentence: *I want to expose you this paper with an address* . . . when suddenly a dog's bark was heard quite near them, and two men with guns in their hands approached across the clearing.

The men who headed toward them were apparently hunters. They wore broad-brimmed hats and skin jackets on which the fur still clung at the seams. They were un-kempt, fully bearded, and were accompanied by two fierce curs whose hair stood on end. As they neared the Swedish immigrants they lifted their guns threateningly. The dogs barked furiously, and the frightened children began to yell.

A commotion of indescribable fear broke out among the travelers at the strangers' unexpected behavior. The women pressed their children to them and huddled to-gether, the men looked irresolutely from one to the other, feeling for their knives. The strangers acted and spoke roughly, and although the immigrants couldn't understand their words, they understood their guns: the men ordered them not to move and seemed ready to lay hands on them. Karl Oskar and Jonas Petter fingered their knives—their guns were still in their chests in Stillwater—and wondered what kind of ruffians they had encountered. What did the men want? If they were hunters, they ought to pursue their game and let peaceful folk alone. This Karl Oskar and Jonas Petter told them in Swedish.

A third man was now approaching across the clearing. He was shorter than the other two, but he too had a gun and was dressed like them. His trousers had great patches over the knees. He carried two rabbits by their hind legs, blood dripping from their headless bodies. He looked more threatening than either of the other two hunters.

The unarmed group of men, women, and children was now surrounded by three men with guns, apparently hun-ters of peaceful human beings. Now they were indeed in danger and they huddled close together like a herd of

201

game, stalked and encircled by hounds. What could they do?

The dogs rushed to the third hunter and licked the blood dripping from his rabbits. Then, suddenly, one of the immigrant women rushed after the dogs, calling in fury at the top of her old voice: "You bastard! Don't you know how to behave?"

It was Fina-Kajsa, the oldest and most decrepit of the women. She rushed forward in an insane rage as if threatening the ruffian. But suddenly she stopped and stared at the man, and the hunter with the rabbits pushed back his broad-brimmed hat; he too stopped and stared; his chin fell, leaving his mouth open.

Fina-Kajsa took a few steps forward: "Shoot your paltry rabbits, but leave peaceful folk alone! Have you no shame at all, boy? To meet your old mother with a gun!"

The hunter's chin fell another inch. He dropped his rabbits on the ground.

"Throw down your shooting iron too," Fina-Kajsa ordered him.

"Mother!"

"I had expected you to greet me like a decent man. And here you and your pack of friends aim guns. . . ."

"Mother—I didn't expect you!"

"I thought I would never get here. But here you see me as I am, Anders my son."

"Mother—you're here!"

"I thought America had no end!"

"Where's Father?"

"He lies on the bottom of the sea."

"Is Father *dead?*"

"As dead as the rest on the bottom of the sea! And the grindstone he had brought for you lies there too."

"Did Father bring me a grindstone?"

"The stones are cheap on Oland. Here is our old iron pot! Here, right in my hand! They broke one leg. . . . Anders . . . if you don't recognize your mother you at least remember our old pot!"

"Yes, yes! You bring our old *gryta!* Yes, yes. . . . Welcome, Mother!"

Mother and son had found each other, and the group around them listened in silence.

202

They had reached Taylors Falls; they were only a short distance from Anders Mansson's home.

He told them he had been out with his two neighbors to shoot some rabbits for supper. And now they also heard the explanation for the strange behavior of the woman and the other two hunters: The settlers here were afraid of cholera, and all newcomers were met and questioned before they were allowed to enter the settlement. If anyone arrived from a contaminated region he was put into a shed near the falls where he was fumigated with sulphur and tar for a few days before he was let out. Weak people could not stand the ordeal of being smoked like hams, some only lasted a day before fainting. But it was a fact that in this manner they had so far avoided the sickness in Taylors Falls.

Fina-Kajsa pointed out to the group what might have happened to them if she hadn't been along to recognize Anders. And turning to her son she asked: "But what kind of sickness ails you? Your face blooms like a red rose!"

"It's the heat, Mother."

Anders Mansson greatly resembled his father, whom they all remembered from the beginning of their journey, and whom they had helped bury in the North Sea. Anders was a thickset man with broad, somewhat stooping shoulders. He was almost bald, his complexion was red, his nut-brown eyes restless, avoiding a direct look at them. At first he had looked threatening, but now they discovered he was shy to a fault.

Twilight was upon them, they had arrived none too soon. They walked down a slope, through a grove of green trees, and arrived at a level, low-lying piece of ground. They could see water, a lagoon or small tarn, bordered by tall grass. Near the water was tilled ground, they saw a yellowed stubble field with some rye shocks. These were Anders Mansson's fields which he himself had cleared. By now it was too dark to see how far the fields extended. A cabin stood in the flat meadow, with a few lindens and elms around it. There were other cabins across the rye field.

Anders Mansson approached the small cabin of roughly

hewn logs; it was situated like a hay barn in the meadow.

"So this is your hay shed," said Fina-Kajsa.

"Hay shed?" the son repeated, as if not remembering what the Swedish word meant.

Anders opened the door, and Fina-Kajsa stuck in her head to inspect the hay crop in her son's shed.

"Did you get much hay this summer?" she asked. She couldn't see any hay at all, but in the dim light she espied pieces of furniture; clothing and tools hung on pegs around the walls: "You keep your hay shed empty!"

"Yes—no—You see, Mother, I have no hay in this house—"

"Do you have people living in the barn?"

"I live here myself."

"Isn't this your hay barn?"

"No, Mother. It is my house."

"But why do you live in the barn? Where's your main house?"

"I have built this cabin for my own use. Welcome to my home, Mother! We must boil these rabbits for supper."

And Anders Mansson took out his hunting knife and began to skin and clean his game.

Fina-Kajsa turned to her Swedish traveling companions: "My son is the same! Here he stands lying to my face. He won't show us his home. He's telling stories. All of you can see this is nothing but a barn. A small barn."

The rest of the immigrants had at first, like the old woman, taken this cabin for a hay barn, since it sat in the middle of a field. Also it was rather small, not more than fifteen or sixteen feet square. And the door, cut through the logs without a jamb, was as low as a barn door. Kristina whispered to Karl Oskar: This house was exactly like their meadow barn which had burned down when lightning struck it.

But by and by they all understood that Anders Mansson had led them to his main house; this barn was his home. All understood this, but none mentioned it—none except his mother.

"Anders! Don't fool me any longer! Show me your house!" she commanded.

"This is my house, Mother! Come into my house, all you *Svenskar!* I'll fix you a good supper tonight."

And the immigrants obeyed him and entered his humble abode; fatigue had overcome them to the very marrow of their bones, and they climbed with great contentment over the log serving as threshold, happy and pleased to be in a house, under a roof, having reached a shelter where they could rest.

But old Fina-Kajsa sat down on her pot outside the cabin, she remained there, repeating more and more severely, "Take me to your house!"

While all the others gathered in the cabin, and darkness fell, she remained there, sitting on her iron pot. At length Anders went outside and half carried, half dragged his mother over the threshold.

The group from Ljuder had now reached the end of their long journey. All but the widow Fina-Kajsa Andersdotter from Oland. She had not yet arrived: she had not yet seen the home her son had described in his letters. It had come to pass as she had predicted so often during the journey: she would never arrive.

XIII

Distant Fields Look Greenest

The arrival of the Swedish immigrants in Taylors Falls was a momentous occurrence. The whole population of the village consisted of only thirty-odd people, and with the fifteen new arrivals it was increased in one day by half. Until now there had been only four women in the settlement; with the arrival of Fina-Kajsa, Kristina, Ulrika, and Elin their number had doubled. Previously there had been only three families, the rest were single men.

Taylors Falls had been named for an American, Jesse Taylor, who was the first white man to settle here, twelve years earlier; he had built a sawmill at the falls. He had since died, but the mill was operated by an old Irishman named Stephen Bolles who had also started a flour mill. A German couple, the Fischers, had recently opened a combined inn and store, consisting of two log cabins connected by a roofed passage. Mr. and Mrs. Fischer also kept a bull to serve the settlers' cows. A general store was owned and operated by a Scot, Mr. Abbott, who was the postmaster as well, with the post office located in the store. The largest building in the settlement was occupied by the Stillwater Lumber Company.

Besides Fina-Kajsa's son, two other Swedes lived in Taylors Falls, one man and one woman—Samuel Nojd

and Anna Johansdotter, the latter known as *Svenska*
Anna, or Swedish Anna. Samuel Nojd was a fur hunter by
trade, and Swedish Anna was cook in a logging camp a
few miles north of the village. With fifteen newcomers the
Swedish population in this part of the St. Croix River Valley increased six-fold at once.

Anders Mansson offered the use of his cabin to his
homeless countrymen until they could build living quarters
for themselves or for as long as they wished to stay. Helping them thus he was only repaying a debt: "You have
cared for my mother," he said.

And should they feel too cramped in his cabin, they
might sleep at German Fischer's inn; lodging there would
cost only ten cents a night for each person; they would, of
course, have to sleep with other people, but never more
than four in the same bed; and the host was quite strict
and let no one wear his boots in bed. The Fischers were
particular and cleanly people and maintained good order
at their inn.

There were now sixteen persons living in Anders Mansson's small cabin; but they had become accustomed to
close quarters during their voyages; indeed, they had been
more cramped in the holds. Here they could let their children run outside in the daytime and could themselves go
out whenever they wished, so they need not jostle each
other in the house all the time. Since Anders Mansson was
kind enough to let them use his house, they accepted
gratefully. In this way they saved a dollar and fifty cents a
day, the amount it would have cost them if all had been
forced to sleep at the inn. And Fina-Kajsa's son felt proud
that they considered his cabin good enough; he was well
pleased with it himself. During his first winter in Taylors
Falls he had lived with thirteen other people in a cabin
half as large as this one. He said it was only nine feet
square, and only six feet from the ground to the roof, and
it had no flooring.

The travelers could now rest for a few days until their
belongings arrived. The men helped Anders Mansson harvest his crop. His fields were smaller than they had realized; he had broken barely eight acres. He owned a team
of oxen and two cows as well. But he would only keep one
cow for the winter; he intended to butcher the other one,

for she was too old to breed. Each time he milked his cows all four women came to watch him: they had never before seen a man do the milking.

As soon as the news spread of the arrival of guests at Anders Mansson's, the two other Swedes in the settlement came to visit the immigrants from their homeland. Samuel Nojd, the fur hunter, was a friendly, talkative man of about fifty, but he mixed so many English words with the Swedish that they understood only half of what he said. He had been in North America more than ten years, he had moved from place to place, and soon he would move away from this river valley: desirable fur-bearing animals were getting scarce hereabouts. He advised his countrymen to take land on the prairies instead of here.

Swedish Anna was in her forties, a buxom woman with big arms and a voluminous bosom. She was the picture of health, capable and unafraid, as a woman cooking for men in a logging camp should be. She showed also a tender, motherly side: she was much concerned over the small Swedish children and was surprised that the babies could have survived the long journey in such good health. Swedish Anna was a widow who had emigrated alone from Ostergotland; Samuel Nojd came from Dalecarlia.

Counting the new arrivals, there were now immigrants from four Swedish provinces in this valley; and the Smalanders, of course, were in the majority.

The newcomers were eager for information and at every opportunity questioned those who had arrived earlier: How was life for settlers in this St. Croix Valley, and how should they go about the business of getting settled? Anders Mansson, himself a homesteader, could best advise them; but he was a man of few words; much probing was required to learn anything from him. This much they discovered: The Territory was almost as large as all of Sweden, yet hardly more than two hundred settlers had taken up land and begun tilling it. Most of these lived to the south in Washington County. The Territory was as yet surveyed only along the rivers. To the west and southwest the whole country was still unsurveyed and unclaimed—it lay there free and open to the first claimant.

There was indeed space for all, land in abundance. But many of the inhabitants of the river valley took land only for the timber, said Anders Mansson. They did not clear fields, they cut down the forest and sold the lumber for a high profit. They left the soil untouched and grew rich from the forest. Most of the newcomers had only one desire: to get rich quickly.

The farmers from Ljuder said they had not come for that purpose. They were merely seeking to earn a living, they intended to break land, build houses, settle down: they had come to live on their land as settlers of this country, where they hoped in time to better their condition.

But they must begin from the very beginning and find everything a farmer needed, ground and house, chattel and cattle. And they were filled with concern at learning how much livestock cost: a cow, thirty dollars, a yoke of oxen, one hundred dollars. Hogs and poultry also fetched sky-high prices; Anders Mansson had only recently bought a laying hen in St. Paul for five dollars, but she had died of loneliness, and so he was unable to treat them to eggs. The exorbitant prices were explained in this way: domestic animals were also immigrants into the Territory, and as rare as the settlers themselves.

One evening, as all were gathered together in Anders Mansson's cabin, Karl Oskar asked his advice: What should a man in his predicament do? He had sold his farm in Sweden, but most of the money had been spent on the journey, and he was now practically a pauper. He had only ninety dollars left in cash. A farmer needed first of all a team of oxen, and he didn't even have enough money for that! And how could he buy land with the small sum he had left?

"You don't pay for the land before it's put on the market," Anders Mansson explained. "To begin with, you must sit down on the claim as a squatter."

And he explained what the word *squatter* meant—a settler who built his house on land that had not yet been surveyed or sold. That was why he needn't pay anything for the claim to begin with. Later, when the land had been surveyed, the government would put it up at auction and he would have priority because he had been there first. Anyone wanting to take a claim as squatter need only locate and mark the place he wanted and report it to the land office in Stillwater. Then he could remain in security on the land until it was offered for public sale. It might be several years before he need begin paying for the land.

This arrangement sounded generous to Swedish peasant ears—no one could ask for better conditions.

"I came here as a squatter myself," said Fina-Kajsa's son. "To squat means to sit on one's haunches."

"Skvatter . . . skvatter . . ." Karl Oskar attempted to pronounce the word, but its sound had something degrading in it, it sounded like a reproach to his poverty. "Yes, I guess I too must be such a one. An impoverished farmer, arriving in America . . ."

The other two farmers were better off than he; Danjel had four hundred dollars left from the sale of his farm Karragarde, and Jonas Petter had about two hundred and fifty dollars left of his traveling money. Karl Oskar had the least for a new start. But Anders Mansson advised all three to take squatters' claims on unsurveyed land, then they could use their cash for livestock and implements. Each settler could claim a hundred and sixty acres, the American acre being a little less than the Swedish acre.

Karl Oskar thought: The manor at Krakesjo at home had only seventy-five acres of tilled fields. If all the land he could take here were tillable, he would have fields for two manors!

Anders Mansson also told them the price they would have to pay when the land went on sale: one dollar and twenty-five cents for each acre. This sounded like a most reasonable price for such rich and fertile land as they had seen on their walk from Stillwater. A farmer would undoubtedly be able to manage and prosper here as soon as he got started.

Anders Mansson continued: All products from the fields commanded high prices: bread, butter, pork, milk, eggs, cheese. Consequently, broken ground was highly valuable. If they were able to clear and plant the fields, and hold on to them, they would soon be well off. He himself had experienced great adversity during the four years after his arrival; the first summer his crop had suffered from drought, the second year a forest fire had spread to his fields and part of his rye had burned while in the shocks; last year it was the grasshoppers, which appeared in such swarms that they darkened the sun and left nothing but bare ground behind them. Each fifth year was a hopper year, when every green blade was eaten, and last summer they had even devoured his jacket and the scythe handle which he happened to leave in the field; he could only be grateful they hadn't eaten him too.

Karl Oskar had closely inspected Mansson's fields and he did not think the Olander was an industrious farmer; he had suffered adversity, yes—but why hadn't he broken more land in four years? All he had to do was to plow this stone-free ground. Nor had he built a threshing barn as yet, in spite of all the lumber around him. Mansson threshed his crops in wintertime on the ice of the small lake. But that was a poor way to handle grain. Karl Oskar thought something must be wrong with Fina-Kajsa's son, he seemed to lack energy and an enterprising spirit.

"The first years are hard ones for settlers," Anders Mansson assured them. He continued: There were no roads anywhere out here in the wilderness, and it was not until last year that he had been able to buy a yoke of oxen in St. Paul. Before he got the team his chores had been endless; he himself had carried or pulled everything that had to be moved. A settler without a team had to use his own back, be his own beast of burden.

Fina-Kajsa looked searchingly at her son: "You've grown hunchbacked here in America, Anders. Have you carried something that was too heavy?"

"No longer, Mother. I carry nothing more now."

He straightened his bent shoulders. Then he sat silent a while and replied only in monosyllables as they tried to glean more information about his four settler years. He seemed to avoid their questions and said at last, in an effort to clarify everything to them: He had had his difficulties at times, but he had managed, one way or another.

Jonas Petter questioned him to the very point: "Do you regret your emigration?"

"Oh no, *nej!* Never! I don't mean that!" he assured them eagerly. "I have no such thoughts any longer."

"I think you have been ailing, you look so old," Fina-Kajsa said.

"The weather here is hard on one's health," the son exclaimed quickly. "If you intend to stay long in Minnesota Territory, it is well to take care of your health from the very beginning. I was sick the two first summers because I hadn't taken care of myself."

The first year he had felt lonely in America, and his

211

thoughts had returned to Sweden at times. But the second year he had begun to like the country, and the third year he actually felt at home, and ever since, he had liked it more and more; in every respect the new country was better than the old.

And now he would soon get his American papers and become a "sitter." "Sitter" was Anders Mansson's word for citizen.

"I have already got my first *najonal-paper.*"

From his Swedish chest Anders Mansson produced a large paper, which he proudly showed his guests, but as it was printed in English, only Robert was able to glean some of its contents. They would all in due time get such papers, and then they too would become "sitters" in North America.

Anders Mansson's house guests understood plainly that he was unwilling to tell all of what had happened to him out here. He was a taciturn man and seemed to have a secret, something that weighed on his mind.

The newcomers hoped to profit by the experience of those who had come before them. Already they were aware that their own problems would be greater because they had arrived at this inopportune season; it would be a whole year before they could harvest anything from the earth. Somehow they must sustain life during this long year of waiting; above all, they must manage to live through the winter.

2

In time their belongings arrived at Taylors Falls, having been freighted by the lumber company's barge; but they were dismayed at the great cost: thirty dollars! Karl Oskar, Danjel, and Jonas Petter must pay ten dollars each.

"Those dirty dogs!" exclaimed Karl Oskar, but aside from voicing his disgust he could do nothing about the price.

Anders Mansson was of the opinion that the lumber company took advantage of settlers as often as possible. A barrel of flour cost ten dollars in Stillwater, and fifteen in Taylors Falls, because the company charged five dollars for freight.

But the settlers had waited impatiently for their goods;

now they had their own tools and needn't wait another day to go out and find land; without delay they must seek out their places for settling.

The clothes chests from Sweden were opened. Karl Oskar first of all dug up his axes from the bottom of his chest.

"You have two axes!" Anders Mansson exclaimed in surprise. "Then you are not poor."

Karl Oskar had only brought along one heavy ax and one hand ax. He still had no felling ax.

"If you have an ax all your own you are ahead of the rest of us."

The settlers often owned an ax together, using it in turn, every second day, or every second week, according to agreement. Sometimes three might own one ax together. Anders Mansson knew a settler who had owned no tools except a knife and one-half of an ax when he arrived. Seeing all the tools Karl Oskar had brought from Sweden, he said with respect in his voice: A well-off man has arrived here.

Fina-Kajsa's son had promised to go with them and point out places suitable to settle on. It was decided that Arvid and Robert should remain at home with the women and children while the men were away looking for land. Following their guide's advice, they now made themselves ready for the expedition: they took food for three days, and each carried a copper container of water, as it was said they might get chills and fever from the stagnant water in the forest. Besides axes, they took their guns. In these regions no one went far from home without a weapon of some kind, and a settler was as much dependent on his loaded gun as a limping man is on his staff.

They were to walk through regions where Indians had their favorite hunting grounds; as yet their fall hunt hadn't begun, but they moved their wigwams constantly and had no permanent camp. Anders Mansson had never been annoyed by the Chippewas, the tribe roaming in the forests near Taylors Falls; during the winter, Indians often came into his cabin to warm themselves, and they sat hours on end by the fire without saying a single word. Many times they had brought him venison. But the savages were never to be relied on; no one knew what they might do, or when they had murder on their minds. A trader, James Godfrey by name, living alone in his cabin not far from Taylors Falls, had been scalped by the Indians one night last winter as he lay in bed. It was thought that the trader had taken advantage of the Indians in some deal and that they had murdered him in revenge. The Chippewas never disturbed anyone unless they themselves had been disturbed or cheated.

So one morning at dawn the Swedish farmers set out to find new homes.

Smalanders had always looked down on Olanders, yet here walked three Smalanders guided by an Olander. They headed southwest down the broad valley. Their guide told them that if they continued in this direction they would find the most fertile soil in the whole river valley. A road had been begun from Taylors Falls, and they followed this clearing as far as it ran, then they had to find their own way, using their axes to cut through the worst thickets. The farther away from the river they walked, the fewer pine trees and more leafy wood they found. The birches here were mostly river birch, growing near water. The newcomers asked their guide the names of the trees that were unknown to them. He pointed out cedars and walnut trees, and they tried to remember the color of the bark and the shape of leaves and trunks. In a bog they discovered larches which they at first assumed to be some kind of pine tree. But the needles were softer, and they were told that these trees lost their needles in winter and made fine lumber. The deeper they penetrated into the lush valley, the larger and more numerous grew the sugar maples, from which sap was tapped in spring. From the rich, sweet maple sap sugar and sirup were made.

The three Smaland farmers missed only one leaf-tree in this new forest—the alder tree, which supplied them with material for wooden shoes at home. And when they were told that no alders grew here, they wondered which one of the other trees might supply them with wood suitable for shoes. Their leather shoes would soon be worn out, and they would be forced to use the same kind of footgear they had worn in Sweden.

The land-seekers walked leisurely through the fertile valley, they did not walk straight ahead, they turned off to left or right, they made side trips, they observed everything they saw, particularly evaluating the soil. They walked as their forefathers once had walked through their homeland, countless thousands of years ago; they sought what their forebears had sought before a single turf had been turned in that parish where later generations had cultivated their fields. And they compared the American forest with the one at home and felt proud when they discovered that this enormously rich growth lacked one tree which was found in the forest of the land they had left.

They saw game frequently: rabbit ears stuck up in the grass, big fat squirrels scampered about and jabbered like magpies, near streams and lakelets they saw flocks of wild geese. Gnawed saplings indicated the presence of elk. Once a furred animal ran up a tree, and Jonas Petter recognized the hairy thief who had tried to steal their food the night they camped in the forest. He was told it was a raccoon, a harmless little animal that abounded in that country.

The forest shone luminously green, the grass stood tall in open places, an abundance of wild fruit and berries weighed down the branches of trees and bushes this beautiful August day.

"The Lord's sun has never shone on a more pleasing countryside," said Danjel Andreasson.

And where the land-seekers wandered now they had only to choose: they could stop wherever they wished and each stake out one hundred and sixty acres of land.

From time to time, Karl Oskar measured the depth of the topsoil with a small shovel he had brought along. Black mold lay on clay bottom; red clay on hard ground, blue clay on low-lying ground. In a few places he found sand mixed with the clay. But in practically every place he dug, he found topsoil to a depth of two feet, sometimes nearly three feet.

"More likely earth can't be found in the whole of creation," Jonas Petter said.

But they were also looking for clean drinking water; they had been warned that some of the stagnant pools and tarns were full of insects and small animals which caused dangerous sicknesses. If they were unable to locate a spring or running stream near their place of settling, they would have to dig wells for drinking water, and Anders

Mansson maintained that this would be a heavy, long-drawn-out undertaking: once he had had to dig a well twenty-five feet deep.

He showed them all the lakes he was familiar with. The greatest lake in this region lay farther to the southwest and was called Ki-Chi-Saga; it was an Indian name, said to mean "Great and Beautiful Lake." Anders Mansson himself had never roamed the forest as far as Ki-Chi-Saga, but he knew a Swede, Johannes Nordberg, who had reached the big lake last autumn. Nordberg was a farmer from Helsingland who had embraced Erik Janson's new religion and had accompanied him to Illinois. Later he had fallen away from that sect and had left the colony on the prairie to look for a new place in which to settle in the north. He was said to be the first white man ever to see Lake Ki-Chi-Saga, and he had told Mansson that the finest land and the richest soil he had ever seen in this valley lay around it. He had gone back to Illinois but had promised to return last spring with many of Janson's deserters to settle near the lake with the Indian name. As yet nothing had been heard of him.

However, added the guide, fine soil was obtainable much nearer. They needn't go so far to find good places for settling.

The immigrants made no haste in choosing a site, but inspected the land carefully as they walked along. The heat also forced them to move slowly; they breathed heavily in the muggy atmosphere. They sought to refresh themselves with the water they had brought with them, but it was already tepid in the copper containers and did not quench their thirst.

In the depth of the forest they suddenly came upon a strange mound, and their guide told them this was an old Indian grave. They stopped and looked in wonder: earth had been thrown up in a great pile, and grass had grown over it. The mound had oval sides, narrowing at the top, and resembled a giant beast whose legs had sunk into the ground, an animal stuck in the forest and unable to move for so long that grass had grown on its back. And inside this huge body rested the dead savages, in the midst of their forest hunting grounds; they had never known Christ or the Gospel, throughout life they had been heathens, and so after death were lost souls. But peaceful seemed their camp, lying here in the thickest part of the wild forest, green and thriving was the grass covering their grave.

The peasants from Sweden stood a long time gazing at this mound built by human hands, rising like a round, green-furred animal-body, and they sensed that they beheld something immeasurably ancient, something from the long-past time of witches, trolls, and sagas. In this barrow where the country's native hunters returned to dust, the immigrants sensed vaguely that inexplicable something which makes women and children shudder in the dark. Before encountering these savage people in life, they had come upon them in death, they had met the dead before the living.

The strangers from faraway Sweden knew nothing of the answer the Chippewa chief had given the whites when they had asked the price of the tribal hunting grounds: "Fill this valley with gold until it lies even with the hills! Yet we will not take your gold for the graves of our fathers. Wait still a little longer, until all my people are dead. Then you may take our whole valley, and all our graves, and keep your gold as well."

The men who had traveled thousands of miles to take over the Chippewas' land, and who measured the topsoil of the Indians' hunting grounds, gazed in wonder at the grave in the forest; they stood there timidly, glancing about suspiciously, as though listening to the oldest saga of all sagas in the world.

3

The land-seekers rested in the shade of some maples and ate from their knapsacks: bread and cold rabbit. They took off their shirts, wet and clammy with perspiration, and spread them to dry on the bushes. But as they sat with their upper bodies bare, the mosquitoes attacked them in great swarms and bit them furiously. They made a fire to drive away the plague, but Anders Mansson said the best way to protect oneself was to cover the whole body with mud; while sleeping in the forest one could in this way rest peacefully.

Anders Mansson had been a homesteader for some time, he seemed to have much useful information. Jonas Petter asked him how it went with men in these womanless regions. He remembered the little shoemaker in Stillwater who had looked with such longing at the women in their company. There was only one woman to each twenty men in the American wilderness; what did the men here do?

Jonas Petter put this question to Anders Mansson, but he looked away and answered only with an embarrassed grin. He was shy with people, especially with women; he had probably never touched a woman, Jonas Petter guessed. Fina-Kajsa had once asked her son, in the presence of all, why he hadn't married yet. Anders Mansson had said nothing and had only grown redder in the face than he usually was.

Jonas Petter went on. He almost wished he had been turned into a woman here in America, as they were the only ones who needn't sleep alone. Even Ulrika seemed to think she might get married out here; she had said she need only choose among the men ready for marriage.

"Well, why wouldn't a man marry Ulrika?" Anders Mansson asked. "She is healthy and well shaped. How long since her last husband died?"

Jonas Petter and Karl Oskar exchanged glances: unmarried Ulrika of Vastergohl was taken for a widow here, as she had arrived without a husband but with a daughter. And here people might think whatever they wished, let them think her husband was dead. Ulrika herself had said, when questioned by Swedish Anna if her menfolk had died: Yes, of course her menfolk had died, all her menfolk had passed away from her forever, none would return, she had none left. And people in Taylors Falls now believed that Ulrika had been married and widowed many times, and none of her group would tell the truth about her carryings-on at home; all had agreed that everything discreditable that had happened in the land of Sweden, no matter whom it concerned, must be forgotten, buried, and lost in this new country.

Jonas Petter had almost let the cat out of the bag, but he saw Karl Oskar's warning glance, and hastened to explain: Concerning Ulrika's widowhood, he knew only what she herself had said—all her menfolk had left her forever, they were dead to her. And how long it was since the last one passed away, that Jonas Petter couldn't say. But this much he knew: Ulrika was free and open to marriage.

Thus Jonas Petter avoided the truth without telling a lie.

Anders Mansson nodded and seemed satisfied with this information. Such an elegant and handsome woman as Ulrika, he said, would soon be married here in Minnesota Territory.

4

Later in the afternoon the four Swedes reached a small, longish lake with low shores overgrown with reeds and grass. Oaks, Maples, lindens, and ash trees were scattered in this region, but the ground nearest the lake was even and ready to till, sloping gently toward the water.

"Here it's easy to break land," said their guide. "This is a fine place for homesteading."

They walked around the lake, a distance of only a few miles, and inspected the ground everywhere. Yes, the earth was easy to break; one need only turn it with the plow. The topsoil was two and a half feet deep in some places. Material for building grew everywhere close by.

Danjel and Jonas Petter were at once satisfied with the location and inclined to stake claims here. Karl Oskar admitted that the topsoil was excellent, but the ground nearest the lake was low and swampy, full of muddy pool and quagmires.

"It's a mosquito hole," he said.

Jonas Petter replied that the mosquitoes swarmed about every place and that they shouldn't let this factor influence their decision. And when they discovered a spring with clear, translucent water under a fallen tree near by, he and Danjel were in enthusiastic accord: At this little lake they had found all they wanted, here they wished to settle.

Anders Mansson advised neither one way nor another. The lake was about seven or eight miles as the crow flies from Taylors Falls, and he didn't think they would want to be farther away from people.

"It is far enough," Danjel said. "Let us all three take claims here. This is a good place for us to live."

They laid down their burdens at the edge of the forest and rested in the shade to talk it over. Danjel continued: As they had come from the same place at home, they

219

oughtn't to separate now, they ought to stick together. If they settled here, close to each other, they could help each other and enjoy each other's company. To begin with, they could even use each other's tools and teams.

Jonas Petter also wanted them to build close together, like a village at home; to live like villagers would be more enjoyable here in the wilderness than to live alone.

Then it was Karl Oskar's turn to voice his thoughts: Just because there was so much space out here, they must not settle on top of each other, elbow each other and build their homes corner to corner as farmers did in Sweden. He thought they should live a little apart. They could do as they pleased, but he wanted to settle in a place some distance from the others. He didn't, of course, mean to be so far away that they couldn't see each other and help each other when needed.

Danjel wanted them to remain one family, as they were at present; the first Christians whom he tried to imitate, had owned all things in common. But Karl Oskar wanted to think this over, and he would obey no head except his own. Even though Danjel well knew that his sister's daughter's husband never followed any advice, he now seriously tried to persuade him: "Don't seek any farther! Be satisfied with this fair land."

"I might find some more likely a little farther on."

"We should be satisfied when the Lord has shown us this."

Jonas Petter said: "Don't be a fuss-pot, Karl Oskar! This place is good enough!"

But Karl Oskar turned to Anders Mansson and asked him for more information about the region near the lake with the Indian name. That farmer from Helsingland who inspected the soil, hadn't he said that the richest farm land in this whole valley was beside that lake? Karl Oskar would like to see for himself if this were actually the truth before he chose his own land. How far from here would it be to the lake?

Anders Mansson didn't think it was more than two miles from where they now were to Lake Ki-Chi-Saga, but he couldn't say for sure. The country to the west and southwest had not yet been explored, no one except Indians and an occasional pelt trader had been farther. But streams ran in that direction, and if he followed one of these, he would undoubtedly reach Lake Ki-Chi-Saga.

Karl Oskar looked thoughtfully at the fields in front of him: he did not wish to appear displeased with what he saw, but he had once and for all made up his mind that he would have the best soil in North America, wherever it was to be found. And now it was said that the soil was even better at the other lake. Why be satisfied with the next best if the very best was within reach? Suppose he took a claim here—and then for the rest of his life had to regret not having gone a few miles farther. He couldn't know until he had seen the other place. He was to settle down for the rest of his life, he wanted to choose carefully, find a place that he liked so well he would never want to leave it. He had traveled many thousands of miles, all the way from Sweden. He had strength left to go a few miles farther.

The farmer from Korpamoen was so stubborn that nothing could change his mind once he got an idea in his head, and Danjel and Jonas Petter could only wish him good luck when he said he would go on farther by himself. They had firmly decided to settle down here as squatters.

"Cut marks in the trees," said Anders Mansson. "That means you have taken a claim."

Danjel and Jonas Petter each blazed a maple; then Anders Mansson carved in each blazed tree a ten-inch-high letter, C: this indicated that the land at the lake had been claimed, anyone coming later would see it.

But Karl Oskar picked up his pack again—there were still some hours before sunset, and if it were only a few miles to the lake with the peculiar name, he thought he might get there before dark. He would be back by tomorrow noon, if they cared to wait for him, but if he were delayed they had better return to Taylors Falls without him; he was sure he could find his way back alone.

As he disappeared among the thick tree trunks, Jonas Petter looked after him and said: The old proverb was right—distant fields look greenest. . . .

5

Karl Oskar Nilsson walked alone through the wilderness. He continued directly southwest, and when the trees did not shade him, the sun shone right in his face, burning him like a flame. Progress became more difficult, he had to use his ax often to get through. He reached a swamp where he sank down to his boot tops, he circled giant trees, seemingly yards around the base, he climbed over fallen trees whose upturned roots towered house tall, he walked around deep black water holes like wells, he tore his way through tangles of ferns and bushes, he fought thorny thickets which clawed his hands and face until they bled. At times he walked on the bottom of the forest ocean with the sky barely visible, at other times—while craning his neck to look up at the tall trees—he was reminded of the church steeple at home, which, as a little boy, he had thought reached into the very heavens.

Karl Oskar mused to himself that probably he was the first white man ever to go through the forest at this place.

The ground had been tramped by hunters and game, by soft moccasins and light cloven hoofs, by the pursued and the pursuer. But now came a man, lumbering along in heavy boots, who was neither Indian nor deer, neither hunter nor hunted. Cautiously he took one step at a time, treading firmly on the unknown ground. He had entered this forest on a new mission, a mission that had brought no one here before: Karl Oskar Nilsson was the first one to enter here with a farmer's purpose of planting and harvesting.

In spite of the many obstacles hindering his progress, he felt in high spirits. During the whole journey from Sweden he had lived closed in with other people, forced to be part of a group. Here he had miles of space in every direction, he didn't hit his head on a ceiling, his elbows against walls, he didn't jostle anyone if he moved. Here he walked along as if the whole wide wilderness were his own, to do with as he pleased; wherever he wished, he could choose his land, blaze a trunk: "This earth is mine!" he thought.

He was in high spirits because he was the first one here, because he knew a freedom which none of those would have who came after him. He walked through the forest as if he had a claim to everything around him, as if he now were taking possession and would rule a whole kingdom. Here he would soon feel at home and know his way.

Now he was searching for Ki-Chi-Saga; the name was like a magic formula, like a word from an old tale about an ancient, primeval, moss-grown, troll-inhabited forest. He spelled the word and tried to pronounce the three syllables he had heard Anders Mansson utter; the foreign name had a magic lure; he would not return until he had seen this water.

He reached a rushing stream, which he followed; the creek, with all its turns, indicated the direction he must go. To make doubly sure of his way back, he blazed occasional trees with his ax as he had done all day.

Karl Oskar followed the brook until dusk began to fall. But he had not reached a lake, large or small. Fatigue from the long walk during the hot day overtook him, and he decided to find a place to camp for the night. In the morning he would continue his search for Ki-Chi-Saga. Perhaps the distance was greater than Mansson had guessed, perhaps the brook had led him astray—who knew for sure that it emptied into the lake? But he didn't think he had gone far since leaving his countrymen, he had walked slowly and been delayed by having to cut his way through thickets.

He sat down to rest on a fallen tree; he ate a slice of bread and some meat and drank water from his container, water he had taken from the spring where the other men were. The landscape was different here, it was now more undulating and open. Should he lie down and sleep under this tree trunk, or should he try to go on? His feet had gone to sleep in his boots, his injured leg ached. Another day would come tomorrow—the land around him would not run away if he rested here for the night.

A flock of birds, large and unfamiliar to him, flew overhead, their wings whizzing in the air. They were quite low, barely above the treetops—they slanted their wings and descended and he lost sight of them. He guessed they were water birds—the lake must be near by!

This action of the birds made him decide to go on. After a few hundred paces he reached a knoll with large hardwood trees amid much greenery, behind which daylight shone through. He hurried down a slope and was in an open meadow. Now he could see: the meadow with its tall, rich grass sloped gently toward glittering water; the lake lay in front of him.

At first glimpse he was disappointed: this was only a small lake, it was not the right one. But as he approached he discovered that it was only an arm of a lake. Through a narrow channel it connected with other arms and bays and farther on the water expanded into a vast lake with islands and promontories and channels as far as his eyes could see. He had arrived.

All that he saw agreed with what he had heard—this lake must be Ki-Chi-Saga. Staggering with fatigue, he walked down to inspect it. He must complete his mission before night fell.

The shores had solid banks without any swamps, and he could see sandy beaches. Here and there, the topsoil had clay in it. The stream, his guide, emptied into the west end of the arm, near a stand of tall, slender pines. To the east a tongue of land protruded, overgrown with heavy oaks. A vast field opened to the north between the lake and the forest's edge, open, fertile ground covered with grass. He went over to inspect the tongue of land with leaf-trees: besides the oaks there were sugar maples, lindens, elms, ash trees, aspens, walnut and hazel trees, and many other trees and bushes he did not recognize. The lake shores were low and easily accessible everywhere. Birds played on the surface of the water splashing, swimming in lines, wriggling about like immense feathered water snakes, and there were ripples and rings from whirling, swirling fins.

Karl Oskar measured the sloping meadow with his eyes. It must be about fifty acres. He supposed a great deal of this ground once had been under water, the lake had at one time been larger. The soil was the fattest mold on clay bottom, the finest earth in existence. He stuck his shovel into the ground—everywhere the topsoil was deep, and in one place he did not find the red clay bottom until he had dug almost three feet down.

Earlier in the day he had seen the next best; he had gone on a little farther, and now he had found the best. He had arrived.

He felt as though this soil had been lying here waiting just for him. It had been waiting for him while he, in another land, had broken stone and more stone, laid it in piles and built fences with it, broken his equipment on it; all the while this earth had waited for him, while he had wasted his strength on roots and stones; his father had labored to pile the stone heaps higher and higher, to build the fences longer and broader, had broken himself on the

224

stones so that now he must hobble along crippled, on a pair of crutches for the rest of his life—while all this earth had been lying here waiting. While his father sacrificed his good healthy legs for the spindly blades that grew among the stones at home, this deep, fertile soil had nurtured wild grass, harvested by no one. It had been lying here useless, sustaining not a soul. This rich soil without a stone in it had lain here since the day it was created, waiting for its tiller.

Now he had arrived.

In the gathering dusk Karl Oskar Nilsson from Korpamoen appraised the location of the land: Northward lay the endless wilderness, a protection against winter winds; to the south the great lake; to the west the fine pine forest; to the east the protruding tongue of land with the heavy oaks. And he himself stood in the open, even meadow, the grass reaching to his waist, hundreds of loads of hay growing about him, covering the finest and most fertile topsoil; he stood there gazing at the fairest piece of land he had seen in all of North America.

Now he needn't go a step farther. Here lay his fields, there grew the timber for his house, in front of him lay the water with game birds and fish. Here he had fields, forest, and lake in one place. Here things grew and throve and lived and moved in whatever direction he looked—on the ground, in trees and bushes, on land and water.

At last he had found the right spot: this was the place for a farmer's home. Here he must live. And he would be the first one to raise his house on the shores of Lake Ki-Chi-Saga.

He turned left to the stand of oaks and selected the biggest tree he saw. He cut wide marks with his ax; then he took out his red pencil, his timberman's pencil from home, and wrote on the wood: *K. O. Nilsson, Svensk.*

This would have to do; if it wasn't sufficient, he must do it over some other time. The red letters on the white blaze in the oak could be seen a long way and would tell anyone passing by that this place was claimed. Besides, he wasn't able to do more, not today. After the few cuts with the ax he suddenly felt tired, more tired than he had ever felt in his life. He sank down under the tree, heavily, and laid his pack beside him—his gun, ax, water keg, knapsack, all; he had forced himself to walk a long way, and now he had no more strength, he fell at last under the tree on which he had just printed his name.

He felt he couldn't move, couldn't do another thing this evening; he was too tired to make a fire, to gather moss for a bed, to take off his boots, open the knapsack, eat. He was too tired to do anything at all, even to chase away the mosquitoes—he no longer felt their smarting bites. He didn't care about anything now, he was insensible to everything except the need to rest his body: he stretched out full length on his back, on the ground under the big oak, with his coat as a pillow.

He was satisfied with his day; he had persevered and reached his destination before the end of the day. He had found what he so long had striven to find. And this evening he rested, unmindful of all the dangers of the wilderness—he rested with the assurance of having arrived home, protected by his own tree, on his own land: The farmer from the Stone Kingdom had arrived in the Earth Kingdom which he would possess.

He went to sleep at once, his weary body fell into the well of oblivion, peace, and renewal. Karl Oskar Nilsson slept heavily and well during his first night on the shore of Lake Ki-Chi-Saga, where he was to build a farmer's life from its very beginning.

XIV

A Smaland Squatter

The next morning Karl Oskar returned to the small lake where the other three settlers awaited him, and before nightfall the four of them were back at Anders Mansson's cabin in Taylors Falls.

The following day the men began to stake out and cut a road through to their claims, so as to be able to move their belongings and whatever they might need for the settling. Their clearing work began where the logging road ended; they continued past the small lake where Danjel and Jonas Petter had decided to settle, all the way to Lake Ki-Chi-Saga. They were five menfolk. Five axes cut all day long, through thickets and groves, felling and chopping and clearing. They built a road, digging here, filling there, until wagon wheels could roll along over the ground. The distance from Taylors Falls to Lake Ki-Chi-Saga was estimated to be ten miles, and it took the five men ten days to make a passable clearing.

Then it took three days to haul boards from the Taylors Falls mill to their places of settling. With these boards they intended to raise huts in which to live while building their log houses. For the hauling they hired Anders Mansson's oxen, which moved so slowly on the newly cleared road that a whole day was required for each load.

Their almanac indicated to the Swedish settlers that the

year had reached the last week of August. Only two months remained before winter would come to the St. Croix Valley; they were told that snow and cold weather would begin early in November. But the autumns were mild in the river valley—during all of September and most of October pleasant weather was said to prevail. For another two months people could live in huts and sheds without discomfort or danger from cold. And during this time they must build more permanent houses, able to withstand all weathers. They had not one day to lose if they were to have comfortable log houses before winter set in with its severe cold and blizzards.

First they must build a shanty on each claim. "Shanty" was Anders Mansson's name for a shed. Jonas Petter was an experienced carpenter and timberman, and in three days he had built his small hut on the shores of the little lake; then he helped Danjel and Arvid build a larger one for Danjel's family to move into. As soon as this was done they began felling timbers for their log houses.

Karl Oskar chose as the site for his first home the oak grove where he had slept during his first night at Lake Ki-Chi-Saga. With Robert as helper he soon raised a hut of rough boards, about nine feet square in size; he made the roof of young lindens, on top of which he laid bark and sod. This work took him and Robert four days. There were not sufficient boards left for flooring, and the two brothers stamped down the ground and covered it with a thick layer of hay, which they gathered from the meadow. They had left an opening to the south, facing the meadow, and now Karl Oskar hammered through a door, which he hung on hinges he had made of willow wattles; then he cut open a few holes to let in light. He did not bother with a fireplace, as it would be difficult to get rid of the smoke. Instead, he built a makeshift cooking place of clay, sand, and a few stones outside near the door. This could be used as long as the warm season lasted. But he had to search widely along the shores before he found enough stones. To search for stones was a new and unusual occupation for the farmer from Korpamoen!

The family's first home in North America was now ready, and they could move in under their own roof. Kristina and the children had remained with Anders Mansson and had not yet seen their new home. Karl Oskar prepared his wife cautiously: "It's only a simple weather break: soon I'll raise a sturdy log house."

She looked forward to being in her own home where she could have her own say; this had long been her fervent desire.

Karl Oskar borrowed the oxen from Anders Mansson for the moving, and their belongings made a big load. Besides their things from Sweden, they must bring a supply of foodstuffs, which Karl Oskar had bought from Mr. Abbott, the Scot, in Taylors Falls: one barrel of rye flour for bread, one sack of salt, a few pounds of sugar, and other necessities for the household; he had also bought various articles needed for the building of the main house. He had dug deep into his cash, spending almost twenty-five dollars. The barrel of flour would last a long time for bread baking, but he had bought no meat or pork: for more substantial food they must depend on game from the forest and fish from the lake.

It was a pleasant morning in early fall when the family from Korpamoen set out for Lake Ki-Chi-Saga. The weather was now cooler, with mild sunshine over the green forest wilderness; perfect weather for moving. Kristina and the children rode on the wagon, Karl Oskar and Robert walked on either side of the load, holding on to it now and then to prevent the wagon from turning over. Karl Oskar drove, holding the thongs in one hand and steadying the load with the other. The new road was rough and the wagon was no soft-rolling spring carriage: it was entirely made of wood.

The wheels of Anders Mansson's ox wagon consisted of four trundles sawed from a thick oak log. The axles fitted into holes in these rough blocks and had pins of wood on their ends, like the pins in a single-horse pull shaft. The front wheels were a little smaller than the back pair; the wagon tree connecting the two pairs had holes in it to lengthen or shorten the wagon, if required. The dry wooden axles groaned as the trundles turned, they squeaked loudly at the friction of wood against wood. And the clumsy wheels jolted and rolled heavily over hollows and stumps.

The children yelled in delight; they had not been on a

wagon pulled by a team since leaving the horse wagons in Karlshamn last spring. But Kristina was not so well pleased to sit on this jouncing, shaking wooden vehicle. And was this clearing through the forest called a road? Even a person walking would find it difficult to get through between stumps and thickets. She wondered that the wheels were able to roll at all, she sympathized with the whining, whimpering wagon; if she had been a wagon she too would have complained about being forced through this wild woodland.

Karl Oskar explained that the wagon was not greased; Anders Mansson did not keep his implements in good order. Nor had he himself been able to find any fat—animal tallow, or such—to use this morning for greasing the axles. The wagon reminded him that iron was as scarce here as wood was abundant.

Kristina called the vehicle "The Whimpering Wagon," but the day they hauled the boards to the claim, Robert had already named it "The Screech Cart."

The riders on the big load were soundly shaken; the wagon jolted and bumped, almost worse than a ship on a stormy sea—it rolled and pitched more than the *Charlotta*. After a few miles Kristina felt sick: "No! I want no more swinging! Neither on water nor land!"

She stepped down from the load and walked. She was afraid of being badly shaken; it might injure the child she carried in her. Only ten or eleven weeks remained before she would be in childbed, and she might have a miscarriage if she weren't careful. She would rather walk than sit on a load that shook like a threshing floor, even though she had begun to be heavy of foot.

The ox wagon crept along the wretched road, squeaking and screeching. The load nearly turned over many times—only through the efforts of the two men was it kept upright. The oxen moved at a snail's pace, and Kristina walked on one side and kept an eye on her children.

The trail skirted a glen in the depths of the forest, and here stood a strange pole which the Indians had erected. The settlers stopped to let the oxen rest while they inspected it. Karl Oskar and Robert had seen this image before—now they wanted to show it to Kristina. The pole was made from a cedar tree and stood taller than a man.

But it did not represent a man—it ended in a snarling wolf's head.

The wooden image in the midst of the forest seemed to Kristina a phantom, and she was afraid to go near it. Robert guessed it was some kind of god whom the Indians worshiped when they gathered here—remnants of huts were to be seen close by. Kristina knew that heathens lacked knowledge of even the first of God's Ten Commandments, she knew they worshiped images, but she couldn't understand how they could worship so horrible an image as this one—a wolf with ravenous jaws. She urged the group to continue their journey: the savages must revere their image; should they happen to arrive and find people gaping at the pole, they might do harm. And since she had seen what horrible idols heathens made unto themselves, she thanked her Creator from the bottom of her heart for letting her be born in a Christian land.

The plodding ox team pushed on sluggishly, step after step, and the wooden wheels rolled along, turning slowly while the axles cried out. Robert said the noise hurt his ears, particularly the injured one. To Kristina, the four wooden wheels sang a song about impoverished wanderers: their long-drawn-out wail was to her a song of their own tribulations, of their eternal struggle, of loneliness in the wilderness. Long had their journey taken, long would it be before they had a home. As slowly as these wheels turned on their axles, keeping up their constant groans of complaint—so slowly would they manage to establish a home.

But Karl Oskar, walking beside the wagon and urging on the team, said many times: "If these were only my oxen and my wagon!"

The complaint of the ungreased wheels did not dishearten him. He was stimulated, in high spirits at being able again to drive a wagon, however much it groaned—but he drove someone else's team, someone else's wagon. A settler who owned a team had improved his situation. If this had been his own team and his own wagon, then the squeaking wheels would have been a beautiful tune. If he had been the owner of this team and this wagon, he would be walking along listening to a happy song—a song of persistence, tenacity, and reward—a song of comfort to the ears of a settler.

Their newly built road made a circuitous turn to Jonas Petter's and Danjel's settlement, lengthening the distance to Lake Ki-Chi-Saga. Karl Oskar had cleared a short cut to his own land which he now followed, thus lessening the distance by one mile. From Taylors Falls to Ki-Chi-Saga the road was now only nine miles.

Therefore, they did not drive by the smaller lake where their companions from Sweden had settled. Kristina knew full well that Karl Oskar had taken his claim farthest away —she had known this a very long time, long before he knew it himself. She had known it before they left Sweden —she had guessed he would search for a settling place as far away as he could within America's borders.

How far away from people must they now settle down? She thought the road to their new home was long and tedious. But Karl Oskar explained to her, they hadn't actually driven very far; it was the oxen, they were so slow and lazy that it took a long time to reach the claim. That was all. They could have traveled this road faster by foot.

Kristina asked: Wouldn't they be there soon?

Karl Oskar answered: Only a little stretch farther.

Some time elapsed, and then she asked again: How much farther? . . . Oh, not very much; they would be there presently. . . . But when they had driven on some distance, her patience ran out: now she insisted that he must tell her exactly how much of the road was left.

He said he couldn't tell her exactly, he hadn't measured the road in yards, feet and inches. Moreover, they were now supposed to count in American measurements, so he couldn't compute the distance.

Kristina flared up: "Don't try to make a fool of me! You'd better figure out that distance!"

He had jested with her about the road length only because she had asked so many times. He said, "Don't be angry, Kristina. I didn't mean anything."

"You might at least have talked it over with me before you went so far away for land!"

"But I had to make the decision alone. You couldn't have gone with us out here in the woodlands."

"How far do you intend to drag us? Speak up now!"

"I've told you before—I've selected the best earth there is hereabouts."

"But the road to it—it's eternal."

Karl Oskar assured her that when she arrived she would forget the tiresome journey to the wonderful land he had chosen. She must have confidence in his choice, she must rely on him here in America as she had done in Sweden.

But she was still vexed: he mustn't think she would always endure his whims. He never asked anyone's advice, he always thought he knew best. It was time for him to realize that he was nothing but a poor, wretched, fallible human; he too could make mistakes and wrong decisions.

"But I often ask your advice, Kristina. . . ."

"Maybe sometimes. But then you do as you please!"

His wife was touchy in her advanced pregnancy, she was easily upset, but he mustn't let this affect his temper, he must handle her carefully. She angered him at times, but when he controlled himself, she soon calmed down.

Suddenly he heard a cry from Kristina. He reined in the team with all his might. Little Harald had fallen off the wagon.

Robert picked up the boy before his mother reached him. Luckily the child had fallen into a mass of ferns, so soft that no damage was done. He cried only a few tears, caused more by fright than hurt. But now Kristina climbed onto the load in order to hold Harald in her arms the rest of the way. She was regretting her earlier outbreak: it was as if God had wished to give her a warning by letting her child fall off the wagon.

They now came onto more open, even ground, and Kristina no longer had to "ride a swing." She looked over the landscape and saw many flowers; the countryside was fair and pleasingly green; she caught herself comparing it with the prettiest parts of her home village, Duvemala in Algutsboda Parish.

In a moment the wagon rolled slightly down a wide meadow toward a lake. The ground sloped gently, and in no time they had reached the shore. The team came to a stop on an outjutting tongue of land.

Karl Oskar threw the thong across the back of the left ox: they had arrived. According to his watch, it had taken more than five hours to move their load from Taylors

233

Falls. But that was because of the sluggish oxen; a good walker could cover the distance in three hours; their home here was not at the end of the world!

Kristina climbed down from the oxcart and looked about in all directions: this then was the lake with the strange name, Ki-Chi-Saga. The sky-blue water with the sun's golden glitter on its waves, the overflowing abundance of green growth around the shores, all the blossoms and various grasses in the wild meadow, the many lush leaf-trees, the oaks and the sugar maples, the many birds on the lake and in the air—this was a sight to cheer her. This was a good land.

"The ground is easy to break," Karl Oskar said. "There isn't any finer!"

He hoped she would forget the long road and feel better as she saw the place where they would build their new home.

"You've found a nice place, Karl Oskar. It looks almost as nice as home in Duvemala."

Kristina had compared the shores of Lake Ki-Chi-Saga with the village where she was born and had grown up; it was the highest praise she could give. Looking at Karl Oskar she knew he had expected more, probably he had expected her, on seeing the land, to break out in loud praise and grateful joy as if they had arrived in the Garden of Eden. But all the while the thought would not leave her that here they must live like hermits in the midst of savages and wild beasts.

Karl Oskar pushed the whip handle into the ground and said the topsoil was as deep as the whip handle was long. He had measured all over—it was the same everywhere.

"Such pretty flowers in the meadow," she said.

She saw things above ground, while Karl Oskar was anxious to impress her with what was under the surface; the growth came from below, down in the black mold which they couldn't see, down there would grow the bread.

"There are only flowers and weeds now," he said. "Bread will grow here from now on. You can rely on that, Kristina!"

This was Karl Oskar's promise for the future, an earnest and binding promise to wife and children: here the

234

earth would give life's sustenance to them all, and his was the responsibility of breaking the land whence it would come.

The ox wagon with their possessions had come to a stop in front of the newly built board shed, and Karl Oskar and Robert began to unload; soon they were struggling with the heavy America chest. Kristina stood at the open door which hung there on its willow hinges; the children hovered around her.

She knew now how people lived out here when they began with the earth from the very beginning. Like Anders Mansson's old mother, she too had taken his house for a meadow barn at first sight; it was so exactly like those rickety sheds on moors and meadows at home in which the summer hay was harvested. At first, she had been unable to accept that it was a farmer's house and home. But at least it had been a solid house, built of logs. Here she stood in front of a still smaller hut, roughly thrown together of unfinished boards; this could not even be called a barn, it looked more like a tool house or a woodshed.

But then—what had she expected? Kristina looked at the shanty Karl Oskar had built for them; she realized her husband had done the best he could with a few boards, as yet she couldn't expect anything better. Seeing how people lived out here, it would have been impossible to ask for anything better, to insist on a more comfortable house. No one could conjure forth a real home in a few days; she must be satisfied with a hut.

Karl Oskar looked at his wife, anxiously wondering what she might say about his cabin. Deep down he was a little ashamed not to be offering her a better home in the new country. They had traveled such a long way to come here—and at last they stood in front of a small board shed, hurriedly nailed together in a few days. She might not think it much of an achievement; even though he had prepared her in advance, he was afraid she might be disappointed:

"It's only a *shanty,* as they call it here," he said.

The very sound of the English word emphasized to Karl Oskar better than anything he could say in Swedish that this was a makeshift. He added, "The shanty will give us protection until the house is ready."

"It'll do as long as the weather is decent," said Kristina, and felt the walls. "You put it up fast," she added.

Karl Oskar had done carpentry work as a youth, helping his father, but he did not consider himself proficient. He could have built himself a hut of twigs and branches and saved the cost of the boards, but it would have been too wretched, he thought; and then the mosquitoes, they would have come in everywhere through the brush; boards were more of a protection in every way.

Now he was pleased Kristina had found no fault with his cabin; it was the first house he had made all by himself, however it had turned out. He himself knew how poor it was. But she had said not one belittling word about the shanty, however clumsy or crooked or warped it was. She had only praised him for his handiness and speed.

He said that in the beginning they must live like crofters, without flooring in their house, it couldn't be helped. But see all the land they had! They might live like cotters but they had better and larger fields than the biggest farmer in Ljuder; they had reason to be well satisfied.

"And next time, Kristina, just wait and see! Next time we shall timber a real house! A real home! Just wait and see. . . ."

And he waved his hands in the direction of the pine stand across the meadow where the lumber still stood—couldn't she just see their sturdy, well-timbered house! Back there grew the walls for it, it was rooted, it wouldn't run away from them, it was well anchored in their own ground—no one could take their future home away from them!

Karl Oskar had moved in as a squatter, a man possessing the land without having to pay for it as yet. A squatter was a man staying close to the ground, and he too would need to stay close to the ground in the beginning; but not for long! No longer than he absolutely had to! He guessed Anders Mansson had squatted so long on his land that it had made him stoop-shouldered. Karl Oskar would be careful to avoid this; he had decided, if health and strength remained his, that only a short time would elapse before he would begin to rise, rise up to his full stature; on his own land he could rise to a man's stature, to the proud independence of a free farmer.

236

So far, he had always kept his resolutions; as far as it depended on him, this one would be kept also.

For a time they would have to live in a board shed, without windows, without fireplace, the black earth for their floor. As Kristina now entered her new home she had to stoop to get through the door. Here they were now moving in with all their possessions, her children were already playing about in the hay inside, the hay for beds which all of them would sleep on; the children had great fun digging holes in the hay, tumbling about, screaming and laughing. They were already at home, acting as if they had lived here all their lives.

Johan called out to his mother, in jubilation: "Now we live in a house, Mother! Our house in America!"

Yes, she answered the boy, they were now living in a house, at last in their own house; no longer need they crowd in among others, they could at last be their own masters, do as they pleased in their own home. From today on they had a home of their own to live in. And for this they must be grateful to God.

But deep inside her Kristina was also grateful for something else: that no one at home, neither her parents, nor her sisters, nor any other person from the old country need ever see this shanty, her first home in North America.

XV

. . . To Survive with the
Help of His Hands

In the wilderness at Lake Ki-Chi-Saga in Minnesota Territory Karl Oskar and Kristina were to begin again as tillers of the soil; they must begin their lives anew.

During the journey their hands had rested. Often they had wished to have something to do. Now all at once the settler's innumerable chores crowded upon them; all were important, but all were not equally important; all could not be performed at one time, some must be put off. To find shelter, warmth, and food for the winter at hand—these were the most urgent tasks and took precedence over all others.

For the time being they settled in their shanty, much smaller than Anders Mansson's cabin, but now they were only six people instead of sixteen, and this hut was their own. In the center of the earth floor sat the large clothes chest, half as long as the shanty itself and occupying much of the space. At home it had been called the America chest, here it was called the Swedish chest. It was their one piece of furniture in their first American home. The chest bore the scars of its emigration adventure; it had been used roughly on the journey, in New York one corner had been smashed in, it was marred and scratched all over. But within its oaken planks, held together with heavy iron bands, it had protected its owner's indispensable belongings. Men who had had to handle the chest, lifting it by its clumsy iron handles, had been surprised by its weight, and cursed and complained about what it might contain.

The clothes chest contained exactly the articles which the owners could not be without if they were to survive in the wilderness—so thought Kristina as she now unpacked them all. How could they withstand the winter's cold without the woolen garments she now lifted from the chest? Camphor and lavender had protected them against moths and mildew; she found to her satisfaction that all the pieces of clothing were unharmed, though they had been packed this long time, from spring to autumn. Carefully Kristina handled woolen jackets, wadmal coats, linen sheets. She could have caressed the well-known pieces of clothing from home, in gratefulness that they had followed her out here, that they were ready for her now that she would need them. And it seemed almost incredible that they could be here with her in these foreign surroundings, so far away from home; they were like strangers here, they belonged to another home, in another country.

It was so long since she had packed the chest, she could not remember what was in it, and now she found objects she had not expected; she made discoveries, many times she was pleasantly surprised: Did she pack *that?* Had she brought along *this* also? What luck!

She found her carding combs, her wool shears, her sewing basket with balls of yarn, knitting needles, tallow candles which she herself had dipped last Christmas, her tablecloth of whole linen, woven by herself as part of her dowry, the small bottle of Hoffman's Heart-Aiding Drops, children's playthings. All these came now as unexpected gifts, at a moment when she needed them. She was most pleased when she found the swingletree which Karl Oskar had decorated with red tulips—his betrothal gift to her: through this her youth was brought back to her, such a long time ago, she thought—her betrothal time.

In the Swedish chest were also Karl Oskar's carpenter tools; without them he could not have attempted to build a house for his family. Had he known how expensive tools were out here, he would have brought along much more edge iron: planes, augers, chisels, more axes. He also regretted not having more powder and shot, for it was costly

239

to load a gun here. For once Robert had shown foresight —his hooks, fish traps, nets, and other fishing gear would come in handy for them, living as they did on the shores of a lake.

The odor of the camphor and lavender that had kept the packed clothing in good condition filled the shanty as the lid of the chest was thrown open. It was pleasing to Kristina—it smelled like *home*.

It had been in late March that she packed the America chest—it was in early September that she unpacked the Swedish chest. During all the months in between she had been moving; she had traveled from spring to autumn, and she had experienced so much during this time that it seemed more like years than months since she had left home. Was it only last spring that she had packed her possessions? To Kristina it seemed the packing had taken place in another life, in another world. And it was indeed true—they were living a new life, in a new world.

Many were the memories awakened in her as she unpacked the chest; every object was linked with some happening at home, some experience with people close to her, friends or relatives. The wool cards had been given her by her mother when she moved into her own home, the sewing basket she had bought at the fair the first spring she was married, the knitting needles had occupied her hands during winter evenings in company of friends around the fire. So many intimate things were here thrust upon her; from the old clothes chest she now unpacked Sweden.

And with these objects came many thoughts of little value to her—rather, they annoyed her. She knew that nothing could be more futile than to let her thoughts wander back and dwell on what once had been and never could be again. Her family must begin anew, they could not bury themselves in memories of the past. She had taken it as a warning when Karl Oskar had said: If their thoughts were too much on their old homeland, on things they had once and for all given up, this would hinder their success in the new country.

From that point of view, it had been disturbing to open the lid of the America chest—now the Swedish chest: their old home and their life there had thrust itself upon her; yet, it was as distant as ever.

But the chest *was* the only piece of furniture in the hut.

240

And now she used it as a table; she spread food on the lid, and it became the family's gathering place at every meal. And the old homeland odor remained; the chest occupied the center of the shanty and smelled of camphor and lavender—a lingering reminder of Sweden.

2

Karl Oskar arranged his work according to the sun; he began early, before it was too warm, rested during the noon heat, and continued his work in the afternoon and into the cool evening as late as daylight would permit him. He was felling pines near the stream for house timbers. He felled the straightest and most suitable trees, stripping them of bark so the logs would dry while there was still warmth in the air. He cut young lindens, which he rough-hewed for a roof and floor boards; he dug sod for the roof, he gathered and dried the birch and pine bark that was to hold the sod, he collected the stringy linden bark for ropes, he burned debris and cleared roads, he built a simple baking oven near the shanty, he dug a hole in the ground where they could keep food in a cool place and where it was protected from wild animals and insects, and he daily performed innumerable small chores. But even though he used the last reflected rays of the sun, the day was not long enough for him, he wished to do still more. And he complained because he had only two hands.

"Be satisfied with your two hands!" Kristina said. "You might have had only one."

So much of the work was new to him, he was constantly learning new ways, he was ever improving the knowledge of his hands. All that specially skilled workmen had done for him at home, he himself must do here as best he could. Necessity was the best teacher, his father had said, and necessity forced a settler to try his skill at all kinds of work.

Karl Oskar had always learned easily and quickly imitated others. Now everything depended on his hands' knowledge—unable to help himself with his hands, a settler would soon perish in this wilderness.

Kristina too must learn new ways: how to make beds without bedsteads, wash without proper soap, keep food without a cellar. And she was much concerned about their clothing, badly worn during the journey; some garments

241

were completely worn out, all were soiled, all must be
darned and patched, mended and washed. Her bridal quilt
had fared ill in the hold of the *Charlotta,* it was spotted
and torn and would never be the same; Kristina took this
very hard. The working clothes for every member of the
family needed attention, they must last a long time; she
must be careful of every single garment, as she thought it
might be a long time before new things could be obtained
to cover their bodies.

Their soft-soap jar from Sweden was empty, and Kristina could wash nothing clean. Karl Oskar tried to help
her: he boiled a mixture of rabbit fat and ashes, he
thought this might be strong enough to eat away the dirt.
And most of the dirt did wash away in the soap he had invented.

Kristina's greatest concern was to keep dirt and vermin
away, to keep grownups and children clean. During their
journey cleanliness had been neglected, and this had troubled her. One evening as she sat outside the shanty and
watched Karl Oskar and Robert, who busied themselves
stacking firewood, the thought came to her that she should
cut the hair of her unkempt menfolk; they looked uncivil-
ized, bringing shame to all Sweden, should anyone happen
to see them.

She went inside and fetched her wool shears: "Come
here! Your heads need attention!"

"You—a woman—you can't cut men's hair!" exclaimed
Robert scornfully.

"I used to shear the sheep at home."

"Hmm," grunted Karl Oskar. He took off his cap and
sat down on the chopping block. "Better begin with the
old ram, then."

"When I shear frisky rams I usually tie their legs. Shall
I do the same with you?"

Kristina's wool shears mowed mercilessly through Karl
Oskar's thick locks, which fell from his head and gathered
in piles on the ground. She guessed he gave at least a
pound of wool.

Karl Oskar hardly recognized his own head as he
looked in a piece of mirror-glass; his hair was cut in steps,
marking each shear bite, just the way sheep looked after
the shearing. But he was well pleased to be rid of the thick
mat of hair which had been uncomfortable in the heat.

Robert sorely felt the degradation of having his hair cut by a woman. But he insisted that Kristina cut his hair as short as she possibly could; this would save his scalp from the knives of the Indians. Samuel Nojd, the pelt man in Taylors Falls, had related how some of his companions a few years earlier had been scalped by the savages; only one man in the group had escaped, and this because he was completely bald; the Indians thought he had already been scalped.

Robert's hair was cut according to his instructions, and his head looked something like a scraped and scalded hog; this would undoubtedly make the Indians believe he had no scalp. But he would not be secure for long, his hair soon would grow out again.

Kristina also cut Johan's and Harald's hair quite short, but this was less from fear of Indians than of head lice, which were thus discouraged from building their nests.

The children had improved so much since the journey's end, she was happy to see. Their little bodies and limbs were now quite firm, their eyes clear, and their pale cheeks had bloomed since arriving here. They spent most of their time in the open. Food at the moment was fresh and plentiful; wild fruit and berries grew in abundance near the shanty. The family fare had lately changed fundamentally: they had fresh meat at every meal, fish or game which they seldom had enjoyed in Sweden, except on rare occasions. The countryside abounded with rabbits, which supplied most of the meat, as well as fat for many uses. Robert learned to catch them by hand; he ran after the fat animals until they tired and crouched, when he grabbed them. In this way he saved powder and shot for larger game. Ducks and wild geese kept to the lake and could only be obtained through shooting; but it was child's play to catch fish in Lake Ki-Chi-Saga, where life bubbled below the surface. They would put a pot over the fire, go down to the lake, and return with the fish before the water was boiling. They caught pike and perch, but these were the only fish they recognized. The pike had black backs with yellow stripes, and a narrower body than those at home. The perch had enormous jaws and were less tasty than the Swedish variety. Among the unfamiliar fish suitable for food was one called whitefish, delicious either boiled or fried. Whitefish resembled roach in color, but had longish bodies like pike.

243

The catfish was ugly, with long whiskers, and purred like a cat when pulled out of water. A short, fat fish, the color of perch but with blood-red eyes, was called bass, Anders Mansson told them.

One morning at daybreak as Karl Oskar stepped out of the shanty, his eyes fell on an unusually large stag with immense antlers drinking from the lake less than fifty yards from him. He picked up his gun—always near by and loaded with a bullet—and fired at the buck. The animal fell where it stood, shot through the heart. The fallen stag with the multipronged antlers was heavy, as much as Karl Oskar could handle by himself, but he managed to hang his prey by the hind legs to a pole between two trees. He skinned and drew the animal before Kristina was up; when she came out to prepare the morning meal, Karl Oskar surprised her by pointing to his morning kill—she had not even heard the shot! He cut a few slices from the carcass, which she fried for their breakfast.

The weather was still warm, and meat would not keep long; if only they had had vessels to salt it in, they could have had meat for the whole winter.

At Lake Ki-Chi-Saga there was little concern about meat at this time of year. But bread they must use sparingly. They had paid dearly for the flour in Taylors Falls. Kristina herself cut the loaf and divided the slices at each meal: the menfolk doing the heavy work rated two slices each, while she and the chilrren had to be satisfied with one slice apiece. This made eight slices to a meal and left little of a loaf. The flour in the barrel shrank with alarming speed; here it was easier to find meat for the bread than bread for the meat.

Anders Mansson had given them a bushel of potatoes, and they had bespoken a barrel for their winter supply. Butter, cheese, and eggs they must do without, since they had no cows or chickens. And milk! As yet they had no milk. Always, it seemed, they missed the milk. The children often pleaded for it, for sweet milk, as they had during the long journey.

Kristina looked out over the vast, grassy meadow: there grew fodder for thirty cows! But they owned not one. If she had only one—one lone cow to milk mornings and evenings! In Sweden they had owned cows but were often short of fodder—here they had fodder but no cows. Why must this be so? And how could her children survive the winter in good health without milk?

Why hadn't Karl Oskar thought about this? He was the one who managed and decided for all of them. She spoke to him: "You must get a cow, to give us milk for the winter."

To her surprise, he didn't answer at once; he turned away, embarrassed.

"Why haven't you bought one already?"

"Kristina—I should have told you before. I am sorry. . . ."

He looked pained, as though pressed to admit something shameful. He looked away from her and spoke with obvious effort: "We have nothing to buy a cow with."

It wasn't easy for him, but now he had managed to say it; he should have told her before, since she would have to know sooner or later.

"Nothing to buy it with! Are things as bad for us as that?"

"Most of our money is already gone."

And he explained to her: When they arrived in Taylors Falls he had had ninety silver dollars in his belt. Ten dollars he had had to give the greedy wolves who freighted their goods from Stillwater; besides the barrel of flour and other foodstuff, he had bought a load of boards, some nails, a felling ax, and a few essentials for the building; these supplies had cost more than fifty dollars; now he had only thirty-eight dollars and a few cents left in his purse. Yes, they had had great expenses, everything they had bought was unchristian dear; and yet, Anders Mansson had not requested any payment for either their lodging with him or the loan of the oxen. He must repay him by doing favors in return, by and by. Yes, the money had gone awfully fast. But he had bought only essentials, things they couldn't do without.

It had originally been his intention to buy both oxen and cows as soon as they arrived. But he hadn't known the price of cattle; a good cow cost thirty dollars, almost as much as they had left. And he still had to buy a few essentials for the house-building if they expected to have shelter for the winter. And next spring he would have to buy seed

245

grain. He must lay aside money for the seed. If they had nothing to plant next spring, all their troubles in emigrating would have been in vain.

That was how things were with them. They had already spent so much that a cow was out of the question; and yet, he had been as careful as he could with his outlays.

"Have I bought anything unimportant, Kristina?"

"No—I can't say that you have. But a cow that gives milk is as important as anything else."

"Not as important as the house!"

"But a whole, long, milkless winter, Karl Oskar! How can the children live through the winter without a drop of milk?"

And she added: The children had lately gained in weight and strength, but without milk, there might be nothing left of their little bodies by spring. She had heard him say many times that above all they must keep healthy through the winter. To do this, they needed a cow. They had been poor at home, but they had always had a drop of milk for the children, all year round.

Karl Oskar repeated: First of all they must build a house; they could get along without a cow, but not without a house. If the children were given other food they would survive the winter without milk, but if they were forced to live in the shanty, they would freeze to death. And she mustn't forget that they awaited yet another tender life— that one, too, would need a warm shelter, that new life must be saved through the winter. They couldn't live in a shed with a newborn baby through the winter; they couldn't live in this hovel where daylight shone through the cracks, where it would be as cold inside as outside.

He was right; but she insisted that she too was right. They must save their lives, and the question was how best to do this. Timbered walls gave protection against cold, milk against hunger and illness. They needed the cow as well as the house, she was not going to give in on this point—they must have the indispensable cow. Couldn't he at least look about for one? Now that they had land, mightn't they be allowed some delay in payment, wouldn't people trust them?

He answered, as yet they had no paper on their claim; an impoverished squatter was not trusted for anything out here. The Scot in Taylors Falls wouldn't give him credit for a penny's worth. Moreover, how could they expect to be trusted, strangers as they were? No one knew what sort of people they were. Here in America a newcomer must show that he could help himself, before he could expect help from others.

Kristina thought this sounded uncharitable; a person unable to help himself needed help above all others.

"Isn't there *any* way we could get a cow?"

"It looks bad. I can't buy without money."

But she had made up her mind to have her own way, that he understood. She said, as a rule he made the decisions alone, but there were times when he must listen to her. He had persuaded her to emigrate.—She had never before reminded him of that, but he often reminded himself of it and felt the responsibility he had assumed. If she had wanted to, she could have said: You never told me we would be without milk out here! You never mentioned in advance that we must be without a cow. Had you mentioned that fact the time you persuaded me, then perhaps I mightn't be here now.

Karl Oskar thought long over her words about the children and the milkless winter. It could be a question of life or death. He handled their money, he was the one who had to choose—and the choice stood between two indispensables; there was no choice. How could he decide—when life or death might depend on his decision?

3

Robert was not very deft with his hands, he had never learned anything about carpentry, he had no feeling for working with wood. Karl Oskar could rely on him for only the simplest chores. Together they had felled the timbers and prepared the logs, and after this was finished Karl Oskar told his brother to grub hoe the meadow. His feeling was that the two of them, as brothers, ought to stick together, that Robert should remain and help him until he was of age and could take a claim for himself; he would pay his brother for this as soon as he could. Robert was now eighteen, in a few years he could choose his own farm from the thousands of acres that lay here waiting on the shores of Lake Ki-Chi-Saga.

"I'll never take land!" exclaimed Robert with conviction.

"What do you mean? Wouldn't you like to be on your own?"

"Yes! That is exactly what I want! Here in America everyone decides for himself. That's why I wanted to come here."

Karl Oskar stared at his brother in surprise: Didn't Robert want to be the owner of one hundred and sixty acres of this good earth? Was he so shiftless that he wouldn't claim all the land he could on such favorable conditions?

"If you don't take land before it's claimed, you'll regret it," Karl Oskar insisted.

"Maybe. But I don't think so."

And Robert thought to himself as he said this: Karl Oskar was not his guardian, he had never promised to serve as farm hand for his brother here in America; he had paid for his emigration with his own inheritance, which Karl Oskar had kept; he didn't owe his brother anything, he was not bound to him in any way.

Yet here his brother put a hoe in his hand and asked him to break land! He felt almost as though he were back home again, in his old farm-hand service; he had cleared land many long days, back in Sweden—now it was the same here. The tools he had thrown away in Sweden he had had to pick up again. And the American grub hoe Karl Oskar had bought was much heavier than the one at home. What advantage had there been in his emigration if everything was to be the same as before? To stoop all day long until his back ached in the evenings—this he had done enough of in Sweden. He had not emigrated to America in order to hoe.

Robert could not understand his brother's joy in squatting on a piece of land that required so much labor—a patch to plow, seed, and harvest, year after year, as long as he was able, all his life. A patch of soil he could never get rid of. Robert only wanted to do the kind of work that would liberate him from work. Only the rich man had no master, only the rich were free to do as they pleased; and no one would grow rich from hoeing the earth, even if he hoed to the end of eternity.

Never, never would Robert become a squatter. While he hoed for his brother he kept listening to his left ear: through that ear the Atlantic Ocean had called to him, and he had listened to the call and crossed the ocean. He had come here to get away from cruel masters, from the servant law, from drudgery with hoe and spade—and now he turned the clods and lived the same life he had fled from. Again he heard the humming call in his ear: *Come! Don't stay here!*

In New York Harbor he had seen a ship with a red banner, its soft-sounding girl-name beckoning him: *Angelica.* In his ear he could now hear that name again, the name of the speedy, copper-plated ship with her singing and dancing passengers. Why hadn't he stepped on board and joined them? Why hadn't he gone with the *Angelica?*

In the New World there were other fields than farmers' fields. And Robert listened so intently to his own ear that he didn't hear when Karl Oskar spoke to him; his brother had to repeat his words.

"Have you lost your hearing?"

"No. But I only hear in English."

The fact was that Robert would not admit his hearing was bad. He now explained to Karl Oskar that he tried to close his ears to the Swedish language, he wished he could listen to English only; in that way he would learn the language sooner.

Robert also wished to consult a doctor about his deafness, but he must wait until he could speak English fluently in order to explain the nature of his ear illness. In the language book there was not a single word about bad hearing under the heading: *Conversation with a Physician.* There was instruction about what to say when seeking a doctor for malaria: *I shiver and my head aches. I have vomited the whole night.* Another sentence concerned immigrants with sprained ankles; there was also one for those with irregular voiding, and lastly one for people who didn't know what was the matter with them, since they were sick in every way. For immigrants with other ailments there was no help to be found in the book; it was of no use to one who must say: *I don't hear well with my left ear.*

And a youth of barely eighteen would feel ashamed to

go to a doctor and say: "My hearing is getting bad." At the height of his youth to admit that he was hard of hearing, like an old man of eighty!

He still hoped that the climate of North America would heal his ear. This he knew, however: the weather in Minnesota Territory was so far of little help. His ear alone told him so; in fact, it told him to leave! He must travel farther, farther west.

There were other fields in this new land where he now labored with his grub hoe—there were gold fields in the New World.

Why must he hoe turf here, when in another place he could hoe gold? What pleasure could he get from crops that might grow here? Why hadn't he sought the fields where a crop of gold could be harvested? A gold harvester need not work in the earth year after year. He would get rich from one single crop—he would become free.

And again and again Robert heard a song that had remained in his ear, a song he had heard sung in a foreign language by the deck hands on the Mississippi steamer while darkness fell over the broad river—a song about the winds of the earth and the waves of the sea. It was the song of promised freedom his ear had sung to him, long ago in Sweden; then the ocean's roar in his ear had called him to cross the sea: *Come!*

This time too he must obey that call.

4

Now in late September the weather was cooler. The air no longer felt oppressive, it was easier to breathe. It was fine working weather.

But climatic changes were violent and sudden; without any warning a thunderstorm would blow up, booming and shaking the earth. The bolts blinded one's eyes, the rain fell, lashing the face like a whip, pouring from the heavens in barrelfuls; in no time at all, every hole and hollow would be filled with water, while the stream rose over its banks in its rush toward the lake. And when the wind blew, it swept across the ground as mercilessly as a giant broom with its handle in the heavens. No weather in America was just right; all was immoderate.

As autumn progressed the leaves of the trees changed

250

color, making the forest seem more beautiful than ever. There stood the red mountain ash, surrounded by brown walnut trees, the green aspens among the golden-yellow lindens. The oak—the master tree of the forest—still kept its leaves green, as did the aspen and the poplar. Here grew white oak, black oak, red oak, and now they could recognize the different types. The white oak grew in Sweden also, its leaves turned brown in fall. The leaves of the other oaks now took on a dark-red sheen resembling blossoms; the settlers said that it looked as though these oaks bloomed in autumn.

The meadow grass remained as fresh and green as before. It bothered Karl Oskar that this splendid fodder would wither away to no use. He said to Kristina, if only they could send home a few loads to the poor cow his parents kept in Korpamoen!

It had been impressed upon him ever since childhood that the growth of the earth must be tended and gathered. Once, as a small boy, he had stepped on the head of a rye sheaf; his father had then unbuttoned his pants and switched him with a handful of birch twigs: he must learn to respect the earth's growth.

Now he made a handle for the scythe blade he had brought from Sweden and cut the grass on the plot he intended to hoe. Here he could mow as wide a sweep as his arms could reach, here he need not rake the straws together in swaths, the hay fell in one long thick swath behind him. In a few side swings, he had enough for one feeding of a full-grown cow; in a day, he could gather enough fodder to feed a cow through the winter. In Korpamoen, he had struggled with the hay harvest a whole month, picking the short thin blades from between the stones with the point of his scythe. He had labored from sunup to sundown, mowed and sharpened and cut against stones—yet he had gathered such a small amount of hay that he had been forced to half-starve his cattle.

As yet he had no cattle to feed, but he couldn't help saving some of this good fodder. It might be of some use. And he made a row of haystacks along the shore. It was good hay weather; what he cut one day, he turned the next, and stacked the third day. Stacked hay was not as good as barn hay, and he decided to build a shed later in the fall after the house was ready.

251

His work with the scythe over this even ground was a joy, and every day he felt more and more remorseful over the six years he had wasted on his stone acres in Korpamoen. He had left that farm poorer than when he took over; it had gone backward instead of ahead for him; he had put in thousands of days of futile labor on the paternal home: these were lost years. He had wasted his youthful strength in the land where he was born, and he realized that had he instead spent those six years of labor in this country, he would by now have been a well-to-do farmer.

However, at twenty-seven he still had his manhood years ahead of him, and his manhood strength he would give to the new country. Here he would earn something in return; here he worked with a greater zest than at home, because the reward was greater. He felt his ability to work had increased since settling here, his physical strength had grown. The very sight of the fertile land stimulated him and egged him on to work. Also, he enjoyed a sense of freedom that increased his endeavor to such a degree that he was surprised at himself when evening came and he saw all he had done during the course of one single day: that much he had never managed in one day in Sweden!

However great the inconveniences out here, he felt vastly happier than he had in the old place. Here no one ruled him, no officials insisted that he bow to them, no one demanded that he obediently and humbly follow a given path, no one interfered with his doings, no one advised him, no one rebuked him for refusing advice. He had seen no one in authority, nobody had come to tell him what he must do; here he had met not a single person to whom he must defer; he was his own minister and sheriff and master.

At home, people struggled to get ahead of each other until they were full of evil wounds that never would heal; their minds grew morbid, festering boils corroded their souls; they went about bloated by grudges and jealousy. Most of them were afraid, bowing in cowardice to the great lords who sat on high and ruled as they saw fit. No one dared decide for himself, no one dared walk upright; it was too much of an effort, their backs were too weak. They dared not be free, were incapable of freedom. That required courage, entailed responsibility and worry as well; anyone trying to decide for himself in the old country

252

was derided, mocked, slandered, pushed out. For the Swedish people could not endure someone who attempted what the rest of them dared not do, or were incapable of.

Here no one cared what he did, nor need he care what others did. Here he could move as he pleased, with his body and with his soul. Nowhere could he be freer than here. Here a farmer ruled himself—though in return, a demand was put on him that might scare many away: he must take care of himself—he must survive with only the help of his hands.

But a man unable to improve his situation, with such generous freedom, such fertile soil—such a man was good for nothing in the world.

XVI

At Home on Lake Ki-Chi-Saga

The homesteader's ax cut its way through the land—
through trunk and timber, through beam and board,
through shingle and shake, through branch and bramble.
Clearing, splitting, shaping, it cut its way. There was the
felling ax with the long handle and the thin blade, eating
its way through the heart of the tree, leaving the stump
heads even and smooth. There was the dressing ax with
the short handle and the broad blade, shaving trunks and
timbers while the chips flew in all directions; there was the
splitting ax with the heavy hammer and the thick blade,
forcing its blunt nose into the wood, splitting logs into
planks and scantlings. Then there was the short, light,
hand ax, clearing the thickets, brambles, and bushes. Narrow axes and broad, thin and thick, light and heavy. From
early morning to late evening the echo of the axes sounded
over the shores of Lake Ki-Chi-Saga—a new sound, the
sound of peaceful builders in the wilderness.

With the ax as foremost tool—with the ax first, with the
ax last—the new home was raised.

Karl Oskar and Kristina had chosen the site for their
log house among some large sugar maples at the edge of
the forest on the upper meadow, the distance of a long
gunshot from the lake shore. Here their home would be
protected by the forest on three sides, while the fourth

254

overlooked the bay of the lake. Their house was to be twenty feet long and twelve feet wide, and placed the same way as farmhouses in Sweden: the gables to east and west, the long sides to north and south. The back of the house would then be toward the forest and the cold north winds, while the front opened on the lake and the warm south sun.

Karl Oskar had promised to help Danjel and Jonas Petter, and they in turn would help him raise his house the second week in October. The green, peeled logs were too heavy for two men to handle; three or four would be needed. But Karl Oskar alone prepared all the timbers and laid a footing for his house. For the foundation, he selected the thickest pines he had cut, and with the aid of Anders Mansson's oxen, dragged the clumsy logs to the building site. For floor boards he used young linden trees which he split in two, to be laid with the flat side upward. He hewed and smoothed the edges of these to make them fit as tight as possible, in order to avoid big cracks in the floor. For roof boards he cut straight elms—there were enough trees to choose from in the forest, and he selected what he thought most suitable for each need. Oak logs would have lasted longer for house timbers, but they were hard to work with, and pine would last long enough. He had no intention of living in this house of peeled logs for all eternity.

He cut sod for the roofing—sod was used for roofing at home in Smaland, and it took less time than to split shakes. Kristina said she was afraid the sod might not withstand the violent rains here—the earth might blow away in the merciless winds. Karl Oskar replied that he would put on shakes next summer if the roof did not withstand the weather. She must not worry, he would see to it that they did not sleep under a leaking roof.

He had to buy odds and ends for the building and carry them on his back from Taylors Falls. He bought everything in Mr. Abbott's store, except sash, which he ordered from Stillwater. Everything of iron was absurdly expensive; he paid a full dollar for a pair of hinges for the door. And the price of nails was equally high. But wood could substitute for iron in many instances, and he made pegs of ash—in Sweden used for rake teeth and handle wedges—to take the place of nails. Without cash, he was forced to be inventive. Each time he had to buy something he searched his mind: Couldn't he make it with his own hands?

October—the almanac's slaughter month—had arrived, but the only slaughter which took place at Lake Ki-Chi-Saga was the occasional killing of rabbits and deer. The days sped by, the weeks flew, only one month remained of the autumnal season of grace, with its mild weather, permitting them to live in the shanty. Winter was fast approaching, and Karl Oskar had promised his wife their new log house would be ready to move into in good time before her childbed.

The third week in November, Kristina's forty weeks would be up, if she had counted aright. It seemed to her as though this pregnancy had lasted longer than any of the previous ones; she had been through so much during this tedious year, her twenty-fifth. She had gone through the usual period of expectancy during a hard journey, carrying the child within her from Sweden to the new land. Perhaps this was why she felt the period had been longer this time than any of the others. And now she was as big as the time she had carried the twins; she wondered if she would again give birth to two lives. As things were with them at the moment, twins would be inconvenient; she had not even had time to prepare swaddling clothes for one baby.

Her movements became more cumbersome every day, every day she felt heavier. She could walk only short distances; her chores were confined to the shanty and its immediate vicinity. But she never let her children entirely out of sight. At home she had let them run free, but here she never knew what kind of snakes might hide in the thick, tall grass; what kind of biting, stinging, flying creatures infested the air. All around the cabin she saw hordes of creeping, crawling little animals she had never found at home, and as yet she could not distinguish between the dangerous ones and the harmless. In the meadow, the men had killed snakes with yellow and silver-gray stripes; these vipers lifted their egg-shaped heads from the ground, open mouthed, their blood-red stingers protruding exactly like those of the poisonous snakes at home. She tried to keep the children where the grass had been mowed and where they could watch where they stepped. A few times the children had been frightened by a gray, furry animal the size of a dog, with thick legs and a short tail, which they thought was a lynx or small wolf. Large, fat, gray-brown squirrels called gophers played around the shanty in great numbers, their heads sticking up everywhere in the grass; one could hardly avoid stepping on them, and they looked as if they might bite; they frightened the children, but they were harmless. There were flying squirrels, too, with skin stretched between their legs. They flew about in the trees, waving their long tails like sails. They came and ate out of one's hand, like tame animals; the children liked them.

The little creature who made the persistent screeching sound had at last been discovered, and they had been told its name—cricket. It was gray-brown, smaller than a grasshopper, and difficult to see on the ground; its wings were so small it couldn't fly but jumped about like a grasshopper. This small thing screeched loudly all night through, and because of its noise they called it "the screechhopper." If a cricket happened to get into the shanty at night, Kristina had to find it and kill it before she could get a wink's sleep.

However small an animal might be in America, it always caused trouble. But the rodents, devouring Kristina's food, were the greatest nuisance of all. Rats and ratlike vermin were everywhere, running in and out of their holes, hiding underground. Kristina found it did little good to hide food in a hole in the ground, she still found rat dirt in it, and her heart ached when she had to throw away rat-eaten pieces of food. If only they could get hold of a cat to catch the rats. But Karl Oskar had no idea where they might find one. In Taylors Falls, he had seen only one cat; probably cats were as expensive as other animals; perhaps a cat would cost five dollars, like a hen. It would be a long time before they would have all the domestic animals they needed.

One day Johan came rushing into the shanty holding tight in his arms a small, black-furred animal: "Look Mother! I've found a cat!"

The boy held out the animal toward Kristina. The long-haired creature had a white streak along its back, and it was the size of a common cat.

"Is it a wildcat?" Kristina asked.

The little furry beast fretted and sputtered, Johan had great difficulty holding it. He said he had found it in a hole outside the cottage.

"You wanted a cat, Mother! But we have no milk for it."

His prey stared at him, its eyes glittering with fury.

"Be careful! He might scratch you!" Then Kristina sniffed the air: a horrible smell overwhelmed her.

"Have you done something in your pants, boy?"

"No!"

"Then you must have stepped in something."

She inspected the clothing and shoes of the boy but could see nothing to explain the smell.

"Is it the cat?"

"No, he isn't dirty either."

And she could see that its coat was clean. Johan looked at the paws, but these too were clean.

"No, he hasn't stepped in anything either."

Kristina put her nose to the little animal. Such a disgusting smell overcame her that she jumped backward, almost suffocating. The cat was alive, yet it smelled as if it had been dead a long time. She held her nostrils with her thumb and forefinger, crying: "Throw the beast out!"

"But it's a cat!" Johan wailed.

"Throw it out this minute!"

"But he will catch the rats. . . ."

She grabbed the boy by the arms and pushed him and his pet out through the door. Johan loosened his hold, and the animal jumped to the ground and disappeared around the corner of the shanty.

Johan looked at his empty hands and began to cry; the beautiful cat with a white stripe on its back and tail, he had caught it for his mother and now it was gone and he couldn't catch it again.

Kristina was rid of the nasty-smelling animal, but the evil stench remained in the hut. And little Johan smelled as bad as the cat! She told him to stay outside until the smell was gone.

When Karl Oskar came home he stopped in the door, sniffing: "What smells so bad in here?"

"Johan dragged in some creature."

She described the animal, and guessed it must be a wildcat.

"Disgusting the way cats smell in America!" she said. "You can't have them in the house here."

"It must have been a baby skunk," Karl Oskar said. "Their piss stinks, I have heard. I guess it pissed on him."

And he pinched the boy on the ear: hadn't he told him not to touch any animals or try to catch them? He must leave them alone, big or little, however tame they seemed.

He turned to Kristina: "Now we have to wash the child's clothes or we'll never get rid of the stink."

Kristina undressed the boy to his bare skin. Then she wrapped him in one of his father's coats, which hung all the way to the ground and made him stumble when he walked. His own clothes were boiled in ash lye. They had to boil them a long time before the smell of skunk disappeared. But in the shanty the odor remained. The baby skunk had left behind him such a strong smell that for weeks it lingered; it drove the settlers outside, and for many days they ate in the open, near the fire where the food was prepared.

All this trouble had been caused by a little cat that was no cat at all. If the animals hereabouts didn't bite with their teeth or scratch with their claws, Kristina said, they smelled so bad that they drove people from their homes. They must all be doubly careful in the future.

Indeed, they must be on their guard about everything in North America.

2

It was about one hour's walk from Lake Ki-Chi-Saga to the settlement of Danjel and Jonas Petter. When settling down, Danjel Andreasson had said he did not wish to live in a nameless place, nor in a place with a heathenish name. He had therefore named his home New Karragarde, after the old family farm in Sweden, and it was his belief that through the revival of this name his old family homestead would blossom to new life in the New World. The little lake near his home he called Lake Gennesaret, a reminder of the Holy Land; the shores of Lake Gennesaret in the Biblical land had once carried the imprint of Jesus' footsteps; the Lord had wandered about there, preaching the Gospel, and His disciples had enjoyed good fishing in its water. The lake near Danjel's house resem-

259

bled the Biblical Gennesaret in that it was blessed with many fish. A brook emptying into the lake he called Childron.

The men had many errands back and forth, and often walked the road between the two settlements, but the women seldom met after they had settled on different claims. It was dangerous for a woman to walk alone through the wilderness; besides, Kristina was unable to walk any distance at this time. Week after week passed and no one came. No callers arrived at the hut on Lake Ki-Chi-Saga. The young wife missed people, she looked for callers and awaited guests, without exactly knowing whom she looked for or might expect.

One day Swedish Anna came to visit them; she accompanied Karl Oskar, who had been in Taylors Falls, and she stayed overnight. Kristina had met her only once—the woman from Ostergotland was practically unknown to her, and yet she felt she had known her for years: someone had come to whom she could talk. Swedish Anna brought a coat she had made for little Harald; she was fond of children, she had had two of her own in Sweden, but they were both dead, she said. Kristina was touched to the bottom of her heart by the gift, and she wished her guest could have remained several days, even though she could offer her only a poor sleeping place in a shed. When Anna had left, Kristina thought how kind God had been in creating some people in such a way that they could speak the same language.

She missed her countrymen who now lived at a distance —and most of all, she found, she missed Ulrika. She wondered about this: she actually felt lonesome for the Glad One! How could this be? Now she realized she had enjoyed Ulrika's company. There was something stimulating about her, she was never downhearted; many times during the journey Kristina had felt Ulrika's presence as a help: she realized it now. And during the final weeks they had grown quite intimate. Ulrika had confided to her all she had had to go through in life, ever since that day when, as a four-year-old orphan, she had been sold at auction to the rich peasant of Alarum, called the King of Alarum. He had been known in the village as her kind, good foster father. When she was fourteen years old, he had raped her, and for years afterward, as often as he felt inclined. Each time she had received two pennies from the "King," but when she had saved enough for a daler, her foster mother had taken the money away from her, saying she had stolen it and ought to be put in prison.

And she *had* been put in prison: the honored and worthy farmer had taught her how to sell her body, she had become the parish whore, banished from church and Sacrament, and at last imprisoned for unlawful communion. But the King of Alarum—who had raped a child and used her for his aging body's lust—when he died, he had been given the grandest funeral ever seen in Ljuder Parish.

Kristina could remember how as a little girl she had been to the church when this funeral took place. The church had been filled to the last pew, people standing in the aisles, the organ had played long and feelingly, the coffin had been decked with the finest wreaths, and the dean himself had stood at the altar, lauding the dead one and extolling his good deeds in life. The memory of the "King" still was held in respect at home, and his tombstone was the tallest one in the whole churchyard.

Then the truth about him had been revealed to Kristina. And Ulrika said that she was only one of his victims, he had seduced and ruined many girls before they were of age. But the mighty ones could do whatever they wanted to in that hellhole, Sweden. Two of the jurors at her trial ought to have been in prison themselves, they had stolen money entrusted to them as guardians of orphans; and one owed her four daler for having committed what was known as whoring, not punishable in men. This she had told the judge and had pointed out that the law ought to be the same for all. But he gave her fourteen days extra on bread and water for having insulted the jury. And she had never received the four daler.

Ulrika was straightforward and said whatever came to her mind to whomsoever she met, even mighty lords. She could not help it, she was made that way. But in Sweden such honesty brought only misery; if you told the truth there, you were put in prison.

Having believed that justice ruled in her homeland, Kristina was deeply disturbed by Ulrika's confidence. How rash and unjust her condemnation of Ulrika had been! She had listened to what other women said about the Glad One. No woman had a right to judge Ulrika and

261

hold her in contempt unless she herself had been sold at auction as a four-year-old, and raped at fourteen. Kristina felt she could no longer rebuke Ulrika for her adultery before coming to live with Danjel. Vanity and self-righteousness were as sinful as whoring, and she had committed these sins many times. But that day in the steam wagon, when she had shared her food with the onetime parish harlot and her daughter, then her eyes had been opened: she had approached Ulrika, and Ulrika had approached her. When at last she had accepted Ulrika—something she felt now she should have done from the very beginning—she had discovered that this so-called bad woman was honest and could be a good friend.

Ulrika had changed, too, since people had changed their behavior toward her. Here she was no longer the parish whore. Here she was honored and treated like other women. Kristina was still bothered by the ugly words Ulrika liked to use, but now she knew they belonged to her old way of talking. The ugliest names invented for parts of men's and women's bodies, and for their conjugal acts, were part of the life she had led. The King of Alarum had taught them to her. But from Ulrika, Kristina learned that a person's way of speaking had nothing to do with that person's heart.

Now at Lake Ki-Chi-Saga, she discovered that she longed for Ulrika to come and visit her in her loneliness.

To the north lived the people who spoke her language; but in the other three directions there were no people of her own color. Their nearest neighbors were copper colored. The Indians had recently gathered in great numbers to make camp on one of the islands in Lake Ki-Chi-Saga, and every evening after dark she could see their fires. On that island now lived her nearest neighbors.

These Indians were said to be docile and peaceful, they would never commit atrocities against white people—but they were also said to be treacherous and unreliable, always watching their chance to scalp and kill the whites! Thus, the varying reports: they were kind, gave the settlers food, and helped them in need; they were bloodthirsty and cruel and blinded the eyes of their prisoners with spears before burning them in the campfires. They were as innocent as children, yet they murdered the settlers' wives and babies. How could a newcomer know which was the truth?

From time to time they could hear piercing, long-drawn-out yells from the Indian camp. Only wild beasts yelled like that. But these were not wolf howls, these were human sounds, and as such they were terrifying. These yells through the night would frighten the most courageous, and lying there in the shanty listening to them, the settlers were inclined to believe the evil things they had heard of the brown skins.

The immigrants on Lake Ki-Chi-Saga had met and escaped so many dangers on their journey that they could scarcely imagine any worse in store for them. Yet now it seemed that their settling here might be as calamitous as their journey. The wild, heathenish people in the neighborhood filled them with insecurity.

Almost every day Karl Oskar met Indians in the forest, but they had not spoken to him or annoyed him; they only seemed curious, stopping and staring at him. He guessed the Indians were inquisitive. One day, some of their women came to look at the shanty. They carried children in pouches on their backs. One old woman looked hideous, with a face like gray-brown, cracked clay; the mosquitoes hung in droves on her wrinkled face. All the women were thin and looked wretched. Kristina felt sorry for them and wondered if the Indian men tortured them. Comparing her situation with theirs, she felt fortunate in her poverty. These poor creatures lived in the lowliest hovels, under matting hung on a few raised poles; next to their pitiable shelters, her own hut was like a castle. She did not understand how they could survive the winters in such dwellings.

Karl Oskar felt it unwise to mingle with the Indians in this vast wilderness, and he did not intend to get too close to them. Probably they considered him an intruder. But he had not come here as a thief, he intended to obtain his land honestly from the government of the country, who in turn had bought it from the brown skins. The Indians were too lazy to cultivate the ground. The whites here called them lazy men. And since they did not wish to till the land themselves, they could hardly object if others came and did so. The tiller of the soil had a right to it above all others; it would be a cruel injustice to hungry people if this fertile land—capable of feeding so many— should be allowed to lie fallow, producing only wild grass.

In the end, the family decided, all they heard of the heathens indicated that they could not be trusted. Though now they left the settlers in peace, there was no assurance of future safety. Karl Oskar always carried his gun when he went into the forest, and he kept it at hand when working near the shanty.

The building of Danjel's house had begun, and now Karl Oskar went there to help, as Danjel would help him in return. One day while he was away, and Kristina was alone in the shanty, she suddenly was frightened into immobility: a face had appeared in the opening at the back of the shanty! At first she didn't realize it was a human face: it looked like a furry animal skin. She saw a black, thick, stringy mat of hair, a dark oily skin splotched with red streaks. But when she discovered something moving under the mat of hair—a pair of coal-black eyes peering at her—then she realized it was a human face looking in through the opening. Human eyes were looking at her. She fled outside with such a loud outcry that she frightened herself.

Robert heard her, in spite of his deafness, and came running from the clearing. As they looked through the shanty door, the face in the opening disappeared. Turning around, they saw an Indian running into the woods.

That evening, when Kristina told Karl Oskar about the Indian, he said he would send Robert to work on Danjel's house tomorrow. Now that he knew the savages were sneaking about their house, he wanted to stay close by; he dared not leave his family alone with the Indian camp so near.

It could be that the savages had no evil intentions, that they were only curious about the strangers who had moved in on their land—though no one could know for sure what they had in mind. But as Kristina listened to the outlandish yells from the camp on the island, she was filled with a deep sense of compassion. The Indians frightened her, but they were, after all, unchristian, they did not know their Creator, they did not know the difference between good and evil, they lived in darkness, according to their own limited knowledge—who could blame the poor creatures for anything? She herself could not condemn them. She was only grateful she had not been born one of them.

Here among the savages she could only trust to God's protection.

3

Unexpectedly they had a change in the weather. One morning they awakened in their hut shivering—frozen through and through by a cold wind. An icy northwester was sweeping through their shanty, they felt as though the walls had fallen down during the night, as if they were lying in the open. The merciless wind seemed to strip them naked, it penetrated their thick woolen clothing, pinched their skin until it hurt, clawed with sharp talons, and blew right into their bodies.

When they looked out through the door at this weather, it seemed as if the crust of the earth might blow away. The grass lay flat to the ground like water-combed hair on a head. At the edge of the forest great trees were blown over, the exposed roots stretching heavenward like so many arms. All the haystacks in the meadow had blown over. They wondered that their little shanty still stood.

Now they could not use their fireplace, which lay to windward of the storm; but they managed to make a fire on the lee side of an enormous oak trunk. When they walked against the wind, they had to stoop in order to move. The unrelenting northwester swept away anything not tied to the earth.

Kristina said that none among them had ever known what a wind was, until they came to North America.

The children were blue-red from the cold; Lill-Marta and Harald coughed, and the noses of all three were running. Kristina put an extra pair of woolen stockings on each of them and wrapped them in woolen garments; she herself bundled up as much as she could, until she felt wide as a barrel; she was now in her last month. But clothes did not help against this ferocious wind, big and little shivered and shook; nothing helped. In the daytime they could get some warmth from the fire behind the oak, but how were they to keep warm inside the shanty during the nights if this weather continued?

"Has the winter come so soon?" Kristina wondered.

"It couldn't come so suddenly," Karl Oskar said anxiously. "It would be too bad for us—the house not yet ready. . . ."

They had heard of the unexpected changes in temperature hereabouts, and that the thermometer could fall forty degrees in one minute (but American degrees were said to be shorter than Swedish ones). Now the sudden cold and wind had come upon them while the timbers for the house still lay and waited. The men would come as soon as they had put the roof on Danjel's house. It was expected to be ready in a week or so. Now Karl Oskar tightened the shanty as best he could; he nailed extra pieces of boards to the windward side and closed all cracks and holes with moss and wet clay. Inside, he laid a ring of stones for a fireplace and cut a hole in the roof for the smoke; now they could heat their hut. During the second night they were able to keep a fire alive, and they covered themselves with every piece of clothing they had, but the cold still penetrated—they froze miserably. The children whined and whimpered in their sleep like kittens. Many times during the night Kristina rose and put a kettle on the fire and boiled a meat soup, which they drank to warm their insides—though nothing could help their outsides.

In the morning the hurricane died down a little, but toward evening it increased again, with heavy showers of hail. Inch-long pieces of ice, hard as stones, fell and remained in drifts on the ground. But on the third morning the wind abated, and by evening the storm had spent itself.

After the three days' frightful weather the sun warmed them again. The hail drifts melted away, the air was so still that not the smallest leaf moved, and the grass that had been combed flat rose again. Mild, late-fall weather reigned once more.

But the new settlers in the shanty on Lake Ki-Chi-Saga had experienced the touch of the blizzard on their bodies, they felt as if they had been saved from death. The winter had discharged a warning shot to show what miserable shelter they had against the cold north winds; to survive, they would need a tighter, better house, and soon.

And early one Monday morning their helpers arrived and began to raise the house. They were three carpenters

—Karl Oskar, Danjel, and Jonas Petter—with two helpers, Robert and Arvid. Now there were rushed days for Kristina, who must prepare food for all of them over a fire in the open, while she kept an eye on the children. But the break in their loneliness was welcome, now there was life on their place with the menfolk building, and new strength came into her as she saw their house rise on the foundation timbers. Back there, under the great sugar maples, the walls of their new home grew, higher for each meal she prepared for the builders. Often she walked back to watch them and felt as if she herself were participating in the building.

The house was to be eight feet high at the eaves. The timbers were roughhewn, and now the men smoothed the upper and under sides of the logs to make them lie close together. Karl Oskar would later fill the cracks with moss, which he intended to cover with a mixture of clay and sand. The timberman's most complicated task was the fitting of the logs together at each corner. "When a corner you can lay, you get a timberman's pay" was an old saying at home, often quoted to a carpenter's helper. Karl Oskar had learned building from his father, but he did not feel he was a master; working now as a timberman, he was glad his house had only four corners.

The long, heavy logs were hoisted into place on the wall by the combined strength of all five men; each log was fastened to the underlying timber by means of thick pegs driven into the lower log and fitted into auger holes in the next one above. There was a racket all day long from three ax hammers; three axes were busy, three timbermen timbered. And the sound of axes against wood was no languid, depressing sound, it was bold, fresh, stimulating—it was a promise, an assurance of security. Here something took place of lasting import—not for a day, or a year, but for future times; here a human abode was raised. And the echo from the timbermen's axes rang out over the forest in the clear autumn air, it was thrown from tree to tree—the axes cut and hammered, and the echo returned from the other side of the lake.

Jonas Petter was the master among the three timbermen; his ax corrected and finished where the others had begun. And in rhythm with his ax blows against the timbers, he sang "The Timberman's Song," which his father

267

and grandfather before him had sung at house-building in
the homeland, a song that had been sung through centuries when walls were raised for Swedish peasant houses, a
song always sung to the music of ax and hammer—a song
stimulating to the timberman, suitable for singing at his
work, and now for the first time sung in Minnesota Territory:

> What's your daughter doing tonight?
> What's your daughter doing tonight?
> What's your timberman's daughter doing tonight?
> Timberrim, timberram, timberammaram—
> What's your daughter doing tonight?

> Your daughter is making a bed,
> Your daughter is making a bed,
> Your daughter is making a timberman's bed—
> Timberrim, timberram, timberammaram—
> Your daughter is making a bed.

> Who shall sleep in your daughter's bed?
> Who shall sleep in your daughter's bed?
> Who shall sleep in your daughter's timberman's bed?
> Timberrim, timberram, timberammaram—
> Who shall sleep in your daughter's bed?

> I and your daughter, that's who
> I and your daughter, that's who
> I and your timberman's daughter that's who. . . .

"The Timberman's Song" was fully ten verses long;
Jonas Petter knew only three verses and part of the fourth;
his father had sung the song to him when they worked as
timbermen together, and he had managed to sing it from
beginning to end while he set one log in place. The verses
Jonas Petter had forgotten described the occupation in the
timberman's bed; but he couldn't for the life of him remember how it went, except that in the timberman's bed
was made a timberman's tyke, by a timberman's "stud."
But, asked Jonas Petter, could there be anything easier
than to be a stud, when you had the bed and the woman?
He thought it might be more difficult not to.

The three men timbered up the house walls in five days,

and on the sixth they put on the rafters and laid the roofing. Robert and Arvid handed up the turf, each piece fastened to a long pole, and the three men laid the sod over a layer of bark. So the house was ready with four walls and a roof.

The timbermen's work was done, a house had been built in the same number of days as God had required in the beginning for the Creation. The seventh day arrived, and the almanac indicated it was a Sunday; and the timbermen kept the Sabbath and rested on the seventh day, while they inspected their handiwork; they found it good, strong, suitable for human habitation. A new home had been built, a solid, sturdy log house on secure footing, not to be felled by wrestling winds. It had been built to stand, by men who had built houses for farmers in Sweden, who had timbered the way their forebears had timbered through the centuries. A new house, of ancient construction, was built in a new land, on the shore of Lake Ki-Chi-Saga. His helpers had done their part, but the long, tedious work of completion remained for Karl Oskar before they could move in. First he laid the flooring; he placed the split linden trunks with the flat side up and fastened them to the joist logs with a wooden peg in each end. The planks were smooth hewn, and the floor turned out as even as it could be from hand-hewn boards. Through the front wall he cut a hole for a door, three feet wide and six and a half feet high; he wanted to be able to step over his threshold into his new home in America without having to bend his neck. He made the door of oak, heavy and clumsy as a church door; it would be a chore for the smaller children to open. He hung it by the strong, expensive hinges—the ones that had cost a whole dollar. Then he made a simple wooden latch for the outside, but on the inside he fitted heavy timbers for bolts, so that they could lock themselves in securely against their brown neighborfolk, if need be. He cut three holes for windows—one larger one, to the right of the door at the front, and a small one in each gable; the glazed sash, sent for from Stillwater, was fitted into these. He would have liked to let more of God's clear daylight into his house, but he could not afford any more of the expensive glass.

Next in turn was the fireplace where the food was to be prepared; it would also be the source of heat and of light at night. He had lately worked as carpenter, timberman, and roofer, now he must also do a mason's work, and this worried him. He asked Jonas Petter to help him, and with his skillful neighbor's aid, he built a fireplace and chimney of stone, clay, and sand. Later, with less urgency, he would build a bake oven beside the fireplace.

The fireplace took up one corner of the house; in each one of the three remaining corners, Karl Oskar built a bedstead: one for Kristina and himself, one for the children, and one for Robert. Six feet from each gable and five feet from the side walls, he fastened posts to the floor on which he placed timbers long enough to be secured to the gable walls; this made the bed frames. Crossing these timbers and fitting between the wall logs he laid thinner scantlings for the bed bottom. He had seen beds built this way in an American settler's house in Taylors Falls and he liked them; they were easy to make, yet ingenious and practical. During the coming winter he would make such furniture as they absolutely needed when he was forced to sit inside by the fire.

Karl Oskar brought Kristina over to their new house for a tour of inspection, to show her all he had done. He explained that everything was on the rough side—walls, windows, floor, door, and ceiling. There were no perfectly smooth surfaces—but he had done the best he could. And nothing was intended for looks, anyway, all was done to keep out rain, wind, cold. It could not be helped if the walls were a little rough, if the floor wasn't quite even, if the door hung askew. Yes, the door did hang somewhat crooked, but she must remember the old saying: "Out of plumb is dumb, but a little lean cannot be seen." Many planks might be poorly fitted, for he had used mostly pegs, he hadn't driven a hundred nails into the whole house) the price of nails had worried him so much that he had thought a long while before using one.

Their new house was built roughly, but he was sure it would provide them with comfort and shelter.

Kristina said that this house was like a castle, it was heaven compared to the shanty! And she was well pleased with all she saw, especially their new beds; these were the most comfortable sleeping places they had since leaving home.

Karl Oskar assured her he would make the house still

more comfortable for her. On the long back wall, between the beds, he intended to place an oak log, which would make an excellent sofa; next to the fireplace he intended to build shelves, he would drive pegs into the logs to hang clothes on, and as soon as he had time he would make her a table, surely before Christmas. By and by they would be quite comfortable in this house.

Kristina was aware of the rough timbers in the cabin, the unfinished walls; she saw better than her husband all that was crooked and out of line, but she had been deeply worried that the house would not be finished before winter came. How glad she was now that she could move into it! They had wandered about so long and had to change shelter and sleeping places so often—how wonderful it would be to settle down under a real roof, be within four solid walls, live in a house where they could stay!

Yes, Kristina was satisfied with their house of rough-hewn logs, even though Karl Oskar said: "Wait till next time! Next time I'll build a real . . ."

Even before they had moved into their new house he was planning the next one: This forest had timber enough for real mansions; as soon as he had improved his condition, he would build something larger and finer than any farmhouse in all Ljuder Parish! It would be at least two stories high, of the finest timber, elegantly finished.

Yes, he assured his wife, she could rely on him; their next house would be well finished, both inside and outside.

4

Karl Oskar made a cross in the almanac on the twenty-eighth of October—that was the day they moved into the new log house.

They invited their countrymen at the other settlement for a housewarming, and Anders Mansson and his mother were also asked. All the guests came in Anders Mansson's ox wagon—the ungreased wooden wheels, ever moaning and squeaking, announced their arrival half an hour before the wagon emerged from the forest. Now the new house was filled with people jostling for seats. Karl Oskar had made a few chairs from sawed-off oak blocks, leaving a back rest sticking up, somewhat rounded to fit the back of a full-grown person. These made solid seats, but for the party he had to roll in ordinary blocks as well, and still some of the guests had to sit on the beds.

So they were again together, sixteen of them, all born in the same land, all speaking the same language. They had settled in different places, made up separate households, and had no possessions in common except their language, and this united them and held them together in their new country. They felt almost like close relatives. However kind and friendly people may be, if they are unable to speak a common language, they remain strangers. Today, no strangers had come to visit Karl Oskar and Kristina; their visitors seemed like blood relations.

Kristina had prepared a venison dinner; she had peeled the potatoes before boiling them, as was the custom at parties at home. She had boiled a whole kettle of cranberries; these berries were now ripening in great quantities in the bogs hereabouts, and they had a pleasing sour-fresh taste. To a housewarming the guests were supposed to bring gifts of food, and Ulrika had cooked the moving-in porridge, made of rice; she came with a large earthen bowl full of it. Jonas Petter had brought a keg of American brannvin. There were not as many dishes or as much of everything as was customary at housewarmings in Sweden, but all felt that they were sitting down to a great feast.

Karl Oskar and Kristina had invited their guests before they had a table; the food was served on top of their Swedish chest, around which they all sat down. Their guests said they too were still using their chest lids for food boards.

Ulrika had not been stingy when she cooked the housewarming porridge, it was sugar-sweet and won praise from all; before they knew it they had reached the bottom of the earthen bowl. As a young girl, Ulrika had occasionally worked as cook's helper at Krakesjo manor; she had learned cooking well and was handy at both stove and oven, when she had anything to cook with.

Today, for once, the settlers felt entitled to many dishes at the same meal, and they ate steadily and solemnly. At last the coffeepot was taken down from its hook over the fire, and a delicious odor of coffee spread through the cabin. Robert proudly showed the coffee grinder he had made for Kristina: he had hollowed out a stone to make a

272

mortar with another stone for pestle, to crush the coffee beans. He had seen the Indians use such mills—their coffee now was ground Indian-wise.

All ate to their full satisfaction, and when Ulrika wanted to rise, the chair clung to her behind. She had eaten so much that she couldn't get out of the chair, she blamed Karl Oskar who had made the seat too narrow for a grown woman; he ought to be old enough to know that women were broader across the behind than men; God had created them that way in order to make them lie steady on their backs those times when they obeyed His commandment to increase and replenish the earth.

Jonas Petter poured the American brannvin, and all drank—even the children were given a few drops each. Anders Mansson said the whisky was stronger than Swedish brannvin; at first it burned the tongue a little, but later it felt good in the stomach. Some people had a hard time getting accustomed to the taste of whisky, some had to keep at it persistently, it might take years; he himself had already become accustomed to it. The whisky was made from Indian corn, "Lazyman's Grain" as it was called. He had planted this corn for the first time last spring.

"At home the brannvin is white, why is it brown here?" Kristina asked.

"They haven't strained it carefully," said Ulrika. "There's mash in it."

Jonas Petter had his own opinion: "It's the color of cow piss but it tastes mighty good!"

Kristina and Ulrika both thought Swedish brannvin was sweeter and milder; this tasted pungent. But old Fina-Kajsa liked American brannvin better than Swedish: "Brannvin should be felt in the throat! It mustn't slip down like communion wine!"

Anders Mansson's mother had changed much since she had found her son; at times she sat silently by herself, staring straight ahead for hours, hardly hearing if she were spoken to. At other times she seemed to have lost her memory. Believing herself still on the journey, she kept mumbling, downhearted and confused: "Oh me, oh my! We'll never get there! Oh me, oh my!"

She could forget everything around her to such an extent that she wasn't aware she had reached her son three months ago. The long journey seemed to have been too much for her head. But at other times she pulled herself together and worked all day long like a young woman, running her son's house and cooking for him the delicious Oland dumplings which he had been without so long in America. Since he now could get the dumplings here, Anders Mansson said, there was nothing left in Sweden to go back to.

After their feast, the settlers grouped themselves around the hearth where a great fire of dry pine boughs was burning. And sitting there, to let the "food die in the stomach," they began to talk of Sweden and of people in their home community: It was now the servants' "Free Week" at home, all crops were in, the potatoes picked, the fields plowed. The bread for the winter was in the bins, the cattle in the byre. Those at home lived in an old and settled land, they had their food for the winter. And they could not help but compare their own situation: they were farmers without crops, without grain bins, without pork barrels, without livestock. And ahead of them lay the earth's long resting season, when the ground gave nothing.

But Sweden had already begun to fade into the vague distance; it seemed far away in time and space. Heaven seemed closer than Sweden. Their old homes had taken on an aspect of unreality, as does everything at a great distance.

They began speaking of the loneliness of the great wilderness, and Jonas Petter said: "Is there one among us who regrets the emigration?"

The question caught them unaware, and a spell of silence fell over the group. A puzzling question had been asked—a poser—which required a great deal of thought before they could answer it; it was like a riddle to be solved. Do I regret my emigration? It was an intrusive question, forcing itself upon them, knocking at each one's closed door: a demand to open and show what was hidden inside.

Ulrika was the first to answer. She stared at Jonas Petter, almost in fury: "Regret it! Are you making fun of me? Should I regret having moved to a country where I'm accepted as a human being? I'd rather be chopped to sausage filling than go back to Sweden!"

"It was to be," Danjel Andreasson said. "We were

274

chosen to move here. We shall harbor neither regret nor fear."

"I regret one thing!" spoke up Karl Oskar. "I regret I didn't emigrate six years ago, when I first came of age."

"You are not yet of age—your Guardian still lives in Heaven," Danjel said. "His will has been done."

"But the Lord's servant—the dean—advised against my emigration."

"Then it was an evil spirit that spake through him," Danjel retorted calmly.

"Well—I'm here! And no one can get me away from here! As surely as I sit on this chopping block!" Karl Oskar spoke with great emphasis.

He was settled now, he and his family had moved into their house, furnished with sturdy beds and seats he had made. Beginning this very day, he felt settled and at home in North America.

Jonas Petter said: Life in the wilderness had its drawbacks, but things would improve by and by, as they improved themselves. It had been well for them to travel about and see how great the earth was, how vast its seas and countries. At home, people thought Sweden made up the whole world; that was why folk there were so conceited.

"They should read geography books," interrupted Robert.

"That they should, instead of poking their noses into everyone else's business," agreed Jonas Petter. If anyone hiccoughed in Sweden, folk picked it up and ran with it until it was heard throughout the whole county. His father knew an old morning hymn which all should follow:

> Peaceful walk and do thy bit,
> Obey thy Lord, on others spit!

This psalm Jonas Petter's father used to sing every morning before he began his day, and if they obeyed it, they would be happy through all their days, and at last pass to the beyond in contentment.

Judging from the replies to Jonas Petter's question, no one regretted his emigration. And the settlers began to talk of work to be finished before winter set in. Karl Oskar intended to dig a well before the frost got into the earth; he had not been able to find a spring in the vicinity, they had been using brook water, which didn't seem to hurt them; it was running water, but it wasn't quite clear in color or taste.

The talk around the fire was suddenly interrupted by Kristina, who was seized by a fit of weeping. This happened unexpectedly and without forewarning. No one had said a word to hurt or upset her. She herself had been silent a long time. She had not joined in their talk about Sweden, but she had listened. Karl Oskar now asked in consternation if she was in pain. But she only shook her head—he mustn't pay any attention to her. And she continued to cry and sob, she put both her hands to her face and wept without saying why. No one could comfort her, as no one knew what ailed her. They asked many times if she were ill: No, she was not ill. . . .

Karl Oskar felt embarrassed and didn't know what to say to the guests; but they would understand she was sensitive now. . . .

"You're worn out, I guess?" he said kindly.

Danjel patted his niece on the shoulder: "Lie down and rest, Kristina. We too must seek the comfort of our homes."

"I am acting like a fool. Forgive me, all of you. . . ."

Fearing that the guests were departing because of her behavior, Kristina pleaded with them to remain, trying to swallow her sobs: "To blubber like this . . . I don't understand it. Pay no heed to it; it will soon be over."

But their guests must start on their homeward road to be back before dark. Anders Mansson did not wish to drive the new road after nightfall; he went out and yoked the team to the wagon, while Ulrika washed the dishes and picked up her empty earthen bowl; Jonas Petter left his keg with at least half a quart still splashing in it.

Karl Oskar accompanied his guests a bit of the way, walking up the slope. The housewarming had ended on an unhappy note, too suddenly. And he was worried over Kristina's peculiar behavior; if she wasn't sick, she must be crying for some other reason, and this reason she had kept secret from him. He must know what it was, she must tell him what ailed her.

When he returned to the house, Kristina had dried her tears. She began to speak of her own will: "I couldn't help it, Karl Oskar."

"I guess not."

"I assure you, it was nothing. . . ."

"One can be sad and weep. But why did you have to weep just this day?"

"It irks me terribly—with all the guests . . ."

Karl Oskar wondered if after all she wasn't a little disappointed with the log house. Had she expected their new home to be different—better and roomier? He tried to comfort her by telling her about the house he intended to build next time: "You wait and see our next house, Kristina! Next housewarming you won't cry!"

"Karl Oskar—I didn't cry because of . . ."

No, he mustn't think she shed tears because their house wasn't fine enough! He mustn't think she was so ungrateful! That would have been sinful of her. No, the house was good, she had told him she was pleased with their new home. And she hadn't complained before, when there might have been reason—she hadn't said a word when they shivered and froze in the shed. Why should she be dissatisfied now when they had moved into a warm, timbered house? No, she had everything she could want, this last year she had learned to be without; before they managed to get under this roof, she had learned to value a home; she had thanked God Who had let them move in here, well and healthy and all of them alive, after the dangers they had gone through.

But she couldn't help it—something had come over her today, making her cry. Before she knew it the tears had come to her eyes, as if forced out. She didn't know what it was—she only felt it was overpowering. And she couldn't tell him how much it disturbed her that this had happened at their housewarming, on that longed-for day when they moved in. . . .

Karl Oskar was satisfied with her explanation: no wonder she was a little sensitive, unable to keep her tears, the condition she was in. She needed comforting words and he went on talking of their next housewarming: "Just wait and see our next house! Then we'll be really at home here on Lake Ki-Chi-Saga!"

277

5

When Kristina went to bed the first evening in the log house, the first time in the new, comfortable bed, with her husband beside her, she remained awake a long while: Had she lied to him today? Didn't she know what had come over her and made her cry? It had come over her many times before, although never so overpoweringly as today. It used to come when she had nothing to busy herself with, nothing to occupy her mind. Usually it soon passed, but it came back, it always came back. And of course it would come back today, with all the others sitting there talking about it! Indeed, they forced it to come. They sat and reminisced about the old country and the people at home, they made everything come to life so vividly, everything she had given up with a bleeding heart to follow her husband.

Now they were at last settled, now they would stay here forever, *at home* on Lake Ki-Chi-Saga, as Karl Oskar put it. So strange it sounded, to have her home linked to that name. She was to be at home here for the rest of her life— but she wasn't at home. This house was her home, but it was so far away. . . .

Here was *away* for Kristina—Sweden was *home*. It ought to be just the opposite: the two places should change position. She had moved, but she could not make the two countries move, the countries lay where they had lain before—one had always to her been *away,* the other would always remain *home.*

And she knew for sure now, she had to admit it to herself: in her heart she felt she was still on a journey; she had gone away but hoped one day to return.

Home—to Kristina, this encompassed all that she was never to see again.

XVII

Guests in the Log House

The settlers at Lake Gennesaret had moved into their log house a few weeks before their countrymen on Lake Ki-Chi-Saga. Jonas Petter would build his house next summer, and in the meantime he lived with Danjel. He had begun to fell timbers to let them season for his building, and Robert helped him with the felling; he was doing exchange work for his brother. To avoid the hour-long walk from Ki-Chi-Saga and back, he stayed in Danjel's house during the week and went home only Saturdays.

One Saturday afternoon Robert arrived at his brother's settlement leading a cow behind him with one of Karl Oskar's linden-fiber ropes. He tied the cow to the sugar maple at the door and called Kristina.

She came out, looked at the cow, and rubbed her eyes. "What kind of creature is that? Did you run across a stray cow in the forest?"

"No. I've led her from Taylors Falls."

Kristina inspected the animal more closely: It was one of Anders Mansson's cows, the one that wouldn't get with calf, which he intended to butcher.

Karl Oskar also came out and stood there by Kristina laughing to himself: Was she surprised? She could thank Fina-Kajsa for this, the old woman had suggested lending her son's cow for the winter; the cow had once more been taken to German Fischer's bull in Taylors Falls, and as it now appeared she was with calf, it would be a shame to butcher her. Anders Mansson and his mother had enough milk from the other cow, and as Karl Oskar had gathered plenty of hay to feed her, he could keep her through the winter; he was to bring her back to the owner at calving time next spring. The cow still gave a couple of quarts of milk a day and would not go dry for several months.

"The animal is old, of course," he concluded.

The cow was badly saddle-backed and had an enormous stomach; she must have borne fifteen calves at least in her day. But Kristina threw her arms around the neck of the animal: she had a milch cow, even though it was only borrowed, and they would have milk for the children during most of the winter. And she patted the cow, caressed her, felt above the udder for the milk arteries, and said they were good, for an old cow: she could easily increase her milk if she were fed and cared for.

Karl Oskar was as pleased as Kristina with the cow. He thought that this time his wife had enforced her will in spite of him.

Here in Minnesota people had miserable shelters for their cattle; the Swedish settlers thought it a wonder they didn't freeze to death during the winters. Karl Oskar led his borrowed cow to the lately vacated shanty. The cow moved into the house they themselves had occupied until a few days before. Their old home was turned into a byre! They would let the cow graze in the meadow until the snow began to fly, but they would be careful to put her in the shanty every night.

Anders Mansson was the owner of one young and one old cow. Both had American names—the young one was called Girl and this one was called Lady, which was supposed to be a title like Mrs. in America. Large-bellied Lady was a calm, easygoing, friendly animal, grazing peacefully and contentedly, never trying to run off to the woods. She became a pleasant companion to Kristina and the children in their isolation; it seemed almost that they had acquired a new member of the family, and this member contributed to the family sustenance. Lady was always called by name, like a human being, a respected woman of noble lineage. And Robert pointed out that women were

280

scarce out here and a noble name for a cow showed how highly men valued women in North America.

2

The night frosts had begun. The grass stood silvery in the mornings; winter was lurking outside their timbered house.

One late afternoon, at twilight, Kristina was alone inside their log house with Lill-Marta and Harald. Karl Oskar had gone to the lake to examine some willow snares he had placed in the shore reeds near a point where the pike often played, and Johan had run after him; the boy was always at the heels of his father. Kristina poured water into a pot and hung it over the fire, as Karl Oskar would soon be back with the fish for their evening meal. She hoped he would find pike in the snares, pike tasted better than any other fish in the lake; whitefish and perch were good too, but the catfish with its round head and long beard was so ugly that the sight of it did not whet the appetite.

Lill-Marta was playing on the floor and Harald was still taking his nap in the children's bed. Kristina was busy at the hearth with her back to the door when the girl suddenly began to scream.

"What's the matter with you, Lill-Marta?"

The child answered with another yell, still louder.

"Did you hurt yourself, child dear?"

The girl was sitting on the floor, staring wide-eyed toward the door.

Kristina turned quickly. The door was open and two figures stood inside the threshold. She could barely see them in the dim light, and at first she couldn't determine whether they were men or women; she saw only two skin-covered bodies which had somehow got inside. But how had they opened the door? She hadn't heard it open, nor had there been any other noise, or sound of steps.

The startling sight near the door made her back up so quickly that she almost stepped into the fire. Then she rushed to pick up the child on the floor—her heart stopped beating and felt cramped in her breast, and fear spread over her whole trembling body, as if it had been drenched with ice water.

The two figures at the door peered at her with black-currant eyes, set deep under low foreheads. And now she recognized who the guests were: their nearest neighbors had come to pay a call.

But what did they want here? Why had they come to her?

She called to them: "Go outside!"

The two Indians remained immobile inside the threshold. In her fear, she had forgotten they couldn't understand a word she said.

Harald awoke and sat up in his bed, rubbing the sleep from his eyes. With the girl in her arms Kristina cautiously stole back to the children's bed in the corner, she walked slowly backward, she dared not turn her back to the Indians. With one child in her arms she stood protectingly in front of the other.

"What do you want? Please go outside!"

Uncomprehending, the Indians remained, and again she remembered that she spoke to deaf ears: What use was there in talking to savages who didn't understand her?

"Karl Oskar! Karl Oskar! Come quick!"

She kept on calling, she yelled as loud as she could, she must yell loud enough for him to hear her down at the lake. Karl Oskar wasn't far away, perhaps he was already on his way back, he ought to hear her calls. . . .

Then she stopped calling; she might anger them by yelling, it might be better to keep quiet and pretend she wasn't afraid of them. If she only knew their errand. What could they want of her?

The unwelcome guests did not leave, they moved from the door toward the hearth, and in the light of the fire Kristina had a good look at them.

The Indians were dressed in soft brown-red skins, and their feet were shod in the same kind of hides. Their faces were deceptively alike, except that one had a flat nose. Their cheeks were beardless. On their cheekbones were painted red, bloodlike streaks, and black hair hung in tufts from their heads, gleaming as if greased with fat. Both Indians had red animal tails dangling from the backs of their necks, they looked as if they had live squirrels sitting behind their ears. From their squirrel tails to their moccasins, they looked furry and ragged; they hardly resembled human beings. And they had sneaked into the house on soft paws like wild beasts.

The Indians looked around the cabin, they inspected the pot over the fire, the chest, the clothes hanging on the wall. Meanwhile they spoke in low voices to each other; their words sounded like short, guttural grunts.

She could not take her eyes off their red-streaked faces. Their eyes burned like black coals under their brows, they looked cruel and treacherous. Long knives hung at their sides; they might stick their knives into her and the children, any moment. The Indian with the pushed-in nose seemed to her the more dangerous of the two.

Kristina kept silent now, she no longer called for help, no use frightening her children. She stood at the corner of the bed, as far from the intruders as possible, with her two little ones pressed close to her. The children too kept silent, their round eyes staring at the strange, uncouth creatures.

They had left the door open; could she pick up Harald and the girl and escape through the door? Would she dare run past the two savages?

The flat-nosed Indian pointed to Karl Oskar's gun which hung on the gable wall above the clothes chest; now both Indians stood looking at the gun with their backs toward Kristina. Now she must run by them out of the house! She gathered her strength, took a firm hold of her children, measured the distance with her eyes . . . it was only a few steps. . . .

But suddenly the Indians turned toward her again. They had managed to lift Karl Oskar's muzzle-loader off the pegs; both held the gun, one had the butt, the other the barrel.

What did they want with the gun? It was loaded. What were they about to do, did they want to steal it? Why didn't Karl Oskar come? What was he doing all this time?

Now the flat-nosed Indian alone held the shooting piece; he lifted the weapon to firing position, level with his shoulder; he stood with his back to the gable end of the house and aimed toward Kristina!

He intended to fire—he was going to shoot her and the children! She was looking right into the gun barrel, and there was no place to flee now; she pushed against the logs

283

but she couldn't creep through the wall. She stood petrified, a target.

"No! No!" she screamed.

She wanted to tell them they could have the gun, if only they wouldn't shoot her and the children. The children! Quickly she pushed them behind her; now she protected them with her own body, now the bullet must first go through her. If she only could have called to them: Don't shoot! Let us live! Don't kill us here now!

But they wouldn't understand her.

The flat-nosed Indian again held the butt, while the other one held up the barrel, helping his friend to aim the heavy weapon. It was clear they wanted to try the gun by firing a shot; the flat-nosed Indian was fingering the hammer, trying to cock it.

Pressed against the wall, Kristina crouched over her children, she couldn't move any farther, she was trembling and weak with fright. The poor children—she couldn't ask the savages to spare them, they wouldn't understand. But Someone else understood and would listen to her; she stammered forth a prayer: "Dear God! If I die now, what will become of my children? My little, innocent children? Dear God, help me!"

Lill-Marta and Harald, squeezed between her body and the wall, began to whimper. But the visitors paid no attention to Kristina and the children, they were busy with the gun. Now both of them were fingering the hammer. The gun had a hard action. Kristina followed their motions with wide-open, frozen eyes. And she saw they had managed to cock the gun. Then she didn't see anything more.

Black and red clouds covered her eyes. She closed them, her whole body numb with terror. Karl Oskar! What *are* you doing out there? Why don't you come?

Karl Oskar! Perhaps he had encounterd the Indians before they came in! Could they have done him any harm? Was that why he didn't come? Suppose he were lying out there . . .

"Dear sweet God! Help him! Help us!"

Kristina closed her eyes and waited. She waited for the shot, she waited for the lead bullet. . . . She must die. This was the end for her on earth. And she prayed incoherently and silently that her merciful Father would receive her, wretched, sinful creature that she was, and let

284

her children live unharmed in this world: the poor children . . . dear God, let them live, my poor children. . . .

Her trembling lips moved, but she kept her eyes closed and waited, waited through an eternity. It was silent in the house. She heard nothing. As yet no shot had been fired from the gun. It remained silent.

Kristina kept her eyes closed and waited. . . . Until a child's voice said: "Open your eyes, Mother! Why do you keep your eyes shut?"

Then she opened her eyes and looked about her, all around the cabin, as if awakening from a long, bad dream. Lill-Marta sat on the floor with her playthings as before, and little Harald stood in the open door and looked out. No one else was in sight. She was alone in the house with her children. The callers had gone: the two Indians had gone their way with the gun. They had come into the house soundlessly, they had left in equal silence—stolen away on their soft moccasins like animals slinking back into the forest. They had not fired a shot. . . .

But when she tried to walk, she felt the floor sway under her: the planks sank steeply under her feet, she took one step into a depth—she fell full length to the floor and knew nothing more.

3

Karl Oskar came in, Johan at his heels; he carried a few pike strung through the gills on a branch; he threw the fish on the floor in front of the hearth. It was cold inside the cabin and he wondered why the door had been left open. Then he discovered Kristina, stretched out on the floor at the other end of the room.

He hurriedly soaked a towel in the water pail and laid it on his wife's forehead. In a few minutes she opened her eyes and sat up, confused and questioning: What was it? Why was she on the floor?

"You fainted," Karl Oskar said.

She still felt dizzy, she put her hand to her forehead and began to remember: Karl Oskar had returned—at last!

"What were you doing? Why did you stay away so long?"

"So long? I was only gone a short while."

He looked at his watch: he had examined the snares

285

and moved them a bit, but he hadn't been gone a half hour.

"A half hour?" Kristina was surprised. In that time she had suffered death, spent time in eternity. "I called you." Her dulled senses were clearing: "The Indians came. Two awful ones! They took your gun."

Karl Oskar looked at the wall—the gun was still there where he had hung it. As Kristina noticed this, she said: "I was so confused—I thought they stole the gun. But they cocked it."

Karl Oskar took down his muzzle-loader and examined it; he couldn't see that anyone had touched it.

"Did they handle it?"

"They aimed it."

"At you? Oh Lord in Heaven!"

"I thought they would shoot me and the children."

"God, they must have frightened you! No wonder you fainted!"

She related what had taken place in the cabin the few minutes he was gone. And as Karl Oskar listened, a cold perspiration broke out on his forehead. While he had been gone less than half an hour, the greatest disaster he could imagine had nearly befallen him: he might have returned to find wife and children dead on the cabin floor.

"Oh Lord my God! What an escape!"

Kristina said: First she had called him. Then she had prayed God to help her, and He had listened to her prayer and sent the savages away from their house without harming her or the children. Never before in her life had she realized so fully as today how all of them were under the protection of their Creator.

"They left the gun. I don't understand it. What did they want in here?"

Karl Oskar suggested that the Indians were curious: they hadn't come to murder anyone, they only wanted to see how the new settlers lived. But they handled shooting irons like children—the gun might easily have gone off and killed her!

"This must never happen again," he said.

They had had a serious warning today. She must bolt the door carefully whenever he was out, even if only for a short time. And they must rig up a loud bell so she could call him when there was danger.

286

"I hope you didn't hurt yourself?"

"No. I feel perfectly well again."

She had looked very pale when he saw her lying on the floor, but now her color had come back. She busied herself with her chores, they must have their evening meal at last. She stirred up the fire under the pot and Karl Oskar went outside for more wood.

She sat down to clean the fish. But as she stuck the knife into the first pike belly, she felt a jerking convulsion grip her: an intense pain began in the small of her back and spread through her whole lower body. It felt as if she had stuck the knife into her own belly instead of into the fish.

When Karl Oskar came back with the wood, he saw she had grown pale again, her very lips were bluish. And her hand with the knife trembled as she cut the entrails from the pike.

"Is something wrong?"

"Nothing much. It'll soon be over."

"But you've pain?"

"It will soon pass."

She went on cleaning the fish, she cleaned all the pike, and the pain abated. She had told Karl Oskar the truth—the pain had passed.

But what she hadn't said was that it would soon be upon her again; she had recognized the pain.

And it did come back—an hour later, when they sat around the chest lid eating their supper. The same pain returned, radiating from the small of her back, shooting and cutting through her lower body. This time it lasted longer than before. Her appetite was gone, but she forced herself to swallow a few bites of the boiled fish.

Karl Oskar looked uneasily at his wife: "How do you feel, Kristina?"

"I don't feel so well, after the fainting spell."

"Eat! That will bring back your strength."

She tried for a moment to persuade herself that it was only the after-effect of fainting. And the pain eased, but in a little while it came again for a third time, and now it seized her so violently that she had to let a few moans escape her lips. She panted and drew in her breath with difficulty.

"Take some drops!" Karl Oskar urged.

He found the bottle of Hoffman's Heart-Aiding Drops,

287

which Kristina had hidden with great care: he poured a tablespoonful and gave it to her. She swallowed the drops without a word. But by now she knew: no drops would help her, this would not pass, this would come back many times, and more intense each time it came—until it was over. She remembered it well; after all, she had experienced it four times before. And she regretted immediately having taken the heart-aiding drops, they couldn't help her in any way; those drops had been wasted on her; they might better have been used for the children, when they ailed. Foolish of her. . . . Why had she believed something would help? The first time might have been a mistake—but now. . . . Why didn't she tell Karl Oskar the truth?

"It's my time, Karl Oskar."

"Do you think so?"

"Yes. It couldn't be anything else."

He looked at her in foolish surprise. "But—isn't it too soon?"

"Fourteen days too soon."

"Yes, that's what I thought. . . . Then we must get someone right away!"

He had just finished pulling off his boots, now he pulled them on again quickly. Where could he find a woman to help? Who out here could act as midwife? At home she had had both her mother and mother-in-law at her childbeds. But here—a married woman, a settler woman who spoke their language—there was hardly a one. An unmarried woman who had never borne children would not be good for much. He had had it in mind to suggest to Kristina—as long as she herself hadn't mentioned it—that they ought to bespeak a woman to help her in childbed, before it was too late. Fina-Kajsa was too old, her hands trembled, and her head wasn't always clear. He had thought of Swedish Anna, who was a widow and had reached ripe age—she should be able to help a life into the world.

But it was a long way to fetch her from Taylors Falls—a three-hour walk by daylight. And would she come with him through the wilderness tonight? This had happened so suddenly, night was falling, and this too was bad luck.

"I had better get Swedish Anna. But it will take a few hours."

"You needn't go so far," Kristina said. "Get Ulrika."

"What? Ulrika of Vastergohl?"

"Yes. I asked her at the housewarming."

"You want the Glad One to be with you?"

"She promised me."

Karl Oskar was stamping on his right boot, and he stopped, perplexed: The Glad One was considered as good as anyone here, no one spoke ill of her now. Both he and Kristina had made friends with her, had accepted her in their company. But he had not imagined that his wife would call for Ulrika of Vastergohl to be with her at childbed, he had not thought she would want her so close. Yet she had already bespoken her—the woman she had wanted to exclude as a companion on their journey. She would never have done this at home; there a decent wife would never have allowed the public whore to attend her at childbirth.

Kristina rose and began preparing the bed: "Don't you think Ulrika can manage?"

"Yes! Yes, of course! I only thought . . ."

But he never said what his thought was. It was this: he had accepted Ulrika, but hardly more. He could not forget that, after all, she had been the parish whore in Ljuder, and he was surprised that Kristina seemed to have forgotten. Perhaps it was as well, perhaps it was fortunate that she was within call when a midwife was needed. She should know the requirements at such a function, she had borne four children of her own, she should know what took place at childbirth. Ulrika had health and strength, she was cleanly. She would probably make a good midwife. She could help a wedded woman, even though all her own children had been born out of wedlock. What wouldn't do at home would have to do here; here each one did as best he could, and they must rely on someone capable, regardless of her previous life.

Karl Oskar now was surprised at himself for not having thought of Ulrika. "I shall fetch her as fast as I can run."

"It's already dark. It won't be easy for you."

He said he could find the road to their neighbors' settlement, he had walked it often enough. But it was too bad that Robert was staying with Danjel, or he could have sent him instead. Now he must leave Kristina and the children alone—and just after they had been frightened by the Indians. She must bolt herself in, to be safe. Would she be able to push in the bolts after he left? It would be almost two hours before he could get back.

"Can you hold out till I get back?"

"I think I can. But be sure to bring Ulrika with you."

Karl Oskar cut a large slice of bread for each of the children, to give them something to gnaw on while he was gone. He stopped a moment outside the door while Kristina bolted it, and then he took off.

Outside it was pitch-dark. Karl Oskar had made himself a small hand lantern out of pieces of glass he had found in Taylors Falls: he had fitted these into a framework of wood. But the tiny tallow candle inside burned with so weak a flame that the lantern helped him but little. Later there might be a moon, but at the moment the heavens were cloaked in dark clouds, not letting through a ray. He must hurry, he hadn't time to look for obstacles, he strode along fast, stumbled on roots, slipped into hollows; thorns stung him and branches hit him in the face; he was drenched with perspiration before he was halfway to Danjel's. A few times he had to stop to get his breath. It was difficult to hurry in his heavy boots.

Karl Oskar was panting and puffing like a dog in midsummer when at last he espied the light from Danjel's cabin; he had never before covered the distance between the two settlements in so short a time.

He arrived as the Lake Gennesaret people were preparing for bed. Danjel, shirt-clad only, opened the door for him. Looking at Karl Oskar's face he guessed the caller's errand: "It's Kristina? She must be ready."

"Yes."

Ulrika of Vastergohl was sitting on the hearth corner darning socks in the light from the fire. She stood up: "How far has it gone?"

"I don't know. The pains came right after dusk."

"Had the birth-water come?"

"I don't know."

"It's probably just begun."

"It came on somewhat suddenly. Two Indians came in and frightened her. That might have brought it on."

"It's always sudden," Ulrika told him.

She gathered up the worn socks and put them away; then she threw a woolen shawl over her shoulders and was ready. Danjel handed her a bottle of camphor drops and a large linen towel.

Robert asked if he should go with them, but Ulrika said: "There's no need for any more menfolk." She glanced at Karl Oskar, who stood there anxious and pale: "No—no more chickenhearted males!"

And out into the darkness went Karl Oskar in Ulrika's company; he went ahead through the forest and tried to light their way with his lantern. Now he couldn't walk fast, partly because he was tired, partly because of Ulrika.

Soon the moon broke through the clouds, and the moonlight was of more help than the lantern.

Ulrika talked almost incessantly: Yes, menfolk were soft at a woman's childbirth; they used as excuse that they couldn't bear to see a poor woman suffer. . . . Hmm. . . . The truth was, probably, they suffered from bad conscience—those who had a conscience; they themselves had put the woman in childbirth pain.

Karl Oskar answered her in monosyllables, mostly he listened. Whatever was said of Ulrika in Vastergohl she was a fearless and plucky woman. This was well—such a one was needed at a childbed.

Ulrika continued: She herself had been delivered four times, but at her childbeds no man had needed to see her suffer; least of all the fathers of the children, for they had kept themselves far, far away. They had kept away at the birth and after; indeed, she had never heard from them again. It was best for them, of course; they were wise; they wanted to partake of the sweet tickling, but not of the sour suffering. Men were always quick to be on their way; and she had been too proud to ask their whereabouts. No one could ever accuse her of having run after men. It was the menfolk who had never left her in peace, they had tempted and promised and lured her in every way; and that poor excuse for a man who didn't do the right thing of his own will was not worth running after.

Yes, Ulrika knew the menfolk; the only one who might know them better was God the Father Himself, Who had made them. She had been with many; she knew what cowards they were toward women, how they tried to shirk their responsibility for what they had done, how they lied and accused others, how they wriggled and squirmed— those men. She knew how they shammed concern and acted the hypocrite, their tongues sweet and soft until they got a woman on her back, and how afterward—having been let in to enjoy the feast—they grew cheap and penurious and unkind: turned back into the useless cowards they actually were.

There might be a few real men; the best that could happen to a woman in this world was to be married to a real man, one she could rely on when she needed him.

"You are a man with a will, Karl Oskar. And you take care of your brats as well as your woman," said Ulrika.

The man who received this praise felt somewhat embarrassed.

The Glad One went on: Kristina was a fine, honest woman, she did not begrudge her a good man. She, Ulrika, had accommodated many married men who were in need of her, but she would never go to bed with Kristina's husband, no, not even for a whole barrel of gold.

This annoyed Karl Oskar and he rebuffed her tartly: "I've never asked you, have I?"

"You were pretty hot on me at sea. You can't deny that. No one fools me about such things."

Karl Oskar felt his cheeks burn; even his ears smarted: once on the ship he had used Ulrika—in his dreams. But no one could help what he dreamed. And even if there had been times when he felt himself tempted by the Glad One's attractive body, he was too proud to go where other men had been before. Better not pay any attention to what she was saying, it wasn't a penny's worth. It was just like Ulrika to talk of bed play when they were on their way to a woman in childbirth. His own wife to boot! He would not be dragged into a quarrel with the woman he had fetched to help. . . .

Ulrika went on heedlessly. She nudged Karl Oskar in the side and told him it was nothing to be ashamed of that he was hot on women, particularly as he had been forced to go without for such a long time—his wife had been ill, and pregnant, these were long-drawn-out obstacles, trying his patience. But any man of Kristina's she, Ulrika, would never help, however badly in need he might be.

What she said was true; it struck him to the quick. But he did not answer. He had a sense of relief as the surface of Lake Ki-Chi-Saga glittered in the moonlight ahead of them.

A hundred yards from the cabin they stopped short at the sound of a scream. Both listened intently; it wasn't a bird on the lake, it was a human voice, a voice Karl Oskar recognized: "It's Kristina!"

He ran ahead as fast as his legs could carry him. He hammered with his fists on the door, which was bolted from the inside; he could hear his wife's shrieks, she was in her bed, unable to open the door. How would he get in?

"Kristina! Can you hear me?"

Ulrika came up to his side, panting: "Have you locked her in?"

"Yes. And I don't think she is able to open . . ."

"Break a window."

Karl Oskar picked up a piece of firewood and was ready to break the nearest window when he heard Johan inside: the boy was trying to open the heavy bolts. The father directed the boy, told him how to lean against the door while he pulled the bolts, and he and Ulrika tried to pull the door toward them. After a few eternity-long minutes, the door swung open on its hinges.

Kristina was lying on her side in the bed, her body twisting as she shrieked and moaned.

"Kristina! How is it?"

"It's bad. Where is Ulrika? I've been waiting so . . ."

"We hurried as much as we could." Karl Oskar took hold of his wife's hand: it was clammy with perspiration; her eyes were wide open, she turned them slowly to her husband: "Isn't Ulrika with you?"

Ulrika had thrown off her shawl and now stepped up to the bed, pushing Karl Oskar aside: "Here I am. Good evening, Kristina. Now we'll help each other."

"Ulrika! God bless you for coming."

"How far along are you? Any pushing pains yet?"

"Only the warning pains, I think. But—oh, my dear, sweet Ulrika! Why did you take so long?"

The fire in the corner had died down, Lill-Marta and Harald were huddled on their bed with their clothes on, asleep, but Johan was up and about, his eyes wide open, full of terror: "Why does Mother cry so?"

"She has pain."

"Is her nose going to bleed again, as on the ship?"

"You can see for yourself—her nose doesn't bleed."

293

There had been one night on the *Charlotta* which Johan never would forget. "Will Mother die?"

"No—she won't die. Go to bed and be a good boy."

"Father—is it true? Mother won't die tonight?"

"She is just a little sick. She'll be well again tomorrow morning when you wake up."

Ulrika pulled down the blanket and felt Kristina's body with her hands, lightly touching her lower abdomen; then she asked: Had the birth-water come, and how long between the last pains? While Karl Oskar undressed the children and tucked them in, and rekindled the fire, the two women spoke together: they understood each other with few words, they had gone through the same number of childbeds, four each; they were united and close through their like experience.

"It feels large," said Ulrika after the examination.

"I have thought—perhaps it's twins."

"Haven't you had twins before?"

"Lill-Marta's twin brother was taken from us when he was fourteen days old."

"It runs in the family. Karl Oskar. Get me some light. Heat water over the fire. Be of some use!"

Ulrika assumed command in the cabin, and Karl Oskar speedily performed as he was told to do. It was not his custom to take orders, but tonight at his wife's childbed he was glad someone told him what to do.

From dry pine wood he made such a roaring fire that it lighted the bed where Kristina lay, comforted by her helping-woman in between the pains. She had not had time to sew anything for the child, not the slightest little garment; she had had so many other things to do this fall. And she had thought it would be another two weeks yet; it came too early according to her figuring; no, not a single diaper—and suppose she had twins!

"No devil can figure out the time," said Ulrika. "A brat will creep out whenever God wants him to."

Kristina had hoped it would happen in warm daylight; then she could have sent her children out to play. Now they had to stay inside and listen to her moans; but she couldn't help that.

The next pain came and she let out piercing screams, filling the small cabin with her cries. Johan began to sob; the father took him on his knee and tried to comfort him.

294

Karl Oskar had never before been present at childbirth; at home the women had taken care of everything and never let him inside until all was over. He didn't feel too much for other people—sometimes his insensibility made him feel guilty—but his wife's cries of agony cut right through him, he could scarcely stand it.

"You look pale as a curd, Karl Oskar," said Ulrika. "Go outside for a while. You're of no use here. I'll put the boy to bed."

He obeyed her and went out. It was now about midnight. He went down to the shanty near the lake and gave Lady her night fodder. Then he remained in the shanty with the cow, who stood there so calm and undisturbed, enjoying her own pleasant cow-warmth. The closeness of the animal in some way comforted him. And he didn't feel cold here—Lady warmed him too. The cow chewed her good hay peacefully and rhythmically, and he scratched her head and spoke to her as if she were a human. He confided his thoughts to Lady, it eased him somehow to talk: Yes, little cow, things are strange in this world. The Glad One is inside helping Kristina . . . and I stand here . . . I can't help her. How many times I've wished to be rid of Ulrika! And Kristina herself thought she would bring disaster. Instead, she is our great comfort. Yes, little cow, we never know our blessings. It happens, this way or that, strange things, one never could have dreamed of at home. One can't explain it.

Karl Oskar Nilsson spent most of the night in the byre, lost and baffled, talking to his borrowed cow; he felt he had been sent to "stand in the corner," he didn't know what to do with himself. He had been told to go out—he was driven out of his own house and home. The Ljuder Parish whore was master in his house tonight.

4

After a few hours he went to inquire how the birth was progressing. Kristina lay silent, her eyes closed. Ulrika sat by the bed, she whispered to him: He must walk quietly, she had just gone through another killing pain. Things went slowly, the brat did not seem to move at all. The real birth-water hadn't come yet, and the pushing pains had not yet set in. This birth didn't go according to rule, not as

295

it should; something was wrong. Perhaps she had been frightened too much by the Indians, perhaps the fright had dislodged something inside her. The birth had come on too suddenly—the body was not yet ready for delivery, it did not help itself the way it should when all was in order. This appeared to be a "fright-birth," and in that case it would take a long time. But there was no use explaining to him; he wouldn't understand anyway.

"I wonder how long . . ."

No one could say how long it would take; maybe very long; Kristina might not be delivered tonight. And Ulrika told him to go to bed. There was no need for his roaming about outside, like a spook.

Johan had at last fallen asleep. Karl Oskar stretched out in Robert's bed; he didn't lie down to sleep, he lay down because he had nothing else to do. He had been sitting up late for several evenings, writing a letter to Sweden, but he couldn't work on that tonight.

Kristina had dozed off between the pains; she moaned at intervals: "Ulrika . . . Are you here?"

"Yes. I'm here. You want something to drink?"

Ulrika gave her a mug of warm milk into which she had mixed a spoonful of sugar.

Kristina dozed again when the pains abated. She had always had easy births—what she went through this night surpassed all the pain she had ever experienced in her young life. But she felt succor and comfort close by now: a little while ago she had been lying here alone in the dark, alone in the whole world, alone with her pains, no one to talk to—no one except her whimpering children. Now she had Ulrika, a compassionate woman, a sister, a blessed helper.

There was so much she wanted to tell Ulrika, but she didn't have the strength now, not tonight. She had lived with Ulrika in bitter enmity—she remembered that time when Ulrika had called her a "proud piece." Ulrika had been right. She had been proud. Many times, at home, she'd met unmarried Ulrika of Vastergohl on the roads without greeting her. She was the younger of the two, she should have greeted her first with a curtsy. Instead she had stared straight ahead as if not seeing a soul. She had behaved like all the other women, she had learned from

296

them to detest and avoid the Glad One. She had acted the way all honorable, decent women acted toward Ulrika. But when she had met the King of Alarum, she had greeted him and curtsied deeply, for so did all honorable women. One must discriminate between good and evil people.

Yes, all this she must tell Ulrika—some other time—when she was able to, when this agony was over. Oh, why didn't it pass? Wouldn't she soon be delivered? Wouldn't God spare her? It went on so long . . . so long. . . . "Oh, help! Ulrika, help!"

The pains were upon her; she felt as if she were bursting into pieces, splitting in halves lengthwise. A wild beast was tearing her with its claws, tearing her insides, digging into her, digging and twisting. . . .

Ulrika was near, bending over her. The young wife threw herself from side to side in the bed, her hands fumbling for holds. "Oh! Dear God! Dear God!"

"The pushing pains are beginning," Ulrika said encouragingly. "Then it'll soon be over."

"Dear sweet, hold me! Give me something to hold on to!"

Kristina let out piercing cries, without being aware of it. The billowing pains rose within her—and would rise still higher, before they began to subside. In immeasurable pain she grasped the older woman. She held Ulrika around the waist with both arms and pressed her head into the full bosom. And she was received with kind, gentle arms.

Kristina and Ulrika embraced like two devoted sisters. They were back at humanity's beginning here tonight, at the childbed in the North American forest. They were only two women, one to give life and one to help her; one to suffer and one to comfort; one seeking help in her pain, one in compassion sharing the pain which, ever since the beginning of time, has been woman's fate.

5

"It will be over soon now. Come and hold her."

Ulrika was shaking Karl Oskar by the shoulder; he had dozed off for a while. The night was far gone, daylight was creeping in through the windows.

The midwife was calling the father—now she would see what use he could make of his hands.

Kristina's body was now helping in the labor, Ulrika said. Her pushing muscles were working, she was about to be delivered. But this last part was no play-work for her; Karl Oskar might imagine how it would hurt her when the child kicked itself out of her, tearing her flesh to pieces, breaking her in two. While this took place it would lessen her struggle if she could hold on to him, as she, Ulrika, had to receive the baby and couldn't very well be in two places at the same time.

Karl Oskar went up to the head of the bed and took a firm hold around his wife's shoulders.

"Karl Oskar—" Kristina's mouth was wide open, her eyes glazed. She tossed her head back and forth on the pillow. She stretched her arms toward her husband and got hold of his body, pressing herself ever closer to him, seeking a solid stronghold.

"Hold on to me. . . ." The words died in a long, moaning sigh.

"The head is coming! Hold her firmly. I'll take the brat." Ulrika's hands were busy. "A great big devil! If it isn't two!"

Karl Oskar noticed something moving, something furry, with black, shining, drenched hair. And he saw a streak of dark-red blood.

The birth-giving wife clung convulsively to her husband, seeking his embrace in her deepest agony. Severe, slow tremblings shook her body, not unlike those moments when her body was joined with his—and from moments of lust had grown moments of agony.

While the mates this time embraced, their child came into the world.

A hair-covered crown appeared, a brow, a nose, a chin —the face of a human being: Ulrika held in her hands a living, kicking, red-skinned little creature.

But the newcomer was still tied to his mother.

"The navel cord!" Ulrika called out. "Where did I put the wool shears?"

For safety's sake she had rinsed Kristina's wool shears in warm water in advance; they had seemed a little dirty and rusty, and one was supposed to wash everything that touched the mother's body during childbirth. Oh, yes, now she remembered—she had laid the shears to dry near the fire.

"On the hearth! Hand me the wool shears, Karl Oskar!"

With the old, rusty wool shears Ulrika cut the blood-red cord which still united mother and child.

Then she made that most important inspection of the newborn: "He is shaped like his father. It's a boy!"

Kristina had given life to a son, a sturdy boy. His skin was bright red, he fluttered his arms and legs, and let out his first complaining sounds. From the warm mother-womb the child had helterskelter arrived in a cold, alien world. The mother's cries had died down, the child's began.

Ulrika wrapped the newborn in the towel Danjel had sent with her: "A hell of a big chunk! Hold him and feel, Karl Oskar!"

She handed the child to the father; they had no steel-yard here, but she guessed he weighed at least twelve pounds. Ulrika herself had borne one that weighed thirteen and a half. She knew; the poor woman who had to squeeze out such a lump did not have an easy time. Ulrika had prayed to God to save her—an unmarried woman—from bearing such big brats; the Lord ought to reserve that honor for married women, it was easier for them to increase mankind with sturdy plants. And the Lord had gracefully heard her prayer—He had taken the child to Him before he was three months old.

Thus for the first time Karl Oskar had been present at childbed—at the birth of his third son—his fourth, counting the twin who had died.

Yes, Ulrika was right, his son weighed enough. But he lacked everything else in this world: they hadn't a piece of cloth to swaddle him in; his little son was wrapped at birth in a borrowed towel.

Ulrika warmed some bath water for the newborn, then she held him in the pot and splashed water over his body while he yelled. And her eyes took in the child with satisfaction all the while—she felt as if he had been her own handiwork.

She said: "The boy was made in Sweden, but we must pray God this will have no ill effect on him."

Kristina had lain quiet after her delivery. Now she asked Karl Oskar to put on the coffeepot.

She had put aside a few handfuls of coffee beans for her childbed; Ulrika had neither drunk nor eaten since her arrival last evening, they must now treat her to coffee.

"Haven't you got anything stronger, Karl Oskar?" Ulrika asked. "Kristina must have her delivery schnapps. She has earned it this evil night."

The delivery schnapps was part of the ritual, Karl Oskar remembered; he had given it to Kristina at her previous childbeds. And this time she needed it more than ever. There were a few swallows left in the keg of American brannvin Jonas Petter had brought to the housewarming.

"I think you could stand a drink yourself," Ulrika said to Karl Oskar.

She finished washing the baby and handed him to the impatient mother. Meanwhile Karl Oskar prepared the coffee and served it on top of an oak-stump chair at Kristina's bedside. He offered a mug to Ulrika, and the three of them enjoyed the warming drink. The whisky in the keg was also divided three ways—to the mother, the midwife, and the child's father. And the father drank as much as the two women together, and he could not remember that brannvin had ever tasted so good as this morning.

While the birth had taken place inside the log house, a new day had dawned outside. It was a frosty November morning with a clear sun shining from a cloudless sky over the white, silver-strewn grass on the shore of Lake Ki-Chi-Saga.

The newly arrived Swedes in the St. Croix Valley had increased their number by one—the first one to be a citizen in their new country.

XVIII

Mother and Child

The child is handed to the mother—it had left her and it has come back.

All is over, all is quiet, all is well.

Kristina lies with her newborn son at her breast. She lies calm and silent, she is delivered, she has changed worlds, she is in the newly delivered woman's blissful world. It is the Glad One—the public whore of the home parish—her intimate friend, who has delivered her. But it is the child—in leaving her womb—who has delivered her from the agony; the child is her joy, and her joy is back with her, is here at her breast.

Mother and child are with each other.

The mother tries to help the child's groping lips find a hold on her breast. The child feels with its mouth aimlessly, rubs its nose like a kitten; how wonderfully soft is its nose against the mother's breast; as yet it seeks blindly. But when the nipple presses in between its lips, its mouth closes around it; the child sucks awkwardly and slowly. Gradually the movements of the tiny lips grow stronger— it answers her with its lips: it answers the mother's tenderness and at the same time satisfies its own desires.

The mother lies joyful and content. The newborn has relieved her of all her old concerns, as he himself now has become all her concern. Now it is he who causes her anxiety: she hasn't a single garment ready to swaddle his naked body, not even a piece of cloth, not the smallest rag. What can she use for swaddling clothes?

A child could not arrive in a poorer home than this, where nothing is ready for it, it could not be given to a poorer mother. Wretched creature! Arriving stark naked, to such impoverished parents, in a log house in the wilderness, in a foreign land! Wretched little creature. . . .

But a child could never come to a happier mother than Kristina, and therefore its security is the greatest in the world.

At her breast lies a little human seedling, entrusted to her in its helplessness and defenselessness. It depends on her if it shall grow up or wither down, if it shall live or die. And at this thought a tenderness grows inside her heart, so strong that tears come to her eyes. But they are not tears of sorrow, they are only the proof of a mother's strong, sure feeling for her newborn child.

When God gave her this child in her poverty, He showed that He could trust her. And if the Creator trusted her, then she could wholeheartedly trust Him in return. From this conviction springs the sense of security and comfort which the child instills in the mother.

Poor little one—happy little one! Why does she worry? Why is she concerned about him? She *has* something fine to swaddle him in! Why hadn't she thought of it before? She should have remembered at once: her white petticoat, the one she never uses, because it is a piece of finery. Her petticoat of thick, fine linen, woven by herself, her bridal petticoat! As yet she has used it only once—at her wedding. And for what can she use it here in the forest? Here she'll never go to weddings, here she'll never be so much dressed up as to need such a petticoat. She can cut it to pieces and sew diapers from it; it is large, voluminous, it will make many diapers. And she must use it because she has nothing else. But isn't it the best thing she could ever find for protection of her child, that delicate little body, with its soft, tender skin? Her own bridal petticoat!

How happy the woman who can cut up her best petticoat for her child.

So much for the clothing. Food for the child the mother has herself. Milk for the child runs slowly as yet, only a few white drops trickling. And Kristina aids the newborn's blindly seeking mouth, pushes her nipple into blindly seeking lips which do not yet quite know how to hold and close and suck, to receive the mother's first gift.

All is well, all is over, all is quiet. Now mother and child rest in mutual security.

XIX

The Letter to Sweden

North America at Taylors Falls Postoffice in
Minnesota Teritory, November 15, Anno 1850

Dearly Beloved Parents,
May all be well with you is my Daily wish.

I will now let you know how Our Journey progressed, we were freighted on Steam wagon to Buffalo
and by Steam ship further over large Lakes and
Rivers, we had an honest interpreter. On the river
boat Danjel Andreasson lost his youngest daughter in
that terrible pest the Cholera. The girl could not live
through it. But the rest of us are in good health and
well fed. Nothing happened on the journey and in
August we arrived at our place of settling.

We live here in a Great Broad valley, I have
claimed and marked 160 American acres, that is
about 130 Swedish acres and I will have *delasjon*
with the payment until the Land is offered for Sale.
It is all fertile Soil. We shall clear the Land and can
harvest as much Hay as we want. We live at a fair
Lake, full of fish and my whole farm is overgrown
with Oak, Pine, Sugar Maples, Lindens, Walnuts,
Elms and other kinds whose names I do not know.

I have timbered up a good house for us. Danjel and his Family settled near us in the valley, also Jonas Petter. Danjel no longer preaches Ake Svensson's teaching, nor is he making noise about his religion, he is pious and quiet and is left in peace by Ministers and Sheriffs. Danjel calls his place New Karragarde.

Our beloved children are in good health and live well, I will also inform you that we have a new little son who made his first entry into this world the seventh of this November, at very daybreak. He is already a *sitter* as are all who are born here. We shall in time carry him to Baptism but here are ministers of many Religions and we dare not take the Lord's Supper for fear it is the wrong faith. Here is no Religious Law but all have their free will.

Scarcely any people live in this Valley, rich soil is empty on all sides of us for many miles which is a great shame and Sin. We have no trouble with the indians, the savages are curious about new people but harm no one. They have brown skin and live like cattle without houses or anything. They eat snakes and grasshoppers but the whites drive away the indians as they come.

There is a great difference between Sweden and America in food and clothing. Here people eat substantial fare and wheat bread to every meal. Newcomers get hard bowels from their food but the Americans are honest and helpful to their acquaintances and snub no one if ever so poor. Wooden shoes are not used, it is too simple for the Americans. They honor all work, menfolk milk cows and wash the floor. Both farmers and Ministers perform womanwork without shame. In a town called Stillwater we were given quarters with a priest who did his own chores.

I have nothing of importance to write about. Nothing unusual has happened to us since my last letter. Things go well for us and if health remains with us we shall surely improve our situation even though the country is unknown to us. I don't complain of anything, Kristina was a little sad in the beginning but she has now forgotten it.

305

We hope soon to get a letter from you but letters are much delayed on the long way. Winter has begun in the Valley and the mail can not get through because of the ice on the river. I greet you dear parents, also from my wife and children, and Sister Lydia is heartily greeted by her Brother. My Brother Robert will write himself, he fools with writing easier than I. Kristina sends her greetings to her kind parents in Duvemala. Nothing is lacking her here in our new settlement.

The year is soon over and we are one year nearer Eternity, I hope these lines will find you in good health.

Written down hastily by your devoted son
Karl Oskar Nilsson

PART THREE

To Keep Alive
Through the Winter

XX

The Indian in the Treetop

Some distance west of the creek which empited into Lake
Ki-Chi-Saga a sandstone cliff rose high above the forest
pines. The cliff had the copper-brown color of the Indians,
and its shape strongly resembled the head of an Indian.
Seen from below, a broad, smooth, stone brow could easily be recognized. Under the forehead lay two black eye
holes, well protected by the formidable forehead boulders.
Between the eyes a protruding cliff indicated a handsome
Indian nose. The upper lip was formed by a ledge, and
under it opened a broad indentation; this was the mouth,
a dark gap. Below the mouth opening was a chin ledge.
Even the neck of the Indian could be discerned below the
chin and on top of the head grew maple saplings and el-
derberry bushes which the Indian in summer carried like a
green wreath on his head.

This cliff in the forest was visible from afar and served
as a landmark. The Swedish settlers at Lake Ki-Chi-Saga
soon referred to it as the Indian-head.

In the caves and holes of the rock, animals found protection and hiding places, and those forest creatures which
sought refuge in rain and storm within the Indian's jaws
could rest there in comfort. But on the deer path below
could be seen great boulders, which from time to time had
fallen from the cliff. And near some of these blocks were

309

whitened, disintegrating bones, remnants of animal skeletons; perhaps, as a forest beast had run by below, the Indian had spit out a stone from his mouth and crushed it.

This Indian was of stone, and as dead as a stone, but the white bones indicated that he could be trusted as little as a living Indian.

When Robert passed the Indian-head he trod lightly and stole quickly by, lest a boulder be loosed by his step and come crashing down on him. No one knew when the Indian might hurl a stone at a passer-by, human or beast.

In the beginning, Robert was as much afraid of the Indians as he was curious about them. But as time went by his curiosity increased and his fear diminished. The Indians seemed so friendly that they might in time become a nuisance. They frightened people sometimes with their terrifying appearance, they liked to deck themselves in all kinds of animal parts, but as yet they had done no harm to the Swedish settlers.

Karl Oskar despised the Indians for their laziness and called them useless creatures. Kristina pitied them because they were so thin and lived in such wretched hovels; and both she and Karl Oskar were grateful not to have been created Indians.

No one knew what the copperskins thought of their white neighbors, for no one understood their language. Robert guessed they considered their pale brethren fools to waste their time in work. He had begun to wonder which one of the two peoples could be considered wiser, the whites or the browns, the Christians or the heathens. The Indians were lazy, they did not till the earth, and what work they did was done without effort. He had watched them fell trees: they did not cut down the tree with an ax, they made a fire around it and burned it off at the root. The Christian hewed and labored and sweated before he got his tree down. But the heathen sat and rested and smoked his pipe until the fire burned through and the tree fell by itself, without a single ax blow.

The Indians did not waste their strength in work; they spared their bodies for better use, they saved their strength for enjoyment. At their feasts they danced for three weeks at a stretch—it was just as well they had rested beforehand. But Karl Oskar and the other peasants in Smaland had accustomed themselves to tiresome labor and drudgery every day, they would not have been able to dance for even one week, so worn out were they. The heathens wisely economized their body strength so that they were capable of more endurance than the Christians.

The Indians were vain, they decorated themselves with buffalo horns, they greased their hair with bear fat, they smeared red clay over their faces. At times they painted their whole bodies so red they resembled blood-stained butchers; in such things they were childish. But in other ways they were so clever one might take them for magicians; their bows were simple and useless looking—only a piece of skin stretched between the two ends of a broken-off branch—yet their arrows killed game in its tracks; Robert had once seen an Indian shoot a big buck with his bow and arrow. The brownskins' flint arrows were short, but they sharpened them against a peculiar stone called Indian-stone until their points grew so sharp they would penetrate hide and flesh and shatter bone.

The Indians were childish in another way—they believed dead people could eat and drink; they carried food and drink to the graves of their relatives.

But in one way they were much wiser than the whites: they did not hoe the earth.

Robert had once seen the picture of an Indian girl in a book; she was so beautiful he would have liked to make her his wife, could he have found her. But the young women he had seen here among the Chippewas were almost all ugly: they had short legs, clumsy bodies, broad, square faces with thick noses. The older women had such rough skin that they were almost repulsive. Yet white menfolk were said to desire Indian women. Samuel Nojd, the fur trapper, had related that in the old days there were French trappers so burning with lust they couldn't pass a female in the forest. They had raped every Indian woman they had encountered, however ugly or old she might be. And this caused them no more concern than shooting an animal.

However, Nojd said, the trappers had grown less eager to attack Indian women after the Sioux had taken a gruesome revenge on one white man. They had tied him to a pole, and for a whole night they sharpened their knives in front of him, now and then calling out to him: "You may live until our knives are sharp!" At intervals they tested

311

their knives by cutting off a piece of his skin. At daybreak the knives were sharp—and the trapper insane. Then the Indians stuck their well-honed knives into his breast, cutting loose his heart, as slowly as they could, and the man lived a long while with his heart dangling outside him like a big red blossom. This had taken place near the Indian cliff. Later the savages had buried the trapper in the cave called the mouth of the Indian-head. Every day at dawn the trapper's agonized cries could still be heard, Samuel Nojd concluded.

The Sioux, who from time to time roamed through these regions, were much more cruel than the Chippewas. But Robert did not avoid the Indians because of their cruelty or their heathenish ways; rather, he admired and esteemed them for their wisdom and their easy way of living. Had he himself been given brown skin instead of white, he would not have been forced either to cut timber in the forest or grub hoe the earth.

2

The night frost grew sharper; each morning the meadow resembled a field of glittering white lilies. An intense storm had in a single day shaken the leaves from the trees, carrying them into the air like clouds of driven snow; afterward the surface of Lake Ki-Chi-Saga shone golden yellow with all the floating leaves from the naked forest on its shores. After the storm came the cold, and land and water were soon frozen hard. On the lake the mirror-clear ice crust thickened each night, and in the ground the frost dug deeper, not to release its hold until spring.

No one could work frozen ground, and Robert put away his grub hoe for the winter. He must now help his brother cut fence rails; in the spring Karl Oskar would fence the part of his land he intended to cultivate, and thousands of rails were needed.

Robert and Arvid visited each other every Sunday; either Robert would walk over to the settlement at Lake Gennesaret, or Arvid would come to Ki-Chi-Saga. Usually they went down to the lake shore, where they made a fire; here the two friends from Sweden could sit undisturbed in intimate talk.

Robert had told Arvid when he first decided to leave his

312

Swedish service and emigrate to North America. Now he again had a secret of a similar nature, and Arvid was the only one he confided in. One frosty Sunday, as they sat feeding their fire on the lake shore, he began: "Can you keep your mouth shut?"

"I never say anything. You can rely on me."

"I carry a great secret—no one knows it; I'm going to run away from here as soon as I can."

Arvid was astonished: "What's that you say? You want to leave your brother?"

"Karl Oskar is not my master."

"I thought you two brothers would stay together."

"I shall travel far away and dig gold."

"Dig up gold? The hell you will! And you haven't told anyone?"

"Such a plan must be kept secret."

Robert explained: It wasn't that his brother treated him badly, Karl Oskar neither kicked nor hit him; but the work was no different from the drudgery he had endured while a hired hand in Sweden; it was equally depressing and heavy; the days dragged along with the same monotony. He could not stand it much longer, he had never wanted to be a day laborer, he knew a shorter way to riches, and here in America no one could stop him from traveling wherever he wished.

"Do you know where the gold lies?" Arvid asked.

"Yes. In California. Farthest away to the west."

"Is California a—a broad land?"

"Broader than Minnesota."

"Do you know the exact place? I mean, where the gold lies?"

"No. I'll have to look and ask my way, I guess."

"Is the gold spread all over? Or is it in one place?"

"It's spread all over."

Arvid thought about this for a while, then he said: Gold was supposed to glitter, it should be easy to see it, if one looked sharp. But if California was bigger than Minnesota, and if the gold was spread all over that broad country, then Robert might have a troublesome, long-drawn-out journey before he found it; he would have to walk over the whole country and look everywhere.

Robert realized that Arvid did not know anything about the gold land; he had only heard the name. He must ex-

313

plain to his friend about that country, since he wished to share his plans for the future with Arvid.

And so Robert began a simple explanation of California. He told Arvid all he had read and heard, besides much he had neither read nor heard but which he knew must be so, without exactly knowing how he knew it. And perhaps the things he knew in this way were the most important.

In California the valuable metal called gold was almost as common as wood in Minnesota. Gold was used for all kinds of tools, implements, and furniture, because it was cheaper than iron or wood. Rich people used gold chamber pots. The gold grew in that country on fields called gold fields. It grew quite near the surface. Only a light hoe was needed to reach it, not a heavy ten-pound grub hoe such as he labored with here. In some places no hoe at all was required—there were those who had dug up as much as fifty thousand dollars' worth of gold with a tablespoon. The only tool needed was a wooden bowl in which to wash the gold to remove the dirt. And if you couldn't afford a bowl, you might wash the gold in your hat; an old, worn-out hat was all one needed to gather a fortune. And when the gold had been washed clean of earth and other dirt, until it shone and glittered according to its nature, one had only to put it in a skin pouch and carry it to the bank, and then return to withdraw the interest each month. All gold pickers with good sense did this; the others squandered their gold in gambling dens, or ruined themselves with whores.

One needn't pick up a great deal of gold in order to get rich. About a hundred pounds would be right, or as much as one could carry on one's back; about two bushels would be right.

"How big might the gold clods be?" Arvid asked.

"They are of different weights."

The gold grew in pieces of all sizes, from about half a pound to twenty-five pounds weight, Robert explained. There were chunks as large as a human head, while others were tiny as dove eggs. There was also a still smaller kind, about the size of hazelnuts, and these lumps were most prevalent and easiest to find. But they were such a nuisance to pick that he did not intend to bother with them; for himself he would choose the larger chunks, then he

314

wouldn't have to bend his back too often; by picking the twenty-five-pound pieces one could save one's strength in the gold fields.

Nor would Robert gather such a great fortune that it would be a burden to him. He wanted a medium-sized fortune that would be easy to look after and not bring him eternal damnation; he did not intend to build himself a castle, or buy expensive riding horses, or marry some extravagant woman with a desire for diamonds and pearls. He only wished to gain enough of a fortune to live for the rest of his life without drudgery, or labor, or masters.

Robert wanted to weigh up for himself a hundred pounds of the California gold; then he would return completely satisfied. Perhaps he might even return to Sweden and buy himself a manor house. He had heard of two farm hands from Smaland who had dug gold in California and then returned home and bought great estates. They had each brought home a sack of gold, which they had exchanged for Swedish coin. But Robert thought he would be satisfied with a smaller estate, about two hundred acres or so; the larger ones required too much attention and could easily become a burden to their owners. Robert would get himself an overseer; and he would pay his hands well—a thousand daler a year, and they would be let off work at six o'clock, Saturdays at five.

"You are good to them," said Arvid.

"Having served as farm hand myself I know what they deserve," said Robert modestly.

"And . . . was it your thought to travel alone to California?"

"No. That's what I wanted to tell you: the two of us should go together."

There should be two, because the road was so awfully long. And two would find the gold much more easily than one. True enough—gold glittered and shone, but four eyes could see twice as much as two; and two would be safer against robbers and thieves.

"Are you coming with me, Arvid?"

It was the same question Robert had once before asked his friend, one night long ago in a stable room in their homeland. Then it had concerned North America, and so great had been Arvid's surprise at Robert's daring and ingenuity that he had been speechless for a long moment.

Now the question concerned a journey to the land of gold in North America, and that land also lay so far away that the sun needed extra hours to reach it in the mornings.

Robert repeated his question: "Are you coming with me, Arvid?"

"I want to—that you must know. But I'm in Danjel's service."

"He cannot keep you here! Not in America."

"But I owe my master for the journey here."

Danjel Andreasson had paid the expense for his servant's emigration, and Arvid felt it would be dishonest to leave him before he had repaid Danjel through his work. But he too knew full well that no master could keep him longer than he wanted to stay; no servant law was in force here, no sheriff fetched runaway farm hands.

"You can pay Danjel what you owe him when you come back from California!" said Robert. "You can just hand him a chunk of gold."

Yes, returning from the gold fields Arvid would be so well-to-do that he need never again lift his hand in work, neither with ax, hoe, nor any other tool. He had only to carry his gold to the bank and each month withdraw sufficient interest to pay his expenses; there would be plenty of money to pay Danjel.

Moreover, the two youths had once and for all promised each other to stick together in America.

"I haven't forgotten that promise," said Arvid, deeply moved. "I want to follow you, that you must know. But I must talk to Danjel before I shake your hand on it."

Robert already felt sure he could persuade Arvid to go with him to California.

"You mustn't whisper a word to anyone! I don't intend to tell Karl Oskar until the day before I leave!"

He had already figured out the way to take: They would board the *Red Wing* next time the packet steamer came to Stillwater, then the boat would carry them down the Mississippi to St. Louis, the same way they had traveled last summer. By helping to load wood and wash dishes, they would not have to pay a cent for their transportation on the *Red Wing*. From St. Louis they could walk dryshod all the way to California, following the great highways that led to the West.

"Isn't there any—any ocean in between?" Arvid asked with some concern.

Robert assured him there was not; only solid land, mostly dry, sandy stretches where they could walk comfortably to the home of the gold in the New World.

Robert had long been listening to his left ear, its persistent humming and ringing urging him on: *Come! Come!* A new land far away called him again, and having obtained his friend's promise of company, he would soon follow the call.

But the winter was to interfere with his plans; the frost grew in intensity, soon the whole St. Croix River was covered with solid ice. The *Red Wing*'s bell no longer was heard in Stillwater; indeed, no craft would be seen on the river until next spring when the ice had broken up; the inhabitants of the St. Croix Valley were separated from the outside world by the frozen river.

For the rest of the winter Robert was shut up in Minnesota Territory.

3

Early one Sunday morning, Robert picked up his brother's gun and went into the forest. New-fallen snow, three or four inches deep, covered the ground; it was fine hunting weather. Not far from the cabin he came on the tracks of an elk, and hunting fever seized him. The elk could not be very far away—Karl Oskar had not yet shot an elk—think if he could shoot this big animal and be the first one to bring home all the meat!

The elk tracks led past the Indian-head, and Robert stopped a moment to look up at the cliff. The stone Indian stared back at him with his unchanging, black eye holes. As long as this cliff had existed—for thousands of years—those deep, inscrutable eyes had looked out over the forest; the Indian stood guard for his brown-skinned people, an eternal watchman over the hunting grounds hereabouts. But his green wreath was now withered, the bushes on top of his head had lost their leaves, the wind whipped the naked, dry branches; only above the Indian's left ear some limbs still carried their leaves—like eagle feathers stuck behind his ear.

Every time Robert looked at the enormous face of this cliff, a strange sensation of uneasiness stole over him; there was something threatening in the stone Indian's eternal immobility; he felt like a sneaking intruder on the age-old hunting grounds of the savages.

Suddenly he crouched, holding his breath: he had discovered a living Indian close by.

Below the cliff, hardly a gunshot from where he stood, a human figure huddled in the top of a small birch. His face was turned away from Robert, but he could see skinny legs, partly covered by tattered skins which fluttered in the wind. And near his hands Robert could clearly see a bent branch—the Indian's bow!

For a long minute he grew cold and hot in quick succession. An Indian lurking in the tree, with his bow and sharp arrows! Whom could this sly brownskin be waiting for? White intruders who trespassed on his hunting grounds? Was he waiting for Robert? Was that why he had climbed the birch? The Indians were said to surprise their prey from treetops. . . .

Robert held on to his gun butt with trembling fingers. Apparently he had discovered the Indian before being seen himself; why not fire first? But if he missed? An Indian could shoot a score of arrows in a minute. And already Robert could feel them penetrate his body—twenty arrows all over his body! Hadn't he seen one single Indian arrow kill a huge buck? If he should miss—he could see himself dead.

But perhaps the Indian too was after elk. Perhaps he too had seen the fresh tracks? If he were waiting for game, then Robert might be able to sneak away before being seen. As yet there had been no threatening move.

Robert threw himself down in the snow and began hitching himself away on his elbows, his gun above his head. In this way he moved some twenty yards until he reached a thicket, behind which he crouched cautiously; now the man in the tree could not see him. He wasn't sure if an arrow had pursued him—a bow did not give a report like a gun, and he didn't hear too well.

He waited a few minutes but nothing happened. Carefully he separated the branches to peek through: the Indian was still sitting in the tree, he didn't seem to have moved the least bit, he still held his bow in the same position. Indians could sit for hours in a tree, as immobile as stones; he must still be waiting, watching the trail below the cliff.

Robert was now sure the Indian had not yet seen him, and if he could get away a little farther he would be beyond reach of an arrow.

As he began to steal away he heard a rustle in the thicket. He listened. Was it the wind? Or a rabbit? Or was it an arrow? He heard the sound again; some branches moved close by his head where he lay on the ground. It must have been an arrow striking in the thicket, the Indian must have discovered him when he peeked through a moment before.

For a third time there was a rustle in the bush, the branches quivered; now he could clearly hear the whizz of an arrow through the air!

He grew panicky; his heartbeats throbbed in his ears, he felt choked. He aimed the gun in the general direction of the Indian and fired. The report echoed loudly against the cliff, the shot must have been heard for miles. It was so loud that it deafened him and echoed inside his eardrums. What had he done? He had fired the gun in fright, without exactly knowing why. Now all the Indians in the vicinity would be warned, now they would all come after him!

Seized by an overwhelming fear, Robert took to his heels. He ran as if the devil were after him. He ran toward the cabin the shortest way he knew, he slunk between the trunks of a thick stand of timbers; he was conscious of leaving tracks behind for his pursuers to follow, but he was too scared to look back; the Indians could run twice as fast as white men, and they had fresh snow tracks to follow. But Robert dared not look to find out if they followed him; he did not stop to consider that if an Indian had pursued him he would immediately have been overtaken.

He didn't even slow down as he reached the lake shore and saw the cabin, he rushed panting in through the door and sank down on his bed. It was some time before he recovered his breath sufficiently to speak, and Karl Oskar and Kristina watched him and wondered what had happened.

Robert had brought back no game. But Karl Oskar knew that he often missed with his shots and as he now looked at the gun he could see that it had been fired; a little annoyed at this waste of powder and bullet, he asked: "What have you been shooting at?"

"I shot—an Indian."

"You lie!"

"No. No. But he shot at me first."

And by and by Robert breathed easier and could stammer out his story: He had almost been shot to death, near the Indian cliff. A brownskin had been sitting in wait for him in a tree. Robert had sought protection behind some bushes, but the Indian had shot several arrows at him. He had had to defend himself and he had fired a shot at the Indian. Then he had run home as fast as he could.

"Did no one come after you?"

"Not as far as I could see. That's why I'm sure I shot him."

Karl Oskar grew more concerned. But he controlled himself, he didn't want to say anything that might frighten Kristina. He took Robert outside and questioned him in detail about everything that had taken place below the cliff.

Since the Indian had not pursued him, Robert was sure his bullet had hit him, he had seen him fall down from the tree like a fat woodcock.

"Did you really see him fall?" asked Karl Oskar.

"Well—I ran as fast as I could. . . ."

"But you don't know for sure if you hit him? I hope to God you didn't!"

And Karl Oskar told his brother what he had not wanted to say in Kristina's presence: If he had shot an Indian, he had brought disaster on all of them.

He had many times admonished Robert to avoid the Indians and never in any way to disturb them. All had been well so far, they had lived in peace with the Chippewas. If it was true that Robert had been waylaid and attacked with arrows, and had defended himself, then he was within his rights. But if he had wounded or killed a peaceful Indian, then revenge-hungry tribe members would make them all pay for it; then their copper-colored neighbors would soon come and call on them.

"I only hope you missed him!" Karl Oskar repeated.

The next few days Karl Oskar went in constant fear that the Indians would appear at the cabin for revenge. He tried to figure out how he might summon help in time. He had heard of Fort Snelling, near St. Paul, where the Americans kept a company of soldiers to protect the whites. But it was thirty miles to the fort, and long before a message could reach there the Indians would have had time to murder them and burn down their house. There was this about the savages, they could never be relied on; no one could predict what they would do.

But then one day something happened to allay his fears: The Indians on the island in Lake Ki-Chi-Saga broke up their camp and moved away; brownskins no longer lived in their vicinity. It was the custom of the Chippewas to live in winter quarters some forty or fifty miles to the south.

4

Some weeks went by, and Karl Oskar had almost forgotten about Robert's encounter with the Indian in the tree. Then one day, having picked up his gun to follow some forest birds, he happened to pass the Indian cliff. Snowdrifts had now piled on the Indian-head, giving him wintry eyebrows, and a crown of glittering snow. In summer this Indian had a green wreath, in winter a white crown. But Karl Oskar's alert eyes espied something else: A birch tree grew below the cliff, and something was fastened to the top of the birch.

He walked toward it to investigate; someone was hanging in the treetop, a human being, an Indian. This Indian could not move, however, he was frozen stiff. The wind had swept away the snow, but no odor tainted the air—the frost was protecting the corpse from decay.

Robert's Indian was still hanging in his tree. He had hung there for weeks; he was stone dead. The shot had hit him then, the calamity Karl Oskar feared had taken place. But the rest of the tribe must not have discovered what had happened to one of their members, they must not have found his body. Or why hadn't they come for revenge?

Then he discovered something else in the treetop, something he couldn't understand at first. He walked around the tree, looking up; he climbed a stone to see better, and suddenly the mystery was solved; now he knew why they had been spared a visit from revengeful neighbors: *The Indian in the tree had been hung there!* His neck was pierced through by the top of the birch, which had been sharpened and stuck through the neck like a spear. The top of the young tree was bent like a bow, the Indian was strung up through his neck, like a dead .fish on a forked stick.

And now Karl Oskar remembered what he had heard about the Indians, how they preserved the bodies of their dead in wintertime, when the digging of a grave in the frozen ground was too hard work. They strung up the corpses in trees, high enough above ground to be safe from beasts. The dead one had been placed there by his own tribe!

He left the Indian in the tree and walked home; he had no desire to disturb the body, he did not wish to interfere with the doings of the Indians. But now he knew the truth about his brother's adventure: Robert had been attacked by an Indian who was strung up in a tree, he had run for his life from a dead Indian.

Walking home, Karl Oskar recalled Robert's story on the *Charlotta* about the captain's slave trade. That time he had greatly doubted his brother's veracity; this time he knew that Robert had invented the story, he had proof that his brother was a liar.

As soon as he reached home he called Robert aside: "Did you say the Indian in the tree shot an arrow at you?"

"Yes! He shot several arrows, right into the bush where I hid!" Robert assured him.

"Did any of the arrows hit you?"

"No. Luckily enough, the bush protected me."

"Yes, I understand. I guess the Indian had poor aim. And I don't wonder—you see, he was dead. He's still hanging dead in the tree. The top is stuck right through his neck!"

Karl Oskar took Robert with him to the tree with the Indian. This was his proof, and he turned to Robert, sterner than ever: "You're a damned liar! The Indian never shot a single arrow at you!"

"But I could hear them rustle in the bush!"

"I think it was the wind."

"It was arrows! I'm sure! I could hear them!"

"You don't hear very well. And you invent lies! You spin yarns! Now I want you to tell me the truth."

322

"But it is the truth! I swear it, Karl Oskar."

To Robert, his story of the Indian in the treetop was irrevocably the truth. The brownskin had shot at least three arrows at him, with his own ears he had heard them whizz through the thicket. And how could Karl Oskar know that the Indian wasn't alive when he shot at Robert? Moreover, he couldn't remember if the Indian had been sitting in exactly that tree; perhaps it was another Indian, in another tree. He, Robert, had seen a living Indian, with a bow, he could not alter his story in the least, for he had told the truth.

Robert's behavior angered and worried Karl Oskar; not only did the boy lie, he was so thoroughly dishonest that he stubbornly insisted his lies were true. He insisted he had been attacked by the Indian and that he had run for his life.

Now Karl Oskar spoke sternly, with fatherly concern: Was Robert so hardened that he believed his own fabrications? Didn't he know the difference between truth and lies? If he continued to invent and tell tales like this, people would soon believe not a single word he said, no one would have confidence in him. And if no one could rely on him, he would have a hard time getting along in America. He must be careful about what he said, or disaster might follow.

He must realize that Karl Oskar felt responsible for him as an older brother, now that he was in a foreign country without his parents to look after him. Didn't he think his own brother was concerned for his welfare? Why couldn't he admit that he had lied, and promise never to do it again? He ought to do it for his own sake, for his own good!

But Robert admitted nothing. His ear had heard the Indian's whizzing arrows in the bush; at least three times his ear had heard them, and this remained the truth to him.

Karl Oskar could get nowhere. Robert had a weak character, and no persistence in work or effort. He hadn't a farmer's feeling for the earth, he did what he was told, but unwillingly, without joy or pleasure. At work he often acted as if he neither saw nor heard, as if walking in his sleep in full daylight. Karl Oskar had long been aware of these shortcomings in his brother, but he had hoped they would disappear as he grew older and his common sense increased. A settler in this new land needed a sturdy character, persistence, clear vision; he couldn't walk about in his sleep. . . . To these faults, Robert had lately added this infernal habit of lying, more dangerous than all the rest—it might bring him to utter ruin.

After this happening, Karl Oskar's concern about Robert increased; he thought it might have been better if his brother had remained in Sweden.

XXI

The Swedish Settlers' Almanac

November passed with changing weather—cold days followed milder ones. Little snow fell. But in early December the first blizzard broke, beating the cabin walls for four days.

All living creatures sought their lairs for shelter against the fierce north wind. The snow did not fall on the ground, it was driven down violently, flung by the forceful sling of the storm. Man and beast trying to move against this wind must crouch, almost creep along. And the north wind brought in its wake a cold that penetrated bone and marrow, that made the blood stop in its course.

During this blizzard no one ventured outside unless forced by necessity. It was an undertaking even to open the door. Karl Oskar had to go to the shanty morning, noon, and evening, to give Lady water and fodder. It was hardly more than a hundred steps between the cabin and the small stable, yet the first day of the blizzard he almost lost his way. The snow beat into his eyes so that he could not see, everything around him was snow, hurled, whirling snow; he walked in a thick, gyrating snow cloud, fumbling about like a blind person. He could not see one step ahead of him, he lost his sense of direction, and wandered about a long time before he found the cabin.

In the raging blizzards of this country he could lose his

way a few steps from his house. And should he get lost on his way between cabin and stable there was the danger of freezing to death in the snow.

Karl Oskar felt the need of something to guide him between his two houses, and from the linden bark he had saved he now twisted a rope, fastening one end to the cabin and the other to the shanty. While walking the short distance he never let go of the rope; each time he opened the door and faced the blizzard he felt like a diver descending to the bottom of the sea and holding to a guide rope—without it he might have been lost.

During the blizzard Karl Oskar milked Lady every day. The cow still gave little at each milking—only one quart —but this was sufficient for the children; the grownups had to do without. He had never before sat on a milking stool, and now he learned a chore which in this country was usually performed by the menfolk. Strong hands were needed to squeeze the milk from the teats, and he wondered why milking had always been considered woman's work.

Now that the feared winter had come Kristina spent most of her time within the house; she had regained her strength and resumed her household tasks but she dared not go outside. She said the snow, like everything else, was different here: at home the snowflakes fell soft as wool on one's face, here they were hard and sharp and pricked like awl points.

Karl Oskar had made sure they need not freeze in the house this winter; outside the door he had stacked firewood in high piles, logs from dry pines long dead on root, excellent wood that gave much heat. As long as the fire was kept burning it was warm in the house. He had also split pitch wood in great quantity to be used for lighting the cabin; these splinters were stuck in the wall between the logs and used as candles, but they had to be watched carefully to avoid setting fire to the house.

Their home was now taking on the appearance of a carpenter shop. Karl Oskar spent much time making furniture and tools—chairs, food vessels, snow shovels, hay forks, rakes. He busied himself long after the others had gone to bed. Being handy with wood, he could use it for many purposes; a settler beginning from the very beginning had to use it for almost everything.

326

He had already worked as lumberman, carpenter, mason, roofer, rope maker—now he attempted a new handicraft: that of shoemaker. Their leather shoes were wearing out and they couldn't buy new ones; he must make wooden shoes for his family. No alder trees grew in this forest so he decided to use elm; the American elm was softer than the Swedish and easy to work with. But wooden shoes could not be made comfortable and light without years of experience. He had neither experience nor the proper tools; the shoes that came from his hands were clumsy and ill fitting though they could be worn. He made one pair of wooden shoes for each member of his family except the baby, who would not need shoes until he could walk. For his newborn son he made a cradle—a dug-out log which he fastened to rockers.

Then he began to make a table. He had made up his mind to have a fine table, solid and well made, a durable piece of furniture, a table he could ask visitors to sit down to without feeling ashamed. And he worked long and carefully on this piece of furniture. He cut a block from the thickest oak he could find and made a table top; to this he fastened a smaller log for footing. He planed the top until it shone; now they would not get splinters in their fingers when eating. The leg logs also caused him great labor, the table must stand evenly on the floor without leaning or limping.

And he took his time with the table, time hung heavily upon him during these winter days and long evenings. And when he rested he got into the habit of fingering the three books they had brought from Sweden: the Bible, the psalmbook, and the almanac. Two thick books and one thin; the thick ones contained spiritual fare, they were the soul's guide to eternity; the thin book was their guide in this transitory world. Karl Oskar had used the almanac most often, and now in the last month of the year it was badly worn and soiled. Each Sunday he or Kristina read the text in the psalmbook, and each Sunday Karl Oskar also looked in the almanac to determine where they were in the calendar year. He had marked the days of this year which they must remember: April 6, when they felt their home; April 14, when they said farewell to their homeland in Karlshamn; June 23, when they arrived in North America; and July 31, when they reached Minnesota Territory.

327

After their arrival here he had put a cross in the almanac on the day they moved into their house, the day when his third son was born, and the day Lady had been taken to the bull at Fischer's, the German's.

The year 1850 was nearing its end, and when the old year ended, the almanac too would come to an end. They could not obtain a new Swedish almanac, and they could not read an American one. Karl Oskar wondered how they would manage to keep track of days and weeks and months in the year to come. He must invent some means. To make an almanac that would last a single year was harder than to make a table that would last for generations. But without the almanac he would feel lost in time.

2

Yuletide was near—a strange Yule for Kristina, a Christmas in another world, a Christmas without Yule chores. No pig to butcher, no ale to brew, no great-bake to bake. But they must nevertheless celebrate the holiday and honor the Saviour's birth like Christian people. She said to Karl Oskar, this year they must not think of the outside—food, drink, and material things. They must celebrate Christmas in their hearts; this year must be a Christmas for their souls.

She scoured the cabin floor until it was shining white, she washed their underclothes in ash lye, so that all could change for the holiday, she hung fresh pine boughs on the walls and decked the cabin inside as best she could. Of a pine top with upright branches Karl Oskar made a five-armed candlestick, an ingenuity which his wife praised greatly. He had promised they would celebrate Christmas at a table, and he kept his promise: on Christmas Eve itself he gave the table the last finishing touches with his plane. He was proud of his handicraft, the first piece of real furniture he had ever made, particularly when, at the final inspection, Kristina said: This sturdy oak table would undoubtedly last so long that not only they themselves but their children and grandchildren as well could eat their meals at it throughout their whole lives.

While they had eaten their meals at the chest lid Karl Oskar had felt like a pauper sitting in a corner of someone else's house, eating handed-out food. Now, as he put his feet under his own table, his self-confidence increased: Now he had settled down, now he had become his own master in the new land.

They used their new table for the first time at the Christmas Eve dinner. And Kristina too was pleased—to gather for a feast around a table was something quite different from sitting down to a meal at the old chest lid. The five-armed candleholder was put in the center of the table; they had saved only three candles for Christmas, so two arms were left empty, but the three burning candles spread Yule light in their house. They had bought a pound of rice for the Christmas porridge, and with it they used sweet milk. It was their only Christmas dish, but they ate it with a deep sense of holiday spirit. Its smell and taste brought to their minds recollections of this Holy Eve's celebration at home. Long-ago Christmases now entered their cabin, Christmas Eves with the whole family gathered; and their thoughts lingered on those who at other Yuletides had sat down at table with them. Relatives at home in Sweden tonight seemed more alive than ever, and they spoke of the letter from Sweden which they had been waiting for so long. How much longer before they would hear from parents and relatives? The expected mail from Sweden had not had time to arrive before the river froze and the packets stopped coming for the winter. Now it could not arrive until spring, and that was a long time to wait.

Tonight Karl Oskar remembered his parents as he had seen them that last morning—when he had looked back from the wagon seat for a final glimpse of them as he left the old home: father and mother, looking after the departing ones, standing on the stoop close together, immobile as two statues. To him they would always remain in that position; they could not move or walk away; they stood there, looking after their departing sons; they stood like two dead objects, hewn in stone. His parents could never again resume life in his mind's eye. Perhaps this was because deep within him he knew he would never again meet them on this earth.

A thought came to him—it remained a thought only, which he would not utter: his father and mother might already be dead and buried, without his knowledge. . . .

After the meal Kristina opened the Bible and read the second chapter from St. Luke which in her home had always been read by her father on Christmas Eve in commemoration of the Saviour's birth:

"And so it was, that, while they were there, the days were accomplished that she should be delivered.

"And she brought forth her first-born son, and wrapped him in swaddling clothes, and laid him in a manger; because there was no room for them in the inn. . . ."

Kristina read the Christmas Gospel for all of them, but after a few verses she felt as though she were reading it for herself only: it concerned her above all, it concerned her more than the listeners. Mary's delivery in the stable in Bethlehem reminded her of the childbed she had but recently gone through. It seemed that Mary's time too had come suddenly and unprepared for, even though her days were accomplished: Mary had been on a journey, and perhaps they had been delayed, unable to reach home in time. And Mary had been poor, even more impoverished than she herself. Kristina had borne her child in a human abode, in a well-timbered house—Mary had lain on straw in an animal shelter, in a stall. Kristina had enjoyed the comfort of a kind and helpful midwife, but the Bible said not one word about any help-woman for Mary in the stable. And she wondered whence the Saviour's mother had obtained the swaddling clothes she wrapped about her child before she placed it in the manger. Had she prepared them in advance and brought them along on the journey to Bethlehem? The Bible was so sparing with details that she often wondered and questioned while reading. She guessed Mary must have had as much concern about the clothing of her first born as she herself had had for her child. Perhaps Mary too had been forced to cut up her petticoat to prepare the swaddling clothes for Jesus.

For the first time in twenty years Kristina slept on Christmas morning; ever since early childhood she had gone with her parents on this morning to the early service, which took place hours before daylight, the church illuminated with many candles. But here also they would revere Christmas Day, and Second Christmas Day: all work in the house ceased. They had carried in enough firewood before the holiday, all they had to do was to tend the fire and prepare food.

On Third Christmas Day they had unexpected guests. Swedish Anna and Samuel Nojd came driving a team of

330

oxen and a dray which they had borrowed from the lumber company; holidays were the time for visits among their countrymen, and they were eager to see the first child born to Swedish settlers in the St. Croix Valley. The boy was now seven weeks old, he was in splendid health, he nursed heartily and cried for more. The mother had enough milk for him, and he was hungry—both facts made Kristina's heart glad. What more could she ask? Suppose she had been without milk, or the child without appetite?

Swedish Anna looked at the tender child as if beholding a miracle of God; she wanted to hold the baby in her arms the whole time she was there. And for luck each of the guests gave the child a coin—a whole silver dollar each!

The parents were in great perplexity about having their last born baptized; so far as they knew, there was not a single Swedish minister in the whole Territory. Karl Oskar wished Danjel Andreasson to conduct the baptism: he was experienced in religious matters, he lived as piously as any minister. In Sweden Dean Brusander had once forbidden them to invite Danjel to be godfather to Harald, because Danjel had been excluded from the church; but the dean had no power over them here, and they ought to compensate Danjel for this insult—they ought to ask him to perform the Sacrament of Holy Baptism for their last-born son.

Kristina was much devoted to her uncle and thought as highly of him as Karl Oskar, but she worried about his earlier heresy and wondered if he weren't still a little confused in religious matters. And she had always felt that the rites of Holy Baptism should be performed by an ordained minister in frock and collar.

Karl Oskar argued: If Danjel read the ritual according to their own Swedish psalmbook, following every word, then it must be valid; they themselves had been baptized in accordance with these instructions.

Kristina asked if a baptism by an American minister wouldn't have the same effect as a baptism by the Swedish clergy. She had thought of Pastor Jackson in Stillwater, who had been so kind to them last summer when they landed from the steamboat. She turned to Swedish Anna: Was there anything wrong in having a child baptized in English? Wouldn't Jesus accept it equally well? Weren't all tongues the same to the Lord?

331

Swedish Anna looked at her in consternation: "You must be out of your mind! Do you want your child to be a Baptist?"

"Baptist?"

"Pastor Jackson is a Baptist! I thought you knew!"

"No, I didn't know that. But Anna—are you sure?"

"Ask anyone in Taylors Falls!"

Yes, it was true, insisted Swedish Anna: Pastor Jackson was minister of the Baptist Church in Stillwater. He was a sectarian, an Anabaptist, a heretic, an Antichrist preacher. Of all sectarians, the Baptists were the most dangerous, because they rebaptized grown people and robbed them of their Christian grace, bringing them eternal damnation.

And Swedish Anna paled in terror, hovering over the cradle of the unbaptized baby as if trying to protect him against evil powers. "If you let Pastor Jackson baptize the child, you hand him over to the devil instead of to Jesus!"

By now Kristina's concern was as great as Swedish Anna's. But she was also confused: How could the pastor in Stillwater be a false teacher, baptizing people to eternal damnation, eternal fire? Of all the Americans she had met he was the kindest and most helpful; there had been no end to his thoughtfulness for their comfort last summer. And now she related how good he had been to her and the children and all of them. How could he be an evil person, an Anabaptist, sent by Satan?

"That is exactly what he is!" Swedish Anna assured her with inflexible determination. "All Baptists are tools of the devil!"

And this Kristina ought to have realized: That time last summer, he had only tried to snare the newcomers with his false religion, so that he might baptize them and snatch them from Jesus. *That* was why he had given them food and lodging! That was why he had pretended kindness, while the devil sat in his heart and roared with laughter at the easily lured Swedish souls! That was how the Baptists gained their adherents—through deceit and falsity! And Kristina ought to know that devilish evil powers always decked themselves in sheep's clothing while stealing souls! Had she looked closer, she might have seen the cloven hoof of Pastor Jackson, hidden in his boot!

Swedish Anna picked up the unbaptized child from its crib and held it firmly and protectingly in her arms: Before this child were turned over to a false priest, she herself would steal it from the parents!

Moreover, the Baptists only baptized grown people.

Still Kristina could not entirely understand; she grew more confused. She felt in her heart that she had not heard the whole truth about the minister in Stillwater, even if it were true he preached a false religion: he too might have been led astray; perhaps in his honest simplicity he believed what he taught.

After this there was no further talk between Karl Oskar and Kristina about taking their son to Stillwater. But they were not concerned only about the child—it was high time they found a minister for themselves as well; their souls needed a nourishing sermon. And Kristina ought to be churched after childbirth; she felt the need of entering a temple to thank God for His grace in giving her a child; she needed His blessing, His comfort, she wished to seek Him in His temple. When a woman was touched by the minister's hand, she was cleansed and purified after her childbed. And all of them needed the Sacrament of Communion after the long journey from the home church. She tried to tell herself that the Lord would overlook their delay and not consider it an unforgivable sin, since they were settled in this wilderness and unable to reach His table—but often, nevertheless, she prayed for forgiveness, worrying over their inability to partake of the Sacrament: though God must look kindly on her, she sometimes said to herself, else He wouldn't have entrusted a new life to her care.

The boy was now so old the parents could no longer keep him unbaptized with a clear conscience. It was their duty to give the child to their Lord and Saviour. They therefore agreed to let Danjel perform the ritual in their home on New Year's Eve. Kristina wished to invite Ulrika of Vastergohl as godmother, to hold the child at the baptism. After some hesitation, Karl Oskar gave his consent.

The father made a neat little bowl of ash wood for the baptismal water. The christening robe Kristina sewed from leftover pieces of her bridal petticoat, which she washed and starched in potato water until it shone. A child should wear a snow-white robe when the Saviour received him at baptism.

They had never before had a christening performed at

home, and now they felt as though they were going to church in their own house. They dressed themselves in their best clothes. The floor was swept and the cabin put in order. They could not afford a feast this time; no guests were invited except the officiant and the godmother. Besides, it was difficult now in the middle of the winter to get from one house to another. This time they would have only a simple christening ale; the important thing was that the child be baptized according to the clear Lutheran confession.

And on New Year's Eve in late afternoon the christening took place in the log house. Parents, christening officiant, and godmother stood gathered around the new table, on which was spread their only linen cloth, brought from their old home. Before the holy act Kristina had given the breast to the baby; she held him a long while and let him suck out every drop of milk she had so that he would keep silent while receiving the Sacrament. He was now satisfied and content as she handed him to the godmother, and he lay goodnaturedly in Ulrika's comfortable arms.

Ulrika herself realized fully the importance of her function here; she stood solemn and silent and let Danjel do the talking today.

Kristina had asked her uncle to perform the christening word for word as it was printed in the psalmbook on the page *About Baptism*. And Danjel did as he had been asked to do—he used only the printed words of the book, not a single one of his own. He read *Our Father* and the Christian doctrine into which the child was to be baptized, he read every one of the Tenets of the Faith, from beginning to end. And with his hand laid gently on the little one's head, he asked according to the book: "Child! Do you wish to be baptized in this faith?"

The babe in Ulrika's arms was so filled with his mother's milk that part of his last meal began to run out of his mouth in little runnels. Down his chin it dripped—he spluttered all over his godmother's blouse. And to the officiant's question he answered only with a satisfied belching.

But Ulrika answered for the baby in the psalmbook's own words, which she had learned by heart in advance: Yes, he wanted to be baptized in this faith! Then Danjel

334

Andreasson picked up the boy from the godmother, three times he dipped his hand into the water in the wooden bowl and sprinkled it over the downy head: He was baptizing a human soul in the name of the Holy Trinity.

The child suddenly began to yell, annoyed at this wetting, even though Kristina had been careful to warm the water so it would be neither too hot nor too cold for his delicate scalp. But Ulrika, with motherly care, stuck her thumb into the baby's mouth and the little one sucked and kept his silence.

According to the ritual, Danjel now turned to Ulrika: In case of the parents' inability or absence, it was the godmother's duty to watch over the child, to see that it faithfully kept the promise it had today given in baptism. And she answered her "Yes" in a loud voice and promised to obey all God asked of her. And the parents observed all was performed to the very last word as was written in the psalmbook. Everything at this baptism was done right.

Thus the christening was accomplished: the pure Evangelical-Lutheran Church had one more adherent in the St. Croix Valley.

The budding American citizen in the settlement on Lake Ki-Chi-Saga had been given the name Nils Oskar Danjel. He was to be called Danjel. He had one name from his father, one from his grandfather, and one from the man who had baptized him. All three were good Swedish names. Ulrika had wished to add a fourth, an American name, because he was born in America; but the parents thought they would wait to use such a name until they had another child to christen. The boy, after all, had had his beginning in Sweden.

After the Sacrament was over, the godmother prayed a silent prayer to the Lord of Heaven for her foster son: Would the Almighty ever keep His hands over him, so that no disadvantage might come to him and no evil befall him, even though he was begotten in Sweden.

So ended the year of our Lord 1850. It had been the most unusual year yet in the lives of the immigrants.

3

The new year 1851 opened with blizzards, followed by heavy snowfalls over the Territory. The snow piled so high

335

around the cabin that they could not see through the windows; it reached to the eaves. Karl Oskar Nilsson's log cabin lay there at the edge of the forest like a tall snowdrift, little resembling a human habitation. Inside, the cabin's owners lived as in a mine, deep in the ground.

They had heard the story of one settler who had hung his cabin door swinging outward; after a heavy snowfall he had been unable to open it; for three weeks he had been locked inside his house and had almost starved to death before the snow melted and he managed to get out. At home all entrance doors swung inward; the locked-in settler could not have been a Swede.

After the heavy snowfall the men had a new chore—to shovel the snow from the door, make paths to the shanty, the lake, the water hole at the brook. They also cleared away the snow from the windows, but the tall drifts against the walls were left undisturbed, as they were a protection against winds and helped to keep the warmth inside.

After the blizzards followed a time of even, strong winter. The air was crystal clear and like hoarfrost to breathe. The cold dug and tore with its sharp frost claws; the hard snow crust, strong enough to carry full-grown men on its glittering back, now made the wilderness easily accessible. During the stillness of the nights, cracking sounds could be heard as the frost sharpened under a starlit sky.

They must ever be on guard against freezing to death. In the cabin the fire was kept alive day and night. If the embers should die down for a few hours toward morning they would feel the cold when awakening. The children were not very anxious to crawl out of their beds until the fire was burning brightly. All of them—big and little—huddled around the hearth with its blessed fire.

Outside, all animals had sought invisible hideouts. The lake birds had long ago disappeared, and so had the rabbits, the squirrels, and the gophers. The crickets no longer drove their ungreased wagon wheels; the screechhopper had been heard in the grass until late in November but now at last it was silenced. And the settlers at Lake Ki-Chi-Saga wondered how any of the delicate forest creatures could survive such a winter, such unmerciful cold; here even able-bodied people found it hard to survive.

The almanac had come to an end with the old year, and with it Swedish time had ended for the immigrants. They had no guide for days and weeks, nothing to indicate name days and holidays.

Now an idea came to Robert: He could take the old almanac for 1850 and from this figure the days of the new year. He could write a new almanac for the whole year 1851. In Sweden it ʋas forbidden by law to use any almanac except the one printed and sold by the government, but North America had a friendly government; here people could live according to their own almanac, free from persecution or punishment. And once Robert had written one almanac he might make copies of it and sell them to other Swedes who might be equally lost in time.

Karl Oskar gave his brother a few sheets of paper which he had bought when he wrote the last letter to Sweden. Robert folded each sheet twice, cut it up and sewed the pages together into a small book about the size of the old almanac. Then he filled each page with his writing in ink; this work helped him while away the long winter evenings.

Within a week Robert had his almanac ready, an almanac that would last for a whole year. He labored long on the letters of the front page to make them look like those of the old almanac.

All almanacs were prefaced with a chapter on some subject of interest to the reader; for Anno 1850, this chapter was entitled: "Watering of Meadows and Fertilizing Same." Robert also began his almanac with a chapter of general interest and information; he wrote a description of North America which he had long had in mind and for which he had gathered notes. In his description he had changed and corrected all earlier, false descriptions of the New World.

ALMANAC
FOR THE YEAR
AFTER OUR LORD'S BIRTH
1851

Which Year is Considered to be the Fivethousandeighthundredfiftythird from the Creation.

At Stockholm Horizon
59 degr. 20 and one-half min Lat.
Without
His Royal Maj.'s Permission or Instruction
Written, issued and sewn together
by
Axel Robert Nilsson from Sweden.
In the Year 1850 Emigrated to
N. America

In Accordance with His Majesty's Pleasure and Decree of August 10, 1819, the small Almanacs are hereafter to be sold, cut and bound, for 4 Skilling Banco apiece, which in American money is 3 cents Silver; whosoever dares increase this price or whosoever at the sale of almanacs offers them uncut or unbound at 4 Sk. apiece, will be fined 33 Riskdaler 16 Skilling Banco for each offence.

A New Description of the United States of North America
Truthfully written down after personal inspection on the spot. Begun during a Steamship Journey on the Mississippi July 27, 1850.

First Part
A skipper named Christoffer Columbus was the first white man to discover the United States of North America. Columbus arrived in the Northamerican Republic almost four hundred years before me, and he showed other Immigrants and Skippers the way here. He was later put into prison and severely punished.

North America is a very large and spacious land. If the whole Kingdom of Sweden were moved over here, it would hardly be noticed. Here the sun sets each evening six hours later than in Sweden, which is caused by all clocks and watches being six hours late. But the country is so large and broad that the sun hasn't time to set everywhere at the same hour; far to the west in North America it does not set until many hours after dark.

The inhabitants of North America all speak English, due to the fact that they made themselves free of England's tyranny by melting the lead of the English King's statue in New York and making bullets of him. The English tongue is also called the language of the stutterers,

338

because a stuttering person can speak it most easily. Most of the words are very short, and if they are too long they are bitten off in speech, and a stutterer will easier remember to bite off a word at the right moment.

Watercourses are in many places full of diseases, and the summers are often warm and unhealthy. It is better to take land in the forest, where the lakes are full of fish, than to settle on the prairies, where the rivers are full of fevers and chills. One can buy a horse and wagon and travel comfortably through North America, but this is expensive and takes a long time, for the country is large. Instead one can without danger to life ride on the Steam Wagon. Then one does not need a guide, for the Steam Wagon follows the road without concern to the rider. Two ruts are in North America called a road. Steamships move on all rivers faster than the current. They are also called Packets because they freight packets of mail. During the winter, ice lies on top of the running water, closing all passage of ships.

The rumors concerning white immigrants being sold as slaves in North America and sent to the Infidel Turk are without foundation. This I have been able to ascertain on the spot. Black people are offered for sale at their full price, but whites are not in demand and without value.

Second Part

The oldest Americans in this country are savages and called Indians. They do not have red skins as so falsely has been written before; they are brown. Because they are of a different color than the white Americans, they do not wish to live orderly or work. When the browns are killed they sometimes make great objections and attack white settlers. The tame Indians go about free everywhere with gray blankets over their heads.

The Indians are heathens but do not eat people as heathens are accustomed to, in their simple-mindedness, but live on wild seed called rice which grows among the reeds of the lakes. The grains are small and consequently it takes a long time to eat one's sufficiency. For solid fare the Indians use the same food as John the Baptist in the desert: fried grasshoppers and wild honey and other larger and smaller animals. But when they meet a dangerous rattlesnake in the forest they say to him in all friendliness: Go your way and I will go mine! Him they do not kill.

The Indians live from hunting and such tilling as does not require work. On small patches they grow a grain which has no heads but a kind of rootstock, because this grain saves labor and requires no threshing with flail. The Indians paint their axes in all colors. But they do not use the axes for cutting trees or wood, only for smashing skulls of people and animals. When the Indian sees an enemy near by, he immediately cuts off the scalp and hangs it with the hair to dry outside his tent when the weather is fine. The one who hangs out the greatest number of scalps is highest in the tribe. Scalps without hair are without value and are not counted. Bald people are not scalped but allowed to run about.

The Indians are very clever at shooting with arrows. Even when they have climbed a tree and had their neck pierced through with the tree top they are able to shoot many arrows. In such cases, however, they seldom hit their aim. The men are the wisest and most intelligent among the Indians. The women do all the work.

Third Part

All people in North America call each other *you*, regardless of position, riches, or situation. The word is the same as the Swedish *du* (thou) and is pronounced like the Swedish *jo* (yes); this word can be used to anyone without danger. It is not forbidden to remove one's hat in greeting but it is degrading in the North American Republic and not used.

In this country it is not—as in Sweden—considered distinguished or fine to show one's great fortune in a round and fat body; in North America a skinny person is considered and honored as much as a fat one.

The livestock of North America enjoy so much good grazing that their horns sometimes are invisible in the tall grass. All cattle are big, beautiful, and very expensive. Even the women of North America are scarce and of high value.

Examinations in the Catechism are not held in the North American Republic. This I have ascertained after investigations on the spot. Authorities in America are not like in Sweden—eternal and mighty. This is so because it

340

is not as in Sweden—put in its place by God. Government exists maybe but is not seen. Those in Power do not use the Catechism to keep the populace in obedience. No one need obey another unless he murders or steals. If anyone obeys anyone else in North America then it is because he is still too much Swedish.

The way from Sweden to North America is one-fourth the circumference of the globe, which prevents most Swedes from moving here.

Not in one word have I departed from the truth in this my Description of North America in the Almanac of Anno 1851.

1851 JANIARIUS 1851

Give, O Lord, Success and Joy!

Days	Moon	Weather	G. St.
	Christ's Circumcision Luke:2.		
1. Friday	New Year 9.0 .)	First qu.	20
2. Saturday, Abel	10.28		

XXII

"Mother, I Want Bread!"

One of the Swedish homesteads had been given a name—
New Karragarde—and Danjel suggested that Karl Oskar
ought to follow his example and call his farm New Korpamoen, after his childhood home in Sweden. But Karl
Oskar answered: Korpamoen was the last name he would
wish to give his new home; he had no desire to be thus
constantly reminded of the six years he had thrown away
among the stone piles in Sweden. He did not wish for a
new Korpamoen in America, he had had enough of the
old one; they would find a more suitable name for their
home in due time—the christening of a piece of land was
not so urgent as the christening of a baby; it was, after all,
only a patch of earth, not a human soul.

Danjel also felt they ought to change the name of Ki-
Chi-Saga. How could they live near a lake with such an
outlandish heathen name? Couldn't they think of some
pious Swedish word which a Christian could take in his
mouth without distaste? Karl Oskar replied that as he
lived on a small arm of the lake, he felt it would be presumptuous for him to change the name of the whole lake.
As yet he was the only settler here; when he had neighbors
on the shores, they would all think of a new name for
Lake Ki-Chi-Saga.

The winter had made it easier for the Swedish settlers to

342

visit back and forth. The frozen snow made a firm road, and they gave each other a hand whenever needed. Ulrika came frequently to the log house at Ki-Chi-Saga to see how her godson fared after his christening. Once she was accompanied by Swedish Anna, and the two women had a violent dispute about sectarians and heretics. Swedish Anna began: "I'm ever thankful to the Lord for saving the child from that Anabaptist in Stillwater!"

Ulrika flared up and threatened dire happenings if Swedish Anna dared say ill of Pastor Jackson. No one could have anything but good to say about that man; he was so helpful, kind, merciful, that it was hard to believe he was a minister; he had even taken the pail from her hands and fetched water himself. It was nobody's business what religion he preached, Lutheran or Baptist, Methodist or Jansonist. When a man like Jackson preached, any religion became the right one. Swedish Anna need not bring up the subject again. Ulrika herself had been a sectarian ever since she came to live with Danjel; she would have been happy to have her godson baptized by Jackson in Stillwater, nay, she wouldn't hesitate for a moment to have such a minister baptize her too!

Swedish Anna started in horror: Ulrika had been led astray from the true Lutheran religion, had been snared already by the Evil One in his heresies! Didn't she know that only the Lutherans had the right religion and lived according to the Ten Commandments of the stone tablets?

How did the Lutherans live in Sweden! exclaimed Ulrika. God's commandments were only for paupers and simple folk! The ministers never dared say one word against the nobles, or correct them in any way. If the high and mighty lords broke every one of God's commandments a hundred times a day, they would never be rebuked from the pulpit. And if the Bishop from Vaxio on his visits to the parishes raped every parsonage maid until the bottom fell out of the bed, not one priest in the whole chapter would object. Yes, if the Swedish King himself should break God's commandments, and if besides this he were degenerate and committed vices against nature, all the priests would still bow to him, as low as ever, and praise him, and pray for him every Sunday according to the words of the prayer book—even though they knew the truth, for it was the King who gave them the parishes.

343

Such were the Lutheran clergy in Sweden, Ulrika stated, and such they would remain.

But Swedish Anna was a strict Lutheran; the two women could not be friends.

During the Christmas holidays Jonas Petter had gossiped to Kristina that Anders Mansson intended to marry Ulrika of Vastergohl. Next time Ulrika came to visit, Kristina asked her if this were true.

"It's true. Mansson wants to marry me."

"May I congratulate you on your luck, Ulrika?"

"No!" exclaimed the Glad One. "I have no intention of marrying Mansson!"

"But he is a good and kind man," insisted Kristina.

"He's good and kind. But he isn't a man. No, he's not for me."

Kristina felt sorry in some way for Fina-Kajsa's son; he had lived alone for so long in this wilderness; and he was sparing with his words, closemouthed, as if carrying a great sorrow. Perhaps he regretted his emigration even though he wouldn't admit it. Karl Oskar had many times remarked that something must be wrong with Anders Mansson, he had done so little to improve his homestead. He barely managed—this winter he had borrowed thirty dollars from Danjel; having been here almost five years, Mansson ought to have reached a stage when borrowing no longer was necessary—if he had the right stuff in him. There must be some secret about Anders Mansson, Karl Oskar had said, but he was unable to guess what it was.

Ulrika admitted that Fina-Kajsa's son had been good to all of them when they arrived last summer without a roof over their heads; he was a kindhearted man; and he had a home to offer her. But each time she shook his hand she felt he wasn't exactly the way men should be. Something was missing, either in his head, or in his spine, or between his legs; something was missing that a man should have. Ulrika said this was only her feeling, but she usually felt aright: she had learned to know menfolk inside and out. Moreover, here in America there were so many men to choose from she needn't take the first suitor to approach her. She had not been here long, she wanted time to think it over before she chose her man. God would surely help her find the right one when the time came to stand as bride.

344

But Ulrika had consoled Anders Mansson to the best of her ability. Thus, she had promised never to divulge his rejected proposal, and she had held to her promise—she was not the sort of low person who would brag about being in demand. But Anders Mansson had made the mistake of asking Jonas Petter to intercede for him, and that loosemouthed gossip had of course not been able to keep it to himself. Jonas Petter also would undoubtedly have proposed to her, if he hadn't already had a wife in Sweden; she could feel that he was much in need of a woman. Ulrika knew menfolk, she knew them all right. . . .

While the snow crust still held, Karl Oskar, Danjel, and Jonas Petter walked through the forest to Stillwater to register their claims of land. The Swedish settlers used the few English words they had picked up when they reported to the land office that they were squatters within the Minnesota Territory; they were also able to tell in a general way where their claims were located. A man in the office told them that next summer a surveyor would be sent to their part of the forest.

While in Stillwater they also bespoke and paid for seed grain for the coming spring. Karl Oskar spent the last of his cash for rye, barley, and potatoes; the last of the money he got from the sale of his farm and livestock in Sweden was now spent for spring seed, from which he hoped to reap a fall harvest to feed them next winter.

From Stillwater, Danjel and Jonas Petter continued south to St. Paul in order to buy in partnership a yoke of oxen, while Karl Oskar, now without funds, returned home. Five days later his neighbors came back with a pair of young oxen, measuring eleven and a half hands, which they had bought for seventy-five dollars. The animals had been part of a herd, driven from Illinois to St. Paul. They were unbroken and could not yet be used for hauling. Karl Oskar was promised the loan of the team for the spring plowing.

During the walk from St. Paul in the intense cold, Jonas Petter's nose became frostbitten, and he had had to stay over in Stillwater for a few days to seek a doctor.

The winter was far gone, and the food supply was running low for the settlers at Lake Ki-Chi-Saga. They were near the bottom of the flour barrel, and Kristina reduced their bread rations to one thin slice apiece at every meal.

345

They were now on their last bushel of potatoes, and these too had to be rationed. They still had some frozen venison, and this was not yet rationed. Fresh meat was seldom on the table—the game seemed to have disappeared in the dead of winter. Indians used dogs to hunt, but without a dog a hunter usually returned without game. And Lady, their borrowed cow, had almost gone dry; she gave only half a quart a day.

Fishing, too, had become difficult after the snow had piled high on the lake ice. Earlier in the winter they had caught a great many pike without any fishing gear, using only an ax. They would walk over the clear ice until they espied fish, and then hit the ice above them with the ax hammer; the pike were stunned, turning up their white bellies, and it was easy to break the ice and pull them out. After the snow covered the lake several feet deep, Karl Oskar and Robert had to cut holes through the ice for fishing. It was mostly catfish they caught this way, standing at the holes with their fingers stiff from cold. Catfish had an unpleasant, oily taste, and no one liked them as well as the other lake fish. Robert detested them, with their round, catlike heads, actually purring like cats; after an evening meal of catfish he complained about being unable to sleep—the cat kept purring in his stomach the whole night through!

"Better to have a fish purr in you than to have your stomach purr from emptiness," answered Karl Oskar.

Kristina boiled the catfish, she fried it, salted it, dried it, made soup from it, she tried in all ways to make it taste good. They ate catfish at almost every meal, it was their only fresh winter food, and when the venison was gone, it would be their only animal food. The fish was ugly to look at, its taste was not appetizing, but Kristina said it would be ungrateful to speak ill of this creature, which had the same Creator as they themselves; hungry people ought to eat without complaint whatever they could find. And the catfish was faithful to them; when everything else on land and in the water failed them, they always had the bearded, purring fish. It came as a gift from God and helped them sustain life through the winter.

Robert's almanac indicated they were now in February. And each day the settlers asked themselves the same question: How long would it be before the ground grew green?

When would the ice break up? How long before spring came?

They had put this question to Anders Mansson, he had spent several years here, he ought to know. He had answered: Spring varied from year to year, it might vary by many weeks. He remembered one spring when the frost had gone out of the ground the last week in March, another year he had not started his plowing until the second week of April. The ice on the St. Croix River usually broke up toward the end of March, and spring in the St. Croix Valley was counted from the day when the river flowed free.

So they must fight the winter, perhaps another two months.

The settlers in the log cabin at Ki-Chi-Saga kept their house warm with their constant fire, they were well protected against the winter weather, no longer were they afraid of the cold; but they began to fear hunger.

2

Kristina knew from experience: it was always harder to satisfy a hungry family in winter than in summer. All were hungrier and ate more in winter. During the cold part of the year a human body needed rich, nourishing food to keep the blood active and warm in the body. And as the food grew scarce, her family grew hungrier than any winter before. She too—her stomach ached all day long, she wakened during the nights with the pain. And she was in charge of their food—before she herself ate she must see to it that the others had something on their plates.

At meals she left the table a little before the others or she might be tempted to eat so much that the children would have too little. She was so careful of the flour she hardly dared use a few pinches for gravy; it must be saved for bread. But however she skimped and saved, she could not make the barrel deeper than it was. The time came when she swept the barrel bottom clean to have sufficient flour for a baking. And the moment arrived when the loaves from this baking were eaten. Now she had nothing more to bake with. Now they were breadless.

That day when they sat down at table there was no bread. No one said a word about it, no one asked about

347

the missing bread. How could questions help them? The men had long dreaded the day when bread would be missing—it was no surprise to them. Nevertheless, Karl Oskar and Robert glanced from time to time at the empty place on the board where the bread used to lie. Did they think it would suddenly appear?

At the next meal little Johan began to complain: "Mother! I want bread! Where's the bread?"

"There is no bread, child," said the mother.

"Mother, you must bake," Johan told her. "I want bread."

None of the others at the table said a word, but the boy kept repeating: "Mother! Why don't you bake?"

No other food satisfies a human stomach like bread, no food will keep hunger away like bread. Nothing can take the place of bread for grownups or children, but a growing child-body suffers most from the lack of it.

And a mother suffers when she must deny her own child who hangs on to her skirts and cries persistently: "Mother, I want bread!"

It was the same at every meal. No one said anything except the child, but it was almost more than Kristina could endure. She knew only too well how things were with them; they had used all their money. At length she had to speak to Karl Oskar: Their children must have bread to stay healthy until spring; growing children needed bread. Couldn't he manage to get hold of a small sack of flour— only a very small sack?

This problem had been ever in his mind since the bread had been missing from the table; one sack of flour. . . . But their last money had been spent for seed grain which Karl Oskar had ordered for spring. The seed grain was more important to them than anything else—it was next year's crop. If they had spent the seed money for this winter's food, they would starve to death next winter.

Kristina argued: It did not matter which winter they starved to death—this one or next. What help would their spring seed be to them if they couldn't survive until spring? How could they put the seeds in the ground if they themselves were already under the ground?

Karl Oskar said he would go to Danjel and ask for a loan. This was the only way out. He would not be trusted by anyone else. Here everyone asked for cash. If he wanted to buy a penny's worth in a store, the owner would first ask if he had cash. *Cash* was an American word he now understood quite well, he had learned what it meant. Cash! Cash! Cheap for cash! How many times he had heard it! It began to sound like the rustle of paper bills. He could hear the same rustle in the voice of Mr. Abbott, the Scots storekeeper in Taylors Falls: "Do you have cash, Mr. Nilsson?" A settler's life—or death—depended on *cash*.

He was embarrassed to borrow from Danjel again; he still owed his wife's uncle one hundred daler for the mortgage interest on Korpamoen; his lost years at home still weighed him down. And now Danjel wasn't much better off than he was himself; Danjel too had a large family to feed, he had bought a half share in the ox team, he had lent thirty dollars to Anders Mansson, he was very generous to Ulrika and her daughter, he helped people without being asked. He had been extravagant with the cash he had on arrival, he too would soon be impoverished.

But Karl Oskar went to Danjel, and came back with five shining coins in his hand: five silver dollars: "Now we can buy a sack of flour!"

Kristina said: As long as there was one single human being who felt for his neighbor, the world was not lost.

The settlers in Taylors Falls had bought their winter supplies in early autumn, and Mr. Abbott had run out of flour long before Christmas; new supplies would not arrive until the river opened. Karl Oskar must therefore go to Stillwater for his sack of flour. This would not be so long a trip as the settlers' first walk to Taylors Falls. After all, Karl Oskar and his family now lived nine miles nearer Stillwater. Besides, the walk through the forest was shorter than the wandering way by the river; still, it was at least six miles longer than the walk to Taylors Falls. He had already carried home many burdens from Mr. Abbott's store, both on his back and in his hands. During the last half year he had struggled with more burdens than in his whole previous life. But the road northeast through the forest to Taylors Falls was only nine miles; southeast to Stillwater it was fifteen; and to walk that distance back and forth in one day, and carry a sack of flour on his return walk, would be a hard day's work. And he must start out early enough to reach home while it was still daylight.

The following morning, one hour before daybreak, Karl Oskar set off with an empty sack under his arm. Johan woke up and called happily to his father in the door: "Buy flour, Father! Then Mother can bake!"

"Be careful of your nose," admonished Kristina. "Remember what happened to Jonas Petter in this cold winter."

But the weather was now mild, had been for almost a week; the snow had thinned down, it was hardly more than a foot deep; the cold was not noticeable, the sky was hazy, with a flurry of snow now and then. Karl Oskar had walked through the forest to Stillwater only once before, but he had taken notice of landmarks and was sure he would find his way. He followed the east shore of Lake Ki-Chi-Saga, almost in a southerly direction; he passed by places he recognized—a fallen giant trunk over a brook, a deserted wigwam, an oak hill with an Indian pole, a mound like a bread loaf. Having crossed the brook, he followed an Indian trail until he reached the logging road used by the Stillwater lumber company, and from there on he could not lose his way.

The walk to Stillwater was easy; his whole burden was an empty sack, he walked with good speed and arrived before noon. He went to visit Pastor Jackson, the kind minister, as he had done last time he was in town. Pastor Jackson had now moved into a comfortable new house near the little whitewashed wooden church where he preached. But Jackson's door was locked, and no one opened for him. The minister must be on one of his many preaching journeys through the Territory.

Karl Oskar walked around and inspected the Baptist church. This was the first non-Lutheran church he had been close to. It was a simple building of wood, made of timbers faced with boards—it was the smallest God's House he had ever seen. He sat down on a bench outside the church and ate what he had brought with him—a piece of venison and a few boiled potatoes, which he gulped down without feeling satisfied. Then he walked the street at the river's edge and looked at the signs and tried to read the inscriptions: *Pierre's Tavern; Abraham Smith,*

Barber and Druggist; James Clark, Hardware—Tools.
Outside some houses horses stood hitched—the farmers
near Stillwater were already so well off that they used
horses.

He studied particularly one large sign in front of a ram-
shackle shed:

CHRISTOPHER CALDWELL
PHYSICIAN AND HOUSE-BUILDER
CARPENTER AND BLACKSMITH

Caldwell was the name of the doctor who had taken
care of Jonas Petter's frostbitten nose; this must be his
house. Jonas Petter had said that the doctor had built his
own house. He was a very learned doctor who could heal
all kinds of ailments, he was also a carpenter and a capable smith. He had been busy shoeing a horse when Jonas
Petter arrived, and after attending to the horse's hoofs he
had cared for Jonas Petter's frostbitten nose. He administered equally well to the needs of people and livestock.
Such learned and capable doctors were not available in
Sweden. Karl Oskar thought he must remember the doctor's name; in case any of his family should be sick he
would seek Dr. Caldwell.

But he must attend to his errand in town, he must buy
his sack of flour and get on his way homeward.

He entered the finest and largest store he saw: Harrington's General Store. He knew that *store* was the American
name for a shop, but he could not understand the meaning
of the word *general*. In Swedish, general meant a high military man; perhaps the owner had been a general in the
army.

Behind the long, high counter of Harrington's General
Store stood two clerks dressed exactly alike: they wore
gray cotton shirts, white aprons, and bowlers; the clerks in
America kept their hats on inside; apparently they did not
stand on ceremony with the customers.

While the two clerks waited on some fat men in skin
jackets, Karl Oskar looked around the store. He espied a
small wooden barrel with an inscription: *Kentucky
Straight Whisky Pure 14 G.* Karl Oskar had learned the
American measurements for both fluid and solid goods

and he understood that the barrel contained fourteen gallons of the strong American brannvin. But in this country he could not afford brannvin; at home in Sweden he had distilled his own spirits.

Many articles of food were displayed in the store; on the counter lay heaps of fat sausages, dried and smoked; large, shining, yellow cheeses were piled on top of each other, breads of many sizes and colors were displayed. Over the counter hung hams and pieces of meat, whole sides of pork, short ribs; a steelyard in its chain hung near the meat, as if calling out: "I'll weigh up all of this for you!"

On the floor stood boxes full of eggs and fish in wooden buckets; in a corner were sacks full of flour, rice, peas, beans; in smaller boxes were stick candy, nuts, dried berries, and fruit; on the shelves lay bundles of all kinds of fabrics in all colors, rows of earthenware and china vessels. On small shelves in the window were jars and bottles of all shapes and sizes, round, flat, oblong, and square, containing salves, drops, and other medicines. From the ceiling hung pots and pans, pails and baskets, saddles and yokes, wheels, saws, guns, hats, boots, skin jackets; on the floor stood plows, churns, fire pokes, axes, hoes, spades, shovels. Karl Oskar felt that if he looked carefully in all the corners of this store he wouldn't find lacking a single object a person would need or wish for in this world; his eyes lingered on tobacco pouches and pipes, snuff boxes, powder horns, books as large as Bibles and as small as almanacs, hymnbooks, playing cards, dice. The store offered for sale everything a beginner might want in the wilderness for his spiritual and bodily needs.

In this store there was ten times as much as in Mr. Abbott's store in Taylors Falls, and Karl Oskar sighed as he beheld all the accumulated fortune; a feeling of hunger came over him: his eyes saw and his nose smelled all the tempting food—the fresh bread, the smoked hams and sausages, the fat cheeses. The people in Stillwater had sold their forests and grown rich from all the lumber, they could afford to buy anything they wanted in this store. . . . It must be an old general or some other very high person who owned this store and all it contained.

But Karl Oskar was only a poor squatter—the multitude of good things was not for him. He had come to buy

352

a sack of flour which he must carry fifteen miles on his back; he was an impoverished settler without bread.

One of the clerks came up to him and Karl Oskar held up his empty sack, pointed toward the rye flour in the corner, and said: "Five dollar!"

He held out the five fingers of his right hand. The clerk kept up a constant flow of talk, the words spilling from his mouth with such speed that Karl Oskar was unable to understand a thing he said. He could explain his needs to Mr. Abbott in Taylors Falls, they understood each other's language. But each time he met a new American the same thing happened to him: he could neither understand nor be understood. It was as though he had to learn English anew whenever he met a stranger; he felt each time equally foolish and annoyed, standing there tongue-tied. As yet, however, he had not met a single American who poked fun at a newcomer because of his language difficulties. Instead, all were eager to help him, trying to guess what he wanted to say.

The clerk filled a wooden measure twice and emptied the rye flour into Karl Oskar's sack: "Five dollars' worth," he said.

Karl Oskar lifted the sack—it weighed about a hundred pounds, was probably about two bushels. He had hoped to get another twenty-five pounds for his five silver dollars. He tried two English words: "No more?"

The clerk shook his head. "No! This is cheap because of cash."

Karl Oskar could only comfort himself with the thought that the sack would be easier to carry; he should be able to manage only two bushels. He swung the sack onto his back.

"Too heavy to carry! Have you oxen outside?" asked the clerk.

Karl Oskar heard the word oxen, the clerk must think he had a team outside; he shook his head, "No, no— *farval!*" In his confusion, he said good-by to the clerk in Swedish.

Karl Oskar Nilsson started on his way home from Stillwater with a hundred pounds of flour on his back. Now the weather was clear and colder. There was no wind, the snow crunched and squeaked under his booted feet, all indications were for strong frost tonight.

353

He stopped to pull on his woolen mittens. As always here, the change in weather had come on suddenly; no one could have guessed in the morning that it would freeze before night. He had left his thick wadmal coat at home and wore only his short sheepskin jacket, as it was easier to walk when dressed lightly. Now he regretted not having brought the heavy coat as well.

In the store he had handled the flour sack like a light burden, swinging it onto his back with the greatest of ease. And during the first part of his return walk he was little aware of its weight. But after a few miles the sack began to sag down his back, he felt it against his thighs; time and again he stopped to shove it up onto his shoulder. The sack grew heavier the longer he walked; the flour seemed to increase in weight the farther he got from the store.

He had carried sacks twice as heavy in Sweden, but never such a long distance; the more he thought about it, the more he realized that this was rather a heavy burden for such a long road. Apparently he must pay twice for his flour—first in money, then in backache.

The crooked sled tracks showed him the way through the forest; here and there on the glittering snow lay fresh ox dung, like dark loaves of bread on a white platter, and here and there were yellow stains from ox urine; axes could be heard at a distance, a logging camp must be close by.

The sack grew heavier, his right boot chafed his heel, the cold increased. But Karl Oskar gave himself no time to sit down and rest, he tramped on; he must not lose time, he hurried his steps to cover the stretch between the end of the logging road and Lake Ki-Chi-Saga before dusk; once at the lake he could follow the shore all the way home, but he had several miles yet to walk through deep wilderness, and he would have trouble finding his way after dark.

The logging road came to an end. From here on he had only his own tracks of the morning to follow. Some snow must have fallen in the forenoon, in places his tracks were filled up.

Mostly he kept his eyes on his own boot prints but he found familiar landmarks—he passed a deserted wigwam; as soon as he reached the brook with the wind-fallen oak trunk over it, he would be close to the lake.

354

Karl Oskar walked on, his boots crunching in the snow; he struggled with his sack up steep hills, down inclines; he forced his way through thorny thickets, he bent low under trees and branches, with the sack on his back. Dusk fell sooner than he had expected, and he found it more and more difficult to follow the tracks which showed him the way. The frost sharpened, his fingers went numb inside the thick mittens; his boot still chafed his heel, and the sack sagged all the way down to his legs. The sack would not follow him docilely any longer, it crept down below his waist, down the back of his legs, it wanted to get down on the ground. He felt the sack on his shoulders, on his back, against his legs, his knees, in his feet, in his hands.

After a few hours' walk the flour weighed two hundred pounds—had they given him four bushels instead of two? And he had yet a long way to go—his burden would grow heavier still.

The cloak of darkness spread quickly among the trees, it soon grew so dense that he could not see the marks of his steps from the morning. The snow shone white; otherwise everything in the forest was black, dark as the inside of a barrel with the lid on. No longer did Karl Oskar waste his time in looking for his earlier tracks; he followed his nose, he tried to walk northward; to the north lay the lake, and at the lake lay his home.

But he hadn't yet come to the brook with the tree trunk over it, and this began to worry him; he had crossed the brook quite a stretch after leaving the lake shore. What had happened to the brook? It was frozen over so he couldn't hear it.

Now he walked more slowly, plodding along among the trees. In the dark he could not see the low-hanging branches which hindered his path, snatching at the flour sack on his back like so many evil arms. He held on to his burden with stiff, mittened fingers; time and again he tore his face on twigs and thorns, he could not see in front of him. There would be a moon later, the stars already shone brightly, twinkling through the tall treetops. But nothing lighted his way except the snow, and the snow no longer showed him the way by his morning footprints—not even with the stars out.

The wanderer struggled through the dark with the flour on his bent back. But he did not reach a lake, he did not

355

find a brook, and the forest grew thicker around him. He had not brought his watch—he never brought it along on walks in the forest for fear he might lose it—and he did not know how much time he had spent on the homeward trek. But many hours must have elapsed since he had left the logging road; if he had followed the right path he ought to have reached Lake Ki-Chi-Saga long ago.

At each step he hoped to see the forest come to an end, he hoped to see a white field—the snow-covered lake surface. As soon as this happened he would only have to follow a shore line until he reached a newly built log cabin where his wife and children were waiting for him. But instead he seemed to go deeper and deeper into the forest.

He repeated to himself, over and over: If I walk straight ahead, I must come to the lake. I'm walking straight forward, I'm on the right road! But the hours went by and the thick forest around him testified to his mistake.

At last the stiff fingers inside the mittens lost their hold: Karl Oskar let his sack drop onto the snow and sat down on it. The truth had now been forced upon him: he was wandering aimlessly, he did not know in what direction home was—he was lost.

3

He rested a while, sitting on his sack, his legs trembling with fatigue and cold. He was worn out from the many hours' struggle with the flour: he had weakened sooner than he had expected because his stomach was empty. Hunger smarted his stomach, in his limbs and back was an ache of fatigue, but most terrible was the pain of cold after he had sat a while. The cold embraced his body from head to heel, crept like icy snakes up his legs, penetrated his groin, dug into chest and throat, pinched his ears, nose, and cheeks. But he remained sitting, letting it overtake him; he was forced to rest.

He had told Kristina he would return well before bedtime. She would be sure to sit up and wait for him, darning stockings or patching clothes. She was waiting, not only for him but also for the flour—she would surely wish to set the dough this very evening, so she could bake tomorrow.

And here he sat on their flour and didn't know in which direction he should carry it.

He had wandered about in a black forest like a child playing blindman's buff. Perhaps he had strayed too much to the left, or to the right; when he thought he had been walking northward, he might have walked southward; hoping to get nearer to his home, he had perhaps gone farther and farther away from it.

There was only one thing to do: He must walk on! He couldn't camp in the forest, the cold was too intense. He couldn't make a fire, he had brought no matches. If he lay down to sleep it would surely be his eternal sleep.

Walk on! He must warm himself by moving. Sitting on the sack, his whole body shivered and shook with cold. He rose, stamped his feet, rubbed his nose, ears, and cheeks; he was not going to endure the cold that came with immobility any longer—he must move on.

Karl Oskar resumed his walk at random; he must walk in some direction, and one way was as good as another. Damned bad luck! If only he had been able to reach the lake before dark. He had walked as fast as he could, but that damned sack—it had sagged and delayed him. But now what was he doing? Cursing the sack with their bread flour—the bread that was missing from their table, the bread that would satisfy the hunger of their children! He must be out of his mind, he must be crazy from fatigue and hunger.

"Father is buying flour—Mother will bake bread!"

Put the sack under a tree and walk unhindered? But it would not be easier to find his way without his burden. And he might never again find his flour. Better carry it as far as he was able. . . . But his back felt broken, and his legs wobbled. He had carried it for many hours, an eternal road. He staggered; again and again the burden on his back sagged down, down to his thighs, to his legs, again and again his hold on the sack loosened, his fingers straightened out; his back wanted to throw off the burden, his fingers wanted to let it go.

Karl Oskar no longer walked; he reeled, tottering among the tree trunks. But he dared not sit down to rest in this cold; he dared not remain still because of the frost— yet he could not walk because of exhaustion. Which must he do—sit down, or go on? One he dared not, the other he was barely able to do.

He struggled along at random, stumbling, fumbling,

stooping with his burden. He bumped against the trees, he could not see where he was going. He found no landmarks, no lake, no brook; perhaps he had crossed the brook without knowing it? A few times the forest opened up and he walked across a glade—then he was instantly in deep forest again.

Suddenly he hit his head against something hard. He lost hold of the sack and tumbled backward.

Very slowly he struggled to his feet in the snow; above him he vaguely saw an animal, a head appeared a few yards away. A bear, a wolf, or could it be a lynx? The beast was snapping at him with enormous jaws, below fiery red eyes. It was quite close—Karl Oskar crouched backward and pulled out his knife.

He crept a few more steps backward; the beast did not come after him, it did not move. He could discern the upright ears, the sharp nose, the neck—it must be a wolf —the eyes glittered in the dark. He expected a leap, he crouched and held his breath. But the wolf too remained immobile.

He yelled, hoping to frighten the beast: "Go to hell, you devil!"

But the beast did not make the slightest move, it seemed petrified in one position, its ears upright, its eyes peering. And a suspicion rose within Karl Oskar; he approached the animal cautiously. Now he was close enough to touch it—and it wasn't furry or soft, it was cold and hard: it was a wolf image on a pole.

His body sagged after the tension: an Indian pole, an image with glittering eyes and toothy jaws; it could startle anyone in the dark. Or—was he so far gone from struggling that he could be frightened by wooden poles?

His head ached; he felt a bump on his forehead from the encounter with the post; blood was oozing from his face and hands, torn by branches and thorns. He took off his mittens and licked the blood from his fingers; it felt warm in his mouth. He needed something warm this bitterly cold night.

With great effort he managed to get the sack onto his back again and continued his walk, lurching, stumbling. It had lightened a little in the forest, more stars had come out. High above the snowy forest and the lost settler with his burden glittered a magnificent, starry heaven. The

firmament this night seemed like a dark canopy of soft felt
spread by God above the frozen earth, and sprinkled with
silvery sparks.

The wanderer below walked with bent head, stooped
under his sack; he did not look up toward the heavenly
lights. He carried the heavy fruit of the earth on his back.
His steps were stumbling and tottering, he did not know
where they would lead him. Home—in which direction lay
the house where wife and children waited for him? Was he
carrying their bread home—or away from home?

Suddenly he came upon large boot prints in the snow.
They were his own! He felt his heart beat in his throat:
then he had walked here in the early morning. He inspected the tracks more closely—and discovered they
were quite fresh. He had been here only a short while
ago. . . .

He was walking in a circle, in his own tracks. He wasn't
carrying the bread away from his family, neither was he
carrying it home.

But he must keep going, no matter where, to escape
freezing. He staggered on. His foot caught in something—
a root, a windfall, a stump—and he fell again, forward
this time, with the hundred-pound sack on top of him. He
lay heavily in the snow, sunk down, slumped, like a bundle of rags. After a few minutes he tried to remove the
sack. Slowly, with endless effort, he managed to roll it off
his back. In a sweet sensation of deliverance he stretched
out full length in the snow, with the flour sack for a pillow.

4

The fruit of the earth is good and sustaining, the fruit of
the earth is indispensable, but heavy to carry on one's
back.

How comfortable to lie on it, instead. Better to lie
upon flour than kill oneself by carrying it . . . when one
doesn't know where to carry it. And it has grown overpoweringly heavy, five hundred pounds. There is lead in
the sack, five hundred pounds of lead—too much for one's
back—better lie here and rest on the sack . . . better than
to carry it . . . when one doesn't even know the way
home. . . .

The cold is dangerous and evil, the cold has sharp teeth,

digging like wolf's fangs into flesh and bone, the cold has tongs that pinch and tear and pierce. The skin burns like fire. But it is good to rest . . . better to be cold a little than struggle with the burden. . . . Don't be afraid of a little cold! Nothing is worse than to be afraid, Father used to say. Nothing is dangerous to him who is fearless. No, he isn't afraid. A settler needs courage, good health, good mind. . . . Father didn't say that—he has learned that himself—he has learned it now. . . .

Father has grown a great deal since he last saw him—that time on the stoop, with Mother. He is six feet tall, entirely straight; the way he stands here, he isn't a cripple any longer, he must have thrown away his crutches—no, he still has one crutch, but he doesn't lean on it, he shakes it at his oldest son: ". . . and you take your children with you! You not only take your children, you take my grandchildren, and my grandchildren's children! You drag the whole family out of the country! You are as stubborn as your nose is long, it will lead you to destruction!"

The sack—that damned flour sack! Here . . . here it is, under . . . how soft it is. Rye flour is the best pillow. With a whole sack of rye flour . . . sustain life until spring . . . not die this winter. Where is the loaf? Why isn't it on the table?

"Mother! Bake some bread!"

Now Father is speaking sternly, shaking his crutch: What kind of fool are you, Karl Oskar? Why do you wander about here in the forest with such a sack of flour on your back? You have a team of oxen in Korpamoen, why don't you drive to the mill, like other farmers? Sit up and ride, the way sensible people do, rest on your flour sack the whole way. Wouldn't that be better than carrying flour miles through the forest? No one can call you a wise farmer, Karl Oskar! Here you struggle like a wretched crofter! You have no sense about providing food for your family. A hell of a fool is what you are! Never satisfied at home, hmm—you must emigrate. . . . People should see you now, lying in a snowdrift! What would they say? No —don't show yourself to anyone, Karl Oskar. Crawl into the snow, hide yourself in the drift! Hide well. Let no one in the whole parish see you. . . .

"Be careful of your nose in this cold," Kristina says. She is concerned, she is a good wife. She is thinking of his nose because Jonas Petter's became frostbitten. But she means: Be careful of your life! Watch out against freezing to death. Don't stop too long. Don't lie down in the snow, whatever you do—don't lie down in the snow! I'm going to bake, this evening, as soon as you get home. I need the flour. . . .

"You've come at last!" she says. "Then I'll set the dough, knead it tonight. We'll heat the oven tomorrow morning, rake out the coals, put in the bread; you made a good oven for me, even though it doesn't give quite enough top-heat. . . . A hundred pounds, two bushels, three bushels? It'll last till spring. But the sack! Where is the sack? Did you forget the sack? You come home without flour?"

"The sack lies back there in the woods, but I know where I hid it—I buried it in the snow. How could I do anything so silly? I must go back at once and find it."

"Go at once and get the sack. Hurry, Karl Oskar! Hurry before it's too late!"

"It's already too late for you," says Father, and now he leans on both of his crutches; now he is a helpless cripple again, a wizened, dried-up old man. And he complains: "It's too late, Karl Oskar. You won't have time, you won't find the sack, you've lost it! How could you forget the sack in the snow, far out in the woods? Don't you know your children are in it? Don't you know they are all bundled up in there? How could you take your children to North America and carry them in a sack on your back? You must have known that such a burden would be too heavy. You must have realized you could never get home. That long road. . . . I told you you couldn't manage. And then you dropped them in the snow. Now it's too late to find them. They must be frozen to death, starved to death by now. . . . Didn't I tell you things would go ill with you in North America? But you wouldn't listen to my warning, you wouldn't listen to your parents. You were always stubborn and headstrong."

No! No! He must defend himself, he must tell Father the truth: It was because of the children he had emigrated —above all for their sake. He had brought his wife and three children with him, but he had also brought with him a pair of worn-out little shoes that had belonged to a fourth child. Didn't Father remember Anna? She died.

361

She was hungry too long. Of her he had only the little shoes left, and he had taken them with him from Korpamoen; they would always remind him of his child, they would make him remember the hunger that snatched her away from him. Father must know, he must remember: the famine year, the famine bread, the poor beggars, all those who starved to death? If not, he would show Father Anna's shoes. They are here in the sack! I put them into the sack. There isn't another thing in the sack. . . .

When he lost his little girl he had been in despair. Father must remember how he had searched for knot-free boards for the coffin. It was lowered into the earth, but her shoes were left. At times he picks them up, holds them in his hands: her small feet have been in them, her little feet have romped about in them, she has taken many steps in them, up and down, a thousand times. Anna's feet. . . . *Father, it hurts to die. Don't let God come and take me! I want to stay here with you.* . . . No, it mustn't happen again, it mustn't happen to his other children, he must take them away from the tormenting hunger—out here. And now he is here with his sack; and it has grown heavier and heavier, until he has fallen with it. He is crawling on his knees in the snow, with the burden on his back. But it's burning hot in the snow, it smarts, smarts. . . .

And his own father is also here in America—he hasn't written a letter, although he learned to write while sitting inside as a cripple. He has come here himself and speaks severe words to his eldest son: "I warned you, your mother warned you, friends and neighbors warned you. But you had to do it. You were self-willed, stubborn, listened to no one. Therefore things went as they did; now you lie here. . . . You dragged away my children, my grandchildren. Where are your own children? Where do you keep them? Have you taken care of them? Have you found them yet? Do you remember the place where you buried them in the snow? Be careful of your nose in this cold!"

Father will buy flour, Mother will bake bread. . . . Where is the bread? . . . It's *my* son! But you are my son. And things have come to pass as you wanted them to. Karl Oskar, are you looking for bread on your own table? You're as stubborn as your nose is long. You couldn't rest until you got to North America. You wanted to get here to fetch that sack of flour, to wander about with the sack. . . . It wasn't much to travel so far for—not much for one who wanted to improve things for himself. . . . But I told you it was a long way to travel, that you never would find your way, wouldn't be able to carry it all the distance, it's too heavy . . . and what a cold night! Not even a beggar would be out in this weather. . . .

I'll succeed! I'll improve myself! And Karl Oskar swings the sack onto his back again and waves good-by to his father and mother, who stand on the stoop looking after him. He walks lightly with his burden, through the narrow gate, onto the road, and then he looks back: Father and Mother stand there. He calls to them but they do not answer. They remain standing on the stoop, deaf, dumb, lame. Never more in his life will they move. They will remain standing there forever, looking after him, the son who walked out through the gate, who emigrated. For all time they will stand there; they do not hear when he calls, but he must tell them, he must call louder: "It wasn't because I was stubborn and wouldn't listen to you, nor was I dissatisfied. That you must remember! I didn't emigrate because of this, do you hear me, Father and Mother? *I didn't want to make any more coffins.* No coffins for my little ones. Remember that! That was why I emigrated."

But Father and Mother do not listen, they do not hear. And they cannot move. They are only wooden images, put up by the Indians. The red eyes staring at him aren't human eyes; the Indians have put animal heads on Father's and Mother's bodies! They have cut off the heads of his parents and have replaced them with wolf heads! That's why they stand immobile without hearing him when he shouts at them: "Can you hear me?"

He shouts and yells, he has to, he can no longer endure tht intense smarting from the fire, he shrieks as he lies there among the scorching firebrands of the bitter-cold snow. . . .

5

Karl Oskar Nilsson sat up and felt his face with his hand: Where was he? Was he at home with his father, defending his emigration? Or had his father come here? Was he in two countries at the same time? Wasn't he walking homeward with a—*the sack!*

His befuddled mind cleared: He had gone to sleep on his sack in the snow. But the cold had bitten him badly, and he had shouted himself awake. He jumped to his feet, violently, as if attacked by a swarm of hornets; he was like a madman—he jumped about, kicking, stamping the ground. He flailed his arms, slapped his hands and face, beat his body with his fists. For several minutes he pummeled himself—and his blood pumped faster, his body heat was returning.

He must have dozed off for a little while; he might never have awakened! How could he have lain down this bitterly cold night? How could he have forgotten to guard against the treacherous temptation of rest?

He could not have been asleep long, yet he had had time to dream evil dreams, listen to many voices; they had told him things he probably had thought to himself, when alone; and all the while he had felt the smarting cold, burning his skin like firebrands. Thank God, he had not lost sensation—he was not frostbitten yet. But a few moments more, in that hole in the snow. . . . The ice-cold shroud of frost-death was down there—it would soon have soothed his pains, would soon have made him slumber forever!

But he was still alive. He loosened his stiff joints, he forced his body to move again. And once more he swung the flour sack onto his back. Fury boiled within him as he made ready to carry it farther; he gained strength from his seething anger, from adversity's bitterness. Many times before he had enjoyed the gift of strength from vexation, and this time it was more welcome than ever. Who said he wasn't able? Those spiteful neighbors in Sweden, how they would enjoy his misfortunes if they knew! He could just hear them say: Karl Oskar couldn't succeed! What did we tell you?

He was enraged. In a wild frenzy he began to kick the big stump that had tripped him. His feet felt like icicles in his boots. But suddenly he stopped and stood still: Who could have felled a great tree here in the wilderness? The stump was fresh and cut by an ax!

He dropped his sack, bent down, brushed away the

364

snow and examined the stump carefully. It was a low stump, not cut by a straight-standing American. This stump was cut by a Swede! He recognized the stump—*he had felled this tree himself*. It was the great oak he had cut down here, their food table! And that oak had grown on a knoll close behind their house—only a few hundred yards from home. . . .

Now he would find his way; he was practically there.

But Karl Oskar walked the remaining distance slowly. He was exhausted; and he must have carried the sack much farther than fifteen miles, for he was approaching his house from the wrong direction! He could see the yellow light from a window greeting him between the trunks of the sugar maples. There stood his house, a fire burning on the hearth. With infinite slowness he dragged his feet the last steps. The sack's weight had increased again, this last stretch.

In a low voice Karl Oskar called Kristina's name. He heard her pull the bolt on the inside of the door. With great effort he managed to lift his feet over the high threshold and dump the sack onto the floor. He put down his burden for the last time, with a dull thud. And then he slumped down on a stump chair near the fire, limp, jointless, weak; he dropped a full sack on the floor and sank into the chair like a discarded, empty sack.

"You're late," said Kristina. "I've been worried about you."

"It was a long way."

"I guess so. And cold tonight. Did it bother you?"

"A little. The last stretch."

"You should have taken your other coat."

"But it was so mild when I left."

He was thawing out near the fire. He wondered how his feet had fared—perhaps his toes were frostbitten. He must go out and get a shovelful of snow, then he would melt some fat and rub his limbs, first with snow, then with fat.

Kristina had already opened the sack. She dipped into it for some flour which she strained between her fingers: "Good rye flour! You must have almost three bushels."

"Thereabouts, I guess."

"You had enough to carry!"

"About right for me."

"Now we'll have bread till spring. And we've been promised potatoes."

She related how Danjel had come to visit today and offered to lend them a bushel of potatoes, Jonas Petter too had promised them a bushel; they could pay back in the fall when they harvested their own.

"That's well," Karl Oskar said. "They are kind."

"It's hardest for us," Kristina said. "We're the poorest. Danjel wondered if we would survive the winter."

"We shall manage!"

Karl Oskar had taken off his boots and socks and sat with his bare feet near the fire: his toes itched and burned, feeling was returning. There was a spell of silence, and he thought: It could have happened that the next letter to reach Ljuder Parish, probably written by Danjel, would have said Karl Oskar Nilsson from Korpamoen had frozen to death in the forest a short distance from his house. One cold night February last. His body was found on a sack of flour which he had carried on his back from the store, many Swedish miles away. The exhausted man hadn't been able to reach home, he had lain down to rest in the severe cold, on his sack, had fallen asleep, and had never awakened.

But this piece of news would not reach Sweden now. It would not gladden those hearts who had predicted ill for him out here. What had happened to him this winter night in the wilderness would not happen again. Bread was necessary for life, but one mustn't give life to get it.

Kristina was putting food on the table for her husband; she would set the dough before they went to bed and she would get up early to heat the oven. . . .

Johan awakened in his bed in the corner; he yelled with delight as he saw his father sitting at the hearth: "Father is back!"

He jumped out of bed and ran to sit on Karl Oskar's knee: "Father has brought flour! Mother can bake bread!"

Karl Oskar sat silent, stroking his son's head clumsily with his frost-stiff fingers.

"You must be hungry, Karl Oskar," Kristina said. "It's all ready for you."

He sat down to his supper, and he ate quietly but he was satisfied in his silence; tomorrow the missing loaf of bread would again be in its place on their table.

366

XXIII

The Letter from Sweden

This was the longest of all winters for the settlers; they counted the days and waited for spring.

March had his cap full of snow, shaking it over the earth in a final blizzard. But after the snowstorm came mild weather with a south wind blowing day after day. The snow carpet thinned, the lake ice soon lay blueish bare. The night frost was still with them, but the sun warmed the air in daytime; no longer need they keep the hearth fire alive through the night.

One day Johan came rushing in from the meadow, calling out loudly before he reached the threshold. What had happened? In his hand the boy held a little flower, pulled up by its roots.

"Look Mother! A *sippa!* I've found a spring *sippa!*"

He had found the flower near the brook. All in the cabin crowded around to see it. It was a spindly little flower, hardly three inches tall, with liver-brown leaves and a blue crown on a thin stem. Below the crown was a circle of heart-shaped green leaves. It must be a *sippa*, but it was the smallest one any of them had ever seen. Kristina said the Swedish *sippa* had a wider crown, and this flower had no smell. Karl Oskar and Robert could not remember how it was with the *sippas* at home in that respect, but she insisted they had a fragrance: all flowers in the homeland were fragrant.

However small the flower was, it must be a *sippa*. In both Sweden and America the hepatica was the first flower to appear in spring, and this was a singular discovery for the settlers. The flower grew near a brook in Minnesota, just as in Smaland. In some way it seemed to link the two countries, to bring home closer.

Kristina filled a cracked coffee cup with water and put the little bloom on the window ledge: the first message of spring had come to them.

One more March shook his cap, but this time it was a wet snowfall, soon turning into heavy rain. For a few days the earth was washed with melting snow. The calls of water birds were heard from the lake: this was the second spring message.

The ground was bare, but ice still covered the St. Croix River. Robert went about in a dream, waiting. During the nights he lay awake in his bed, listening to the changing sounds in his left ear. He could hear one sound that impatiently called him away from here, he could hear the muffled roar of a mighty water which as yet ran under the winter's icy roof but soon would burst into open daylight and swell in its spring flow; it would bring a vessel with eagle feathers on the bow, a ship to carry him away. Soon he would travel downstream on that great water which was forever wandering on to the sea: Robert was waiting for the *Red Wing* of St. Louis.

Karl Oskar and Kristina were waiting for the same boat: they were waiting for a letter from Sweden.

A year would soon have passed since they had left the homeland, and as yet they had not heard one word from their parents and families.

Karl Oskar had written a letter to Sweden last summer, and another last fall, and now in spring they waited for an answer. During the fall Robert had written a letter for Kristina to her parents in Duvemala, and she was now waiting for an answer. When she had learned to read in school, she ought to have asked to be instructed in writing also, then she could now have written herself to her relatives and friends at home. But her father had been of the opinion that a female could make no use of the art of writing—it was always the menfolk who drew up sales

368

contracts, wrote auction records and other important papers. She now deeply regretted having let her father decide for her. But how could she know when going to school as a little girl what she must go through in life? How could she then have imagined that one day she would emigrate to North America? At that time she didn't even know this land existed! It was only two years ago that she had first heard the name North America.

Karl Oskar was helping Jonas Petter cut fence rails, in order to earn a few dollars to enable him to buy food supplies from Mr. Abbott's store in Taylors Falls. He also helped his neighbors to break in their newly bought oxen, and to build a wagon of wood with oak trundles for wheels, a replica of Anders Mansson's ox wagon. Having no team, Karl Oskar needed no wagon, but by helping his neighbors he gathered knowledge that would be useful when he made his own.

Danjel's first journey with his new team and wagon was when he drove Ulrika and her daughter to Stillwater, where Elin was to seek work. He drove on a new road which the lumber company had cleared through the forest during the past winter. Ulrika returned to the settlement without her daughter, and a few days later she walked to Ki-Chi-Saga and related to Kristina what had taken place on their journey to Stillwater.

Elin had remained in town as maid to an upper-class American family. Pastor Jackson had found her a position with one of the richest men in his congregation, a high lord who ruled the lumber company. Elin was to receive eight dollars a month besides food and lodging, and all she had to do was wash dishes, scrub floors, and do laundry. She would not be called on to do a single outside chore, not even carry in water and wood. This was quite different from Sweden, where the maids had to do the menfolk's chores as well, and were paid one daler a month. Here not even half as much work was required—yet her wages were twenty times as high! For eight dollars made about twenty daler.

Ulrika praised God Who had helped her and her daughter to America, and next to the Lord she praised Pastor Jackson who had negotiated the position for Elin.

On this visit Ulrika had been able to speak with Pastor Jackson. She had understood about half of the words he said, and he had understood a little more than half of her words. For the rest they had guessed, and nearly always guessed right. The Glad One was quick-witted and learned easily, she had picked up so many English expressions that Kristina was surprised. She herself had learned hardly a single word yet.

But Ulrika was bold and resourceful, she talked to every American she met. She was often spoken to by American menfolk who—as menfolk will—let their eyes rest on an attractive woman. In this way she had opportunity to practice the foreign tongue. Because of her shapely body she learned English faster than women who were spoken to less often. She told Kristina she was already dreaming in English, and in her dreams men spoke whole long sentences in English to her. But it still happened that she dreamed wrong about some words.

Jonas Petter had gossiped that unmarried Ulrika of Vastergohl had a new suitor, Samuel Nojd, the fur trader from Dalcarlia. Kristina now asked if the gossip were true.

"Yes. Nojd has proposed."

"He too! And you have answered him?"

"He got the same answer as Mansson. And the same comfort!"

Ulrika explained: She was just, she treated all her suitors alike. Here in America all people should be treated alike since there weren't four classes of people as there were in Sweden, but only one class, a human class. Samuel Nojd had offered her a home in St. Paul, where he intended to open a store for meat—sausages, hams, steaks, and such. He was going to give up his fur trapping. But she had never liked the Dalcarlian, nothing was ever right for him, he complained wherever he lived, complained of the food and houses and people. That was why she had given a new name to the pelt hunter; in Swedish his name meant Samuel Satisfied, *she* called him Samuel Mis-Nojd, Samuel Dissatisfied. If she married him, he would soon be dissatisfied and complain of her too. Nor did she think he was a desirable man for bed play. He acted like a man, but he liked to live in dirt, he didn't keep himself clean, he stank at a yard's distance. He stank of old slaughter, he smelled of fat, blood, and entrails. All his work had to do with slaughter, skinning animals, tanning their hides. She wouldn't mind working in his store in St. Paul—she had heard two thousand people lived in that city—and she would willingly sell his meat and sausage and ham at great profit. But she would not in her marriage bed have a husband who stank like an entrail slinger.

No, she would never become Mrs. Samuel Nojd, she had thanked him and said no to the offer.

"I wonder who your next suitor will be," said Kristina.

"I've had one since Nojd," Ulrika reported. "That Norwegian in Stillwater made a try for me."

Thomassen, the little Norwegian shoemaker whom they had met last summer, had dropped in at Pastor Jackson's last time she was there. He had asked if she were married, the man obviously meant business. Ulrika had never seen so lustful a man, he was so hot he had to walk stooped over. But he was such a little man, so spindly, she might have trouble finding him in bed. And before he had time to propose she had made it clear to him that she had no desire to become a shoemaker's wife in Stillwater. If she were to marry any man outside her own countrymen, then he must be an American. There were not many Swedes to choose from in Minnesota, nearly all the unmarried ones had already proposed to her, so she guessed she would be forced to marry an American.

Jonas Petter had said to Kristina that Ulrika of Vastergohl was now the most sought-after woman in the whole St. Croix Valley. And Kristina answered that this was not surprising: Every unmarried man was looking for a wife, and Ulrika had the fortune to be shaped in such a way that she attracted and tempted menfolk. She was good-looking, still young, and looked younger than she was; she had a healthy, blooming appearance, and since arriving in America she had blossomed out in both soul and body. She was capable in all she did, she cooked good food, she was companionable, always in good temper and high spirits. No one had ever seen the Glad One weep. Those who knew her well could not imagine her shedding tears. Who wouldn't wish such a wife?

Jonas Petter predicted Ulrika would be married before full summer.

Kristina said to Ulrika: "I wonder who will finally get you?"

"I myself don't bother to wonder," replied Ulrika, full of confidence. "I leave everything to the Lord's decision."

371

Before Elin went to Stillwater and accepted her position with the high American family, she and Robert had studied a chapter from his language book: "Advise for Swedish servant-folk in America." She must learn to understand the commands of the mistress, otherwise she would perform her duties wrongly and be driven from service the very first day. Together they read the most important sentences concerning her duties, they read them in English, over and over, until the servant-girl-to-be knew them by heart. The instructions began with the first day and went on for the whole week:

Good morning, Missus! I am the new servant girl.— Welcome, change clothes and feel at home!—What time am I expected down in the morning?—You must get up at six o'clock. Clean out the ashes in the stove. Hand me the pot, I'll show you how to make oatmeal. Empty the slop bucket and tidy the maid's room. Eat your own breakfast. Leave no food on the dining-room table while you sweep and dust. Wash dishes and pots. Tomorrow is washday. Everything must be ironed Tuesday morning. After dinner on Sunday you may go to church. You must be back at half past nine. Wednesday you must clean upstairs. Now eat your own dinner. . . .

They went through the whole week of a maid in an upper-class American family.

By now Elin had learned to move her lips less, and she kept her tongue far back in her mouth while speaking English. She had improved greatly since her mother had been teaching her what she picked up in her conversations with American menfolk.

When Elin had served as nursemaid at home in Ljuder, the master had held morning prayers for all the maids and farm help every day. Each one had been required to repeat by heart the verses in the Catechism from Titus, Second Chapter, before they were allowed to eat breakfast: "Exhort servants to be obedient unto their own masters, and to please them well in all things; not answering again; not purloining, but shewing all fidelity; that they may adorn the doctrine of God our Saviour in all things."

Elin thought as an American maid she would now be required to read these verses and she wanted to learn them in English. But Robert told her: The Americans did not require their servants to obey the Catechism. Moreover, no one out here had to obey the authorities, who weren't put in their place by God. She herself could see from the book that servants were treated justly in America. The master and mistress bade them welcome! They asked servants to feel at home and gave them time off to go to church! Nay, the mistress was even so noble that she told her maid to eat! Both breakfast and dinner! Had anyone in Sweden ever heard a master or a mistress ask a servant to eat?

When Elin accepted the position in Stillwater, Robert stayed at home and waited. He waited for a secret message Elin had promised to send him. And one Saturday, the third week in March, it came: The ice had broken up on the St. Croix River, and in Stillwater they were looking for the first steamer.

The next day, Sunday, Robert walked to Danjel's and spoke to Arvid. They were ready, they had long been ready, they had been waiting. And when Robert came home in the evening he announced to Karl Oskar: "Tomorrow morning Arvid and I shall walk to Stillwater. We're taking the steamboat."

"The steamboat?"

"We shall journey to the gold fields in California."

"What are you talking about? What do you want to do there?"

"Dig gold, of course."

"Dig gold?" Karl Oskar thought that Robert had invented some tale to deceive him.

"We decided last fall. We were only waiting for the ice to melt."

"Are you serious?"

Robert assured him he was in earnest. Karl Oskar began to wonder if Robert and Arvid might have met an American who wanted to lure them away on some adventure; but as he listened to his brother he realized the gold-digging fancies had originated entirely with Robert. The boy had heard rumors about a land of gold far to the west, and he believed all he heard. He lived entirely in his imagination. And even though Arvid was a full-grown man, he was as credulous and gullible as Robert, and equally childish. And these two intended to undertake a long journey in

373

this vast, dangerous country. Karl Oskar could easily see the outcome of such a venture! He must avert his young brother's fancy.

"You couldn't manage alone, Robert! You're too young and too weak as yet."

"To dig gold isn't heavy work. It's easier than grub hoeing!"

"*If* you found some gold. *If* your fancies came through. But California lies far away, in the back end of America. How will you get there?"

"We'll work on the steamboat to St. Louis. Then we can walk the highway. I have a map and I know English. Don't worry about me, Karl Oskar."

Arvid was coming to Ki-Chi-Saga to meet Robert the following morning. Danjel had said he would not keep his servant against his will. Arvid had already worked for him a whole year, that was enough for the transportation from Sweden. Danjel was decent about everything, he let Arvid have his free will.

"This will come to a terrible end!" Karl Oskar almost shouted his words at Robert. If his brother had been strong and handy and tough! But Robert was a weak, inexperienced, timid boy. He ran from dead Indians and could hear the whizz of arrows that had never been shot. And his hearing was bad. He was filled with his own imagination; he was possessed by his own fancies. He was walking with open eyes into his own destruction!

Karl Oskar recalled that Robert had been odd as a boy at home: he was at least twelve years old before he stopped running after rainbows, trying to catch them with his hands. Robert was fascinated by the glittering colors and never realized that however far he ran the rainbow remained equally far away. Karl Oskar had never run to catch a rainbow.

It was pure folly for Robert to start out. And Karl Oskar pleaded with him and warned him. He was trying to talk him out of the gold-digging notion, not because he wanted Robert as a helper on the farm—he could take care of himself—it was for Robert's own sake. He could not with a clear conscience let his younger brother set out on so reckless, danger-fraught a journey. Here in a foreign country he felt in a father's place toward his brother. Had Robert thought of all the perils he and Arvid might encounter?

374

They must travel through vast stretches of wilderness, they didn't know the roads, they could easily become lost; they didn't know people, they could be swindled and cheated; they might even be killed.

"You can't manage alone! Believe what I say. You're only eighteen!"

"You were only fourteen when you left home," retorted Robert.

"That's true. But that was at home, that was different."

"When you were fourteen you said to Father: 'I'll go! I've decided for myself!' And you left."

"Yes—but that was in Sweden."

"You went off on your own at fourteen. Haven't I the right to do the same at eighteen?"

Robert had put his older brother in a position where he was unable to answer. Ever since he was fourteen he *had* decided for himself, done as he pleased, traveled where he wished. He could not deny his brother the same right.

"You can't stop me, Karl Oskar," Robert said.

He had already gathered together his belongings. They were not many, they made only a small bundle. Persuasion and warning words were lost on him, no one could tie him down or tether him like an animal. And as Karl Oskar could not stop him by force, he could not stop him in any other way. From now on Robert must decide for himself and take the responsibility for his own life. Karl Oskar sought to ease his conscience—he had done all in his power, there was nothing more to do.

Kristina was as much disturbed as Karl Oskar but she agreed with him: they must let Robert do as he wanted. What else could they do?

Robert had saved five dollars; he had earned four of them as day laborer for Danjel, and one dollar had been his profit from the almanacs he had made at New Year and sold to the Swedish settlers in the St. Croix Valley. Of the eight dollars Karl Oskar had earned from rail splitting for Jonas Petter, he had only five left, and these he gave to Robert. It was the only help he could offer, the only cash he had to give when his brother left home. Kristina began to prepare a good-sized food basket for the boy; that was all she could do. He might be hungry many times and need many meals before he reached the California gold fields.

Robert said: He was going to California because he wanted to become rich while still young and able to enjoy his riches. But he would not forget Karl Oskar and Kristina when he returned from the gold fields. He would share his gold—first of all, he would give Karl Oskar money for a pair of oxen, a real draft team, then he wouldn't need to carry such heavy burdens long distances through the wilderness. And for Kristina he would buy cows, fine milch cows that would give milk enough for all of them. This family had been kind to him, he would remember them. This they could rely on: he would not keep all his fortune for himself, he was not like that—he would share.

Monday morning before daybreak Arvid arrived at the log house—he was ready to walk with Robert through the forest to Stillwater.

Robert had ten dollars in his pocket, his bundle of worldly possessions on his back, and food for ten days. As he shook hands with his brother in good-by, he said he had been lying awake during the night—his ear had bothered him—and he had made a decision: When he returned from California he would journey back to Sweden for a time and buy Krakesja Manor from Lieutenant Rudeborg and give this estate to his father and mother. They had such a little room, and their reserved rights in Korpamoen were very poor. It would be well for them in their old age to live in a manor. They had earned this, he thought; they would have more room in a mansion. Yes, he would not forget father and mother at home, Karl Oskar could rely on that—this was the last thing he wanted to say before they parted.

Karl Oskar and Kristina stood outside the log house door and looked after Arvid and Robert. The two disappeared into the forest. Karl Oskar and Kristina asked the same question of themselves: Would they see the boys ever again?

3

The river was open, its water flowed free—this was the final harbinger of spring in the St. Croix Valley.

In bays and inlets of Lake Ki-Chi-Saga the spawn-bellied pike began their play among belated, melting ice floes. Now the settlers again had fresh fish at every meal, good sustaining fare. And the rabbits emerged from their winter shelters and ate the green grass in the meadow; the rabbits were not so fat as last fall, but their meat tasted better. Food worry diminished each day. The weather was mild with a warming sun, the sap rose under the bark of the tree trunks. Karl Oskar took his auger and drilled holes in the sugar maples near the log house, and the running sap filled the containers he placed below the holes. From it they boiled a sweet sirup which they spread on bread instead of butter; the children were overjoyed with this delicious food. Useful trees grew around their house —with nourishment flowing under their bark.

People and animals came to life again, the shores of Lake Ki-Chi-Saga teemed with fresh, young growth. A new joy burst forth in all growing things—the joy of having kept alive through the winter.

Robert and Arvid had boarded the *Red Wing*, the spring's first steamer to Stillwater. The packet also brought the year's first mail to the Territory—it should include a letter from Sweden.

Kristina talked every day about this letter which they had been waiting for so long, and she begged Karl Oskar to go to the post office in Taylors Falls and ask about it. But the walk would require half a day, and now all his days were busy—the frost would soon be out of the earth, and he had begun to make a plow for the turning of the meadow. At last, however, he gave in to his impatient wife —early one morning he took off on the nine-mile walk to Taylors Falls to inquire in the Scotsman's store about the letter from Sweden.

There was always a paper nailed to the outside of the door of Mr. Abbott's store, a list of the names of people who had letters inside: *Letters remaining at the Post Office in Taylors Falls, Walter H. Abbott, Postmaster.*

How many times Karl Oskar had stopped on the steps of the store and read through that list, searching for his own name! As yet it had never been there. He had read the name of every other inhabitant of Taylors Falls and thereabouts, but not his own, or Danjel's, or Jonas Petter's. He had read the names of other settlers until he learned to recognize them, but he had always missed his own name. Many times he had wondered how it would feel to find his own name written down, and be counted among the fortunate people who had letters inside in the custody of storekeeper and postmaster Walter H. Abbott.

And today his name was on the list! Indeed, it was the first one, it stood at the top of the list! He counted all the names, there were seventeen below his. It was as though his letter were the most important of all. For a moment he felt he was better than the others who had letters inside. His name was written in the Scot's firm hand, with large, round, clear letters, easy to read: *Mr. Karl Oskar Nilsson.* Here he was called *Mr.* like the others. That meant the same as *Lord* in Sweden. He was a lord here, like all Americans. But the Mr. before his name seemed strange to him. In some way it did not belong before a name like his, it belonged before Jackson and Abbott and other American names, but not before Karl Oskar Nilsson.

However, the letter from Sweden had arrived.

Karl Oskar opened the door and went inside. Mr. Abbott stood in his place behind the counter. He was a tall, scrawny man with sharp features and piercing eyes. He always wore the same serious look, his features were in some way incapable of change. And the strangest thing about him was that he could talk without seeming to move his lips. He was held among the settlers to be a good man, very exact in his business. He gave the customers full weight, though not an ounce more. He was an honest trader, but no one was ever granted delay in payment; in his store trading was done for cash only.

Karl Oskar had not come to buy anything, he was penniless since he had given Robert his last five dollars. That was one reason he had delayed going to the store— he could buy nothing to bring home. He could only fetch the letter.

Before he had time to ask for it, the postmaster-storekeeper behind the desk said to him: "I have a letter for you, Mister Nilsson."

Mr. Abbott pulled out a long drawer under the counter and looked through a stack of letters until he found a small, square, gray-blue envelope: "Here it is! Yes, Mr. Nilsson."

Karl Oskar's face lit up, he recognized the letter: it was the kind of envelope they used at home. He stretched out his hand for the letter.

378

"Fifteen cents." The tall Scot held the letter between his thumb and forefinger, but he did not give it to the Swede on the other side of the counter: "Fifteen cents, sir."

"What mean you, Mr. Abbott?" Karl Oskar spoke his halting English. Why didn't the postmaster hand over his letter? Did he want money because he had held it so long? What was the meaning of this charge?

"You have to pay fifteen cents in postage due, Mr. Nilsson."

The postmaster of Taylors Falls still held the little gray-blue envelope between the thumb and forefinger of his right hand while he pointed with his left forefinger to some stamps on the letter. And Karl Oskar still stood with his hand outstretched for the letter from Sweden.

Then he thought he understood: the freight for the letter had not been paid. He must redeem it with fifteen cents. But he did not have even one cent.

"Yes, sir?" Mr. Abbott was waiting, expressionless. He held the letter firmly in his hand, as if afraid Karl Oskar might try to snatch it. Mr. Abbott was not a man to be taken by surprise.

"No—No—" The Swedish settler struggled with the language of the new land. "I can—can not today—no—have . . . not one cent!" Karl Oskar pulled out his pockets—empty!

A trace of pity was discernible in the postmaster's voice: "No cash, Mr. Nilsson? Sorry, I have to keep your letter." And he replaced it in the drawer under the counter.

Karl Oskar, who had stretched out his hand for the letter from Sweden, had to pull it back empty—he thrust it into his empty pocket.

The storekeeper at the other side of the counter scrutinized him sharply: Karl Oskar looked foolishly at the floor. He could not redeem the letter he had come to fetch. . . . "No cash, Mr. Nilsson?" He had heard those words so many times, he knew what they meant. *Cash*—the word still sounded to him like the rustle of paper money, the fingering of piles of dollar bills. It was one word in the foreign language which he did not like, he could not get by it, he always bumped against it like a stone wall—cash! It was the word of permanent hindrance, the word for the settler's greatest obstacle.

Mr. Abbott looked at Karl Oskar's feet, at his shoes. To save his boots, already quite worn, Karl Oskar now wore his wooden shoes even for walks to the village. People in Taylors Falls stared at his feet in the wooden shoes, they had never seen such footgear. They apparently thought that people who wore wooden shoes were impoverished and wretched, he could see in Mr. Abbott's eyes. The Scot pitied the woodenshod settler, the poor Swede who did not have even fifteen cents to pay for his letter from the homeland.

If there was one thing Karl Oskar detested above all else it was to be pitied. "All right!" he said, as if the letter did not concern him. And he felt he pronounced those words like an American.

"Sorry," Mr. Abbott repeated. "But I have to keep the letter."

News from Sweden, the first in a year, again lay hidden in the postmaster's drawer. All that the settlers had wanted so long to know about their relatives at home—if they were well or ill, if all were alive, or if someone were dead—this long-awaited news was pushed back among the letters in the drawer. There it must remain until the fee was paid. Karl Oskar had nothing to reproach the postmaster with, it was not his fault if the addressee lacked the fifteen cents. The mail company granted no delay in payments. Mr. Abbott worked for the mail company, he did only his duty when he kept the letter.

Karl Oskar nodded a silent good-by and walked toward the door.

"Sorry!" Mr. Abbott said, for the third or fourth time.

His expression was still unchanged, but there was sadness in his voice. The postmaster was sorry for Karl Oskar, because he was unable to redeem his letter. *Sorry,* he heard that word often when Americans talked, it sounded as if they were constantly grieving for others. But he had sometimes heard the word uttered so lightly and unconcernedly that he wasn't sure real sorrow was always felt. This time, however, he believed Mr. Abbott was genuinely sorry he had had to leave without the letter.

The day had been almost wasted. A walk to Taylors Falls and back was tiresome, his wooden shoes were heavy and clumsy, his feet always felt sore after a long walk. Must he now walk back nine miles without the letter?

But Anders Mansson lived in the village only half a mile away; he could borrow the fifteen cents from him, go back to Mr. Abbott's postoffice, and lay the money on the counter!

The Mansson fields lay deserted today, all was quiet. Fina-Kajsa sat in the sun outside the cabin, patching one of her son's skin coats. She sat slumped and her glassy eyes wandered listlessly as if following something far away in the forest. She did not look at the work in her hands, she stared in front of her as if in deep worry; perhaps she was still brooding over the journey of disappointment she had undertaken to her son's fine mansion in Minnesota; as yet she had not arrived.

Her cream-pitcher lips moved vaguely in answer as Karl Oskar greeted her and asked for Anders.

"He lies flat-back today."

"Flat-back?"

"Yes. He lies flat on his back inside."

Fina-Kajsa's voice sounded hollow. Karl Oskar looked at her in surprise. Did Anders Mansson lie in bed on a weekday for no reason, without working? Or had something happened to him? "Is he ailing? Is that why—"

The mother gave no answer, she only pointed to the door meaningfully: Go inside! And he entered the tiny cabin into which the whole group of Swedish newcomers had packed themselves last year.

A strong, sweet odor struck him as soon as he was over the threshold and in the stuffy air of the cabin. It was a work day, the middle of the day—but Anders Mansson lay in his shirt on his bed, stretched out on his back, sleeping and snoring. The door creaked loudly on its ungreased hinges, and Karl Oskar clumped noisily on his wooden shoes, but the sleeper was not awakened by these sounds. Anders Mansson had not lain down for a light nap, he was sunk in deep slumber.

Karl Oskar went to the bed. As he leaned over the sleeper the rancid-sweet odor grew stronger. He discovered its source: his foot struck a wooden keg that lay overturned on the floor near the bed.

It was a whisky keg, rolling in a dark-brown wet spot on the floor, where some of the contents had run out. But not much had been wasted: Karl Oskar suspected that the keg had been practically empty when it was turned over.

381

And the man who had emptied it now lay on the bed after his drinking bout, with open, gaping mouth, breathing noisily in deep jerky snores. His breath rattled in his throat, and his chest heaved slowly up and down. It seemed as if each new breath might choke him, stick in his throat, and be his last.

Anders Mansson was dead drunk today, a day in the middle of the week; he lay unconscious on his bed in full daylight, he lay flat-back as his mother had said. But his face bloomed red, his cheeks blossomed.

"Why are you so red in the face?" Fina-Kajsa had asked her son when they arrived last summer. And Karl Oskar remembered one time when he met Fina-Kajsa at Danjel's; he had asked about Anders, and she had answered: "He lies flat-back at home." He had wondered what she meant.

He looked at Anders Mansson with disgust and pity: he slept a drunkard's sleep and nothing would wake him now, nothing but time could stop that rattle in his throat. But his face looked healthy and red; "if you have red cheeks you are far from dead," the saying was. . . .

Karl Oskar walked slowly out of the cabin. The drunkard's mother was still sitting outside; he had nothing to say to her.

But she asked: "Was it something you wanted with Anders?"

"Nothing to speak of. Just wanted to look in as I passed by."

"He wakes up toward evening."

"Well . . . is that so? Does he often—"

"As often as he has money to buy drinks with." Old Fina-Kajsa spoke to the air in a low, hollow voice—without reproach or sorrow. "He got started on it when he lived alone."

"I suppose so."

"He ailed from lonesomeness."

"I see."

Karl Oskar felt embarrassed and ashamed, as though he had surprised her son during some natural but private occupation which concerned no one except himself and which usually is not performed in sight of others.

Fina-Kajsa continued: "Anders says he grew lonesome

here. He says it can affect one's head, to emigrate and grow lonely. . . ."

Karl Oskar searched for words of comfort for the old one. But strangely, comforting words were far away when needed. He could not find a single one—he had nothing to say to Fina-Kajsa. He greeted her from Kristina, and then went his way. The old woman remained sitting, her vacant eyes staring over the wilderness forest.

He son who lay flat-back on his bed had grown lonesome . . . hmm. . . .

Now Karl Oskar knew why Anders Mansson had been unable to improve his circumstances during his years in the Territory—now he knew the secret of Fina-Kajsa's son.

4

Karl Oskar could now go to Lake Gennesaret and borrow the fifteen cents from his neighbors, but then he would not have time for a second walk back to Mr. Abbott's store. He must let the letter from Sweden remain in the post-office drawer for the time being; after all, it was not floating in the lake, Postmaster Abbott had it in safekeeping.

Karl Oskar walked straight back home. Kristina met him in the door: "Did you get the letter? What did it say? Are they well?" Three anxious questions, and she found time for a fourth before her husband had said a word: "Hasn't the letter come?"

"It has come. But it must be redeemed. It costs fifteen cents."

"You couldn't redeem it?"

"No."

"You walked all the way for nothing?"

"Yes."

Kristina had been waiting eagerly for his return, she was sure he would bring the letter from Sweden. Now she felt like a child who is chased away from the Christmas tree after waiting long at the door.

A silence fell between husband and wife. And Karl Oskar felt another question coming, but this one his wife need not utter. He said he had not wished to borrow from anyone in Taylors Falls, he was too proud to ask for a loan of fifteen cents; he did not wish to advertise his poverty among all the Swedes in the St. Croix Valley. Their letter was in good hands in the store, they need not worry, no one would take it away from them.

"Did you see the writing on the letter?"

"No, I wasn't that close."

"You don't know who wrote it?"

"No. It could be my father, or it might be yours. One or the other, I guess."

A few days passed. Spring had come to the valley. The ice on the river had broken up, the steamboat had come with the letter from Sweden; it now lay in a drawer in the post office in Taylors Falls and could be redeemed for fifteen cents. Kristina thought, what luck that the sun and the warmth came to people without having to be redeemed; had they been forced to pay fifteen cents for the spring, the winter would still be with them.

Karl Oskar and Kristina said nothing more about the letter, but their thoughts hovered around it. They could not get it off their minds, they wondered and mused: What was in the letter? A whole year had run away since they had climbed on the wagon for the drive to Karlshamn—how much might have happened in that time! And everything that had happened was written in that letter, and the letter had finally almost reached them, it was only a few miles away, yet as far away as ever. It cost fifteen cents!

Kristina thought it would have been better not to know about the letter. It would have been better if Karl Oskar had kept quiet about it. Now she was wrought up and worried about news from home. It was so close, yet not within her reach.

Karl Oskar was resigned to waiting patiently until the time he could redeem it, and he thought Kristina should do the same. He was busy all day long making his new breaking plow. He was making it entirely of wood, and he must have it ready when the frost left the ground. He had been promised he might borrow his neighbors' oxen and he was anxious to begin the plowing. A plow was far more important to him than a letter. He talked about it every time he came inside for a meal, it was on his mind early and late. It was the first time he had made a plow, the farmer's most important implement, and it required clever hands. He cut and carved, he chiseled and dug, he tried

384

various kinds of wood, discarded and began anew, improved and finished each part from day to day. The blade must have the right curve, the pull tree the right turn, the shafts and handles the right angles. The plow body must be light, sensitive to the steering hands of the plower, it must cut its way easily through the sod. He would follow this plow in its furrow for a long time, he would follow it every day until the whole meadow was turned into a field. The new plow would give them the field for their bread to grow in.

But Kristina wished to hear no more of the plow he was making, she wanted to talk of the letter they must redeem.

Karl Oskar was too proud to borrow a mere fifteen cents from his neighbors. If a poor man could afford nothing else, at least he could afford his pride. This was a lesson he had learned in Sweden. But it might be that this lesson was neither good nor useful for an impoverished settler here in the wilderness. He could not live by his pride. And whence would he get the fifteen cents if he did not borrow it from Danjel or Jonas Petter?

A few more days went by and Karl Oskar kept busy at his plow. Then Kristina could wait no longer: Did he intend to get the letter soon? He replied that the letter was in good hands, Mr. Abbott would not give it to anyone else, she must not be impatient, the work on the plow was much more urgent.

Kristina made her own decision: She would go to her uncle and borrow fifteen cents.

Without Karl Oskar's knowledge she would set out early next morning through the forest to Danjel's settlement. She would show her stubborn husband that *she* could redeem the message from Sweden. His pride could not keep her letter from her any longer!

Strangers rarely came to the log house at Lake Ki-Chi-Saga. Occasionally a pelt trader might walk by. But the day Kristina had made her decision a stranger dropped in on them.

He was a man from the lumber company in Stillwater; he had walked through the forest staking out new roads and had lost his way. The stranger arrived at the new settlement as the family was sitting down to the noonday meal and he was asked to share their dinner: Would he be satisfied with their simple food?

385

Karl Oskar and the American could barely make each other understood, but he seemed a kind man. He thanked them for the dinner and before he left he patted Johan on the head and gave him a coin.

The stranger was hardly outside the door before Kristina turned to the boy and looked at the gift. It was a ten-cent piece.

She turned the thin coin in her hand, deeply disappointed. It was not enough, she was still five cents short. She would still have to borrow, and a five-cent loan would reveal their poverty more than a fifteen-cent one.

"That was close!"

"You mean. . . . ?" Karl Oskar gave his wife a quick glance.

"You know what I mean!"

"But you wouldn't take the coin from the boy?"

Johan was pulling his mother's arm: "I want my money, Mother!"

"Give it to the boy," said the father. "It's the first coin he's ever had."

Kristina handed the child his coin: 'But we could have borrowed it if it had been a fifteen-cent coin."

Johan meanwhile held the ten-cent piece tightly in his closed fist: "It's my money! He gave it to me!"

Karl Oskar said he would never have had the heart to rob the boy of the first money he had owned in his life.

Kristina flared up: "Then go and find fifteen cents! You're impossible! Wait and wait and wait! How long must we wait? When are you getting the letter? Shall we leave it there till Christmas?"

"I'll fetch it tomorrow morning."

"That I must see before I believe it! You're like a stubborn horse! My patience has come to an end!" Her cheeks flashed red from indignation, her eyes seemed to shoot sparks.

Karl Oskar let her anger spend itself and did nothing to interrupt her. When she had finished, he said calmly as before: Early tomorrow morning he would take the dried stag skin to Mr. Fischer in Taylors Falls. He had thought they would use it for clothing but now they must sell it; they could not get along without cash any longer. He might get two dollars for the skin, he would have enough for both the letter and some groceries.

386

"Why didn't you sell the skin long ago? Why have you waited?"

She was interrupted by the door swinging open. The stranger who had given money to Johan was back. He stopped at the threshold and pointed to the lake shore, rolling a lump of tobacco in his hand while he talked.

Karl Oskar listened eagerly and tried to understand. He recognized the word hay. The stranger pointed to the haystacks in their meadow—three stacks were still left, Lady had been unable to eat all the hay before they returned her to Anders Mansson. The stranger had come back because he had discovered their hay—now Karl Oskar understood.

He accompanied the man to the meadow. Shortly, he returned to the house with three large silver coins in his hand: the lumber company in Stillwater was short of hay for their teams, and the man bought the three remaining haystacks for three dollars.

Never was a seller more satisfied with a transaction. "I felt it in my bones last fall when I cut the hay! I knew it would come in handy!" said Karl Oskar.

That very day he went to fetch the letter from Taylors Falls, and this time he carried it with him when he returned. He had recognized his father's big writing on the envelope but he carried it home with the seal unbroken, he wanted to break it in Kristina's presence, he wanted her to listen when he read it for the first time.

As soon as he was inside the door they sat down on either side of their table. It was the middle of the week, but both had a feeling of reverence, a Sunday mood. Karl Oskar picked up the bread knife, the sharpest one they had in the house and he cut the seal slowly and carefully so as not to harm the letter.

It was a small sheet, narrow and written full from top to bottom. The letters were stiff, crooked, and broken— they were reminders of the pain-stiffened, crooked fingers that had formed and written them.

The letter from Sweden brought the following message to the reader and the listener:

Dear Son, Daughter-in-Law and Children,
    Our dearly loved Ones, May you be well is our constant Wish!

We have received your letter and its message that you have arrived alive and in health, Which is a great Joy to us. Now I will write to let you know how we are—we all have God's great gift of health and all is well.

Much evil and good has happened since we parted. The churchwarden in Akerby fell of a wagon and was killed last summer near the hill at Abro mill, Oldest Son took over home, on my Homestead all work and chores progress in due order, the farmer who supplies our Reserved Rights is penurious, but otherwise kind, this year has had fine weather and good crops.

Mother and I do not go to other places much, we keep busy at home, most the time I keep close to the fire as you know. You have had your free will and have deserted home, we hope you all have success, it must be un-Christian hard for you in the beginning in a new land. Mother wonders if you have any Minister to preach God's clear Word to you, your God is with you also in a foreign country. Turn to Him when your own strength fails.

Have no concern and do not worry for Us, We greet your little children and your good wife from Our Hearts. Her parents and Sisters in Duvemala are well and wish the same to Kristina in North America. I have paid the freight for this letter, hope it is sufficient. You can afford it as little as I in a strange country.

You are every hour in our Thoughts, I invoke the Lord's blessing upon you, our dear ones in this world.

Written Down by your Father

Nils Jakob's Son

Korpamoen in Ljuder Parish October 9 in the year of Our Lord 1852. Let no outsider see my scribble.

XXIV

Unmarried Ulrika of Vastergohl Weeps

Karl Oskar reread the letter from Sweden three times before Kristina was satisfied. Only after that did he have an opportunity to tell her the great news he had heard today in Taylors Falls: Ulrika of Vastergohl was going to enter into holy matrimony with Mr. Walter H. Abbott, she was to move to Taylors Falls as wife to the postmaster and storekeeper.

This he had heard and it had come from Swedish Anna, who was not one to spread untrue gossip. She herself would move to New Karragarde as housekeeper for Danjel and Jonas Petter in Ulrika's place.

Mr. Abbott had often of late visited the Swedish settlement at Lake Gennesaret, according to Swedish Anna. And Ulrika had treated him to food—the most delicious food she could cook—sweet cheese, pork omelet, cheesecake. She had offered him all her choice dishes. And Mr. Abbott had been so taken by the Swedish fare that he wished for it on his table at every meal. In order to have the good food daily, he must keep the cook in his house, and so he had proposed to Ulrika. Swedish Anna had hinted that the impending marriage was some piece of witchery: Ulrika had bewitched Mr. Abbott with the food she had given him. She had taken advantage of a poor man who never before had known how food should taste.

Ulrika could thank her Creator that the preparation of decent food was not as yet known in America.

Swedish Anna had spoken as though Ulrika had committed a heinous crime in offering Mr. Abbott her Swedish dishes.

The Taylors Falls postmaster and storekeeper was a well-to-do man, nothing in the way of worldly goods was missing from his house. There might be other women besides the Glad One who would have liked to be in charge of a store full of good wares. Karl Oskar suspected that Swedish Anna spoke in jealousy when she belittled Ulrika.

Kristina had seen Mr. Abbott behind his counter last summer. His head, on a lanky, loose-limbed body, almost reached the ceiling; she remembered his big hands, covered with black hair, his broad, flat feet. He was always dressed in a motley coat with long tails, his shirt neck open. Everyone said he was honest in his dealings. Kristina thought he had a hardened heart, denying the poor settlers credit for a single cent; but she would not call him stingy—many times he had given her sugar sticks for her children.

Kristina said to Karl Oskar: Next Sunday he must stay home alone and look after their offspring. She would go to Uncle Danjel's and wish Ulrika of Vastergohl well on her coming marriage.

2

She started out on her walk early in the morning. It was the first time she had walked alone from Ki-Chi-Saga to the settlement at Lake Gennesaret. Karl Oskar had advised against it—but this time she wanted to go by herself through the clearing; sometime she must learn to walk alone, in a place where she would live for the rest of her life. She would feel like a penned-in animal if she could never leave her home without being followed and guarded like a herd beast. She could not lose her way—there only was one road to follow.

The Indians had returned and had been around the lake, but she tried to suppress her fear of the copperskins with this thought: If God protects me, I need not be afraid to walk alone through the forest. If God does not protect me, I would not be safe in the greatest company of people.

The forest had been washed clean by the mild spring rains, the grass was sprouting, the leaf-trees were budding, the air smelled fresh and good, of foliage and bark and buds, of earth and mold. Kristina stepped lightly over the wretched road, she breathed with an easy heart. For long stretches she could imagine she walked through the woodlands at home in Duvemala. Here grew the same trees, though they were larger, more wild looking than at home. She was more at home with trees and bushes than with people, and did not feel lonely in her walk through the woods.

But she never forgot the dangers that might lurk in the forest. Any moment she might encounter something frightening. Last time Swedish Anna came to visit she had seen a cut-off human foot in the road. It was tied to a post stuck in the ground, a bloody foot with a brown skin—an Indian foot. It was a gruesome sign put there by the savages—Swedish Anna thought it meant war between the Chippewas and the Sioux.

Nor did Kristina forget the snakes which had come out of their holes in the spring sunshine and might lie in wait for her. But neither humans nor animals molested her on her Sunday walk, she saw neither snakes nor maimed human feet.

When she reached Danjel's house, she found Ulrika alone. Jonas Petter had made a small skiff, and he and Danjel had taken the children onto the lake; they hoped to catch some fish for dinner.

Ulrika had returned the evening before from a visit with her daughter in Stillwater. Elin was satisfied in her service, her duties were light and her American master and mistress were kind to their servants. Ulrika had also visited Pastor Jackson in his new house, and she had been to his church and heard him preach.

Kristina noticed at once that Ulrika was not herself today. She did not seem as lively or hearty as usual, she had a serious look on her face, her motions and bearing were different, there was something inscrutable about her. She had a new expression, a thoughtful, solemn look. Perhaps it was caused by the great change which her imminent marriage would bring her.

She took out her knapsack and began carefully folding

garments and placing them in it. So she was already busy with her moving.

"I'm packing up a little," she said.

"Yes. I've already heard about it. You're moving to Taylors Falls to be the storekeeper's wife!"

Ulrika looked up quickly, with a strange, serious glance. She did not answer. Kristina wished her well in her marriage, she repeated her words twice. But Ulrika seemed not to appreciate this good wish, rather, it pained her. She did not acknowledge it, she did not say thank you. She seemed embarrassed and annoyed as she picked up a well-washed and newly ironed shift—Kristina guessed this shining white garment might be her bridal shift.

What was the matter with the Glad One today? Kristina scarcely recognized her. She was always jolly and in high spirits, and this was surely the time for rejoicing. Something must be wrong.

A worrying thought came to Kristina: Perhaps the marriage with Mr. Abbott was off? Had something come between them? Had the suitor regretted his proposal and taken it back? Something had happened. But Ulrika was packing her clothes—was she moving away from Danjel in any case? Kristina asked outright.

"Yes, I'm moving away," Ulrika said, as she spread her clean shift on the table. "But not to Taylors Falls! I am not going to be Storekeeper Abbott's wife."

"Then it isn't true?"

"It *was* the truth. Or almost the truth." Ulrika's voice trembled slightly in a way Kristina had never heard before. "It was as close to the truth as anything can be. I could have married Mr. Abbott. But now I've changed my mind."

"What in the world—"

"Everything has changed for me."

Kristina held her breath: Ulrika must mean that the suitor had changed his mind. Someone might have slandered Ulrika to Mr. Abbott, someone might have told him about her life in Sweden. It must be some Swede—who could it be? Who would be so cruel? Who had betrayed Ulrika?

"Has something come between you?"

"Yes, something came between."

Anger rose within Kristina. Never would she shake hands with the dastard who had ruined Ulrika's marriage plans. "Some wicked, jealous gossip has spoiled it?"

"No," said Ulrika. "It was not a human being."

"No human being?"

"It was God Himself."

"What do you mean?"

"God came between. He did not want me to marry Mr. Abbott."

Ulrika folded the sleeves of her shift. She turned toward Kristina, her full bosom heaving inside her tight bodice: "The Lord stepped in and averted the marriage."

Kristina was confused; Ulrika did not seem to feel she had lost a great opportunity; rather, the Glad One spoke as though a great disaster had nearly overtaken her, which at the last moment God had prevented.

Ulrika explained: Mr. Abbott was the American she had exchanged more English words with than anyone else; she understood him better than anyone, what she had learned of the new language she had learned from him. Ever since New Year's she had known that the postmaster wanted to marry her. Shortly before Christmas, when she went to shop in his store, he had walked part way back with her and helped carry her food basket. He did the same thing again and again, and one evening he had walked all the way to their house and stayed overnight. He had eaten with them, she had offered him the same fare she gave to Danjel and Jonas Petter, but never had she seen a man so grateful for food. He had said she was an expert at cooking, and a few weeks ago he had proposed. He said he needed a housekeeper, and she needed a home —if they married, both would have what they needed.

Abbott was a courteous and fine man, he acted toward her the way all American men acted toward women. How many pounds he had carried for her from Taylors Falls! Even a choosy woman could accept such a man. But she wasn't quite satisfied with the way he had proposed; he ought to have said: I need a human being in my home during the daytime, and a woman in my bed at night! But he hadn't said that. He had only said he needed a housekeeper and cook. If he had proposed the other way, then she would have accepted him at once. Instead she asked

393

for some time to think it over—and this she had done in such a way that he undoubtedly took it for half a promise to marry him.

She needed not only a home, she needed also a man, she hadn't slept with a man for more than three years. She was in her prime, her youthful blood still flowed warm in her body. And when she married, she wanted to marry a man who cared more for what a woman could give in bed than what she could offer at the table. She had long wished for a man who would rather starve at table than fail to appreciate what a woman could give with her soul and body. She wanted, too, a man to help her physically and spiritually, a man she could always rely on. She was afraid a marriage with Mr. Abbott would turn out badly.

That was why she had asked for time to think it over. And yesterday, as she came through Taylors Falls on her way from Stillwater, she had stopped in to see Mr. Abbott in his store and told him: She was honored by his proposal, but she could not accept, because the Lord Jesus would not give His sanction to their wedlock.

Kristina stared at Ulrika, more confused than before: Ulrika had declined to become a storekeeper's wife, she had refused the splendor of Mr. Abbott's store, she had rejected the kind man who had helped carry her burdens homeward!

"Are you serious?"

"I've never been more serious."

"But you're packing! Are you still moving away from Danjel?"

"Yes. I'm moving away. To Stillwater. A miracle has happened to me." She spoke the last sentence with great emphasis.

Something new lit up Ulrika's features, a light shone in her eyes, an unusual gravity was in her voice: "Listen to me, Kristina. You're the first to know: I'm going to be baptized. I'm going to be baptized by a Baptist."

"Oh . . . now I understand. You've changed your religion."

"No! I haven't changed. I've been on the right road. But only now have I come close to God. And for this I can thank Pastor Jackson."

"Ah . . . it's he who has made you a Baptist?"

"Yes. My husband-to-be will baptize me."

394

"What?"

"I'm marrying Pastor Jackson in Stillwater."

And Ulrika turned again to the table where her new-washed linen shift still lay spread.

Kristina was lost in astonishment. But not for long. Her surprise lessened as she thought the news over. She ought to have guessed from the very beginning, she should have foreseen, after all Ulrika's talks of Pastor Jackson and her visits with him, after all the praise Ulrika had lavished on the minister.

"Are you surprised?"

"No!" Kristina answered. "This is the best thing that could happen to you! A likelier man couldn't be found. With Pastor Jackson, I don't even need to wish you well!"

Yes, that was how things were; God had come between Ulrika and Mr. Abbott. And he had chosen another husband for her.

Ulrika was to be married in the Baptist Church in Stillwater this spring. But before she married Pastor Jackson she would be baptized at the great baptism which the church performed in the St. Croix River every spring.

"It's a God's miracle!" said the Glad One. "You don't even understand it, Kristina."

Her hand lightly touched the white shift on the table, slowly, tenderly, like a caress. Kristina had guessed right —it was her bridal shift.

Ulrika went on: Three years ago she had been converted by Danjel, but ever since that time she had felt something missing. She had shed her old body, but she had never felt quite at home in the new one. She had known something was missing from her rebirth in Christ. Since meeting Jackson she had spoken many times to Danjel about the Baptists and had asked him if a new baptism might give new comfort to her soul. Danjel no longer believed God had entrusted him with the care of any soul except his own. Since he had gone astray in self-righteousness, he felt he could lead no one else along the right road. And he had told her she had her own free will in religious matters. She knew best what God asked of her, he would not rebuke her if she turned Baptist and enjoyed a new christening.

Now Ulrika felt a rechristening was just what she needed. Only the Baptists were entirely reborn into this world. To rid herself completely of the old flesh-body, she must again go through baptism, which should never be undertaken until a person was full grown in mind and body. Now she felt old enough, her mind wasn't likely to grow any more, she was as wise as a woman in her position and of her age would ever be; the time had arrived for her rechristening into the Baptist faith. And the crown of the miracle was the fact that her husband-to-be would baptize her with his own hands.

The baptism would take place as soon as the river water grew warmer. Many other persons would be immersed at the same time as she. All would be fully dressed, but baptism for a rebirth required the whole body to be under water. They were to wade into the river until the water stood above their shoulders. Pastor Jackson would hold on to her neck and push down her head, while he read the baptismal prayer. It would take only a few moments with the head under water to make it binding, he had told her. Then the newly baptized must hurry home and put on dry clothes and drink warm milk or steaming coffee so as not to catch cold. But later in the spring the St. Croix River would be warmer, so there would be less risk of getting sick.

". . . but I can't explain it! I can't tell you any more! Oh, Kristina, I am chosen. I am."

And as Ulrika was talking in great exhilaration she suddenly stopped short—she rested her elbows against the table and broke out in loud weeping.

She slumped down onto a chair as if her legs had given way under her, she began to cry so violently that her whole body shook, she put her hands to her face, the tears dripped between her fingers and fell onto the shift on the table.

"Ulrika, my dear!" Kristina had never seen Ulrika of Vastergohl cry, no one had ever seen her shed a tear. No one had imagined she could weep, she was such a strong, fearless woman. Kristina realized that something profound had happened to her. "Ulrika! You never weep!"

Copiously Ulrika's tears ran while from trembling lips she stammered forth: She was not sad, she was happy. Her tears were tears of joy. She never cried when she was sad, only when she was happy. That was why she had never wept before, she had never been hapy, never in all her life until now. What had there been for her to be happy over? Nothing—ever! Until now!

The Glad One wept. She soaked her wedding linen in tears.

Kristina sat silent and looked at her. Ulrika continued to sob. Long had she carried her tears, long had she saved them, now the moment had come when she spent her savings. It was as though all the tears she had kept back through all the years were now gathered in force, breaking through in one great torrent—as though she wished at one single time to weep tears for all the happiness which had been denied her throughout life.

At length she became aware of her tears dripping onto the white garment; then she put her apron to her eyes and wept into her apron. Her blooming cheeks were washed in her flood of tears, she wiped them away with the apron.

Kristina sat silent; one who weeps for joy needs no comfort. She was glad for Ulrika's sake, she would have liked to weep also, to show that she shared her happiness.

When the Glad One's tears at last began to give out and her tongue regained its former use, she told Kristina why she began to weep after these many years: It was because of God's all-forgiving love which she had experienced through her husband-to-be—through Henry. When he had asked her to be his wife—and he had spoken very slowly and clearly so that she would understand the English words—she had at once recognized who he was: he was the mate God had chosen and saved for her, and who had long been waiting for her here in North America. Then she had felt that she too must show him who she was— God demanded this of her, forced her to it. She had told him she was a great sinner, that she had lived in sin and shame in her homeland, that she had felt at home in her sin-body and enjoyed its pleasures. She was a sister of the Bible harlot who had been brought to Jesus for judgment. She had met a Lord's Apostle who had repeated Christ's words: Go, and sin no more! And for three years she had done repentance, for three years she had not let a single man near her.

Henry had told her that God had already informed him she had been a great sinner. But one forgiven by God had nothing to fear from mortals. Who was he to judge her? He himself was a great sinner, forgiven by God. They

397

were alike, she and he. The old life was past, blotted out through the rebirth. And if some part of her old sin-body still clung to her, she would be cleansed in the baptism he would give her later in spring when the river water was a little warmer.

It was because of God's love, all-forgiving love, that Ulrika of Vastergohl now wet her bridal linen with her tears.

But only a person who knew what sin was could rightly understand her joy. Sin was like a wasp, a big, angry, buzzing hornet. Or like a bee. Sin had sweet honey in its mouth, and a sharp, piercing sting in its end. First it lured a mortal with its honey sweetness, then it stung with its stinger. Sin had led her astray with its delightful sweetness, but how bitterly it had then stung her! Nothing in this world could sting such deep wounds as sin!

But people too had hurt her. How much evil she had suffered from them! Ever since she had borne her first child she had been called *unmarried* Ulrika of Vastergohl. It was even written down in the church book. She had been born unmarried, she couldn't help it. God had created her unmarried, He had created her in such a way that she bore children easily, she couldn't help that either. And later she couldn't get married, later, when she had lost that which men required in a bridal bed. That too she couldn't help. She had never had a maidenhead to save, since it had been stolen from her as a little girl, before she was fully developed.

But now she had been sleeping alone in her bed so long, now she had spared her body so long that the old marks of sin must be obliterated. She had been with no man for such a long time, she had a feeling something had grown inside her, her maidenhead had at last had a chance to develop, to come back to her. She felt like a virgin, like an expectant and trembling virgin, now that she was to step into a bridal bed. And this too made her happy, this too was something to shed tears of joy over; this too was a miracle. She who was called the Glad One had never until now been glad.

Voices were heard outside the cabin, and Ulrika of Vastergohl rose quickly. "The men are coming with fish for dinner. I can't sit here and bawl!" She picked up her wedding shift and folded it quickly. "I must put on the potato pot!"

398

Hurriedly she dried the last tears with the corner of her apron. Now she had wept and enjoyed it, she had wept to her heart's content. Now she had completed her joy-weeping over the passing of the old, the coming of the new.

3

Kristina started for home in the early afternoon; little Danjel must be waiting for her in his cradle. She had nursed her last born generously before leaving in the morning, but he must be howling with hunger by now, he was such a lusty child.

Her uncle Danjel had bought two cows this spring, and one had recently calved. As they were milkless at Ki-Chi-Saga, he now gave his niece a pail of milk. Kristina was overjoyed at the gift; she must save every drop for her children; she must walk carefully on the rutty road so the precious milk would not splash out.

Ulrika whispered to her that she had more confidences to share, she couldn't speak freely with Danjel and Jonas Petter listening, so she would accompany her a bit on the way and help her carry the milk pail.

Kristina told her she was much pleased that no one now could go to Pastor Jackson and slander his wife-to-be, no evil person could ruin this marriage. After all the sufferings Ulrika had gone through she had earned her happy lot as wife of the minister in Stillwater, and nothing should interfere.

Ulrika answered: She herself had always maintained that the best that could happen to a woman in this world was to marry a man she could rely on. Henry had a new house, he could offer her all she needed of worldly goods. With Mr. Abbott she would have had more than she needed, if she had been looking for things of this world only and wished to live in the flesh. Pastor Jackson earned his daily bread, but nothing more. Here in the Territory a minister earned no great sums for looking after souls. People spent most of their money on their bodies. Pastor Jackson was paid three pounds of pork for a very long sermon, a pat of butter for a wedding, a dozen eggs for a prayer for the sick. No one could get rich from such puny contributions. And he endured hardships and suffered want when he traveled about in this wilderness. He preached in the open, in log cabins and barns, in woodsheds and hovels, in logging camps and hunters' huts, in all sorts of dens and nests. He preached from morning to night, every hour of the day, the whole week through—it was only on Sundays he preached at home in his church. But that was the way an honest minister should preach, according to the words in the Acts: "The Lord of heaven and earth dwelleth not in temples made with hands."

But she would have an easy life as the minister's wife in Stillwater. Henry washed dishes and kept the house clean, scrubbed the floors, carried in water and wood. All she need do was cook the food and run the house. The rest of the time she could stay inside and keep herself clean. The Americans wanted clean, neat wives, the men did all the chores to save their womenfolk from getting bent backs, crooked limbs, or wrinkled faces while still in their days of youth. Swedish menfolk could not ruin their women quickly enough, with slave labor and the roughest work—this gave them a good excuse when they later went to younger, better-looking women. . . .

"Are you coming to my wedding, Kristina?" asked Ulrika.

Kristina said she was sorry, but she couldn't leave the children long enough to journey all the way to Stillwater. Karl Oskar would stay home in her place if she asked him, but he couldn't give the little one the breast.

"I'll come to your first christening instead! Then I won't be nursing the baby any longer."

"You'll have to wait a long while. You'll have to wait till the child is grown. Then his father will baptize him in the river."

Since Ulrika had carried Kristina's child to baptism, she ought in turn to carry Ulrika's. But she had forgotten the parents' religion—their child would not be christened until full grown.

"Henry intends to ask the Lord for many children," said Ulrika of Vastergohl.

"You aren't too old yet."

"I should say not! I can bring forth brats another ten years!"

"And you give birth easily, you told me."

"Much more easily than you last time!"

400

Pastor Jackson did not hope for such a great blessing as Jacob—to father twelve tribes—but he would consider it a particular grace from God if he might be the father of half as many—six.

Ulrika went on: First of all she would pray to God for a son who could walk in his father's footsteps as minister. She herself could never become a priest, she felt women weren't good enough. Yet God allowed women to bear males for the holy priesthood. It wasn't forbidden women to take part in the making of priests, they were permitted to carry them inside their bodies for a whole nine months. And it was Ulrika's great desire to make use of that opportunity: She had never thought she would marry a priest, but she surely had wished to make one.

And if by the Highest One's Grace she were permitted to see the day when this took place, she would write a letter to Dean Brusander in Ljuder, who had excluded her from church and sacrament, and she would tell him: Great Lord's gifts were required in a minister, but now she had done something the Mr. Dean could not do—she had made a priest!

So she would write. And as Ulrika mused on this, walking at Kristina's side, helping to carry the milk pail through the forest, an expression of deep contentment and happy expectation lighted her face.

"There was something you wanted to tell me," Kristina reminded her.

"So there is! I'll tell you."

And after making Kristina promise to keep it to herself until after the wedding, Ulrika confided in her: *She had bought a hat.*

The transaction had taken place yesterday in Stillwater; for the time being she had hidden the hat under her bed in the log house. She had wanted to show it to Kristina, but the men had come, and she did not wish Jonas Petter to see it—he would poke fun at her. In Sweden everyone ridiculed a woman of the simple sort if she wore anything but a shawl on her head. The noble women could not bear it if anyone besides themselves wore a hat. But here in North America a woman was not denied a hat, here she could wear whatever she wanted without fear of heckling.

And so for her wedding she had bought a beautiful hat, with long plumes and blooms and ribbon bands. She would show it to Kristina another time. It was so elegant the imagination could not grasp it.

Ulrika would put on her hat the day she was married. And once she had her hat on, *unmarried* Ulrika of Vastergohl would be no more.

4

Spring found these changes among the new settlers in the St. Croix Valley: Robert's and Arvid's whereabouts were unknown, they were on their way to the far-off land of California; Ulrika and her daughter Elin had moved away from Danjel to Stillwater, and Swedish Anna moved to the Lake Gennesaret settlement in Ulrika's place, to run the household for Danjel and Jonas Petter.

It was a warm, sunny spring day when Ulrika was baptized in the St. Croix River. The following Saturday she was married in the little whitewashed wooden church in Stillwater and became Mrs. Reverend Henry O. Jackson.

She was the first Swedish bride in the St. Croix Valley. She was to be the mother of a flock of children, the founder of a fine new family; a strong, enduring family: One day her great-grandchildren would speak of their descent from the noble family of Vastergohl in Sweden, whence their female ancestor a hundred years earlier had emigrated.

XXV

"At Home" Here in America—
"Back There" in Sweden

The sun's arc climbed, the days lengthened, but the evenings had not yet begun to lighten. The sun departed, darkness came in its place, but no twilight under a pale heaven lingered over the earth. Kristina waited: Spring was as yet only beginning.

April came and brought sun-warm days to the shores of Lake Ki-Chi-Saga, but the evenings remained almost as dark as in winter. Kristina still waited.

And when at last she realized her waiting was futile, her thoughts wandered to a land where the evenings in spring were light.

After the many chores which each day fell to her with their unchanging sameness, her body was tired as she lay down on her bed in the evening. But her mind and soul would not rest, she lay awake with her thoughts. Outside the small log-house windows the night was dark, but she lay with her eyes wide open and gazed into the darkness where nothing could be seen.

As spring progressed, with darkness still prevailing, her sleepless hours increased. She still gazed through the darkness—toward that land where evenings were light in spring.

Memories reawakened, images stood clear. She and her sisters sat "twilighting" at the window; they used to delay lighting the candles, by the light of the spring evening they would sit talking in hushed voices to each other. They never spoke aloud at "twilighting"—the gathering dusk of an April evening called for whispered talk. Outside by the gable the great rosebush brushed against the window, with its tender green growth and swelling buds. Later in summer the roses would be out, and then the bush would cover the whole window with its fragrant blooms. Against the evening sky the young Astrachan apple tree stood out clearly—she had planted it herself as a companion for the lonely rosebush. Each autumn she had dug around the little tree; it had carried its first apples the last fall they were at home—big juicy apples with transparent skin; how many times she had gone out just to look at the apples; and how delicious they had been.

Would her apple tree bloom this spring? Would it bear apples in the fall? And would there be gooseberries on the bushes she had planted against the cellar wall? Those berries were as big as thumbs, and dark red when ripe; their taste was sweet as sugar.

A year had passed since the April evening she had said good-by to her parents and sisters at the gate of her childhood home. She—the departing one—had stood outside the gate, they—whom she would part from—had stood inside. Her mother had said: "Don't forget, our dear daughter, we want to meet you with God." Her father had stood bent against the gatepost, he said nothing, he stood with his face turned away, holding on to the post as if seeking support.

She had left, and they had remained; never more in this world would she see them.

That evening had been light, one whole long twilight that still lit her way home on sleepless nights. . . . It had rained during the day, but cleared toward evening. There had been a spring fragrance over black fields and green meadows as she walked away from the farm where she was born.

And since that evening a year had completed its cycle, the year's great wheel had made a complete turn and carried her far away in the world, thousands of miles away. She had emigrated and now she lived so far away that only her thoughts could carry her back. Here she lay in her bed, next to her husband, in her new home, and peered

404

into the darkness, looking for the land where the evenings were light in spring.

She traveled the way back, she traversed the great waters and the immense stretches of land. She retraced the road that separated her from her old home. She could see that road in her mind, bit by bit, mile by mile. And the mile she remembered at home was a long mile, six times as long as the American mile, it took her two or three hours to walk it. And as she gazed into the dark outside the cabin window she felt the distance increase a thousand times. She measured mile after mile, she counted as she traveled, ten, twenty, thirty . . . until she tired of her journey, and yet she had retraveled so small a part. Her thoughts would never reach the thousand-mile mark, her journey must end, the immense distance stifled her imagination. And after a while she grew dizzy, her tired eyes vainly penetrating the darkness—she was unable to fathom the road that separated her from her homeland.

That road she would never again travel.

Longing for home gripped Kristina in its vise more forcibly as spring came with no twilight. And the evening hours when she lay awake became the time of day she most feared.

2

What was the matter with Kristina? What did she long for? Didn't she live here, have her home here—wasn't she at home? How could she long for home when she was already at home?

Karl Oskar had said, *"Here at home* on Lake Ki-Chi-Saga I'll build a large house next time!" *Here at home*—but she felt as though she were away, as though she were in a foreign place. She always said, *"Away here in America—back home in Sweden."* So she thought, so she spoke. But this was not right, and her saying it wasn't right, when her home would be here forever. She should say just the opposite, exchange the countries: This was home, Sweden was away.

And she tried, she tried to think and say the opposite. She said to herself: At home here in America—back there in Sweden. She repeated this, again and again. Her mouth learned to say it, but her heart wouldn't accept it. Next

405

time, she forgot herself, again she used the words *back home—away here*. Something inside her refused the change, something she could not force. She still thought and talked as she had when she first arrived. She could not make the countries change place—back home would always remain *home* to Kristina.

What *was* the matter with her? Kristina put the question to herself, and Karl Oskar too asked her. Nothing was the matter with her, she answered. Did she lie when she said this? Did she speak the truth? She was satisfied with her lot here, she complained of nothing; she had husband and children with her, they were all in good health, they had their sustenance, everything essential, everything they needed to sustain life. They could forget their temporary inconveniences, finding comfort in the good promises the future held out for them in the new land.

Kristina lacked nothing, yet she missed something. It was hard to understand.

What did she miss? What did she long for? Why did she lie awake so long in the evenings thinking about the rosebush and the Astrachan tree at home in Duvemala? Did she miss the bushes and trees of the home village? There were enough bushes and trees and plants growing around their new home, they grew more profusely than in Sweden, and they bore quantities of fruit and berries, much richer fruit than the trees and bushes in Sweden. She should be well satisfied with all the good things here.

Why did she long so for home? Perhaps it was weakness, a softness in her. Perhaps some childishness remained in her, had remained in her too long: When she had been a married woman, mother of several children, she had secretly put up a swing in the barn and gone there to play. That had been childish. And now it was childish of her to think of rosebushes and trees she had planted in her parental home—to regret that she never again would taste apples from her tree, never see her rosebush bloom outside the gable.

Now she was a grown woman—and she wanted to be a grown woman, she did not wish Karl Oskar to see how childish and weak she was, she did not want to act like a silly girl. That was why she hadn't confided in him. Not a single human being knew what stirred within her as she lay awake these spring nights in her bed.

It was only natural that she longed to see her loved ones, that she missed the life she had been born into and bred up in. Everything focussed in those clear pictures of home—the apple tree and the rosebush in the twilight, all that her longing made vivid in the dark: the family gatherings, familiar customs and ways, the Sundays on the church green, spring and autumn fairs, the year's festivities and holidays, the seasons in the farm-year cycle. Here in the wilderness all was different, here people had other customs, and she lived like a bewildered stranger among people whom she could not reach with her tongue, and who could not reach her with their own speech.

She saw the sunshine, the light of the moon, and the stars in the heavens—it was the same sun, the same moon, and stars she had seen at home. The heavenly lights had accompanied her on her emigration and shone on her here. They were lit at home too and shone over the people she had left behind. Sun, moon, and stars revealed to her that though she was in a foreign land she still shared the firmament with those at home. But she was away, and she would remain away. In this country she would live out the rest of her allotted days, few or many, broken soon or stretching into late old age. Here she would live, here she would die, here she would lie in her grave.

And this was the way it was with Kristina: she could not reconcile herself to the irrevocable. She had emigrated for life, yet it seemed she was still on a journey that would eventually bring her home again.

And night after night she lay awake and measured the road she never again would journey.

3

During daylight her chores occupied her thoughts, in the daytime, she could defend herself. But when she lay wide awake at night, waiting for sleep to engulf her, she was open and unprotected; and then longing and sorrow stole over her. Her evening prayer sometimes brought calm to her mind and helped her go to sleep. Karl Oskar always went to sleep immediately, usually as soon as his head hit the pillow, and often she said her prayer after he had gone to sleep; she wanted only God to hear her.

One evening she made an addition to her usual prayer:

407

She prayed God that He might once more let her see her home and her loved ones. For God nothing was impossible. If He wanted to, He could stretch out His omnipotent arm and move her from North America back to Sweden.

Afterward she lay awake; in her thoughts she was with those at home sitting "twilight." No, her evening prayer did not always help her.

She felt Karl Oskar's hand on the quilt, slowly seeking hers. "Kristina . . ."

"I thought you were asleep, Karl Oskar."

"Something wakened me. Maybe a screechhopper."

"There is no hopper in here tonight." She must have wakened him saying her prayer. "Have you been awake long?"

"No. Just a little while."

She hoped he hadn't heard her prayer.

His hand had found hers: "What is the matter with you, Kristina?"

"Nothing. Nothing is the matter with me. Go back to sleep!"

But her voice was thick and disturbed, so sad that it troubled him. Her voice denied the words she uttered. Her voice said: Yes, there is something wrong. Don't go to sleep, Karl Oskar! Stay awake and help me!

And she was afraid he might hear her voice rather than her words.

"But why do you lie awake this late?" he persisted.

"Oh, I don't know. It's silly and childish. . . ."

She wanted to be strong, as strong and hardy as he.

"Are you—sad? Is something wrong, Kristina?"

"No . . . I don't know how to explain. . . ."

He gripped her hand in his own big, hard hand, he held her hand so tightly that it hurt her. "Aren't we friends, the best of friends, as before?"

"Yes, Karl Oskar, of course."

"But then you must tell me everything. If you fight something, I might help you. Good friends help each other."

She did not answer. A silence fell between them.

Then he said—and his words were firm and determined: "If you want God's arm to move you back, then I'll hold you here with my arm!"

408

He meant what he said. So, not only God had heard her this evening.

"Yes. Now you know, Karl Oskar." She said this with a slow, hesitating sigh. Then she added: "There isn't much more to say. It was a childish wish that came over me as I said my prayer."

"I began to wonder that time last fall when you cried at the house-warming party. Since then I have wondered how things stood with you. And lately I've felt you don't like it here. You're brooding."

"I like it here. It isn't that. I don't know myself what it is. I'll tell you, and let me hear what you think. . . ."

And suddenly she wanted to confide in her husband, she wanted him to know and understand. It was painful for her to keep such a thing as this a secret, it wore on her mind to suffer a sorrow which she had to hide every moment, had to hide even from her own husband. And hadn't she and Karl Oskar been joined together in order to lighten life's burdens for each other, to comfort each other in trouble? Shouldn't he know why she lay awake nights, what she thought of and played with in her imagination—that she traveled the road back home, bit after bit, mile after mile?

Now he must have the whole explanation: She was not dissatisfied with their new home, or their new country. She felt as he did: They would improve themselves and find security here, if health remained and they managed to struggle through a few hard years. But one country could not be like another country. America could never become Sweden to her. She could never bring here what she missed from childhood and youth in the homeland. She was only twenty-six, and when she thought of all the coming years out here, all the years left of her life, this unexplainable pain stole over her and kept her awake. Only lately had she understood what it meant to move for life. It was something for a soul to ponder. And so at last, this evening, she had prayed for help from the Almighty's arm —wouldn't He stretch it out. . . . Yes, that was all.

"Kristina—"

He had not let go her hand, now he held on to it so tightly that it hurt her: he held on as though someone were trying to snatch her out of their bed, to take her away from his side. But he said nothing now.

She asked: "Karl Oskar—don't you ever feel a longing for your old home?"

"Maybe. At times. Now and then. . . ."

Yes, he must admit, a longing came over him too. It seemed to come over all emigrants at times. But he always drove it away at once. He was afraid it might burden his mind. He needed his strength for other matters. He needed all his strength to improve their lives out here. He was careful, he couldn't spend his strength pondering over what he had left forever. Just the other day, he had seen how dangerous it could be to dig oneself down in thoughts and musings—he had seen a man lying on a bed of wretchedness. . . .

Yes, she knew it well: What she worried over could never change. All her musing and thoughts were of no avail, served no purpose. . . . "But I can't help it, Karl Oskar!"

"No, I guess not." He rose. "I'll fetch something for you."

He stepped onto the floor, and she could hear him as he walked barefoot toward the fireplace corner. She heard him stir in the Swedish chest. What was he fetching for her? Drops? Did he think the Four Kinds of Drops or Hoffman's Heart-Aiding Drops would help her? There was hardly a spoonful left in either bottle, although she had used them sparingly.

Karl Oskar came silently back to the bed, he had something in his hand which he gave his wife. It was not drops, it was a pair of tiny, worn-out, broken shoes, a child's shoes.

She accepted them in bewilderment, she recognized them in bewilderment. "Anna's old shoes."

"Yes. They help me to remember. If I sometimes feel downhearted a little . . ."

"You mean—?"

"Perhaps the shoes can help you too."

"Karl Oskar!" Her voice grew thick again.

"Do you remember the winter the child died? You do, don't you?"

"Yes. It was the winter when I agreed—to the emigration. I have almost regretted it at times. But I still agree. I don't blame you a bit, Karl Oskar. You remember what I said that night on the ship?"

He remembered well, he remembered nothing better: She had said she had nothing to reproach him for, nothing to forgive him for. They were the best of friends. He could remember nothing more clearly than that. For that was the night when he thought she would die.

That time it had been she who had taken his hand and kept it firmly in hers. And there between them on the quilt had lain the old shoes, made by the village shoemaker in their home parish, made for their child's feet—made for Anna, who had time to wear out only one pair of shoes while she lived on earth. And now they had the shoes here in America, still aiding them—they reminded the parents of what they had gone through in the homeland: Because of hunger the little girl's life had been so short she had never needed more than one pair of shoes.

Karl Oskar said: Here in Minnesota was their home, here their home would remain. Here they had their children and all they owned, all that belonged to them in this world. In Sweden they owned not even a wooden spoon any longer, in Sweden they were homeless. This was their home.

And if Kristina still felt that she was away, then he would help her all he could to make *away* become *home* to her: "There is something I've long had in mind to tell you," he said. "One day our children will thank us for emigrating to America."

"You think that? You believe so?"

"I feel it. I know it."

"Maybe. But who knows?"

"I know it's true. I'm sure, Kristina. Our children will thank their parents for bringing them to this country when they were little."

"But no one can know."

Karl Oskar persisted: Every time he looked at this countryside and realized how much it could give to them, he felt assured of this: The children would be grateful to their parents. She must think ahead, of their children, and their children's children in time, of all the generations after them. All the ones who came after would feel and think and say that she had done right when she moved from Sweden to North America.

On that thought he himself often lingered, it was a great help to him when his struggles at times seemed heavy and

411

endless. It gave him renewed strength when he slackened. Couldn't the same thought comfort her when she was depressed, longing for home?

"You may be right, Karl Oskar," she said. "But we know nothing of the day we haven't seen."

There was one more matter Karl Oskar had thought over and which he now wanted to discuss with his wife: It was high time they gave a name to their home.

They had lived here an autumn and a winter and soon spring would be over. They ought to name their homestead now that they were settled and would never move away. That day last fall when they had moved in she had said that the place here with the lake reminded her of Duvemala, that it was almost as beautiful as her home village. He had thought about this many times. They could name their home after her childhood home in Algutsboda Parish. And since he had heard her talk tonight, he was even more confirmed in that thought: They must name their home in the new land Duvemala. How did she like that? What did she think of moving the name of her parental home over here?

"I—you must know I like it!"

Kristina was overjoyed. Now she took hold of his hand and held it tightly. It was a good idea, this name for their home. She would never have thought of it herself—the name of her own village!

"Duvemala . . . we don't live at Ki-Chi-Saga any longer, we live in Duvemala. How lovely it sounds." Her voice was clear, no longer thick and uncertain.

"That settles the name, then," said Karl Oskar, with the intonation of a minister at baptism.

Kristina thought, from now on she would live in Duvemala. And she would again try to make herself believe she was at home here.

So the first home on Lake Ki-Chi-Saga in Minnesota Territory was named, and the name was given late of an evening in spring as the couple who had built it lay awake in their bed and talked. They talked long to each other; the wife confessed her childish longing and spoke of the light spring nights at home, of the rosebush and the Astrachan tree and the gooseberry bushes and all the things that came to her mind at this time of evening.

It was nearly midnight, and they still lay awake. Karl Oskar said, now they must sleep. If they didn't go to sleep soon, they would wake up tired next morning. And the morrow would bring heavy work—he himself would begin the most important task of the next years: the wooden plow he had made with his own hands, with great difficulty, was at last finished, and the ox team was waiting for him at his neighbor's on Lake Gennesaret. Tomorrow he would begin to plow the meadow, the earth that was to become their good and bearing and nourishing field.

"Do you remember, Kristina? Tomorrow is an important day to remember."

"No. Isn't it a usual workday?"

"It is the fourteenth of April. The day we went on board ship in Karlshamn."

Tomorrow, a year would have passed since they had tramped their homeland soil for the last time. Tomorrow they would put the plow into American soil for the first time.

Karl Oskar immediately fell into deep sleep, but Kristina lay awake yet a while. She listened to the sounds from the bed at the opposite corner of the cabin—short, quick breaths, the light rustle of children's breathing in sleep. It reminded her of Karl Oskar's words tonight: their children would be grateful to the parents for having emigrated with them while they still were little and had their lives ahead of them.

It might be so, perhaps he was right. But one couldn't say for sure, no human could know this for sure—it would be better not to predict anything in advance.

What she could predict, what she did know for sure, was that her children would never have to go through the pain of longing which she now went through. They carried no memories from the homeland, her longing would never afflict them, no vivid memories from a past life in another country would plague them. Once they were grown they would never know any other life than the one lived here. And their grandchildren in turn would know even less of another way of life. Her children and her children's children would never, as she did, remember trees and bushes they had planted in a far-off land, they would not ask, Do they still bud and bloom in spring, do they carry their fruit

413

in fall? They would never, as she did, lie awake nights and gaze into the dark for that land where spring evenings are light.

The ones she had borne into the world, and the ones they in turn would bear, would from the beginning of their lives say what her own tongue was unable to say: *At home* here in America—*back there* in Sweden. With this thought, listening to her children's breathing, Kristina went to sleep.

XXVI

A Letter to Sweden

Duvemala at Taylors Falls Postoffice in
Minnesota Teritory Northamerica
June 4 1851.

Dearly Beloved Parents
May all be well with you is my daily Wish

Father's letter came some time ago, I thank you for
it. I have not written to you because of great over-
sight, it was a joy to learn you are alive and in good
health, the same good holds true for your son and
Family in Northamerica.

It has been a struggle right along but all things
turn out well for us, I plowed a five acres field on my
land last spring, I have seeded the earth with three
bushels of rye and two bushels of barley. Besides I
have planted four bushels of potatoes, the american
bushel is half time larger than the Swedish. All crops
in the field grow and thrive it is a joy for the eye to
behold.

I wonder if you will ask Kristina's parents to send
us seeds from the Astrakan apple in Duvemala, we
wish to plant a new astrakan apple tree here in Minnesota then we can have the same sort of apples, they
were so fresh in eating as we well remember, and then
we will have moved something from there over here.

Sweden has good apple seeds and here is good soil to sprout and grow in, so it might grow to be a large tree in time, with many blooms.

As you see from this letter our abode now carries the name Duvemala, Kristina holds that name dear I suppose, here it will soon be for her like in her childhood home, we have already full summer and warm weather, I sweat on my hands while I write this the sweat drops upon the paper, I have not much to write about, nothing has happened to us.

Our children are well and healthy, there is long space between my letters but they will not stop, I live far away but no day has come to its end without my thoughts on my dear Home and You my kind parents, your son never forgets his home.

Kindly overlook my poor writing written down hastely by your devoted Son

Karl Oskar Nilsson